Also available in Random House Large Print

THE SECRET PILGRIM

THE
NIGHT
MANAGER

THE NIGHT MANAGER

A novel by

JOHN LE CARRÉ

Published by Random House Large Print
in association with Alfred A. Knopf, Inc.
New York 1993

Library of Congress Cataloging-in-Publication Data
Le Carré, John, 1931—
    The night manager : a novel / by John le Carré. — 1st large print ed.
        p. cm.
    ISBN 0-679-74728-1
    1. Large type books.   I. Title
[PR6062.E33N5 1993]
823′.914—dc20   93-1880 CIP

Manufactured in the United States of America
First Large Print Edition

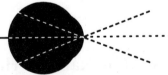

This Large Print Book carries the
Seal of Approval of N.A.V.H.

*For Helga Macazek,
the bravest of the brave,
in belated gratitude for
a lifetime shared*

THE
NIGHT
MANAGER

ONE

ON A SNOW-SWEPT January evening of 1991, Jonathan Pine, the English night manager of the Hotel Meister Palace in Zurich, forsook his office behind the reception desk and, in the grip of feelings he had not known before, took up his position in the lobby as a prelude to extending his hotel's welcome to a distinguished late arrival. The Gulf war had just begun. Throughout the day, news of the Allied bombings, discreetly relayed by the staff, had caused consternation on the Zurich stock exchange. Hotel bookings, which in any January were low, had sunk to crisis levels. Once more in her long history Switzerland was under siege.

But the Meister Palace was equal to the challenge. Over all Zurich, "Meister," as the hotel was affectionately known to taxi drivers and habitués, presided physically and traditionally alone, a staid Edwardian aunt perched on her own hilltop, gazing down on the folly of hectic urban life. The more things changed in the valley, the more Meister stayed herself, unbending in her standards, a bastion of civilized style in a world intent on going to the devil.

Jonathan's point of vantage was a small recess between the hotel's two elegant showcases, both of them displaying ladies' fashions. Adèle of the Bahnhofstrasse was offering a sable stole over a female dummy whose only other protection was a gold bikini bottom and a pair of coral earrings, price on application to the concierge. The clamor against the use of animal furs these days is as vocal in Zurich as in other cities of the Western world, but the Meister Palace paid it not a blind bit of notice. The second showcase—by César, likewise of the Bahnhofstrasse—preferred to cater for the Arab taste, with a tableau of lusciously embroidered gowns and diamanté turbans and jeweled wristwatches at sixty thousand francs a shot. Flanked by these wayside shrines to luxury, Jonathan was able to keep a crisp eye on the swing doors.

He was a compact man but tentative, with a smile of apologetic self-protection. Even his Englishness was a well-kept secret. He was nimble and in his prime of life. If you were a sailor you might have spotted him for another, recognized the deliberate economy of his movements, the caged placing of the feet, one hand always for the boat. He had trim curled hair and a pugilist's thick brow. The pallor of his eyes caught you by surprise. You expected more challenge from him, heavier shadows.

And this mildness of manner within a

fighter's frame gave him a troubling intensity. You would never during your stay in the hotel confuse him with anybody else: not with Herr Strippli, the creamy-haired front-of-house manager, not with one of Herr Meister's superior young Germans, who strode through the place like gods on their way to stardom somewhere else. As a hotelier Jonathan was complete. You did not wonder who his parents were or whether he listened to music or kept a wife and children or a dog. His gaze as he watched the door was steady as a marksman's. He wore a carnation. At night he always did.

The snow, even for the time of year, was formidable. Fat billows swept across the lighted forecourt like white waves in a tempest. The chasseurs, alerted for a grand arrival, stared expectantly into the blizzard. Roper will never make it, Jonathan thought. Even if they let his plane take off it can never have landed in this weather. Herr Kaspar has got it wrong.

But Herr Kaspar, the head concierge, had never got anything wrong in his life. When Herr Kaspar breathed "Arrival imminent" over the internal speaker, only a congenital optimist could imagine that the client's plane had been diverted. Besides, why else would Herr Kaspar be presiding at this hour, except for a big spender? There was a time, Frau Loring had told Jonathan, when Herr Kaspar would maim for two francs and strangle for five. But old age is a different state. These days, only the richest pickings were able to lure Herr Kaspar from the pleasures of his evening television.

Hotel's full up, I'm afraid, Mr. Roper, Jonathan rehearsed in another last-ditch effort to fend off the inevitable. *Herr Meister is desolated. A temporary clerk has made an unpardonable error. However, we have managed to obtain rooms for you at the Baur au Lac,* et cetera. But that wishful fantasy too was stillborn. There was not a great hotel in Europe tonight that boasted more than fifty guests. The wealthiest of the earth were bravely hugging the ground, with the one exception of Richard Onslow Roper, trader, of Nassau, the Bahamas.

Jonathan's hands stiffened, and he instinctively flicked his elbows as if to ready them for combat. A car, a Mercedes by its radiator, had entered the forecourt, the beams of its headlights choked with swirling snowflakes. He saw Herr Kaspar's senatorial head lift and the chandelier glint on its pomaded rivers. But the car had parked on the far side of the forecourt. A taxi, a mere city cab, a no one. Herr Kaspar's head, now glowing with acrylic light, sank forward as he resumed his study of the closing stock prices. In his relief, Jonathan allowed himself a ghostly smile of recognition. The wig, the immortal wig: Herr Kaspar's one-hundred-and-forty-thousand-franc crown, the pride of every classic concierge in Switzerland. Herr Kaspar's William Tell of a wig, Frau Loring called it: the wig that had dared to raise itself in revolt against the millionaire despot Madame Archetti.

Perhaps to concentrate his mind while it was tearing him in so many directions, or perhaps because he found in the story some hidden relevance to his predicament, Jonathan recounted it to himself yet again, exactly as Frau Loring, the head housekeeper, had recounted it the first time she made him cheese fondue in her attic. Frau Loring was seventy-five and came from Hamburg. She had been Herr Meister's nanny and, as rumor had it, Herr Meister's father's mistress. She was the keeper of the legend of the wig, its living witness.

"Madame Archetti was the richest woman in Europe in those days, *young* Herr Jonathan," Frau Loring declared, as if she had slept with Jonathan's father too. "Every hotel in the world was after her. But Meister was her favorite until Kaspar made his stand. After that, well, she still came, but it was only to be seen."

Madame Archetti had inherited the Archetti supermarket fortune, Frau Loring explained. Madame Archetti lived off the interest on the interest. And what she liked at the age of fifty-something was to tour the great hotels of Europe in her open English sports car, followed by her staff and wardrobe in a van. She knew the names of every concierge and headwaiter from the Four Seasons in Hamburg to the Cipriani in Venice to the Villa d'Este on Lake Como. She prescribed them diets and herbal remedies and acquainted them with their horoscopes. And she tipped them on a scale scarcely to be imagined, provided they found favor.

And favor was what Herr Kaspar found in bucketloads, said Frau Loring. He found it to the tune of twenty thousand Swiss francs each annual visit, not to mention quack hair remedies, magic stones to put beneath his pillow to cure his sciatica, and half kilos of Beluga caviar on Christmas and saints' days, which Herr Kaspar discreetly converted to cash by means of an understanding with a famous food hall in the town. All this for obtaining a few theater tickets and booking a few dinner tables, on which of course he exacted his customary commission. And for bestowing those pious signals of devotion that Madame Archetti required for her role as chatelaine of the servant kingdom.

Until the day Herr Kaspar bought his wig.

He did not buy it rashly, said Frau Loring. He bought land in Texas first, thanks to a Meister client in the oil business. The investment flourished, and he took his profit. Only then did he decide that like his patroness he had reached a stage in life where he was entitled to shed a few of his advancing years. After months of measuring and debate, the thing was ready—a wonder wig, a miracle of artful simulation. To try it out he availed himself of his annual holiday on Mykonos, and one Monday morning in September he reappeared behind his desk, bronzed and fifteen years younger as long as you didn't look at him from the top.

And no one did, said Frau Loring. Or if they did they didn't mention it. The amazing truth was, no one mentioned the wig at all. Not Frau Loring, not André, who was the pianist in those days, not Brandt, who was the predecessor of Maître Berri in the dining room, not Herr Meister senior, who kept a beady eye for deviations in the appearance of his staff. The whole hotel had tacitly decided to share in the glow of Herr Kaspar's rejuvenation. Frau Loring herself risked her all with a plunging summer frock and a pair of stockings with fern-pattern seams. And things continued happily this way until the evening Madame Archetti arrived for her customary month's stay, and as usual her hotel family lined up to greet her in the lobby: Frau Loring, Maître Brandt, André and Herr Meister senior, who was waiting to conduct her personally to the Tower Suite.

And at his desk Herr Kaspar in his wig.

To begin with, said Frau Loring, Madame Archetti did not permit herself to notice the addition to her favorite's appearance. She smiled at him as she swept past, but it was the smile of a princess at her first ball, bestowed on everyone at once. She permitted Herr Meister to kiss her on both cheeks, Maître Brandt on one. She smiled at Frau Loring. She placed her arms circumspectly round the undeveloped shoulders of André the pianist, who purred, "Madame." Only then did she approach Herr Kaspar.

"What are we wearing on our head, Kaspar?"

"Hair, Madame."

"Whose hair, Kaspar?"

"It is mine," Herr Kaspar replied with bearing.

"Take it off," Madame Archetti ordered. "Or you will never have another penny from me."

"I cannot take it off, Madame. My hair is part of my personality. It is integrated."

"Then dis-integrate it, Kaspar. Not now—it is too complicated—but for tomorrow morning. Otherwise nothing. What have you got at the theater for me?"

"Othello, Madame."

"I shall look at you again in the morning. Who is playing him?"

"Leiser, Madame. The greatest Moor we have."

"We shall see."

Next morning at eight o'clock to the minute Herr Kaspar reappeared for duty, his crossed keys of office glinting like campaign medals from his lapels. And on his head, triumphantly, the emblem of his insurrection. All morning long a precarious hush prevailed in the lobby. The hotel guests, like the famous geese of Freiburg, said Frau Loring, were aware of the imminent explosion even if they did not know its cause. At midday, which was her hour, Madame Archetti emerged from the Tower Suite and descended the staircase on the arm of her prevailing swain, a promising young barber from Graz.

"But where is Herr Kaspar this morning?" she asked in Herr Kaspar's vague direction.

"He is behind his desk and at your service as ever, Madame," Herr Kaspar replied in a voice that, to those who heard it, echoed for all time in the halls of freedom. "He has the tickets for the Moor."

"I see no Herr Kaspar," Madame Archetti informed her escort. "I see hair. Tell him, please, we shall miss him in his obscurity."

"It was his trumpet blast," Frau Loring liked to end. "From the moment that woman entered the hotel, Herr Kaspar could not escape his destiny."

And tonight is my trumpet blast, thought Jonathan, waiting to receive the worst man in the world.

· · ·

JONATHAN WAS WORRYING about his hands, which as usual were immaculate and had been so ever since he had been the subject of spot fingernail inspections at his army school. At first he had kept them curled at the embroidered seams of his trousers, in the posture drummed into him on the parade ground. But now, without his noticing, they had linked themselves behind his back with a handkerchief twisted between them, for he was painfully conscious of the sweat that kept forming in his palms.

Transferring his worries to his smile, Jonathan checked it for faults in the mirrors either side of him. It was the Smile of Gracious Welcome that he had worked up during his years in the profession: a sympathetic smile but a prudently restrained one, for he had learned by experience that guests, particularly very rich ones, could be tetchy after a demanding journey, and the last thing they needed on arrival was a night manager grinning at them like a chimpanzee.

His smile, he established, was still in place. His feeling of nausea had not dislodged it. His tie, self-tied as a signal to the better guests, was pleasingly insouciant. His hair, though nothing to match Herr Kaspar's, was his own and, as usual, in the sleekest order.

It's a different Roper, he announced inside his head. *Complete misunderstanding, whole thing. Nothing whatever to do with her. There are two, both traders, both living in Nassau.* But Jonathan had been going back and forth through that hoop ever since half past five this afternoon, when, arriving in his office for duty, he had heedlessly picked up Herr Strippli's list of the evening's arrivals and seen the name Roper in electronic capitals, screaming at him from the computer printout.

Roper R. O., party of sixteen, arriving from Athens by private jet, expected 2130 hours, followed by Herr Strippli's hysterical annotation: *"V* VIP!" Jonathan called up the public relations file on his screen. Roper R. O. and the letters *OBG* after him, which was the coy house code for bodyguard, *O* standing for "official" and official meaning licensed by the Swiss federal authorities to bear a sidearm. Roper, OBG, business address Ironbrand Land, Ore & Precious Metals Company of Nassau, home address a box number in Nassau, credit assured by the Zurich Bank of Somebody. So how many Ropers were there in the world with the initial R and firms called Ironbrand? How many more coincidences had God got up His sleeve?

"Who on earth is Roper R. O. when he's at home?" Jonathan asked of Herr Strippli in German while he affected to busy himself with other things.

"He's a British, like you."

It was Strippli's maddening habit to reply in English though Jonathan's German was better.

"Not like me at all, actually. Lives in Nassau, trades in precious metals, banks in Switzerland—

why's that like me?" After their months of incarceration together, their quarrels had acquired a marital pettiness.

"Mr. Roper is actually a very important guest," Strippli replied in his slow singsong as he buckled his leather overcoat in preparation for the snow. "From our private sector he is number five for spending and chief of all English. Last time his group was here, he was average twenty-one thousand seven hundred Swiss francs a day, *plus* service."

Jonathan heard the soggy chatter of Herr Strippli's motorbike as, snow notwithstanding, he puttered down the hill to his mother. Easy, he told himself. Roper has taken his time, you can do the same. He sat at his desk for a while, his head hidden in his hands, like someone waiting for an air attack. Finally he sat upright and, with the composed expression of someone taking his time, gave his attention to the letters on his desk. A soft-goods manufacturer in Stuttgart was objecting to the bill for his Christmas party. Jonathan drafted a stinging response for signature by Herr Meister. A public relations company in Nigeria was inquiring about conference facilities. Jonathan replied regretting there were no vacancies.

A beautiful and stately French girl named Sybille who had stayed at the hotel with her mother complained yet again of his treatment of her. "You take me sailing. We walk in the mountains. We have beautiful days. Are you so very English that we cannot also be more than friends? You look at me, I see a shadow fall across your face. I am disgusting to you."

Feeling a need to move, he launched himself on a tour of the construction work in the north wing, where Herr Meister was building a grill-room out of old arolla pine rescued from the roof of a condemned treasure in the city. No one knew why Herr Meister wanted a grillroom, no one could recall when he had started it. The numbered panels were stacked in rows against the unrendered wall. Jonathan caught their musky smell and remembered Sophie's hair on the night she walked into his office at the Queen Nefertiti Hotel in Cairo, smelling of vanilla.

Herr Meister's building works could not be held to blame for this. Ever since seeing Roper's name at half past five that afternoon, Jonathan had been on his way to Cairo.

· · ·

HE HAD GLIMPSED her often but never spoken to her: a languid dark-haired beauty of forty, long-waisted, elegant and remote. He had spotted her on her expeditions through the Nefertiti's boutiques or being ushered into a maroon Rolls-Royce by a muscular chauffeur. When she toured the lobby the chauffeur doubled as her body-guard, hovering behind her with his hands crossed over his balls. When she took a *menthe frappé* in

Le Pavillon restaurant, dark glasses shoved into her hair like driving goggles and her French newspaper at arm's length, the chauffeur would sip a soda at the next table. The staff called her Madame Sophie, and Madame Sophie belonged to Freddie Hamid, and Freddie was the baby of the three unlovely Hamid brothers who between them owned a lot of Cairo, including the Queen Nefertiti Hotel. Freddie's most celebrated accomplishment at twenty-five was to have lost half a million dollars at baccarat in ten minutes.

"You are Mr. Pine," she said in a French-flavored voice, perching herself on the armchair on the other side of his desk. And tilting her head back and viewing him on the slant: "The flower of England."

It was three in the morning. She was wearing a silk trouser suit and a topaz amulet at her throat. Could be legless, he decided: proceed with caution.

"Well, thank you," he said handsomely. "No one's told me that for a long time. What can I do for you?"

But when he discreetly sniffed the air around her, all he could smell was her hair. And the mystery was that though it was glistening black it smelled blond: a vanilla smell and warm.

"And I am Madame Sophie from penthouse number three," she continued, as if to remind herself. "I have seen you often, Mr. Pine. Very often. You have steadfast eyes."

The rings on her fingers antique. Clusters of clouded diamonds set in pale gold.

"And I have seen *you,*" he rejoined, with his ever-ready smile.

"You also *sail,*" she said, as if accusing him of an amusing deviation. The *also* was a mystery she did not explain. "My protector took me to the Cairo Yacht Club last Sunday. Your ship came in while we were drinking champagne cocktails. Freddie recognized you and waved, but you were too busy being nautical to bother with us."

"I expect we were afraid of ramming the jetty," said Jonathan, recalling a rowdy bunch of rich Egyptians swilling champagne on the club veranda.

"It was a pretty blue boat with an English flag. Is it yours? It looked so royal."

"Oh my goodness no! It's the minister's."

"You mean you sail with a priest?"

"I mean I sail with the second man at the British Embassy."

"He looked so young. You both did. I was impressed. Somehow I had imagined that people who work at night are unhealthy. When do you sleep?"

"It was my weekend off," Jonathan replied nimbly, since he did not feel inclined, at this early stage in their relationship, to discuss his sleeping habits.

"Do you always sail on your weekends off?"

"When I'm invited."

"What else do you do on your weekends off?"

"Play a little tennis. Run a little. Consider my immortal soul."

"*Is* it immortal?"

"I hope so."

"Do you believe so?"

"When I'm happy."

"And when you are unhappy, you doubt it. No wonder that God is so fickle. Why should He be constant, when we are so faithless?"

She was frowning in rebuke at her gold sandals, as if they too had misbehaved. Jonathan wondered whether after all she was sober and merely maintained a different rhythm from the world around her. Or perhaps she does a little of Freddie's drugs, he thought: for there were rumors that the Hamids traded in Lebanese hash oil.

"Do you ride horseback?" she asked.

"I'm afraid not."

"Freddie has horses."

"So I hear."

"Arabs. Magnificent Arabs. People who breed Arab horses are an international elite. You know that?"

"So I have heard."

She allowed herself a pause for meditation. Jonathan availed himself of it:

"Is there something I can do for you, Madame Sophie?"

"And this minister, this Mr. . . ."

"Ogilvey."

"Sir Something Ogilvey?"

"Just Mister."

"He is a friend of yours?"

"A sailing friend."

"You were at school together?"

"No. I wasn't at that kind of school."

"But you are of the same class, or whatever the expression is? You may not breed Arab horses, but you are both—well, my God, what does one say?—both gentlemen?"

"Mr. Ogilvey and I are sailing companions," he replied with his most evasive smile.

"Freddie also has a yacht. A floating bordello. Isn't that what they are called?"

"I'm sure not."

"I'm sure *yes*."

She made another pause while she reached out a silk-clad arm and studied the underside of the bracelets on her wrist. "I would like a cup of coffee, please, Mr. Pine. Egyptian. Then I shall ask a favor of you."

Mahmoud the night waiter brought coffee in a copper pot and poured two cups with ceremony. Before Freddie came along she had belonged to a rich Armenian, Jonathan remembered, and before that an Alexandrian Greek who owned dubious concessions along the Nile. Freddie had laid siege to her, bombarding her with bouquets of orchids at impossible moments, sleeping in his

Ferrari outside her apartment. The gossip writers had printed what they dared. The Armenian had left town.

She was trying to light a cigarette, but her hand was shaking. He struck the lighter for her. She closed her eyes and drew on the cigarette. Lines of age appeared on her neck. And Freddie Hamid all of twenty-five, Jonathan thought. He put the lighter on the desk.

"I too am British, Mr. Pine," she remarked, as if this were a grief they shared. "When I was young and unprincipled I married one of your countrymen for his passport. It turned out he loved me deeply. He was a straight arrow. There is no one better than a good Englishman and no one worse than a bad one. I have observed you. I think you are a good one. Mr. Pine, do you know Richard Roper?"

"I'm afraid not."

"But you must. He is famous. He is beautiful. A fifty-year-old Apollo. He breeds horses, exactly as Freddie does. They even talk of opening a stud farm together. Mr. Richard Onslow Roper, one of your famous international entrepreneurs. Come."

"Not a name to me. I'm sorry."

"But Dicky Roper does a lot of business in Cairo! He is English, like you, very charming, rich, glamorous, persuasive. For us simple Arabs, almost too persuasive. He owns a splendid motor yacht, *twice* the size of Freddie's! How come you do not know him, since you are also a sailor? Of course you do. You are pretending, I can see."

"Perhaps if he has a splendid motor yacht he doesn't have to bother with hotels. I don't read the newspapers enough. I'm out of touch. I'm sorry."

But Madame Sophie was not sorry. She was reassured. Her relief was in her face as it cleared and in the decisiveness with which she now reached for her handbag.

"I would like you to copy some personal documents for me, please."

"Well now, we do have an executive services bureau directly across the lobby, Madame Sophie," Jonathan said. "Mr. Ahmadi usually presides at night." He made to pick up the telephone, but her voice stopped him.

"They are confidential documents, Mr. Pine."

"I'm sure Mr. Ahmadi is perfectly dependable."

"Thank you, I would prefer that we use our own facilities," she retorted, with a glance at the copier standing on its trolley in the corner. And he knew she had marked it on her journeys through the lobby, just as she had marked him. From the handbag she drew a wad of white paper, bundled but not folded. She slid it across the desk to him, her ringed fingers splayed and rigid.

"It's only a very *small* copier, I'm afraid, Madame Sophie," Jonathan warned, rising to his feet. "You'll have to hand-feed it. May I show you how, then leave you to yourself?"

"We shall hand-feed it together, please," she said, with an innuendo born of tension.

"But if the papers are confidential . . ."

"You must please attend me. I am a technical idiot. I am not myself." She picked up her cigarette from the ashtray and drew on it. Her eyes, stretched wide, seemed shocked by her own actions. "You do it, please," she ordered him.

So he did it.

He switched on the machine, inserted them—all eighteen of them—and skim-read them as they reappeared. He made no conscious effort to do this. Also he made no conscious effort to resist. The watcher's skills had never abandoned him.

From the Ironbrand Land, Ore & Precious Metals Company of Nassau to the Hamid InterArab Hotels and Trading Company of Cairo, incoming dated August the twelfth. Hamid InterArab to Ironbrand, outgoing, assurances of personal regard.

Ironbrand to Hamid InterArab again, talk of merchandise and items four to seven on our stock list, end user to be Hamid InterArab's responsibility and let's have dinner together on the yacht.

The letters from Ironbrand signed with a tight flourish, like a monogram on a shirt pocket. The InterArab copies not signed at all, but the name Said Abu Hamid in oversized capitals below the empty space.

Then Jonathan saw the stock list, and his blood did whatever blood does when it sets the surface of your back tingling and makes you worry how your voice will sound when you next speak: one plain sheet of paper, no signature, no provenance, headed "Stock available as of October 1st 1990." The items a devil's lexicon from Jonathan's unsleeping past.

"Are you sure one copy will be enough?" he inquired with that extra lightness that came to him in crisis, like a clarity of vision under fire.

She was standing with her forearm across her stomach and her elbow cupped in her hand while she smoked and watched him.

"You are adept," she said. She did not say what in.

"Well, it's not exactly complicated once you get the hang of it. As long as the paper doesn't jam."

He laid the original documents in one pile, the photocopies in another. He had suspended thought. If he had been laying out a dead body he would have blocked his mind in the same way. He turned to her and said, "Done," overcasually, a boldness he in no way felt.

"Of a good hotel one asks everything," she commented. "You have a suitable envelope? Of course you have."

Envelopes were in the third drawer of his

desk, left side. He selected a yellow one, A4 size, and guided it across the desk, but she let it lie there.

"Please put the copies inside the envelope. Then seal the envelope very effectively and put it in your safe. Perhaps you should use some sticky tape. Yes, tape it. A receipt is unnecessary, thank you."

Jonathan had a specially warm smile for refusal. "Alas, we are forbidden to accept guests' packages for safekeeping, Madame Sophie. Even yours. I can give you a deposit box and your own key. That's the most I can do, I'm afraid."

She was already stuffing the original letters back into her bag as he said this. She snapped the bag shut and hoisted it over her shoulder.

"Do not be bureaucratic with me, Mr. Pine. You have seen the contents of the envelope. You have sealed it. Put your own name on it. The letters are now yours."

Never surprised by his own obedience, Jonathan selected a red felt-tipped pen from the silver desk stand and wrote PINE in capitals on the envelope.

On your own head be it, he was telling her silently. I never asked for this. I never encouraged it.

"How long do you expect them to remain here, Madame Sophie?" he inquired.

"Perhaps forever, perhaps a night. It is not known. It is like a love affair." Her coquettishness deserted her, and she became the supplicant. "In confidence. Yes? That is understood. Yes?"

He said yes. He said of course. He gave her a smile that suggested he was a tiny bit surprised that the question needed to be raised.

"Mr. Pine."

"Madame Sophie."

"Concerning your immortal soul."

"Concerning it."

"We are all immortal, naturally. But if it should turn out that I am not, you will please give those documents to your friend Mr. Ogilvey. May I trust you to do that?"

"If that is what you want, of course."

She was still smiling, still mysteriously out of rhythm with him. "Are you a permanent night manager, Mr. Pine? Always? Every night?"

"It's my profession."

"Chosen?"

"Of course."

"By you?"

"Who else?"

"But you look so well by daylight."

"Thank you."

"I shall telephone you from time to time."

"I shall be honored."

"Like you, I grow a little tired of sleeping. Please do not escort me."

And the smell of vanilla again as he opened the door for her and longed to follow her to bed.

· · ·

STANDING TO ATTENTION in the gloom of Herr Meister's permanently unfinished grillroom, Jonathan watched himself, a mere walk-on character in his overcrowded secret theater, as he goes methodically to work on Madame Sophie's papers. For the trained soldier, trained however long ago, there is nothing startling about the call to duty. There is only the automaton's drill movement from one side of the head to the other:

Pine standing in the doorway of his office at the Queen Nefertiti, staring across the empty marble hall at the liquid crystal digits above the lift as they stammer out its ascent to the penthouses.

The lift returning empty to the ground floor.

Pine's palms tingling and dry, Pine's shoulders light.

Pine reopening the safe. The combination has been set—by the hotel's sycophantic general manager—at Freddie Hamid's date of birth.

Pine extracting the photocopies, folding the yellow envelope small and slipping it into an inside pocket of his dinner jacket for later destruction.

The copier still warm.

Pine copying the copies, first adjusting the density button a shade darker for improved definition. Names of missiles. Names of guidance systems. Techno-babble that Pine cannot understand. Names of chemicals Pine cannot pronounce yet knows the use of. Other names that are as deadly but more pronounceable. Names like Sarin, Soman and Tabun.

Pine sliding the new copies inside tonight's dinner menu, then folding the menu longways and slipping it into his other inside pocket. The copies still warm inside the menu.

Pine placing the old copies in a fresh envelope indistinguishable from its predecessor. Pine writing PINE on the new envelope and placing it in the same spot on the same shelf, the same way up.

Pine reclosing the safe and locking it. The overt world restored.

Pine eight hours later, a different kind of servant, seated buttock-to-buttock with Mark Ogilvey in the cramped cabin of the minister's yacht while Mrs. Ogilvey in the galley, wearing designer jeans, runs up smoked salmon sandwiches.

"Freddie Hamid buying dirty toys from Dicky Onslow Roper?" Ogilvey repeats incredulously, leafing through the documents a second time. "What the hell's that about? Little swine would be safer sticking to baccarat. The ambassador's going to be absolutely furious. Darling, wait till you hear this one."

But Mrs. Ogilvey has heard this one already. The Ogilveys are a husband-and-wife team. They spy in preference to having children.

· · ·

I LOVED YOU, thought Jonathan uselessly. Meet your past-tense lover.

I loved you but betrayed you instead, to a pompous British spy I didn't even like.

Because I was on his little list of people who would always do their bit when the bugle went.

Because I was One of Us—Us being Englishmen of self-evident loyalty and discretion. Us being Good Chaps.

I loved you but never quite got around to saying so at the time.

Sybille's letter rang in his ears: I see a shadow fall across your face. I am disgusting to you.

No, no, not disgusting at all, Sybille, the night manager hastened to assure his unwelcome correspondent. Just irrelevant. The disgust is all my own work.

TWO

HERR KASPAR AGAIN lifted his famous head. The throb of a powerful motor became discreetly audible above the beating of the wind. He rolled up his bulletins from the beleaguered Zurich stock exchange and slipped an elastic band over them. He dropped the roll into his investment drawer, locked it and nodded to Mario, the head chasseur. He eased a comb from his back pocket and skimmed it through his wig. Mario scowled at Pablo, who in turn simpered to Benito, the ridiculously pretty apprentice from Lugano, who was probably favoring both of them. All three had clustered inside the lobby for shelter, but now, with Latin bravado, they breasted the storm, buttoning their capes at the neck as they grabbed their umbrellas and trolleys and vanished, swallowed by the snow.

It never happened, Jonathan thought, watching each signal of the car's approach. There is only the snow, racing over the forecourt. It's a dream.

But Jonathan was not dreaming. The limousine was real, even if it was floating on a white void. A stretch limousine, longer than the hotel, was berthing at the front entrance like a black liner nosing into dock, while the chasseurs in their capes scurried and pranced to make it fast, all but the impertinent Pablo, who in a moment of inspiration had unearthed a curling broom and was delicately picking the snowflakes from the red carpet. For one last blessed moment, it was true, a gust of snow did blank everything out, and Jonathan was able to imagine that a tidal wave had swept the liner back to sea, to founder against the crags of the surrounding hilltops, so that Mr. Richard Onslow Roper, and his officially licensed bodyguards, and whoever else made up the party of sixteen, had perished to a man in their private *Titanic* in the memorable Great Storm of January 1991, God rest their souls.

But the limousine had returned. Furs, well-grown men, a beautiful long-legged young woman, diamonds and gold wristbands and castles of matching black luggage, were emerging like plundered booty from its plush interior. A second limousine had joined it, now a third. A convoy of limousines. Already Herr Kaspar was propelling the swing doors at the speed best suited to the party's progress. First an untidy brown coat of camel hair loomed into the glass and was cautiously rotated into focus, a grimy silk muffler dangling over its collar, surmounted by a soggy cigarette and the pouchy stare of a scion of the English upper classes. No fifty-year-old Apollo he.

After the camel hair came a navy blue blazer in his twenties, the blazer single-breasted for the cross-draw, and eyes shallow as paint. One OBG, thought Jonathan, trying not to answer their malign stare; one more to follow, and a third if Roper's scared.

The beautiful woman had chestnut hair and wore a quilted coat of many colors that reached almost to her feet, yet she managed to appear slightly underdressed. She had Sophie's comic slant to her, and her hair, like Sophie's, fell to either side of her face. Someone's wife? Mistress? Anyone's? For the first time in six months, Jonathan felt the devastating, irrational impact of a woman he instantaneously desired. Like Sophie she had a jeweled brilliance and a kind of dressed nakedness. Two strings of splendid pearls set off her neck. Diamond bracelets peeked from her quilted sleeves. But it was the vague air of shambles, the raggedy smile and unselfconscious carriage, that appointed her an instant citizen of Paradise. The doors swung open again, disgorging everyone at once, so that suddenly an entire leftover delegation of the English affluent society was ranged under the chandelier, each of its members so sleekly groomed, so sun-rich, that together they seemed to share a corporate morality that outlawed sickness, poverty, pale faces, age and manual labor. Only the camel hair coat, with his disgracefully battered suede boots, remained a voluntary outcast from their ranks.

And at their center, yet apart from them, The Man, as only The Man could be after Sophie's furious descriptions of him. Tall, slender and at first glance noble. Fair hair stirred with gray, swept back and flicked into little horns above the ears. A face to play cards against and lose. The stance that arrogant Englishmen do best, one knee cocked, one hand backed against the colonial arse. *Freddie is so weak,* Sophie had explained. *And Roper is so English.*

Like all deft men, Roper was doing several things at once: shaking hands with Kaspar, then clapping him with the same hand on the upper arm, then using it to blow a kiss to Fräulein Eberhardt, who went pink and waved at him like a menopausal groupie. Then finally fixing his overlord's eye on Jonathan, who must have been strolling toward him, though Jonathan himself had no direct evidence of this except that Adèle's dummy had been replaced first by the newsstand, then by the flushed features of Fräulein Eberhardt at the reception desk, and now by The Man himself. *He has no qualms,* Sophie had said. *He is the worst man in the world.*

He's recognized me, thought Jonathan, waiting for the denunciation. He's seen my photograph, listened to my description. In a minute he'll stop smiling.

"I'm Dicky Roper," a lazy voice announced as the hand closed round Jonathan's and briefly owned it. "My chaps booked some rooms here. Rather a lot of 'em. How d'you do?" Belgravia slur, the proletarian accent of the vastly rich. They had entered each other's private space.

"How very good to see you, Mr. Roper," Jonathan murmured, English voice to English voice. "Welcome back, sir, and poor you, what a perfectly ghastly journey you must have had. Wasn't it rather heroic to venture aloft at all? No one else has, I can tell you. My name's Pine. I'm the night manager."

He's heard of me, he thought, waiting. Freddie Hamid told him my name.

"What's old Meister up to these days?" Roper asked, his eyes slipping away to the beautiful woman. She was at the newsstand, helping herself to fashion magazines. Her bracelets kept falling over her hand, while with the other she continually pushed back her hair. "Tucked up with his Ovaltine and a book, is he? *Hope* it's a book, must say. Jeds, how you doing, darling? Adores magazines. Addict. Hate the things m'self."

It took Jonathan a moment to realize that Jeds was the woman. Not Jed a single man, but Jeds a single woman in all her varieties. Her chestnut head turned far enough to let them see her smile. It was puckish and good-humored.

"I'm just *fine,* darling," she said bravely, as if she were recovering from a knock.

"Herr Meister is unavoidably tied up to-night, I'm afraid, sir," said Jonathan, "but he does enormously look forward to seeing you in the morning when you're rested."

"You English, Pine? Sound it."

"To the core, sir."

"Wise man." The pale gaze wanders away again, this time to the reception desk, where the camel hair coat is filling in forms for Fräulein Eberhardt. "You proposing marriage to that young lady, Corky?" Roper calls. "That'll be the day," he adds to Jonathan in a lower tone. "Major Corkoran, my assistant," he confides with innuendo.

"Nearly there, Chief!" Corky drawls, and lifts a camel hair arm. He has squared his legs and pushed out his rump like somebody about to play a croquet shot, and there is a tilt to his haunches that, by nature or intent, suggests a certain femininity. A heap of passports lies at his elbow.

"Only got to copy a few names, God's sake. Not a fifty-page contract, Corks."

"It's the new security, I'm afraid, sir," Jonathan explains. "The Swiss police insist. There seems to be nothing we can do."

The beautiful Jeds has chosen three magazines but needs more. She has perched one slightly scuffed boot pensively on its long heel, with the toe pointing in the air. Sophie used to do the same. Mid-twenties, Jonathan thinks. Always will be.

"Been here long, then, Pine? Wasn't here last time round, was he, Frisky? We'd have noticed a stray young Brit."

"No way," said the blazer, eyeing Jonathan through an imaginary gun slit. Cauliflower ears, Jonathan noticed. Blond hair, going on white. Hands like axheads.

"I make it six months, Mr. Roper, almost to the day."

"Where were you before that?"

"Cairo," Jonathan replied, light as a spark. "The Queen Nefertiti."

Time passes, like time before a detonation. But the carved mirrors of the lobby do not shatter at the mention of the Queen Nefertiti Hotel, the pilasters and chandeliers hold still.

"Likee, did you? Cairo?"

"Loved it."

"What made you leave the place, then, if you were so high on it?"

Well, *you* did, actually, Jonathan thinks. But he said instead: "Oh, wanderlust, I suppose, sir. You know how it is. The drifting life is one of the attractions of the trade."

Suddenly everything was in motion. Corkoran had detached himself from the reception desk and, cigarette held wide, was advancing on them with high steps. The woman Jeds had chosen her magazines and was waiting, Sophie-like, for someone to do something about paying for them. Corkoran said, "On the room bill, heart." Herr

Kaspar was unloading a wad of mail into the arms of the second blazer, who ostentatiously explored the bulkier packages with his fingertips.

"High bloody time, Corks. Hell's happened to your signing hand?"

"Wanker's colic, I should think, Chief," said Major Corkoran. "Could be limp wrist," he added, with a special smile for Jonathan.

"Oh, *Corks*," said the woman Jeds, giggling.

Out of the corner of his eye Jonathan spotted Mario, the head doorman, wheeling a stack of matching luggage to the service lift, using the paddling gait with which porters hope to imprint their images on the fickle minds of clients. Then he saw his own fragmented reflection passing him in the mirrors, and Corkoran's beside him, carrying his cigarette in one hand and the magazines in the other, and he allowed himself a moment of officious panic because he couldn't see Jeds. He turned and saw her and caught her eye and she smiled at him, which in his startling resurgence of desire was what he craved. He caught Roper's eye also, because she was hanging from Roper's arm, holding it in both her long hands while she almost trod on his feet. The bodyguards and the affluent society trailed behind them. Jonathan noticed a blond male beauty with his hair tied at the nape, a plain wife scowling beside him.

"Pilots'll be along later," Corkoran was saying. "Some crap about the compass. If it's not the compass, it's the bogs won't flush. You a permanency here, darling, or just a one-night stand?"

His breath smelled of the day's good things: the martinis before lunch, the wines with it and the brandies afterwards, washed down by his foul French cigarettes.

"Oh, I think as permanent as one can be, in this profession, Major," Jonathan replied, altering his manner a little for an underling.

"Goes for us all, heart, believe me," said the Major fervently. "Permanently temporary. Jesus."

Another film cut, and they were traversing the great hall to the tune of "When I Take My Sugar to Tea," played by Maxie the pianist to two old ladies in gray silk. Roper and the woman were still entwined. You're new to each other, Jonathan told them sourly, out of the corner of his eye. Or else you're making up after a quarrel. *Jeds,* he repeated to himself. He needed the safety of his single bed.

Yet another cut, and they were standing three deep before the ornate doors of Herr Meister's new Tower Suite lift, the affluent society twittering in the background.

"Hell happened to the *old* lift, Pine?" Roper was demanding. "Thought Meister was a sucker for old things. Bloody Swiss would modernize Stonehenge if they got a chance. Wouldn't they, Jeds?"

"Roper, you can't make a scene about a *lift,*" she said in awe.

"Try me."

From far away, Jonathan hears a voice not unlike his own, enumerating the advantages of the new lift: a security measure, Mr. Roper, but also an attractive extra feature, installed last autumn for the sole convenience of our Tower Suite guests. . . . And as Jonathan talks, he dangles between his fingers the golden master key created to Herr Meister's personal design, decked with a golden tassel and capped with this rather amusing golden crown.

"I mean, doesn't it remind you of the pharaohs? It's *quite* outrageous, really, but I can assure you that our less sophisticated guests *adore* it," he confides, with a camp little smile that he has never vouchsafed to anyone before.

"Well, *I* adore it," says the Major, offscreen. "And I'm *bloody* sophisticated."

Roper balances the key in his palm as if to cost its melt weight. He studies both sides, then the crown, then the tassel.

"Taiwan," he pronounces and, to Jonathan's alarm, slings it at the blond blazer with cauliflower ears, who catches it low down and fast on his left side, shouting "Mine!" as he dives.

Beretta .09 automatic with safety catch at the "on," Jonathan records. Ebony finish, holster-carried under the right armpit. A left-handed OBG, with a spare magazine in his belt bag.

"Oh, well *played,* Frisky, heart. Good *catch,"* Corkoran drawls, and there is relieved laughter from the affluent outfield, led by the woman, who squeezes Roper's arm and says *honestly, darling,* though in Jonathan's clouded ear it at first sounds like *policy, darling.*

Now everything is in slow motion, everything is happening under water. The lift takes five at a time; the rest must wait. Roper strides in, drawing the woman after him. Roedean and model school, Jonathan is thinking. Plus a special course that Sophie had also taken in how to do that with your hips when you walk. Then Frisky, then Major Corkoran without his cigarette, finally Jonathan. Her hair is soft as well as chestnut. She is also nude. That is to say, she has slipped off her quilted coat and slung it over her arm like an army greatcoat. She wears a man's white shirt with Sophie's puffy sleeves rolled to the elbows. Jonathan starts the lift. Corkoran stares disapprovingly upward like a man peeing. The girl's hip rides carelessly against Jonathan's flank in cheerful friendship. *Get off,* he wants to tell her irritably. *If you're flirting, don't. If you're not flirting, keep your hip to yourself.* She smells not of vanilla but of white carnations on Commemoration Day at cadet school. Roper stands behind her, wide hands resting possessively on her shoulders. Frisky gazes blankly downward at the faded bite mark on her neck, at her unsupported breasts inside the expensive shirt. Like Frisky, no doubt, Jonathan has a disgraceful urge to scoop one out.

"Now why don't I go ahead and show you all the new goodies Herr Meister's put in for you since your last visit?" he suggests.

Perhaps it's time you gave up manners as a way of life, Sophie had said to him as she walked beside him in the dawn.

He went ahead, indicating the suite's priceless advantages: the amazing low-flush bar . . . the thousand-year-old fruit . . . the very *latest* in superhygienic jetstream loos, does everything for you except clean your teeth. . . . All his whimsical little jokes, whisked out and polished for the delectation of Mr. Richard Onslow Roper and this long-waisted, funny-faced, unpardonably attractive woman. How dare she be so beautiful at a time like this?

· · ·

MEISTER'S LEGENDARY TOWER hovers like an inflated dovecote over the magic peaks and valleys of the hotel's Edwardian roof. The three-bedroom palace inside it is built on two floors, a pastel experience in what Jonathan confidingly calls Swiss Franc Quatorze. The luggage has arrived, the chasseurs have received their largesse, Jeds has retired to the master bedroom, from which issue the far sounds of female singing and running water. The singing is indistinct but provocative, if not downright bawdy. Frisky the blazer has stationed himself at a telephone in the landing and is murmuring orders to someone he disdains. Major Corkoran, armed with a fresh cigarette but minus his camel hair, is in the dining room, talking slow French on another line for the benefit of somebody whose French is worse than his. His cheeks are fluid as a baby's, the dabs of color very high. And his French is French French, no question. He has slipped into it as naturally as if it were his mother tongue, which perhaps it is, for nothing about Corkoran suggests an uncomplicated provenance.

Elsewhere in the suite, other lives and conversations are unfolding. The tall man with the ponytail is called Sandy, we learn, and Sandy is talking English on another telephone to somebody in Prague called Gregory, while Mrs. Sandy sits in a chair with her overcoat on, glowering at the wall. But Jonathan has banished these secondary players from his immediate consciousness. They exist, they are elegant, they revolve in their far periphery around the central light of Mr. Richard Onslow Roper of Nassau, the Bahamas. But they are chorus. Jonathan's guided tour of the splendors of the palace is complete. It is time he took his leave. A graceful wave of the hand, an endearing exhortation—"Please to be sure to enjoy every *bit* of it"—and in the normal way he would have descended smoothly to ground level, leaving his wards to enjoy their pleasures by themselves as best they could at fifteen thousand francs a night including tax, service and continental breakfast.

But tonight is not the normal way, tonight is

Roper's night, it is Sophie's night, and Sophie in some bizarre way is played for us tonight by Roper's woman, whose name to everyone but Roper turns out to be not Jeds but Jed—Mr. Onslow Roper likes to multiply his assets. The snow is still falling, and the worst man in the world is drawn toward it like a man who is contemplating his childhood in the dancing flakes. He stands cavalry-backed at the center of the room, facing the French windows and the snow-clad balcony. He holds a green Sotheby's catalogue open before him like a hymnal from which he is about to sing, and his other arm is raised to bring in some silent instrument from the edge of the orchestra. He sports a learned judge's half-lens reading spectacles.

"Soldier Boris and his chum say okay Monday lunchtime," Corkoran calls from the dining room. "Okay Monday lunchtime?"

"Fix," says Roper, turning a page of the catalogue and watching the snow over his spectacles at the same time. "Look at that. Glimpse of the infinite."

"I adore it every time it happens," says Jonathan earnestly.

"Your friend Appetites from Miami says why not make it the Kronenhalle—food's better." Corkoran again.

"Too public. Lunch here or bring his sandwiches. Sandy, what does a decent Stubbs horse make these days?"

The pretty male head with the ponytail pokes round the door. "Size?"

"Thirty by fifty inches."

The pretty face barely puckers. "There was a good'un went at Sotheby's last June. *Protector in a Landscape.* Signed and dated 1779. A lulu."

"Quanta costa?"

"You sitting comfortably?"

"Come off it, Sands!"

"A million two. Plus commish."

"Pounds or bucks?"

"Bucks."

From the opposite doorway, Major Corkoran is complaining. "The Brussels boys want half in cash, Chief. Bloody liberty, if you ask me."

"Tell 'em you won't sign," Roper retorts, with an extra gruffness that he apparently uses for keeping Corkoran at arm's length. "That a hotel up there, Pine?"

Roper's gaze is fixed on the black window-panes where the childhood snowflakes pursue their dance.

"A beacon, actually, Mr. Roper. Some sort of navigational aid, I gather."

Herr Meister's treasured ormolu clock is chiming the hour, but Jonathan for all his customary nimbleness is unable to move his feet in the direction of escape. His patent evening shoes remain embedded in the deep pile of the drawing room carpet as solidly as if they were set in cement. His mild gaze, so at odds with the pugilistic brow, remains fixed on Roper's back. But Jonathan sees him in only a part of his mind. Otherwise he is not in the Tower Suite at all but in Sophie's penthouse apartment at the top of the Queen Nefertiti Hotel in Cairo.

. . .

SOPHIE TOO has her back to him, and it is as beautiful as he always knew it was, white against the whiteness of her evening gown. She is gazing, not at the snow, but at the huge wet stars of the Cairene night, at the quarter-moon that hangs from its points above the soundless city. The doors to her roof garden are open; she grows nothing but white flowers—oleander, bougainvillea, agapanthus. The scent of Arabian jasmine drifts past her into the room. A bottle of vodka stands beside her on a table, and it is definitely half empty, not half full.

"You rang," Jonathan reminded her with a smile in his voice, playing the humble servant. Perhaps this is our night, he was thinking.

"Yes, I rang. And you answered. You are kind. I am sure you are always kind."

He knew at once that it was not their night.

"I need to ask you a question," she said. "Will you answer it truthfully?"

"If I can. Of course."

"You mean there could be circumstances in which you would not?"

"I mean I might not know the answer."

"Oh, you will know the answer. Where are the papers that I entrusted to your care?"

"In the safe. In their envelope. With my name on it."

"Has anybody seen them except myself?"

"The safe is used by several members of the staff, mostly for storing cash until it goes to the bank. So far as I know, the envelope is still sealed."

She allowed her shoulders to slump in a gesture of impatience but did not turn her head. "Did you show them to anyone? Yes or no, please. I am not judgmental. I came to you on an impulse. It would not be your fault if I made a mistake. I had some sentimental vision of you as a clean Englishman."

So did I, thought Jonathan. Yet it did not occur to him that he had a choice. In the world that mysteriously owned his allegiance, there was only one answer to her question.

"No," he said. And he said again, "No; no one."

"If you tell me it is the truth, I shall believe you. I wish very much to believe there is one last gentleman on earth."

"It's the truth. I gave you my word. No."

Again she seemed to disregard his denial or find it premature. "Freddie insists I have betrayed him. He entrusted the papers to my care. He did not want them kept in his office or at home. Dicky

Roper is encouraging Freddie in his suspicions of me."

"Why should he do that?"

"Roper is the other party to the correspondence. Until today, Roper and Freddie Hamid were proposing to become business partners. I was present at some of their discussions on Roper's yacht. Roper was not comfortable to have me as a witness, but since Freddie insisted on showing me off to him, he had no choice."

She seemed to expect him to speak, but he kept his silence.

"Freddie visited me this evening. It was later than his usual hour. When he is in town, it is his custom to visit me before dinner. He uses the car park lift, out of respect for his wife, he stays two hours, then he returns to dine in the bosom of his family. It is my somewhat pathetic boast that I have helped to keep his marriage intact. Tonight he was late. He had been talking on the telephone. It appears that Roper has received a warning."

"A warning from whom?"

"From good friends in London." A spurt of bitterness. "Good for Roper. That is understood."

"Saying what?"

"Saying that his business arrangements with Freddie are known to the authorities. Roper was careful on the telephone, saying only that he had counted on Freddie's discretion. Freddie's brothers were not so delicate. Freddie had not informed them of the deal. He was wishing to prove himself to them. He had gone so far as to set aside a fleet of Hamid trucks under a pretext in order to transport the merchandise through Jordan. His brothers were not pleased about that either. Now, because Freddie is frightened, he has told them everything. He is also furious to be losing the esteem of his precious Mr. Roper. So *no?*" she rehearsed, still staring into the night. "Definitely *no*. Mr. Pine has no suggestions about how this information could have reached London or come to the ears of Mr. Roper's friends. The safe, the papers—he has no suggestions."

"No. He hasn't. I'm sorry."

Until then she had not looked at him. Now at last she turned and let him see her face. One eye was closed entirely. Both sides were bloated out of recognition.

"I would like you to take me for a drive, please, Mr. Pine. Freddie is not rational when his pride is threatened."

. . .

NO TIME has passed. Roper is still absorbed in the Sotheby's catalogue. Nobody has smashed *his* face into a pulp. The ormolu clock is still chiming the hour. Absurdly, Jonathan checks its accuracy against his wristwatch and, finding himself able to move his feet at last, opens the glass and advances the large hand until the two agree. Run for cover, he tells himself. Flatten. The invisible radio is playing Alfred Brendel playing Mozart. Offstage, Corkoran is once more talking, this time in Italian, which is less assured than his French.

But Jonathan cannot run for cover. The enraging woman is coming down the ornamental staircase. He does not hear her at first, because she is barefooted and dressed in Herr Meister's complimentary bathrobe, and when he does, he can hardly bear to look at her. Her long legs are baby pink from the bath, her chestnut hair is brushed out like a good girl's over her shoulders. A smell of warm *mousse de bain* has replaced the Commemoration Day carnations. Jonathan is nearly ill with desire.

"And for additional refreshment, allow me to recommend your private bar," he advises Roper's back. "Malt whisky, personally selected by Herr Meister, the vodkas of six nations." What else? "Oh, and twenty-four-hour room service for you and yours, naturally."

"Well, I'm *ravenous,*" says the girl, refusing to be ignored.

Jonathan allows her his hotelier's passionless smile. "Well now, do please ask them for *anything* you want. The menu is merely a compass, and they *adore* being made to work." He returns to Roper, and a devil drives him one step further. "And English-language cable news in case you want to watch the war. Just touch the green knob on the little box, then nine."

"Been there. Seen the movie, thanks. Know anything about statuary?"

"Not much."

"Me neither. Makes two of us. Hullo, darling. Good bath?"

"Gorgeous."

Crossing the room to a low armchair, the woman Jed folds herself into it, picks up the room service menu and pulls on a pair of completely circular, very small and, Jonathan is angrily convinced, totally unnecessary gold-framed reading spectacles. Sophie would have worn them in her hair. Brendel's perfect river has reached the sea. The hidden quadraphonic radio is announcing that Fischer-Dieskau will sing a selection of songs by Schubert. Roper's shoulder is nudging against him. Out of focus, Jed crosses her baby-pink legs and absentmindedly pulls the skirt of her bathrobe over them while she continues to study the menu. Whore! screams a voice inside Jonathan. Tramp! Angel! Why am I suddenly prey to these adolescent fantasies? Roper's sculpted index finger is resting on a full-page illustration.

Lot 236, Venus and Adonis in marble, seventy inches high excluding pediment. Venus with her fingers touching Adonis's face in adoration, contemporary copy of Canova, unsigned, original at the Villa La Grange, Geneva, estimated price £60,000–£100,000.

A fifty-year-old Apollo wishes to buy Venus and Adonis.

"What's *roasty,* anyway?" says Jed.

"I think you're looking at *rösti,*" Jonathan replies in a tone laced with superior knowledge. "It's a Swiss potato delicacy. Sort of bubble and squeak without the squeak, made with lots of butter and fried. If one's ravenous, perfectly delicious. And they do it *awfully* well."

"How do they grab you?" Roper demands. "Likee? No likee? Don't be lukewarm—no good to anyone. . . . Hash browns, darling; had 'em in Miami. . . . What do you say, Mr. Pine?"

"I think it would *rather* depend where they were going to live," Jonathan replies cautiously.

"End of a floral walk. Pergola over the top, view of the sea at the end. West-facing, so you get the sunset."

"Most beautiful place on earth," says Jed.

Jonathan is at once furious with her. Why don't you shut up? Why is your blah-blah voice so near when you are speaking from across the room? Why does she have to interrupt all the time instead of reading the bloody menu?

"Sunshine guaranteed?" asks Jonathan, with his most patronizing smile.

"Three hundred and sixty days a year," says Jed proudly.

"Go on," Roper urges. "Not made of glass. What's your verdict?"

"I'm afraid they're not me at all," Jonathan replies tautly, before he has given himself time to think.

Why on earth does he say this? Probably it is Jed's fault. Jonathan himself would be the last to know. He has no opinion of statues; he has never bought one, sold one, scarcely paused to consider one, unless it was the awful bronze of Earl Haig looking at God through binoculars from the side of the saluting base on one of the parade grounds of his military childhood. All he was trying to do was tell Jed to keep her distance.

Roper's fine features do not alter, but for a moment Jonathan does wonder whether after all he is made of glass. "You laughing at me, Jemima?" he asks, with a perfectly pleasant smile.

The menu descends, and the puckish, totally undamaged face peers comically over the top of it. "Why on *earth* should I be?"

"Seem to remember you didn't much care for them either, when I showed 'em to you in the plane."

She sets the menu on her lap and with both hands removes her useless glasses. As she does so, the short sleeve of Herr Meister's bathrobe gapes, and Jonathan to his total outrage is offered a view of one perfect breast, its slightly erect nipple lifted to him by the action of her arms, the upper half golden-lit by the reading lamp above her.

"Darling," she says sweetly. "That's utter, total, unadulterated balls. I said her *bum* was too big. If you like big bums, have her. Your money. Your bum."

Roper grins, reaches out and grabs hold of

the neck of Herr Meister's complimentary bottle of Dom Pérignon, and wrenches.

"Corky!"

"Right here, Chief!"

The moment's hesitation. The corrected voice. "Give Danby and MacArthur a bell. Shampoo."

"Will do, Chief."

"Sandy! Caroline! Shampoo! Hell *are* those two? Fighting again. Bores. Give me the queers every time," he adds, in an aside to Jonathan. "Don't go, Pine—party's just warming up. Corks, order up another couple of bottles!"

But Jonathan goes. Somehow semaphoring his regrets, he gains the landing, and as he looks back, Jed is flapping a zany goodbye at him over her champagne glass. He responds with his most glacial smile.

"Night night, old love," Corkoran murmurs as they brush past each other on their separate ways. "Thanks for the tender loving care."

"Good night, Major."

Frisky the ash-blond OBG has installed himself on a tapestried throne beside the lift and is studying a paperback of Victorian erotica. "Play golf, do we, sweetheart?" he asks as Jonathan flits by.

"No."

"Me neither."

I shoot the snipe with ease, Fischer-Dieskau is singing. *I shoot the snipe with ease.*

· · ·

THE HALF-DOZEN dinner guests sat bowed over their candlelit tables like worshipers in a cathedral. Jonathan sat among them, basking in a determined euphoria. This is what I live for, he told himself: this half-bottle of Pommard, this *foie de veau glacé* with vegetables of three colors, this hotel silver with its bruised old face, twinkling wisely up at me from the damask cloth.

Dining alone had always been his particular pleasure, and tonight, in deference to the war's depletion, Maître Berri had promoted him from his single-seater by the service door to one of the high altars at the window. Gazing down over the snow-clad golf links to the city lights prickling along the lakeside, Jonathan doggedly congratulated himself on the satisfying completeness of his life till now, the early uglinesses he had left behind.

That wasn't easy for you up there with the egregious Roper, Jonathan my boy, the school's gray-jawed commandant told his best cadet approvingly. *And that Major Corkoran is a real piece of work. So was the girl, in my opinion. Never mind. You were firm, you fought your corner. Well played.* And Jonathan actually managed to bestow a congratulatory smile on his reflection in the candlelit window as he recalled his every fawning phrase and lustful thought in the order of its shameful appearance.

Suddenly the *foie de veau* turned to ash in his

mouth and the Pommard tasted of gunmetal. His bowels writhed, his vision blurred. Rising from the table in a flurry, he mumbled something to Maître Berri about a forgotten duty, and made it just in time to the men's room.

THREE

JONATHAN PINE, orphaned only son of a cancer-ridden German beauty and a British sergeant of infantry killed in one of his country's many post-colonial wars, graduate of a rainy archipelago of orphanages, foster homes, half-mothers, cadet units and training camps, sometime army wolf-child with a special unit in even rainier Northern Ireland, caterer, chef, itinerant hotelier, perpetual escapee from emotional entanglements, volunteer, collector of other people's languages, self-exiled creature of the night and sailor without a destination, sat in his sanitary Swiss office behind reception, smoking his third unusual cigarette and pondering the sage words of the hotel's revered founder that hung framed alongside his imposing sepia photograph.

Several times in the last months Jonathan had taken up his pen in an effort to free the great man's wisdom from its tortuous German syntax, but his efforts had always foundered against some immovable dependent clause. "True hospitality gives to life what true cooking gives to eating," he began, believing for a moment that he had it. "It is the expression of our respect for the essential basic value of every individual creature entrusted to our care in the course of his travail through life, regardless of his condition, of mutual responsibility in the spirit of humanity invested in the—" Then he lost it again, as he always did. Some things were best left in the original.

His eye returned to Herr Strippli's tarty television set, squatting before him like a man's handbag. It had been playing the same electronic game for the last fifteen minutes. The aerial bomber's sights center on a gray fleck of building far below. The camera zooms closer. A missile speeds toward the target, enters and descends several floors. The base of the building pops like a paper bag, to the unctuous satisfaction of the newscaster. A bull's-eye. Two more shots for no extra money. Nobody talks about the casualties. From that height there aren't any. Iraq is not Belfast.

The image changed. Sophie and Jonathan are taking their drive.

· · ·

JONATHAN IS DRIVING, and Sophie's pulped face is partly hidden by a headscarf and dark glasses. Cairo is not yet awake. The red of dawn is coloring the dusty sky. To smuggle her out of the hotel and into his car, the undercover soldier has taken every precaution. He set out for the pyramids, not knowing she had a different spectacle in mind. "No," she says. "Go that way." A fetid oozing pillow of filth hangs over the crumbling tombs of Cairo's city cemetery. On a moonscape of smoking cinders amid shanties of plastic bags and tin cans, the wretched of the earth are crouched like Technicolor vultures, picking through the garbage. He parks the car on a sand verge. Lorries thunder past them on their way to and from the rubbish dump, leaving stink in their wake.

"This is where I brought him," she says. One side of her mouth is ridiculously swollen. She speaks through a hole in the other side.

"Why?" says Jonathan, meaning: Why are you now bringing me?

" 'Look at these people, Freddie,' I told him. 'Each time someone sells weapons to another tin-pot Arab tyrant, these people starve a little more. Do you know the reason? Listen to me, Freddie. Because it is more fun to have a pretty army than to feed the starving. You are an Arab, Freddie. Never mind that we Egyptians say we are not Arabs. We are Arabs. Is it right that your Arab brothers should be the flesh to pay for your dreams?' "

"I see," says Jonathan, with the embarrassment of an Englishman when faced with political emotion.

" 'We do not *need* leaders,' I said. 'The next great Arab will be a humble craftsman. He will make things work and give the people dignity instead of war. He will be an administrator, not a warrior. He will be like you, Freddie, as you could be if you grew up.' "

"What did Freddie say?" says Jonathan. Her

smashed features accuse him every time he looks at them. The bruises round her eyes are turning to blue and yellow.

"He told me to mind my own business." He catches the choke of fury in her voice, and his heart sinks further. "I told him it *was* my business! *Life and death* are my business! *Arabs* are my business! *He* was my business!"

And you warned him, he thinks, sickened. You let him know you were a force to be reckoned with, not a weak woman to be discarded at his whim. You let him guess that you too had your secret weapon, and you threatened to do what I did, without knowing I'd done it already.

"The Egyptian authorities will not touch him," she says. "He bribes them, and they keep their distance."

"Leave town," Jonathan tells her. "You know what the Hamids are like. Get out."

"The Hamids can have me killed as easily in Paris as in Cairo."

"Tell Freddie he must help you. Make him stick up for you against his brothers."

"Freddie is frightened of me. When he is not being brave he is a coward. Why are you staring at the traffic?"

Because it's all there is to stare at apart from you and the wretched of the earth.

But she does not wait for an answer. Perhaps deep down this student of male weakness understands his shame.

"I should like some coffee, please. Egyptian." And the brave smile that hurts him more than all the recrimination in the world.

He gives her coffee in a street market and drives her back to the hotel car park. He telephones the Ogilveys' house and gets the maid. "Him out," she shouts. What about Mrs. Ogilvey? "Him not there." He telephones the embassy. Him not there either. Him gone to Alexandria for regatta.

He telephones the yacht club to leave a message. A drugged male voice says there is no regatta today.

Jonathan telephones an American friend named Larry Kermody in Luxor: Larry, is that guest suite of yours empty?

He telephones Sophie. "An archaeologist friend of mine in Luxor has a spare flat," he says. "It's in a place called the Chicago House. You're welcome to use it for a week or two." He searches for humor in the silence. "It's a kind of monk's cell for visiting academics, stuck onto the back of the house, with its own bit of rooftop. Nobody need even know you're there."

"Will you come also, Mr. Pine?"

Jonathan does not allow himself a moment's hesitation. "Can you dump your bodyguard?"

"He has already dumped himself. Freddie has apparently decided I am not worth protecting."

He telephones a travel agent who does business with the hotel, a beery-voiced Englishwoman called Stella. "Stella, listen. Two VIP guests, incognito, want to fly to Luxor tonight, expense no object. I know the whole place is shut up. I know there are no planes. What can you do?"

A long silence. Stella is psychic. Stella has been in Cairo too long: "Well, I know *you're* very important, darling, but who's the girl?" And she gives a foul, wheezing laugh that chokes and whistles in Jonathan's ear long after he has rung off.

· · ·

JONATHAN AND SOPHIE sit side by side on the flat roof of the Chicago House, drinking vodka and staring at the stars. On the flight she has barely spoken. He has offered her food, but she wants none. He has put a shawl over her shoulders.

"Roper is the worst man in the world," she announces.

Jonathan's experience of the world's villains is limited. His instinct is to blame himself first and others afterwards.

"I guess anyone in his business is pretty frightful," he says.

"He has no excuse," she retorts, unappeased by his moderation. "He is healthy. He is white. He is rich. He is wellborn, well educated. He has grace." Roper's enormity grows as she contemplates his virtues. "He is at ease with the world. He is amusing. Confident. Yet he destroys it. What is missing in him?" She waits for him to say something, but in vain. "How does he come to be like this? He was not dragged up in the back streets. He is blessed. You are a man. Perhaps you know."

But Jonathan doesn't know anything anymore. He is watching the outline of her battered face against the night sky. *What will you do?* he was asking her in his mind. *What will I?*

He switched off Herr Strippli's television set. The war ended. I loved you. I loved you with your smashed face as we walked at arm's length among the temples of Karnak. *Mr. Pine,* you said, *it is time to make the rivers flow uphill.*

. . .

IT WAS two a.m., the hour at which Herr Meister required Jonathan to make his rounds. He began in the lobby, where he always began. He stood at the center of the carpet where Roper had stood, and listened to the restless night sounds of the hotel, sounds that by day were lost in the hubbub: the throb of the furnace, the growl of a vacuum cleaner, the clink of plates from the room-service kitchen, the footfall of a waiter on the back stair. He stood where he stood every night, imagining her stepping from the lift, her face repaired, her dark glasses shoved into her black hair, crossing the lobby and pulling up before him while she quizzically examines him for flaws. "You are Mr. Pine. The flower of England. And you betrayed me." Old Horwitz the night concierge was sleeping at his counter. He had laid his cropped head in the crook of his arm. You're still a refugee, Horwitz, thought Jonathan. March and sleep. March and sleep. He set the old man's empty coffee cup safely outside his reach.

At the reception desk, Fräulein Eberhardt had been relieved by Fräulein Vipp, a grayed, obliging woman with a brittle smile.

"Can I see tonight's late arrivals, please, Fräulein Vipp?"

She handed him the Tower Suite registration forms. Alexander, Lord Langbourne, alias no doubt Sandy. Address: Tortola, British Virgin Islands. Profession, according to Corkoran: Peer of the realm. Accompanied by wife, Caroline. No reference to the long hair tied at the nape, or to what a peer of the realm might do apart from being a peer. Onslow Roper, Richard. Profession: Company director. Jonathan leafed briskly through the rest of the forms. Frobisher, Cyril: Pilot. MacArthur, Somebody, and Danby, Somebody Else: Company executives. Other assistants, other pilots, bodyguards. Inglis, Francis, from Perth, Australia—Francis, hence Frisky, presumably: Physical-training instructor. Jones, Tobias, from South Africa—Tobias, hence Tabby: Athlete. He had left her till last deliberately, like the one good photograph in a batch of misses. Marshall, Jemima W. Address, like Roper's, a numbered box in Nassau. British. Occupation—rendered with a particular flourish by the Major—*Equestrienne.*

"Can you do me copies of these, Fräulein Vipp? We're conducting a survey of Tower Suite guests."

"Naturally, Mr. Pine," said Fräulein Vipp, taking the forms to the back office.

"Thank you, Fräulein Vipp," said Jonathan.

But in his imagination it is himself that Jonathan sees, laboring over the photocopier in the Queen Nefertiti Hotel while Sophie smokes and watches him: *You are adept,* she says. Yes, I am adept. I spy. I betray. I love when it is too late.

Frau Merthan was the telephone operator, another soldier of the night, whose sentry box was an airless cubicle beside reception.

"Guten Abend, Frau Merthan."

"Good morning, Mr. Jonathan."

It was their joke.

"Gulf war running nicely, I trust?" Jonathan glanced at the bulletins dangling from the newsprinter. "Bombing continues unabated. One thousand missions already flown. Safety in numbers, they say."

"So much money to spend on one Arab," said Frau Merthan with disapproval.

He began tidying the papers, an instinctive habit that had been with him since his first school dormitory. As he did so his eye caught the faxes. One sleek tray for incoming, contents to be distributed in the morning. One sleek tray for out-going, waiting to be returned to their senders.

"Lots of telephone activity, Frau Merthan? Panic selling across the globe? You must be feeling like the hub of the universe."

"Princesse du Four must call her cousin in Vladivostok. Every night, now that things are better in Russia, she calls Vladivostok and speaks to him for one hour. Every night she gets cut off and must be reconnected. I think she is looking for her prince."

"How about the princes in the Tower?" he asked. "They seemed to be living on the telephone from the moment they got in there."

Frau Merthan tapped a couple of keys and peered at the screen through her bifocals. "Belgrade, Panama, Brussels, Nairobi, Nassau, Prague, London, Paris, Tortola, England somewhere, Prague again, more Nassau. All direct. Soon it will be only direct and I shall have no job."

"One day all of us will be robots," Jonathan assured her. Leaning over Frau Merthan's counter he affected a layman's curiosity.

"Does that screen of yours show the actual numbers they ring?" he asked.

"Naturally; otherwise the guests complain immediately. It's normal."

"Show me."

She showed him. Roper knows the wicked people everywhere, Sophie had said.

In the dining room, Bobbi the odd-job man was balanced on an aluminum ladder, cleaning the droplets of a chandelier with his spider mop. Jonathan trod lightly in order not to disturb his concentration. In the bar, Herr Kaspar's nymphet nieces in trembling smocks and stone-washed jeans were replenishing pot plants. Bouncing up to him, the elder girl displayed a pile of muddy cigarette stubs in her gloved palm.

"Do men do this in their own homes?" she demanded, lifting her breasts to him in saucy indignation. "Put their fag ends in the flowerpots?"

"I should think so, Renate. Men do the most unspeakable things at the drop of a hat." Ask Ogilvey, he thought. In his abstraction, her pertness annoyed him unreasonably. "I'd watch out for that piano if I were you. Herr Meister will kill you if you scratch it."

In the kitchens, the night chefs were preparing a dormitory feast for the German newlyweds on the Bel Étage: steak tartare for him, smoked salmon for her, a bottle of Meursault to revive their ardor. Jonathan watched Alfred the Austrian night waiter give a sensitive tuck with his fine fingers at the napkin rosettes and add a bowl of camelias for romance. Alfred was a failed ballet dancer and put "Artist" in his passport.

"They're bombing Baghdad, then," he said with satisfaction while he worked. "That'll teach them."

"Did the Tower Suite eat tonight?"

Alfred took a breath and recited. His smile was becoming a little young for him. "Three smoked salmon, one fish and chips English style, four fillet steak medium, and a double dollop of carrot cake and *Schlag,* which you call *Rahm.* Carrot cake is what His Highness has for a religion. He told me. And from the Herr Major, on His Highness's instructions, a fifty-franc tip. You English always tip when you're in love."

"Do we indeed?" said Jonathan. "I must remember that." He ascended the great staircase. Roper's not in love; he's just rutting. Probably hired her from some tarts' agency, so much a night. He had arrived at the double doorway to the Grande Suite. The newlyweds were also newly shod, he noticed: he in patent black with buckles, she in gold sandals flung impatiently where they lay. Impelled by a lifetime of obedience, Jonathan stooped and placed them side by side.

Reaching the top floor, he put his ear to Frau Loring's door and heard the braying of a British military pundit over the hotel's cable network. He knocked. She was wearing her late husband's dressing gown over her nightdress. Coffee was glugging on a ring. Sixty years of Switzerland had not altered her High German by a single explosive consonant.

"They are children. But they are fighting, so they are men," she announced in his mother's perfect accents, handing him a cup.

The British television pundit was moving model soldiers round a sandbox with the fervor of a convert.

"So the Tower Suite is full of whom to-night?" asked Frau Loring, who knew everything.

"Oh, some English mogul and his cohorts. Roper. Mr. Roper and party. And one lady half his age."

"The staff say she is exquisite."

"I didn't look."

"And quite unspoilt. Natural."

"Well, they should know."

She was studying him the way she always did when he sounded casual. Sometimes she seemed to know him better than he knew himself.

"You are glowing tonight. You could light a city. What is going on inside you?"

"I expect it's the snow."

"So nice the Russians are on our side at last. No?"

"It's a great diplomatic achievement."

"It's a miracle," Frau Loring corrected him. "And like most miracles, nobody believes in it."

She handed him his coffee and sat him firmly in his usual chair. Her television set was enormous, bigger than the war. Happy troops waving from armored personnel carriers. More missiles racing prettily to their mark. The sibilant shuffle of tanks. Mr. Bush taking another encore from his admiring audience.

"You know what I feel when I watch war?" Frau Loring asked.

"Not yet," he said tenderly. But she seemed to have forgotten what she had meant to say.

Or perhaps Jonathan does not hear it, for the clarity of her assertions reminds him irresistibly of Sophie. The joyful fruition of his love for her is forgotten. Even Luxor is forgotten. He is back in Cairo for the final awful act.

· · ·

HE IS standing in Sophie's penthouse, dressed— what the hell does it matter what I wore?— dressed in this very dinner jacket, while a uniformed Egyptian police inspector and his two plainclothes assistants eye him with the borrowed stillness of the dead. The blood is everywhere, reeking like old iron. On the walls, on the ceiling and divan. It is spilled like wine across the dressing table. Clothes, clocks, tapestries, books in French and Arabic and English, gilt mirrors, scents and ladies' paint—all have been trashed by a gigantic infant in a tantrum. Sophie herself is by comparison an insignificant feature of this havoc. Half crawling, perhaps toward the open French windows leading to her white roof garden, she lies in what the Army First Aid Manual used to call the recovery position, with her head on her outstretched arm, a counterpane draped across her lower body, and over the upper part the remnants of a blouse or nightdress, of which the color is unlikely ever to be known. Other policemen are doing other things, none with much conviction. One man is leaning over the parapet of the roof garden, apparently in search of a culprit. Another is fiddling with the door of Sophie's wall safe, making it plop as he works it back and forth across its smashed hinges. Why do they wear black holsters? Jonathan wonders. Are they night people too?

From the kitchen a man's voice is talking Arabic into the telephone. Two more policemen guard the front door, leading to the landing, where a bunch of first-class cruise passengers in silk dressing gowns and face-cream stare indignantly at their protectors. A uniformed boy with a notebook takes a statement. A Frenchman is saying he will call his lawyer.

"Our guests on the floor below are complaining about the disturbance," Jonathan tells the inspector. He realizes he has made a tactical mistake. At a moment of violent death it is neither natural nor polite to explain one's presence.

"You was friends with thisser woman?" the inspector asks. A cigarette hangs from his lips.

Does he know about Luxor?

Does Hamid?

The best lies are told face-to-face, with a touch of arrogance: "She liked to make use of the hotel," Jonathan replies, still fighting for a natural tone. "Who did this? What happened?"

The inspector shrugs a prolonged, disinterested shrug. *Freddie is not normally troubled by the Egyptian authorities. He bribes them, and they keep their distance.*

"You was having sex with thisser woman?" the inspector asks.

Did they see us board the plane?

Follow us to the Chicago House?

Bug the flat?

Jonathan has found his calm. He can do that. The more terrible the occasion, the more certainly can his calm be relied upon. He affects a certain irritation: "If you call the odd cup of coffee sex. She had a bodyguard. He was employed by Mr. Hamid. Where is he? Has he disappeared? Perhaps the bodyguard did it."

The inspector appears unimpressed. "Hamid? What is Hamid, please?"

"Freddie Hamid. The youngest of the Mr. Hamids."

The inspector frowns as if the name is not agreeable to him, or not relevant, or not known. Of his two assistants, one is bald, the other ginger-haired. They wear jeans and bomber jackets and a lot of facial hair. Both are listening intently.

"What you talk with thisser woman? You are political with her?"

"Small talk."

"Small?"

"Restaurants. Social gossip. Fashion. Mr.

Hamid sometimes took her to the yacht club, here or in Alexandria. We'd smile at each other. Wave good morning."

"You killer this woman?"

Yes, he replies in his mind. *Not in quite the way you think, but yes, I definitely killered her.*

"No," he says.

The inspector hitches his black belt with both his thumbs at once. His trousers are also black, his buttons and insignia gold. He loves his uniform very much. An acolyte is addressing him, but the inspector pays him no attention.

"She ever tell you that someone wish to killer her?" the inspector asks Jonathan.

"Of course not."

"Why, please?"

"If she had done I would have reported it to you."

"Okay. You go now."

"Have you contacted Mr. Hamid? What are you going to do?"

The inspector touches the peak of his black cap in order to give authority to his theory. "Was burglar. Crazy burglar killer woman. Maybe drug."

Bleary-eyed medics in green overalls and sneakers are arriving with a stretcher and a body bag. Their leader wears dark glasses. The inspector grinds the stub of his cigarette into the carpet and lights another. A camera is flashing, operated by a man in rubber gloves. Everyone has raided the properties chest in order to wear something different. Lifting her onto the stretcher, they turn her over, and one white breast, much diminished, slips free of its torn covering. Jonathan notices her face. It has been almost obliterated, perhaps by kicks, perhaps by a pistol butt.

"She had a dog," he says. "A Pekingese."

But even as he speaks he spots it through the open doorway to the kitchen. It lies on the tiles, straighter than it has ever lain before. A gash like a zipper runs along its underbelly from its throat to its back legs. Two men, Jonathan thinks dully: one to hold, one to cut; one to hold, one to beat.

"She was a British subject," Jonathan says, using the past tense to punish himself. "You'd better call the embassy."

But the inspector is no longer listening. The bald assistant takes Jonathan by the arm and starts to lead him to the door. For a moment— but it is long enough—Jonathan feels the heat of combat race across his shoulders, down his arms and into his hands. The assistant feels it also and steps back as if he has received a shock. Then he smiles dangerously in kinship. As he does so, Jonathan feels the panic taking hold of him. Not of fear, but of permanent and inconsolable loss. I loved you. And never even admitted it, to you or to myself.

. . .

FRAU MERTHAN was dozing beside her switchboard. Sometimes very late she rang her girlfriend and whispered dirty to her, but not tonight. Six incoming faxes for the Tower Suite lay waiting for the morning, together with the originals of last night's outgoing. Jonathan eyed but did not touch them. He was listening to Frau Merthan's breathing. He passed his hand tentatively across her closed eyes. She let out a piggish snore. Like a skilled child stealing from his mother's shopping bag, he coaxed the faxes from their trays. Will the copier still be warm? Has the lift returned empty from the top floor? *You killer her?* He touched a key on Frau Merthan's computer, then another, then a third. *You are adept.* The computer peeped, and he had another disconcerting vision of Roper's woman descending the Tower Suite stairs. Who were the Brussels boys? Who was Appetites from Miami? Who was Soldier Boris? Frau Merthan turned her head and growled. He began writing down the telephone numbers while she went on snoring.

· · ·

EX–JUNIOR LEADER JONATHAN PINE, a sergeant's son trained to fight in all weathers, crunched down the snowy footpath beside a hillside stream as it bubbled and tumbled through the woods. He was wearing an anorak over his dinner jacket and a pair of light climbing boots over his midnight-blue socks. His patent-leather evening shoes dangled in a plastic bag at his left side. All round him in trees and gardens and along the bank, the snow's tracery sparkled under a perfect blue sky. But Jonathan for once was indifferent to such beauty. He was heading toward his staff apartment in the Klosbachstrasse, and the time was eight-twenty in the morning. I shall eat a serious breakfast, he decided: boiled eggs, toast, coffee. Sometimes it was a pleasure to serve oneself. Perhaps a bath first to restore him. And over breakfast, if he could get himself onto a single track, he would decide. He slipped a hand inside his anorak. The envelope was still in place. Where am I going? A fool is someone who does not learn by experience. Why do I feel battle-bright?

Approaching the house that contained his apartment, Jonathan discovered that his step had settled to a marching rhythm. Far from relenting, it conveyed him instead to the Römerhof, where a tram waited for him with its doors ominously open. He rode in it without any opinion as to his behavior, the alien brown envelope stabbing at his chest. Alighting at the main railway station, he allowed himself with the same passivity to proceed once more on foot as far as an austere building in the Bleicherweg, where a number of countries, among them his own, maintained consular and commercial representatives.

"I'd like to speak to Wing Commander Quayle, please," Jonathan said to the big-jawed

Englishwoman behind the bulletproof window. He extracted his envelope and slid it under the glass. "It's a private matter. Perhaps you'll tell him I'm a friend of Mark Ogilvey from Cairo. We sailed together."

. . .

WAS THE AFFAIR of Herr Meister's wine cellar partly responsible for Jonathan's decision to vote with his feet? A short while before Roper's arrival, Jonathan had been incarcerated in it for sixteen hours, and he recalled the experience as an introductory course in death.

Among the extra duties entrusted to Jonathan by Herr Meister was the preparation of the monthly inventory of the fine-wine cellar, which lay deep in the blue rock underneath the oldest part of the hotel. Jonathan customarily undertook this task on the first Monday of each month, before beginning the six-day break to which he was by contract entitled in lieu of weekends. On the Monday in question, his routine did not vary.

The insurance value of the fine wines had recently been set at six and a half million Swiss francs. The cellar's security devices were of a commensurate complexity. One combination and two inertia locks had to be released before a fourth, a spring lock, would yield. A baleful video camera eyed each suitor as he approached. Having successfully negotiated the locks, Jonathan embarked upon his ritual count, beginning as usual with the 1961 Château Pétrus, offered this year at four thousand five hundred francs a bottle, and graduating to the ten-thousand-franc magnums of 1945 Mouton Rothschild. He was in the middle of his calculations when the lights went out.

Now Jonathan loathed the dark. Why else does a man elect to work at night? As a boy he had read Edgar Allan Poe and shared every hell endured by the victim of "The Cask of Amontillado." No mining disaster, no collapsed tunnel or story of alpinists trapped in a crevasse, but had its separate gravestone in his memory.

He stood motionless, deprived of orientation. Was he upside down? Had he had a stroke? Had he been blown up? The mountaineer in him braced himself for impact. The blinded sailor clung to the wreckage. The trained combatant edged toward his invisible adversary without the comfort of a weapon. Wading like a deep-sea diver, Jonathan began feeling his way along the wine racks, in search of a light switch. Telephone, he thought. Did the cellar have a telephone? His habit of observation was a hindrance to him. It was retrieving too many images. The door: had the door a handle on the inside? By brute mental force he managed to recall a buzzer. But the buzzer needed electricity.

He lost his hold upon the cellar's geography and began circling the racks like a fly inside a black lampshade. Nothing in his training had equipped him for anything as awful as this. No endurance marches, hand-to-hand-combat courses or deprival exercises were of the least avail. He remembered reading that goldfish had such short memories that each circuit of the bowl was a brand-new thrill for them. He was sweating, he was probably weeping. He yelled several times: Help me! It's Pine! The name tinkled to nothing. The bottles! he thought. The bottles will save me! He contemplated hurling them into the darkness as a means of rousing help. But even in his dementia his self-discipline won the day, and he could not muster the irresponsibility to smash bottle after bottle of Château Pétrus at four and a half thousand a go.

Who would notice he was missing? So far as the staff knew, he had left the hotel for his monthly six days off. The inventory belonged technically to his free time, a bad bargain wheedled out of him by Herr Meister. His landlady would assume he had decided to sleep at the hotel, a thing he did occasionally when there were spare rooms. If no chance-millionaire came to his aid by ordering a bottle of fine wine, he would be dead before anyone noticed his absence. And millionaires were grounded by the impending war.

Willing himself into a calmer state, Jonathan sat to attention on what felt like a cardboard crate and strove with all his might to make order of his life till now, a last tidying before he died: the good times he had had, the lessons he had drawn, the improvements he had wrought upon his personality, the good women. There were none. Times, women, lessons. None. None but Sophie, who was dead. Look at himself how he might, he saw nothing but half-measures, failures and undignified withdrawals, and Sophie was the monument to all of them. In childhood he had struggled night and day to be an inadequate adult. As a special serviceman he had cloaked himself in blind obedience and, with occasional lapses, endured. As a lover, husband and adulterer, his record was quite as thin: a burst or two of wary pleasure, followed by years of abuse and craven apology.

And gradually it dawned on him, if a dawning can take place in total blackness, that his life had consisted of a run of rehearsals for a play he had failed to take part in. And that what he needed to do from now on, if there was going to be a now on, was abandon his morbid quest for order and treat himself to a little chaos, on the grounds that while order was demonstrably no substitute for happiness, chaos might open the way to it.

He would leave Meister's.

He would buy a boat, something he could manage single-handed.

He would find the one girl he cared about and love her in present time, a Sophie without the betrayal.

He would make friends.

He would find a home. And, for want of parents of his own, become a parent himself.

He would do anything, absolutely anything, rather than cringe any longer in the gloom of servile equivocation where, as it now seemed to him, he had wasted his life, and Sophie's.

His savior was Frau Loring. With her customary vigilance, she had noticed him through her net curtains on his way to the cellar, and realized belatedly that he had not returned. When the posse arrived to release him, shouting "Herr Pine! Herr Jonathan!" and led by Herr Meister wearing a hair net and armed with a twelve-watt car lamp, Jonathan was not, as might have been expected, mad-eyed with terror but at his ease.

Only the English, they assured one another as they led him to the light, were capable of such composure.

FOUR

THE RECRUITMENT of Jonathan Pine, former undercover soldier, by Leonard Burr, former intelligence officer, was conceived by Burr immediately after Jonathan presented himself to Wing Commander Quayle but only accomplished after tense weeks of Whitehall infighting, despite the mounting clamor from Washington and Whitehall's perpetual urge to earn merit in the fickle corridors of Capitol Hill.

The title of Jonathan's part of the project was first Trojan, then hastily changed to Limpet—the reason being that while some members of the joint team might not know much about Homer's wooden horse, they all knew that Trojan was the brand name of one of America's most popular condoms. But Limpet was fine. A limpet attaches itself through thick and thin.

Jonathan was a godsend, and nobody knew this better than Burr, who from the moment the first reports from Miami started landing on his desk had been beating his brains for some way, *any* way, into the Roper camp. But how? Even Burr's mandate to operate hung by a thread, as he discovered when he took his first soundings about the feasibility of his plan.

"My master is a bit *chary,* frankly, Leonard," a mandarin called Goodhew confided skittishly to Burr over the secure telephone. "Yesterday it was all about the cost, today he's not keen on aggravating an uneasy situation in a former colony."

The Sunday papers had once described Rex Goodhew as Whitehall's Talleyrand without the limp. But as usual they had it wrong, for Goodhew was nothing that he seemed. If there was a separateness about him, it came of virtue, not intrigue. His mangy smile, flat cap and bicycle concealed nothing more sinister than a high-minded Anglican of reforming zeal. And if you were ever lucky enough to penetrate his private life, you found, instead of mystery, a pretty wife and clever children who adored him.

"Uneasy, my Aunt Fanny, Rex!" Burr exploded. "The Bahamas is the easiest country in the hemisphere. There's hardly a bigwig in Nassau isn't up to his ears in cocaine. There's more bent politicians and shady arms dealers on that one island—"

"Steady down, Leonard," Rooke warned him, from across the room. Rob Rooke was Burr's restraining hand, a retired soldier of fifty with grizzled hair and a rugged, weather-beaten jaw. But Burr was in no mood to heed him.

"As to the rest of your premise, Leonard," Goodhew resumed, undaunted, "which personally I thought you presented with *tremendous* brio, even if you were a *trifle* long on adjectives, my master called that 'reading tea leaves with a dash of special pleading for good measure.' "

Goodhew was referring to his minister, a silky politician not yet turned forty.

"Tea leaves?" Burr echoed in furious bewilderment. "What's he bleating about tea leaves for? That's a five-star, chapter-and-verse, verifiable report from a highly placed informant of American Enforcement. It's a miracle Strelski ever showed it to us! What's *tea leaves* about that?"

Once more Goodhew waited for Burr to finish his tirade. "Now for the *next* question—my master's again, Leonard, not mine, so don't shoot the messenger! When do you propose to advise our friends across the river?"

He was referring this time to Burr's former service and present rival, which traded in Pure Intelligence from a grim tower block on the South Bank.

"Never," Burr retorted belligerently.

"Well, I think you should."

"Why?"

"My master regards your old colleagues as realists. Far too easy, in a small, very new and, dare he say it, *idealistic* new agency such as yours, not to see beyond one's fence. He'd feel more comfortable if you had the River boys aboard."

The last of Burr's self-restraint gave way. "You mean your master would like to see someone else bludgeoned to death in a Cairo flat, is that it?''

Rooke had risen to his feet and was standing like a traffic policeman, his right hand raised for "halt." On the telephone, Goodhew's flippancy gave way to something harder.

"What *are* you suggesting, Leonard? Perhaps you'd better not explain."

"I'm suggesting nothing. I'm telling you. I've *worked* with your master's realists, Rex. I've lived with them. Lied with them. I *know* them. I *know* Geoffrey Darker. And I *know* his Procurement Studies Group. I *know* their houses in Marbella, and their second Porsches in the garage, and their unstinted devotion to the free market economy, provided it's *their* freedom and somebody *else*'s economy. Because I've *been* there!''

"Leonard, I will not hear you, and you know I won't."

"And I *know* there's more crookery in that shop, more bad promises to keep, more lunching with the enemy, and gamekeepers turned poachers, than is healthy for my operation, or my agency!''

"Just stop," Rooke advised quietly.

As Burr slammed down the telephone, a sash window slipped its ancient fastening and toppled like a guillotine. Patiently, Rooke folded a used brown envelope, raised the sash and wedged it in place.

Burr was still sitting with his hands buried in

his face, speaking through his splayed fingers. "What the hell does he want, Rob? One minute I'm to frustrate Geoffrey Darker and all his wicked works, the next he's ordering me to collaborate with Darker. What the bloody hell does he *want?*"

"He wants you to ring him back," said Rooke patiently.

"Darker *is* wicked. You know that, I know that. On a clear day, so does Rex Goodhew. So why do we have to ponce around pretending Darker's a realist?"

Burr rang Goodhew back nonetheless, which was only proper because, as Rooke constantly reminded him, Goodhew was the best and only champion he had.

In appearance Rooke and Burr could scarcely have been more different: Rooke the military parade horse in his nearly good suits, Burr as slovenly in his manner as his speech. There was a Celt in Burr somewhere, an artist and a rebel—Goodhew said a gypsy. When he troubled to dress himself for an occasion, he only contrived to look more disreputable than when he wasn't bothering. Burr, as he would tell you himself, was the other kind of Yorkshireman. His forebears were not miners but handloom weavers, which meant they had owned their lives instead of being vassals in a corporate endeavor. The blackened sandstone village where Burr had grown to manhood was built onto a south-facing hillside, with each house looking at the sun and each attic window stretched to catch the most of it. In their solitary lofts, Burr's forefathers had woven all alone and all day long, while the womenfolk downstairs chattered and did the spinning. The men led lives of monotony in communion with the sky. And while their hands mechanically performed the daily drudgery, their minds took off in all sorts of startling directions. In that one small town, there are tales to fill a book about the poets, chess players and mathematicians whose brains grew to fruition in the long daylight of their attic eyries. And Burr, all the way to Oxford and beyond, was the inheritor of their collective thrift, their virtue and their mysticism.

So that it was somehow written in the stars, from the day Goodhew plucked Burr from the River House and gave him his own under-financed, underwanted agency, that Burr should appoint Richard Onslow Roper as his personal Antichrist.

· · ·

OH, there had been others before Roper. In the dying years of the Cold War, before the new agency was a twinkle in Goodhew's eye, when Burr was already dreaming of the post-Thatcher Jerusalem and even his most honorable colleagues in Pure Intelligence were casting about for other people's enemies and jobs, there were few insiders who did not remember Burr's vendettas against such renowned illegals of the eighties as the gray-suited billionaire "scrap-metal dealer" Tyler, who flew standby, or the monosyllabic "accountant" Lorimer, who made all his calls from public pay phones, or the odious Sir Anthony Joyston Bradshaw, gentleman and occasional satrap of Darker's so-called Procurement Studies Group, who ran a vast estate on the fringes of Newbury and rode to hounds with his butler mounted at his side, equipped with stirrup cup and foie gras sandwiches.

But Richard Onslow Roper, said the Burr-watchers, was the adversary Leonard had always dreamed of. Everything Leonard was looking for to appease his Fabian conscience, Dicky Roper possessed in trumps. In Roper's past there was neither striving nor disadvantage. Class, privilege, everything Burr loathed, had been handed to Roper on a salver. Burr even had a special voice for talking about him: "our Dicky," he would call him, with a shove of his Yorkshire accent; or, for variety, "the Roper."

"He's tempting God, is our Dicky. Everything God's got, the Roper's got to have two of, and it'll be the undoing of him."

Such obsession did not always make for balance. Embattled in his shoestring agency, Burr had a tendency to see conspiracy everywhere. A file had only to go missing, a permission be delayed, for him to scent the long arm of Darker's people.

"I tell you, Rob, if the Roper committed daylight armed robbery in full view of the Lord Chief Justice of England—"

"The Chief Justice would lend him his jemmy," Rooke suggested. "And Darker would have bought it for him. Come on. Lunch."

In their dingy offices in Victoria Street, the two men would prowl and brood till late into the evenings. The Roper's file ran to eleven volumes and half a dozen secret annexes, flagged and cross-referred. Put together, it documented his steady glide from the gray or semitolerated arms deal all the way to what Burr called dark black.

But the Roper had other files: at Defence, the Foreign Office, the Home Office, the Bank of England, the Treasury, Overseas Development, the Inland Revenue. To obtain them without arousing curiosity in the circles where Darker might have allies required stealth and luck, and occasionally Rex Goodhew's devious connivance. Pretexts had to be invented, unwanted papers requested, in order to confuse the scent.

Gradually, nevertheless, an archive was assembled. First thing in the morning a policeman's daughter called Pearl would trundle in a metal trolley with the purloined records patched and bandaged like casualties of war, and Burr's little team of dedicated assistants would resume its work. Last thing at night she trundled them back to their cell. The trolley had a wonky wheel, and you could hear it whistling down the linoleum corridor. They called it Roper's tumbril.

. . .

BUT EVEN in the midst of these exertions, Burr never took his mind's eye off Jonathan. "Don't let him risk his hand now, Reggie," he urged Quayle over the secure telephone while he champed and waited for what Goodhew sarcastically referred to as his master's official, final maybe. "He's not to go stealing any more faxes or listening at key-holes, Reggie. He's to tread water and act natural. Is he still angry with us over Cairo? I'll not flirt with him till I know I can have him. I've been that road before." And to Rooke, "I'm telling no one, Rob. He's Mr. Brown for the lot of them. Darker and his friend Ogilvey have taught me a lesson I'll not ignore."

As a further desperate precaution, Burr opened a decoy file for Jonathan, gave it a ficti-tious name, fronted it with the particulars of a fictitious agent, and surrounded it with a conspic-uous secrecy, which he hoped would draw the eye of any predator. Paranoia? Rooke suggested. Burr swore it was no more than a sensible precau-tion. He knew too well the lengths that Darker would go to in order to do down a rival—even one as humble as Burr's tin-pot outfit.

Meanwhile in his neat script Burr added note

after note to Jonathan's fast-expanding dossier, which he kept in an untitled folder in the dreariest corner of the registry. Through intermediaries, Rooke drew the army papers on Jonathan's father. The son was barely six years old when Sergeant Peter Pine won his posthumous Military Medal in Aden for "outstanding courage in the face of the enemy." A press cutting showed a ghostly child displaying it on the breast of his blue mackintosh outside the palace gates. A weeping aunt escorted him. His mother was not well enough to attend. A year later she too was dead.

"Those are usually the chaps who love the army best," Rooke commented in his simple way. "Can't think why he gave it up."

By the age of thirty-three, Peter Pine had fought the Mau Mau in Kenya, chased Grivas across Cyprus and battled with guerrillas in Malaya and northern Greece. Nobody had a bad word to say of him.

"A sergeant and a gentleman," Burr the anticolonialist told Goodhew wryly.

Returning to the son, Burr pored over reports of Jonathan's progress through army foster homes, civilian orphanages and the Duke of York's Military School in Dover. Their inconsistency quickly incensed him. *Timid,* ran one; *plucky,* another; *a solitary, a grand mixer,* an *inward* boy, an *outgoing* one, *a natural leader, lacks charisma,* back and forth like a pendulum. And once, *very involved with foreign languages,* as if this were a morbid symptom of something better left alone. But it was the word *unreconciled* that got Burr's goat.

"Who the hell ever decreed," he demanded indignantly, "that a sixteen-year-old boy of no fixed abode, who's never had a chance to know parental love, should be *reconciled?*"

Rooke took his pipe from his mouth and frowned, which was about as near as he came to indulging in an abstract argument.

"What does cabby mean?" Burr demanded from deep in his reading.

"Street wise, among other things. Pushy."

Burr was at once offended. "Jonathan's not *street wise.* He's not wise at all. He's putty. What's a roulement?"

"A five-month tour," Rooke replied patiently.

Burr had come upon Jonathan's record in Ireland, where, after a succession of special training courses, for which he had volunteered, he had been assigned to close observation duties in the bandit country of South Armagh.

"What was Operation Night Owl?"

"I haven't the foggiest idea."

"Come on, Rob. You're the soldier in the family."

Rooke rang the Ministry of Defence, to be told the Night Owl papers were too highly classified to be released to an unchartered agency.

"Unchartered?" Rooke exploded, blushing darker than his mustache. "What the devil do they think we are? Some Whitehall bucket shop? Good Lord!"

But Burr was too preoccupied to relish Rooke's rare outburst. He had fixed upon the image of the pale boy wearing his father's medal for the convenience of photographers. Burr was by now molding Jonathan in his mind. Jonathan was their man, he was sure of it. No cautious words from Rooke could soften his conviction.

"When God finished putting together Dicky Roper," he told Rooke earnestly over a Friday evening curry, "He took a deep breath and shuddered a bit, then He ran up our Jonathan to restore the ecological balance."

· · ·

THE NEWS Burr had been praying for came exactly a week later. They had stayed in to wait for it. Goodhew had told them to.

"Leonard?"

"Yes, Rex."

"May we agree that this conversation is not taking place? Or not until after Monday's meeting of the Joint Steering Committee?"

"If you like."

"Here's the bottom line. We've had to toss them a few trinkets, or they'd have sulked. *You* know how the Treasury is." Burr didn't. "Number one. It's an Enforcement case, one hundred percent. Planning and execution to be yours exclusively, the River House to provide support in aid, theirs not to reason why. Do I hear shouts of hooray? I don't think I do."

"How exclusive is exclusively?" said Burr the wary Yorkshireman.

"Where you have to use outside resources, you obviously take pot-luck. One can't, for instance, expect the River boys to run a telephone check for one and not take a peek at the product before they lick the envelope. Can one?"

"I'll say one can't. What about our gallant American Cousins?"

"Langley, Virginia, like their counterparts across the Thames, will remain outside the charmed circle. It's like to like. The *Lex Goodhew*. If Pure Intelligence is to be held at bay in London, then it stands to reason that their opposite numbers in Langley must also be held at bay. Thus have I argued, and thus has my master heard me. Leonard . . . ? Leonard, are you sleeping there below?"

"Goodhew, you're a bloody genius."

"Number three—or is it D? My master in his capacity as minister responsible will nominally hold your tiny hand, but only with the thickest possible gloves, because his latest phobia is scandal." The flightiness disappeared from Goodhew's voice, and the proconsul came through. "So nothing direct from you to him at all, thank you, Leonard. There's one route only to my master, and that's me. If I'm putting my reputation at risk, I don't want you muddling. Agreed?"

"How about my financial estimates?"

"What do you mean, how about them?"

"Have they been approved?"

The English damn fool returned: "Oh my goodness no, you silly boy! They have *not* been approved. They have been *endured* through gritted teeth. I've had to carve them up between three ministries *and* cadge some extra from my aunt. And since I personally shall be cooking the books, will you please account to *me* for your money as well as for your sins?"

Burr was too excited to bother with any more fine print. "So it's the green light," he said, as much for Rooke as for himself.

"With more than a dash of amber, thank you," Goodhew retorted. "No more snide digs at the Darker Procurement octopus, or silly talk about secret servants feathering their own nests. You're to be all honey with your American Enforcement buddies, but you will be, anyway, and you're not to lose my master his safe seat or his shiny car. How would you like to report? Hourly? Three times a day before meals? Just remember we didn't have this conversation until after Monday's *agonized* deliberations, which on this occasion are a formality."

· · ·

YET IT WAS not till the U.S. Enforcement team actually set foot in London that Burr allowed himself to believe he had won the day. The American policemen brought a whiff of action with them that washed away the taste of interdepartmental haggling. Burr liked them at first sight, and they liked him, better than they liked the less winnable Rooke, whose army back stiffened as soon as he sat down with them. They warmed to Burr's blunt language and his short way with bureaucracy. They liked him better still when it became clear that he had forsaken the unsavory preserves of Pure Intelligence for the hard tack of defeating the enemy. Pure Intelligence for them meant all things bad, whether it resided in Langley or the River House. It meant turning a blind eye to some of the biggest crooks in the hemisphere for the sake of nebulous advantages elsewhere. It meant operations inexplicably abandoned in midstream and orders countermanded from on high. It meant callow Yale fantasists in button-down shirts who believed they could outwit the worst cut-throats in Latin America and always had six unbeatable arguments for doing the wrong thing.

First of the enforcers to arrive was the celebrated Joseph Strelski from Miami, a tight-jawed American-born Slav in training shoes and a leather jacket. When Burr had first heard his name five years before, Strelski had been leading

Washington's uncertain campaign against the illegal arms traffickers who were Burr's declared foe. In his fight against them, he had crashed head-on with the very people who should have been his allies. Hastily transferred to other duties, Strelski had enlisted himself in the war against the South American cocaine cartels and their appendages in the States: the crooked percentage lawyers and silk-shirt wholesalers, the arm's-length transportation syndicates and money launderers, and what he called the no-see-'em politicians and administrators who cleared the path and took their cut.

The dope cartels were now Strelski's obsession. America spends more money on dope than food, Leonard! he would protest, in a taxi, in a corridor, across a glass of 7-Up. We're talking the cost of the entire Vietnam war, Rob, every year, untaxed! After which he would rattle off the prevailing dope prices with the same enthusiasm with which other addicts quote the Dow-Jones index, starting with raw coca leaves at a dollar a kilo in Bolivia, rising to two thousand for a kilo of base in Colombia, to twenty thousand a wholesale kilo in Miami, to two hundred thousand a kilo at street. Then, as if he had caught himself being a bore again, he would pull a hard grin and say he was damned if he knew how anyone could pass up a profit of a hundred dollars to a dollar. But the grin did nothing to quench the cold fire in his eyes.

This permanent anger seemed to make Strelski almost physically unbearable to himself. Each morning early and each evening, whatever the weather, he went jogging in the royal parks, to Burr's simulated horror.

"Joe, for God's sake, have a big slice of plum pudding and sit still," Burr urged him, with mock severity. "You're giving us all heart attacks, just thinking about you."

Everyone laughed. Among the enforcers it was that kind of locker-room atmosphere. Only Amato, who was Strelski's Venezuelan-American sidekick, refused to smile. At their conferences, he sat with his mouth clamped into a grimace and his wine-black eyes staring into the horizon. Then suddenly on the Thursday he was beaming like an idiot. His wife had had a little girl.

Strelski's unlikely other arm was an overweight, meat-faced Irishman named Pat Flynn from U.S. Customs: the kind of policeman, Burr told Goodhew with relish, who typed his reports with his hat on. Legend attached to Flynn, and with reason. It was Pat Flynn, said the word, who had invented the first pinhole-lens camera, known as a pole camera and disguised as a junction box, that could be fixed to any stray telegraph post or pylon in a matter of seconds. It was Pat Flynn who had pioneered the art of bugging small boats from under water. And Pat Flynn had other skills, Strelski confided to Burr while the two men strolled together one early evening in St. James's Park, Strelski in his jogging gear and Burr in his crumpled suit.

"Pat was the one who knew the one who knew the one," said Strelski. "Without Pat, we'd never have gotten to Brother Michael."

Strelski was talking about his most sacred and delicate source, and this was holy ground. Burr never ventured onto it except at Strelski's invitation.

. . .

IF THE ENFORCERS bonded closer every day, the espiocrats from Pure Intelligence did not take lightly to their role as second-class citizens. The first exchange of gunfire occurred when Strelski let slip his agency's intention of putting Roper behind bars. Knew the very prison he had in mind for him, he cheerfully informed the company. "Sure do, sir. Little place called Marion, Illinois. Twenty-three and a half hours a day in solitary lock-down, no association, exercise in cuffs, food off a tray they shove at you through a slit in the cell. Ground floor's toughest, no views. Top floor's better, but the smell's worse."

Icy silence greeted this revelation, broken by an acid-voiced solicitor from the Cabinet Office.

"Are you sure this is the sort of thing we should be discussing, Mr. Strelski?" he asked with courtroom arrogance. "I had rather understood that an identified rogue was of more use to society when he was left at large. For as long as he's out and about, you can do what you want with him: identify his conspirators, identify *their* conspirators, listen, watch. Once you lock him up, you have to start the same game all over again with someone new. Unless you think you can stamp out this sort of thing altogether. Nobody here thinks that, do they? Not in this room?"

"Sir, in my submission there's basically two ways you can go," Strelski replied, with the respectful smile of an attentive pupil. "You can be exploitative, or you can enforce. Be exploitative, that's a never-ending story: that's recruiting the enemy so that you catch the next enemy. Then recruit the *next* enemy so that you catch the next one, ad infinitum. Enforce, that's what we have in mind for Mr. Roper. A fugitive from justice, in my book you apprehend him, you charge him under the International Trafficking in Arms regulations, and you lock him up. Exploitation, in the end you get to ask yourself who's being exploited: the fugitive, or the public, or justice."

"Strelski is a maverick," Goodhew confided to Burr with undisguised pleasure as they stood on the pavement under umbrellas. "You're two of a kind. No wonder the legal people have misgivings."

"Me, I've got misgivings about legal people."

Goodhew glanced up and down the rain-swept street. He was in sparkling mood. The previous day, his daughter had won a scholarship to South Hampstead, and his son, Julian, had been accepted by Clare College, Cambridge. "My master is having a severe case of the croup, Leonard. He has been talking to people again. Worse than scandal, he now fears he will look a bully. He is offended by the notion that he is instigating a wide-flung plot, mounted by two powerful governments against a lone British trader locked in battle against the recession. His sense of fair play tells him you are being disproportionate."

"Bully," Burr echoed softly, remembering Roper's eleven volumes of file, the tons of sophisticated weaponry lavished upon unsophisticated people. "Who's the bully? Jesus."

"Leave Jesus out of it, thank you. I need a counterblast. For Monday at first light. Brief enough to go on a postcard, no adjectives. And tell your nice man Strelski I *adored* his aria. Ah. We're saved. A bus."

· · ·

WHITEHALL IS A JUNGLE, but like other jungles, it has a few watering holes where creatures who at any other hour of the day would rip each other to pieces may assemble at sunset and drink their fill in precarious companionship. Such a place was the Fiddler's Club, situated in an upper room on the Thames Embankment and named after a pub called the Fiddler's Elbow, which used to stand next door.

"*I* think Rex is in the pay of a foreign power, don't you, Geoffrey?" said the solicitor from the Cabinet Office to Darker, while together they drew themselves a pint from the keg in the corner and signed a chit. "Don't you? *I* think he's taking Frog gold to undermine the effectiveness of British government. Cheers."

Darker was a small man, as men of power often are, with hollowed cheeks and sunken, steady eyes. He dressed in sharp blue suits and lots of cuff, and this evening he wore brown suede shoes as well, which gave a hint of Ascot to his gallows smile.

"Oh, Roger, however did you guess?" Goodhew replied with willed cheerfulness, determined to take the sally in good part. "I've been on the take for years, haven't I, Harry?"—passing the question down the line to Harry Palfrey. "How else could I afford my shiny new bicycle?"

Darker continued smiling. And since he had no sense of humor, his smile was a little sinister, even mad. Eight men and Goodhew sat at the long refectory table: a Foreign Office mandarin, a baron from Treasury, the Cabinet Office solicitor, two squat-suited earthlings from the Tory middle benches, and three espiocrats, of whom Darker was the grandest and poor Harry Palfrey the most derelict. The room was fuggy and smoke-stained. Nothing commended it other than its handiness to Whitehall, to the House of Commons and to Darker's concrete kingdom across the river.

"Rex is dividing and ruling, if you ask me, Roger," said a Tory earthling who spent so much of his time sitting on secret committees that he was often mistaken for a civil servant. "Power mania got up as constitutional cant. He's deliberately eroding the citadel from within, aren't you, Rex? Admit it."

"Sheer balderdash, thank you," Goodhew replied lightly. "My master is merely concerned to drag the intelligence services into the new era and help them to set down their old burdens. You should be grateful to him."

"I don't think Rex has *got* a master," the mandarin from the Foreign Office objected, to laughter. "Has anyone ever seen the wretched fellow? I think Rex makes him up."

"Why are we so squeamish about drugs, anyway?" a Treasury man complained, his thin fingertips propped together like a bamboo bridge. "Service industry. Willing buyer, willing seller. Vast profits to the Third World, *some* of it's going to the right places, must be. We accept tobacco, booze, pollution, pox. Why are we such prudes about drugs? *I* wouldn't mind an order for a couple of billion quids' worth of arms, even if there *was* a bit of cocaine on the bank notes; I'll tell you that for nothing!"

A drenched voice cut through their merriment. It came from Harry Palfrey, a River House lawyer now on permanent loan to Darker's Procurement Studies Group. "Burr's real," he warned huskily, with no particular prompting from anybody. He was drinking a large Scotch, not his first. "Burr does what he says."

"Oh my *God,*" cried the Foreign Office in horror. "Then we're *all* for the high jump! Right, Geoffrey? Right?"

But Geoffrey Darker just listened with his eyes and smiled his mirthless smile.

· · ·

YET OF ALL those present at the Fiddler's Club that night, only the leftover lawyer Harry Palfrey had any notion of the scope of Rex Goodhew's crusade. Palfrey was a degenerate. In every British organization there is always one man who makes an art form of going to the devil, and in this one respect Harry Palfrey was the River House's prize exhibit. Whatever he had done well in the first half of his life, Palfrey had systematically undone in the second—whether it was his law practice, his marriage or the preservation of his pride, of which the last shameful tatters lingered in his apologetic grin. Why Darker kept him on, why anybody did, was no mystery at all: Palfrey was the failure who made everyone look successful by comparison. Nothing was too humble for him, nothing too demeaning. If there was scandal, Palfrey was ever willing to be slaughtered. If murder was to be done, Palfrey was on hand with a bucket and cloth to mop up the blood and find you three eyewitnesses to say you were never there. And Palfrey, with the wisdom of the corrupt, knew Rex Goodhew's story as if it were his own—which in a sense it was, since he had long ago made the same perceptions as Goodhew, even if he had never had the courage to draw the same conclusions.

The story was that after twenty-five years before the Whitehall mast, something inside Goodhew had discreetly snapped. Perhaps it was the ending of the Cold War that had caused it. Goodhew had the modesty not to know.

The story was that one Monday morning Goodhew woke as usual and decided with no premeditation that for far too long, in the misused name of freedom, he had been sacrificing scruple and principle to the great god expediency, and that the excuse for doing so was dead.

And that he was suffering from all the bad habits of the Cold War without their justification. He must mend his ways or perish in his soul. Because the threat outside the gates had gone. Decamped. Vanished.

But where to begin? A perilous bicycle ride supplied him with his answer. On the same rainy February morning, the eighteenth—Rex Goodhew never forgot a date—he was cycling from his home in Kentish Town to Whitehall as usual, weaving between the choked columns of commuter cars, when he experienced a silent epiphany. He would crop the secret octopus. He would give away its powers to separate, smaller agencies and make each of them separately accountable. He would deconstruct, decentralize, humanize. And he would begin with the most corrupting influence of all: the unholy marriage between Pure Intelligence, Westminster and the covert weapons trade, presided over by Geoffrey Darker of the River House.

. . .

How DID Harry Palfrey know all this? Goodhew had told him. Goodhew, out of his Christian decency, had invited Palfrey to Kentish Town at summer weekends to drink Pimm's in the garden and play silly cricket with the kids, well aware that, in his shabby, grinning way, Palfrey was near the dangerous edge. And after dinner, Goodhew had left Palfrey at the table with his wife so that he could pour out his soul to her, because there is nothing that dissolute men like better than confessing themselves to virtuous women.

And it was in the afterglow of one such luxurious unbaring that Harry Palfrey, with pathetic alacrity, volunteered to become Goodhew's informant on the backstairs machinations of certain wayward barons at the River House.

FIVE

ZURICH huddled low beside the lake, shivering under a freezing gray cloud.

"My name's Leonard," Burr announced, hauling himself out of Quayle's office chair like someone about to intervene in a brawl. "I do crooks. Smoke? Here. Poison yourself."

He made the offer sound so much like a jovial conspiracy that Jonathan obeyed at once and—though he smoked rarely and always regretted it afterwards—took a cigarette. Burr drew a lighter from his pocket, cocked it and fired it at Jonathan's face.

"I expect you think we let you down, don't you?" he said, going for the point of most resistance. "You and Ogilvey had quite a how-d'you-do before you left Cairo, if I'm correct."

I thought you let *her* down, Jonathan almost replied. But his guard was up, so he gave his hotelier's smile and said, "Oh, nothing terminal, I'm sure."

Burr had thought carefully about this moment and decided on attack as his best defense. Never mind he harbored the worst suspicions of Ogilvey's part in the affair: this was no moment to suggest he was speaking for a divided house.

"We're not paid to be spectators, Jonathan. Dicky Roper was flogging some very high-tech toys to the Thief of Baghdad, including a kilo of weapons-grade uranium, which had fallen off the back of a Russian lorry. Freddie Hamid was laying on a fleet of relief trucks to smuggle the stuff through Jordan. What were we supposed to do? File and forget?" Burr was gratified to see Jonathan's face set in the kind of rebellious obedience that reminded him of himself. "There's a dozen ways the story could have leaked without anybody pointing the finger at your Sophie. If she'd not shot her mouth off at Freddie she'd be sitting pretty to this day."

"She wasn't my Sophie," Jonathan put in too fast.

Burr affected not to hear. "Question is, how do we nail our chum? I've a couple of ideas on that subject if you're interested." He gave a warm smile. "That's right. You've spotted it, I can see. I'm common Yorkshire. And our chum Mr. Richard Onslow Roper, he's quality. Well, that's *his* tough luck!"

Jonathan laughed dutifully, and Burr was grateful to find himself on dry land the other side of Sophie's murder. "Come on, Jonathan, I'll buy you lunch. You won't mind us, Reggie? Only we're strapped for time, see. You've been a good scout. I'll pass the word."

In his haste, Burr failed to notice his cigarette

burning in Quayle's ashtray. Jonathan stubbed it out, sorry to be saying goodbye. Quayle was a bluff, twitchy soul, with a habit of beating his mouth with a handkerchief that he whipped, Services style, from his sleeve; or of suddenly offering you biscuits from a tax-free tartan tin. In the weeks of waiting, Jonathan had come to rely on their quaint, inarticulate sessions. And so, he realized as he left, had Reggie Quayle.

"Thanks, Reggie," he said. "Thanks for everything."

"My dear chap! Pleasure all mine! Travel well, sir. Keep your arse to the sunset!"

"Thanks. You too."

"Got transport okay? Wheels? Whistle you up a barouche? All fixed? Jolly good. Wrap up warm, now. See you in Philippi."

"You always thank people for doing their job, do you?" Burr asked as they stepped onto the pavement. "I suppose you learn to, in your trade."

"Oh, I think I like to be polite," Jonathan replied. "If that's what you mean."

· · ·

As ALWAYS for an operational encounter, Burr's field manners had been meticulous. He had chosen his restaurant in advance; he had inspected it the night before: an out-of-town lakeside trattoria, unlikely to attract the Meister set. He had chosen his corner table and for ten cautious Yorkshire francs to the headwaiter reserved it in one of his work names, Benton. But he was taking no chances.

"If we bump into someone you know and I don't, Jonathan, which as you are no doubt aware is Sod's Law in this game, don't explain me. If you're driven to it, I'm your old barrackmate from Shorncliffe and switch to the weather," he said, thus incidentally demonstrating that he had done his homework on Jonathan's early life. "Doing any climbing these days?"

"A bit."

"Where?"

"Bernese Oberland mainly."

"Anything spectacular?"

"Quite a decent Wetterhorn during the cold spell if you like ice. Why? Do you climb?"

If Burr recognized the mischief in Jonathan's question, he chose to ignore it. "Me? I'm the fellow who takes the lift to the second floor. How about your sailing?" Burr glanced at the window, where the gray lake smoldered like a bog.

"It's all pretty much kiddie stuff round here," said Jonathan. "Thun's not bad. Cold, though."

"And painting? Watercolors, wasn't it? Still dabble, do you?"

"Not often."

"But now and then. What's your tennis like?"

"Middling."

"I'm serious."

"Well, good club standard, I suppose."

"I thought you won some competition in Cairo."

Jonathan gave a modest blush. "Oh, that was just some exiles' knockabout."

"Let's do the hard work first, shall we?" Burr suggested. He meant: let's choose our food so that we can talk in peace. "You're a bit of a cook yourself, aren't you?" he inquired as they hid their faces in the overlarge menus. "A man of parts. I admire that. There's not a lot of Renaissance blokes about these days. Too many specialists."

Jonathan turned the page from meat to fish to dessert, thinking not of food but of Sophie. He was standing before Mark Ogilvey in his grand ministerial house in Cairo's green suburbs, surrounded by fake eighteenth-century furniture assembled by the Ministry of Works, and Roberts prints assembled by Ogilvey's wife. He was wearing his dinner jacket, and in his mind it was still coated with Sophie's blood. He was shouting, but when he heard his voice it sounded like a sonar echo. He was cursing Ogilvey to hell and back, and sweat was running down the undersides of his wrists. Ogilvey was wearing his dressing gown, a mousy brown thing with a drum major's frayed gold frogging on the sleeves. Mrs. Ogilvey was making tea so that she could listen.

"Watch your language, do you mind, old

boy?" said Ogilvey, pointing at the chandelier to remind him of the risk of microphones.

"Damn my language! You've killed her, do you hear me? You're supposed to protect your sources, not have them beaten to death!"

Ogilvey sought refuge in the only safe answer known to his profession. Grasping a crystal decanter from a silver-plate tray, he removed the stopper with a practiced flick.

"Old boy. Have a drop of this. You're barking up the wrong tree, I'm afraid. Nothing to do with us. Or you. What makes you think you were her only confidant? She probably told her fifteen best friends. You know the old saying: Two people can keep a secret provided one of 'em's dead? This is Cairo. A secret's what everyone knows except you."

Mrs. Ogilvey chose the same moment to enter with her pot of tea. "He may *just* think he's better with this, darling," she said in a voice pregnant with discretion. "Brandy does odd things to one, when one's het up."

"Actions have consequences, old boy," Ogilvey said, handing him a glass. "First lesson in life."

A crippled man was limping between the tables of the restaurant on his way to the lavatory. He had two walking sticks and was assisted by a young woman. His rhythm discomforted the diners, and nobody was able to go on eating until he was safely out of sight.

. . .

"So THAT NIGHT our chum arrived was pretty much all you saw of him, then," Burr suggested, shifting the topic of conversation to Roper's stay at Meister's.

"Apart from good morning and good evening, yes. Quayle said don't press my luck, so I didn't."

"But you did have one more casual conversation with him before he left."

"Roper asked me if I skied. I said yes. He said where. I said Mürren. He asked me how the snow was this year. I said good. He said, 'Pity we haven't got time to pop up there for a few days; my lady's dying to have a shot at it.' End of conversation."

"She was there too, then—his girl—Jemima? Jed?"

Jonathan affects to search his memory while he secretly celebrates her unfurrowed gaze on him. *Are you* frightfully *good at it, Mr. Pine?*

"I think he called her *Jeds*. Plural."

"He's got names for everyone. It's his way of buying them."

It must be absolutely gorgeous, she says, with a smile that would melt the Eiger.

"She's quite a looker, they say," said Burr.

"If you like the type."

"I like all types. What type's she?"

Jonathan acted world-weary. "Oh, I don't know. Good spread of O-levels . . . floppy black hats . . . the millionaire urchin look. . . . Who is she, anyway?"

Burr seemed not to know, or not to care. "Some upper-class geisha, convent school, rides to hounds. Anyway, you got along with him. He won't forget you."

"He doesn't forget anyone. He had all the waiters' names off pat."

"It isn't everyone he asks for their opinion on Italian sculpture, though, is it? I found that rather encouraging." Encouraging to whom or why, Burr did not explain, and Jonathan was not disposed to ask. "He still bought it, though. The man or woman wasn't born yet who could head off the Roper from buying something he fancies." He consoled himself with a large mouthful of veal. "And thanks," he continued. "Thanks for all the hard work. There's some choice observation in those reports of yours to Quayle I've not seen bettered anywhere. Your left-handed gunman, timepiece on the right wrist, changes his knife and fork over when he tucks into his food—I mean, that's classic, that is."

"Francis Inglis," Jonathan recited. "Physical-training instructor from Perth, Australia."

"His name's not Inglis, and he doesn't come from Perth. He's a British ex-mercenary, is Frisky, and there's a price on his nasty little head. It was him taught Idi Amin's lads how to extract voluntary confessions with the aid of an electric cattle prod. Our chum likes them English, and he likes them with a dirty past. He doesn't fancy people he doesn't own," he added as he carefully sliced his roll down the middle and spread butter on it. "Here, then," he went on, jabbing his knife in Jonathan's direction. "How come you got the names of his visitors, with you only working nights?"

"Anyone proposing to go up to the Tower Suite these days has to sign in."

"And hanging around the lobby of an evening?"

"Herr Meister expects it of me. I hang around, I ask whatever I want. I'm a presence; that's why I'm there."

"So tell us about these visitors of his," Burr suggested. "There was this Austrian, as you call him. Three separate visits to the Tower Suite."

"Dr. Kippel, address Vienna, wore a green loden coat."

"He's not Austrian, he's not Kippel. He's a humble Pole, if a Pole's ever humble. They say he's one of the new czars of the Polish underworld."

"Why on earth should Roper be messing with the Polish underworld?"

Burr gave a regretful smile. His purpose was not to enlighten Jonathan but to tantalize him. "How about the thickset fellow with the glittery gray suit and eyebrows, then? Called himself Larsen. Swedish."

"I simply assumed he was a Swede called Larsen."

"He's Russian. Three years ago he was a big shot in the Soviet Ministry of Defense. Today he runs a flourishing employment agency, pimping East Bloc physicists and engineers. Twenty thousand dollars a month, some are pulling in. Your Mr. Larsen takes his cut both ends. As a sideline he traffics in military hardware. If you're looking to buy a couple of hundred T-72 tanks or a few Scud missiles at the Russian back door, Mr. Larsen is your man. Biological warheads come extra. What about your two military-looking Brits?"

Jonathan remembered two loose-limbed men in British blazers. "What about them?"

"They come from London, all right, but they're not Forbes and Lubbock. Belgium is where they're based, and they're purveyors of military trainers to the leading crazies of the world."

The Brussels boys, Jonathan was thinking as he began to follow the threads that Burr was deliberately weaving before his memory's eye. *Soldier Boris.* Who's next?

"This one ring any bells? You didn't describe him, not in as many words, but I thought he might be one of those suited gentlemen our chum received in the ground-floor conference room."

While Burr was speaking he had drawn a

small photograph from his wallet and passed it across the table for Jonathan's inspection. It showed a tight-mouthed man in his forties with saddened shallow eyes and unnaturally waved black hair and an incongruous gold cross hanging over his Adam's apple. It had been taken in bright sunlight and, to judge by the shadows, with the sun directly overhead.

"Yes," Jonathan said.

"Yes what?"

"He was half the size of anyone else, but they deferred to him. Carried a black briefcase that was too big for him. Wore risers."

"A Swiss? A Brit? Pin him down."

"More a Latin American of some sort." He handed back the photograph. "Could be anything. Could be Arab."

"His name is Apostoll, believe it or not, Apo for short." And Appetites for long, thought Jonathan, once again remembering Major Corkoran's asides to his chief. "Greek, first-generation American, doctor of law at Michigan, magna cum laude, crook. Offices in New Orleans, Miami and Panama City, all places of impeccable respectability, as you are no doubt aware. Remember Lord Langbourne? Sandy?"

"Of course," Jonathan replied, recalling the unnervingly beautiful man with the ponytail and the sour wife.

"He's another bloody lawyer. Dicky Roper's,

actually. Apo and Sandy Langbourne do deals together. Very lucrative deals."

"I see."

"No, you don't, but you're getting the idea. How's your Spanish, by the by?"

"All right."

"Should be more than all right, shouldn't it? Eighteen months at the Ritz in Madrid, with your gifts, it should be bloody perfect."

"I've let it go a bit, that's all."

An interval while Burr sat back in his chair and let the waiter clear away their plates. Jonathan was surprised to rediscover excitement: the feeling of edging toward the secret center, the pull of action after too long away.

"You're not going to be a pudding traitor, are you?" Burr asked aggressively as the waiter handed them each a plastic-coated card.

"Good Lord, no."

They settled for a purée of chestnut with whipped cream.

"And Corky, Major Corkoran, your brother soldier, his gofer," said Burr, in the tone of one who has left the best until the end. "What did you make of him, then? Why are you laughing?"

"He was amusing."

"What else is he?"

"The gofer, as you say. The majordomo. He signs."

Burr leapt on the word as if it were the one he

had been waiting for all lunch. "What does he sign?"

"Registration forms. Bills."

"Bills, letters, contracts, waivers, guarantees, company accounts, bills of lading, checks," said Burr excitedly. "Waybills, freight certificates, and a very large number of documents saying that everything his employer ever did wrong wasn't done by Richard Onslow Roper but by his loyal servant Major Corkoran. Very rich man, Major Corkoran. Hundreds of millions to his name, except he's signed them all away to Mr. Roper. There's not a dirty deal the Roper does but Corky puts his signature to it. 'Corks, come over here! You don't have to read it, Corks old boy, sign it, there's a good lad. You've just earned yourself another ten years in Sing Sing.' "

The force with which Burr delivered this image, combined with the jagged edge to his voice as he imitated Roper's, gave a jolt to the easy rhythm of their conversation.

"There's not a paper trail worth a damn," Burr confided, his pale face close to Jonathan's. "You can go back twenty years, I don't care, you'll not find Roper's name on anything worse than a church donation. All right, I hate him. I'll admit it. So should you, after what he did to Sophie."

"Oh, I have no problem about that."

"You don't, eh?"

"No. I don't."

"Well, keep it that way. I'll be right back. Hold everything."

Fastening the waistband of his trousers, Burr went off for a pee, leaving Jonathan mysteriously elated. *Hate* him? Hate was not an emotion he had so far indulged. He could do anger; certainly he could mourn. But hate, like desire, seemed a lowly thing until it had a noble context, and Roper with his Sotheby's catalogue and his beautiful mistress had not yet provided one. Nevertheless, the idea of hate, dignified by Sophie's murder—of hate turned perhaps to revenge—began to appeal to Jonathan. It was like the promise of a distant great love, and Burr had appointed himself its procurer.

· · ·

"So why?" Burr continued cozily, settling back into his chair. "That's what I kept asking myself. Why's he doing it? Why does Mr. Jonathan Pine the distinguished hotelier risk his career pinching faxes and snitching on a valued client? First Cairo, now again in Zurich. 'Specially after you were cross with us. Quite right. I was cross with us too."

Jonathan pretended to address the question for the first time. "You just do it," he said.

"No, you don't. You're not an animal, all instinct. You *decide* to do it. What drove you?"

"Something stirred, I suppose."

"What stirred? How does it *stop* stirring? What would stir it again?"

Jonathan took a breath but for a moment did not speak. He had discovered that he was angry, and didn't know why. "If a man's peddling a private arsenal to an Egyptian crook . . . and he's English . . . and you're English . . . and there's a war brewing . . . and the English are going to be fighting on the other side—"

"And you've been a soldier yourself . . ."

"—you just do it," Jonathan repeated, feeling his throat clog.

Burr pushed aside his empty plate and leaned forward across the table. " 'Feeding the rat'— isn't that the climbers' expression? The rat that gnaws inside us, telling us to take the risk? It's quite a big rat, yours is, I suppose, with that father of yours to live up to. He was undercover too, wasn't he? Well, you knew that."

"No, I'm afraid I didn't," said Jonathan politely as his stomach turned.

"They had to put him back into uniform after he was shot. They didn't tell you?"

Jonathan's hotelier smile, cast iron from cheek to cheek. His hotelier voice, iron soft. "No. They didn't. Really not. How strange. You'd think they would, wouldn't you?"

Burr shook his head at the enigmatic ways of civil servants.

. . .

"I MEAN, you did retire quite early, when you work it out," Burr resumed reasonably. "It's not everyone gives up a promising army career at twenty-five in favor of being a night flunky. Not with all the sailing and climbing and Outward Bound activities in the world. What made you choose hoteling, for heaven's sake? Of all the ways you could have gone, why that one?"

To submit, thought Jonathan.

To abdicate.

To rest my head.

Mind your own fucking business.

"Oh, *I* don't know," he confessed with a self-negating smile. "For the quiet life, I suppose. I expect I'm a bit of a closet sybarite, if I'm honest."

"Well now, I don't believe that, as a matter of fact, Jonathan. I've been following you very closely these weeks and thinking about you in some depth. Let's talk army a bit more, can we? Because I was very impressed by some of the things I read about your military career."

Great, thought Jonathan, now very lively in his mind. We're talking Sophie, so we're talking hate. We're talking hate, so we're talking hoteling. We're talking hoteling, so we're talking army. Very logical. Very rational.

All the same, he could find no fault with Burr. Burr was from the heart, which was his saving. He might be clever. He might have mastered the grammar of intrigue, he had an eye for human strength and failing. But the heart still led, as Goodhew knew and Jonathan could feel, which was why he permitted Burr to wander in his private kingdom and why Burr's sense of mission was beginning to throb like a war drum in Jonathan's ear.

SIX

IT WAS mellow time. Confidence time. They had agreed on a glass of plum spirit to wash down their coffee.

"I had a Sophie once," Burr recalled, not altogether truthfully. "Surprised I didn't marry her, come to think of it. I usually do. My current one's called Mary, which always strikes me as a bit of a comedown. Still, we've been together, oh, must be five years now. She's a doctor, as a matter of fact. Just a GP, parish priest with a stethoscope. Social conscience the size of a somewhat enlarged pumpkin. Seems to be panning out quite well."

"Long may it last," said Jonathan gallantly.

"Mary's not my first wife, mind. She's not my second, to be frank. I don't know what it is about me and women. I've aimed up, I've aimed down, I've aimed sideways; I never get it right. Is it me, is it them? I ask myself."

"I know what you mean," said Jonathan. But inside himself he had become watchful. He had no natural conversation about women. They were the sealed envelopes in his desk. They were the friends and sisters of the youth he had never had, the mother he had never known, the woman he should never have married, and the woman he should have loved and not betrayed.

"I seem to get to the root of them too fast and wear them out," Burr was complaining, once again affecting to open his heart to Jonathan in the hope of receiving the same favor in return. "It's kids are the problem. We've each got two of our own, and now we've got one between us. They take the spice out of it. You never did kids, did you? You steered clear of them. Wise, I call that. Shrewd." He took a sip of Pflümli. "Tell us a bit more about *your* Sophie," he suggested, though Jonathan had so far told him nothing.

"She wasn't mine. She was Freddie Hamid's."

"But you screwed her," Burr suggested equably.

. . .

JONATHAN IS in the bedroom of the little flat in Luxor, with the moonlight sloping between the half-closed curtains. Sophie is lying on the bed in her white nightgown, eyes closed and face upward. Some of her drollness has returned. She has drunk a little vodka. So has he. The bottle stands between them.

"Why do you sit the other side of the room from me, Mr. Pine?"

"Out of respect, I imagine." The hotelier's smile. The hotelier's voice, a careful composite of other people's.

"But you brought me here to comfort me, I think."

This time, no answer from Mr. Pine.

"Am I too damaged for you? Too old perhaps?"

Mr. Pine, normally so fluent, continues to preserve a dread silence.

"I am worried for your dignity, Mr. Pine. Perhaps I am worried for my own. I think you sit so far away from me because you are ashamed of something. I hope it is not me."

"I brought you here because it was somewhere safe, Madame Sophie. You need a pause for breath while you work out what to do and where to go. I thought I could be helpful."

"And Mr. Pine? He needs nothing, I suppose? You are a healthy man, assisting the invalid? Thank you for bringing me to Luxor."

"Thank you for agreeing to come."

Her large eyes were fixed upon him in the moonlight. She did not easily resemble a helpless woman grateful for his help.

"You have so many voices, Mr. Pine," she resumed, after too long. "I have no idea anymore who you are. You look at me, and you touch me with your eyes. And I am not insensitive to your touch. I am not." Her voice slipped a moment; she straightened herself and seemed to regroup. "You say one thing, and you are that person. And I am moved by that person. Then that person is called away, and somebody quite different takes his place. And you say something else. And I am moved again. So we have a changing of the guard. It is as if each person in you can only stand a little while of me, and then he has to go and get his rest. Are you like this with all your women?"

"But you are not one of my women, Madame Sophie."

"Then why are you here? To be a boy scout? I don't think so."

She fell silent again. He had a sense that she was deciding whether to abandon pretense. "I would like one of your many people to stay with me tonight, Mr. Pine. Can you arrange that?"

"Of course. I'll sleep on the sofa. If that's what you wish."

"No. It's not at all what I wish. I wish you to sleep with me in my bed and make love to me. I wish to feel that I have made at least one of you happy and that the others will take heart from his example. I cannot have you so ashamed. You accuse yourself much too much. We have all done bad things. But you are a good man. You are many good men. And you are not responsible for my misfortunes. If you are part of them"—she was standing now, facing him, her arms at her sides—"then I should wish you to be here for better reasons than shame. Mr. Pine, why do you insist on keeping yourself so far away from me?"

In the fading moonlight her voice had

become louder, her appearance more spectral. He took a step toward her and found that the distance between them was no distance at all. He stretched out his arms to her, tentatively because of her bruises. He drew her carefully to him, slid his hands under the halter of her white nightgown, spread his palms and lightly flattened them against her naked back. She laid the side of her face against his; he smelled the vanilla again and discovered the unexpected softness of her long black hair. He closed his eyes. Clutching each other, they toppled softly onto the bed. And when the dawn came, she made him draw the curtains so that the night manager no longer did his loving in the dark.

"That was all of us," he whispered to her. "The whole regiment. Officers, other ranks, deserters, cooks. There's no one left."

"I don't think so, Mr. Pine. You have hidden reinforcements, I am sure."

· · ·

BURR WAS still waiting for his answer.

"No," said Jonathan defiantly.

"Why ever not? Never pass one up, me. Did you have a girl at the time?"

"No," Jonathan repeated, coloring.

"You mean mind my own business?"

"Pretty much."

Burr seemed to like being told to mind his own business. "Tell us about your marriage, then.

It's quite funny, actually, thinking of you being married. It makes me uncomfortable, I don't know why. You're single. I can feel it. Maybe I am too. What happened?"

"I was young. She was younger. It makes me uncomfortable too."

"She was a painter, wasn't she? Like you?"

"I was a Sunday dauber. She was the real thing. Or thought she was."

"What did you marry her for?"

"Love, I suppose."

"You suppose. Politeness, more likely, knowing you. What did you leave her for?"

"Sanity."

No longer able to keep the flood of memory at bay, Jonathan abandoned himself to the angry vision of their married life together dying as they watched it: the friendship they no longer had, the love they no longer made, the restaurants where they watched happy people chat, the dead flowers in the vase, the rotting fruit in the bowl, her paint-caked easel propped against the wall, the dust thick on the dining table while they stared at each other through their dried tears, a mess not even Jonathan could tidy up. It's just me, he kept telling her, trying to touch her and recoiling as she recoiled. I grew up too quickly and missed women on the way. It's me, not you at all.

Burr had made another of his merciful leaps.

"So what took you to Ireland?" he suggested

with a smile. "Was that running away from her, by any chance?"

"It was a job. If you were in the British Army—if you wanted to be a real soldier, useful, live ammunition after all the training rounds—Ireland was where you had to be."

"And you did want to be useful?"

"Wouldn't you at that age?"

"I still do," Burr replied.

Jonathan let the implicit question lie.

"Were you hoping you might get killed?" Burr asked.

"Don't be absurd."

"I'm not being absurd. Your marriage was on the rocks. You were still a kid. You thought you were responsible for all the world's ills. I'm just surprised you didn't do big game or join the Foreign Legion. What did you get up to over there, anyway?"

"Our orders were to win Irish hearts and minds. Say good morning to everyone, pat the kiddies. A bit of patrolling."

"Tell about the patrolling."

"Boring VCPs. Nothing to it."

"I'm not much of a one for initials, I'm afraid, Jonathan."

"Vehicle Control Points. You'd pick a blind hill or a corner, then pop up out of a ditch and hold up the cars. Occasionally you'd come across a player."

"And if you did?"

"You got through on the Cougar, and your controller told you which course of action to take. Stop and search. Wave him through. Question him. Whatever they wanted."

"Any other jobs on the menu, apart from VCPs?"

The same blandness, as Jonathan made a show of remembering. "Buzzing around in a helicopter a bit. Each group had a piece of land to cover. You'd book your Lynx, take a bivibag, camp out for a couple of nights, then come home and have a beer."

"How about contact with the enemy?"

Jonathan gave a deprecating smile. "Why should they come out and fight us when they could blow us up in our jeeps by remote control?"

"Why indeed?" Burr always played his best cards slowly. He sipped his drink, he shook his head and smiled as if it were all a bit of a conundrum. "So what were these special duties you got up to, then?" he asked. "All those special training courses you did, that wore me out just reading about them? I get frightened every time I see you pick up a spoon and fork, to be frank. I think you're going to skewer me."

Jonathan's reluctance was like a sudden slowing down. "There were things called Close Observation Platoons."

"Which were?"

"The senior platoon in each regiment, artificially created."

"Out of?"

"Anyone who wanted to join."

"I thought they were the elite."

Short, tight sentences, Burr noticed. Monitored as he spoke them. Eyelids down, lips tense.

"You were trained. You learned to watch, recognize the players. Make hides, get in and out of them in darkness. Lie up for a couple of nights. In lofts. Bushes. Ditches."

"What weapons did they give you?"

Jonathan shrugged as if to say, Who cares? "Uzis. Hecklers. Shotguns. They teach them all. You select. Sounds exciting from the outside. Once you're into it, it's just a job."

"What was your choice?"

"Heckler gave you the best chance."

"Which brings us to Operation Night Owl," Burr suggested, with no change in the inflection of his voice. And sat back to watch the no-change in Jonathan's expression.

. . .

JONATHAN WAS talking in his sleep. His eyes were open, but his mind was in another country. He had not expected lunch to be a tour of the worst parts of his life.

"We had a tip-off that some players were coming across the border into Armagh to relocate a stash of weapons. RPGs." This time Burr did not ask what the initials meant. "We lay up for a couple of days, and finally they showed. We took out three. The unit was pretty chuffed. Everyone went round whispering 'three' and holding up three fingers at the Irish."

"I'm sorry?" Burr seemed not to have heard. *"Take out* in this context meaning *killed?"*

"Yup."

"Did you do the *taking out* yourself? Single-handed, as it were?"

"I was part of it, sure."

"Of the fire team?"

"Of a cutoff group."

"Of how many?"

"We were a pair. Two. Brian and me."

"Brian."

"He was my oppo. Lance corporal."

"What were you?"

"Corporal. Acting sergeant. Our job was to catch them when they ran."

His face had grown a harder skin, Burr noticed. The muscles round the jaw were flexed.

"It was absolute luck," Jonathan said with clean-and-press casualness. "Everyone dreams of taking out a terrorist. We got the chance. We were just *terribly* lucky."

"And you took out three. You and Brian. Killed three men."

"Sure. I told you. Luck."

Rigid, Burr noticed. Rigid ease and deafening understatement.

"One and two? Two and one? Who scored highest?"

"One each and one shared. We quarreled over it at first, then settled on half each. Hard to tell who bags who in the heat of battle quite often."

Suddenly Burr didn't need to prod him anymore. It was as if Jonathan had decided to tell the story for the first time. And perhaps he had.

"There was this clapped-out farmhouse right on the border. The owner was a subsidies cowboy, smuggling the same cows over the border and claiming farming subsidies both sides. He had a Volvo and a brand-new Merc and this slummy little farm. Intelligence said three players would be coming across from the South after the pubs had closed, names supplied. We hunkered down and waited. Their cache was in a barn. Our hide was a bush a hundred and fifty yards away from it. Our brief was to sit in our hide and watch without being watched."

That's what he likes to do, thought Burr: watch without being watched.

"We were to let them go into the barn and collect their toys. When they left the barn we were to signal their direction and get out unobserved. Another team would throw up a roadblock five miles on, hold a random check, pretend it was all sheer chance. That was to protect the source. Then they'd take them out. Only trouble was, the players weren't planning to drive the weapons anywhere. They'd decided to bury them in a ditch ten yards from our hide. Sunk a box into the ground in advance."

He was lying on his belly in the sweet moss of a South Armagh hillside, gazing through light-intensifiers at three green men lugging green boxes across a green moonscape. Languidly the man on the left rises on his toes, lets go his box and spins gracefully round, his arms extended for the cross. *That dark green ink is his blood. I'm taking him out, and the silly bugger isn't even complaining,* Jonathan decides as he becomes aware of the bucking of his Heckler.

"So you shot them," Burr suggested.

"We had to use our initiative. We each took one, then we both took the third. The whole thing lasted seconds."

"Did they shoot back?"

"No," said Jonathan. He smiled, still rigid. "We were lucky, I suppose. Get your first shot in, you're home free. That all you want to know?"

"Ever been back since?"

"To Ireland?"

"To England."

"Not really. Neither."

"And the divorce?"

"That was all taken care of in England."

"By?"

"Her. I left her the flat, all my money and whatever friends we had. She called that fifty-fifty."

"You left her England too."

"Yes."

Jonathan had finished speaking, but Burr was still listening to him. "I guess what I *really* want to know, Jonathan," he resumed at last, in the commonplace voice he had used for most of their discussion, "is whether you'd be at all attracted by the idea of having another go. Not at marriage. At serving your country." He heard himself say it, but for all the response he got he could have been staring at a granite wall. He beckoned for the bill. And then: To hell with it, he thought; sometimes the worst moments are the best. So he said it anyway, which was his nature, while he counted Swiss bank notes into a white saucer.

"Suppose I asked you to trash your whole life till now in favor of a better one," he suggested. "Not better for you maybe, but better for what you and I are pleased to call the common good. A five-star unimpeachable cause, guaranteed to improve the lot of mankind or your money back in full. Bye-bye to the old Jonathan, enter the new blue improved product. Resettlement afterwards, a new identity, money, the usual. There's a lot of people I know might find that quite attractive. I'm not sure *I* mightn't, to be frank, except it wouldn't be fair on Mary. But who've you got to be fair to except yourself? Nobody, not so far as I know. You'll be feeding the rat three meals a day, hanging on by your fingernails in force-twelve gales, there's not a scrap of you won't be used, not an hour you won't be frightened stiff. And you'll be doing it for your country, same as your dad, whatever you thought of Ireland. Or Cyprus, for that matter. And you'll be doing it for Sophie, too. Tell him I need a receipt, will you? Benton. Lunch for two. What do I give? Another five? I won't ask you to sign for me, not like some. Let's move."

· · ·

THEY WERE strolling beside the lake. The snow had disappeared. An afternoon sun shimmered on the steaming pathway. Teenaged drug addicts, huddled in costly overcoats, gazed at the disintegrating ice. Jonathan had thrust his hands into the pockets of his overcoat, and he was listening to Sophie congratulating him on his gentleness as a lover.

"My English husband was also very gentle," she was saying while she drew her fingers admiringly over his face. "I had preserved my virginity so jealously that it took him days to persuade me I was better off without it." Then a presentiment seized her, and she drew him against her for protection. "Just remember you have a future, Mr.

Pine. Never again renounce it. Not for me or for anyone. Promise me."

So he had promised her. As we promise anything in love.

Burr was talking about justice. "When I get to run the world," he announced comfortably to the steaming lake, "I'm going to hold the Nuremberg Trials Part Two. I'm going to get all the arms dealers and shit scientists, and all the smooth salesmen who push the crazies one step further than they thought of going, because it's good for business, and all the lying politicians and the lawyers and accountants and bankers, and I'm going to put them in the dock to answer for their lives. And you know what they'll say? 'If *we* hadn't done it someone else would have.' And you know what I'll say? I'll say, 'Oh, I see. And if you hadn't raped the girl some other fellow would have raped her. And that's your justification for rape. Noted.' Then I'd napalm the lot of them. Fizz."

"What's Roper *done?*" Jonathan asked in a kind of angry frustration. "Apart from . . . Hamid, all that."

"It's what he's doing now that matters."

"If he stopped today. How bad is he? How bad's he been?"

He was remembering Roper's shoulder riding unconsciously against him. *Pergola over the top, view of the sea at the end.* He remembered Jed: *Most beautiful place on earth.*

"He plunders," said Burr.

"Where? Who?"

"Everywhere and everyone. If the deal is bent, our chum is in there cutting it, and getting Corkoran to sign for him. He's got his white operation, and that's Ironbrand: venture capital, hairy land deals, minerals, tractors, turbines, commodities, a couple of tankers, a bit of corporate raiding. Offices in the whitest part of Nassau, smart young men with short-back-and-sides, tapping at computers. That's the part that's in deep trouble, and that's the part you've read about."

"I'm afraid I haven't."

"Well, you should have done. His last year's results were bloody awful, and this year's will be worse. His shares are down to seventy from one sixty, and three months ago he took a bold position on platinum just in time to see it go through the floor. He's not seriously concerned; he's just desperate." He drew breath and began again. "And tucked underneath his Ironbrand umbrella he's got his little uglies. There's the five Caribbean classics—money laundering, gold, emeralds, wood from the rain forests, arms and more arms. There's phony pharmaceuticals, phony aid packages with bent health ministers and fake fertilizers with bent agricultural ministers." The anger in Burr's voice was like a slowly rising storm, and the more alarming because it didn't break. "But weapons are his first love. Toys, he calls them. If you're into power, there's nothing like toys to feed the habit. Don't ever believe that crap about 'just another commodity,' 'service industry.' Arms are a drug, and Roper's hooked. Trouble with arms is, everyone thought they were recession-proof, but they're not. Iran-Iraq was an arms dealers' charter, and they thought it would never end. Since then it's been downhill all the way. Too many manufacturers chasing too few wars. Too much loose hardware being dumped on the market. Too much peace about and not enough hard currency. Our Dicky did a bit of the Serbo-Croat thing, of course—Croats via Athens, Serbs via Poland—but the numbers weren't in his league and there were too many dogs in the hunt. Cuba's gone dead; so's South Africa—they make their own. Ireland isn't worth a light, or he'd have done that too. Peru, he's got a thing going there, supplying the Shining Path boys. And he's been making a play for the Muslim insurgents in the southern Philippines, but the North Koreans are in there ahead of him and I've a suspicion he's going to get his nose bloodied again."

"Well, who lets him?" Jonathan asked aggressively. And when Burr for once was taken aback: "It's a hell of a lot to get away with, isn't it, with people like you breathing down his neck?"

For a moment longer Burr was stuck for a rejoinder. Exactly the same question, with its disgraceful answer, had been coursing in his own mind as he spoke: *The River House lets him,* he wanted to say. *Whitehall lets him. Geoffrey Darker and his pals in Procurement Studies let him. Goodhew's master puts his telescope to both blind eyes and he lets him. If his toys are British, anyone will let him do anything he bloody likes.* But his good luck delivered a distraction:

"Well, I'm damned!" he exclaimed, grasping Jonathan's arm. "Where's *her* father, then?"

Watched by her boyfriend, a girl of about seventeen was rolling up the leg of her jeans. Patches like wet insect bites covered her calf. She inserted the needle and didn't wince. But Burr winced for her, and his disgust sent him into himself for a while, so that they walked a distance in silence while Jonathan for a moment forgot Sophie and remembered instead Jed's endless baby-pink legs coming down Meister's ornamental staircase, and her smile as she just happened to catch his eye.

· · ·

"So WHAT is he?" Jonathan asked.

"I told you what he is. He's a bastard."

"What's his background? What makes him run?"

Burr shrugged. "Father a small-time auctioneer and valuer in the shires. Mother a pillar of the local church. One brother. Private schools the parents couldn't afford—"

"Eton?"

"Why should he be?"

"It's that voice. No pronouns. No articles. The slur."

"I've only ever overheard him on the telephone. That'll do me fine. He's got one of those voices that make me vomit."

"Is Roper the elder or younger brother?"

"Younger."

"Did he go to university?"

"No. In too much of a hurry to screw up the world, most likely."

"Did his brother?"

"Yes. Are you being clever? The brother joined the family firm. It went down in the recession. Now he's pig-farming. So what?" He cast Jonathan an angry sideways look. "Don't you bloody start making excuses for him now, Jonathan," he warned. "If the Roper had gone to Eton and Oxford and had half a million a year of his own, he'd *still* be screwing up the world. He's a villain, and you'd better believe it. Evil exists."

"Oh, I know, I know," said Jonathan, placating him. Sophie had said the same.

"So what he's done is, he's done the lot," Burr resumed. "We're talking high-tech, mid-tech, low-tech and bugger-all-tech. He hates tanks because they've a long shelf life, but at a price he'll bend his rules. We're talking boots, uniforms, poison gas, cluster bombs, chemicals, MREs—that's meals ready to eat—inertial navigation systems, fighter airplanes, signal pads, pencils, red phosphorus, grenades, torpedoes, custom-built submarines, motor torpedo boats, fly killer, guidance systems, leg irons, mobile kitchens, brass buttons, medals and regimental swords, Metz flashguns and spook laboratories got up as chicken batteries, tires, belts, bushings, ammo of all calibers, both U.S. and Sov compatible, Red Eyes and other shoulder-held launchers such as Stingers, and body bags. Or we were—because today we're talking glut and national bankruptcies and governments offering better terms than their own crooks. You should see his warehouses. Taipei, Panama, Port of Spain, Gdansk. He used to employ close to a thousand men, did our chum, just to polish the equipment he was storing while the price went up. Always up, never down. Now he's reduced to sixty men, and prices are through the floor."

"So what's his answer?"

It was Burr's turn to become evasive. "He's going for the big one. One last bite of the apple. The deal to end all deals. He wants to turn Ironbrand around and hang up his boots in a blaze of glory. Tell me something."

Jonathan was not yet accustomed to Burr's abrupt changes of direction.

"That morning in Cairo when you took Sophie for a drive. After Freddie had smacked her about."

"Well?"

"Do you think anyone rumbled you at all, spotted you with her, put two and two together?"

Jonathan had asked himself the same question a thousand times: at night when he roamed his darkened kingdom in order to escape his inner self, by day when he couldn't sleep but flung himself instead against the mountains, or sailed his boat to nowhere.

"No," he retorted.

"Certain?"

"Certain as I can be."

"Did you take any other risks with her? Go anywhere together where you could have been recognized?"

It gave Jonathan a mysterious pleasure, he discovered, to lie for Sophie's protection, even though it was too late.

"No," he repeated firmly.

"Well, you're clean then, aren't you?" Burr said, unconsciously echoing Sophie again.

. . .

SHARING A QUIET SPELL, the two men sipped Scotch together in a coffeehouse in the old town, a place with no night or day, among rich ladies wearing trilby hats to eat cream cakes. Sometimes the catholicity of the Swiss enchanted Jonathan. This evening it seemed to him they had painted their entire country in different shades of gray.

Burr began telling an amusing story about

Dr. Apostoll, the distinguished lawyer. It began jerkily, almost as a blurt, as if he had intruded upon his own thoughts. He should not have told it, which he knew as soon as he had embarked on it. But sometimes when we are nursing a great secret we can think of nothing else.

Apo's a voluptuary, he said. He had said it before. Apo's screwing everything in sight, he said, don't be fooled by that prissy demeanor; he's one of those little men who's got to prove he's got a bigger willie than all the big men put together. The secretaries, other people's wives, strings of hookers from the agencies—Apo's into the whole thing.

"Then one day, up gets his daughter and kills herself. Not nicely either, if there is a nicely. A real murder job on herself. Fifty aspirin washed down with half a bottle of pure bleach."

"Whatever did she do that for?" Jonathan exclaimed in horror.

"Apo had given her this gold watch for her eighteenth birthday. Ninety thousand dollars' worth from Cartier's in Bal Harbour. You couldn't find a better watch than that one anywhere."

"But what's wrong with giving her a gold watch?"

"Nothing, except he'd given her the same watch on her seventeenth and forgotten. The girl wanted to feel rejected, I suppose, and the watch tipped the scales for her." He made no pause. He did not raise his voice or change his tone. He wanted to get away from the story as fast as possible. "Have you said 'yes' yet? I didn't hear."

But Jonathan, to Burr's discomfort, preferred to stay with Apostoll. "So what did he do?" he asked.

"Apo? What they all do. Had himself born again. Came to Jesus. Burst into tears at cocktail parties. Do we sign you up or write you off, Jonathan? I never was one for long courtships."

The boy's face again, green for red as it split and spread with each fresh wave of shot. Sophie's face, smashed a second time when they killed her. His mother's face, tilted with her jaw wide open, before the night nurse pushed it shut and bound it with a piece of cheesecloth. Roper's face, coming too close as it leaned into Jonathan's private space.

But Burr too was having his own thoughts. He was berating himself for painting Apostoll so large in Jonathan's mind. He was wondering whether he would ever learn to guard his stupid tongue.

. . .

THEY WERE in Jonathan's tiny flat in the Klosbachstrasse, drinking Scotch and Henniez water, and the drink was doing neither of them good. Jonathan sat in the only armchair, while Burr roamed the room in search of clues. He had fingered the climbing gear and studied a couple of

Jonathan's cautious watercolors of the Bernese Oberland. Now he stood in the alcove, working his way through Jonathan's books. He was tired, and his patience was beginning to run out, with himself as well as Jonathan.

"You're a Hardy man, then," he remarked. "What's that about?"

"Exile from England, I suppose. My shot of nostalgia."

"Nostalgia? Hardy? Bollocks. Man as mouse and God as uncaring bastard, that's Hardy. Hullo. Who've we got here? Colonel T. E. Lawrence of Arabia himself." He held up a slim volume in a yellow dust jacket, waving it like a captured flag. "The lonely genius who wished only to be a number. Forsaken by his country. Now we're getting warm. Written by the lady who fell in love with him after he was dead. Your hero. Well, he would be. All that abstinence and flawed endeavor, beans out of the can; he's a natural. No wonder you took that job in Egypt." He looked at the flyleaf. "Whose initials are these? Not yours." But by the time he asked, he knew.

"My father's, actually. It was his book. Will you put it back, please?"

Noticing the edge to Jonathan's voice, Burr turned round. "Have I touched a nerve? I believe I have. Never occurred to me that sergeants read books." He was probing the wound deliberately. "Officers only, I'd have thought books were."

Jonathan was standing in Burr's path, blocking him in the alcove. His face was stone pale, and his hands, instinctively freed for action, had risen from his sides.

"If you could put it back on the shelf, please. It's private."

Taking his time, Burr replaced the book on the shelf among its companions. "Tell us something," he suggested, announcing another change of topic as he ambled past Jonathan to the center of the room. It was as if their conversation of a moment ago had never taken place. "Do you handle hard cash at all at that hotel of yours?"

"Sometimes."

"Which times?"

"If we get a late-night departure and somebody pays cash, we handle it. The reception desk is closed between midnight and five a.m., so the night manager stands in."

"So you'd take the cash off them, would you, and you'd put it in the safe?"

Jonathan lowered himself into the armchair and folded his hands behind his head. "I might."

"Suppose you stole it. How long before anybody noticed?"

"End of the month."

"You could always put it back for accounting day and take it out after, I dare say," said Burr thoughtfully.

"Meister's pretty watchful. Nothing if not Swiss."

"I'm building up a legend for you, you see."

"I know what you're doing."

"No, you don't. I want to get you inside Roper's head, Jonathan. I believe you can do it. I want you to lead him to me. I'll never nail him else. He may be desperate, but he doesn't drop his guard. I can have microphones up his arse, overfly him with satellites, read his mail and listen to his telephones. I can smell him, hear him and watch him. I can send Corkoran to jail for five hundred years, but I can't touch the Roper. You've four more days before you're due back at Meister's. I want you to come to London with me in the morning, meet my friend Rooke and hear the deal. I want to rewrite your life from day one and make you love yourself at the end of it."

Tossing an air ticket onto the bed, Burr placed himself at the dormer window, parted the curtains and stared out at the dawn. There was more snow in the air. The sky was dark and low. "You don't need time to think about it. You've had nothing but time since you jacked in the army and your country. There's a case for saying no, same as there's a case for digging a deep shelter for yourself and living in it for the rest of your life."

"How long would it take?"

"I don't know. If you don't want to do it, a week's too long. Do you want another sermon?"

"No."

"Want to call me in a couple of hours?"

"No."

"How far have you got, then?"

Nowhere, Jonathan thought as he opened the ticket and read the time of departure. There's no such thing as a decision. There never was. There's whether you've had a good day or a bad day, there's going forward because there's nothing behind and running because if you stand still any longer you'll fall over. There's movement or there's stagnation, there's the past that drives you, and the regimental chaplain who preaches that only the obedient are free, and the women who say you have no feelings but they can't live without you. There's a prison called England, there's Sophie whom I betrayed, there's an Irish boy without a gun who kept looking at me while I shot his face off, and there's a girl I've scarcely spoken to who puts *equestrienne* on her passport and annoyed me so much that weeks later I'm still raging at her. There's a hero I can never be worthy of who had to be put back into uniform to be buried. And a sweaty Yorkshire Pied Piper whispering in my ear to come and do it all again.

. . .

REX GOODHEW was in fighting fettle. He had spent the first half of the morning successfully arguing Burr's cause to his master, and the second half addressing a Whitehall seminar on the misuses of secrecy, ending with a pleasurable shoot-out with a young fogy from the River

House, barely old enough to tell his first lie. Now it was lunchtime in Carlton Gardens, a low sun hit the white façades, and his beloved Athenaeum was a stroll away.

"Your chap Leonard Burr is putting himself about a bit, Rex," said Stanley Padstow of the Home Office with an anxious smile, falling in beside him. "I don't think I quite realized what you were letting us in for, to be honest."

"Oh dear," said Goodhew. "Poor you. What sort of putting about, exactly?"

Padstow had been up at Oxford at the same time as Goodhew, but the only thing Goodhew remembered about him was that he had seemed to have a mission to the plainer girl.

"Oh, nothing much," said Padstow, trying to sound light. "Using my staff to launder his file requests. Persuading the registrar to lie in her teeth for him. Taking senior police officers to three-hour lunches at Simpson's. Asking us to vouch for him when they get cold feet." He was glancing all the time at Goodhew but failing to catch his eye. "But it's all right, is it? It's just that, with these chaps, one never absolutely knows. Does one?"

There was a small delay while they negotiated themselves out of earshot of a flock of nuns.

"No, Stanley, one doesn't," said Goodhew. "But I did send you a detailed confirmation in writing, top secret for your very own file."

Padstow struggled yet more valiantly for the

throwaway tone. "And devilish frolics in the West Country—I mean, that's all going to be covered, is it? Only your letter didn't seem to make that totally clear."

They had reached the Athenaeum steps.

"Sounds fine to *me,* Stanley," Goodhew said. "Para three of my letter, as I recall, covers West Country frolics to the hilt."

"Murder not excluded?" Padstow asked urgently below his breath, as they stepped inside.

"Oh, I don't think so. Not as long as nobody gets hurt, Stanley." Goodhew's voice changed tone. "And it's compartmentation, isn't it?" he said. "Nothing to the River boys, nothing to anyone except Leonard Burr and, when you're worried, me. That's all right for you, is it, Stanley? Not a strain?"

They ate at separate tables. Goodhew treated himself to steak-and-kidney pie and a glass of the club's claret. But Padstow ate very fast, as if he were counting his bites against the clock.

SEVEN

JONATHAN ARRIVED at Mrs. Trethewey's post office store on a bleak Friday, calling himself Linden, a name he had picked out of the air when Burr invited him to suggest one. He had never met a Linden in his life, unless he was unconsciously recalling something on his German mother's side, a song or poem she had recited to him on her seemingly eternal deathbed.

The day had been sullen and damp, an evening that began at breakfast. The village lay a few miles from Land's End. The blackthorn on Mrs. Trethewey's granite hedge was hunchbacked from the southwesterly gales. The bumper stickers in the church car park told strangers to go home.

There is larceny to returning covertly to your own country after you have abandoned it. There is larceny to using a brand-new alias and being a new version of yourself. You wonder whose clothes you have stolen, what shadow you are casting, whether you have been here before as someone else. There is a sense of occasion about your first day in the part after six years as your undefined self in exile. Some of this freshness may have shown in Jonathan's face, for Mrs. Trethewey has always afterwards maintained that she observed a cockiness about him, what she called a twinkle. And Mrs. Trethewey is not given to romancing. She is a clever woman, tall and stately, not country to look at at all. Sometimes she says things that make you wonder what she might have been if she'd had the education they get these days, or a husband with more under his hat than poor old Tom, who dropped dead of a stroke in Penzance last Christmastime after a touch too much charity at the Masonic Hall.

"Jack Linden, he was *sharp,* now," she will say in her didactic Cornish way. "His eyes was nice enough when you first looked at them; merry, I dare say. But they was all over you and not the way *you're* thinking, Marilyn. They saw you far and close at the same time. You'd think he'd stole something before he ever come in the shop. Well, he had. We know that now. Same as we know a lot else we'd sooner not."

It was twenty past five and ten minutes to closing, and she was running up her totals on the electronic till before watching *Neighbors* on TV with Marilyn, her daughter, who was upstairs minding her little girl. She heard his big motorbike—"one of them real *growlers.*" She saw him bump it onto its stand and take off his helmet and smooth down his nice hair though it didn't need it, more a way of relaxing himself, she guessed. And she believed she saw him smile. An emmet, she thought, and a cheerful one at that. In West

Cornwall emmet means foreigner, and a foreigner is anyone who comes from east of the river Tamar.

But this one could have been an emmet from the moon. She'd a good mind to turn the notice round on the door, she says, but his looks stopped her. Also his shoes, which were the same as her Tom's used to be, polished like conkers and wiped carefully on the mat as he came in, not what you expected from a motorcyclist at all.

So she went on with her totals while he drifted round the shelves without bothering to take a basket, which is men all over whether they're Paul Newman or plain as mud: come in for a packet of razor blades, end up with their arms full, anything but take a basket. And very quiet on his feet, soundless almost, him being so light. You don't think of motorbike people being quiet as a rule.

"You from up-country then, are you, my dove?" she asked him.

"Oh, well, yes, I'm afraid I am."

"There's no need to be afraid, my darling. There's plenty of nice people come from up-country, and there's plenty down here I wish would *go* up-country." No answer. Too busy with the biscuits. And his hands, she noticed, now he'd pulled his gloves off: groomed to a turn. She always liked well-kept hands. "What part are you from, then? Somewhere nice, I hope."

"Well, nowhere, really," he confessed, pert as

may be, taking down two packets of digestives and a plain crackers and reading the labels as if he'd never seen them.

"You can't be from Nowhere Really, my robin," Mrs. Trethewey retorted, following him along the racks with her eyes. "You may not be Cornish, but you can't be just air. Where you from, now?"

But where the villagers tended to come smartly to attention when Mrs. Trethewey put on her stern voice, Jonathan merely smiled. "I've been living *abroad,*" he explained, as if humoring her. "I'm a case of the wanderer returned."

And his voice the same as his hands and shoes, she recounts: polished like glass.

"What part of abroad, then, my bird?" she demanded. "There's more than one abroad, even down here. We're not *that* primitive, though there's a lot may think we are, I dare say."

But she couldn't get past him, she says. He just stood there and smiled and helped himself to tea and tuna and oat cakes, calm as a juggler, and every time she asked a question he made her feel cheeky.

"Well, I'm the one who's taken the cottage at the Lanyon, you see," he said.

"That means you're barking mad, then, my darling," said Ruth Trethewey comfortably. "Nobody who wasn't mad would want to live out on the Lanyon, sitting in the middle of a rock all day."

And this farawayness in him, she says. Well, he was a sailor, of course, we know that now even if he put it to a bad use. This fixed grin he had while he studied the tinned fruits like he was learning them by heart. *Elusive,* that's what he was. Like soap in the bath. You thought you had him, then he'd slipped through your fingers. There was something about him, that's all she knows.

"Well, I suppose you have a name at least, if you've decided to join us," said Mrs. Trethewey in a kind of indignant despair. "Or did you leave that abroad when you come home?"

"Linden," he said, getting out his money. "Jack Linden. With an *i* and an *e*," he added helpfully. "Not to be confused with Lyn*don* with a *y.*"

She remembers how carefully he loaded everything into his saddlebags, one for this side, one for that side, like trimming his boat. Then kick-started his bike, with his arm up to say goodbye. You're Linden of the Lanyon, she decided, as she watched him ride up to the crossroads and tilt neatly to the left. From Nowhere Really.

"I've had a Mr.-Linden-of-the-Lanyon-with-an-*i*-and-an-*e* in the shop," she told Marilyn when she went upstairs. "And he's got a motor-bike bigger than a horse."

"Married, I suppose," said Marilyn, who had a baby girl but would never talk about the father.

And that was who Jonathan became, from his first day until the news broke: Linden of the Lanyon, another of those migrant English souls who seem almost by gravity to sink further and further westward down the peninsula, trying to escape their secrets and themselves.

The rest of the village's intelligence about him was gathered piecemeal by those near-supernatural methods that are the pride of any good network. How he was rich, which was to say he paid cash and paid it almost before it was owed—in new fives and tens counted like playing cards onto the lid of Mrs. Trethewey's deep-freeze. Well, we know where he got *that* from, don't we? No wonder it was cash!

"Say when, please, Mrs. Trethewey," Jonathan would call as he went on dealing out the bank notes. Shocking really to think they weren't his. But money has no smell, they say.

"Now, that's not my job, Mr. Linden," Mrs. Trethewey would protest. "That's your job. I can take all you've got of those and more." In the country, jokes fare best by repetition.

How he spoke all the foreign languages in the world, leastways German. Because when Dora Harris at the Count House had a lady German hiker go poorly on her, Jack Linden got to hear about it somehow and rode down to the Count House and talked to her, with Mrs. Harris sitting on the bed for respectability. Then stayed till Dr.

Maddern came, so he could translate the girl's symptoms to him, some of them very intimate, said Dora, but Jack Linden knew all the words. Dr. Maddern said he must have special knowledge to know words like that at all.

How he strode the cliff path in the early mornings like a man who couldn't sleep; so that Pete Hosken and his brother out at sea, lifting their lobster pots off Lanyon Head at dawn, would glimpse him on the clifftop, striding out like a trooper, most often with a pack on his shoulders: and what the hell would he put in a pack at that hour of the day? Drugs, I suppose. Well, they must have been. We know that too.

And how he worked the cliff meadows, up and down with his pick, till you'd think he was punishing the earth that bore him: that fellow could have made an honest living as a workman any day. Vegetables he was tilling, so he said, but didn't never stay long enough to eat them.

And cooked all his own food, said Dora Harris; gourmet by the smell of it, because when the southwesterly was mild enough he could make her mouth water from half a mile off, same with Pete and his brother out to sea.

And how he was sweet on Marilyn Trethewey, or more likely she was sweet on him— well, Linden, he was sweet on everybody, to a point, but Marilyn hadn't smiled for three winters, not till Jack Linden gave her reason.

And how he fetched old Bessie Jago's groceries for her twice a week on his motorbike from Mrs. Trethewey's—Bessie living on the corner to Lanyon Lane—arranging everything tidy on her shelves, not dumping the tins and packets on the table for her to sort out afterwards. And chattered to her all about his cottage, how he was slurrying his roof with cement and fitting new sashes to his windows and laying a new path to his front door.

But that was all he talked about, not a word about himself at all, where he'd lived or what he'd lived off, so that it was quite by accident they learned he had an interest in a boat business in Falmouth, a firm called Sea Pony, specialists in chartering and leasing sailing yachts. But not very highly regarded at all, said Pete Pengelly, more a hangout for water cowboys and druggies from up-country. Pete spotted him sitting in their front office one day when he took his van up to fetch a reconditioned outboard from Sparrow's boatyard next door: Linden was sat at a table, said Pete, talking to a big, fat, sweating, bearded bugger with curly hair and a gold chain round his neck, who seemed to run the place. So that when Pete got to Sparrow's he asked old Jason Sparrow outright: What's up with Sea Pony next door, then, Jason? Looks like they've been taken over by the Mafia.

One's Linden, the other's Harlow, Jason told Pete. Linden's from up-country, and Harlow, he's the big fat bearded bugger, Australian. The two of them bought the place for cash, said Jason, and haven't done a damn thing by it except smoke cigarettes and sail pleasure yachts up and down the estuary. Linden, he's some sailor, Jason conceded. But that Harlow, the fat one, he doesn't know his arse from his rudder. Mostly they quarrel, said Jason. Or Harlow does. Yells like a bloody bull. The other one, Linden, he just smiles. There's partners for you, said Jason with contempt.

So that was the first they heard of Harlow. Linden & Harlow, partners and enemies.

A week later, at lunchtime in the Snug, the same Harlow became flesh, and a bigger lump of it you never saw, eighteen stone, twenty. In he walked with Jack Linden and sat down right there in the pine corner next to the darts board where William Charles sits. Filled the whole damn bench, he did, and ate three pasties. And there the two of them stayed till afternoon closing time, heads together over a map, murmuring like a pair of bloody pirates. Well, we know why. They were plotting it.

And now turn your back and Jumbo Harlow dead. And Jack Linden vanished and not a bloody goodbye for anyone.

· · ·

VANISHED SO FAST that most of them only ever got to grips with him in their memories. Vanished so thoroughly that if they hadn't had the press cuttings pinned to the Snug wall they might have believed he never passed their way at all; that the Lanyon valley was never cordoned off with orange tape guarded by two dirty-minded young coppers from Camborne; that the plainclothes detectives never trampled over the village from milking time till dusk—"three cars' worth of the buggers," says Pete Pengelly; that the journalists never poured down from Plymouth, even London, women some of them and others who might as well have been, bombarding everyone with their stupid questions, from Ruth Trethewey right down to Slow-and-Lucky, who's a penny short of a pound and walks his Alsatian dog all day, the dog as daft as Lucky is, but more teeth: what did he wear, then, Mr. Luck? what did he talk about? did he never act violent with you at all?

"First day of it, we didn't hardly know the bloody difference between coppers and reporters," Pete likes to recall, to the laughter of the Snug. "We was calling the reporters sir and telling the coppers to bugger off. Second day, we was telling the whole lot of 'em to bugger off."

"He never bloody did it, boy," growls shrunken William Charles from his place beside the darts board. "They never proved nothing. You don't find no corpse, you got no bloody murderer. That's the law."

"They found the blood, though, William,"

says Pete Pengelly's younger brother, Jacob, who got three A-levels.

"Bugger blood," says William Charles. "Drop of blood didn't never prove nothing. Some bugger up-country cuts hisself shaving, police jumps up and calls Jack Linden a murderer. Bugger 'em."

"Why'd he run away, then? Why'd he flit off in the middle of the night if he never killed nobody?"

"Bugger 'em," William Charles repeats, like a beautiful Amen.

And why'd he leave poor Marilyn looking like a snake bit her, staring up the road all day in case his motorbike come back? *She* wouldn't tell the police no nonsense. Told them she'd never heard of him, and bugger it! Well, she would.

On it flows, back and forth, a checkered stream of puzzled reminiscence: at home as they sit dog-tired from the plow before their flickering television sets, on fogged-out evenings in the Snug as they sip their third beers and gaze at the plank floor. Dusk falls, the mist rolls in and sticks to the sash windows like steam, there's not a breath. The day's wind stops dead, the crows go quiet. On one short stroll to the pub you smell warm milk from the dairy, paraffin stoves, coal fires, pipe smoke, silage and seaweed from the Lanyon. A helicopter is plodding out to Scilly. A tanker is lowing in the sea fog. The church tower's chimes bang in your ear like a boxing gong. Everything is single, everything a separate smell or sound or piece of remembering. A footstep in the lane snaps like a broken neck.

"Tell you *one* thing, boy," Pete Pengelly pipes up as if butting in on a lively argument, though nobody has spoken a word about anything for minutes. "Jack Linden must have had some damn good reason. Jack, he had a reason for everything he ever done. You tell me if he didn't."

"He was some man in a boat too," concedes young Jacob, who like his brother fishes small boats out of Porthgwarra. "He come out with we one Saturday, didn't he, Pete? Never spoke a bloody word. Said he'd take a fish home. I offered to clean it for him, didn't I? Oh, I'll do it, he says. Lifted the fish straight off the bloody bone. Skin, head, tail, flesh. Cleaned it better than a seal."

"How 'bout sailing, then? Channel Islands to Falmouth single-handed in half a bloody gale?"

"Australian bugger got no more'n what he deserved," says a voice from the corner. "He was more rough than ever Jack was by a mile. You see his hands, then, Pete? Dear God, they was big as marrows."

It takes Ruth Trethewey to lend the philosophical touch, though Ruth will never talk about the Marilyn side and shuts anybody up who tries it in her company. "Every man has his personal devil waiting for him somewhere," declares Ruth, who since her husband's death will occasionally flout the male domination of the Snug. "There's no man here tonight who hasn't got murder in his heart if the wrong person tempts him to it. You can be Prince Charles, I don't care. Jack Linden was too polite for his health. Everything he'd got locked up in him come out all at once."

"Damn you, Jack Linden," Pete Pengelly announces suddenly, flushed with drink, while they sit there in the respectful silence that always follows one of Ruth Trethewey's insights. "If you walked in here tonight I'd buy you a bloody beer, boy, and shake you by the bloody hand same as I did that night."

And next day Jack Linden will be forgotten, perhaps for weeks. His amazing sea voyage is forgotten, so is the mystery of the two men in a Rover car who were said to have called on him at the Lanyon the night before he flitted—and several times before that, according to one or two who ought to have known.

Yet the press cuttings are still pinned to the Snug wall, the blue crags of Lanyon valley still weep and smolder in the poor weather that seems always to hang over them, the gorse and daffodils still flourish side by side on the banks of the Lanyon River, which is no wider these days than a fit man's stride. The darkened lane twists beside it on its way to the stubby cottage that was Jack Linden's home. The fishermen still steer a healthy berth round Lanyon Head, where brown rocks lurk like crocodiles at low water and the currents can suck you under on the quietest days, so that every year some fool cowboy from up-country, with a girlfriend and a rubber dinghy, diving for bits of wreck, dives his last or has to be lugged to safety by a rescue helicopter from Culdrose.

There were bodies enough in Lanyon Bay, they say in the village, long before Jack Linden added his bearded Australian to the score.

· · ·

AND JONATHAN?

Jack Linden was as much a mystery to himself as to the village. A dirty drizzle was falling as he kicked open the front door of the cottage and dumped his saddlebags on the bare boards. He had ridden three hundred and thirty miles in five hours. Yet as he tramped from one desolate bare room to another in his motorcycling boots and gazed out of the smashed windows at the apocalyptic landscape, he smiled to himself like a man who has found the palace of his dreams. I'm on my way, he thought. To complete myself, he thought, remembering the oath he had sworn in Herr Meister's fine-wine cellar. To discover the missing parts of my life. To get it right with Sophie.

His training in London belonged to another room in his mind: the memory games, the camera games, the communications games, the ceaseless drip of Burr's methodical instruction. Be this, never be that, be your natural self but more so. Their planning fascinated Jonathan. He enjoyed their ingenuity and the paths of contrary reasoning.

"We'll reckon on Linden lasting the first round," Burr had said through Rooke's pipe smoke, as the three men sat together in the Spartan training house in Lisson Grove. "After that we'll find you someone else to be. You still up for this?"

Oh, he was up for this! With his rekindled sense of duty, he had cheerfully participated in his impending destruction, adding touches of his own that he considered more faithful to the original.

"Hang on a sec, Leonard. I'm on the run and the police are looking for me, okay? You say make a dash for France. But I'm an Ireland man. I'd never trust a border while I'm hot."

And they heeded him, and penciled in a hellish extra week of lying low, and were impressed, and said as much behind his back.

"Keep him on a tight lead," Rooke advised Burr in his role as custodian of Jonathan's army persona. "No pampering. No extra rations. No unnecessary visits to the front line to buck him up. If he can't take it, the sooner we find out the better."

But Jonathan could take it. He had always

taken it. Deprival was his element. He longed for a woman, a woman he had yet to meet, someone with a mission like his own, not a frivolous equestrienne with a rich patron: a woman with Sophie's gravitas and heart, and Sophie's undivided sexuality. Rounding a corner on his cliff walks, he would let his face light up with a smile of delighted recognition at the notion that this unmet paragon of female virtue would be waiting for him: Oh, *hullo,* Jonathan, it's *you.* Yet too often, when he examined her features more closely, she bore an uncomfortable similarity to Jed: Jed's wayward, perfect body, Jed's puckish smile.

· · ·

THE FIRST TIME Marilyn Trethewey came to visit Jonathan was to deliver a case of mineral water that was too big to go on his motorbike. She was finely molded like her mother, with a strict set jaw and jet-black hair the color of Sophie's, and ruddy Cornish cheeks and strong high breasts, for she could not have been a day more than twenty. Spotting her striding behind her pram down the village street, always alone, or standing apart at the till in her mother's shop, Jonathan had wondered whether she was even seeing him, or merely resting her gaze on him while she saw something different in her mind.

She insisted on carrying the case of bottles to the front door, and when he made to take it from her, she shrugged him off. So he stood on his own doorstep while she went into the house and set the box on the kitchen table, then took a long stare round the living room before coming back outside.

"Dig yourself in," Burr had advised. "Buy a greenhouse, plant a garden, form lifelong friendships. We need to know you had to tear yourself away. If you can find a girl to leave dangling, so much the better. In a perfect world you'd make her pregnant."

"Thanks very much."

Burr caught his tone and gave him a swift sideways glance. "What's the matter, then? Taken a vow of celibacy, have we? That Sophie really got to you, didn't she?"

A couple of days later Marilyn came again, this time without anything to deliver. And instead of her habitual jeans and scruffy top, she had got herself up in a skirt and jacket, as if she had a date with her solicitor. She rang the bell, and as soon as he opened the door she said, "You gon' leave me be, then, right?" So he took a step back and let her past him, and she placed herself at the center of the room as if testing his reliability. And he saw that the lace cuffs of her blouse were shaking, and he knew that it had cost her a lot to get this far.

"You like it here, then, do you?" she asked him in her challenging way. "All by your own?" She had her mother's quick eye and untutored shrewdness.

"It's meat and drink to me," said Jonathan, taking refuge in his hotelier's voice.

"What d'you do, then? You can't watch telly all day. You haven't got none."

"Read. Walk. Do a bit of business here and there." So now go, he thought, smiling tensely at her, eyebrows raised.

"You paint, then, do you?" she said, examining his watercolors set out on the table before the seaward window.

"I try."

"I can paint." She was picking through the brushes, testing them for springiness and shape. "I was good at painting. Won prizes, didn't I?"

"Why don't you paint now, then?" Jonathan asked.

He had meant it as a question, but to his alarm she took it as an invitation. Having emptied out the water jar in the sink, she refilled it and sat down at his table, selected a fresh sheet of cartridge paper and, having tucked her hair behind her ears, lost herself to everything except her work. And with her long back turned to him, and her black hair hanging down it, and the sunlight from the window blazing on the top of her head, she was Sophie, his accusing angel, come to visit him.

He watched her for a while, waiting hopefully for the association to fade, but it didn't, so he went outside and dug in the garden until dusk. He returned to find her wiping down the table just as she had done at school. Then she propped her unfinished painting against the wall, and instead of sea or sky or cliff, it showed a dark-haired, laughing girl—Sophie as a child, for instance, Sophie long before she married her perfect English gentleman for his passport.

"Come again tomorrow, then?" she asked in her clipped, aggressive way.

"Of course. If you wish. Why not?" said the hotelier, making a mental note to be in Falmouth. "If I have to be out, I'll leave the door open."

And when he returned from Falmouth he found the painting of the girl completed, and a note telling him gruffly that it was for him. After that she came most afternoons, and when she had finished her painting she sat herself opposite him in the armchair across the fire and read his copy of *The Guardian.*

"World's in a damn good mess, then, in't it, Jack?" she announced, rattling the paper. And he heard her laugh, which was what the village was beginning to hear too. "It's a bloody pigsty, Jack Linden. You take my word for it."

"Oh, I do," he assured her, careful not to return her smile for too long. "I absolutely do, Marilyn."

But he began urgently to wish her gone. Her vulnerability scared him. So did his sense of distance from her. Not in a thousand years, he assured Sophie in his mind. I swear.

. . .

ONLY OCCASIONALLY, in the early mornings, for he woke most often with the dawn, did Jonathan's operational resolve threaten to collapse, and for a black hour he became the plaything of a past that reached much further back than Sophie's betrayal. He remembered the prickle of uniform against his child's skin and the khaki collar sawing at his neck. He saw himself sleeping at attention in the iron cot of his barrack room, waiting for reveille and the first falsetto orders of the day: Don't stand like a bloody butler, Pine, get your shoulders back, boy! *Right* back! More! He relived his fear of everything: of the mockery when he failed and the envy when he won; of the parade ground and the games field and the boxing ring; of being caught when he stole things for his comfort—a penknife, a photograph of someone's parents; of his fear of failure, which meant failing to ingratiate himself; of being late or early, too clean, not clean enough, too loud, too quiet, too subservient, too cheeky. He remembered learning to be brave as an alternative to cowardice. He remembered the day he struck back, and the day he struck first, as he taught himself to lead from weakness into strength. He remembered his early women, no different from his later ones, each a bigger disillusionment than the last as he struggled to elevate them to the divine status of the woman he had never had.

Of Roper he thought constantly—he had only to fish him from the pockets of his memory to feel a surge of purpose and direction. He could not listen to the radio or read a newspaper without detecting Roper's hidden hand in every conflict. If he read of a massacre of women and children in East Timor, it was Roper's guns that had committed the outrage. If a car bomb exploded in Beirut, Roper had supplied it, and probably the car as well: *Been there. Seen the movie, thanks.*

After Roper, it was Roper's people who became the object of his fascinated indignation. He thought of Major Corkoran alias Corky alias Corks, in his grimy muffler and disgraceful suede boots: Corky the signer, Corky who could get five hundred years in jail anytime Burr chose.

He thought of Frisky and Tabby and the misty company of retainers—of Sandy Lord Langbourne, with his gold hair bound at the nape; of Dr. Apostoll on his risers, whose daughter had killed herself for a Cartier watch; of MacArthur and Danby, the gray-suited executive twins from the nearly respectable side of the operation—until collectively the Roper household became a kind of monstrous First Family for him, with Jed his First Lady in the Tower.

"How much does she know about his business?" Jonathan asked Burr once.

Burr shrugged. "The Roper doesn't boast and doesn't tell. Nobody knows more than he needs to. Not with our Dicky."

An upper-class waif, thought Jonathan. A

convent-school education. A faith rejected. A locked-up childhood like mine.

· · ·

JONATHAN'S ONLY confidant was Harlow, but between operational confidants there are limits to what either can confide. "Harlow is a walk-on," Rooke warned, during a night visit to the Lanyon. "He's only there for you to kill. He doesn't know the target, and he doesn't need to. Keep it that way."

Nevertheless, for this stage of the journey the murderer and his mark were allies, and Jonathan strove to make a bond with him.

"You a married man, Jumbo?"

They were sitting at the scrubbed pine table in Jonathan's kitchen after returning from their planned appearance at the Snug. Jumbo shook his head regretfully and took a pull of beer. He was an embarrassed soul, as big men often are, an actor or a grounded opera singer with a huge barrel chest. His black beard, Jonathan suspected, had been grown expressly for the part and would be gratefully removed as soon as the show ended. Was Jumbo a genuine Australian? It didn't matter. He was an expatriate everywhere.

"I shall expect a lavish funeral, Mr. Linden," said Jumbo gravely. "Black horses, a sparkling carriage and a nine-year-old catamite in a top hat. Your health."

"And yours too, Jumbo."

Having drained his sixth can, Jumbo slapped on his blue denim cap and lumbered to the door. Jonathan watched his crippled Land-Rover hobble up the winding lane.

"Who on earth was that?" said Marilyn, arriving with a pair of fresh mackerel.

"Oh, he's just my business partner," said Jonathan.

"Looked more like bloody Godzilla on a dark night to *me*."

She wanted to fry the fish, but he showed her how to bake it in foil, with fresh dill and seasoning. Once, as a dare, she tied his apron round him, and he felt her strong black hair brush against his cheek and waited for the smell of vanilla. Stay away from me. I betray. I kill. Go home.

· · ·

ONE AFTERNOON Jonathan and Jumbo took the plane from Plymouth to Jersey and in the little port of St. Hélier made a show of inspecting a twenty-five-foot yacht that was moored on the far side of the harbor. Their journey, like their joint appearance at the Snug, was intended for display. In the evening, Jumbo flew back alone.

The yacht they inspected was called *Ariadne,* and according to her log she had arrived from Roscoff two weeks earlier, sailed by a Frenchman named Lebray. Before Roscoff she was in Biarritz and, before that, open seas. Jonathan spent two days fitting her out, provisioning her and preparing the chartwork. On the third day he took her to sea to get the feel of her and boxed the compass for himself while he was about it, for at sea as on land he trusted no one's work but his own. At first light on the fourth day he set sail. The area forecast was good, and for fifteen hours he cruised nicely at four knots, reaching for Falmouth on a southwesterly. But by evening the wind had turned blustery and by midnight it had freshened to a six or seven, throwing a big ground swell that had the *Ariadne* pitching. Jonathan reduced sail and ran before the weather for the safety of Plymouth. As he passed the Eddystone Lighthouse the wind veered westerly and fell, so he changed course to Falmouth once more and beat west, hugging the shore and short-tacking to avoid the heavy weather. By the time he reached harbor he had been sailing hard for two nights without sleep. Sometimes the sounds of the storm deafened him. Sometimes he heard no weather at all and wondered if he was dead. The beam sea and the close-hauling had rolled him about like a boulder; his body creaked and his head rang hollow with the solitude of the sea. But throughout the journey he thought of nothing he afterwards remembered. Or nothing but his own survival. Sophie was right. He had a future.

"You been somewhere nice, then?" Marilyn asked him, staring at the fire. She had taken off her cardigan. She wore a sleeveless blouse, buttoned down the back.

"Just a trip up-country."

He realized with dread that she had been waiting for him all day. Another painting stood on the chimneypiece, very like the first. She had brought him fruit, and freesias for the vase.

"Well, thank you," he said politely. "That's super of you. Thanks."

"You want me, then, Jack Linden?"

She had lifted her hands to the back of her neck and unfastened the top two buttons of her blouse. She took a step to him and smiled. She began weeping, and he didn't know what to do. He put his arm round her and led her to her van and left her there to weep till she was ready to drive home.

· · ·

THAT NIGHT, an almost metaphysical sense of his uncleanliness descended over Jonathan. In his extreme solitude, he decided that the fake murder he was about to commit was an externalization of the real murders he had already committed in Ireland and the murder he had committed against Sophie; and that the ordeal that awaited him was a mere foretaste of a lifetime of penance.

For the days that remained to him, a passionate fondness for the Lanyon took possession of his heart and he rejoiced in every fresh example of the cliff's perfection: the seabirds wherever they put themselves, always in the right place, the hawks lying on the wind, the setting sun melting into black cloud, the fleets of small boats clustered over the shoals below, while the gulls above made a shoal of their own. And when darkness came, there were the boats again, a tiny city in the middle of the sea. With each last hour, this urge to be assumed into the landscape—hidden in it, buried in it—became almost unbearable.

A storm got up. Lighting a candle in the kitchen, he stared past it into the swirling night, while the wind crackled in the window frames and made the slate roof chatter like an Uzi. In the early morning, when the storm dropped, he ventured outdoors to wander over last night's battlefield—then, Lawrence-like, leapt helmetless onto his motorbike, drove up to one of the old hill forts and scanned the coastline till he made out some landmark that pointed to the Lanyon. That is my home. The cliff has accepted me. I will live here forever. I will be clean.

But his vows were in vain. The soldier in him was already polishing his boots for the long march toward the worst man in the world.

· · ·

IT WAS during these final days of Jonathan's tenure of the cottage that Pete Pengelly and his brother, Jacob, made the mistake of going lamping at the Lanyon.

Pete tells the story cautiously, and with visitors present he won't tell it at all, for there's confession to it and a certain rueful pride. Lamping for rabbits in those parts has been a hallowed sport for fifty years and more. With two motorcycle batteries in a small box strapped against your hip, an old car spotlamp with a close beam, and a bunch of spare six-volt bulbs, you can mesmerize a whole convocation of rabbits for long enough to pick them off in salvos. No law and no battalions of strident ladies in brown berets and ankle socks have succeeded in putting a stop to it, and the Lanyon has been a favored hunting ground for generations—or was, until four of them went up there one night with guns and lamps, led by Pete Pengelly and his younger brother, Jacob.

They parked at Lanyon Rose, then picked their way along the river-bed. Pete swears to this day they were quiet as rabbits themselves and hadn't used the lamps but found their way by full moon, which was why they'd chosen that night. But when they came out on the cliff, careful to keep below the horizon, there stood Jack Linden not half a dozen paces uphill from them, his bare hands lifted from his sides. Kenny Thomas afterwards kept on about his hands, so pale and prominent in the moonlight, but that was the effect of the occasion. The knowing recall that Jack Linden never had big hands. Pete prefers to talk about Linden's face, which was set, he says, like a chunk of bloody blue elvan rock against the sky. You'd have broken your fist on it. There is no dispute about what took place after that.

"Excuse me, but where do you gentlemen think you're going, if I may ask?" says Linden with his customary respectfulness but no smile.

"Lamping," says Pete.

"Nobody's lamping here, I'm afraid, Pete," says Linden, who had only set eyes on Pete Pengelly a couple of times but seemed never to forget a name. "I own these fields, you know that. I don't farm them, but I do own them, and I let them be. That's what I expect other people to do as well. So I'm afraid lamping is out."

"It is, is it, Mr. Linden?" Pete Pengelly says.

"Yes, it is, Mr. Pengelly. I won't have sitting game shot on my land. It's not fair play. So why don't you all please empty your guns and go back to the car and go home and no hard feelings?"

At which Pete says, "To hell with you, boy," and the other three gather to Pete's side so that they are all four bunched and looking up at Linden, four guns against one fellow with the moon behind him. They had come straight on from the Snug, all of them, and were the better for a beer or two.

"Get out of our bloody way, Mr. Linden," says Pete.

Then he makes the mistake of fidgeting his gun under his arm. Not pointing it at Linden: he swore he would never have done that, and those who know Pete believe him. And the gun was broken: Pete would never in his life have walked with a closed and loaded gun at night, he says. Nevertheless, as he fidgeted the gun, making it clear that he meant business, it is possible he snapped the breach shut by mistake; he will grant you that. Pete does not claim to have a precise and accurate memory of everything that happened, because the world by then was turning on its head around him, the moon was in the sea, his arse was on the other side of his face, and his feet were the other side of his arse, and the first useful information Pete could put together was that Linden was standing over him emptying the cartridges from his gun. And since it is true that big men fall harder than small men, Pete had fallen very hard indeed, and the impact of the blow, wherever it had hit him, had robbed him not only of his breath but of his will to get up.

The ethics of violence required that it was now the turn of the others, and there were still three of them. The two Thomas brothers had always been quick with their fists, and young Jacob played wing forward for the Pirates and was broad as a bus. And Jacob was all set to go in after his brother. It was Pete, lying in the bracken, who ordered him off.

"Don't touch him, boy. Don't you ever bloody go near him. He's a bloody witch. Go back to the car, all of us," he said, climbing slowly to his feet.

"Empty your guns first, please," says Linden.

On Pete Pengelly's nod the three men emptied the cartridges from their guns. Then all four trooped back to the car.

"I'd have bloody killed him!" Jacob protested as soon as they had driven off. "I'd have broke the bugger's legs for him, Pete, after what he done to you!"

"No, you wouldn't, my handsome," Pete replied. "But he'd have broke yours for sure."

And Pete Pengelly, they say in the village, changed his manners from that night on, though perhaps they are a little hasty to link cause with effect. Come September month, Pete married a sensible farmer's daughter from St. Just. Which is why he is able to look back on the episode with distance and tell about the night Jack Linden damn near did for him the way he did for that fat Aussie.

"I'll tell you one thing, boy. If Jack *did* do him in, he made some neat job of it, that's for sure."

But there's a better ending to it than that, even if Pete sometimes keeps it to himself like a thing too precious to share. The night before Jack Linden disappeared, he walked into the Snug and laid a bandaged hand on Pete Pengelly's shoulder and bought him a bloody beer, man. They talked for ten minutes, then Jack Linden went on home. "He was puttin' it right with himself," Pete insists proudly. "You bloody listen to me, boy. Jack

Linden was setting his bloody house straight after he done his business with the Aussie."

Except that his name wasn't Jack Linden by then, which was something they couldn't properly get used to, and perhaps they never will. A couple of days after his disappearance, Linden-of-the-Lanyon-with-an-*i*-and-an-*e* turned out to be Jonathan Pine of Zurich, wanted by the Swiss police on suspicion of embezzlement at a fashionable hotel where he had been a trusted employee. "Sailing Hotelier on the Run," the *Cornishman* sang, over a photograph of Pine alias Linden. "Police seek Falmouth boat trader in case of missing Australian. 'We are treating this as a drug-related murder inquiry,' says CID chief. 'The man should be easily identified by his bandaged hand.' "

But Pine was not a man they knew.

. . .

YES, BANDAGED. And wounded. Wound and bandage were both integral features of Burr's plan.

Jack Linden's hand, the same as he had laid on Pete Pengelly's shoulder. A lot of people, not just Pete Pengelly, had seen that hand bandaged, and the police, at Burr's instigation, made a fair fuss of who they all were, which hand it was, and when. And when they'd got the who and the when and the which, then, being police, they wanted the why. Which is to say, they wrote down the conflicting versions that Jack had given for having his right hand done up in a big gauze bandage, professional, and the fingertips tied together like asparagus. And with Burr's help, the police made sure these found their way into the press.

"Trying to fit a new pane of glass at my cottage," Jack Linden told Mrs. Trethewey on the Thursday as he paid her out his cash wrong-handed for the last time.

"Teach me to help out a friend," Jack had remarked to old William Charles when the two of them chanced to meet at Penhaligon's garage, Jack for petrol for the bike, William Charles for passing the time. "Asked me to pop by and help him mend his window. And now look." Then shoved his bandaged hand at William Charles like a sick dog with his paw, because Jack could make a joke of anything.

But it was Pete Pengelly who got them hot and bothered. "Of course it was in his bloody woodshed, boy!" he told the detective sergeant. "Trimming a pane of bloody glass, he was, up at the Lanyon in his woodshed, and the cutter slipped, blood all over the place. He put a bandage on it, bound it tight and drove himself one-handed to hospital on his bike, blood running up his sleeve all the way to Truro, told me! You don't make that up, boy. You bloody *do* it."

But when the police dutifully inspected the Lanyon woodshed, they found no glass, no cutter and no blood.

Murderers lie, Burr had explained to Jonathan. Too consistent is too dangerous. If you don't err, you won't be criminal.

The Roper checks, Burr had explained. Even when he's not suspicious, he checks. So we give you these little murderer's lies, to make the untrue murder true.

And a nice scar speaks volumes.

· · ·

AND AT SOME POINT in these last few days, Jonathan broke all the rules and, without Burr's consent or knowledge, visited his former wife, Isabelle, in search of atonement.

I'll be passing through, he lied, telephoning her from a Penzance call box. Let's have lunch somewhere quiet. Riding his motorbike to Bath, wearing only the left glove because of his bandaged hand, he rehearsed his lines to her until they became a heroic song in his mind: You'll read things about me in the papers, but they won't be true, Isabelle. I'm sorry about the bad times, Isabelle, but there were good times too. Then he wished her luck, imagining she would do the same for him.

In a men's lavatory he changed into his suit and became a hotelier again. He hadn't seen her for five years, and he barely recognized her when she strode in twenty minutes late and blamed the bloody traffic. The long brown hair she used to brush down her naked back before they went to bed was cut to a practical brevity. She wore chunky clothes to hide her shape and carried a zip bag with a cellular telephone. And he remembered how, by the end, the telephone had been the only thing she could talk to.

"*Christ,*" she said. "*You* look prosperous. Don't worry, I'll switch it off."

She's become a blurter, he thought, and remembered that her new husband was something in the local hunt.

"Well, stone the crows," she shouted. "Corporal Pine. After *all* these years. What on *earth* have you done to your hand?"

"Dropped a boat on it," he said, which apparently was sufficient explanation. He asked her how business was. In his suit it seemed the right sort of question to ask. He had heard she had gone into interior design.

"Bloody awful," she replied heartily. "What's Jonathan up to, anyway? Oh my Lord," she said, when he told her. "You're in the leisure industries too. We're doomed, darling. You're not *building* them, are you?"

"No, no. Brokering. Ferrying. We've got off to quite a decent start."

"Who's *we,* darling?"

"An Australian chum."

"Male?"

"Male and eighteen stone."

"What are you doing for sex? I always thought you might be queer. You're not, though, are you?"

It was a charge she had made often in her day, but she seemed to have forgotten this.

"Good Lord no," Jonathan replied with a laugh. "How's Miles?"

"Worthy. Very sweet. Banking and good works. He's got to pay off my overdraft next month, so I'm being nice to him."

She ordered a warm duck salad and Badoit and lit a cigarette. "Why did you give up hoteling?" she asked, blowing smoke in his face. "Bored?"

"Just the lure of the new," he said.

We'll desert, the captain's untamable daughter had whispered as she spread her sublime body over his. *If I have to eat one more army dinner I'll blow up this whole barracks single-handed. Fuck me, Jonathan. Make me a woman. Fuck me and take me somewhere I can breathe.*

"How's the painting doing?" he asked, remembering how they had both worshiped her great talent, how he had abased himself in order to elevate it, cooked and carried and swept for her, believing she would paint the better for his self-denial.

She snorted. "My last exhibition was three years ago. Sold six out of thirty, all to Miles's rich friends. Probably needed someone like you to make a basket case out of me. *Jesus,* you led me a dance. What the hell did you want? I wanted to be van Gogh—what did *you* want? Apart from being the army's answer to Rambo?"

You, he thought. I wanted you, but you weren't there. He could say none of it. He wished he could be worse-mannered. Bad manners are freedom, she used to say. Fucking is bad manners. But there was no point to her argument anymore. He had come to ask forgiveness for the future, not the past.

"Anyway, why didn't you want me to tell Miles I was seeing you?" she asked accusingly.

Jonathan pulled the old false smile. "I didn't want us to upset him," he said.

For a magic moment he saw her as he had first possessed her in the days when she was the belle of his regimental depot: the crisp rebellious face tilted in desire, lips parted, the angry smolder in her eyes. Come back, he shouted in his heart. Let's try again.

The young ghost vanished and the old one reappeared.

"Why on *earth* don't you pay in plastic?" she asked as he counted out the bank notes with his left hand. "Far easier to tell where the pennies are going, darling."

Burr was right, he thought. I'm a single man.

EIGHT

HUNCHED IN the passenger seat of Rooke's car as they plunged through the gathering Cornish dusk, Burr pulled his overcoat collar more tightly about his ears and returned his soul to the suite of windowless rooms on the outskirts of Miami where not forty-eight hours earlier the covert action team for Operation Limpet had been holding its exceptional Open Day.

. . .

COVERT ACTION teams do not normally admit espiocrats and other sophists to their midst, but Burr and Strelski have their reasons. The atmosphere is of a Holiday Inn sales conference held in battle conditions. Delegates arrive singly, identify themselves, descend in steel elevators, identify themselves again and greet each other carefully. Each wears his name and occupation on his lapel, even if some names have been chosen only for this day and some occupations are so obscure that old hands pause to work them out. DEP DR OPS CO-ORDS, reads one. SUPT NARCS & FMS SW, reads another. And between them, like refreshing smiles of clarity, U. S. SENATOR, FEDERAL PROSECUTOR or U. K. LIAISON.

The River House is represented by an enormous Englishwoman in perfect curls and Thatcherite twin set, known universally as Darling Katie and officially as Mrs. Katherine Handyside Dulling, Economic Counselor of the British Embassy in Washington. For ten years Darling Katie has held the golden key to Whitehall's special relationship with America's numberless intelligence agencies. From Military to Naval to Air to State through Central and National to the omnipotent murmurers of the White House palace guard—from the sane to the harmlessly mad to the dangerously ridiculous—the secret overworld of American might is Katie's parish, to explore, bludgeon, bargain with and win to her celebrated dinner table.

"Do you hear what he called me, Cy, this *monster* here, this *thing?*" Katie bellows to a tight-lipped senator in a double-breasted suit, while she holds an accusing finger, pistol-like, to Rex Goodhew's temple. "A *femagogue!* Me! A *femagogue!* Isn't that the most politically incorrect thing you ever *heard*? I'm a mouse, you beast. A wilting violet! And calls himself a Christian!"

Jolly laughter fills the room. Katie's iconoclastic boom is the theme music of insiders. More delegates arrive. Groups break up, re-form. "Why, Martha, *hullo!* . . . Walt, *hi*. Good to see you. . . . Marie, great!"

Someone has given the signal. A dry clatter

as delegates toss their paper cups into trash bags and troop to the projection room. The lowliest, led by Amato, head for the front rows. Farther back, in the expensive seats, Darker's deputy in Procurement Studies, Neal Marjoram, shares cozy laughter with a ginger-headed American espiocrat whose name card reveals him only as "Central America—Funding." Their laughter fades with the lights. Somebody funny says, "Action!" Burr takes a last look at Goodhew. He is leaning back in his chair, smiling at the ceiling, like a concertgoer who knows the music well. Joe Strelski embarks on his address.

· · ·

AND JOE STRELSKI as a purveyor of disinformation is word perfect. Burr is bemused. After a decade of deception, it has never occurred to him until today that the best deceivers are the bores. If Strelski were wired from head to toe with lie detectors, Burr is convinced, the needles would not flinch. They would be too bored. Strelski speaks for fifty minutes, and by the time he has finished, fifty are as much as anyone can take. In his word-heavy monotone, the most sensational intelligence is turned to ash. The name of Richard Onslow Roper barely escapes his lips. In London he had used it without compunction. Roper is our target; Roper is the center of the web. But today in Miami, before a mixed audience of Purists and Enforcers, Roper is relegated to obscurity, and when Strelski trails a halfhearted slide show of the cast, it is **Dr. Paul Apostoll** who gets star billing as *known to us for the last seven years as the cartels' principal intermediary and dealmaker in this hemisphere.* . . .

Strelski now logs the wearisome process of pinpointing Apostoll as *the primary axis of our initial investigations* and offers a labored account of *the successful activities of agents Flynn and Amato* in placing a bug in the doctor's New Orleans offices. If Flynn and Amato had repaired a leaking pipe in the men's room, Strelski could not have sounded less thrilled. With a superbly tedious sentence, read from a prepared text, unpunctuated and full of false emphases, he hastens his audience on its way to sleep:

"The basis for Operation Limpet is intelligence indicators from a variety of technical sources to the effect that the three leading Colombian cartels have signed a mutual nonaggression deal with each other as a prerequisite to providing themselves with a military shield commensurate with the financial muscle available and equal to the twin threats foremost in their conceptual thinking." Breath. "These threats are, one"—another breath—"armed interdiction by the United States at the behest of the Colombian government." Almost done, but not quite. "Two, the growing strength of the non-Colombian cartels primarily in Venezuela and Bolivia. Three, the

Colombian government acting on its own account but with the hands-on encouragement of U.S. agencies."

Amen, thinks Burr, transfixed with admiration.

The history of the case appears to interest nobody, which is probably why Strelski supplies it. Over the last eight years, he says—another slump in interest—several attempts have been made by "a variety of parties lured by the cartels' unlimited financial resources" to persuade them to get the habit of buying serious weapons. French, Israelis and Cubans have all pressed their cases, as have a bunch of independent manufacturers and dealers, most with the tacit connivance of their parent governments. The Israelis, assisted by British mercenaries, actually succeeded in selling them a few Galil assault rifles and a training package.

"But the cartels," says Strelski, "well, after a while the cartels kind of lose interest."

The audience knows exactly how the cartels feel.

Screen atmospherics as Dr. Apostoll is discovered on the island of Tortola, in long shot from across the street, seated inside the offices of the Caribbean law firm of Langbourne, Rosen and de Souta, notaries to the nefarious. Two whey-faced Swiss bankers from Grand Cayman are identified at the same table. Major Corkoran sits between them, and to Burr's secret pleasure the signer is holding a drawn fountain pen in his right hand. Across the table from him sits an unidentified Latin American. The languid male beauty next to him, hair tied prettily at the nape, is none other than Lord Langbourne, alias Sandy, legal adviser to Mr. Richard Onslow Roper of the Ironbrand Land, Ore & Precious Metals Company of Nassau, the Bahamas.

"Who took this footage, please, Mr. Strelski?" a very legal American male voice demands sharply in the darkness.

"We did," Burr replies complacently, and the company at once relaxes again: Agent Strelski has not, after all, exceeded his territorial powers.

But now even Strelski cannot keep the excitement out of his voice, and for a brief moment Roper's name is fair and square before them.

"In direct consequence of the nonaggression deal to which I have just had reference, the cartels instructed their representative to take soundings with a couple of illegal arms traders in the hemisphere," he says. "What we see here, according to our sources, but filmed unfortunately without sound, is the first overt approach made by Apostoll to hands-off intermediaries of Richard Roper."

As Strelski sits down, Rex Goodhew bobs to his feet. Goodhew plays it straight today. He isn't funny, he uses none of the English linguistic frills that so infuriate Americans. He openly regrets the involvement of British nationals in the affair, some of them with distinguished names. He regrets that they are able to shelter behind the laws of British protectorates in the Bahamas and the Caribbean. He is heartened by the good relations established at working level between the British and American sides. He wants blood, and he wants Pure Intelligence to help him draw it.

"Our shared aim is to catch the culprits and make a public example of them," he declares, with Truman-like simplicity. "With your help, we want to enforce the rule of law, prevent the proliferation of arms in a volatile region and cut off the supply of *drugs*"—in Goodhew's mouth the word sounds like a mild form of aspirin—"which we believe to be the currency in which the arms bill will be paid—to wherever they are destined. To this end, we are asking for your full, unquestioning support-in-aid as intelligence-gathering agencies. Thank you."

Goodhew is followed by the federal prosecutor, an ambitious young man whose voice growls like a racing car engine turning over in the pits. He vows he will "bring this thing to court in record time."

Burr and Strelski take questions.

"How about humint in this one, Joe?" a woman's voice calls at Strelski from the back of the hall. The British contingent is momentarily baffled by this piece of Cousins jargon. *Humint!*

Strelski almost blushes. It is clear he would

have preferred her not to ask. His expression is that of a loser who refuses to admit defeat. "We're working on it, Joanne, believe me. Human sources on a thing like this, you have to wait and pray. We have lines, we have hopes, we have our people in there sniffing, and we believe that somebody out there soon is going to need to buy himself some witness protection, is going to call us up one night and ask us to arrange it for him. It's going to happen, Joanne." He nods determinedly, as if he agreed with himself where nobody else did. "It's going to happen," he repeats, as unconvincingly as before.

It is lunchtime. The smoke screen is in place, even if they cannot see it. Nobody remarks that Joanne is one of Strelski's close assistants. The procession toward the door has started. Goodhew departs with Darling Katie and a couple of espiocrats.

"Now listen, you men," Katie can be heard saying as they leave. "No fobbing me off with two fat-free lettuce leaves, d'you hear? I want meat and three veg and plum duff, or I ain't goin' no place. *Femagogue* indeed, Rex Goodhew. And then you come to us with your begging bowl. I'm going to break your pious neck."

. . .

IT IS EVENING. Flynn, Burr and Strelski sit on the deck of Strelski's beach house, watching the moon path flutter in the wake of returning pleasure boats. Agent Flynn is nursing a large glass of Bushmills single malt. He sensibly keeps the bottle at his side. The conversation is sporadic. Nobody wants to talk out of turn about the day's proceedings. Last month, says Strelski, my daughter was a vegan. This month she's in love with the butcher. Flynn and Burr laugh dutifully. Another silence falls.

"When's your boy cut loose?" Strelski asks quietly.

"End of the week," Burr replies in the same low tone. "God and Whitehall willing."

"With your boy inside pulling and our boy outside pushing, I guess that makes us a closed loop," says Strelski.

Flynn laughs richly, nodding his great dark head like a deaf-mute in the half-darkness. Burr asks what a closed loop is.

"A closed loop, Leonard—that's using every part of the pig except the squeal," says Strelski. Another pause while they sit and watch the sea. When Strelski speaks again, Burr has to lean close to catch his words.

"Thirty-three grown people in that room," he murmurs. "Nine different agencies, seven pols. Must be a couple of 'em telling the cartels Joe Strelski and Leonard Burr don't have a humint source worth shit—right, Pat?"

Flynn's soft Irish laughter is almost drowned by the rustle of the sea.

But Burr, though he keeps it to himself, cannot quite share his hosts' complacency. The Purists had not asked too many questions, it was true. In Burr's uneasy judgment, they had asked too few.

. . .

TWO IVY-COATED granite posts loomed out of the mist. The engraved inscription said Lanyon Rose. There was no house. Farmer probably died before he got round to building it, thought Burr.

They had been driving seven hours. Above the granite hedges and the blackthorn, an uneasy sky was darkening to dusk. The shadows on the pitted track were liquid and elusive, so that the car kept bucking as if it had been hit. It was a Rover and Rooke's pride. His powerful hands wrestled with the steering wheel. They passed deserted farm buildings and a Celtic cross. Rooke switched his headlights to bright, then switched them down again. Since they had crossed the Tamar River they had known only dusk and rolling mist.

The track rose, the mist vanished. Suddenly all they saw through the windscreen was canyons of white cloud. A salvo of raindrops rattled against the car's left side. The car rocked, then tipped over the edge in a free-fall, its nose pointing at the Atlantic. They made the last turn, the steepest. A gust of warring birds clattered over them. Rooke braked to a crawl until the fury passed. A fresh burst of rain hit them. As it cleared, they saw the gray cottage crouching on a saddle of black bracken.

He's hanged himself, Burr decided, catching sight of Jonathan's crooked silhouette as it dangled in the porch light. But the hanged man lifted an arm in greeting and stepped forward into the blackness before switching on his torch. A patch of granite chip made a crude parking place. Rooke climbed out, and Burr heard the two men hailing each other like a pair of travelers. "Good to see you! Great! Christ, what a wind!" Burr in his nervousness stayed stubbornly in his seat, grimacing to heaven while he forced the top button of his overcoat through its hole. The wind was booming round the car, shaking the aerial.

"Get a move on, Leonard!" Rooke yelled. "You can powder your nose later!"

"You'll have to wriggle across, I'm afraid, Leonard," Jonathan said through the driver's window. "We're evacuating you to leeward, if that's all right."

Grabbing his right knee with both hands, Burr navigated it over the gear lever and the driving seat, then did the same for the left. He lowered one city shoe onto the gravel. Jonathan was shining the torch straight at him. Burr made out boots and a seaman's knitted cap.

"How've you been?" Burr shouted, as if they hadn't seen each other for years. "Fit?"

"Well, yes, I think I really am, actually."

"Good lad."

Rooke went ahead with his briefcase. Burr and Jonathan followed him side by side up the hacked path.

"And that went all right, did it?" Burr asked, nodding at Jonathan's bandaged hand. "He didn't amputate it by mistake, then."

"No, no, it was fine. Slice, stitch, wrap it up—didn't take above half an hour, the whole job."

They were standing in the kitchen. Burr's face was still stinging from the wind. Scrubbed pine table, he noticed. Polished flagstones. Polished copper kettle.

"No pain?"

"Not beyond the call of duty," Jonathan replied.

They laughed shyly, strangers to each other.

"I've had to bring you a piece of paper," Burr said, coming as usual straight to what was weighing on his mind. "You're supposed to sign it, with me and Rooke as witnesses."

"What does it say, then?" said Jonathan.

"Humbug's what it says"—laying the blame on a convenient bureaucracy. "Damage limitation. Their insurance policy. We didn't push you, you'll never sue us, you have no case against the government for neglect, malfeasance or rabies. If you fall out of a plane it's your fault. Et cetera."

"Getting cold feet, are they?"

Burr caught the transferred question and turned it back. "Well, are *you*, Jonathan? That's more the point, isn't it?" Jonathan started to protest, but Burr said, "Shut up and listen. This time tomorrow you'll be a wanted man. *Un*wanted is more like it. Anyone who ever knew you will be saying, 'I told you so.' Anyone who didn't will be studying your photograph for evidence of homicidal tendencies. That's a life sentence, Jonathan. It'll never go away."

Jonathan had a stray memory of Sophie among the splendors of Luxor. She was sitting on a plinth, arms around her knees, staring down the aisle of columns. *I need the comfort of eternity, Mr. Pine,* she said.

"I can still stop the clock, if that's what you want, and no harm done except to my ego," Burr continued. "But if you're wanting to pull out and haven't the bottle to say, or if you're being too nice to your Uncle Leonard or some such idiocy, I'll trouble you to get up your courage and declare yourself now, not later. We can have a nice supper, goodbye, drive home, no hard feelings, none that last. We can't do that tomorrow night, or any night after."

Heavier shadows in the face, Burr was thinking. The watcher's stare that stays on you after he's looked away. What have we spawned? He glanced round the kitchen again. Wool pictures of ships in full sail. Bits of treen, Newlyn copperware. A luster plate that read "Thou see'st me, God."

"Are you sure you don't want me to put this stuff in store for you?" Burr asked.

"No, honestly. It's fine. Just sell it. Whatever's easiest."

"You could want it one day, when you settle down."

"Better to travel light, really. And it's all there still, is it—the target, I mean? He's still doing what he's doing, living where he lives and so on? Nothing's changed?"

"Not that I know of, Jonathan," said Burr with a slightly puzzled smile. "And I keep pretty much in touch. He's just bought himself a Canaletto, if that's a guide. And a couple more Arab horses for his stud. And a nice diamond collar for his lady. I didn't know they called them collars. Sounds like a lapdog. Well, I suppose that's what she is."

"Perhaps it's all she can afford to be," said Jonathan.

He was holding out his bandaged hand, and for a moment Burr thought he wanted him to shake it. Then he realized Jonathan was asking for the document, so he delved in his pockets, first his overcoat, then his jacket, and drew out the heavy sealed envelope.

"I'm serious," Burr said. "It's your decision."

With his left hand, Jonathan selected a steak knife from the kitchen drawer, tapped the sealing wax with the handle to break it, then cut open the envelope along the flap. Burr wondered why he bothered to break the wax, unless he was showing off his dexterity.

"Read it," Burr ordered. "Every stupid word as many times as you like. You're Mr. Brown, in case you hadn't guessed. An unnamed volunteer in our employ. In official papers, people like you are always Mr. Brown."

Drafted by Harry Palfrey for Rex Goodhew. Handed down to Leonard Burr for Mr. Brown to sign.

"Just never tell me his name," Goodhew had insisted. "If I've seen it, I've forgotten it. Let's keep it that way."

Jonathan held the letter to the oil lamp in order to read it. What is he? Burr wondered for the hundredth time, studying the hard-soft contours of his face. I thought I knew. I don't.

"Think about it," Burr urged. "Whitehall did. I've had them rewrite it twice." He had one last try. "Just tell me for myself, will you? 'I, Jonathan, am sure.' You know what you're about, you've worked it through. And you're still sure."

The smile again, putting Burr still less at ease. Jonathan was holding out his bandaged hand again, this time for Burr's pen. "I'm sure, Leonard. I, Jonathan. And I'll be sure tomorrow morning. How do I sign? Jonathan Brown?"

"John," Burr replied. "In your usual handwriting." The image of Corkoran the signer with his drawn fountain pen flitted across Burr's inner eye as he painstakingly wrote *John Brown.*

"All done," he said brightly to console him.

But Burr still wanted more of something. Drama, a greater feeling of occasion. He stood up, making an old man's labor of it, and let Jonathan help him out of his coat. They walked together to the parlor, Jonathan leading.

The dining table was set for ceremony. Linen napkins, Burr noticed indignantly. Three lobster cocktails in their glasses. Silver-plate knives and forks like a three-star restaurant. A decent Pommard uncorked to breathe. A smell of roasting meat. What the hell's he trying to do to me?

Rooke was standing with his back to them, hands in pockets, studying Marilyn's latest watercolor.

"I say, I rather like this one," he said in a rare effort at flattery.

"Thanks," said Jonathan.

. . .

JONATHAN HAD heard them approaching long before he saw them. And even before he heard them he knew they were there because alone on the cliff the close observer had learned to hear sounds in the making. The wind was his ally. When the fog came down and all he seemed to hear was the moaning of the lighthouse, it was the wind that brought him the chatter of the fishermen out to sea.

So he had felt the trembling of the Rover's engine before ever its growl rolled down the cliff to him, and he braced himself as he stood waiting in the wind. When its headlights appeared, aimed straight at him, he aimed back at them in his mind, estimating the Rover's speed by the telegraph poles and calculating the distance ahead that he would have to aim if he were sighting a rocket-propelled grenade. Meanwhile a corner of his vision waited on the hilltop in case they had a chase car or were sending in a decoy.

And when Rooke parked and Jonathan walked smiling through the gale with his torch, he had imagined shooting his two guests down the torch's beam, blowing off their green faces in alternate bursts. Players successfully negotiated. Sophie avenged.

But now as they left he was calm and saw different things. The storm had vanished, leaving torn-off shreds of cloud. A few stars lingered. Gray bullet holes made a spray pattern round the moon. Jonathan watched the Rover's tail-lights pass the meadow where he had planted his iris bulbs. In a few weeks, he thought, if the rabbits don't get through the wire, that meadow will be mauve. The tail-lights passed a bull warren, and he remembered how one warm evening, returning from Falmouth, he had surprised Jacob Pengelly and his girlfriend there, stripped of everything except each other, Jacob in transport straining back from her, the girl arched to him like an acrobat.

Next month will be a blue month on account of the bluebells, Pete Pengelly had told him. But this month now, Jack, this one is a gold month getting golder, with the gorse and cowslips and wild daffodils winning against all comers. Just you see if they don't, Jack. Cheers.

To complete me, Jonathan rehearsed to himself. To find the missing parts of me.

To make a man of me, which was what my father said the army did: one man.

To be useful. To stand upright. To rid my conscience of its burden.

He felt sick. Going to the kitchen, he gave himself a glass of water. A brass ship's clock hung above the door, and without pausing to think why, he wound it up. Then he went to the drawing room, where he kept his treasure: a grandmother long-case clock in fruitwood with a single weight, bought of Daphne's in Chapel Street for a song. He pulled the brass chain till the weight was at the top. Then he set the pendulum in motion.

"Reckon I'll go up my Aunt Hilary's in Teignmouth for a bit, then," Marilyn had said, no longer weeping. "Be a break, Teignmouth will, won't it?"

Jonathan had had an Aunt Hilary too, in Wales beside a golf club. She had followed him round the house putting the lights out, and prayed aloud to her dear Lord Jesus in the dark.

· · ·

"DON'T GO," he had begged Sophie, in every way he knew, as they waited for the taxi to take them back to Luxor airport. "Don't go," he had begged her on the plane. "Leave him, he'll kill you, don't take the risk," he had begged her as he saw her into the cab that would take her back to her apartment, and Freddie Hamid.

"We both have our appointments with life, Mr. Pine," she had told him with her battered smile. "There are worse indignities, for an Arab woman, than being beaten by her lover. Freddie is very wealthy. He has made me certain practical promises. I have to consider my old age."

NINE

IT IS Mother's Day as Jonathan walks into Espérance. His third cement truck in four hundred miles has dropped him on the crossroads at the top of the Avenue des Artisans. The signs as he strides down the sidewalk swinging his Third World air bag read MERCI MAMAN, BIENVENUE À TOUTES LES MAMANS and VASTE BUFFET CHINOIS DES MÈRES. The northern sun is an elixir to him. When he breathes, it is as if he is breathing light as well as air. I'm home. It's me.

After eight months of snow, this easy-living gold town in the province of Quebec is hopping in the evening sunshine, which is what the town is famous for among its sister townships strewn along the largest greenstone mineral belt in the world. It hops higher than Timmins to the west in stodgy Ontario, higher than Val-d'Or or Amos to the east, higher by a mile than the dreary white-collar settlements of hydroelectric engineers up north. Daffodils and tulips strut like soldiers in the garden of the white church with its leaden roof and narrow spire; dandelions as big as dollars cover the grass slope below the police station. After their winter's wait beneath the snow, the flowers are as rampant as the town. The shops for the suddenly rich or merely hopeful—the Boutique Bébé with its pink giraffes, the pizza cafés named after lucky miners and prospectors, the Pharmacie des Croyants, which offers hypnotherapy and massage, the neon-lit bars named after Venus and Apollo, the stately whorehouses after vanished madams, the Japanese sauna house with its pagoda and plastic pebble garden, the banks of every color and persuasion, the jewelry stores where the high-graders used to melt the miners' stolen ore and occasionally still do, the wedding shops with their virginal wax brides, the Polish delicatessen advertising "films super-érotiques XXX" as if they were a culinary event, the restaurants open all hours for shift workers, even the notaries with their blackened windows—all sparkle in the glory of the early summer, and *merci Maman* for all of it: *on va avoir du fun!*

As Jonathan glances into shop windows or gratefully upward at the blue heaven and lets the sunlight warm his hollowed face, motorcyclists with beards and dark glasses roar up and down the street, racing their engines and flicking their leather backsides at the girls who sip their Cokes at outdoor tables on the sidewalk. In Espérance the girls stand out like parakeets. The matrons of stodgy Ontario next door may dress themselves like sofas at a funeral, but here in Espérance the hot-blooded Québecois make a carnival every day, in radiant cottons and gold bracelets that smile at you across the street.

There are no trees in Espérance. With forests all around, the townspeople see open space as an accomplishment. And there are no Indians in Espérance, or not so that you'd notice, unless like Jonathan you spot one with his wife and family, loading a pickup with a thousand dollars' worth of provisions from the *supermarché*. One of them stays aboard the truck to guard it, while the rest hang close.

There are no vulgar emblems of wealth in the town either, if you discount the seventy-five-thousand-dollar power yachts in the parking lot beside the Château Babette's kitchens, or the herds of Harley-Davidson motorcycles clustered round the Bonnie and Clyde Saloon. Canadians—French or any other sort—don't care for display, whether of money or emotion. Fortunes are still made, of course, by those who strike it lucky. And luck is the real religion of the town. Everyone dreams of a gold mine in his garden, and a couple of the lucky ones have found just that. Those men in baseball hats and sneakers and bomber jackets who stand about talking into mobile phones: in other towns they would be drug pushers or numbers boys or pimps, but here in Espérance they are the quiet millionaires of thirty. As to the older ones, they eat their lunches out of tin boxes a mile below ground.

Jonathan devours all this in the first minutes of his arrival. In his state of bright-eyed exhaustion, he takes in everything at once, while his heart bursts with the gratitude of a voyager setting foot on the promised shore. It's beautiful. I worked for it. It's mine.

. . .

HE HAD ridden out of the Lanyon at daybreak without looking back, and headed for Bristol for his week of lying low. He had parked his motorbike in a run-down suburb where Rooke had promised to have it stolen, he had taken a bus to Avonmouth, where he found a seamen's hostel run by two elderly Irish homosexuals who, according to Rooke, were famous for not collaborating with the police. It rained all day and night, and on the third day, while Jonathan was eating breakfast, he heard his name and description on the local radio: last seen West Cornwall area, injured right hand, ring this number. While he listened he saw the two Irishmen listening too, their eyes fixed on one another. He paid his bill and took the bus back to Bristol.

Vile cloud rolled over the wrecked industrial landscape. Hand in pocket—he had reduced the dressing to a simple adhesive bandage—he walked the damp streets. Seated in a barber's chair, he glimpsed his picture on the back of someone's evening paper, the photograph that Burr's people had taken of him in London: a likeness deliberately unlike, but still a likeness. He became a ghost, haunting a ghost town. In the cafés and billiard halls he was too white and separate, in the smarter streets too ragged. The churches, when he tried to enter them, were locked. His face when he checked it in mirrors scared him with its hostile intensity. Jumbo's faked death was like a goad to him. Visions of his supposed victim unmurdered and unhunted, carousing serenely in some secret haven, taunted him at all odd moments. Nevertheless, in his other persona, he determinedly shouldered the guilt of his imaginary crime. He bought a pair of leather gloves and threw away his bandage. To buy his air ticket he spent a morning inspecting travel agents before he chose the busiest and most anonymous. He paid in cash and made the booking for two days later, in the name of Fine. Then he took the bus to the airport and changed his booking to the flight that same evening. There was one seat left. At the departure gate a girl in mulberry uniform asked to see his passport. He pulled off a glove and gave it to her with his good hand.

"Are you Pine or Fine, then?" she demanded.

"Whichever you prefer," he assured her, with a flash of the old hotelier's smile, and she grudgingly waved him through—or had Rooke squared them?

When he reached Paris he dared not risk the barrier at Orly, so he sat up in the transit area all night. In the morning he took a flight to Lisbon, this time in the name of Dine, for on Rooke's advice he was trying to stay one jump ahead of the computer. In Lisbon he again made for the docks and again lay low.

"She's called the *Star of Bethel,* and she's a pig," Rooke had said. "But the skipper's venal, which is what you're looking for."

He saw a half-bearded man trailing from one shipping office to another in the rain, and the man was himself. He saw the same man pay a girl for a night's lodging, then sleep on her floor while she lay on her bed and whimpered because she was afraid of him. Would she be less afraid of me if I slept with her? He didn't stay to find out but, leaving her before dawn, walked the docks once more and came upon the *Star of Bethel* moored in the outer harbor, a filthy, twelve-thousand-ton coaling vessel bound for Pugwash, Nova Scotia. But when he asked at the shipping agent's, they said she had a full complement and was sailing on the night tide. Jonathan bribed his way aboard. Was the captain expecting him? Jonathan believed he was.

"What can you do, son?" the captain asked. He was a big, soft-spoken Scot of forty. Behind him stood a barefoot Filipino girl of seventeen.

"Cook," said Jonathan, and the captain laughed in his face but took him as a supernumerary on condition he worked his passage and the captain pocketed his pay.

Now he was a galley slave, sleeping in the

worst bunk and receiving the insults of the crew. The official cook was an emaciated Lascar, half dead from heroin, and soon Jonathan was doing duty for them both. In his few hours of sleep he dreamed the lush dreams of prisoners, and it was Jed without her Meister's bathrobe who played the leading role. Then a sunny morning dawned and the crew were patting him on the back and saying they had never been better fed at sea. But Jonathan would not go ashore with them. Equipped with rations he had set aside, the close observer preferred to make himself a hideaway in the forward hold and lie up for two more nights before sneaking past the dock police.

Alone in an immense and unfamiliar continent, Jonathan was assailed by a different kind of deprivation. His resolve seemed suddenly to drain into the brilliant thinness of the landscape. Roper is an abstraction, so is Jed and so am I. I am dead and this is my afterlife. Trekking along the edge of the uncaring highway, sleeping in drivers' dormitories and barns, scrounging a day's pay for two days' labor, Jonathan prayed to be given back his sense of calling.

"Your best bet is the Château Babette," Rooke had said. "It's big and sloppy, and it's run by a harridan who can't keep staff. It's where you'd naturally hole out."

"It's the ideal place for you to start looking for your shadow," Burr had said.

Shadow meaning identity. Shadow meaning substance, in a world where Jonathan had become a ghost.

. . .

THE CHÂTEAU BABETTE roosted like a tattered old hen amid the razzmatazz of the Avenue des Artisans. She was the Meister's of the town. Jonathan spotted her at once from Rooke's description, and as he approached her he remained on the opposite pavement so that he could take a better look at her. She was tall and timbered and decrepit and, for a former whorehouse, stern. A stone urn stood at each corner of her hideous porch. Flaking naked maidens cavorted on them in a woodland setting. Her hallowed name was blazoned vertically on a rotting wooden board, and as Jonathan started across the road, a sharp east wind made it clatter like a railway train, filling his eyes with grit and his nostrils with smells of *frites* and hair spray.

Striding up the steps, he confidently pushed the ancient swing doors and entered the darkness of a tomb. From far away, as it seemed to him at first, he heard male laughter and caught the stink of last night's dinner. Gradually he made out an embossed copper postbox, then a grandfather clock with flowers on its face that reminded him of the Lanyon, then a reception desk littered with correspondence and coffee mugs and illuminated by a canopy of fairy lights. The shapes of men surrounded him, and it was they who were doing the laughing. His arrival had evidently coincided with that of a bunch of raunchy surveyors from Quebec, who were looking for a little action before taking off next day for a mine up north. Their suitcases and kit bags were flung in a heap at the foot of a wide staircase. Two Slavic-looking boys in earrings and green aprons picked sullenly among the labels.

"Et vous, monsieur, vous êtes qui?" a woman's voice yelled at him above the hubbub.

Jonathan made out the queenly form of Madame Latulipe, the proprietress, standing behind the desk in a mauve turban and cake makeup. She had tilted her head back in order to quiz him and she was playing to her all-male audience.

"Jacques Beauregard," he replied.

"Comment, chéri?"

He had to repeat it above the din: *"Beauregard,"* he called, unused to raising his voice. But somehow the name came easier to him than Linden.

"Pas d'bagage?"

"Pas de bagage."

"Alors, bon soir et amusez-vous bien, m'sieu," Madame Latulipe yelled back at him as she handed him his key. It occurred to Jonathan that she had mistaken him for a member of the surveyors' party, but he saw no need to enlighten her.

"Allez-vous manger avec nous à'soir, M'sieu

Beauregard?" she called, waking to his good looks as he started up the stairs.

Jonathan thought not, thank you, madame. Time he got some sleep.

"But one cannot sleep on an empty stomach, M'sieu Beauregard!" Madame Latulipe protested flirtatiously, once more for the benefit of her raucous guests. "One must have energy to sleep if one is a man! *N'est-ce pas, mes gars?"*

Pausing at the half-landing, Jonathan bravely joined the laughter but insisted nonetheless that he must sleep.

"Bien, tant pis d'abord!" cried Madame Latulipe.

Neither his unscheduled arrival nor his unkempt appearance disturbed her. Unkempt is reassuring in Espérance, and to Madame Latulipe, the town's self-elected cultural arbiter, a sign of spirituality. He was *farouche,* but *farouche* in her book meant noble, and she had detected Art in his face. He was a *sauvage distingué,* her favorite kind of man. By his accent she had arbitrarily ruled him French. Or perhaps Belgian. She was not an expert; she took her holidays in Florida. All she knew was, when he spoke French she could understand him, but when she spoke back at him he looked as insecure as all Frenchmen looked when they heard what Madame Latulipe was convinced was the true, the uncorrupted version of their tongue.

Nevertheless, on the strength of these impulsive observations, Madame Latulipe made a pardonable error. She placed Jonathan, not on one of the floors convenient for receiving lady guests, but in her *grenier,* in one of four pretty attic rooms that she liked to hold in reserve for her fellow bohemians. And she gave no thought to the fact— but then why should she?—that her daughter, Yvonne, had made her temporary refuge two doors down.

. . .

FOR FOUR DAYS Jonathan remained in the hotel without attracting more than his share of Madame Latulipe's consuming interest in her male guests.

"But you have deserted your group!" she cried at him, in mock alarm, when he appeared next morning late and alone for breakfast. "You are not a surveyor anymore? You have resigned? You wish to become a poet perhaps? In Espérance we write many poems."

Seeing him return in the evening, she asked him whether he had composed an elegy today, or painted a masterpiece. She suggested he take dinner, but he again declined.

"You have eaten somewhere else, m'sieu?" she demanded in mock accusation.

He smiled and shook his head.

"Tant pis d'abord," she said, which was her habitual reply to almost everything.

Otherwise he was room 306 to her, no trouble. It was not until Thursday, when he asked her for a job, that she subjected him to closer scrutiny. "What kind of job, *mon gars?*" she inquired. "You wish to sing for us in the disco perhaps? You play the violin?"

But she was already on the alert. She caught his glance and renewed her impression of a man separate from the many. Perhaps too separate. She examined his shirt and decided it was the one he had been wearing when he arrived. Another prospector has gambled his last dollar, she thought. At least we haven't been paying for his meals.

"Any job," he replied.

"But there are many jobs in Espérance, Jacques," Madame Latulipe objected.

"I've tried them," said Jonathan, looking back on three days of Gallic shrugs or worse. "I tried the restaurants, the hotels, the boatyard and the lake marinas. I tried four mines, two logging companies, the cement works, two gas stations and the paper mill. They didn't like me either."

"But why not? You are very beautiful, very sensitive. Why do they not like you, Jacques?"

"They want papers. My social insurance number. Proof of Canadian citizenship. Proof I'm a landed immigrant."

"And you don't have these? None? You are too aesthetic?"

"My passport's with the immigration authorities in Ottawa. It's being processed. They wouldn't believe me. I'm Swiss," he added, as if that explained their incredulity.

But by then Madame Latulipe had pushed the button for her husband.

André Latulipe had been born not Latulipe but Kviatkovski. It was only when his wife inherited the hotel from her father that he had consented to change his name to hers for the sake of perpetuating a branch of the Espérance nobility. He was a first-generation immigrant with a cherub's face and a broad, blank forehead and a mane of premature white hair. He was small and stocky and as fidgety as men become at fifty when they have worked themselves nearly to death and start to wonder why. As a child, Andrzej Kviatkovski had been hidden in cellars and smuggled over snowy mountain passes at dead of night. He had been held and questioned and released. He knew what it was to stand in front of uniforms and pray. He glanced at Jonathan's room bill and was impressed, as his wife had been, that it comprised no extra charges. A swindler would have used the telephone, signed tabs at the bar and in the restaurant. A swindler would have done a midnight flit. The Latulipes had had a few swindlers in their day, and that was what they did.

The bill still in his hand, Latulipe looked Jonathan slowly up and down, much as his wife had done before him, but with insight: at his wanderer's brown boots, scuffed but mysteriously clean; at his hands, small and workmanlike, held respectfully to his sides; at his trim stance and harrowed features and the spark of desperation in the eyes. And Monsieur Latulipe was moved to kinship by the sight of a man fighting for a toehold in a better world.

"What can you do?" he asked.

"Cook," said Jonathan.

He had joined the family. And Yvonne.

. . .

SHE KNEW him immediately: yes. It was as if, through the agency of her appalling mother, signals that might have taken months to exchange were transmitted and received in a second.

"This is Jacques, our very *latest* secret," said Madame Latulipe, not bothering to knock but flinging open an attic bedroom door not ten yards along the passage from his own.

And you are Yvonne, he thought, with a mysterious shedding of shame.

A desk stood at the center of the floor. A wooden reading lamp lit one side of her face. She was typing, and when she knew it was her mother she continued typing to the end, so that Jonathan had to endure the tension of looking at a mop of untidy fair hair until she chose to lift her head. A single bed was shoved along the wall. Stacked baskets of laundered bed sheets took up the remaining space. There was order, but there were no keepsakes and no photographs. Just a sponge bag by the handbasin, and on the bed a lion with a zipper down its tummy for her nightdress. For a sickening moment it reminded Jonathan of Sophie's slaughtered Pekingese. I killed the dog too, he thought.

"Yvonne is our family genius, *n'est-ce pas, ma chère?* She has studied art, she has studied philosophy, she has read every book that was ever printed in the world. *N'est-ce pas, ma chérie?* Now she is pretending to be our housekeeper, she is living like a nun, and in two months she will be married to Thomas."

"And she types," said Jonathan, God alone knew why.

A letter slowly disgorged itself from the printer. Yvonne was looking at him, and he saw the left side of her face in naked detail: the straight, untamed eye, her father's Slavic brow and uncompromising jaw, the silk-fine hairs on the cheekbone, and the side of her strong neck as it descended into her shirt. She was wearing her key chain like a necklace, and as she straightened herself the keys settled with a clink between her breasts.

She stood up, tall and at first glance mannish. They shook hands; it was her idea. He felt no hesitation. Why should he, Beauregard, new to Espérance and life? Her palm was firm and dry.

She was wearing jeans, and again it was her left side that he noticed by the light of the desk lamp: the tight denim creases that stretched from the crotch across her left thigh. After that it was the formal precision of her touch.

You're a retired wildcat, he decided, as she calmly returned his glance. You took early lovers. You rode pillion on Harley-Davidsons while you were high on pot or worse. Now at twenty-something you've reached a plateau, known otherwise as compromise. You're too sophisticated for the provinces but too provincial for the city. You're engaged to marry someone boring, and you're struggling to make him more. You are Jed but on a downward slope. You are Jed with Sophie's gravitas.

She dressed him, with her mother looking on.

. . .

THE STAFF UNIFORMS were hung in a walk-in airing cupboard on the half-landing one flight down. Yvonne led the way, and by the time she opened the cupboard door he knew that for all her outdoor manners, she had a woman's walk—neither the swagger of a tomboy nor the watch-me roll of a teenager, but the straight-hipped authority of a grown and sexual woman.

"For the kitchen, Jacques wears white and only white, and laundered every day, Yvonne. Never the same clothes from one day to the next, Jacques; it is a rule of my house, as everybody knows. At the Babette, one is passionately conscious of hygiene. *Tant pis d'abord."*

While her mother chattered, Yvonne held first the white jacket against him, then the elastic-topped white trousers. Then she ordered him to go into room 34 and try them on. Her brusqueness, perhaps for the benefit of her mother, had an edge of sarcasm. When he came back, her mother insisted that the sleeves were long, which they were not, but Yvonne shrugged and took them up with pins, her hands brushing indifferently against Jonathan's and the warmth of her body mingling with his own.

"You are comfortable?" she asked him as if she didn't give a damn.

"Jacques is always comfortable. He has inner resources, *n'est-ce pas,* Jacques?"

Madame Latulipe wished to know about his extramural preferences. Did Jacques like to dance? Jonathan replied that he was prepared for anything but not perhaps quite yet. Did he sing, play an instrument, act, paint? All these pastimes and more were available in Espérance, Madame Latulipe assured him. Perhaps he would like to meet some girls? It would be normal, said Madame Latulipe: many Canadian girls would be interested to hear of life in Switzerland. Courteously prevaricating, Jonathan heard himself say something mad in his excitement:

"Well, I wouldn't get far in these, would I?"

he exclaimed, so loudly that he nearly broke out laughing, while he continued to hold out his white sleeves to Yvonne. "The police would pick me up at the first crossroads, looking like this, wouldn't they?"

Madame Latulipe let out a peal of the wild laughter that is the signature tune of humorless people. But Yvonne was studying Jonathan with a bold curiosity, eyes on eyes. Was it tactic or was it my infernal calculation? Jonathan wondered afterwards. Or was it suicidal indiscretion that in the first few moments of our meeting I told her I was on the run?

· · ·

THE SUCCESS of their new employee quickly delighted the elder Latulipes. They warmed to him with each new skill that he revealed. In return, Jonathan the more-than-good soldier gave them his every waking hour. There had been a time in his life when he would have sold his soul to escape the kitchens for the elegance of a manager's black jacket. No longer. Breakfast began at six for the men coming back from night shift. Jonathan was waiting for them. An order of twelve-ounce sirloin steak, two eggs and *frites* was nothing out of the way. Spurning the sacks of frozen chips and ill-smelling catering oil favored by his patroness, he used fresh potatoes, which he peeled and parboiled, then fried in a blend of sunflower and peanut oils, only the best quality would do. He got a stockpot going, installed a herb chest, made casseroles, pot roasts and dumplings. He found an abandoned set of steel knives and sharpened them to perfection—no one else must touch them. He revived the old range that Madame Latulipe had variously ruled insanitary, dangerous, ugly or too priceless to be used. When he added salt, he did it in the true chef's way, hand raised high above his head, raining it down from a height. His bible was a tattered copy of his beloved *Le Répertoire de la Cuisine,* which to his delight he had stumbled upon in a local junkshop.

All this Madame Latulipe observed in him at first with an adoring, not to say obsessive, admiration. She ordered new uniforms for him, new hats, and for two pins she would have ordered him canary waistcoats, lacquered boots and cross-garters. She bought him costly pots and double boilers, which he did his best to use. And when she discovered that he employed a common laborer's blowtorch to glaze the sugar surface of his *crème brûlée,* she was so impressed by the blending of the artistic with the mundane that she insisted on marching her bohemian ladies into the kitchen for a demonstration.

"He is so refined, our Jacques, *tu ne crois pas*, Mimi, *ma chère?* He is reserved, he is handsome, he is skillful, and when he wishes he is *extremely* dominating. There! We old ladies may say such things. When we see a fine man, we do not have to blush like little girls. *Tant pis d'abord,* Hélène?"

But the same reticence that she so admired in Jonathan also drove her to distraction. If she did not own him, who did? At first she decided he was writing a novel, but a reconnaissance of the papers on his desk yielded nothing but draft letters of complaint to the Swiss Embassy in Ottawa, which the close observer, anticipating her interest, had composed for her discovery.

"You are in love, Jacques?"

"Not that I am aware, madame."

"You are unhappy? You are lonely?"

"I am blissfully content."

"But to be content is not enough! You must abandon yourself. You must risk everything every day. You must be ecstatic."

Jonathan said his ecstasy was his work.

When lunch was over, Jonathan could have taken the afternoon off, but more often he went down to the basement to help hump crates of empties into the yard while Monsieur Latulipe checked takings: for God help the waiter or bar girl who smuggled in a private bottle to sell at disco prices.

Three evenings a week Jonathan cooked family dinner. They ate it early round the kitchen table, while Madame Latulipe made intellectual conversation.

"You are from Basel, Jacques?"

"Not far from Basel, madame."

"From Geneva?"

"Yes, nearer to Geneva."

"Geneva is the capital of Switzerland, Yvonne."

Yvonne did not raise her head.

"You are happy today, Yvonne? You have spoken to Thomas? You must speak to him every day. When one is engaged to be married, it is normal."

And at around eleven, when the disco hotted up, Jonathan was once more there to lend a hand. The shows before eleven were mere displays of nudity, but after eleven the acts became more animated and the girls gave up putting on their clothes between turns, except for a tinselly apron for their cash and maybe a gown they didn't bother to fasten. When they opened their legs for you for an extra five dollars—a personal service performed at your table, on a stool that the house provided for the purpose—the effect was of a furry burrow belonging to some artificially illuminated night animal.

"You like our floor show, Jacques? You find it cultural? It stimulates you a little, even you?"

"It's very effective, madame."

"I am glad. We should not deny our feelings."

Fights were seldom and had the sporadic quality of skirmishes between puppies. Only the worst of them ended in expulsion. A chair would shriek, a girl would skip back, there was the smack of a fist or the strict silence of two men wrestling. Then out of nowhere André Latulipe was between them like a little Atlas, holding them apart until the company settled again. The first time this happened, Jonathan left him to handle matters in his own way. But when an oversized drunk started to take a swing at Latulipe, Jonathan locked the man's spare arm behind him and led him to the fresh air.

"Where did you learn that stuff?" Latulipe asked as they were clearing bottles.

"In the army."

"The Swiss have an *army?*"

"It's obligatory for everyone."

One Sunday night the old Catholic curé came, wearing a soiled dog collar and a patched frock. The girls stopped dancing and Yvonne ate lemon pie with him, which the curé insisted on paying for out of a trapper's purse bound with a thong. Jonathan watched them from the shadows.

Another night a mountain of a man appeared, with cropped white hair and a cuddly corduroy jacket with leather elbows. A jolly wife in a fur coat waddled at his side. One of Latulipe's Ukrainian waiters gave him a table by the floor; he ordered champagne and two plates of smoked salmon and watched the show with fatherly indulgence. But when Latulipe looked round for Jonathan, to warn him that the superintendent would not expect a bill, Jonathan had vanished.

"You got something against police?"

"Until my passport comes back, yes."

"How come you knew he was police?"

Jonathan smiled disarmingly but offered no reply that Latulipe could afterwards remember.

. . .

"WE SHOULD warn him," Madame Latulipe said for the fiftieth time as she lay sleeplessly in bed. "She is provoking him deliberately. She is up to her old tricks."

"But they never speak. They never look at each other," her husband protested, putting down his book.

"And you don't know why? Two criminals like them?"

"She's engaged to Thomas, and she will marry Thomas," said Latulipe. "Since when was no crime a crime?" he added gamely.

"You are speaking like a barbarian, as usual. A barbarian is a person without intuition. Have you told him he mustn't sleep with the disco girls?"

"He shows no disposition to."

"There you are, then! Perhaps it would be better if he did."

"He's an athlete, for Christ's sake," Latulipe burst out, his Slav temper getting the better of him. "He has other outlets. He goes running. He treks in the bush. He sails. He hires motorbikes. He cooks. He works. He sleeps. Not every man is a sex maniac."

"Then he is a *tapette*," Madame Latulipe announced. "I knew it the moment I saw him. Yvonne is wasting her time. It will teach her a lesson."

"He's not a *tapette!* Ask the Ukrainian boys! He is entirely normal!"

"Have you seen his passport yet?"

"His passport has nothing to do with whether he is a *tapette!* It has gone back to the Swiss Embassy. It has to be renewed before Ottawa will stamp it. He is being tossed back and forth between bureaucracies."

" 'Back and forth between bureaucracies'! Such words always! Who does he think he is? Victor Hugo? A Swiss doesn't talk that way!"

"I don't know how Swiss talk."

"Ask Cici, then! Cici says Swiss are crude. She was married to one. She knows. Beauregard is French, I am certain of it. He cooks like a Frenchman, he speaks like a Frenchman, he is arrogant like a Frenchman, he is cunning like a Frenchman. And decadent like a Frenchman. Of course he is French! He is French, and he is a liar."

Breathing heavily, she stared past her husband at the ceiling, which was sprinkled with paper stars that glittered in the dark.

"His mother was German," said Latulipe, attempting a calmer tone.

"What? Nonsense! Germans are blond. Who told you?"

"He did. Some German engineers were in the

disco last night. Beauregard spoke German with them like a Nazi. I asked him. He speaks English too."

"You must talk to the authorities. Beauregard must be regularized, or he must go. Is it my hotel or his? He is illegal, I am sure of it. He is too conspicuous. *C'est bien sûr!"*

Turning her back to her husband, she switched on her radio, then contemplated her paper stars in fury.

. . .

JONATHAN COLLECTED Yvonne on his Harley-Davidson from the Mange-Quick on the highway north, ten days after Yvonne had dressed him in his whites. They had met in their attic corridor by seeming accident, each having heard the other first. He said it was his day off tomorrow; she asked what he would do with it. Hire a motorbike, he replied. Maybe I'll take in a few lakes.

"My father keeps a boat at his cottage," she said, as if her mother did not exist. Next day she was waiting as arranged, pale but resolute.

The scenery was slow and majestic, with rolling blue forest and a drained sky. But as they pressed north the day darkened and an east wind turned to drizzle. It was raining by the time they reached the cottage. They undressed each other, and a lifetime passed for Jonathan in which for a long while there was no appeasement and no release as he made up for months of abstinence. She fought him without taking her eyes from him except to offer him a different attitude, a different woman.

"Wait," she whispered.

Her body sighed and fell again, then rose, her face stretched and became ugly but did not burst. A cry of surrender escaped her, but from so far off it could have come from the drenched forests that surrounded them or the depths of the gray lake. She mounted him and they began the climb again, peak to peak until they drowned together.

He lay intently beside her, watching her breathing, resenting her repose. He tried to work out whom he was betraying. Sophie? Or just myself as usual? We're betraying Thomas. She rolled onto her side, turning her back to him. Her beauty added to his loneliness. He began caressing her.

· · ·

"HE'S A GOOD MAN," Yvonne said. "Into anthropology and Indian rights. His father's a lawyer working with the Cree. He wants to follow in his footsteps." She had found a bottle of wine and brought it back to bed. Her head was resting on his chest.

"I'm sure I'd like him very much," Jonathan said politely, picturing an earnest dreamer in a Fair Isle pullover penning love letters on recycled paper.

"You're a lie," she said, distractedly kissing

him. "You're some kind of lie. You're all truth, but you're a lie. I don't understand you."

"I'm on the run," he said. "I had a problem in England."

She clambered up his body and put her head beside his. "Want to talk about it?"

"I've got to get hold of a passport," he said. "That stuff about being Swiss is junk. I'm British."

"You're *what?*"

She was excited. She picked up his glass and drank from it, watching him over the brim.

"Maybe we can steal one," she said. "Change the picture. A friend of mine did that."

"Maybe we can," he agreed.

She was fondling him, eyes alight. I've tried everything I could think of, he told her. Explored guest bedrooms, looked in parked cars. No one carries a passport round here. Been down to the post office, got the forms, studied the formalities. Visited the town graveyard looking for dead men of my own age; thought I might apply on their behalf. But you never know what's safe these days: maybe the dead are already in some computer.

"What's your real name?" she whispered. "Who are you? Who are you?"

A moment's wonderful peace descended over him as he made her the ultimate gift. "Pine. Jonathan Pine."

· · ·

ALL DAY they lived naked, and when the rain cleared they took the boat out to an island in the center of the lake and swam naked from the shingle beach.

"He's turning in his thesis in five weeks," she said.

"And then?"

"Marriage to Yvonne."

"And then?"

"Working with the Indians in the bush." She told him where. They swam a distance.

"Both of you?" he asked.

"Sure."

"How long for?"

"Couple of years. See how it goes. We're going to have babies. About six."

"Will you be faithful to him?"

"Sure. Sometimes."

"Who's up there?"

"Cree mainly. He likes Cree best. Speaks it pretty well."

"What about a honeymoon?" he asked.

"Thomas? His idea of a honeymoon is McDonald's and hockey practice at the arena."

"Does he travel?"

"Northwest Territories. Keewatin. Yellowknife. Great Slave Lake. Norman Wells. Goes all over."

"I meant abroad."

She shook her head. "Not Thomas. He says it's all in Canada."

"What is?"

"Everything we need in life. It's all here. Why go further? He says people travel too much. He's right."

"So he doesn't need a passport," Jonathan said.

"Fuck you," she said. "Get me back to shore."

But by the time they had cooked supper and made love again, she was listening to him.

. . .

EVERY DAY or night they made love. In the small hours of morning when he came up from the disco, Yvonne would lie awake waiting for his brushing signal against her door. He would tiptoe to her and she would draw him down on her, her last long drink before the desert. Their lovemaking was almost motionless. The attic was a drum, and every movement clattered through the house. When she started to call out in pleasure, he laid his hand over her mouth and she bit it, leaving teeth marks in the flesh around his thumb.

If your mother discovers us, she'll throw me out, he said.

Who cares, she whispered, gathering herself more tightly round him. I'll go with you. She seemed to have forgotten everything she had told him about her future plans.

I need more time, he insisted.

For the passport?

For you, he replied, smiling in the darkness.

She hated his leaving, yet dared not keep him with her. Madame Latulipe had taken to looking in on her at all odd hours.

"You are asleep, *cocotte?* You are happy? Only four weeks to your wedding, *mon p'tit chou.* The bride must have her rest."

Once when her mother appeared Jonathan was actually lying beside Yvonne in the darkness, but by a mercy Madame Latulipe did not switch on the light.

They drove in Yvonne's baby-blue Pontiac to a motel in Tolérance, and thank God he made her leave their cabin ahead of him, because as she walked to her car, still smelling of him, she saw Mimi Leduc grinning at her from the next-door parking space.

"Tu fais visite au show?" Mimi yelled, lowering her window.

"Uh-huh."

"C'est super, n'est-ce pas? T'as vu le little black dress? Très low, très sexy?"

"Uh-huh."

"I bought it! *Toi aussi faut l'acheter! Pour ton trouss-eauuu!"*

They made love in an empty guest room while her mother was at the supermarket, and in the walk-in airing cupboard. She had acquired the recklessness of sexual obsession. The risk was a drug for her. Her whole day was spent contriving moments for them to be alone together.

"When will you go to the priest?" he asked.

"When I'm ready," she replied, with something of Sophie's quirkish dignity.

She decided to be ready next day.

· · ·

THE OLD curé Savigny had never let Yvonne down. Since childhood she had brought him her cares, triumphs and confessions. When her father struck out at her, it was old Savigny who dabbed her black eye and talked her round. When her mother drove her to dementia, old Savigny would laugh and say, She's just a silly woman sometimes. When Yvonne started going to bed with boys, he never told her to slow down. And when she lost her faith, he was sad, but she went on visiting him each Sunday evening after the Mass she no longer attended, armed with whatever she had filched from the hotel: a bottle of wine or, like this evening, Scotch.

"*Bon,* Yvonne! Sit down. My God, you are glistening like an apple. Dear Heaven, what have you brought me? It's for me to bring presents to the bride!"

He drank to her, leaning back in his chair, staring into the infinite with his leaky old eyes.

"In Espérance we were *obliged* to love each other," he declared, from somewhere in the middle of his homily to intending couples.

"I know."

"It is only yesterday that everyone was a stranger here, everyone missed his family, his country, everyone was a little afraid of the bush and the Indians."

"I know."

"So we drew together. And we loved each other. It was natural. It was necessary. And we dedicated our community to God. And our love to God. We became His children in the wilderness."

"I know," said Yvonne again, wishing she had never come.

"And today we are good townspeople. Espérance has grown up. It's good, it's beautiful, it's Christian. But it's dull. How's Thomas?"

"Thomas is great," she said, reaching for her handbag.

"But when will you bring him to me? If it is because of your mother that you do not let him come to Espérance, then it is time to submit him to the test of fire!" They laughed together. Sometimes old Savigny had these flashes of insight, and she loved him for them. "He must be some boy to catch a girl like you. Is he eager? Does he love you to distraction? Write to you three times a day?"

"Thomas is kind of forgetful."

They laughed again, while the old curé kept repeating "forgetful" and shaking his head. She unclipped her handbag and drew out two photographs in a cellophane envelope and handed one to him. Then handed him his old steel-framed spectacles from the table. Then she waited while he got the photograph into focus.

"*This* is Thomas? My God, he's a pretty boy, then! Why did you never tell me? Forgetful? This man? He's a force! Your mother would kneel at the feet of such a man!"

Still admiring Jonathan's photograph at arm's length, he tilted it to catch the light from the window.

"I'm dragging him off on a surprise honeymoon," she said. "He hasn't got a passport. I'm going to press one into his hand in the vestry."

The old man was already fumbling in his cardigan for a pen. She held one ready. She turned the photographs face down for him and watched him while he signed them one by one, at child's speed, in his capacity as a minister of religion licensed by the laws of Quebec to perform marriages. From her handbag she drew the blue passport application form: *"Formule A pour les personnes de 16 ans et plus,"* and indicated for him the place where he must sign again, as a witness personally acquainted with the applicant.

"But how long have I known him? I've never set eyes on the rascal!"

"Just put forever," said Yvonne, and watched him write down *"la vie entière."*

Tom, she telegraphed triumphantly that night. *Church needs sight of your birth certificate. Send express to Babette. Keep loving me. Yvonne.*

When Jonathan brushed against her door she pretended to be asleep and didn't stir. But when he stood at her bedside she sat up and seized him more hungrily than ever. *I did it,* she kept whispering to him. *I got it! It's going to work!*

.   .   .

IT WAS soon after this episode and at much the same early-evening hour that Madame Latulipe paid her call by appointment on the oversized superintendent of police at his splendid offices. She was wearing a mauve dress, perhaps for half-mourning.

"Angélique," said the superintendent, drawing up a chair. "My dear. For you, always."

Like the curé, the superintendent was an old trailman. Signed photographs on the walls portrayed him in his prime, now in furs handling a dog-sled, now as lone hero in the bush pursuing his man on horseback. But these mementos did the superintendent little service. White chins now hid the once manly profile. A glossy paunch sat like a brown football over the leather belt of his uniform.

"One of your girls got herself into a spot of trouble again?" the superintendent asked with a knowing smile.

"Thank you, Louis, not so far as I know."

"Somebody been putting his hand in the till?"

"No, Louis, our accounts are quite in order, thank you."

The superintendent recognized the tone and erected his defenses.

"I'm glad to hear that, Angélique. There's a lot of it about these days. Not like it used to be at all. *Un p'tit drink?"*

"Thank you, Louis, this is not a social visit. I wish you to make inquiries about a young man whom André has employed in the hotel."

"What's he done?"

"It is more a question of what André has done. He has employed a man with no papers. He has been *naïf."*

"André's a kindly fellow, Angélique. One of the best."

"Perhaps too kindly. The man has been with us already ten weeks, and his papers have not arrived. He has placed us in an illegal situation."

"We're not Ottawa up here, Angélique. You know that."

"He says he is a Swiss."

"Well, perhaps he is. Switzerland's a fine country."

"First he tells André that his passport is with the immigration authorities, then he tells him it is with the Swiss Embassy for renewal, now it is back with another authority. Where is it?"

"Well, *I* haven't got it, Angélique. You know Ottawa. Those fairies take three months to wipe their arses," said the superintendent, imprudently grinning at the felicity of the phrase.

Madame Latulipe colored. Not with a becoming blush, but with a sallow patchy fury that made the superintendent nervous.

"He is *not* Swiss," she said.

"How do you know that now, Angélique?"

"Because I telephoned the Swiss Embassy. I said I was his mother."

"And?"

"I said I was furious at the delay, my son was not permitted to work, he was acquiring debts, he was depressed, if they cannot send his passport they must send a letter of confirmation that everything is in order."

"I'm sure you did it well, Angélique. You're a great actress. We all know that."

"They have no trace of him. They have no Jacques Beauregard who is Swiss and living in Canada; it is all a fiction. He is a seducer."

"He's a *what?*"

"He has seduced my daughter, Yvonne. She is infatuated by him. He is a refined impostor, and his plan is to steal my daughter, *steal* the hotel, *steal* our peace of mind, our contentment, our . . ."

She had a whole list of things that Jonathan was stealing. She had compiled it as she lay awake at night and added to it with each new sign of her daughter's obsession with the thief. The only crime she had omitted to mention was the theft of her own heart.

TEN

THE AIRSTRIP was a green ribbon stretched across the brown Louisiana swamp. Cows grazed at the edge of it, white egrets perched on the cows' backs, looking from the air like dabs of snow. At the far end of the ribbon stood a busted tin shed, which had once been a hangar. A red mud track ran to it from the highway, but Strelski didn't seem sure it was the place, or perhaps he wasn't happy with it. He banked the Cessna and let it slide, then he made a low diagonal pass over the swamp. From his seat in the rear Burr saw an old fuel pump beside the shed and a barbed-wire gate behind it. The gate was shut, and he saw no sign of life until he noticed fresh tire tracks in the grass. Strelski read them at the same moment and seemed to like them, for he opened the throttle, held the turn and came back from the west. He must have said something to Flynn over the inter-com, for Flynn lifted his liver-spotted palms from the submachine gun on his lap and made an un-characteristically Latin shrug. It was an hour since they had taken off from Baton Rouge.

With an old man's grunt, the Cessna touched down and bumped along the causeway. The cows did not lift their heads; neither did the egrets. Strelski and Flynn sprang onto the grass. The causeway was a land bar between steaming mud flats, which trembled to the sound of sucking teeth. Fat beetles trundled in and out of the steam. Flynn led the way toward the shed, the machine gun cradled across his chest as he observed to left and right. Strelski followed with the briefcase and a drawn automatic. After them came Burr with nothing but a prayer, for he had little training in guns and hated them.

Pat Flynn here has done Northern Burma, Strelski had said. Pat Flynn here has done Salvador. . . . Pat is this unlikely Christian. . . . Strelski liked to speak of Flynn with awe.

Burr studied the tire tracks at his feet. Car or plane? He guessed there was a way of telling and was ashamed he didn't know it.

"We've told Michael you're a big Brit," Strelski had said. "Like Winston Churchill's aunt."

"Bigger," said Flynn.

· · ·

"IT'S FATHER LUCAN and it's Brother Michael," Strelski tells Burr the night before, as they sit on the deck of the beach house in Fort Lauderdale. "Pat Flynn here calls the shots. You want to ask Michael something, mostly it pays to have Pat here do it. The guy's a sleazebag and a screwball. Right, Pat?"

Flynn pulls a huge hand across his mouth to hide his gappy smile. "Michael's beautiful," he declares.

"And pious," says Strelski. "Michael is very, very holy—right, Pat?"

"A true believer, Joe," Flynn confirms.

Then, amid much giggling, Strelski and Flynn divulge to Burr the story of Brother Michael's coming to Jesus and to the high calling of Supersnitch—a story, Strelski insists, that would never have had its beginning had not Agent Flynn here chanced to be up in Boston one weekend in Lent, taking a spiritual retreat from his wife and curing his soul with the aid of a case of Bushmills single malt Irish whiskey and a couple of like-minded abstainers from the seminary.

"That right, Pat?" Strelski demands, anxious perhaps lest Flynn fall asleep.

"Dead on, Joe," Flynn agrees, sipping his whiskey and taking a huge mouthful of pizza as he benignly follows the full moon's ascent over the Atlantic.

And Pat here and his reverend brethren have hardly done justice to their first bottle of malt, Leonard—Strelski continues—when in rolls the father abbot himself to inquire whether Special Agent Patrick Flynn of U.S. Customs would have the holiness to grant him a moment of counsel in the seclusion of his private office.

And when Agent Flynn graciously consents

to this proposal, there in the father abbot's office, says Strelski, sits this string-bean Texan kid with ears like ping-pong bats who turns out to be Father Lucan from something called the Blood of the Virgin Hermitage in New Orleans, which, for reasons known only to the Pope, is under the protection of the father abbot in Boston.

And this Lucan, Strelski continues, this kid with the ping-pong-bat ears and the acne, is into recovering lost souls for the Blessed Virgin through personal sanctification and the example of Her Apostles.

In the course of which uphill struggle, says Strelski—while Flynn giggles and nods his red face and yanks his forelock like a fool—Lucan has been hearing the confession of a rich penitent whose daughter has recently killed herself in a particularly disgusting fashion on account of her father's criminal life-style and debauchery.

And this same penitent—says Strelski—in the extreme of his remorse, has confessed his soul so drastically to Lucan that the poor kid has taken his ass full speed to his father abbot in Boston for spiritual guidance and smelling salts: his penitent being the biggest fucking crook Lucan or anybody else has stumbled on in his entire life. . . .

"Penitence, Leonard, in a doper, that's like a very short feast." Strelski has turned philosophical. Flynn is quietly smiling at the moon. "Remorse: I would say that was unknown. By the time Patrick got to him, Michael was already regretting his brief lapse into decency and pleading the First and the Fifth and his sick grandmother. Also whatever he had said was off the record on account of his dementia and grief. But Pat here"—more smiles from Flynn—"Pat with his religion retrieved the situation. He gave Michael exactly two choices. Column A was seventy-to-ninety in a house of permanent correction. Column B, he could play ball with God's legions, earn himself an amnesty, and screw the front row of the Folies-Bergères. Michael communed with his Maker for all of twenty seconds, consulted his ethical conscience, and found it in him to go for Column B."

• • •

FLYNN WAS standing in the tin shed, beckoning Burr and Strelski to come in. The shed stank of bat, and the heat sprang at them like heat out of an oven. There were bat droppings on the broken-down table and on the wood bench and on the collapsed plastic chairs around the table. Bats hugged each other like scared clowns in twos and threes, upside down from the iron girders. A smashed radio stood on one wall, beside a generator with a row of old bullet holes in it. Someone rubbished the place, Burr decided. Someone said, If we're not going to use the place anymore, no one is, and smashed everything that would smash.

Flynn took a last look round outside, then closed the shed door. Burr wondered whether closing the door was a signal. Flynn had brought green mosquito coils. The printed writing on the paper bag said, *Save the globe. Go without a bag today.* Flynn lit the coils. Spirals of green smoke began climbing into the tin roof, making the bats fidget. Spanish graffiti on the walls promised the destruction of the Yanqui.

Strelski and Flynn sat on the bench. Burr balanced one buttock on a broken chair. Car, he decided. Those tracks were car tracks. Four wheels going straight. Flynn laid his machine gun across his knees, crooked a forefinger round the trigger and closed his eyes in order to listen to the chatter of the cicadas. The strip had been built by marijuana smugglers in the sixties, Strelski had said, but it was too small for today's shipments. The dopers of today flew 747 transports with civil markings, hid their stuff in manifested cargo and used airports with state-of-the-art facilities. And for the run home they stuffed their planes with mink coats for their hookers and fragmentation grenades for their friends. Dopers were like anyone else in the transport business, he said: they hated to ride home without a load.

Half an hour passed. Burr was feeling sick from the mosquito coils. Tropical sweat was springing out of his face like shower water, and his shirt was wringing wet. Strelski passed him a plastic bottle of warm water; Burr drank some and mopped his brow with his soaked handkerchief. The snitch re-snitches, Burr was thinking: and we get blown apart. Strelski uncrossed his legs to make his crotch comfortable. He was nursing his .45 automatic on his lap and wore a revolver in an aluminum ankle cup.

"We told him you were a doctor," Strelski had said. "I wanted to tell him you were a duke, but Pat here wouldn't have it."

Flynn lit another mosquito coil, then, as part of the same operation, leveled his machine gun at the door while he moved sideways in silent high strides. Burr didn't see Strelski move at all, but when he turned he discovered him standing flat against the back wall, with his automatic pointed at the roof. Burr stayed where he was. A good passenger sits tight and keeps his mouth shut.

The door opened, flooding the shed with red sunlight. The elongated head of a young man, ravaged by shaving spots, peered round it. Ears like ping-pong bats, Burr confirmed. The scared eyes examined each of them in turn, resting longest on Burr. The head vanished, leaving the door ajar. They heard a muffled cry of "Where?" or "Here?" and a conciliatory murmur in reply. The door was shoved wide, and the indignant figure of Dr. Paul Apostoll, alias Apo, alias Appetites, alias Brother Michael, strutted into the shed, less a penitent than a very small general who has lost his horse. Burr's irritations were forgotten as the magic seized him in its spell. This is Apostoll, he thought, who sits at the right hand of the cartels. This is Apostoll, who brought us the first word of the Roper's plan, who conspires with him, eats his salt, blows the walls out with him on his yacht, and sells him down the river in his spare time.

"Meet the doctor from England," Flynn said solemnly, indicating Burr.

"Doctor, how d'you do, sir," Apostoll replied in a tone of offended gravity. "A little class will make a pleasant change. I surely admire your great country. Many of my forebears are of the British nobility."

"I thought they were Greek crooks," said Strelski, who on Apostoll's appearance had immediately adopted a stance of smoldering hostility.

"On my mother's side," said Apostoll. "My mother was related to the Duke of Devonshire."

"You don't say," said Strelski.

Apostoll didn't hear him. He was speaking to Burr.

"I am a man of principle, Doctor. I believe that as a Britisher you will appreciate that. I am also a child of Mary, privileged to enjoy the guidance of her legionaries. I am not judgmental. I give counsel according to the facts that are supplied to me. I make hypothetical recommendations based on my knowledge of the law. Then I leave the room."

. . .

THE HEAT, the stench, the clatter of the cicadas were forgotten. This was work. This was routine. This was any agent-runner debriefing his joe in any safe house in the world: Flynn in his plain cop's Irish brogue, Apostoll with his courtroom lawyer's truculent precision. He's lost weight, thought Burr, remembering the photographs, noting the sharpened jaw and sunken eyes.

Strelski had taken charge of the machine gun and ostentatiously given Apostoll his back while he covered the open doorway and the airstrip. Lucan sat tensely at his penitent's side, head tilted, eyebrows raised. Lucan wore blue denims, but Apostoll was dressed for the firing squad, in a long-sleeved white shirt and black cotton trousers, and round his neck a gold chain with a figure of Mary holding out her arms. His waved black toupee, artfully awry, was too big for him. It occurred to Burr that he had picked up the wrong one by mistake.

Flynn was doing the agent-runner's housekeeping: What is your cover for this meeting, did anybody see you driving out of town? What time do you have to be back in circulation, when and where shall we meet next? What happened about Annette in the office who you say was trailing you in her car?

Here Apostoll glanced at Father Lucan, who remained staring into the middle distance.

"I recall the matter you mention, and it is resolved," Apostoll said.

"How?" said Flynn.

"The woman concerned conceived a romantic interest in me. I was urging her to join our praying army, and she mistook my purposes. She has apologized, and I have accepted her apology."

But this was already too much for Father Lucan. "Michael, that is not an accurate rendering of the truth," he said severely, removing his long hand from the side of his face in order to speak. "Michael's been two-timing her, Patrick. First he screws Annette, then he screws her roommate. Annette gets suspicious, so she tries to check him out. What's new?"

"Can I take the next question, please?" Apostoll snapped.

Flynn placed two pocket tape recorders on the table and set them going.

"Are the Blackhawks still in, Michael?" Flynn inquired.

"Patrick, I did not hear that question," Apostoll replied.

"Well, I did," Strelski retorted. "Are the cartels still going for fucking combat helicopters? Yes or no. Jesus!"

Burr had seen people play good cop–bad cop before. But Strelski's disgust seemed alarmingly genuine.

"I make it my business not to be in the room when matters of that nature are discussed," Apostoll replied. "To use Mr. Roper's felicitous expression, it is his art to fit the shoe to the foot. If Blackhawks are necessary to Mr. Roper's vision, they will be included."

Strelski scribbled something angry on a pad. "Anybody got a date for finalizing this thing?" he demanded roughly. "Or do we tell Washington, wait another fucking year?"

Apostoll gave a contemptuous laugh. "Your friend must contain his patriotic ardor for instant gratification, Patrick," he said. "Mr. Roper is emphatic that he will not be hurried, and my clients are in full agreement with him. 'What grows well grows slowly,' is an old and tested Spanish proverb. As Latin people, my clients have a very mature sense of time." He glanced at Burr. "A Marian is stoical," he explained. "Mary has many detractors. Their scorn sanctifies her humility."

The to-and-fro resumed. Players and places . . . consignments ordered or delivered . . . money entering or leaving the Caribbean financial laundromat . . . the cartels' latest building project for downtown Miami . . .

Finally Flynn smiled at Burr in invitation: "Well now, Doctor, would there be anything at all by way of an interest of your own that you might be wishing to pursue with Brother Michael here?"

"Well, yes, Patrick, thank you, there is," Burr said courteously. "Being new to Brother Michael—and of course very greatly impressed by the quality of his assistance in this matter—I'd like to ask him first a couple of broad, background questions. If I may. More of texture, shall we say, than content."

"Sir, you are most welcome," Apostoll cut in hospitably, before Flynn could answer. "It is always a pleasure to match intellects with an English gentleman."

Start wide and come in slowly, Strelski had advised. *Wrap it in your British cotton wool.*

"Well, there's a riddle to me in all this, Patrick, speaking as Mr. Roper's fellow countryman," said Burr to Flynn. "What's Roper's secret? What's he got that all the others didn't have? The Israelis, French, Cubans, all of them offered to supply the cartels with more effective weaponry, and all of them except the Israelis came away without a deal. How did Mr. Richard Onslow Roper succeed where everybody else failed in persuading Brother Michael's clients to buy themselves a decent army?"

To Burr's surprise, a glow of unlikely warmth lit Apostoll's scrawny features. His voice acquired a lyrical tremor.

"Doctor, your countryman Mr. Roper is no ordinary salesman. He is an enchanter, sir. A man of vision and daring, a piper of people. Mr. Roper is beautiful because he is beyond the norm."

Strelski muttered an obscenity under his breath, but there was no stopping Apostoll's flow.

"To pass time with Mr. Onslow Roper is a

privilege, sir, a carnival. Many men, coming to my clients, despise them. They fawn, they bring gifts, they flatter, but they are not sincere. They are carpetbaggers looking for a quick buck. Mr. Roper addressed my clients as equals. He is a gentleman, but he is not a snob. Mr. Roper congratulated them on their wealth. On exploiting the asset that nature had given them. On their skill, their courage. The world is a jungle, he said. Not all creatures can survive. It is right that the weak should go to the wall. The only question is, who are the strong? Then he treated them to a film show. A very professional, very competently assembled film show. Not too long. Not too technical. Just right."

And you stayed in the room, Burr thought, watching Apostoll inflate with his story. On somebody's ranch or in somebody's apartment, surrounded by the hookers and the peasant boys with jeans and Uzis, lounging among the leopard-skin sofas and the megasized television sets and the solid-gold cocktail shakers. With your clients. Captivated by the aristocratic English charmer with his film show.

"He showed us the British special soldiers storming the Iranian Embassy in London. He showed us American special forces on jungle training, the American Delta Force, and promotion film of some of the world's newest and smartest weaponry. Then he asked us again who the strong were, and what would happen if the Americans ever got tired of spraying herbicide on Bolivian crops and seizing fifty kilos in Detroit, and decided instead to come and drag my clients from their beds and fly them to Miami in chains and subject them to the humiliation of a public trial under United States law in the manner of General Noriega. He asked whether it was right or natural that men of such wealth should be unprotected. 'You do not drive old cars. You do not wear old clothes. You do not make love with old women. Then why do you deny yourselves the protection of the newest weapons? You have brave boys here, fine men, loyal; I see it in their faces. But I wouldn't think there's five in a hundred of them would qualify for the fighting unit I'm proposing to put together for you.' After that, Mr. Roper described his fine corporation to them, Ironbrand. He pointed to its respectability and diversity, its tanker fleet and transportation facilities, its noted trading record in minerals, timber and agricultural machinery. Its experience in informal transportation of certain materials. Its relations with compliant officials in the major ports of the world. Its familiarity with the creative use of offshore companies. Such a man could cause Mary's message to shine in the darkest pit.''

Apostoll paused, but only to sip some water from the glass that Father Lucan had poured him from a plastic bottle.

"Gone were the days of suitcases packed with hundred-dollar bills, he went on. Of swallowers with olive-oiled condoms in their bellies being hauled off to the X-ray room. Of small planes running the interdiction gauntlet across the Gulf of Mexico. What Mr. Roper and his colleagues were offering them was trouble-free, door-to-door shipment of their product to the emerging markets of Central and Eastern Europe."

"Dope," Strelski exploded, unable to endure any more of Apostoll's circumlocutions. "Your clients' product is *dope,* Michael! Roper is trading guns for refined, processed, nine-nine-nine fucking *cocaine,* calculated at airstrip fucking prices! Mountains of the shit! He's going to ship it to Europe and dump it there and poison kids and ruin lives and make megamillions! Right?"

Apostoll remained aloof from this outburst. "Mr. Roper wished for no cash advances from my clients, Doctor. He would finance all of his side of the bargain out of his own resources. He did not hold out his hand. The trust he bestowed on them transcended the normal trust of man. If they cheated on the deal, he assured them, they could ruin his good name, bankrupt his corporation and turn away his investors forever. Yet he had confidence in my clients. He knew them as good men. The greatest blessing, he said—the greatest guarantee of security from interference—was to finance the entire enterprise *a priori* out of his own pocket until the day of reckoning. That was what he proposed to do. He placed his faith in their hands. Mr. Roper went further. He emphasized that he had no intention of competing with my clients' customary European correspondents. He would enter and leave the chain entirely in accordance with my clients' wishes. Once he had delivered the merchandise to whomever my clients chose to nominate as the recipient, he would regard his task as done. If my clients were reluctant to name such persons, Mr. Roper would be happy to arrange a blind hand-over."

Pulling a large silk handkerchief from his pocket, Apostoll wiped away the sweat that had formed below his toupee.

Now, thought Burr in the hiatus. *Go.*

. . .

"AND WAS Major Corkoran present on this occasion, Michael?" Burr asked innocently.

Immediately, a scowl of disapproval settled over Apostoll's darting features. His voice became snappish and accusing. "Major Corkoran, like Lord Langbourne, was very much in evidence. Major Corkoran was a valued guest. He operated the projector and performed the social honors, he spoke correctly to the ladies, fixed drinks and made himself agreeable. When my clients half-humorously proposed that Major Corkoran remain behind as a hostage until the deal was completed, the idea was warmly received by the ladies. When general heads of agreement were drawn up by myself and Lord Langbourne, Major Corkoran made a droll speech and signed with much flourish on Mr. Roper's behalf. My clients relish a little foolery to lighten the daily burden." He took an indignant breath, and his little fist opened to reveal a rosary. "Unfortunately, Doctor, on the insistence of Patrick and his rough-tongued friend here, I have been compelled to denigrate Major Corkoran in the eyes of my clients to the point where their enthusiasm for him has waned. This is un-Christian behavior, sir. It is bearing false witness, and I deplore it. So does Father Lucan."

"It's just so *shitty,*" Lucan complained. "I don't think it's even *ethical*. Is it?"

"Would you mind telling me, please, Michael, exactly what your clients have so far been told to the detriment of Major Corkoran?"

Apostoll's head was stuck out like an indignant chicken's. The strings in his neck were taut.

"Sir, I am not responsible for what my clients may have heard from other sources. As to what I have told them myself, I have told them precisely what my—" He seemed suddenly to have no word for his handlers. "I have advised my clients in my capacity as their lawyer of certain alleged facts in Major Corkoran's past, which, if true, invalidate his suitability as a nominee in the longer term."

"Such as?"

"I have been obliged to advise them that he has an irregular life-style and uses alcohol and drugs to excess. To my shame, I also told them he was indiscreet, which does not in the least accord with my experience of the Major. Even in his cups, he is the very soul of discretion." He tipped his head indignantly at Flynn. "I was given to understand that the purpose of this distasteful maneuver was to clear away the surrogate figure of Major Corkoran, thereby moving Mr. Roper personally into the firing line. I am obliged to tell you that I do not share the optimism of these gentlemen in that regard, and even if I did share it, I would not consider these actions to be consistent with the ideals of a true legionary. If Major Corkoran is found unacceptable, Mr. Roper will merely procure for himself another signer."

"Is Mr. Roper, so far as you know, aware of your clients' reservations about Major Corkoran?" asked Burr.

"Sir, I am neither Mr. Roper's keeper nor the keeper of my clients. They do not inform me of their inner deliberations. I respect that."

Burr put his hand into the recesses of his sweat-soaked jacket and dragged out a limp envelope, which he tore open while Flynn, in his broadest Irish, explained its contents:

"Michael, what the Doctor has brought with him here is an exhaustive list of Major Corkoran's misdemeanors before his employment by Mr. Roper. Most of the incidents relate to acts of venery. But we also have a couple of cases of riotous behavior in public places, drunk driving, drug abuse and going walkabout for days at a time, plus peculation of army funds. As the guardian of your clients' interest, you are so worried by the rumors you've been hearing about the poor soul that you have taken it upon yourself to cause discreet inquiries to be made over in England, and this is what you've come up with."

Apostoll was already protesting. "Sir, I am a member in good standing of the Florida and Louisiana bars, and a former president of the Dade County Bar Association. Major Corkoran is not duplicitous. I will not be used to frame an innocent man."

"Sit the fuck down," Strelski told him. "And that's bullshit about the bar association."

"He just makes things up," Lucan told Burr in despair. "He's incredible. Every time he says something, he indicates its opposite. Like, if he's giving an example of the truth, it turns out to be a lie. I don't know how to get him out of it."

Burr put in a quiet plea: "If we could just discuss the question of timing, Patrick," he suggested.

· · ·

THEY WALKED back to the Cessna. Flynn led again, his gun across his arms.

"You think it worked?" Burr asked. "You really don't think he guessed?"

"We're too stupid," said Strelski. "Just dumb cops."

"We're assholes," Flynn agreed serenely.

ELEVEN

THE FIRST blow seemed to hit Jonathan in his sleep. He heard the crunch of his jawbone and saw the black lights of a knockout, followed by a long flash of sheet lightning. He saw Latulipe's contorted face glaring at him, and Latulipe's right arm drawn back to hit him a second time. This seemed a silly thing for anyone to be doing: to use the right fist as if it were a hammer working at a nail and leave oneself wide open to retaliation. He heard Latulipe's question and realized he was hearing it for the second time.

"Salaud! Who are you?"

Then he saw the crates of empties he had helped the Ukrainians stack in the yard that afternoon, and heard the striptease music playing through the disco fire exit. He saw a crescent moon hanging above Latulipe's head like a crooked halo. He remembered that Latulipe had asked him to come outside a moment. And he supposed he should hit Latulipe back or at least block the second blow, but indifference or some sense of chivalry stayed his hand, so that the second blow hit him pretty much where the first had, and he had a brief memory of being back at the orphanage and running into a fire hydrant in the dark. But either his head was numb by then or it wasn't a real fire hydrant, because it didn't have half the effect of the first blow, except to open a cut at the corner of his mouth and send a flood of warm blood tracking down his chin.

"Where's your Swiss passport? Are you a Swiss or not? Talk to me! What are you? You fuck up my daughter's life, you lie to me, you drive my wife crazy, you eat at my table, who are you? Why do you lie?"

And this time, as Latulipe pulled back his fist, Jonathan kicked his feet out from under him and laid him on his back, careful at the same time to ease his fall because there was no nice tuft of windblown grass from the Lanyon to cushion him: the yard was paved with good Canadian asphalt. But Latulipe was undeterred and, scrambling gamely to his feet, seized Jonathan's arm and frog-marched him into the dingy alley that ran along the back of the hotel, for years an informal urinal for the male population of the town. Latulipe's Jeep Cherokee was parked at the far end. Jonathan could hear its engine running as they shuffled toward it.

"Get in!" Latulipe ordered. Pulling open the passenger door, he made to force Jonathan into the seat but lacked the skill. So Jonathan climbed in anyway, knowing that at any point in his ascent he could have felled Latulipe with his foot; could probably have killed him, in fact, with a kick to the head, for Latulipe's wide Slav brow was at just the height for Jonathan to smash the temples. By the interior light of the Jeep he saw his Third World air bag lying on the back seat.

"Put on your belt. *Now!*" Latulipe shouted, as if a fastened seat belt would ensure his prisoner's obedience.

But Jonathan obeyed anyway. Latulipe started the engine; the last lights of Espérance disappeared behind them. They entered the blackness of the Canadian night and drove for twenty minutes before Latulipe pulled out a packet of cigarettes and shoved it in Jonathan's direction. Jonathan took one and lit it from the dashboard lighter. Then he lit Latulipe's. The night sky, through the windscreen, was an immensity of rocking stars.

"So?" said Latulipe, trying to maintain his aggression.

"I'm English," Jonathan said. "I quarreled with a man. He robbed me. I had to get out. I came here. It could have been anywhere."

A car overtook them, but it wasn't a baby-blue Pontiac.

"Did you kill him?"

"So they say."

"How?"

Shot him in the face, he thought. With a pump-action shotgun, he thought. Betrayed him. Slit his dog from head to tail.

"They say his neck was broken," he replied, in the same evasive tone as before, for he was overcome by an absurd reluctance to tell yet another lie.

"Why couldn't you have left her alone?" Latulipe demanded in tragic exasperation. "Thomas is a good man. Her whole future waiting for her. Jesus Christ."

"Where is she?"

Latulipe seemed to know no answer except a fierce gulp. They were heading north. Now and then Jonathan caught sight of a pair of headlights in the rearview mirror. They were chase-car lights, the same each time he looked.

"Her mother went to the police," said Latulipe.

"When?" Jonathan asked. He supposed it should have been Why? The chase car was closing on them. Stay back, he thought.

"She checked you out with the Swiss Embassy. They never heard of you. Would you do it again?"

"Do what?"

"This man who robbed you. Break his neck."

"He came at me with a knife."

"They sent for me," Latulipe said, as if that were another insult. "The police. Wanted to know what kind of guy you are. Do you push drugs, make a lot of phone calls out of town, who do you know? They think you're Al Capone. They don't get a lot of action up here. They've got a photo from Ottawa, looks a bit like you. I told them, wait till morning, when the guests are sleeping."

They had reached an intersection. Latulipe drew off the road. He was speaking breathlessly, like a messenger who had run his distance. "Men on the run here go north or south," he said. "Best go west to Ontario. Never come back, understand? You come back, I'll—" He took several breaths. "Maybe this time it will be me who does the killing."

Jonathan took his bag and climbed into the dark. There was rain in the air and a smell of resin from the pines. The chase car passed them, and for a dangerous second Jonathan saw the rear license plate of her Pontiac. But Latulipe had his eyes on Jonathan.

"Here's your pay," he said, shoving a bunch of dollar bills at him.

. . .

SHE HAD driven back along the opposing roadway, then bumped across the center strip to make a U-turn. They sat in her car with the light on. The brown envelope lay on her lap, unopened. The sender's name was printed in the corner: *Bureau des Passeports, Ministère des Affaires Extérieures, Ottawa*. Addressed to Thomas Lamont, care of Yvonne Latulipe, Le Château Babette. Thomas who says it's all in Canada.

"Why didn't you hit him back?" she asked.

One side of her face was swollen, and the eye

was closed. That's what I do for a living, he thought: I obliterate faces.

"He was just angry," he said.

"You want me to take you somewhere? Drive you? Leave you somewhere?"

"I'll just handle it from here."

"You want me to do anything?"

He shook his head. Then shook it again until he knew she had seen.

She handed him the envelope. "Which was better?" she asked harshly. "The fuck or the passport?"

"They were both great. Thanks."

"Come on! I need to know! Which was better?"

He opened the door and climbed out, and saw by the courtesy light that she was smiling brightly.

"You nearly had me fooled, know that? God damn it, nearly got my wires crossed! You were great for an afternoon, Jonathan. Anything longer, I'll take Thomas every time."

"I'm glad I helped," he said.

"So what was it for you?" she demanded, the smile still brilliantly in place. "Come on. Level. Scale of one to nine. Five? Six? Zero? I mean, Jesus, don't you keep a *score?*"

"Thanks," he said again.

He closed the car door and by the glow of the sky saw her head fall forward, then lift again, as she squared her shoulders and turned the ignition. With the engine running, she waited a moment, staring hard ahead of her. He couldn't move. He couldn't speak. She drove onto the highway and for the first couple of hundred yards she either forgot her headlights or didn't bother with them. She seemed to drive on compass in the darkness.

You killer this woman?

No. But I married her for her passport.

A lorry pulled up, and he rode for five hours with a black man called Ed who had problems with his mortgage and needed to talk them through. Somewhere between nowhere and nowhere, Jonathan called the number in Toronto and listened to the cheerful gossiping of the operators as they passed his commission across the forest wastes of eastern Canada.

"My name's Jeremy, I'm a friend of Philip's," he said, which was what he had been saying each week from different pay phones whenever he checked in. Sometimes he could hear the call being rerouted. Sometimes he wondered whether it went to Toronto at all.

"Good *morning*, Jeremy! Or is it evening? How's the world using you, old boy?"

Till now Jonathan had imagined someone enlivening. This time he seemed to be talking to another Ogilvey, false and overbred.

"Tell him I've got my shadow and I'm on my way."

"Then allow me to offer the congratulations of the house," said Ogilvey's familiar.

That night, he dreamed of the Lanyon and of the lapwings flocking on the cliff, rising in their hundreds with stately wingbeats, then falling in a rolling twisting dive, until an unseasonable easterly caught them off their guard. He saw fifty dead and more floating out to sea. And he dreamed he had invited them, then let them die while he went off to find the worst man in the world.

. . .

THIS IS the way safe houses should be, thought Burr. No more tin sheds full of bats in Louisiana swamps. Goodbye to bed-sits in Bloomsbury, stinking of sour milk and the previous user's cigarettes. From now on we'll meet our joes right here in Connecticut, in white weatherboard houses like this one, with ten acres of woodland and leather-lined dens crammed with books on the morality of being mountainously rich. There was a basketball hoop, and an electrified fence for keeping out deer, and an electric zapper that, now evening was upon them, noisily cremated the bugs it lured with its sickly purple glow. Burr had insisted on manning the barbecue and had bought enough meat for several loyal regiments. He had removed his tie and jacket and was basting three enormous steaks in a violent crimson sauce. Jonathan, in swimming shorts, lounged beside the pool. Rooke, arrived from London the day before, sat in a deck chair, smoking his pipe.

"Will she talk?" Burr asked. No answer. "I said, will she talk?"

"What about?" said Jonathan.

"The passport. What do you think?"

Jonathan plunged back into the water and swam a couple of lengths. Burr waited till he had climbed out, then put the question a third time.

"Shouldn't think so," Jonathan said, vigorously toweling his head.

"Why not?" Rooke asked through his pipe smoke. "They usually do."

"Why should she? She's got Thomas," Jonathan said.

They had been putting up with his taciturnity all day. For most of the morning he had walked alone in the forest. When they went shopping he had sat in the car while Burr foraged in the supermarket and Rooke went to Family Britches to buy a Stetson for his son.

"Loosen your girdle, will you?" Burr said. "Give yourself a Scotch or something. It's me. Burr. All I'm trying to do is measure risk."

Jonathan topped up Burr's gin and tonic and poured one for himself. "How's London?" he asked.

"The usual sewer," said Burr. Billows of smoke belched from the steaks. He turned them over and brushed on red sauce to dress the burn.

"How about the old priest chap?" Rooke called from the other side of the pool. "Going to get a bit of a shock, isn't he, when he sees whose photograph he hasn't signed?"

"She says she'll take care of him," Jonathan replied.

"Must be quite a girl," said Rooke.

"She was," said Jonathan, and flung himself into the water again, lunging up and down the pool like a man who could never get clean.

. . .

THEY ATE dinner to the unnerving beat of the zapper's executions. The steak, Burr decided, was really not that bad. Maybe there was only so much you could do to ruin good meat. Now and then he cast a covert glance across the candlelight at Jonathan, who was chatting with Rooke about riding motorbikes in Canada. You're unlocking yourself, he decided with relief. You're coming round. You just needed to talk to us for a while.

They huddled in the den, Rooke at his adventurous best. He had lit the wood stove, and on the table he had spread letters of reference in praise of one Thomas Lamont, and a portfolio of brokers' illustrated prospectuses of private motor yachts.

"This one's called *Salamander*," he said, while Jonathan peered over his shoulder and Burr watched them from across the room. "A hundred and thirty feet, owner's some Wall Street bandit. As of now she's got no cook. This one's called

Persephone, but nobody who's that rich knows how to pronounce her, so the new owner's about to rechristen her *Lolita.* . . . She's two hundred feet, takes a crew of ten plus six protection, two cooks and a majordomo. They're looking for a majordomo, and we think you're perfect for them." A photograph of an agile, smiling man in tennis gear. "This man's Billy Bourne, and he runs a charter and crewing agency in Newport, Rhode Island. Both the owners are clients of his. Tell him you cook and sail and give him your references. He won't check them out, and anyway the people who are supposed to have written them are on the other side of the earth. All Billy cares about is, can you do the job, are you what he calls civilized, and have you got a police record? You can and you are and you haven't. That's to say, Thomas hasn't."

"Is Roper Billy's client too?" Jonathan asked, now out ahead of them.

"Mind your own business," said Burr from his corner, and they all laughed. But beneath the jolly laughter lay a truth they were all aware of: the less Jonathan knew about Roper and his works, the less likely he was to betray himself.

"Billy Bourne's your trump card, Jonathan," said Rooke. "Look after him. As soon as you're paid, make sure you send him his commission. When you're on a new job, be sure to call Billy and tell him how it's going. Play straight by Billy, and he'll open any door you want. Everybody Billy loves loves Billy."

"This is your last qualifying round," said Burr. "After this, it's the final."

Next morning, when Jonathan had had his early swim and everyone was fresh and rested, Rooke got out his magic box: the clandestine radiotelephone with alternating frequencies. First they went into the woods and played hide-and-seek, taking it in turns to cache the box and find it. Then, between briefing sessions, Rooke made Jonathan talk to London, back and forth until he was at home with the system. He showed him how to change the batteries and how to recharge them and how to steal power from the mains. And after the radiotelephone, Rooke produced his other prize exhibit: a subminiature camera got up as a Zippo lighter that was not just idiot-proof, he said, but actually took photographs. In all, they spent three days in Connecticut, which was longer than Burr had intended.

"It's our last chance to talk this through," he kept telling Rooke, as a way of excusing the delay.

Talk what? Through to where? Deep down, as Burr afterwards admitted to himself, he was waiting for an obligatory scene. Yet, as so often with Jonathan, he had no idea how it should have unfolded.

"The equestrienne's still riding high, if that's

any consolation," he said, hoping to cheer Jonathan up. "Hasn't fallen out of her saddle yet."

But the memory of Yvonne must have been hanging too heavy on him, for he barely managed a smile.

"He had a ding-dong with that Sophie woman in Cairo, I bloody know he did," Burr told Rooke as they flew home.

Rooke gave a disapproving frown. He did not hold with Burr's occasional flights of intuition, any more than he believed in blackening a dead woman's name.

. . .

"DARLING KATIE is as mad as a wet hen," Harry Palfrey announced proudly, seated over a whisky in Goodhew's drawing room in Kentish Town. He was gray-haired and ravaged and fifty, with puffy drinker's lips and haunted eyes. He wore a lawyer's black waistcoat. He had come straight from his work across the river. "She's Concording back from Washington, and Marjoram is on his way to Heathrow to meet her. It's a war party."

"Why doesn't Darker go himself?"

"He likes cut-outs. Even if they're his deputy, like Marjoram, he can still say he wasn't there."

Goodhew started to ask something else but thought it better not to interrupt while Palfrey was unburdening himself.

"Katie says the Cousins are waking up to what they've got. They've decided that Strelski lulled them into imbecility in Miami and you and Burr aided and abetted him. She says she can stand on the banks of the Potomac and watch the smoke rising off Capitol Hill. She says everyone is talking new parameters and power vacuums in their own backyard. Filled or created, I can't quite fathom which."

"God, I do hate *parameters,"* Goodhew remarked, buying himself time while he replenished Palfrey's whisky. "I had *formulaic* this morning. It ruined my day. And my master *escalates.* Nothing rises for him, or increases, or grows, or advances, or progresses, or multiplies, or matures. It *escalates.* Cheers," he said, sitting down again.

But as Goodhew spoke these words, a cold shudder passed over him, raising the hair down his spine and causing him to sneeze several times in quick succession.

"What do they *want,* Harry?" he asked.

Palfrey screwed up his face as if he had soap in his eyes, and ducked his mouth to his glass.

"Limpet," he said.

TWELVE

MR. RICHARD ROPER'S motor yacht, the *Iron Pasha,* appeared off the eastern tip of Hunter's Island at six o'clock exactly, prow forward like an attack boat, cut against a cloudless evening sky and growing perceptibly as she advanced toward Deep Bay over a flat sea. In case anybody doubted it was the *Pasha,* her crew had already called ahead by satcom to reserve the long mooring on the outer harbor, and the round table on the terrace for sixteen at eight-thirty, and the front row for the crab races afterwards. Even the menu was discussed. All the adults like seafood. Chips and grilled chicken for the children. And the Chief goes crazy if there isn't enough ice.

It was between seasons, the time of year when you don't see too many big yachts cruising the Caribbean other than the commercial cruise ships out of Nassau and Miami. But if any of those had tried to put in at Hunter's Island, they'd have received no warm welcome from Mama Low, who liked rich yachties and abominated the common herd.

. . .

JONATHAN HAD been waiting for the *Pasha* all week. Nevertheless, for a second or two after he sighted her he fancied himself trapped, and amused himself with the idea of escaping inland to the only town, or hijacking Mama Low's old bumboat, *Hi-lo,* which was anchored, with outboard fitted, not twenty yards from where he was staring out to sea at the *Pasha*'s approach. Twin two-thousand-horsepower diesels, he was rehearsing. Extended afterdeck for helicopter, oversized Vosper stabilizers, seaplane launcher on the stern. The *Pasha* is quite a lady.

But foreknowledge did not ease his apprehension. Until this moment he had pictured himself advancing on Roper, and now Roper was advancing on him. First he felt faint, then hungry. Then he heard Mama Low yelling at him to get his white Canadian ass up here *double quick,* and he felt better. He trotted back along the wooden pier and up the sand track to the shack. His weeks at sea had seen an improvement in his appearance. An oceangoing looseness marked his stride, his eyes had gentled, his complexion had a healthy glow. As he climbed the rise he met the western sun starting to swell before it set, forming a copper rim round its circumference. Two of Mama Low's sons were rolling the famed round tabletop up the stone path to the terrace. Their names were Wellington and Nelson, but to Mama Low they were Swats and Wet Eye. Swats was sixteen and wreathed in fat. He was supposed to be in Nassau studying, but wouldn't go. Wet Eye was lean as a blade, smoked ganja and hated whites. The two had been working on the table for the last half hour, sniggering and achieving nothing.

"Bahamas makes you stupid, man," Swats explained as Jonathan passed by.

"You said it, Swats, I didn't."

Wet Eye watched him, no smile. Jonathan gave him a lazy salute like a wiping clean, and felt Wet Eye's tight gaze follow him up the path. If ever I wake up dead it will be what Wet Eye likes to call his cutlash that has slit my throat, he thought. Then he remembered that he didn't expect to be waking up too many more times on Hunter's Island, dead or otherwise. He took another mental reckoning of the *Pasha*'s position. She had started to turn. She needed a lot of sea.

"Mass' Lamont, you's a lazy white Canadian slob, hear me? You the laziest white slob a poor nigger ever had to hire, an' that's God's truth. You not sick no more, Mass' Lamont. I'm goin' tell that Billy Bourne you just plain fuckin' *lazy*."

Mama Low sat on the veranda beside a tall and very beautiful black girl in plastic curlers known only as Miss Amelia. He was drinking beer out of a can and yelling at the same time. He was "twenty-two stone tall," as he liked to say of himself, "four feet across and bald as a light bulb." Mama Low had told a vice president of the United States to go fuck himself, Mama Low had fathered children as far off as Trinidad and Tobago, Mama Low owned serious real estate in

Florida. He wore a cluster of gold skulls round his huge neck, and in a minute, when the sun set, he would don his churchgoing straw hat with paper roses and "Mama" done in mulberry needlework across the crown.

"You gon' cook them stuff' mussels o' yours tonight, Mass' Lamont?" he yelled as loudly as if Jonathan were still down at the water's edge. "Or you gon' lie about a-fartin' and a-pullin' at your little white fancy?"

"Mussels you ordered, Mama, mussels you get," Jonathan replied cheerfully, as Miss Amelia with her long hands delicately patted the outlines of her hair.

"So where you reck'nin' get them mussels *from?* You thought o' that? The shit you have. You jus' brim *full* o' white man's bullshit."

"You bought a fine basket of mussels from Mr. Gums this morning, Mama. And fifteen crawfish, special for the *Pasha.*"

"From Mr. Gums the kinkajou? I did? Hell now, maybe I did *so.* Well, you go stuff 'em, hear me? Cos we got royalty comin', we got English lords and ladies comin', we got rich little white princes and princesses comin', and we're gon' play fine nigger music to 'em, and we're gon' give 'em a taste of *gen-u-ine nigger livin',* yes *baass.*" He took another pull of his can of beer. "Swats, you gon' push that fuckin' table up them steps or you gon' die of old age?"

Which, plus or minus, was how Mama Low addressed his troops each evening when a half-bottle of rum and the attentions of Miss Amelia had restored his humor after the trials of another day in Paradise.

Jonathan walked round to the washrooms behind the kitchen and changed into his whites, remembering Yvonne, which he did each time he put them on. Yvonne had temporarily supplanted Sophie as the object of his self-distaste. The bubble of nervousness in his stomach had a sexual urgency. His fingertips kept tingling as he chopped the bacon and the garlic. Charges of expectation like electric shocks ran across his back. The kitchen was spotless as a ship's galley and as trim, with stainless steel worktops and a Hobart steel dishwasher. Glancing through the barred window while he worked, Jonathan observed the *Iron Pasha*'s advance in framed shots: her radar mast and satcom dome, then the Carlisle and Finch searchlights. He could make out the red ensign winking on her stern and the gold curtains in the stateroom windows.

"Everyone you love is aboard," Burr had told him in a call to the third public phone cabin on the left as you walk out to sea on Deep Bay pier.

Melanie Rose was singing-along gospel music to the radio while she scrubbed sweet potatoes at the sink. Melanie Rose taught Bible school and had twin daughters by someone called Cecil—pronounced Ceesill—who three months ago had taken a return ticket to Eleuthera and thus far had not used the second half. Ceesill might come back one day, and Melanie Rose lived in the cheerful hope he would. Meanwhile Jonathan had taken Cecil's place as second cook to Mama Low, and on Saturday nights Melanie Rose consoled herself with O'Toole, who was cleaning grouper at the fish table. Today was Friday, so they were starting to get friendly.

"You goin' dancin' tomorrow, Melanie Rose?" O'Toole inquired.

"Ain't no point to dancin' alone, O'Toole," said Melanie Rose with a defiant sniff.

Mama Low waddled in and sat down on his folding chair and smiled and shook his head, as if he were remembering some damned tune he couldn't shake out of it. A voyaging Persian had recently made him a present of a set of worry beads, and he was swinging them round his enormous fingers. The sun had nearly set. Out at sea the *Pasha* was sounding her air horns in salute.

"Oh man, you some damn big feller," Mama Low murmured admiringly, turning to stare at her through the open doorway. "You sho's hell one big white fuckin' millionaire king, Lord King Richard Fuckin' Onslow Fuckin' Roper, sir. Mass' Lamont, you cook nice tonight, mind. Otherwise that Mr. Lord Pasha of Roper he gonna have yo' *ass*. Then us po' niggers gonna help ou'-selves to what's left of that ass, same as nigger pickin's off a rich man's plate."

"What does he make his money from?" Jonathan asked while he toiled.

"Roper?" Mama Low retorted incredulously. "You mean you don't *know?*"

"I mean I don't *know.*"

"Well, sure as hell, Mass' Lamont, *I* don't. And I sure as hell don't *ask*. He's some big company from Nassau that's losin' all its money. Man's as rich as that in recession time, he sure as hell some mighty big crook."

In a short while Mama Low would start creating his hot chili sauce for the crawfish. Then the kitchen would fall into a dangerous hush. The sous-chef was not born yet who dared suggest that the yachties came to Hunter's Island for any other reason than Mama's chili sauce.

* * *

THE *Pasha* is in, her party of sixteen will soon arrive, an atmosphere of battle grips the kitchen as the first diners take their places at the lesser tables. No more brave talk, no more last touches of camouflage paint or nervous checking of the weapons. The unit has become a silent team, relating with eyes and bodies only, weaving round each other like mute dancers. Even Swats and Wet Eye have gone silent in the tension as the curtain rises on another fabled night at Mama

Low's. Miss Amelia, poised at the cash desk in her plastic curlers, is braced for the first bill. Mama Low in his famous hat is everywhere, now rallying his troops in a stream of subdued obscenities, now out front jiggling and dissembling with the hated enemy, now back in the kitchen again, grating out orders made more effective by the suppression of his massive voice:

"Fine white lady, table eight, she some kind o' fuckin' caterpillar. Won't eat nuttin' but fuckin' lettuce leaves. Two Mama's salads, O'Toole! Bastard kid on six, he won't eat nuttin' but fuckin' hamburgers. One kid-sized hamburger, and spit on it! What's *happenin'* to the world, O'Toole? Ain't they got no fuckin' teeth no more? Don't they eat no fish? Wet Eye, take five 7-Ups and two Mama's punch to table one. Move it. Mass' Lamont, you just keep-on goin'-on makin' them mussels, six more dozen ain't too many, hear me, just you be sure you keep back sixteen portions for the *Pasha.* Mussels goes straight to the balls, Mass' Lamont. Ladies 'n' gentlemen gon' screw their hearts out tonight, all on account yo' mussels. O'Toole, where's the dressings, you done drunk them? Melanie Rose, hon', them taters needs turnin' or they'll be sackcloth and ashes before yo' very eyes!"

All this under the protective strains of the six-strong Huntsman's steel band, which roosts on the sprawling roof of the terrace, the sweating faces of the players glistening in the fairy lights, white shirts glowing in the strobes. A boy called Henry is singing calypso. Henry did five years in Nassau prison for pushing coke and came home looking like an old man. Melanie Rose told Jonathan that Henry wasn't any good for lovin' no more, not after his beatings. "Some native people is sayin' that's how come he sing so high," she said with a sad smile.

It's a busy night, Mama Low's busiest in weeks, which explains the extra excitement. Fifty-eight dinners to be served and sixteen coming up the hill—Mama Low has spotted them through his eyeglass—and this is still low season. A whole tense hour goes by before Jonathan is able to do what he likes to do when the lull comes: sluice some cold water over his head and take the measure of his customers through the fish-eye peephole in the swing door.

· · ·

A CLOSE observer's view. Measured, technical, thorough. An in-depth, undeclared reading of the quarry, ahead of any contact with him. Jonathan can do this for days on end, has done it in ditches, hedges, lying up in barns, his face and hands dappled with camouflage paint, real foliage stitched into his battle dress. He is doing it now: I shall come to him when I come to him, and not before.

First the harbor below, with its horseshoe of white lights and small yachts, each a separate campfire sitting on the glass of the sheltered water. Lift your eyeline by a knuckle and there she is: the *Iron Pasha* herself, dressed for a carnival, gold-lit from stem to stern. Jonathan can make out the shapes of the guards, one forward, one aft, and a third lurking in the shadow of the bridge. Frisky and Tabby are not among them. Their duties tonight are on land. His gaze moved in tactical bounds up the sand track and passed under the driftwood archway that announced the sacred kingdom of Mama Low. It scanned the lighted hibiscus bushes and the tattered Bahamian flags dangling at the halfway point either side of the skull and crossbones. It paused at the dance floor where a very old couple held each other close, touching each other's faces unbelievingly with their fingertips. Jonathan guessed they were emigrés still marveling at their survival. Younger dancers pressed together in stationary ecstasy. At a ringside table, he picked out a pair of hard men in their forties. Bermuda shorts, wrestlers' chests. A thrusting way of using their forearms. Is it you? he asked them in his mind—or are you two more Roper leash-dogs?

"They'll probably use a Cigarette," Rooke had said. "Superfast low job, no draft."

The two men had arrived in a new white powerboat shortly before dusk, whether a Cigarette or not he didn't know. But they had the stillness of professionals.

They stood up, smoothing their nether parts and slinging their handbags over their shoulders. One of them threw a Roman wave in Mama Low's direction.

"Sir? Loved it. Oh, nice eating. Brilliant."

Elbows aloft, they waddled down the sand path to their boat.

They were nobodies, Jonathan decided. They belonged to one another. Maybe. Or maybe not.

He shifted his sights to a table of three Frenchmen and their girls. Too drunk, he decided. They had already put away twelve orders of Mama's punch among them, and nobody was pouring his drink into the flower vase. He focused on the mid-deck bar. Against a background of yachting pennants, heads of blue marlin and tail ends of plundered neckties, two black girls in radiant cottons perched on high stools, chatting to two black men in their twenties. Maybe it's you, he thought. Maybe it's the girls. Maybe it's all four of you.

Out of the corner of his eye he glimpsed a low white powerboat heading out of Deep Bay toward the ocean. My two candidates eliminated. Maybe.

He allowed his gaze to begin the climb towards the terrace, where the worst man in the world, surrounded by retainers, jesters, bodyguards and children, was disporting himself in his private Camelot. As his boat now mastered the harbor, so the person of Mr. Richard Onslow

Roper mastered the round table, the terrace and the restaurant. Unlike his boat, he was not dressed for spectacle but had the comfy look of a fellow who had thrown on a few clothes to answer the door to a friend. A navy pullover was slung carelessly over his shoulders.

Nevertheless, he commanded. By the stillness of his patrician head. By the speed of his smile and the intelligence of his expression. By the attention lavished on him by his audience, whether he spoke or listened. By the way everything around the table, from the dishes to the bottles to the candles in their green string jars to the faces of the children, seemed to be ranged toward him or away from him. Even the close observer felt his pull: Roper, he thought, it's me, Pine, the chap who told you not to buy your Italian marbles.

And as he was thinking this, a general cry of laughter went up from the terrace, led by Roper himself and evidently provoked by him, for his bronzed right arm was flung out to make the humorous point and his head was lifted to the woman who faced him across the table. Her carelessly disordered chestnut hair and naked back were thus far all Jonathan could see of her, but he remembered at once the grain of the skin inside Herr Meister's bathrobe, the endless legs and clusters of jewels at the wrists and neck. He felt the surge that had passed through him the first time he set eyes on her, the stab of indignation that someone so young and beautiful should accept the captivity of a Roper. She smiled, and it was her comedian's smile, kooky, slanted and impertinent.

Blocking her from his mind, he allowed his gaze to range the children's end of the table. *The Langbournes have three, MacArthur and Danby one apiece,* Burr had said. *The Roper drafts them to amuse his Daniel.*

Lastly came Daniel himself, aged eight, a tousled, pallid boy with a determined chin. And at Daniel, Jonathan's eye paused guiltily.

"Couldn't we use somebody else?" he had asked Rooke. But he had hit against their iron wall.

Daniel is the apple of the Roper's eye, Rooke had replied, while Burr looked out of the window. Why go for second best?

We're talking five minutes, Jonathan, Burr had said. What's five minutes for a kid of eight?

A lifetime, Jonathan thought, remembering a few minutes of his own.

Meanwhile Daniel is in grave discourse with Jed, whose raggedy chestnut hair divides into two roughly equal parts as she leans downward to address him. The flame of the candle sets a gold fringe on their two faces. Daniel pulls at her arm. She rises, glances at the band above her and calls to somebody she seems to know. Sweeping up her flimsy skirts, she swings one leg then the other over the stone bench, as if she were a teenager vaulting a garden gate. Jed and Daniel scamper hand in hand down the stone staircase. *Upper-class geisha,* Burr had said, *nothing recorded against.* It depends what you're recording, thought Jonathan as he watched her take Daniel in her arms.

· · ·

TIME STOPS. The band is playing a slow samba. Daniel clutches Jed's hips as if he were about to enter her. The grace of Jed's movements is near-criminal. A flurry interrupts Jonathan's reverie. Something dire has happened to Daniel's trousers. Jed is holding them at the waistband, laughing away his embarrassment. Daniel's top button has broken loose, but Jed in an inspired act of improvisation pins him together with a six-inch safety pin borrowed from Melanie Rose's apron. Roper is standing on the parapet, gazing down on them like a proud admiral inspecting his fleet. Catching his eye, Daniel releases Jed long enough to give a child's wave, sawing the air from side to side. Roper responds with a thumbs-up. Jed blows Roper a kiss, then takes Daniel's hands and leans back, mouthing the rhythm for him to follow. The samba quickens. Daniel relaxes, getting the hang of it. The liquidity of Jed's hip movements becomes an outrage against public order. The worst man in the world is too much blessed.

· · ·

RETURNING HIS GAZE to the terrace, Jonathan makes a perfunctory inspection of the rest of the Roper party. Frisky and Tabby sit at opposite sides of the table, Frisky favoring the left draw, Tabby covering the diners and the dance floor. Both men appear larger than Jonathan remembers them. The Lord Langbourne, blond hair still bundled in a ponytail, converses with a pretty English rose while his gloomy wife scowls at the dancers. Across the table from them sits Major Corkoran, lately of the Life Guards, sporting a battered Panama hat with an old Etonian hatband. He is making gallant conversation with an awkward girl in a high-necked dress. She frowns, then blushes and giggles, then corrects herself and takes a stern mouthful of ice cream.

From the top of the tower, Henry the impotent singer breaks into a calypso about a-very-sleepy-girl-who-couldn't-get-to-sleep. On the dance floor, Daniel's chest is cuddled against Jed's mound and his head against her breast, while his hands clutch her hips. Jed lets him rock against her in peace.

"Girl on table six got tits like l'il warm puppy dogs," O'Toole announced, prodding Jonathan in the spine with a tray of Mama's punch.

Jonathan took a last long look at Roper. He had turned his face toward the sea, where a moon path led from his fairy-lit yacht to the horizon.

"Mass' Lamont, sound the Allelujah, sir!"

cried Mama Low, majestically sweeping O'Toole aside. He had donned a pair of ancient jodhpurs and a pith topee, and he was armed with his famous black basket and riding crop. Jonathan followed Mama Low onto the balcony and, white as a target in his chef's tunic and hat, tolled the brass tocsin. The echoes were still booming out to sea as the children of the Roper party came pelting down the path from the terrace, followed at a more becoming pace by the adults, led by Langbourne and a pair of wispy young men of the polo-playing classes. The band played a roll of drums, the perimeter torches were doused, colored spotlights made the dance floor glisten like an ice rink. As Mama Low moved center stage and cracked his whip, Roper and his entourage began taking their reserved places in the front row. Jonathan glanced out to sea. The white motorboat that might have been a Cigarette had vanished. Must have rounded the headland to the south, he thought.

· · ·

"RIGHT WHERE I'm standin' *heah* is the startin' gate! Any nigger crab tries to beat the startin' pistol, that's ten lashes *cold!*"

His pith helmet tipped to the back of his head, Mama Low is giving his celebrated rendering of a British colonial administrator.

"This historic ring right *heah*"—indicating a circular red stain at his feet—"is the finishin' post.

Every crab in this basket *heah* has got a *numbah*. Every crab in this basket *heah* is goin' to run his ass off, or *Ay* am gonna know the reason *whay*. Every crab who doesn't make the finishin' post *heah* will go *right* back into the *chowdah*."

Another crack of the whip. The laughter dwindles to silence. At the edge of the dance floor Swats and Wet Eye are dispensing complimentary rum punches from an elderly perambulator that once bore the infant Low himself. The older children squat cross-legged, the two boys with folded arms, the girls hugging their knees. Daniel is propped against Jed, thumb in mouth. Roper stands next to her. Lord Langbourne takes a flash photograph, distressing Major Corkoran. "Sandy, old love, for Christ's sake, can't we just *remember* it for once?" he says in a murmur that fills the amphitheater. The moon hangs like a pink parchment lantern over the sea. The harbor lights bob and twinkle in a restless arc. On the balcony where Jonathan is standing, O'Toole lays a proprietary hand on Melanie Rose's arse and she wriggles herself obligingly against it. Only Miss Amelia in her curlers spurns the proceedings. Framed in the white-lit window of the kitchen behind them, she is intently counting the cash.

The band plays another roll of drums. Mama Low bows to the black wicker basket, grabs the lid and bears it into the air. The crabs are under starter's orders. Abandoning their perambulator,

Swats and Wet Eye strike out into the audience with their books of tickets.

"Three crabs racin', all crabs is evens!" Jonathan hears Swats yell.

Mama Low is appealing to the spectators for a volunteer:

"I'm *lookin'!* I'm a-*lookin'!*" he cries in an enormous voice of black man's pain. "I'm a-lookin' for a fine white pure Christian chil' who knows his bounden duty by these dumb crabs and won't stand no back-talkin' or insurrection. *You, sir! I'm pinnin' my humble simple hopes on you.*"

His whip is pointing at Daniel, who lets out a serio-comic yell and buries his face in Jed's skirts, then rushes to the back of the audience. But one of the girls is already scampering forward. Jonathan hears the rah-rah voices of the polo boys applauding her.

"Well played, Sally! Sock it to 'em, Sals! Jolly good!"

Still from his place of vantage on the balcony, Jonathan takes a raking glance at the bar, where the two men and their girls are clustered in earnest conversation, resolutely ignoring the dance floor. His gaze glides back to the audience, the band, then the dangerous patches of darkness in between.

They'll come from behind the terrace, he decides. They'll use the cover of the bushes beside the steps. *Just make sure you stay up on the kitchen balcony,* Rooke had said.

The girl Sally or Sals pulls a face and peers into the black basket. The drummer strikes up another roll. Sally reaches one bold arm into the basket, then the other. To shrieks of laughter, she puts her whole head in, emerges with a crab in each hand and places them side by side in the starting gate, while Langbourne's camera whirs and zooms and flashes. She dives in for the third crab, adds it to the starting line and bounds back to her place, to more rah-rah from the polo set. The trumpeter on the tower sends up a hunter's tattoo. Its echoes are still resounding round the harbor as a pistol shot tears the night apart. Caught off guard, Frisky drops into a half-crouch, while Tabby starts to push back the spectators to make himself shooting space, without knowing whom to shoot.

Even Jonathan momentarily searches for the shooter, until he spots Mama Low, sweating under his topee, pointing a smoking starter's pistol at the night sky.

The crabs are off.

· · ·

THEN, casually, it was happening.

No formality, no epiphany, no commotion, no screams—scarcely a sound beyond Roper's curt order to Frisky and Tabby to "stand still and do nothing, *now.*"

If anything was remarkable at all, it was not the noise but the quiet. Mama Low abandoned his harangue, the band stopped playing fanfares and the polo players gave up their frenzied cheers.

And this quiet developed slowly, in the same way that a large orchestra fizzles out at rehearsal, with the most determined players, or the most oblivious, going on for several bars before they too dwindle to a halt. Then for a while all Jonathan noticed were the things you suddenly hear on Hunter's Island when people stop making such a din: bird cries, cicadas, the bubbling of the coral water off Penguin Point, the bray of a wild pony from the cemetery and a couple of tinny wallops of a hammer as some late toiler down in Deep Bay negotiates with his outboard. Then he heard nothing at all, and the quiet became vast and terrible, and Jonathan with his grandstand view from the balcony picked out the two broad-armed professionals who had left the restaurant earlier in the evening and ridden away in their new white Cigarette but were now edging along the lines of the spectators like sidesmen in church, taking their collection of pocketbooks, wallets, purses and wristwatches and little wads of cash from people's back pockets.

And jewelry, Jed's particularly. Jonathan was just in time to see her bare arms lift first to her left ear, then to her right, pushing aside her hair and bowing slightly. Then to her throat to remove her necklace, just as if she were about to climb into someone's bed. Nobody is mad enough to wear jewelry in the Bahamas anymore, Burr had said: unless they happen to be Dicky Roper's girl.

And still no fuss. Everyone understanding the rules. No objectors, no resistance or unpleasantness at all—for the good reason that while one of the thieves was tendering an open plastic briefcase to receive the congregation's offerings, his accomplice was wheeling the beat-up perambulator with the rum and whiskey bottles on it, and the cans of beer in their ice tub. And among the beer and the bottles sat eight-year-old Daniel Roper like a sacrificial Buddha, with an automatic pistol at his head, enduring the first of the five minutes that Burr had said wouldn't matter to a boy his age—and perhaps Burr was right at that, for Daniel was smiling, and sharing the good joke with the crowd, grateful for relief from the scary crab race.

But Jonathan didn't share Daniel's joke. Instead, he saw a flickering of light from somewhere inside his eyes, like a red splash of fury. And he heard a call to battle stronger than any he could remember since the night he had emptied his Heckler at the unarmed green Irishman, so loud that he wasn't thinking anymore, he was only doing. For days and nights—now in the conscious part of his brain, now the unconscious—he had been steeling himself for this moment, relishing it, fearing it, planning it: if they do this, the logical response will be that; if they are here, the place to be is there. But he had not reckoned with his feelings. Until now. Which no doubt was why his first response was not the one that he had planned.

Having stepped as far back into the shadows as the balcony allowed, he slipped off his white chef's hat and tunic, then ran into the kitchen in his shorts, heading for the cash desk, where Miss Amelia sat working on her fingernails. He grabbed her telephone, held the receiver to his ear and rattled the cradle long enough to establish what he already knew, namely that the line was cut. He picked up a dishcloth and, jumping on the central table, removed the neon strip that lighted the kitchen. Meanwhile he ordered Miss Amelia to leave the cash desk exactly as it was and hide herself upstairs, no bellyaching, no trying to take the money or they would come after her. By the glow of the arc lights outside, he then hastened to the work surface where he kept his knife block, selected the most rigid of his carving knives, and ran with it, not back to the balcony but through the scullery to the service door on the south side.

Why the knife? he wondered as he ran. Why the knife? Who am I going to slice up with a knife? But he didn't throw it away. He was glad he had the knife, because a man with a weapon, any weapon, is twice the man he is without one: read the manual.

Once outdoors he kept running southward,

ducking and leaping between the century cacti and the sea-grape trees until he gained the brow of cliff that overlooked Goose Neck. There, panting and sweating, he saw what he was looking for: the white motorboat, moored on the eastern side of the inlet for the men's escape. But he didn't pause to admire the sight. Knife in hand, he ran back to the darkened kitchen. And though the whole exercise had not taken him above a minute, it had been quite long enough for Miss Amelia to make herself scarce upstairs.

From the unlit kitchen window on the north side, Jonathan took stock of the thieves' progress, and blessedly in that time he was able to harness some of his first, murderous anger, for his focus improved and his breathing settled and self-discipline, more or less, was once more his. But where did his anger come from? From somewhere dark and far back in him. It rose and spread over him in a flood, yet its origin was a mystery. And he held on to the knife. *Thumb on top, Johnny, same as buttering bread . . . weave the blade and watch his eyes . . . not too low now, and bother him a little bit with your other hand . . .*

Major Corkoran in his Panama hat had found a chair and was sitting astride it, arms folded along the backrest and chin propped on his arms, watching the thieves as if they were a fashion show. Lord Langbourne had surrendered his camera, but the man with the briefcase no sooner had it than he threw it irritably aside as unacceptable. Jonathan heard a drawled "Oh, *fuck* you." Frisky and Tabby stood like men possessed, rigidly at the alert not five yards from their quarries. But Roper's right arm was still held out to them in prohibition, while his eyes remained fixed on Daniel and the thieves.

As to Jed, she was standing alone without her jewelry at the edge of the dance floor, her body made jagged by the tension, her hands spread on her thighs, as if to stop herself from running to Daniel.

"If it's money you want, you can have it," Jonathan heard Roper say, calmly. "Want a hundred thousand dollars? Have it in cash, got it on the boat, just give me the boy. Shan't send the police after you. Leave you completely alone. Long as I've got the boy. Do you understand what I'm saying? Speak English? Corky, try 'em in Spanish, will you?"

Then Corkoran's voice, obediently passing on the same message in decent Spanish.

Jonathan glanced at the cash desk. Miss Amelia's till stood open. Half-counted piles of money lay strewn across the counter. He stared down the zigzag path that led from the dance floor to the kitchen. It was steep and crudely paved. Only a lunatic would try to push a loaded perambulator up it. It was also floodlit, which meant that anyone stepping into the darkened kitchen would be unsighted. Jonathan slipped the carving knife under his waistband and wiped his sweated palm on the seat of his shorts.

The raiding party was starting up the path. The way in which the captor held his hostage was a matter of crucial interest to Jonathan, because his plan of action depended on it: what Burr had called his plan of plausibility. *Listen like a blind man, Johnny, watch like a deaf one.* But nobody, so far as he remembered, had thought to offer him advice on how one man with a carving knife prizes an eight-year-old hostage from two armed gunmen and survives.

They had made the first leg of the path. Below them the motionless crowd, their faces brilliant under the arc lights, stared after them, not a movement among them, Jed still apart from them, her hair copper in the glow. He was beginning not to know himself again. Bad images of his childhood flooded his vision. Answered insults, unanswered prayers.

First came the bagman, then twenty yards behind him his accomplice, dragging Daniel up the path by his arm. Daniel wasn't joking anymore. The bagman was striding out hungrily, the stuffed briefcase hanging at his side. But Daniel's kidnapper moved in awkward, twisted strides, his upper body turning repeatedly while he menaced the crowd, then the boy, with his automatic pistol. Right-handed, Jonathan recorded, bare-armed. The safety catch at "on."

"Don't you want to negotiate with me?" Roper was shouting up at them from the dance floor. "I'm his father. Why won't you talk to me? Let's do a deal."

Jed's voice, frightened but defiant, with a note of the equestrienne's command: "Why don't you take an adult? You bloody bullies. Take one of us. Take me if you like." And then, much louder, as her fear and anger joined, "Bring him back, you bastards!"

Hearing Jed's challenge, Daniel's captor yanked Daniel round to face her, while he held the pistol to his temple and did the baddy's lines in a sawing Bronx snarl:

"Anybody comes after us, anybody comes up the path, anybody tries to cut us off, I kill the kid, okay? Then I kill whoever. I don't give a shit. I'll kill anybody. So stay down there and shut up."

The blood was pulsing in Jonathan's hands; they were out in front of him, each fingertip throbbing. Sometimes his hands wanted to do the job on their own and pull him after them. Busy footsteps thumped across the wooden deck of the balcony. The kitchen door burst open, a man's fist groped for the light switch and flicked it, to no effect. A hoarse voice panted, "The *fuck,* Jesus Christ, where the fuck? *Shit!*" A bulky figure stumbled toward the cash desk, and stopped midway.

"Anyone in here? Who's in here? Where's the fucking light, for fuck's sake? The *fuck!*"

Bronx, Jonathan recorded again, flattened behind the door to the balcony. A genuine Bronx accent, even when he's out of earshot. The man advanced again, holding the bag out in front of him while he groped with his other hand.

"Anyone in here, get the fuck out, hear me? That's a warning. We got the kid. Anyone makes trouble, the kid gets fucked. Don't mess with us."

But by now he had found the piles of bank notes and was sweeping them into the briefcase. When he had finished he went back to the doorway, and with only the opened door to separate him from Jonathan, he shouted down to his accomplice.

"I'm going on down, Mike! I'll go start the boat, hear me? *Jesus fuck,"* he complained, as if the world were being too hard on him. Then he hurried through the kitchen to the scullery door, which he kicked open, before heading down the path toward Goose Neck. In the same moment Jonathan heard the man called Mike approaching with his hostage, Daniel. Jonathan dried his palm once more on his shorts, drew the knife from his waistband and passed it to his left hand, the sharp edge upward as if to rip a belly from below. As he did so, he heard Daniel sob. One choked or muffled sob, so brief the boy must have caught himself almost before he began it. One half-sob of tiredness, impatience, boredom or frustration, the kind you might hear from any child, whether dirt poor or super-rich, who has a bit of earache or doesn't want to go upstairs to bed until you've promised to come and tuck him up.

Yet for Jonathan it was the cry of his childhood. It echoed in every vile corridor and barrack hut and orphanage and every auntie's spare back room. He restrained himself a moment longer, knowing that attacking blows are better for this moment of delay. He felt his heartbeat slow. He saw the red mist gather across his eyes, and he became weightless and invulnerable. He saw Sophie, her face intact and smiling. He heard the clump of adult feet, followed by the reluctant scuffle of smaller ones, as Daniel's captor came down the two steps from the wooden balcony and reached the tiled floor of the kitchen, dragging Daniel after him. As the man's foot hit the tiles, Jonathan stepped from behind the door and with his right hand seized the arm that held the pistol and gave it a ferocious, breaking twist. Simultaneously, Jonathan screamed: one prolonged cathartic scream, to ventilate, to summon help, to terrorize, to put an end to too much patience for too long. The pistol clattered on the tiles, and he kicked it out of reach. Hauling the man and his damaged arm into the doorway, he grabbed the door, threw his body weight upon it and crushed the arm between the door and jamb. The man called Mike screamed too, but stopped as Jonathan laid the knife blade against his sweating neck.

"Shit, man!" Mike whispered, somewhere

between pain and shock. "Fuck you doing to me? Holy *shit*. You some crazy man or something? Jesus!"

"Run back down the hill to your mother," Jonathan told Daniel. "Off you go. Quick now."

And despite everything that was raging in him, he selected these words with elaborate care, knowing he might have to live with them later. For why should a mere cook know that Daniel's first name was Daniel, or that Jed was not his mother, or that Daniel's real mother was several thousand miles away in Dorset? As he spoke them, he realized that Daniel was no longer listening, but gazing past him toward the other door. And that the bagman, having heard the screaming, had come back to lend assistance.

"Fucker's broken my fucking arm!" the man called Mike was yelling. "Let go my fucking arm, you mad shit! He's got a knife, Gerry. Don't fuck with him. My fucking arm's broke. He broke it two fucking times. He's not kidding. He's crazy!"

But Jonathan went on holding him by the arm that was probably broken, and he kept the knife pressed against the man's thick neck. The head was tipped right back on him with its mouth open, like a head at the dentist's, and the man's sweated hair stroked his face. And with the red mist there before his eyes, Jonathan would have done anything that he felt was necessary, without compunction.

"Walk back down the steps," he told Daniel, quietly so as not to scare him. "Go carefully. Off you go."

At which Daniel did at last consent to take his leave. He turned on his heel and began tripping unevenly down the steps toward the arc lights and the frozen crowd, flapping one hand above his head as if to acknowledge his accomplishment. And this was the consoling image that remained in Jonathan's mind as the man named Gerry hit him with his pistol butt, then hit him again over the right cheek and eye, then yet a third time as Jonathan floated to the ground in veils of Sophie's blood. While he lay on the floor in the recovery position, Gerry dealt him a couple of kicks in the groin for good measure before grabbing his accomplice, Mike, by his remaining arm and—to renewed screams and imprecations—dragging him across the kitchen to the opposite door. And Jonathan was pleased to see the stuffed briefcase lying not too far away, because clearly Gerry couldn't manage a maimed Mike and the loot at the same time.

Then came fresh footsteps and voices, and for a bad moment Jonathan thought they had decided to come back and give him some more of the same, but in his confusion he had mistaken the origin of the sounds, because it was not his enemies who were now gathered round and staring down at him, but his friends, all the people he had fought for and nearly died for: Tabby and Frisky, Langbourne and the polo players, the old couple who touched each other's faces while they danced and the four young blacks from the bar, then Swats and Wet Eye, then Roper and Jed with little Daniel clutched between them. And Miss Amelia, crying, on and on, as if Jonathan had broken her arm too. And Mama Low, yelling at Miss Amelia to shut the fuck up and Miss Amelia screaming, "That poor Lamont." And Roper had noticed it and was taking exception.

"Hell's she calling him Lamont for?" Roper was complaining while he leaned his head this way and that to get a better look at Jonathan's face beneath the blood. "He's Pine from Meister's. The night flunky chap they had. Englishman. Recognize him, Tabby?"

"That's who it is, Chief," Tabby confirmed, kneeling at Jonathan's side and holding his pulse.

Somewhere at the edge of his screen, Jonathan saw Frisky pick up the abandoned briefcase and peer inside.

"It's all here, Chief," he was saying soothingly. "No harm except to life and limb."

But Roper was still crouching over Jonathan, and whatever he saw must have been more impressive than the jewelry, for he kept wrinkling his nose as if the wine were corked. Jed had decided Daniel had seen enough and was walking him sedately down the steps.

"You hear me all right, Pine?" Roper asked.

"Yes," said Jonathan.

"Can you feel my hand okay?"

"Yes."

"Here too?"

"Yes."

"Here?"

"Yes."

"How's his pulse, Tabby?"

"Quite sporting, considering, Chief."

"You still hearing me, Pine?"

"Yes."

"You're going to be okay. Help's on its way. We'll get you the best there is. You talking to the boat there, Corky?"

"On line, Chief."

In the back of his mind, Jonathan had a notion of Major Corkoran holding a portable telephone to his ear, one hand propped on his hip and his elbow raised for extra authority.

"We'll fly him to Nassau on the chopper *now,*" Roper was saying, in the gruff voice he had for Corkoran. "Tell the pilot, then call the hospital. Not that lower-class place. T'other one. Ours."

"Doctors Hospital, Collins Avenue," said Corkoran.

"Book him in. Who's that pompous Swiss surgeon, got a house at Windermere Cay, always trying to put his money in our companies?"

"Marti," said Corkoran.

"Call Marti, get him up there."

"Will do."

"After that, call the coastguards, the police and all the usual idiots. Raise some serious hell. Got a stretcher, Low? Go and get it. You married or anything, Pine? Got a wife or anyone?"

"I'm fine, sir," said Jonathan.

But it was the equestrienne, typically, who had to have the last word. She must have done first aid at convent school. "Move him as little as possible," she was telling someone, in a voice that seemed to float into his sleep.

THIRTEEN

JONATHAN HAD vanished from their screens, missing, believed killed by friendly fire. All their planning, all their listening and watching, all their supposed mastery of the game, lay like a trashed limousine at the roadside. They were deaf and blind and ridiculous. The windowless headquarters in Miami was a ghosthouse, and Burr walked its grim corridors like a haunted man.

Roper's yacht, planes, houses, helicopters and cars were on constant watch; so was the stylish colonial mansion in downtown Nassau where the Ironbrand Land, Ore & Precious Metals Company had its prestigious headquarters. So were the telephone and facsimile lines belonging to Roper's contacts round the globe: from Lord Langbourne in Tortola to Swiss bankers in Zug and semi-anonymous collaborators in Warsaw; from a mysterious "Rafi" in Rio de Janeiro to "Misha" in Prague and a firm of Dutch notaries in Curaçao and an as yet unidentified government official in Panama who, even when speaking from his desk in the presidential palace, affected a drugged murmur and the alias of Charlie.

But of Jonathan Pine, alias Lamont, last

heard of in intensive care at Nassau's Doctors Hospital, not a whisper from any of them.

"He's deserted," Burr told Strelski, through the spread fingers of his hands. "First he goes mad, then he escapes from hospital. A week from now we'll be reading his story in the Sunday newspapers."

Yet everything so perfectly planned. Nothing left to chance, from the moment of the *Pasha*'s departure from Nassau to the night of the faked kidnapping at Mama Low's. The arrival of the cruise guests and their children—the bloodstock English girls of twelve with lolling faces, eating crisps and drawling about gymkhanas, the confident sons with whiplash bodies and the side-of-mouth slur that tells the world to go to hell, the Langbourne family with sullen wife and over-pretty nanny—all had been secretly welcomed, trailed, housed and hated by Amato's watchers, and finally seen aboard the *Pasha,* nothing left to chance.

"You know something? Those rich kids had the Rolls pull up at Joe's Easy, just so they could buy their grass!" Amato the proud new father protested to Strelski over his handset. The story duly entered the legend of the operation.

So did the story of the seashells. On the eve of the *Pasha*'s departure, one of Ironbrand's bright young men—MacArthur, who had made his début with a nonspeaking part at Meister's—

was heard telephoning a dubious banking contact on the other side of town: "Jeremy, in God's name, help me, who sells seashells these days? I need a thousand of the bloody things by yesterday. Jeremy, I'm serious."

The listeners became unusually vocal. *Seashells? Literally* seashells? Shell-like missile? Sea-to-air projectile perhaps? Nowhere in the lexicon of Roper's weaponspeak had anyone before referred to seashells. They were put out of their misery later the same day when MacArthur explained his problem to the manager of Nassau's luxury store: "Lord Langbourne's twin daughters are having a birthday on the second day of the cruise. The Chief wants to hold a shell hunt on one of the uninhabited islands and give prizes for the best collections, but last year nobody found any shells, so this year the Chief is taking no chances. He intends to have his security staff bury a thousand of the things in the sand the night before. So please, Mr. Manzini, where can I get hold of shells in bulk?"

The story had the team in stitches. Frisky and Tabby, launching a night raid on a deserted paddling beach, armed with duffel bags of seashells? It was too rich.

For the kidnapping, every step of the way had been rehearsed. First Flynn and Amato had disguised themselves as yachties and made a field reconnaissance of Hunter's Island. Back in

Florida, they reconstructed the terrain on a tract of dune set aside for them in the training compound at Fort Lauderdale. Tables were laid. Tapes marked the paths. A shack was erected to denote the kitchen. A cast of diners was assembled. Gerry and Mike, the two bad guys, were professional toughs from New York with orders to do what they were told and shut up. Mike the kidnapper was bearish. Gerry the bagman was lugubrious but agile. Hollywood could not have done better.

"Are you gentlemen fully conversant with your orders, now?" Irish Pat Flynn inquired, eyeing the brass rings on each finger of Gerry's right hand. "We're only asking for a couple of friendly belts now, Gerry. More in the line of a cosmetic alteration to the appearance is all that is required. Then we ask you to withdraw with honor. Am I making myself plain, Gerry?"

"You got it, Pat."

Then there had been the fallbacks, the what ifs. All covered. *What if,* at the last minute, the *Pasha* failed to put in at Hunter's? *What if* she put in at Hunter's, berthed, but the passengers decided to have dinner on board? *What if* the adults came ashore to dine, and the kids—perhaps as punishment for some prank—were made to stay aboard?

"Pray," said Burr.

"Pray," Strelski agreed.

But they were not really putting their trust in Providence. They knew that the *Pasha* had never yet passed Hunter's Island without putting in, even if they knew there was bound to be a first time and this would probably be it. They knew that Low's Boatyard in Deep Bay held top-up stores for the *Pasha,* and they knew the skipper stood to take a piece of the stores bill and of the dinner bill at Low's, because he always did. They placed great faith in Daniel's hold upon his father. Daniel had conducted several painful phone calls with Roper in recent weeks about the hellishness of adjusting to divided parents and had singled out the stopover at Hunter's Island as the high point of his forthcoming visit.

"I'm *really* going to get the crabs out of the basket this year, Dad," Daniel had told his father from England only ten days ago. "I don't dream about them anymore. Mums is really pleased with me."

Both Burr and Strelski had had similar upsetting conversations with their children in their time, and their guess was that Roper, though not of the English class that places children high in its priorities, would walk through fire rather than let Daniel down.

And they were right, absolutely right. And when Major Corkoran called Miss Amelia over the satcom to book the terrace table, Burr and Strelski could have hugged each other, which was what the team said they were doing these days anyway.

. . .

IT WAS NOT till around eleven-thirty in the evening of the day itself that they felt the first stirrings of unease. The operation had been scheduled for 2303 hours, or as soon as the crab races had begun. The holdup, the climb to the kitchen, the descent to Goose Neck, had never taken more than twelve minutes in rehearsal. Why on earth hadn't Mike and Gerry signaled "mission accomplished"?

Then the red alarm lit up. Standing with folded arms at the center of the communications room, Burr and Strelski listened to the playback of Corkoran's voice talking in fast order to the ship's captain, the ship's helicopter pilot, Doctors Hospital in Nassau and, lastly, Dr. Rudolf Marti at his home in Windermere Cay. Corkoran's voice was already a warning. It was cool and steady under fire:

"The Chief appreciates you're not in the first-aid business, Dr. Marti. But the skull and side of the face are severely fractured, and the Chief believes they'll have to be rebuilt. And the hospital needs a doctor to refer the patient to them. The Chief would like you waiting at the hospital when he arrives, and he will wish to compensate you generously for your trouble. May I tell him you'll be there?"

A fractured skull and side of face? *Rebuilt?*

What the hell had Mike and Gerry got up to? The relationship between Burr and Strelski was already strained by the time a call from Jackson Memorial Hospital in Miami had them racing there by flashing light, with Flynn riding alongside the driver. When they arrived, Mike was still in the operating theater. Gerry, gray with anger, was chain-smoking in the waiting room, wearing his navy life jacket.

"Fuckin' animal crucified Mike in the fuckin' door," Gerry said.

"So what did he do to *you,* Gerry?" Flynn asked.

"To me, nothin'."

"What did *you* do to *him?*"

"Kissed him on the fuckin' mouth. What do you think, dickhead?"

Then Flynn picked Gerry straight off his chair as if he were a rude child and slapped him hard once across the face, then sat him down again in the same indolent attitude as before.

"You whip him, Gerry?" Flynn asked kindly.

"Fucker went crazy. Played it for real. Held a fuckin' carving knife to Mike's throat, got his arm in the fuckin' door like he's choppin' firewood."

They returned to the operations room in time to listen to Daniel talking to his mother in England over the *Pasha*'s satcom.

"Mums, it's me. I'm all right. I really am."

Long silence while she wakes up.

"Daniel? Darling, you haven't come back to England, have you?"

"I'm on the *Pasha*, Mums."

"Daniel, *really*. Do you *know* the time? Where's your father?"

"I didn't get the crabs out of the basket, Mums. I chickened. They make me sick. I'm all right, Mums. Honestly."

"Danny?"

"Yes?"

"Danny, what are you trying to tell me?"

"Only we were on Hunter's Island, you see, Mums. There was this man who smelled of garlic and took me prisoner, and another man who took Jed's necklace. But the cook saved me and they let me go."

"Daniel, is your father there?"

"Paula. Hi. Sorry about that. He was determined to tell you he's okay. We got held up at gunpoint by a couple of thugs at Mama Low's. Dans was taken hostage for ten minutes, but he's totally unharmed."

"Wait," said Paula. Like his son before him, Roper waited for her to collect herself. "Daniel's been kidnapped and released. But he's all right. Now go on."

"They marched him up the path to the kitchen. Remember the kitchen, up the path on the hill?"

"You're sure all this *happened,* are you? We all know Daniel's stories."

"Yes, of course I'm sure. I saw it."

"At *gunpoint?* They marched him up a hill at *gunpoint?* A boy of eight?"

"They were going for the cash in the kitchen. But there was this cook up there, a white chap, who had a go at them. He winged one, but the other one came back, and they beat him up while Daniel escaped. God knows what would have happened if they'd taken Dans with them, but they didn't. All over now. We even got the loot back. Thank God for cooks. Come on, Dans, tell her how we're giving you the Victoria Cross for gallantry. Here he is again."

. . .

IT WAS five in the morning. Burr sat motionless as a Buddha at his desk. Rooke smoked his pipe and wrestled with the *Miami Herald* crossword. Burr let the phone ring several times before he was able to pick it up.

"Leonard?" said Goodhew's voice.

"Hullo, Rex."

"Did something go wrong? I thought you were going to ring me. You sound as if you're in shock. Did they swallow the bait, then? Leonard?"

"Oh, they swallowed it, all right."

"So what's wrong? You don't sound victorious, you sound funereal. What happened?"

"I'm just trying to work out whether we're still holding the rod."

Mr. Lamont is in intensive care, said the hospital. *Mr. Lamont is stable.*

Not for long. Twenty-four hours later Mr. Lamont had vanished.

. . .

HAS HE discharged himself? The hospital says he has. Has Dr. Marti had him shifted to his clinic? Apparently so, but only briefly, and the clinic gives no information about the destination of discharged patients. And when Amato telephones in the guise of a newspaper reporter, Dr. Marti himself replies that Mr. Lamont has left without leaving an address. Suddenly, outlandish theories are being passed round the ops room. Jonathan has confessed to everything! Roper has rumbled him and dumped him in the sea! On Strelski's orders, the watch on Nassau airport has been suspended. He fears Amato's team is becoming too visible.

"We're engineering human nature, Leonard," says Strelski consolingly, in an effort to lift the burden from Burr's soul. "Can't get it right every time."

"Thanks."

. . .

EVENING COMES. Burr and Strelski sit in a roadside barbecue house with their cellular telephones on their laps, eating ribs and Cajun rice and watching well-fed America come and go. A summons from the telephone monitors has them racing back to headquarters in mid-mouthful.

Corkoran to a senior editor of the leading Bahamian newspaper:

"Old love! It's me. Corky. How are we? How are the dancing girls?"

Coarse intimacies are exchanged. Then the nub:

"Sweetheart, listen, the Chief wants a story killed . . . pressing reasons why the hero of the hour doesn't need the spotlight . . . young Daniel, very hyper boy . . . I'm talking serious gratitude, a mega-improvement to your retirement plans. How about 'a practical joke that came unstuck'? Can you do that, lover?"

The sensational robbery on Hunter's Island is laid to rest in the great cemetery for stories permanently spiked by Higher Authority.

Corkoran to the desk of a senior Nassau police officer known for his understanding of the peccadilloes of the rich:

"Heart, how are we? Listen, in re Brother Lamont, last seen at Doctors Hospital by one of your heavier-footed brethren . . . can we just kind of lose that one from the menu—do you mind? The Chief would greatly prefer the lower profile, feels it's better for Daniel's health . . . wouldn't wish to prefer charges, even if you found the culprits, hates the fuss . . . bless you. . . . Oh, and by the by, don't believe all that crap you're reading about Ironbrand shares going through the floor. . . . Chief's considering a very nice little divi this Christmas; we should all be able to buy ourselves a piece of whatever we like best."

The strong arm of the law agrees to withdraw its claws. Burr wonders whether he is listening to Jonathan's obituary. And from the rest of the world, not a peep.

· · ·

SHOULD BURR RETURN to London? Should Rooke? Logically, it made no difference whether they hung by a thread in Miami or in London. Illogically, Burr needed nearness to the place where his agent was last seen. In the end, he sent Rooke to London and the same day checked out of his steel-and-glass hotel and moved to humbler premises in a sleazy part of town.

"Leonard's putting on the hair shirt while he waits this thing out," Strelski told Flynn.

"Tough," said Flynn, still trying to come to terms with the experience of having his agent immolated by Burr's ewe lamb.

Burr's new cell was a pastel-painted art deco box beside the beach, with a bedside light made out of a chrome Atlas holding up the globe, and steel-framed windows that buzzed to every passing car, and a doped-out Cuban security guard with dark glasses and an elephant gun, lounging in the lobby. Burr slept there lightly, with his cellular phone on the spare pillow.

One dawn, unable to sleep, he took his phone for a walk down a great boulevard. A regiment of cocaine banks loomed at him out of the misted sea. But as he went toward them he found himself in a building site full of colored birds screaming from the scaffolding, and Latinos sleeping like war dead beside their parked bulldozers.

. . .

JONATHAN WAS NOT the only one who had disappeared. Roper too had entered a black hole. Deliberately or not, he had given Amato's watchers the slip. The tap on the Ironbrand headquarters in Nassau revealed only that the Chief was away selling farms—"selling farms" being Roperspeak for "mind your own damn business."

The supersnitch Apostoll, urgently consulted by Flynn, offered no consolation. He had heard vaguely that his clients might be holding a business conference on the island of Aruba, but he had not been invited. No, he had no idea where Mr. Roper was. He was a lawyer, not a travel agent. He was Mary's soldier.

. . .

ANOTHER EVENING CAME, and Strelski and Flynn determined to take Burr out of himself. They collected him from his hotel and, cellular phones in hand, made him stroll among the crowds on the promenade beside the beach. They sat him at a pavement café and fed him margaritas and forced him to take an interest in the people who went by. In vain. They watched muscular blacks in multicolored shirts and gold rings, rolling with the majesty of high life for as long as the highs and the living lasted, their dolls in skin-tight miniskirts and thigh boots toppling between them, their shaven-headed bodyguards in robes of mullah gray to conceal their automatic weapons. A swarm of beachboys on skateboards raced past, and the wiser ladies whisked their handbags out of reach. But two old lesbians in straw trilbies refused to be daunted and marched their poodles straight at them, causing them to veer. After the beachboys came a shoal of long-necked fashion models on roller skates, each more gorgeous than the last. At the sight of them, Burr, who loved women, did for a moment come alive—only to lapse again into his melancholy abstractions.

"Hey, Leonard," said Strelski, making a last gallant effort. "Let's go see where the Roper does his weekend shopping."

In a big hotel, in a conference room protected by men with padded shoulders, Burr and Strelski mingled with the buyers of all nations and listened to the sales talk of wholesome young men with name tags pinned to their lapels. Behind the men sat girls with order books. And behind the girls, in shrines cordoned off with blood-colored ropes, stood their wares, each polished like a loved possession, each guaranteed to make a man of whoever owned them: from the most cost-effective cluster bomb through the all-plastic un-detectable Glock automatic pistol to the latest thing in hand-held rocket launchers, mortars and anti-personnel mines. And for your reading man, standard works on how to build yourself a rocket-propelled gun in your own backyard or make a one-time silencer out of a tubular can of tennis balls.

"About the only thing missing is a girl in a bikini poking her fanny at the barrel of a sixteen-inch fieldpiece," said Strelski as they drove back to the operations room.

The joke fell flat.

. . .

A TROPICAL STORM descends on the city, blackening the sky, chopping the heads off the skyscrapers. Lightning strikes, triggering the burglar alarms of parked cars. The hotel shudders and cracks, the last daylight dies as if the main switch has failed. Jets of rain spew down the windowpanes of Burr's bedroom, black flotsam rides on the scurrying white mist. Billows of wind ransack the palm trees, hurling chairs and plants off balconies. Then disappear, leaving the battlefield to the defeated.

But Burr's cellular phone, ringing in his ear, has miraculously survived the attack.

"Leonard," says Strelski in a voice of suppressed excitement, "get your ass down here fast. We got a couple of murmurs coming out of the rubble."

The city lights bounce back again, shining gaily after their free wash.

. . .

Corkoran to Sir Anthony Joyston Bradshaw, lately unprincipled chairman of a group of derelict British trading companies, and occasional purveyor of deniable arms shipments to Her Majesty's procurement ministers.

Corkoran is telephoning from the Nassau apartment of one of Ironbrand's smart young men, on the mistaken assumption that the line is safe.

"Sir Tony? Corkoran here. Dicky Roper's gofer."

"Fuck do you want?" The voice sounds clotted and half drunk. It echoes like a voice in a bathroom.

"Pressing matter, Sir Tony, I'm afraid. The Chief needs your good offices. Got a pencil?"

While Burr and Strelski listen transfixed, Corkoran struggles to achieve precision:

"No, Sir Tony, *Pine.* Pine like the tree, Pine like a sick dog. P for Peter, I for Item, N for Nuts, E for Easy. That's right. First name Jonathan. Like Jonathan." He adds a couple of harmless details, such as Jonathan's date and place of birth and British passport number. "Chief wants the head-to-toe background check, Sir Tony, please, preferably by yesterday. And mum. All very mum indeed."

"Who's Joyston Bradshaw?" Strelski asks,

when they have heard the conversation to the end.

Seeming to wake from a deep dream, Burr allows himself a cautious smile. "Sir Anthony Joyston Bradshaw, Joe, is a leading English shit. His financial embarrassment is one of the major joys of the current recession." His smile spreads. "Unsurprisingly, he is also a former partner in crime of Mr. Richard Onslow Roper." He warms to his theme. "As a matter of fact, Joe, if you and I were fielding the all-English team of shits, Sir Anthony Joyston Bradshaw would feature high on our batting list. He also enjoys the protection of some other highly placed English shits, some of whom work not too far distant from the river Thames." The relief shone through Burr's strained face as he broke out laughing. "He's alive, Joe! You don't check a corpse, not by yesterday! Head-to-toe background, he says. Well, we've got it all ready for him, and nobody better suited to provide him with it than Tony bloody Joyston Bradshaw! They want him, Joe! He's got his nose into their tent! *You* know what they say, the Bedouin? Never let a camel's nose into your tent, because if you do, you get the whole camel."

But while Burr was rejoicing, Strelski's mind was already on the next practical step.

"So Pat goes ahead?" he said. "Pat's boys can go bury the magic box?"

Burr sobered at once. "If it's okay by you and Pat, it's okay by me," he said.

They agreed on the very next night.

. . .

UNABLE TO SLEEP, Burr and Strelski drove to an all-night hamburger joint called Murgatroyd's on U.S. 1, where a sign said, NO SHOES, NO SERVICE. Outside the smoked-glass windows sat shoeless pelicans in the moonlight, each to his mooring-post along the wooden jetty, like feathery old bombing planes that might never bomb again. On the silver beach, white egrets peered forlornly at their reflections.

At four a.m. Strelski's cellular phone peeped. He put it to his ear, said "yes" and listened. He said, "So get yourselves some sleep." He rang off. The conversation had taken twenty seconds.

"No problem," he announced to Burr, and took a pull of Coke.

Burr needed a moment to believe his ears. "You mean they made it? It's done? They cached it?"

"They beach-landed, they found the shed, they buried the box, they were very quiet, very professional, they got the hell out. All your boy has to do now is speak."

FOURTEEN

JONATHAN WAS BACK in his iron bed at army school after they ripped his tonsils out—except that the bed was huge and white, with the soft down pillows with embroidered edges that they used to have at Meister's, and a small herb pillow for the fragrance.

He was in the motel room one truck ride out of Espérance, nursing his battered jaw with the curtains drawn and sweating out a fever after telephoning a voice that had no name to say he had found his shadow—except that his head was bandaged, he was wearing crisp cotton pajamas, and there was a stitched device on the pocket that he kept trying to read by Braille. Not M for Meister, not P for Pine or B for Beauregard or L for Linden and Lamont. More like a Star of David with too many points.

He was in Yvonne's attic, listening for Madame Latulipe's footfall in the half-light. Yvonne wasn't there, but the attic was—except that this was a bigger attic than Yvonne's, and bigger than the attic in Camden Town that Isabelle had painted in. And it had pink flowers in an old Delft vase, and a tapestry of ladies and gentlemen out hawking. A punkah dangled from a roof beam, making stately turns of its propeller.

He was lying beside Sophie in the apartment in the Chicago House in Luxor while she talked about courage—except that the smell tickling his nostrils was of potpourri, not vanilla. *He said I must be taught a lesson,* she was saying. *It is not I who must be taught a lesson. It is Freddie Hamid and his dreadful Dicky Roper.*

He made out closed shutters slicing sunlight into blades, and layers of fine white muslin curtain. He turned his head the other way and saw a Meister's silver room-service tray with a jug of orange juice, and a cut-glass goblet to drink it from, and a lace cloth covering the silver tray. Across a thickly carpeted floor, he distinguished through the blur of his reduced vision a doorway to a large bathroom, with towels of ascending sizes folded along a rail.

But by then his eyes were streaming and his body was hopping the way it had hopped when he was ten and caught his fingers in somebody's car door, and he realized he was lying on his bandage, and his bandage was on the side of his head that they had smashed and Dr. Marti had repaired. So he rolled his head back to where it had been before he started his close observation, and he watched the punkah going round until the light-spots of pain had cleared and the undercover soldier's gyroscope inside him had begun to right itself.

This is where you get yourself across the bridge, Burr had said.

They'll have to mark the goods, Rooke had said. *You can't just walk up to them with the boy in your arms to everyone's applause.*

Fracture of the skull and cheekbone, Marti had said. Concussion, eight on the Richter scale, ten years' solitary in a darkened room.

Three cracked ribs, could be thirty.

Severe bruising of the testicles following attempted castration with the toe cap of a heavy training boot.

For it seemed that once Jonathan had gone down under the pistol whipping, it was his groin that the man had attacked, leaving among other traces the perfect imprint of a size-twelve boot in his inside thigh, to the raucous amusement of the nurses.

A black-and-white figure flitted across his vision. White uniform. Black face. Black legs, white stockings. Rubber-soled white shoes with Velcro fastenings. At first he had thought she was one person; now he knew she was several. They visited him like spirits, mutely polishing and dusting, changing his flowers and his drinking water. One was called Phoebe and had a nurse's touch.

"Hi, Mist' Thomas. How're *you* today? I'm Phoebe. Miranda, just you go fetch that brush again, and this time you sweep right *under* Mist' Thomas's bed. Yes, *ma'am.*"

So I'm Thomas, he thought. Not Pine. Thomas. Or perhaps I'm Thomas Pine.

He dozed again, and woke to find Sophie's ghost standing over him, in her white slacks, shaking pills into a paper cup. Then he thought she must be a new nurse. Then he saw the broad belt with the silver buckle, and the maddening line of the hips, and the tousled chestnut hair. And heard the Mistress-of-the-Hunt voice, bang on station, no respect for anyone.

"But, *Thomas,*" Jed was protesting. *"Somebody* must love you *terribly.* What about mothers, girlfriends, fathers, chums? Really nobody?"

"Really," he insisted.

"So who's Yvonne?" she asked, as she placed her head within inches of his own, spread one palm on his back and the other on his chest to sit him up. "Is she absolutely *gorgeous?"*

"She was just a friend," he said, smelling the shampoo in her hair.

"Well, shouldn't we be telling Yvonne?"

"No, we shouldn't," he replied, too sharply.

She gave him his pills and a glass of water. "Well, Dr. Marti says you're to sleep for*ever*. So don't think of *anything* except getting better *extremely* slowly. Now, how about distractions— books, a radio or something? Not *quite* yet, but in a day or two. We don't know *anything* about you, except that Roper says you're Thomas, so you'll just have to tell us what you need. There's a *huge* library over in the main house, with masses of *frightfully* learned stuff—Corky will tell you what it all is—and we can get anything you want flown over from Nassau. You just have to yell." And her eyes big enough to drown in.

"Thanks, I will."

She laid a hand on his face to feel his temperature. "We just *never* can thank you enough," she said, keeping it there. "Roper will say it all *far* better than I can when he gets back, but honestly, *what* a hero. Just *so* brave," she said from the door. *"Shit,"* the convent girl added, catching the pocket of her slacks on the handle.

· · ·

THEN HE REALIZED that it wasn't their first meeting since he had arrived here, but their third, and that the first two were not dreams either.

Our first time you smiled at me, and that was fine: you kept quiet and I could think, and we had something going. You had jammed your hair behind your ears, you were wearing jodhpurs and a denim shirt. I said, "Where is this?" You said, "Crystal. Roper's island. Home."

The second time I was feeling vague, and I thought you were my former wife, Isabelle, waiting to be taken out to dinner, because you were got up in a perfectly ridiculous trouser suit with gold frogging on the lapels. "There's a bell right beside your water jug if you need anything," you said. And I said, "Expect my call." But I was thinking: Why the hell do you have to dress up like a pantomime boy?

Her father ruined himself keeping up with the county, Burr said with contempt. *He was serving vintage claret when he couldn't pay the electricity bill. Wouldn't send his daughter to secretarial college because he thought it was infra dig.*

· · ·

LYING ON his safe side, facing the tapestry, Jonathan made out a lady in a broad-brimmed hat and recognized her without surprise as singing Aunt Annie Ball.

Annie was a valiant woman and sang good songs, but her farmer husband got drunk and hated everyone. So one day Annie put on her hat and sat Jonathan beside her in the van with his suitcase in the back, and said they were going for a holiday. They drove late into the evening, and sang songs till they came to a house with BOYS carved in granite over the door. Then Annie Ball started weeping and gave Jonathan her hat as a promise she'd come back soon to get it, and Jonathan went upstairs to a dormitory full of other boys and hung the hat over the corner of his bed to show Annie which boy he was when she returned. But she never did, and when he woke in the morning the other boys in the dormitory were taking it in turns to wear her hat. So he fought for it, and won it against all comers, and rolled it up in newspaper and posted it, with no address, in a red pillar box. He would have preferred to burn it, but he hadn't a fire.

I came here by night as well, he thought. White twin-engined Beechcraft, blue interior. Frisky and Tabby, not the orphanage guardian, searched my luggage for forbidden tuck.

. . .

I HURT him for Daniel, he decided.

I hurt him to get me across the bridge.

I hurt him because I was sick of waiting and pretending.

. . .

JED WAS in the room again. The close observer had no doubt of it. It wasn't her scent, because she wore none, or her sound, because she made none. And for a long time he couldn't see her, so it wasn't sight. So it must have been the sixth sense of the professional watcher, when you know an enemy is present but don't yet know why you know.

"Thomas?"

Feigning sleep, he listened to her tiptoeing toward him. He had a notion of pale clothes, dancer's body, hair hanging loose. He heard a shifting as she drew back her hair and put her ear close to his mouth to hear him breathe. He could feel the warmth of her cheek. She stood again, and he heard slippered feet disappearing down the passage, then the same feet outside, crossing the stableyard.

They say that when she went up to London she scared herself, Burr said. *Got in with a crowd of Hoorah Henries and screwed the field. Bolted to Paris for a rest cure. Met Roper.*

. . .

HE LISTENED to the Cornish gulls and the long echoes from outside the shutters. He smelled the brown salt smell of weed and knew it was low tide. For a while he let himself believe that Jed had taken him back to the Lanyon and was standing barefoot on the floorboards before the mirror, doing the things women do before they come to bed. Then he heard the plop of tennis balls and leisured English voices calling to each other, and one of them was Jed's. He heard a lawn mower, and the yell of rude English children quarreling, and surmised the Langbournes' offspring. He heard the buzz of an electric motor and decided on a skimmer cleaning the surface of a pool. He slept again and smelled charcoal and knew by the pinkish glow of the ceiling that it was evening, and when he dared to lift his head he saw Jed in silhouette before the shuttered window as she peered through it at the last of the day outside, and the evening light showed him her body through her tennis clothes.

"Now, Thomas, what about a little more *food* in your life?" she proposed in a school matron's voice. She must have heard him move his head. "Esmeralda's made you some beef broth and bread and butter. Dr. Marti said toast, but it goes so floppy in the humidity. Or there's chicken breast, or apple pie. *Actually,* Thomas, there's pretty much anything you want," she added, in the startled accents he was becoming accustomed to. "Just whistle."

"Thanks. I will."

"Thomas, it really is *odd,* you not having a *single* person to worry about you in the world. I don't know why it should, but it makes me *frightfully* guilty. Can't you even have a brother? *Everyone's* got a *brother,"* she said.

"Afraid not."

"Well, I've got one *gorgeous* brother and one absolute *pig.* So that cancels them out, *really.* Except I'd far rather have them than not. Even the pig."

She was coming across the room to him. She smiles all the time, he thought in alarm. She smiles like a television commercial. She's afraid we'll switch her off if she stops smiling. She's an actress in search of a director. One small scar on her chin, otherwise no distinguishing marks. Maybe somebody swiped her too. A horse did. He held his breath. She had reached his bed. She was stooping over him, pressing what felt like a piece of cold sticking plaster to his forehead.

"Got to let it cook," she said, smiling more broadly. Then she sat on the bed to wait, tennis skirt parted, bare legs carelessly crossed, the muscles of one calf gently swelling against the shin below. And her skin all one soft tan.

"It's called a fever tester," she explained in a stagy, top-hostess accent. "For some *extraordinary* reason this *entire* house has no proper thermometer. You're *such* a mystery, Thomas. Were those *all* your things? Just one small bag?"

"Yes."

"In the world?"

"I'm afraid so." Get off my bed! Get into it! Cover yourself! Who the hell do you think I am?

"God, you are lucky!" she was saying, this time sounding like a princess of the blood. "Why can't *we* be like that? We take the Beechcraft to Miami just for *one weekend,* and we can *hardly* get our stuff in the hold."

Poor you, he thought.

She talks lines, he recorded in his misery. Not words. Lines. She talks versions of who she thinks she ought to be.

"Perhaps you should use that big boat of yours instead," he suggested facetiously.

But to his fury she seemed to have no experience of being laughed at. Perhaps beautiful women never had.

"The *Pasha?* Oh, that would take *far* too long," she explained condescendingly. Reaching a hand to his forehead, she unpeeled the plastic strip and took it to the shutters to read. "Roper's away selling farms, I'm afraid. He's decided to slow down a bit, which I think is a *frightfully* good idea."

"What does he do?"

"Oh, business. He runs a company, actually. Who doesn't these days? Well, at least it's his *own,*" she added, as if she were apologizing for her lover being in trade. "He did found it. But *mainly* he's just a lovely, darling man." She was tilting the strip, frowning at it. "He's also got *masses* of farms, which is rather more fun, not that I've ever seen any of them. All over Panama and Venezuela and places where you have to have an armed guard to go on a picnic. Not *my* idea of farming, but it's still *land.*" The frown deepened. "Well, it *says* normal, and it *says* clean with alcohol when dirty. Corky could do that for us. No trouble at *all.*" She giggled, and he saw that side of her too: the party girl who is the first to kick off her shoes and dance when things warm up.

"I'll have to be hitting the road pretty soon," he said. "You've been terribly kind. Thanks."

Always play hard to get, Burr had advised. *If you don't, they'll be bored with you in a week.*

"Go?" she cried, making her lips into a perfect O and keeping them there for a moment. "What *are* you talking about? You aren't *nearly* ready to go *anywhere* till Roper gets back, and Dr. Marti said *specifically* that you've got to have simply *weeks* of convalescence. The *least* we can do is build you up. Anyway, we're all dying to know what on *earth* you were doing saving life and limb at Mama's after you'd been someone *totally* different at Meister's."

"I don't think I'm different. I just felt I was getting in a rut. Time I threw away my striped pants and drifted for a while."

"Well, *jolly* good for us you drifted our way, is all *I* can say," said the equestrienne, in a voice so deep that she might have been tightening her horse's girth while she spoke.

"What about you?" he asked.

"Oh, I just live here."

"All the time?"

"When we're not on the boat. Or traveling. Yes. This is where I live."

But her answer seemed to puzzle her. She laid him flat again, avoiding his eye.

"Roper wants me to hop over to Miami for a couple of days," she said as she was leaving. "But Corky's back, and everyone's absolutely *dying* to spoil you *rotten,* and the hot line to Dr. Marti is *wide* open, so I don't think you'll *exactly* fade away."

"Well, remember to pack light this time," he said.

"Oh, I always do. Roper *insists* on shopping, so we always come back with *tons.*"

She left, to his profound relief. It was not his own performance that had tired him out, he realized. It was hers.

. . .

HE WAS woken by the sound of a page turning and made out Daniel in a bathrobe crouched on the floor, with his bottom in the air, reading a large book by a convenient shaft of sunlight, and he knew it was morning, which was why there were brioches and croissants and Madeira cake and homemade jam and a silver teapot beside his bed.

"You can get giant squid sixty feet long," Daniel said. "What do they eat, anyway?"

"Other squid probably."

"I could read you about them if you like." He turned another page. "Do you *like* Jed, actually?"

"Of course."

"I don't. Not *really.*"

"Why not?"

"I just don't. She's soppy. They're all terrifically impressed you saved me. Sandy Langbourne's talking about organizing a collection."

"Who's she?"

"It's a him. He's a lord, actually. Only there's a question mark hanging over you. So he thought he'd better hold off until it's removed one way or the other. That's why Miss Molloy says I'm not to spend too much time with you."

"Who's Miss Molloy?"

"She teaches me."

"At school?"

"I don't go to school, actually."

"Why not?"

"It hurts my feelings. Roper gets in other kids for me, but I hate them. He's bought a new Rolls-Royce for Nassau, but Jed likes the Volvo better."

"Do you like the Rolls-Royce?"

"Yuck."

"What *do* you like?"

"Dragons."

"When are they coming back?"

"The *dragons?*"

"Jed and Roper."

"You're supposed to call him the Chief."

"All right. Jed and the Chief."

"What's *your* name, anyway?"

"Thomas."

"Is that your surname or your Christian name?"

"Whichever you like."

"It's not either of them, according to Roper. It's made up."

"Did he tell you that?"

"I just happened to hear it. Thursday probably. Depends if they stay on for Apo's binge."

"Who's Apo?"

"He's foul. He's got a tart's penthouse in Coconut Grove, which is where he does his screwing. That's in Miami."

So Daniel read to Jonathan about squid, and

then he read to him about pterodactyls, and when Jonathan dozed off, Daniel tapped him on the shoulder to ask whether it would be all right to eat a bit of Madeira cake and would Jonathan like some too? So to please Daniel, Jonathan ate a bit of Madeira cake, and when Daniel shakily poured him a cup of tea he drank some tepid tea as well.

"Coming along, are we, Tommy? They made a right job of you, I will say. Very professional."

It was Frisky, seated on a chair just inside the door, wearing a T-shirt and white ducks and no Beretta, and reading the *Financial Times*.

. . .

WHILE THE PATIENT RESTED, the close observer used his wits.

Crystal. Mr. Onslow Roper's island in the Exumas, one hour's flying time from Nassau by Frisky's right-handed watch, which Jonathan had managed to get a sight of as they loaded him on and off the plane. Slumped in the rear seat, his mind secret-bright, he had watched by white moonlight as they flew over reefs fretted like the tongues of a jigsaw puzzle. A solitary island rose toward them, a cone-shaped hillock at its center. He made out a neat, floodlit airstrip cut into the crest, with a helicopter pad to one side of it, and a low green hangar and an orange communications mast. In his peculiar alertness he looked for the cluster of broken slave houses in the woods that Rooke said marked the spot, but he didn't see one. They landed and were met by a soft-topped Toyota jeep driven by a very big black man who wore string gloves with the knuckles left bare for hitting people.

"He okay for sittin', or you wan' me pull out the back?"

"Just take him nice and slow," Frisky had said.

They drove down an unmade snake track, and the trees changed from blue pine to lush green heart-shaped leaves the size of dinner plates. The track straightened, and by the jeep's headlights he saw a broken sign saying PINDAR'S TURTLE FACTORY and behind the sign a brick sweatshop with the roof torn off and its windows smashed. And at the roadside, shreds of cotton hanging like old bandages from the bushes. And Jonathan memorized everything in order, so that if he ever got out of here and was on the run, he could count them in reverse: pineapple field, banana grove, tomato field, factory. By the burning white moon he saw fields with wooden stumps like unfinished crosses, then a Calvary Chapel, then a clapboard Highway Church of God. Go left at the Highway Church, he thought, as they turned right. Everything was information, everything a straw to clutch as he fought to stay afloat.

A circle of natives sat in the road, drinking from brown bottles. The driver maneuvered respectfully round them, his gloved hand lifted in a calm salute. The Toyota bumped over a plank bridge, and Jonathan saw the moon hanging to his right, with the north star straight above it. He saw flame-of-the-woods and hibiscus and, with the lucidity that was on him, remembered reading that the hummingbird drank from the back of the hibiscus, not the center. But then he couldn't remember whether this made the bird remarkable or the plant.

They passed between two gateposts that reminded him of Italian villas on Lake Como. Beside the gates stood a white bungalow with barred windows and security lights, and Jonathan took this to be a gatehouse of some kind, because the jeep slowed to a crawl as the gates appeared, and two black guards made a leisurely inspection of its occupants.

"This the one the Major say comin'?"

"What do you think he is?" Frisky asked. "A fucking Arab stallion?"

"Just askin', man. Ain't no cause for perturbation. What they do to his face, man?"

"Styled it," said Frisky.

From the gates to the main house was four minutes by Frisky's watch at around ten miles an hour for the speed bumps, and the Toyota seemed to move in a left-handed arc with sweet-smelling water to the left, so Jonathan reckoned a curved driveway about 1.5 kilometers long skirting the shore of a man-made lake or lagoon. As they drove he kept seeing distant lights between the trees and guessed a perimeter fence with halogen lamps, like Ireland. Once he heard the flutter of a horse's feet scampering beside them in the dark.

The Toyota rounded another turn, and he saw the floodlit façade of a Palladian palace, with a central cupola and a triangular pediment supported by four tall pillars. The cupola had round dormer windows like portholes lit from within, and a small tower that shone like a white shrine in the moonlight. On the top of the tower stood a weather vane, with two coursing dogs pursuing a spotlit gold arrow. The bill for the house is twelve million pounds and more to come, Burr had said. Contents insured for another seven, fire only. The Roper doesn't reckon on being robbed.

The palace stood on a grass mound that must have been shaped for it. There was a gravel sweep with a lily pond and a marble fountain, and a hooped marble stairway with a balustrade rising from the sweep to a high entrance with iron lanterns. The lanterns were lit and the fountain was playing; the double doors were made of glass. Through them Jonathan glimpsed a man-servant in a white tunic standing under a chandelier in the hall. The jeep kept going across the gravel, through a cobbled stableyard that smelled of warm horses, past a spinney of euca-lyptus trees and a floodlit swimming pool with a kids' end with a slide, and two floodlit clay tennis courts, and a croquet lawn and a putting green, between a second pair of gateposts, less imposing but prettier than the first, to stop before a redwood door.

And there Jonathan had to close his eyes because his head was splitting and the pain in his groin was driving him nearly mad. Besides, it was time that he played dead again.

Crystal, he repeated to himself as they carried him up the teak staircase. Crystal. A Crystal as Big as the Ritz.

· · ·

AND NOW in his luxurious confinement the unsleeping part of Jonathan still toiled, noting and recording every symptom for posterity. He listened to the day-long flow of black men's voices from outside the shutters, and soon he had identified Gums, who was repairing the wooden jetty, and Earl, who was shaping boulders for a rockery and was an avid supporter of the St. Kitts football team, and Talbot, who was the boatmaster and sang calypso. He heard land vehicles, but their engines had no throat so he divined electric buggies. He heard the Beechcraft plow back and forth across the sky to no routine, and each time it passed he imagined Roper with his half-lens spectacles and Sotheby's catalogue riding home to his island, with Jed beside him reading magazines. He heard the distant whinnying of horses and the scrabbling of hooves in the stableyard. He heard the occasional roar of a guard dog and the yapping of much smaller dogs that could have been a pack of beagles. And he discovered by degrees that the emblem on his pajama pocket was a crystal, which he supposed he might have guessed from the beginning.

He learned that his room, however elegant, was not excused the battle against tropical decay. As he began to use the bathroom he noticed how the towel rail, though polished daily by the maids, grew salt sweat spots overnight. And how the brackets holding the glass shelves oxidized, as did the rivets fastening the brackets to the tiled wall. There were hours when the air was so heavy it defied the punkah and hung on him like a wet shirt, draining him of will.

And he knew that the question mark was still hanging over him.

· · ·

ONE EVENING Dr. Marti paid a visit to the island by air taxi. He asked Jonathan whether he spoke French, and Jonathan said yes. So while Marti explored Jonathan's head and his groin, and hit his knees and arms with a little rubber hammer, and peered into his eyes with an ophthalmoscope, Jonathan answered a string of not very casual questions about himself in French and knew he was being examined about other things than his health.

"But you speak French like a European, Monsieur Lamont!"

"It's how they taught it to us at school."

"In Europe?"

"Toronto."

"But which school was that? My God, they must have been geniuses!"

And more of the same.

Rest, Dr. Marti prescribed. Rest and wait. For what? Until you catch me out?

"Feeling a bit more like ourselves, are we, Thomas?" Tabby asked solicitously, from the seat beside the door.

"A bit."

"That's the way, then," said Tabby.

As Jonathan grew stronger, the guards grew more watchful.

. . .

BUT OF THE house where they were keeping him Jonathan learned nothing, stretch his senses as he might: no doorbells, telephones, fax machines, cooking smells, no scraps of conversation. He smelled honey-scented furniture polish, insecticide, fresh flowers, potpourri and, when the breeze was in the right direction, horses. He smelled frangipani and mown grass, and chlorine from the swimming pool.

Nevertheless, the orphan, soldier and hotelier was soon aware of something familiar to him from his homeless past: the rhythm of an efficient institution, even when the high command was not there to enforce it. The gardeners began work at seven-thirty, and Jonathan could have set his clock by them. The single chime of a tocsin sounded the eleven o'clock break, and for twenty minutes nothing stirred, not a mower or a cutlash, as they dozed. At one o'clock the tocsin sounded twice, and if Jonathan strained his ears he could hear the murmur of native chatter from the staff canteen.

A knock on his door. Frisky opened it and grinned. *Corkoran's as degenerate as Caligula,* Burr had warned, *and as clever as a box of monkeys.*

. . .

"OLD LOVE," breathed a husky, upper-class English voice through the fumes of last night's alcohol and this morning's vile-smelling French cigarettes. "How *are* we today? Not stuck for variety, I must say, heart. We kick off Garibaldi scarlet, then we go blue-based baboon, and today we're a sort of livery, rather stale donkey-piss yellow. Dare one hope we're on the mend?"

The pockets of Major Corkoran's bush jacket were stuffed with pens and male junk. Huge sweat patches reached from his armpits across his gut.

"I'd like to go soon, actually," said Jonathan.

"Absolutely, heart, whenever you like. Talk to the Chief. Soon as they're back. Due season and all that. And we're eating all right and so forth, are we? Sleep the great healer. See you tomorrow. *Chüss.*"

And when tomorrow came, there was Corkoran again peering down at him, puffing at his cigarette.

"Fuck off, will you please, Frisky, old love?"

"Will do, Major," said Frisky with a grin, and he obediently slipped from the room while Corkoran paddled through the gloom to the rocking chair, into which he lowered himself with a grateful grunt. Then for a while he drew on his cigarette without saying a thing.

"Don't mind the fag, do we, old love? Can't do the brainwork if I haven't got a fag between my fingers. It's not the sucking and puffing that I'm hooked on. It's physically holding the little sod."

His regiment couldn't stomach him, so he did five unlikely years in Army Intelligence, said Burr, *which is a misnomer, as we know, but Corky served them proud. The Roper doesn't love him for his looks alone.*

"Smoke ourselves, do we, heart? In better times?"

"A bit."

"What times are they, old love?"

"Cooking."

"Can't hear us."

"Cooking. When I'm taking a break from hoteling."

Major Corkoran became all enthusiasm. "I must say, not a word of a lie. *Bloody* good grub you ran us up at Mama's before you saved the side that night. Were those sauced-up mussels all our own work?"

"Yes."

"Finger-lickin' good. How about the carrot cake? We scored a bull's-eye there, I can tell you. Chief's favorite. Flown in, was it?"

"I made it."

"Come again, old boy?"

"I made it."

Corkoran was robbed of words. "You mean you *made* the carrot cake? Our own tiny hands? Old *love. Heart.*" He drew on his cigarette, beaming admiration at Jonathan through the smoke. "Pinched the recipe from Meister's, no doubt." He shook his head. "Sheer genius." Another enormous draft of cigarette smoke. "And did we pinch anything *else* at all from Meister's while we were about it, old love?"

Motionless on his down pillow, Jonathan affected to be motionless in his mind as well. Get me Dr. Marti. Get me Burr. Get me out.

"Bit of a dilemma, frankly, you see, heart. I was filling in these forms for us at the hospital. That's my job in this shop. For as long as I've got one. Official form-filler. Us military types, about all we know how to do, isn't it? Well, well, I thought. Ho, ho. This is a bit rum. Is he a Pine or is he a Lamont? He's a hero, well we know that, but you can't put *hero* when you've got to put a chap's name. So I put Lamont, Thomas Alexander—I say, old love, I do hope I did right? Born whatnot in Toronto? See page thirty-two for next of kin, except you hadn't got any? Case closed, I thought. Chap wants to call himself Pine when he's a Lamont, or Lamont when he's a Pine, far as I'm concerned, his good right."

He waited for Jonathan to speak. And waited. And drew more cigarette smoke. And still waited, because Corkoran possessed the interrogator's advantage of having all the time in the world to kill.

"But the Chief, you see, heart," he resumed at last, "is hewn of a different tree, as you might say. The Chief, among his many talents, is a stickler for detail. Always has been. Gets on the electric blower to Meister in Zurich. From a call box, actually. Down on Deep Bay. Doesn't always care for an audience. 'How's your nice man Pine these days?' says the Chief. Well, old Meister pops his garters. 'Pine, Pine? *Gott in Himmel!* That bugger robbed me blind! Sixty-one thousand four hundred and two francs, nineteen centimes and two waistcoat buttons, stolen from my night safe.' Lucky he hadn't heard about the carrot cake, or he'd have done you for industrial espionage as well. You with us in there, old love? Not boring you, am I?"

Wait, Jonathan was telling himself. Eyes closed. Body flat. Your head hurts, you're going to be sick. The rhythmic rocking of Corkoran's chair gained speed, then stopped. Jonathan smelled cigarette smoke very close and saw Corkoran's bulk leaning over him.

"Old love? Are you receiving my signals? I don't think we're quite as poorly as we're making out, to be harsh. The leech says we've made a rather impressive recovery."

"I didn't ask to come here. You're not the Gestapo. I did you a favor. Just get me back to Low's."

"But, darling, you did us an *enormous* favor! Chief's totally on your side! Me too. We *owe* you one. Owe you *lots*. Chief's not a fellow to walk away from a debt. Very hung up on you, the way these men of vision get when they're grateful. *Hates* owing. Always prefers to be owed. His nature, you see. How great men are. So he needs to pay you off." He ambled down the room, hands in pockets, reasoning the thing out. "But he's also a tinsy bit *exercised*. In his noddle. Well, you can't blame him, can you?"

"Get out. Leave me alone."

"Seems old Meister pitched him some story to the effect that after busting his safe, you ran away to England and topped a fellow. Codswallop, says the Chief, must be some other Linden; mine's a hero. But then the Chief goes and puts out a few feelers of his own, which is his way. And it turns out old Meister's bang on target." Another lifesaving drag of the cigarette while Jonathan played dead. "Chief hasn't told anyone, of course, apart from yours faithfully. Lot of chaps change their names in life, some do it all the time. But topping a chap, well, that's a bit more private. So the Chief keeps it to himself. Doesn't want to nurse a viper, naturally. Family man. On the other hand, there are vipers and vipers, if you follow me. You could be the non-poisonous variety. So he's deputed me to suss you out while he and Jed do whatever they do. Jed's his virtue," he explained, for information. "Nature's child. You've met her. Tall girl. Ethereal." He was shaking Jonathan's shoulder. "Wake up, do you mind, old love? I'm rooting for you. So's the Chief. This isn't England. Men of the world, all that. Come on, Mr. Pine."

His appeal, though roughly made, had fallen on deaf ears. Jonathan had willed himself into the deep, escaper's sleep of the orphanage.

FIFTEEN

GOODHEW HAD told nobody except his wife.

He had nobody else to tell. On the other hand, such a monstrous story required a monstrous audience, and his dear Hester, alas, was by common consent the least monstrous person on earth.

"Now, darling, are you sure you heard right?" she asked him doubtfully. "You know how you are. You hear a lot of things *perfectly* clearly, but the children *do* have to interpret the television for you. There must have been an *awful* lot of traffic on a Friday in the rush hour."

"Hester, he said exactly what I told you he said. He said it clearly, above the noise of the traffic, into my face. I caught every word. I saw his lips move while he spoke."

"You could go to the police, I suppose. If you're *sure.* Well, of course you are. It's just, I do think you should *talk* to Dr. Prendergast, even if you don't *do* anything."

In a rare fit of anger at the companion of his life, Goodhew took a stiff walk up Parliament Hill to clear his head. But it didn't clear it at all. He simply retold himself the story, as he had done a hundred times already:

The Friday had dawned as any other. Goodhew had bicycled to work early because his master liked to put the week to bed before leaving for the country. At nine o'clock, he received a phone call from his master's private secretary, saying the proposed ten o'clock meeting was canceled because the minister had received a summons to the U.S. Embassy. Goodhew had ceased to be surprised by his exclusion from his master's councils, so he used the morning to catch up on work and lunched on a sandwich at his desk.

At half past three the private secretary called down to ask whether he could step upstairs for a few minutes right away. Goodhew obliged. Spread about his master's office in post-prandial ease, amid coffee cups and the aroma of cigars, sat the survivors of a luncheon party to which Goodhew had not been invited.

"Rex. Well done," said his master expansively. "Sit you down. Who don't you know? Nobody. Jolly good."

His master was younger than Goodhew by twenty years, a rich brawler with a safe seat and a rugger blue, which so far as Goodhew could ascertain was the sum of his educational accomplishment. His eyes were dull, but what he lacked in vision he made up for in ambition. Barbara Vandon from the American Embassy sat to one side of him, and on the other, Neal Marjoram of Procurement Studies, whom Goodhew had always rather taken to, perhaps because of his record in the navy, his trustworthy eyes and air of decent quiet. Indeed, it had always puzzled Goodhew how a man whose honesty was written on his sleeve could possibly survive as Geoffrey Darker's understudy. Galt, another Darker *apparatchik,* sat at Marjoram's elbow and was more in Darker's image: too well dressed, too much the estate agent in the boom. The third member of the River House delegation was a hard-jawed beauty called Hazel Bundy, rumored to share Darker's bed as well as his work load. But Goodhew made a point of never listening to that sort of rumor.

His master was explaining the reason for their meeting, and there was altogether too much buoyancy in his tone. "A bunch of us have been touring the U.K./U.S. liaison machinery, Rex," he said, waving his cigar in a vague arc. "We came up with a couple of rather bothersome conclusions, to be honest, and thought we'd try them out on you. Off the record. No minutes, no pack drill. Discussion about principles. Kicking the ball around. All right by you?"

"Why should it not be?"

"Barbara, darling."

Barbara Vandon was the Cousins' station chief in London. She had studied at Vassar, wintered in Aspen and summered on the Vineyard. Yet her voice was like a shrill scream of deprival.

"Rex, this Limpet thing is right off the wall," she howled. "We're pygmies in this. Totally. The real game is right up *there;* it's *orbital,* and it's *now."*

Goodhew's confusion must have been legible at once. "Barbara feels we're out of step with Langley, Rex," Marjoram explained, aside.

"Who's *we?"*

"Well, us really. The River House."

Goodhew rounded sharply on his master. "You told me this was a discussion about principles—"

"Hang on, hang on!" His master flicked his cigar at Barbara Vandon. "Girl's hardly off the ground. Talk about short fuse. Christ."

But Goodhew would not be put off. "The River House *out of step* with Langley on the Limpet case?" he said incredulously to Marjoram. "The River House isn't even *involved* in the Limpet case, other than supplying support-in-aid. Limpet's an Enforcement case."

"Well, that's what Barbara feels we ought to be discussing," Marjoram explained, with enough distance in his voice to suggest that he didn't necessarily agree.

Barbara Vandon stormed back into the breach: "Rex, we have to do some major, major housecleaning, not just in Langley but right here in U.K.," she resumed, in what was sounding increasingly like a prepared speech. "We have to take this Limpet thing down to basics and begin again from the bottom up. Rex, Langley's been railroaded. Not so much railroaded as shunted into a siding." This time Marjoram did not offer his services as interpreter. "Rex, our pols are not going to buy this. Any day now they will go ballistic. What we have here, Rex, is something that has to be looked at very slowly and carefully from fifty-five ways up, and what do we find? It's a joint operational deal between, *one,* a very fringe, very new British agency—forgive me: fine, dedicated, but fringe—and, *two,* a bunch of Enforcement cowboys from Miami with no geopolitics. It's tail and dog, Rex. The dog is way up here"—her hand was already above her head—"and the tail is *this.* And right now the tail's winning."

A wave of self-recrimination swept over Goodhew. Palfrey warned me, but I didn't take him seriously: *Darker is launching a putsch to recover his lost territories, Rex,* Palfrey had said. *He's proposing to go in behind the American flag.*

"*Rex,*" Barbara Vandon bellowed, so stridently that Goodhew braced himself in his chair, "what we have here is a major geopolitical power shift happening in our own backyard, and it's being handled by amateurs who are not qualified to play in this league, who are running with the ball when they should be passing it, who are out of touch with the issues. The cartels pushing dope, that's one thing. It's a dope problem, and there are people out there whose job it is to deal with that problem. We've lived with that, Rex. We've paid a heavy price for that."

"Oh, top dollar, Barbara, from all one hears," Goodhew agreed gravely. But after four years in London, Barbara Vandon was gun-deaf to irony. She forged on.

"The cartels pushing *pacts* with each other, Rex, making *nice* to each other, buying themselves big-time matériel, training their boys, getting their act together—Rex, that's a different ballpark. There just aren't that number of people in South America who *do* that stuff. In South America, getting your act together is *power.* It's as simple as that. This isn't an assignment for *Enforcement.* This isn't cops and robbers and shooting yourself in the foot. This is *geopolitics,* Rex. And what we have to do here is, we have to be able to go to the Hill and say, 'Guys, we accept the imperatives in this. We have spoken with Enforcement, Enforcement have gracefully backed off, Enforcement will do their *own* thing in the fullness of time, which is their right and duty as cops. Meantime this is geopolitical, this is sophisticated, this has a *lot* of angles and is therefore an *agreed* Pure Intelligence responsibility, we have the way clear for sophisticated input, by tried and trusted professionals in Pure Intelligence, acting to a geopolitical brief.' "

She had evidently finished, for like an actress pleased with her performance, she turned full face to Marjoram as if to ask, How was I? But Marjoram affected a benevolent disdain for her fighting words.

"Well, I do think there's a lot of substance in what Barbara says," he remarked, with that decent, straightforward smile he had. "Obviously, *we* wouldn't stand in the way of a revision of responsibilities between the services. But then the decision is hardly up to us."

Goodhew's face was set in stone. His hands lay lifelessly before him, refusing to participate.

"No," he agreed. "It is *not* up to you at all. It's up to the Joint Steering Committee and no one else."

"Of which your master here is chairman and you, Rex, are secretary, founder and principal benefactor," Marjoram reminded him with another collegial smile. "And, if I may say so, moral arbiter."

But Goodhew would not be mollified, not even by someone as patently conciliatory as Neal Marjoram. "A revision of responsibilities, as you call it, is in no circumstances within the gift of rival agencies, Neal," he said sternly. "Even assuming that Enforcement *were* prepared voluntarily to quit the field, which I gravely doubt, the agencies are not empowered to carve up their responsibilities among themselves without reference to Steering. No side deals. That's one of the things Steering stands for. Ask its chairman"—with a pointed nod at his master.

For a moment nobody asked anybody anything, until Goodhew's master emitted a kind of slurrying grunt which contrived to indicate doubt, irritation and a touch of indigestion at the same time.

"Well, *obviously,* Rex," he said, striking that nasal whinny peculiar to the Conservative front benches, "if the Cousins *are* going to take over the Limpet case on *their* side of the pond, willy-nilly we here on *this* side are going to have to take a cool position about whether to follow suit. Aren't we? I say *if,* because these are informal discussions. Nothing's come through on the formal net so far. Has it?"

"If it has, it hasn't reached me," Goodhew said icily.

"The pace these bloody committees work at, we wouldn't get an answer this side of Christmas, anyway. I mean, come on, Rex, we've got a quorum. You, me, Neal here? Thought we might swing it on our own."

"It's your call, Rex," Marjoram said amiably. "You're the lawgiver. If *you* can't turn it round, who can? It was you who drafted the like-to-like deal: enforcers play with enforcers, spies with spies, no cross-fertilization. The *Lex Goodhew* we called it, quite right too. You sold it to Washington, won the ear of Cabinet, gunned it through. 'Covert Agencies in the New Era': wasn't that the title of your paper? We're only bowing to the inevitable, Rex. You heard Barbara. In a choice between a graceful shimmy and a head-on collision, I go for the shimmy every time. Don't want to see you hoisted on your own petard, or anything."

Goodhew was by now usefully angry. But he was too downy a bird to let his temper get the better of him. He spoke in a reasoned voice, down the table into Neal Marjoram's honest face. He said that the Joint Steering Committee's recommendations to its chairman—another nod at his master—were made in full session, not by an ad hoc quorum. He said it was the Steering Committee's recorded view that the River House was over-extended and should shed more of its responsibilities rather than attempt to win back old ones, and that hitherto the minister as chairman had concurred—"unless you've changed your mind over lunch, of course," he suggested to his master, who scowled through his cigar smoke.

He said that speaking for himself, he would prefer to expand Enforcement so that it could meet its challenges effectively; and he ended by saying that since they were off the record, he personally regarded the activities of the Procurement Studies Group as inappropriate to the new era and derogatory to parliamentary authority, and that at the next meeting of the Steering Committee he intended to move formally for an examination of its activities.

Then he put his hands together in a churchy way as if to say, I have spoken, and waited for the explosion.

None came.

Goodhew's master fished a bit of tooth-pick from his lower lip while he studied the front of Hazel Bundy's dress. *"Ri-ight. Okay,"* he drawled, avoiding everybody's eye. "Interesting. Thanks. Point taken."

"Food for thought *indeed,"* Galt agreed brightly. And smiled at Hazel Bundy, who didn't smile back.

But Neal Marjoram could not have appeared more benign. A spiritual peace had settled over his fine features, reflecting the moral worthiness that was so clearly the man.

"Got a moment, Rex?" he said quietly as they left.

And Goodhew, God help him, was pleased to think that after a bit of healthy give-and-take, Marjoram was bothering to stay behind and make sure there were no hard feelings on either side.

· · ·

GOODHEW GENEROUSLY offered Marjoram his office, but Marjoram was too considerate for that. Rex, you need air to cool you down; let's take a stroll.

It was a sunny autumn afternoon. The leaves on the plane trees shone pink and gold, tourists dawdled contentedly on the Whitehall pavements, and Marjoram bestowed a paternal smile on them. And yes, Hester was right, the Friday rush hour traffic was pretty heavy. But Goodhew's hearing was not affected by it.

"Old Barbara gets a bit wound up," said Marjoram.

"One wonders who by," said Goodhew.

"We told her it wouldn't cut much ice with you, but she would have a go."

"Nonsense. You egged her on."

"Well, what were we supposed to do? Come to you cap in hand and say, Rex, give us Limpet? It's only one case, for goodness' sake." They had reached the Thames Embankment, which seemed to be where they were heading. "It's bend or snap, Rex. You're too holy by half. Just because like-to-like is your baby. A crime's a crime, a spy's a spy and never the twain shall meet. Too black-and-white is your trouble."

"No, Neal. I don't think so. Not black-and-white enough, I fear. If I ever write my autobiography, I shall call it *Half Measures.* We should all be stronger. Not more flexible."

The tone on both sides was still entirely comradely: two professionals, sorting out their differences beside the Thames.

"Picked your moment, I'll grant you," Marjoram said approvingly. "All that *new era* talk earned you a lot of Brownie points around the halls. Goodhew the open society's friend. Goodhew the devolver. Makes you sick. Still, it's a nice bit of turf you carved out for yourself, one must admit. Quite right not to give it up without a fight. So what's it worth to you?"

They were standing shoulder-to-shoulder, staring at the Thames. Goodhew had his hands on the parapet, and rather absurdly he had put on his cycling gloves, because he had recently been suffering the effects of poor circulation of the blood. Not understanding the thrust of Marjoram's question, he turned to him for enlightenment. But all he saw was the saintly profile shining its benediction upon a passing pleasure boat. Then Marjoram turned too, and they were face-to-face and not twelve inches between them, and if the noise of traffic was troublesome, Goodhew by now had no awareness of it at all.

"Message from Darker," Marjoram said through his smile. "Rex Goodhew is in over his head. Spheres of interest he can't know about, doesn't need to, matters of high policy, top people involved, the usual crap. Kentish Town, isn't it, where you live? Squalid little terraced house with net curtains?"

"Why?"

"You've just acquired a distant uncle living in Switzerland. He always admired your integrity. The day the Limpet case is ours, your uncle suffers an untimely death, leaves you three quarters of a million of your own. Pounds, not francs. Tax-free. It's an inheritance. You know what the boys say in Colombia? 'You have the choice. Either we make you rich or we make you dead.' Darker says the same."

"I'm sorry. I'm a little dense today," Good-hew said. "Are you threatening to kill me as well as bribe me?"

"Kill your career, for a start. We can reach you, I should think. If we can't, we'll have to think again. Don't answer now if it's embarrass-ing. Don't answer at all. Just do it. Action before words: the *Lex Goodhew.*" He smiled sympatheti-cally. "Nobody would believe you, would they? Not in your circles. Old Rex is losing his marbles . . . been going on a long time . . . didn't want to say anything. I shan't send you a memo, if you don't mind. I never said a thing. Just a nice stroll by the river after another boring meeting. Have a nice weekend."

. . .

Your premise is absurd, Goodhew had told Burr six months earlier, over one of their little dinners. *It is destructive, it is insidious and I refuse to coun-tenance it, and I forbid you ever to speak of it to me again. This is England, not the Balkans and not Sicily. You can have your agency, Leonard, but you are to renounce for all time your Gothic fantasies about the Procurement Studies Group being run as a multimillion-pound racket for the benefit of Geoffrey Darker and a caucus of bent bankers, brokers and middlemen and corrupt intelligence officers on both sides of the Atlantic.*

Because that way lies madness, he had warned Burr.

That way lies this.

. . .

FOR A WEEK after talking to his wife, Goodhew kept his secret locked up in his head. A man who does not trust himself trusts nobody. Burr telephoned from Miami with the news of Limpet's resurrection, and Goodhew as best he could shared his euphoria. Rooke took over the reins at Burr's offices in Victoria Street. Goodhew bought him lunch at the Athenaeum, but did not confide in him.

Then one evening Palfrey called by with some garbled tale about Darker taking soundings with British arms suppliers about the availability of certain high-tech equipment for use in a "South American type of climate," end user to be advised.

"British equipment, Harry? That's not Roper. He's buying foreign."

Palfrey writhed and sucked his cigarette and needed more Scotch. "Well, it *could* be the Roper, actually, Rex. I mean, if he was covering his backside. I mean, if they're *British* toys—well, no limit to our tolerance, if you know what I mean. Two blind eyes and head in the sand. If they're Brit. Naturally. Flog 'em to Jack the Ripper, if they're Brit." He sniggered.

It was a fine evening, and Palfrey needed movement. So they walked as far as the entrance to Highgate Cemetery and found a quiet bench.

"Marjoram tried to buy me," said Goodhew,

straight out ahead of him. "Three quarters of a million pounds."

"Oh, well, he would," said Palfrey, quite unsurprised. "That's what they do abroad. That's what they do at home."

"There was a stick as well as a carrot."

"Oh, yes, well, there usually is," said Palfrey, delving for a fresh cigarette.

"Who are they, Harry?"

Palfrey wrinkled his nose, blinked a few times and seemed mysteriously embarrassed.

"Just a few clever chaps. Good connections. *You* know."

"I don't know anything."

"Good case officers. Cold heads left over from the Cold War. Scared of being out of a job. *You* know, Rex."

It occurred to Goodhew that Palfrey was describing his own predicament and didn't like doing so.

"Duplicity trained, naturally," Palfrey continued, volunteering his opinion, as usual, in a series of torn-off, shopworn sentences. "Market economy chaps. Peaked in the eighties. Grab it while you can, everybody does it, never sure where the next war's coming from. All dressed up, nowhere to go . . . *you* know. Still got *power,* of course. Nobody's taken *that* away from them. Just a question of where to put it."

Goodhew said nothing, and Palfrey obligingly continued.

"Not *bad* chaps, Rex. Mustn't be too critical. Just a bit marooned. No more Thatcher. No more Russian bear to fight, no more Reds under the bed at home. One day they've got the world all carved up for them, two legs good, four bad. Next day they get up in the morning, they're sort of—well, *you* know. . . ." He finished his premise with a shrug. "Well, nobody likes a vacuum, do they? Not even you like a vacuum. Well, do you? Be honest. You hate it."

"By vacuum you mean peace?" Goodhew suggested, not wishing in the least to sound censorious.

"Boredom, really. Smallness. Never did anyone any good, did it?" Another giggle, another long drink from the cigarette. "Couple of years ago, they were top-notch Cold Warriors. Best seats in the club, all that. Hard to stop running, once you've been wound up like that. You keep going. Natural."

"So what are they now?"

Palfrey rubbed his nose with the back of his hand, as if to correct an itch. "Just a fly on the wall, really, me."

"I know that. What are *they?*"

Palfrey spoke vaguely, perhaps in order to detach himself from his own judgments. "Atlantic men. Never trusted Europe. Europe's a Babel dominated by Krauts. America's still the only place for them. Washington's still their Rome, even if Caesar's a bit of a frost." He made an embarrassed writhe. "Global salvationists. Playing the world's game. World-order boys, having their shot at history and making a few bob on the side, why not? Everybody else does." Another writhe. "They've gone a bit rotten, that's all. Can't blame them. Whitehall doesn't know how to get rid of them. Everyone thinks they must be useful to someone else. No one's got the whole picture, so no one knows there isn't one." More rubbing of the nose. "Long as they please the Cousins, don't overspend, and don't fight each other in public, they can do what they like."

"*How* please the Cousins?" Goodhew insisted, holding his head in his hands as if he had an awful headache. "Spell it out for me, do you mind?"

Palfrey spoke as to a fractious child—indulgently but with an edge of impatience: "The Cousins have *laws,* old boy. Watchdogs breathing down their necks. They hold kangaroo courts, put honest spies in jug, senior officials on trial. The Brits don't have any of that balls. There's Joint Steering, I suppose. But frankly most of you are a bit decent."

Goodhew raised his head, then put it back in his hands. "Go on, Harry."

"Forget where I was, actually."

"How Darker pleases the Cousins when they're having trouble with their watchdogs."

Palfrey was entering the reluctant stage.

"Well. Obvious, really. Some Big Beef in Washington, D.C., ups and tells the Cousins, 'You can't arm the Wozza-Wozzas. That's a law.' Okay?"

"So far, yes."

" 'Right-ho,' say the Cousins. 'Received and understood. We will not arm the Wozza-Wozzas.' An hour later they're on the blower to Brother Darker. 'Geoffrey, old sport, do us a favor, will you? The Wozza-Wozzas need a few toys.' The Wozza-Wozzas are embargoed, of course, but whoever cared a tart's kiss about that, provided there's a few bucks in it for the Exchequer? Darker gets on the blower to one of his trusties— Joyston Bradshaw, Spikey Lorimer or whoever's the flavor of the month: 'Great news, Tony. Green light for the Wozza-Wozzas. You'll have to go in the back door, but we'll make sure it isn't locked.' Then there's the P.S."

"The P.S.?"

Charmed by Goodhew's innocence, Palfrey gave a luminous smile. "The *postscript,* old boy. The sweetener. 'And while you're about it, Tony, old sport, the going rate for introductions is five percent of the action, payable to the Procurement Studies Widows and Orphans Fund at the Bank of Crooks and Cousins Incorporated, Liechtenstein.' It's a cakewalk, long as you're not accountable. Have *you* ever heard of a member of the British Intelligence services caught with his hand in the till? A British *minister* being brought up before the beak for dodging his own regulations? You must be joking! They're fireproof."

"Why does Pure Intelligence want Limpet?"

Palfrey tried to smile, but it didn't work. So he drew on his cigarette and scratched the top of his head instead.

"Why do they want Limpet, Harry?"

Palfrey's slippy eyes scanned the darkening woods in search of rescue or surveillance.

"You'll have to do that one for yourself, Rex. Out of my depth. Yours too, actually. Sorry about that."

He was already getting up when Goodhew shouted at him.

"Harry!"

Palfrey's mouth was pulled crooked in alarm, revealing his ugly teeth. "Rex, for Christ's sake, you don't know how to run people. I'm a *coward*. You mustn't push me or I'll just dry up, or invent something. Go home. Get some sleep. You're too *good,* Rex. It'll be the death of you." He glanced nervously round him and seemed momentarily to relent. "Buy British, darling. That's the clue. Don't you understand *anything* bad?"

. . .

ROOKE SAT at Burr's desk in Victoria Street. Burr sat in the operations room in Miami. Both were clutching secure telephones.

"Yes, Rob," said Burr cheerfully. "Confirmed and reconfirmed. Do it."

"Just let's have that absolutely clear, can we?" said Rooke, with the special tone that soldiers have when they are clarifying orders from civilians. "Just run it by me one more time, do you mind?"

"Put his name out, Rob. Splash it. All of his names. Everywhere. Pine, alias Linden, alias Beauregard, alias Lamont, last seen in Canada on the whatever. Murder, multiple theft, dope running, obtaining and toting a false passport, illegal entry into Canada, illegal exit if there is such a thing, and anything else they can think of to make it interesting."

"So the grand slam?" said Rooke, refusing to be wooed by Burr's joviality.

"Yes, Rob, the grand slam. That's what *everywhere* means, isn't it? An international warrant for Mr. Thomas Lamont, criminal. Do you want me to send it to you in triplicate?"

Rooke replaced the receiver, lifted it and dialed a number at Scotland Yard. His hand felt strangely stiff as he touched the numbers—the way it used to feel in the days when he played with unexploded bombs.

And when he's crossed the bridge, we'll burn it, Burr had said.

SIXTEEN

"*OLD LOVE,*" Corkoran proposed, lighting his first foul cigarette of the day and balancing a porcelain inkstand by way of an ashtray on his lap. "What say we pick the fly shit out of the pepper?"

"I don't want you near me, actually," Jonathan said, in a prepared speech. "I've got nothing to explain and nothing to apologize for. Just leave me alone."

Corkoran lowered himself gratefully into the armchair. They were alone in the bedroom. Frisky had once more been ordered to remove himself.

"Your name's Jonathan Pine, formerly of Meister's, the Queen Nefertiti and other emporia. But you are now traveling as one Thomas Lamont on a bona fide Canadian passport. Except that you don't happen to be Thomas Lamont. Contest? No contest."

"I got the kid back. You've had me patched up. Give me my passport and let me go."

"And *between* being J. Pine of Meister's and T. Lamont of Canada, not to mention J. Beauregard, you were Jack Linden of remotest Cornwall.

In which capacity, you topped a mate of yours, to wit one Alfred alias Jumbo Harlow, an Aussie boat bum with sundry convictions for drug running down under. Whereupon, you did a bunk before the law could have its way with you."

"I'm wanted for questioning by the Plymouth police. That's as far as it ever got."

"And Harlow was your business partner," said Corkoran, writing.

"If you say so."

"Dope-running, heart?" asked Corkoran, glancing up.

"It was a straight commercial venture."

"That's not what the press cuttings say. It's not what our little dickybirds say either. Jack Linden, alias J. Pine, alias you, ran a load of dope for Harlow single-handed from the Channel Islands to Falmouth, what the hacks called an impressive sail. And Brother Harlow, our partner, took the dope to London, flogged it and bilked us out of our cut. Which miffed us. Understandably. So you did what any of us would do when he's miffed with his partner: you topped him. It wasn't the neat piece of necessary surgery it might have been, given your proven skills in the field, because Harlow churlishly offered resistance. So you had a fight. But you won. And when you'd won, you topped him. Hoorah for us."

Stonewall, Burr had said. *You weren't there, it was two other blokes, he hit you first and it was with his consent. Then yield ungracefully and make them think they've got the real you.*

"They've no proof," Jonathan replied. "They found some blood, they never found the body. Now for Christ's sake get out."

Corkoran seemed to have forgotten the whole subject. He was grinning reminiscently into the middle air, all bad thoughts abandoned. "Do you know the one about the chap applying for a job in the Foreign Office? 'Look here, Carruthers,' they say, 'we like the cut of your jib, but we can't overlook the fact that you've done a spot of time for buggery, arson and rape. . . .' *Really* not know it?"

Jonathan groaned.

" 'Perfectly simple explanation,' says Carruthers. 'Loved a girl who wouldn't let me diddle her, so I banged her on the head, raped her, shafted her old dad and set fire to the house.' You *must* have heard it."

Jonathan had closed his eyes.

" 'Okay, Carruthers,' say the selector chaps. 'We knew there'd be a reasonable explanation. Here's the deal. Keep away from the girls in the typing pool, no playing with matches, give us a kiss and you can have the job.' "

Corkoran was really laughing. The chubby wreaths around his neck went pink and shook; merry tears ran down his cheeks. "I feel such a shit, you being in bed, you see," he explained. *"And* the hero of the hour to boot. So much easier if I had you under a bright light with me playing James Cagney and walloping you with a dildo." He adopted the high-flown tones of a court policeman. " 'The wanted man, M'lud, is believed to 'ave a revealin' scar on 'is right 'and!' Show," he ordered in a quite altered voice.

Jonathan opened his eyes. Corkoran was standing at the bedside again, his cigarette held to one side and upward like a grubby yellow wand, and he was holding Jonathan's right wrist in his damp hand, examining the broad scar curling along the back of it.

"Oh dear," said Corkoran. "You can't have done *that* shaving. . . . All right, *be* like that."

Jonathan had snatched back his hand. "He pulled a knife on me," he said. "I didn't know he carried one. He wore it on his calf. I was asking him what was in the boat. I knew by then. I'd guessed. He was a big man. I couldn't trust myself to throw him, so I went for his throat."

"The old Adam's apple, eh? You're quite a brawler, aren't you? Nice to think Ireland's been some use to somebody. Sure it wasn't *your* knife, old love? You do seem quite partial to a knife, from all one hears."

"It was his knife. I told you."

"Who did Harlow flog the dope to—any idea?"

"None. Zero. I was just the sailor. Look, go away. Go and persecute someone else."

"The mule. *Mule* is the term we use. Mule."

But Jonathan kept up his attack. "That's who you are, then, is it? You and Roper? Drug-runners? That's perfect. Home from bloody home."

He dropped back on the pillows, waiting for Corkoran's response. It came with a vigor that found him unprepared. For, with remarkable agility, Corkoran had sprung to his bedside and helped himself to a substantial handful of Jonathan's hair, which he was now pulling very hard indeed.

"*Sweetheart,*" he murmured reproachfully. "Old *love.* Little boys in your position do well to watch their fucking language, actually. *We* are the Ironbrand Gas, Light & Coke Company of Nassau, Bananas, short-listed for the Nobel Prize for Respectability. The question is, who the fuck are *you?*"

The hand relinquished Jonathan's hair. He lay still, his heart thumping. "Harlow said it was a repossession job," he said huskily. "Somebody he'd sold a boat to in Australia who'd welshed on the debt. Jumbo had traced the boat to the Channel Islands through some friends, he said. If I could bring it to Plymouth we could flog it and get ourselves off the hook. It didn't seem such a tall story at the time. I was a fool to trust him."

"So what did we do with the body, old love?" Corkoran inquired chummily, back in his chair. "Dump it down the proverbial tin mine? The great tradition?"

Change the rhythm. Let him wait. The voice gray with despair. "Why don't you just call the police, extradite me, claim the reward?" Jonathan suggested.

Corkoran removed his makeshift ashtray from his lap and replaced it with a buff, army-style folder, which seemed to contain nothing but faxes.

"And Brother Meister?" he inquired. "How did *he* offend?"

"He robbed me."

"Oh, you poor lamb! One of life's true victims. . . . But how?"

"Everyone else on the staff got a piece of the service money. There was a scale, so much for rank and how long you'd been employed. It came to quite a lot each month, even for a newcomer. Meister told me he wasn't obliged to pay it to foreigners. Then I found out he was paying the other foreigners, just not me."

"So you helped yourself from the safe. Well, he was *jolly* lucky you didn't top him too. *Or* unzip his whatnot with your penknife."

"I did overtime for him. Day work. I did the fine-wine inventory on my day off. Nothing. Not even when I took guests sailing on the lake. He charged them a fortune and didn't pay me a cent."

"We left Cairo in a bit of a hurry too, one notices. Nobody quite seems to know why. No hint of foul play, mind. Not a stain on our escutcheon, according to Queen Nefertiti. Or perhaps she just never rumbled us."

Jonathan had that fiction ready. He had worked it out with Burr. "I got mixed up with a girl. She was married."

"She have a name?"

Fight your corner, Burr had said. "Not for you. No."

"Fifi? Lulu? Mrs. Tutankhamen? No? Well, she can always use one of yours, can't she?" Corkoran was leafing lazily through his faxes. "What about the good doctor? Did *he* have a name?"

"Marti."

"Not *that* doctor, silly."

"Then who? What doctor? What is this, Corkoran? Am I on trial for saving Daniel? Where's this leading?"

This time Corkoran waited patiently for the storm to pass. "The doctor who stitched up our hand at Truro Casualty," he explained.

"I don't know what he was called. He was an intern."

"A white intern?"

"Brown. Indian or Pakistani."

"And how did we get ourselves there? To the hospital? With our poor bleeding wrist?"

"I wrapped it in a couple of dishcloths and drove Harlow's jeep."

"Left-handed?"

"Yes."

"The same car we used to remove the body to other premises, no doubt? The law did find traces of our blood in the car. But it seems to have been a bit of a cocktail. There was some of Jumbo's too."

Waiting for an answer, Corkoran was busily writing himself little notes.

"Just get me a lift to Nassau," Jonathan said. "I've done you no harm. I'm not asking for anything. You'd never have known about me if I hadn't been such a fool at Low's. I don't need anything from you, I'm not applying for anything, I don't want money, I don't want thanks, I don't want your approval. Let me go."

Corkoran worked his cigarette while he turned the pages on his lap. "What say we do *Ireland* for a change?" he proposed, as if Ireland were a party game for a wet afternoon. "Two old soldiers having a chin-wag about better times. What could be jollier than that?"

When you come to the true parts, don't sit back, Burr had said. *Better to flounder, forget a little and correct yourself, make them think that's where they should be looking for the lies.*

. . .

"WHAT DID you *do* to that bloke, anyway?" Frisky was asking, with professional curiosity.

It was the middle of the night. He was stretched on a futon across the door, a masked reading light and a heap of pornographic magazines beside his head.

"Which bloke?" said Jonathan.

"The bloke who borrowed little Danny for the evening. Screaming like a stuck pig he was, up there in the cookhouse—they could have heard him in Miami."

"I must have broken his arm."

"Broken it? I think you must have screwed it off him very slowly against the thread. Are you one of these amateur Japanese martial artists, then, one of your hari-suchi merchants?"

"I just grabbed and pulled," said Jonathan.

"Fell to pieces in your hand," Frisky said understandingly. "Happens to the best of us."

The most dangerous moments are when you need a friend, Burr had said.

· · ·

AND AFTER Ireland they reconnoitered what Corkoran called "our days as upwardly mobile flunky," which meant Jonathan's time at catering college, then his days as sous-chef, then as chef and then as graduate to the staff side of the hotel business.

After that again, Corkoran needed to hear about his exploits at the Château Babette, which Jonathan related with scrupulous regard for Yvonne's anonymity, only to discover that Corkoran knew that story too.

"So how in Gawd's name do we come to stick a pin into Mama Low's, old love?" Corkoran asked, lighting himself another cigarette. "Mama's has been the Chief's favorite watering hole for donkeys' years."

"Just somewhere I thought I'd go to ground for a few weeks."

"Keep our head down, you mean?"

"I'd been doing a job on a yacht up in Maine."

"Chief cook and bottlewasher?"

"Majordomo."

Pause while Corkoran rummaged among his faxes. "And?"

"I caught a bug and had to be put ashore. I lay up in a hotel in Boston, then called Billy Bourne in Newport. Billy gets me the work. He said, Why not devil at Low's for a few months, dinners only, take a rest?"

Corkoran licked a finger, fished out whatever he was looking for and held it to the light.

"For heaven's sake," Jonathan muttered, like a prayer for sleep.

"Now, this boat we went sick on, old love. That would have been the *Lolita,* née *Persephone,* built in Holland, owned by Nikos Asserkalian, the celebrated show business personality, God-thumper and crook, two hundred feet of bloody awful taste. Not Nikos; he's a midget."

"I never met him. We were chartered out."

"Who to, my heart?"

"Four California dentists and their women."

Jonathan volunteered a couple of names, which Corkoran wrote down in his scruffy penny notebook, having first flattened it on his ample thigh.

"Balls of fun, were they? Laugh a minute?"

"They did me no harm."

"And you didn't do *them* any?" Corkoran suggested kindly. "Bust their safe or someone's neck, or do a knife job on them or anything?"

"Actually, go to hell," said Jonathan.

Corkoran considered this invitation and seemed to decide it was a good idea. He packed together his papers and emptied his ashtray into the wastepaper basket, making a frightful mess. He peered at himself in the mirror, grimaced and tried to pull his hair straight with his fingers, but it wasn't a success.

"It's too bloody good, dearie," he declared.

"What is?"

"Your story. Don't know why. Don't know how. Don't know where. It's you, I think. You make me feel inadequate." He gave his hair another disastrous yank. "But then I *am* inadequate. I'm a savage little poof in a grownup world. Whereas you—you're just *trying* to be inadequate." He wandered into the bathroom and peed. "Tabby's brought some clothes for you, by the by," he called through the open doorway. "Nothing earthshaking, but they'll clothe our nakedness till the Armanis come through." He flushed, and reappeared in the bedroom. "Left to myself, I'd roast you, actually," he said, zipping himself up. "I'd deprive you, hood you and hang you up by your fucking ankles till the truth fell out of you by gravity. Still, can't have everything in life, can we? Toodle-oo."

. . .

IT WAS the next day. Daniel had decided that Jonathan was in need of entertainment.

"What's a Grecian urn?"

"A pot. A jug. Art form of the ancient Greeks."

"Fifty dollars a week. What goes through a tortoise's brain when it's being hit by a Mercedes?"

"Slow music?"

"Its shell. Corky's talking to Roper in the study. He says he's gone as far as he can go. Either you're squeaky clean or you're the biggest con in Christendom."

"When did they get back?"

"At first light. Roper always flies at first light. They're talking about your question mark."

"With Jed?"

"Jed's riding Sarah. She always rides Sarah as soon as she gets back. Sarah hears her and gets in a rage if she doesn't come. Roper says they're a pair of dykes. What's a dyke?"

"A woman who loves women."

"Roper talked to Sandy Langbourne about you while they were in Curaçao. No one's to discuss you on the telephone. Radio silence on Thomas until further notice. Chief's orders."

"Maybe you shouldn't eavesdrop on people so much. You'll wear yourself out."

Daniel arched his back, flung up his head and yelled at the punkah: "I don't eavesdrop! That's not fair! I wasn't even trying! I just can't help hearing! Corky says you're a dangerous riddle, that's all! You're not! I know you're not! I love you! Roper's going to feel your bones for himself and take a view!"

. . .

IT WAS just before dawn.

"Know the best way to make a bloke talk, Tommy?" Tabby asked from the futon, offering a helpful tip. "Infallible? One hundred percent? Never known to fail? The fizzy-drink treatment. Bung his mouth up so he can't breathe except through his nose. Or her. Get a funnel, if there's one handy. And pour the fizz into his nose. Hits you right in the switchboard, like your brain's boiling. Bloody diabolical."

. . .

IT WAS ten in the morning.

Walking uncertainly at Corkoran's side across the gravel sweep of Crystal, Jonathan had an exact memory of crossing the main courtyard of Buckingham Palace on the arm of his German Aunt Monika the day she took him to collect his dead father's medal. What's the point of prizes when you're dead? he had wondered. And school while you're alive?

A stocky black manservant admitted them. He wore a green waistcoat and black trousers. A

venerable black butler in a striped cotton waistcoat came forward to receive them.

"For the Chief, please, Isaac," said Corkoran. "Dr. Jekyll and Mr. Hyde. We're expected."

The immense hall echoed like a church to
their footsteps. A curved marble staircase with a
gilded handrail rose into the cupola, making three
landings on its way to a blue-painted heaven. The
marble they were walking on was pink, and the
sunlight lifted from it in a rosy dew. Two man-
sized Egyptian warriors guarded an arched doorway of carved stone. They passed through it and
entered a gallery dominated by a gold head of the
sun god Ra. Greek torsos, marble heads, hands,
urns and stone panels of hieroglyphics stood or
lay about in disarray. Brass-bound glass cabinets
ran along the walls, crammed with figurines.
Hand-printed signs declared their provenance:
West African, Peruvian, pre-Columbian, Cambo-
dian, Minoan, Russian, Roman and in one case
simply "Nile."

He plunders, Burr had said.

Freddie likes to sell him stolen artifacts, Sophie had said.

Roper's going to feel your bones for himself,
Daniel had said.

They entered the library. Leather-bound
books reached from floor to ceiling. A rolling
spiral staircase, unmanned, stood by.

They entered a prison corridor between

arched dungeons. From their solitary cells, antique weapons glimmered in the twilight: swords and pikes and maces, suits of armor posed on wooden horses; muskets, halberds, cannon balls and green cannons still barnacled from the sea.

They passed a billiards room and came to the second center of the house. Marble columns supported a wagon roof. A tiled blue pool mirrored them, bordered by a marble concourse. On the walls hung Impressionist paintings of fruit and farms and naked women: can this really be a Gauguin? On a marble chaise two young men in shirtsleeves and twenties baggy trousers talked business across open attaché cases.

"Corky, hi, how's tricks?" drawled one.

"Darlings," said Corkoran.

They approached a pair of high doors of burnished bronze. Before them sat Frisky in a porter's chair. A matronly woman emerged, carrying a shorthand pad. Frisky shoved out his foot at her, pretending to trip her up.

"Oh, you *silly* boy," said the matronly woman happily.

The doors closed again.

"Why, it's the *Major*," Frisky cried facetiously, affecting not to have noticed their arrival till the last minute. "How are *we* today, sir? Hullo there, Tommy. That's the way, then."

"Tit," said Corkoran.

Frisky unhooked a house telephone from the

wall and touched a number. The doors opened to reveal a room so large, so intricate in its furnishings, so bathed with sunlight and blackened by shadow, that Jonathan had a sensation not of arriving but ascending. Through a wall of tinted windows lay a terrace of strangely formed white tables, each shaded by a white umbrella. Beyond them lay an emerald lagoon bordered by a narrow sandbar and black reefs. Beyond the reefs lay the open sea in lakes of jagged blues.

The splendor of the room was at first all Jonathan could take in. Its occupants, if there were any, were lost between the brilliance and the dark. Then, as Corkoran ushered him forward, he made out a swirling golden desk in tortoiseshell and brass, and behind it a scrolled throne covered in rich tapestry frayed with age. And beside the desk, in a bamboo sun chair with wide arms and a footstool, reclined the worst man in the world, dressed in white sailing ducks and espadrilles and a short-sleeved navy blue shirt with a monogram on the pocket. He had his legs crossed and was wearing his half-lens spectacles, and he was reading something from a leather-backed folder that bore the same monogram as his shirt, and he was smiling while he read it, because he smiled a great deal. A woman secretary stood behind him, and she could have been the twin sister of the first.

"No disturbances, Frisky," an alarmingly familiar voice ordered, snapping the leather folder shut and shoving it at the secretary. "Nobody on the terrace. Who's the ass running an outboard in my bay?"

"That's Talbot, fixin' it, Chief," said Isaac from the back.

"Tell him to unfix it. Corks, shampoo. Well, I'm damned. Pine. Come here. Well done. Well done indeed."

He was clambering to his feet, his spectacles perched comically on the tip of his nose. Grasping Jonathan's hand, he drew him forward until, as at Meister's, they had entered each other's private space. And examined him, frowning through his spectacles. And while he did so, he slowly raised his palms to Jonathan's cheeks as if he meant to trap them in a double slap. And kept them there, so close that Jonathan could feel their heat, while Roper posed his head at different angles, peering at him from a few inches' distance until he was satisfied.

"Bloody marvelous," he pronounced finally. "Well done, Pine; well done, Marti; well done, money. What it's for. Sorry not to be around when you arrived. Had a couple of farms to flog. When was the worst?" Disconcertingly, he had turned to Corkoran, who was advancing across the marble floor bearing a tray with three frosted silver goblets of Dom Pérignon. "Here he is. Thought we were running a dry ship. Well?"

"After the operation, I suppose," said Jonathan. "Coming round. It was like the dentist multiplied by ten."

"Hang on. Here's the best bit."

Confused by Roper's scattershot method of talking, Jonathan had failed to hear the music. But as Roper's hand reached out to order silence, he recognized the dying strains of Pavarotti singing "La donna è mobile." All three stood motionless until the music ended. Then Roper lifted his goblet and drank.

"*God,* he's marvelous. Always play it on Sundays. Never miss, do I, Corks? Bloody good luck. Thanks."

"Good luck," said Jonathan, and drank too. As he did so, the sound of the distant outboard cut off, leaving a deep silence. Roper's gaze dropped to the scar on Jonathan's right wrist.

"How many for lunch, Corks?"

"Eighteen, rising twenty, Chief."

"Vincettis coming? Didn't hear their plane yet. That Czech twin-engined thing they fly."

"Coming when last heard of, Chief."

"Tell Jed, name cards. And decent napkins. None of that red loo paper. And track down the Vincettis, yes or no. Pauli come through about those 130s yet?"

"Still waiting, Chief."

"Well, he better be bloody quick, or never. Here you are, Pine. Sit down. Not there. Here, where I can see you. And the Sancerre, tell Isaac.

Cold, for once. Apo faxed the draft amendment yet?"

"In your in-tray."

"Marvelous chap," Roper commented as Corkoran departed.

"I'm sure he is," Jonathan agreed politely.

"Loves to serve," said Roper, with the glance that heterosexuals share.

. . .

ROPER WAS swirling the champagne in his goblet, smiling while he watched it go round and round. "Mind telling me what you want?" he asked.

"Well, I'd like to get back to Low's if I could. As soon as it's convenient, really. Just a plane to Nassau would be fine. I'll make my way from there."

"Not what I mean at all. Bigger question altogether. In life. What do you want? What's your plan?"

"I haven't got a plan. Not at the moment. I'm drifting. Taking time out."

"Balls, frankly. Don't believe you. You've never relaxed in your life, my view. Not sure I have either. I try. Play a bit of golf, do the boat, bit of this and that, swim, screw. But my engine's going all the time. So's yours. What I like about you. No neutral gear."

He was still smiling. So was Jonathan, even though he wondered on what evidence Roper was able to base his judgment.

"If you say so," he said.

"Cooking. Climbing. Boating. Painting. Soldiering. Marrying. Languages. Divorcing. Some girl in Cairo, girl in Cornwall, girl in Canada. Some Australian doper you killed. Never trust a chap who tells me he's not after something. Why'd you do it?"

"Do what?"

Roper's charm was something Jonathan had not allowed himself to remember. Man-to-man, Roper let you know that you could tell him anything, and he would still be smiling at the end of it.

"Go out on a limb for old Daniel. Break a fellow's neck one day, save my boy's the next. You robbed Meister, why don't you rob me? Why don't you ask me for money?" He sounded almost deprived. "I'd pay you. I don't care what you've done; you saved my kid. No limit to my bounty where the boy's concerned."

"I didn't do it for money. You've patched me up. Looked after me. Been good to me. I'll just go."

"What languages y'got, anyway?" Roper asked, reaching for a sheet of paper, looking it over and tossing it aside.

"French. German. Spanish."

"Fools, most linguists. Damn all to say in one language, so they learn another and say damn all in that. Arabic?"

"No."

"Why not? You were there long enough."

"Well, just scraps. Elementary stuff."

"Should have got yourself an Arab woman. Perhaps you did. Did you know old Freddie Hamid while you were there, chum of mine? Bit of a wild chap? Must have done. Family owns the pub you worked in. Got some horses."

"He was on the board of management of the hotel."

"Total monk, you are, according to Freddie. Asked him. Model of discreet behavior. Why did you go there?"

"It was chance. The job was advertised on the notice board at hotel school the day I graduated. I'd always wanted to see the Middle East, so I applied."

"Freddie had a girlfriend. Older woman. Bright. Too good for him, really. Lot of heart. Used to hang around the racecourse and the yacht club with him. Sophie. Ever meet her?"

"She was killed," Jonathan said.

"That's right. Just before you left. Ever meet her?"

"She had an apartment at the top of the hotel. Everyone knew her. She was Hamid's woman."

"Was she yours?"

The clear, clever eyes did not threaten. They appraised. They offered companionship and understanding.

"Of course not."

"Why of course?"

"It would have been madness. Even if she'd wanted it."

"Why shouldn't she? Hot-blooded Arab, forty if a day, loves a tumble. Personable young chap. God knows, Freddie's no oil painting. Who killed her?"

"It was still being investigated as I left. I never heard whether they arrested anyone. Some intruder, they thought. She surprised him, so he knifed her."

"Wasn't you, anyway?" The clear, clever eyes inviting him to share the joke. The dolphin smile.

"No."

"Sure?"

"There was a rumor Freddie did it."

"Was there, though? Why'd he do a thing like that?"

"Or had it done, anyway. She was said to have betrayed him in some way."

Roper was amused. "Not with you, though?"

"I'm afraid not."

The smile still there. So was Jonathan's.

"Corky can't make you out, you see. Suspicious chap, Corks. Got bad vibes about you. Record's one man, you're another, he says. What else have you been up to? Got any more skeletons in your cupboard? Tricks you've pulled that we don't know about? Police don't? More chaps you've topped?"

"I don't pull tricks. Things happen to me and I react. That's how it's always been."

"Well, Christ, you certainly *react*. They tell me you had to identify Sophie's corpse, cope with the coppers. That right?"

"Yes."

"Pretty foul assignment, wasn't it?"

"Someone had to do it."

"Freddie was grateful. Said, if I ever saw you, tell you thanks. Off the record, of course. He was a bit worried he'd have to go himself. Could have been tricky."

Was hate within Jonathan's reach at last? Nothing had altered in Roper's face. The half-smile was neither more nor less. Out of focus, Corkoran tiptoed back into the room and lowered himself onto a sofa. Indefinably, Roper's style altered and he began playing to an audience.

"This boat you came to Canada on," he resumed in his confiding way. "Got a name at all?"

"The *Star of Bethel.*"

"Registered?"

"South Shields."

"How'd you get the berth? Not easy, is it? Bum a berth on a dirty little boat?"

"I cooked."

Seated in the wings, Corkoran was unable to restrain himself. "With one hand?" he demanded.

"I wore rubber gloves."

"How'd you get the berth?" Roper repeated.

"I bribed the ship's cook, and the captain took me on as a supernumerary."

"Name?"

"Greville."

"Your agent chap, Billy Bourne. Crewing agent, Newport, Rhode Island," Roper continued. "How did you bump into Bourne?"

"Everyone knows him. Ask any of us."

"Us?"

"Crew. Catering staff."

"Got that fax from Billy there, Corks? Likes him, doesn't he? Full of balm, far as I remember?"

"Oh, Billy Bourne *adores* him," Corkoran confirmed sourly. "Lamont can do no wrong. Cooks, pleases, doesn't pinch the silver or the guests, there when you want him, fades away when you don't, sun shines out of his fundament."

"But didn't we check some of the other references? They weren't all that clever, were they?"

"A tad fanciful, Chief," Corkoran conceded. "Moonshine, in fact."

"Fake 'em, Pine?"

"Yes."

"That fellow whose arm you smashed up. Ever see him before that night?"

"No."

"Not eating at Low's some other evening?"

"No."

"Never sailed a boat for him? Cooked for him? Run dope for him?"

There was no apparent menace to these questions, no quickening of the flow. Roper's friendly smile remained unruffled, even if Corkoran was scowling and pulling at his ear.

"No," said Jonathan.

"Killed for him, stole with him?"

"No."

"How about his mate?"

"No."

"Occurred to us you could have started out as their inside man and decided to switch sides halfway through. Wondered whether that was the reason you gave him such a working over. Show you're holier than the Pope, get my meaning?"

"That's idiotic," said Jonathan sharply. He gathered strength. "Actually, that's just bloody insulting." And on a more literary note. "I think you should take that back. Why should I put up with this?"

Play the plucky loser, Burr had said. *Never crawl. It makes him sick.*

But Roper appeared not to hear Jonathan's protests. "Form like yours, on the run, funny name, you might not be looking for another brush with the law. Better to earn favor with the rich Brit instead of kidnapping his boy. See our point?"

"I had nothing to do with either of them. I told you. I'd never seen them or heard of them or spoken to them before that night. I got your boy back, didn't I? I don't even *want* a reward. I want out. That's all. Just let me go."

"How did you know they were heading for the cookhouse? Could have been heading anywhere."

"They knew the layout. They knew where the cash was kept. They'd obviously done their reconnaissance. For God's sake."

"With a little help from you?"

"No!"

"You could have hidden yourself away. Why didn't you? Kept out of trouble. That's what most chaps on the run would have done, wouldn't they? Never been on the run myself."

Jonathan let a long silence pass, sighed and appeared to resign himself to the madness of his hosts. "I'm beginning to wish I had," he said, and let his body slump in frustration.

"Corks, what's happened to that bottle? Haven't drunk it, have you?"

"Right here, Chief."

Back to Jonathan: "I want you to stick around, enjoy yourself, make yourself useful, swim, get your strength back, see what we'll do with you. May even find a job for you, something a bit special. Depends." The smile widened. "Cook us a few carrot cakes. What's the matter?"

"I'm afraid I'm not doing that," Jonathan said. "It's not what I want."

"Balls. Course it is."

"Where else have you got to go?" Corkoran asked. "Carlyle in New York? Ritz-Carlton in Boston?"

"I'll just go my own way," Jonathan said, politely but resolutely.

He had had enough. Acting and being had become one for him. He no longer knew the difference. I need my own space, my own agenda, he was telling himself. I'm sick of being someone's creature. He was standing, ready to leave.

"Hell are you talking about?" Roper complained, mystified. "I'll pay you. Not mean. Pay you top whack. Nice little house, other side of the island. He can have Woody's place, Corky. Horses. Swimming. Borrow a boat. Right up your street. Anyway, what're you going to use for a passport?"

"Mine," said Jonathan. "Lamont. Thomas Lamont." He appealed to Corkoran. "It was among my things."

A cloud moved across the sun, making a brief, unnatural evening in the room.

"Corky, sock him the bad news," Roper ordered, one arm outstretched as if Pavarotti had started singing again.

Corkoran shrugged and pulled an apologetic grin. "Yes, well, it's about this Canadian passport of ours, old love," he said. "Thing of the past, I'm afraid. Popped it in the shredder. Seemed the right thing to do at the time."

"What are you talking about?"

Corkoran was working the palm of one hand with the thumb of the other.

"No good getting in a paddy, heart. Doing you a favor. Your cover's blown sky-high. As of a few days ago, T. Lamont is on every watch list in the Western whatnot. Interpol, Salvation Army, you name it. Show you the evidence if you like. Blue chip. Sorry about that. Fact."

"That was *my passport!*"

It was the anger that had seized him in the kitchen at Mama Low's, unfeigned, unbridled, blind—or almost. That was *my* name, *my* woman, *my* betrayal, *my* shadow! I lied for that passport! I cheated for it! I cooked and skivvied and ate dirt for it, left warm bodies on my trail for it!

"We're getting you a new one, something clean," Roper said. "Least we can do for you. Corky, get your Polaroid, take his mug shot. Has to be color these days. Somebody better touch out the bruises. Nobody else knows, understand? Crushers, gardeners, maids, grooms, nobody." A deliberate break. "Jed, nothing. Jed keeps out of all this." He did not say all what. "What did you do with that motorbike you owned—the one in Cornwall?"

"Ditched it outside Bristol," Jonathan said.

"So why didn't you flog it?" Corkoran demanded vindictively. *"Or* take it to France? You could have done, couldn't you?"

"It was an albatross. Everyone knew I rode a bike."

"One more thing." Roper's back was turned to the terrace, and his pistol finger was pointing at Jonathan's skull. "I run a tight ship here. We thieve a little, but we play straight with each other. You saved my boy. But if you step out of line, you'll wish you'd never been born."

Hearing footsteps on the terrace, Roper swung round, prepared to be angry that his order had been flouted, and saw Jed setting out name cards in silver stands on the tables spread about the terrace. Her chestnut hair fell over her shoulders. Her body was hidden demurely in a wrap.

"Jeds! Come over here a minute! Got a spot of good news for you. Name of Thomas. Joining the family for a bit. Better tell Daniel; he'll be tickled pink."

She allowed a beat. She raised her head and turned it, favoring the cameras with her best smile.

"Oh, gosh. *Thomas.* Super." Eyebrows up. Registers misty pleasure. "That's *terribly* good news. Roper, shouldn't we *celebrate* or something?"

. . .

IT WAS the next morning, soon after seven, but in the Miami headquarters it could have been midnight. The same neon lights glowed on the same green-painted brick walls. Sick of his art deco hotel, Burr had made the building his solitary home.

"Yes, it's me," he replied quietly into the red receiver. "And you're you, by the sound of you. How've you been?"

As he spoke, his spare hand slowly rose above his head until the whole arm was stretched toward the shut-off sky. All was forgiven. God was in His heaven. Jonathan was calling his controller on his magic box.

· · ·

"THEY WON'T have me," Palfrey told Goodhew with satisfaction, as they rode round Battersea in a taxi. Goodhew had picked him up at the Festival Hall. We'll have to make it quick, Palfrey had said.

"Who won't?"

"Darker's new committee. They've invented a code name for themselves: Flagship. You have to be on their list, otherwise you're not Flagship cleared."

"So who is on the list?"

"Not known. They're color coded."

"Meaning?"

"They're identified by an electronic band printed into their office passes. There's a Flagship reading room. They go there, they shove their passes into a machine, the door opens. They go in, it shuts. They sit down, read the stuff, have a meeting. The door opens, and they come out."

"*What* do they read?"

"The developments. The game plan."

"Where's the reading room?"

"Away from the building. Far from pry-ing eyes. Rented. They pay cash. No receipts. Probably the upstairs of a bank. Darker loves banks." He kept talking, anxious to unload and go. "If you're Flagship cleared, you're a Mariner. There's a new insiderspeak based on sea lore. If something's a bit wet for circulation, that means it ought to be Flagship classified. Or it's too nauti-cal for non-Mariners. Or somebody's a dry bob, not a wet bob. They've got a kind of outer ram-part of code names to protect the inner bailey."

"Are all the Mariners members of the River House?"

"Purists, bankers, civil servants, couple of MPs, couple of makers."

"Makers?"

"Manufacturers. Arms makers. For Christ's sake, Rex!"

"Are the makers British?"

"Near enough."

"Are they American? Are there American Mariners, Harry? Is there an American Flagship? Is there an equivalent over there?"

"Pass."

"Can you give me *one* name, Harry? Just one way into this?"

But Palfrey was too busy, too pressed, too

late. He hopped onto the curb, then ducked back into the cab to grab his umbrella.

"Ask your master," he whispered. But so softly that Goodhew in his deafness was not absolutely sure.

SEVENTEEN

THERE WAS Crystalside and there was Townside, and though the two were separated by a mere half-mile as the frigate bird flew, they could have been different islands, because between them sat the hillock proudly called Miss Mabel Mountain, the highest point of all the islands far around, which wasn't saying much, with an apron of haze hoisted round her midriff, and the broken-down slave houses at her feet, and her forest where shafts of sun shone like daylight through a broken roof.

Crystalside was meadowed as an English shire, with clusters of umbrella trees that from a distance could have been oak, and English cattle fences, and English ha-has, and vistas of the sea between soft English hilltops artfully landscaped by Roper's tractors.

But Townside was dour and blowy like Scotland with the lights on, with scraggy goat fields on the slant, and tin shops, and a cricket field of blown red dust, with a tin pavilion, and a prevailing easterly that flicked the water in Carnation Bay.

And around Carnation Bay, in a crescent of

pastel-painted cottages, each with its front garden and steps leading to the beach, Roper accommodated his white staff. Of these cottages, Woody's House was unquestionably the most desirable, by virtue of its stylishly fretted balcony and its unspoiled view of Miss Mabel Island in the middle of the bay.

Who Miss Mabel was, God alone knew, though she had left her name on a presumptuous hillock, an uninhabited island, on a defunct bee farm, an abortive cotton industry and a type of lace doily nobody knew how to make anymore. "Some fine old lady from slavin' times," said the natives shyly when the close observer asked. "Best let her memory sleep."

But everyone knew who Woody was. He was Mr. Woodman from England, a predecessor of Major Corkoran from way back, who had come with the first wave when Mr. Roper bought the island, a charming friendly man to the natives till the day the Chief ordered him locked up in his house while the protection asked him certain questions and accountants from Nassau went through the books, tracing Woody's rackets. The whole island was holding its breath by then, because one way or another the whole island had been a partner in Woody's operations. Finally, after a week of waiting, two of the protection drove Woody up Miss Mabel Mountain to the airstrip, and Woody needed both of them because he couldn't walk well. To be exact, his own mother could have been forgiven for stepping over him on the pavement without recognizing her little boy from England. And Woody's House with its fretted balcony and fine view of the bay had stayed empty ever since, as a warning to everyone on the island that while the Chief was a generous employer and landlord and a fine Christian man to the virtuous, not to mention donor and life chairman of the Townside Cricket Club and the Townside Boys Club and the Townside Steel Band, he could also be relied upon to beat the living shit out of anybody who ripped him off.

· · ·

THE COMBINED role of savior, escaped murderer, convalescent houseguest, Sophie's avenger and Burr's spy is not an easy one to master with aplomb, yet Jonathan with his limitless adaptability assumed it with seeming ease.

You give the air of looking for someone, Sophie had said. *But I think the missing person is yourself.*

Each morning after an early jog and swim, he put on a T-shirt and sneakers and a pair of slacks and set off to make his ten o'clock appearance at Crystal. The walk from Townside to Crystalside took him barely ten minutes, yet each time he made it, it was Jonathan who set out and Thomas who arrived. The route led him along a bridle path cut in Miss Mabel's lower slopes, one of half a dozen Roper kept open through the woods. But for most of the year it was a tunnel because of the overhanging trees. A single rain shower left it pattering and dripping for days.

And sometimes, if his intuition had guided him correctly, he would meet Jed on her Arab mare, Sarah, returning from her morning ride in the company of Daniel and Claud the Polish stablemaster and maybe a couple of houseguests. First he would hear the sound of hooves and voices from higher in the woods. Then he would hold his breath as the party trekked down the zigzag path until it appeared at the opening to the tunnel, where the horses broke into a homebound trot, the equestrienne leading and Claud bringing up the rear, and Jed's flying hair turning red and gold in the light patches and making an absurdly beautiful match with Sarah's blond mane.

"Gosh, Thomas, isn't it absolutely *gorgeous?*" Jonathan agrees it is. "Oh, Thomas, Dans was pestering about whether you'd take him sailing today—he's *so* spoilt. . . . Oh, will you *really?*" She sounds almost despairing. "But you spent the *whole* of yesterday afternoon teaching him how to *paint!* You're a darling. Shall I tell him three o'clock?"

Take it down, he wanted to tell her, as a friend. You've got the part, so stop overacting and be real. All the same, as Sophie would say: she had touched him with her eyes.

· · ·

AND OTHER TIMES, if he took an early run along the shore, he might chance to meet Roper in shorts, plowing barefoot through the wet sand at the edge of the surf, sometimes jogging, sometimes walking, sometimes pausing to face the sun and do a few exercises, but all with the mastery he brought to everything: this is my water, my island, my sand, my speed.

"Morning! Marvelous day," he would call, if he was of a mood to play. "Run? Swim? Come on. Do you good."

So they would run, and swim in parallel for a while, talking sporadically till Roper would suddenly wade ashore, collect his towel and, without a word or backward glance, stride off in the direction of Crystal.

· · ·

"OF EVERY tree you may freely eat," Corkoran told Jonathan as they sat in the garden of Woody's House watching Miss Mabel Island darken with the sunset. "The serving wenches, parlor maids, cooks, typists, masseuses, the lady who comes to clip the parrot's claws, even the guests, are yours for the discreet plucking. But if you ever try to lay so much as a you-know-what on Our Lady of Crystal, he'll kill you. So will I. Just for deep background, old love. No offense."

"Well, thanks, Corky," said Jonathan, making a joke of it. "Thanks very much indeed. Having you and Roper baying for my blood would just about complete my luck. Where did he find her, anyway?" he asked, fetching more beer.

"Legend has it, at a French horse sale."

So that's how it's done, thought Jonathan. You go to France, buy a horse and come away with a convent girl called Jed. Easy.

"Who did he have before?" he asked.

But Corkoran's gaze was fixed on the pale horizon. "Do you *know,*" he complained in frustrated marvel, "we tracked down the captain of the *Star of Bethel,* and even *he* can't prove you're lying in your fucking teeth?"

· · ·

CORKORAN'S WARNING is a waste of breath. The close observer has no protection from her. He can watch her with his eyes shut. He can watch her in the candlelit bowl of a silver spoon by Bulgari of Rome, or in the silver candlesticks by Paul de Lamarie that must appear on the Roper dinner table whenever he comes back from selling farms, or in the gilt mirrors of Jonathan's own imagination. Despising himself, he explores her night and day for confirmation of her awfulness. He is repelled by her and therefore drawn to her. He is punishing her for her power over him—and punishing himself for giving way to it. *You're a hotel girl!* he yells at her. *People buy space in you, pay you and check out!* Yet at the same time he is consumed by her. Her very shadow taunts him as

she saunters half-naked across the blushing marble floors of Crystal on her way to swim, sun-
bathe, caress oil onto her skin, turn crookedly
onto her hip, her other hip and then onto her
belly, while she chats with her visiting friend
Caroline Langbourne or gorges herself on her es-
capist bibles: *Vogue, Tatler, Marie-Claire* or the
Daily Express, three days old. And her jester Corkoran in his Panama hat and rolled-up trousers,
sitting ten feet from her, drinking Pimm's.

"Why doesn't Roper take you with him anymore, Corks?" she asks lazily over her magazine,
in one of the dozen voices Jonathan has noted
down for permanent destruction. "He always *used*
to." She turns a page. "Caro, can you *imagine*
anything more awful than being the *mistress* of a
Tory minister?"

"I suppose there's always a Labor minister,"
suggests Caroline, who is plain and too intelligent
for leisure.

And Jed's laugh: the choking, feral laugh
from deep inside her, which closes her eyes and
splits her face in impish pleasure, even when everything else about her is trying its damnedest to
be a lady.

Sophie was a whore too, he thought dismally.
The difference was, she knew it.

. . .

HE WATCHED her as she rinsed her feet under the
electronically controlled tap, first stepping back,

then lifting one painted toe to produce a jet, then shifting to the other foot and the other perfect haunch. Then, without a glance for anyone, walking to the poolside and diving in. He watched her dive, over and again. In his sleep he replayed the slow-drawn act of levitation as her body rose without movement and, everything in line, tilted itself into the water with a splash no louder than a sigh.

"Oh, *do* come on in, Caro. It's *divine.*"

He watched her in all her moods and varieties: Jed the clown, gangly-bodied, legs splayed, cursing and laughing her way round the croquet lawn; Jed the chatelaine of Crystal, radiant at her own dinner table, enchanting a trio of fat-necked bankers from the City with her deafening Shropshire small talk, never a cliché out of place:

"But I mean, isn't it simply *heartbreaking* living in Hong Kong and knowing that absolutely *everything* one's doing for them, all the super buildings and shops and airports and everything, are just going to be *gobbled up* by the *beastly* Chinese? And what about the horse racing? What's going to happen to that? *And* the horses? I mean, *honestly.*"

Or Jed being too young, catching a cautionary glance from Roper and putting a hand to her mouth and saying, "Down!" Or Jed when the party ends and the last of the bankers has waddled off to bed, climbing the great staircase with her head on Roper's shoulder and her hand on his bottom.

"Weren't we absolutely *gorgeous?*" she says.

"Marvelous evening, Jeds. Lot of fun."

"And weren't they *bores?*" she says with a great yawn. *"God,* I do miss school sometimes. I'm so *tired* of being a grownup. Night, Thomas."

"Good night, Jed. Good night, Chief."

. . .

IT IS a quiet family evening at Crystal. Roper likes a fire. So do' six King Charles spaniels who lie in a floppy heap before it. Danby and MacArthur have flown in from Nassau to talk business, dine and leave at dawn tomorrow. Jed perches on a stool at Roper's feet, armed with pen and paper and the circular gold-rimmed spectacles Jonathan swears she doesn't need.

"Darling, do we *have* to have that slimy Greek again, with his dago Minnie Mouse?" she asks, objecting to the inclusion of Dr. Paul Apostoll and his *inamorata* among the guests for the *Iron Pasha*'s winter cruise.

"Apostoll? *El Apetito?*" Roper replies in puzzlement. "Of course we do. Apo's serious business."

"They're not even Greeks, did you know that, Thomas? Greeks aren't. They're jumped-up Turks and Arabs and things. All the *decent* Greeks got wiped out yonks ago. Well, they can bloody well have the Peach Suite and put up with a shower."

Roper disagrees. "No, they can't. They get the Blue Suite and the Jacuzzi, or Apo will sulk. He likes to soap her."

"He can soap her in the shower," says Jed, affecting to show fight.

"No, he can't. He's not tall enough," says Roper, and they all laugh uproariously because it is the Chief's joke.

"Hasn't old Apo taken the veil or something?" Corkoran asks, looking up from an enormous Scotch. "I thought he gave up nooky after his daughter topped herself."

"That was just for Lent," says Jed.

Her wit and bad language have a hypnotic draw. There is something irresistibly funny to everyone, including herself, about her convent-educated English voice enunciating the vocabulary of a navvy.

"Darling, do we actually give a *fart* about the Donahues? Jenny was *pissed as a rat* from the moment she came aboard, and Archie behaved like a total *turd.*"

Jonathan caught her eye and held it with deliberate lack of interest. Jed raised her eyebrows and returned his stare, as if to say, Who the hell are you? Jonathan returned her question at double strength: Who do you think *you're* being tonight? I'm Thomas. Who the hell are *you?*

· · ·

HE WATCHED her in fragments forced upon him. To the naked breast that she had carelessly granted him in Zurich he added a chance view of her entire upper body in her bedroom mirror while she was changing after riding. She had her arms raised and her hands folded behind her neck, and she was performing some sinuous exercise that she must have read about in one of her magazines. As to Jonathan, he had done absolutely everything in order not to look in the direction of her windows. But she did it every afternoon, and there are only so many times that a close observer can force himself to look away.

He knew the balance of her long legs, the satin planes of her back, the surprising sharpness of her athletic shoulders, which were the tomboy bits of her. He knew the white underneath to her arms and the flow of her hips as she rode.

And there was an episode that Jonathan scarcely dared remember when, thinking he was Roper, she called out to him, "Hand me the bloody bath towel *quick.*" And since he was passing their bedroom on his way back from reading Kipling's *Just So Stories* to Daniel, and since the bedroom door was ajar, and since she had not mentioned Roper by name and he honestly believed, or nearly so, that she was calling *him,* and since Roper's inner office on the other side of the bedroom was the constant target of the close observer's professional curiosity, he softly touched the door and made as if to enter, and stopped four feet from the peerless rear view of her naked body as she stood clutching a facecloth to her eye and cursing while she tried to rub away the soap. Heart thumping, Jonathan made his escape, and first thing next morning, uncaching his magic box, he spoke for ten excited minutes to Burr without once mentioning her:

"There's the bedroom, there's his dressing room and then on the other side of the dressing room there's this little office. He keeps his private papers there, I'm sure he does."

Burr took fright at once. Perhaps, even at this early stage, he had an intimation of disaster. "Stay away from it. Too bloody dangerous. Join first, spy later. That's an order."

· · ·

"COMFORTABLE, are you?" Roper asked Jonathan, on one of their jogs along the beach in the company of several spaniels. "Getting your health back? No cockroaches? Get down, Trudy, you silly tart! Hear young Dans did a decent sail yesterday."

"Yes, he really put his heart into it."

"You're not one of these left-wing chaps, are you? Corky thought you might be a pink 'un."

"Good Lord no. It's never crossed my mind."

Roper seemed not to hear. "World's run by fear, you see. Can't sell pipe dreams, can't rule with charity, no good at all. Not in the real world. With me?" But he didn't wait to discover whether

Jonathan was with him or not. "Promise to build a chap a house, he won't believe you. Threaten to burn his place down, he'll do what you tell him. Fact of life." He paused to double-mark time. "If a bunch of chaps want to make war, they're not going to listen to a lot of wet-eared abolitionists. If they don't, doesn't matter whether they've got crossbows or Stingers. Fact of life. Sorry if it bothers you."

"It doesn't. Why should it?"

"Told Corky he was full of shit. Nose out of joint, that's his trouble. Better go gently with him. Nothing worse than a queen with a chip on his shoulder."

"But I do go gently with him. All the time."

"Yeah. Well. No-win situation probably. Hell's it matter, anyway?"

. . .

ROPER RETURNED to the subject a couple of days later. Not of Corkoran, but of Jonathan's presumed squeamishness regarding certain sorts of deals. Jonathan had been up to Daniel's bedroom to suggest a swim, but Daniel wasn't there. Roper, emerging from the royal suite, fell in beside him, and they walked downstairs together.

"Guns go where the power is," he announced without preamble. "Armed power's what keeps the peace. Unarmed power doesn't last five minutes. First rule of stability. Don't know why I'm preaching to you. Army chap, army family. Still, no point in getting you into something you don't like."

"I don't know what you're getting me into."

They crossed the great hall on their way to the patio.

"Never sold toys? Weapons? Explosives? Tech?"

"No."

"Ever bump into it? Ireland or somewhere? The trade?"

"I'm afraid not."

Roper's voice dropped. "Talk about it another time."

He had spotted Jed and Daniel sitting at a table on the patio, playing *L'Attaque.* So he doesn't talk to her about it, thought Jonathan, encouraged. She's another child to him: not in front of the children.

· · ·

JONATHAN is jogging.

He says good morning to the Self-Expression Wash & Beauty Salon, no bigger than a garden shed. He says good morning to Spokesman's Dock, where some weak rebellion had once been quelled and Amos the blind Rasta now lives in his tethered catamaran with its miniature windmill to recharge his batteries. His collie, Bones, sleeps peacefully on deck. Good morning, Bones.

Next comes the corrugated compound called Jam City Recorded & Vocal Music, full of chickens and yucca trees and broken perambulators. Good morning, chickens.

He glances back at Crystal's cupola above the treetops. Good morning, Jed.

Still climbing, he reaches the old slave houses, where no one goes. Even when he comes to the last slave house he does not slow down but jogs straight through its smashed doorway to a rusted oil can that lies on its side in one corner.

Then stops. And listens, and waits for his breathing to settle, and flaps his hands to make his shoulders loose. From among the muck and old rags in the can he extracts a small steel spade and starts to dig. The handset is in a metal box, cached here by Flynn and his night raiders to Rooke's specification. As Jonathan presses the white button, then the black button, and listens to the bird song of space-age electronics, a fat brown rat lollops across the floor and, like a little old lady on her way to church, lollops into the next-door house.

"How are you?" Burr says.

Good question, thinks Jonathan. How am I? I'm in fear, I'm obsessed by an equestrienne with an IQ of 55 when the sun's shining, I'm clinging on to life by my fingernails twenty-four hours a day, which is what I seem to remember you promised me.

He recites his news. On Saturday a big Italian called Rinaldo flew in by Lear and left three hours later. Age forty-five, height six foot one, two bodyguards and one blond woman.

"Did you get the markings on his plane?"

The close observer has written them nowhere but knows them by heart.

Rinaldo owns a palace in the Bay of Naples, he says. The blonde is called Jutta and lives in Milan. Jutta, Rinaldo and Roper ate salad and talked in the summerhouse, while the bodyguards drank beer and sunbathed out of earshot lower down the hill.

Burr has follow-up questions concerning last Friday's visitation of City bankers identified only by their Christian names. Was Tom fat and bald and pompous? Did Angus smoke a pipe? Did Wally have a Scottish accent?

Yes to all three.

And did Jonathan have the impression they had done business in Nassau and come to Crystal afterwards? Or did they simply fly London to Nassau, then Nassau–Crystal in the Roper jet?

"They did business in Nassau first. Nassau's where they do the respectable deals. Crystal's where they go off the record," Jonathan replies.

Only when Jonathan has completed his report on Crystal's visitors does Burr move to welfare matters.

"Corkoran gumshoes after me all the time," says Jonathan. "Can't seem to leave me alone."

"He's a has-been and he's jealous. Just don't

press your luck. Not in any direction. Hear me?" He is referring to the office behind Roper's bedroom. By some feat of intuition, he knows it is still Jonathan's goal.

Jonathan returns the handset to its box and the box to its grave. He treads down the earth, scrapes dust over it, kicks bits of leaf, pine kernels, dried berries over the dust. He jogs down the hill to Carnation Beach.

"Hidah! Mist' Thomas the magnificent, how you do today, sir, in your soul?"

It is Amos the Rasta, with his Samsonite briefcase. Nobody buys from Amos, but that never bothers him. Nobody much comes to the beach. All day long he will sit upright on the sand, smoking ganja and staring at the horizon. Sometimes he unpacks his Samsonite and sets out his offerings: shell necklaces and fluorescent scarves and twists of ganja rolled up in orange tissue paper. Sometimes he dances, rolling his head and grinning at the sky, while Bones, his dog, howls at him. Amos has been blind since birth.

"You been out runnin' up there already, *high* on Miss Mabel Mountain, Mist' Thomas? You been communin' with *voodoo spirits* today, Mist' Thomas, while you was up there doin' your runnin'? You been sendin' messages to those *voodoo spirits,* Mist' Thomas, *high* up on Miss Mabel Mountain?" Miss Mabel Mountain being seventy feet at best.

Jonathan keeps smiling—but what is the point of smiling to a blind man?

"Oh sure. High as a kite."

"Oh sure! Oh boy!" Amos executes an elaborate jig. "I don't tell nothin' to nobody, Mist' Thomas. A blind beggar, he don't *see* no evil and he don't *hear* no evil, Mist' Thomas. And he don't *sing* no evil, no sir. He sell scarves to gentlemen for twenty-five sweet dollar bills and go his way. You like to buy a fine handmade silk *foulard,* Mist' Thomas, for yo' ladylove, sir, in *ex*quisite taste?"

"Amos," says Jonathan, laying a hand on his arm for good fellowship, "if I smoked as much ganja as you do, I'd be sending messages to Father Christmas."

But when he reaches the cricket ground he doubles back up the hill and recaches the magic box in the colony of discarded beehives before taking the tunnel to Crystal.

. . .

Concentrate on the guests, Burr had said.

We must have the guests, Rooke had said. *Everyone who sets foot on the island, we must have his name and number.*

Roper knows the worst people in the world, Sophie had said.

They came in all sizes and durations: weekend guests, lunch guests, guests who dined and stayed and left next morning, guests who did not

take so much as a glass of water but strolled with
Roper on the beach while their protection trailed
them at a distance, then quickly flew away again,
like guests with work to do.

Guests with planes, guests with yachts;
guests with neither, who had to be fetched by
Roper jet or, if they lived on a neighboring island,
Roper chopper, with the Crystal insignia and the
Ironbrand colors of blue and gray. Roper invited
them, Jed welcomed them and did her duty by
them, though it appeared to be a matter of real
pride to her that she knew not the first thing about
their business.

"I mean, why *should* I, Thomas?" she protested, in a gulpy stage voice, after the departure
of a particularly awful pair of Germans. *"One* of
us worrying is quite enough in any household. I'd
far rather be like Roper's investors and say, 'Here
you are, here's my money and my life, and mind
you *bloody* well look after them.' I mean don't
you think it's the *only* way, Corks? I'd never sleep
otherwise—well, would I?"

"Dead right, old heart. Go with the flow, my
advice," said Corkoran.

You stupid little equestrienne! Jonathan raged
at her, while he piously agreed with her sentiments. *You've put yourself in size-twelve blinkers,
and now you're asking for my approval!*

For his memorizing, he filed the guests by
category and dubbed each category with a piece
of Roperspeak.

First came the keen young Danbys and Mac-Arthurs, alias the MacDanbies, who manned the Ironbrand offices in Nassau and went to the same tailor and trailed the same classless accents and came when Roper beckoned and mixed when Roper told them mix, and left in a flurry or they'd never make it to their desks in time next day. Roper had no patience with them; neither had Jonathan. The MacDanbies were not Roper's allies, not his friends. They were his cover, forever twittering about land deals in Florida and price shifts on the Tokyo exchange and providing Roper with the boring outer shell of his respectability.

After the MacDanbies came Roper's Frequent Fliers, and no Crystal party was complete without a smattering of the Frequent Fliers: such as the perennial Lord Langbourne, whose luckless wife minded the children while he danced groin-to-groin with the nanny; such as the sweet young titled polo player—Angus to his friends—and his darling wife, Julia, whose shared purpose in life, apart from croquet at Sally's and tennis at John-and-Brian's and reading housemaids' novels by the pool, was to sit out their time in Nassau until it was safe for them to claim the house in Pelham Crescent and the castle in Tuscany and the five-thousand-acre estate in Wiltshire with its fabled art collection and the island off the coast of Queensland, all of which were presently the property of some fiscal offshore no-man's-land, together with a couple of hundred million to oil the wheels.

And Frequent Fliers are in honor bound to bring their houseguests:

"Jeds! Over here! *You* remember Arno and Georgina, chums of Julia's, dinner with us in Rome, February? Fish place behind the Byron? *Come* on, Jeds!"

Jed frowns the dearest frown. Jed opens first her eyes in incredulous recognition, then her mouth, but holds a beat before she is able to overcome her joyful astonishment. "Gosh, *Arno!* But, darling, you've lost *pounds!* Georgina, *darling,* how *are* you? Super! Gosh. *Hullo!*"

And the obligatory embrace for each of them, followed by a reflective *Mmnh,* as if she were enjoying it a little more than she ought. And Jonathan in his fury actually goes *Mmnh* in imitation of her under his breath, swearing that next time he catches her pretending like this he will leap up and shout: "Cut! One more time, please, Jed, darling. This time for real!"

And after the Frequent Fliers came the Royal & Ancients: the sub-county English debutantes escorted by brain-dead offshoots of the royal brat pack and policemen in attendance; Arab smilers in pale suits and snow-white shirts and polished toecaps; minor British politicians and ex-diplomats terminally deformed by self-importance; Malaysian tycoons with their own cooks; Iraqi Jews with Greek palaces and companies in Taiwan; Germans with Eurobellies moaning about Ossies; hayseed lawyers from Wyoming wanting to do the best by *mah* clients and *mah*self; retired vastly rich investors gleaned from their dude plantations and twenty-million-dollar bungalows—wrecked old Texans on blue-veined legs of straw, in parrot shirts and joky sun hats, sniffing oxygen from small inhalers; their women with chiseled faces they never had when they were young, and tucked stomachs and tucked bottoms, and artificial brightness in their unpouched eyes. But no surgery on earth could spare them the manacled slowness of old age as they lowered themselves into the kids' end of the Crystal pool, clutching the ladder lest they split again and become what they feared to be before they took the plunge at Dr. Marti's clinic.

"My *goodness,* Thomas," Jed whispers, in a strangled aside to Jonathan, as a blue-haired Austrian countess dog-paddles herself breathlessly to safety. "How *ever* old do you suppose *she* is?"

"Depends which bit you're thinking of," says Jonathan. "Averaged out, probably around seventeen." And Jed's lovely laugh—the real one—her bucking, born-free laugh, while she once again touches him with her eyes.

After the Royal & Ancients came Burr's pet hates, and probably Roper's too, for he called them the Necessary Evils, and these were the shiny-cheeked merchant bankers from London with eighties striped blue shirts and white collars and double-barreled names and double chins and double-breasted suits, who said "ears" when they meant "yes" and "hice" when they meant "house" and "school" when they meant "Eton"; and in their train, the bully-boy accountants—the bean counters, Roper called them—looking as if they'd come to extract a voluntary confession, with take-away-curry breath and wet armpits and voices like formal cautions that from here on everything you say will be taken down and faked in evidence against you.

And after them again, their non-British counterparts: Mulder, the tubby notary from Curaçao, with his twinkling smile and knowing waddle; Schreiber of Stuttgart, constantly apologizing for his ostentatiously good English; Thierry from Marseilles, with his pinched lips and toyboy secretary; the bond sellers from Wall Street, who never came in less than fours, as if there really were security in numbers; and Apostoll the striving little Greek-American, with his toupee like a black bear's paw, his gold chains and gold crosses and unhappy Venezuelan mistress toppling uncomfortably behind him on her thousand-dollar shoes as they head hungrily for the buffet. Catching Apostoll's glance, Jonathan turns away but is too late.

"Sir? We have met, sir. I never forget a face," Apostoll declares, whipping off his dark glasses and holding up everybody behind him. "My name is Apostoll. I am a legionary of God, sir."

"Course you've met him, Apo!" Roper cuts in deftly. "We've *all* met him. *Thomas.* You remember *Thomas,* Apo! Used to be the night chap at Meister's. Came west to seek his fortune. Chum of ours from way back. Isaac, give the Doc some more shampoo."

"I am honored, sir. Forgive me. You are English? I have many British connections, sir. My grandmother was related to the Duke of Westminster, and my uncle on my mother's side designed the Albert Hall."

"My goodness. That's wonderful," says Jonathan politely.

They shake hands. Apostoll's is cool as snakeskin. Their eyes meet. Apostoll's are haunted and a little mad—but who is not a little mad at Crystal on a perfect starlit night with the Dom flowing like the music?

"You are in Mr. Roper's employ, sir?" Apostoll persists. "You have joined one of his great enterprises? Mr. Roper is a man of rare power."

"I'm enjoying the hospitality of the house," Jonathan replies.

"You could do no better, sir. You are a friend of Major Corkoran's perhaps? I think I saw you two exchanging pleasantries some minutes back."

"Corky and I are old pals."

But as the group moves on, Roper takes Apostoll quietly aside, and Jonathan hears the words "Mama Low's" spoken with discretion.

. . .

"BASICALLY, you see, Jed," says an evil by the name of Wilfred as they lounge at white tables under a hot moon, "what we at Harvill Maverich are offering Dicky here is the same service as the crooks are offering, but without the crooks."

"Oh, Wilfred, but how *terribly* boring. Wherever will poor Roper get his kicks from?"

And she catches Jonathan's eye again, causing serious mayhem. How does this happen? Who looks first? For this is not affectation. This is not just playing games with somebody her own age. This is looking. And looking away. And looking again. Roper, where are you now we need you?

. . .

NIGHTS WITH EVILS are endless. Sometimes the talk is got up as bridge or backgammon in the study. Drinks are self-serve, the ushers are told to hop it, the study door is guarded by the protection, the servants know to stay away from that side of the house. Only Corkoran is admitted— these days not always Corkoran.

"Corky's fallen from grace a bit," Jed confides to Jonathan, then bites her lip and says no more.

For Jed too has her loyalty. She is no easy frontier-crosser, and Jonathan has warned himself accordingly.

· · ·

"CHAPS COME to me, you see," Roper explains.

The two men are enjoying another of their strolls. This time it is evening. They have played fierce tennis, but neither has won. Roper doesn't bother with scoring unless he is playing for money, and Jonathan has no money. Perhaps for this reason, their conversations flow without constraint. Roper walks close, letting his shoulder ride unconsciously against Jonathan's, as it did at Meister's. He possesses an athlete's carelessness of touch. Tabby and Gus are following at a distance. Gus is the new crusher, recently added to the strength. Roper has a special voice for chaps who come to him:

"'*Meestaire Ropaire,* geeve us state-of-art toys.'" He graciously pauses to allow Jonathan to laugh at his mimicry. "So I ask 'em: 'State of *what* art, old boy? Compared to *what?*' No answer. Some parts of the world, if you gave 'em a Boer War cannon, they'd move straight to the top of the heap." An impatient gesture of the hand moves them there, and Jonathan feels Roper's elbow in his ribs. "Other countries, pots of money, *mad* for high tech, nothing else will do, got to be like the fellow next door. Not *like* him. Better than. *Miles* better. They want the smart bomb that gets *into* the lift, *goes* to the third floor, *turns* left, *clears* its throat, blows up the master of the house but doesn't hurt the television set." The same elbow nudges against Jonathan's upper arm.

"Thing they *never* realize is: you want to play smart, you've got to have the smart backup. *And* the chaps to work it. No good buying the latest fridge and shoving it in your mud hut if you haven't got electricity to plug it into, is it? Well, is it? What?"

"Of course not," says Jonathan.

Roper plunges his hands into the pockets of his tennis shorts and gives a lazy smile.

"Used to *enjoy* supplying guerrillas when I was your age. Ideals before money . . . cause of human liberty. Didn't last long, thank God. Today's guerrillas are tomorrow's fat cats. Good luck to 'em. Real enemies were the big power governments. Everywhere you looked, big governments were there ahead of you, flogging anything to anybody, breaking their own rules, cutting each other's throats, backing the wrong side, making it up to the right side. Mayhem. Us independent chaps got squeezed into the corner every time. Only thing to do, get in ahead of 'em, beat 'em to the draw. Balls and foresight, all we had left to rely on. Pushing the envelope, all the time. No wonder some chaps went off the reservation. Only place to do business. Young Daniel sail today?"

"All the way round Miss Mabel's Island. I didn't touch the rudder once."

"Well done. Cooking another carrot cake soon?"

"Whenever you say."

As they climb the steps to the gardens, the close observer notices Sandy Langbourne entering the guesthouse and, a moment after him, the Langbourne nanny. She is a demure little creature, about nineteen, but at that instant she has the casual larceny of a girl about to rob a bank.

. . .

THERE ARE the days when Roper is in residence, and there are the days when Roper is away selling farms.

Roper does not announce his departures, but Jonathan has only to approach the front entrance to know which kind of day it is. Is Isaac hovering in the great domed hall in his white gloves? Are the MacDanbies milling in the marble anteroom, smoothing their Brideshead hairstyles and checking their zips and ties? They are. Is the protection manning the porter's chair beside the tall bronze doors? It is. Slipping past the open windows on his way to the back of the house, Jonathan hears the great man at his dictating: "No, damn it, Kate! Scratch that last paragraph and tell him he's got a deal. Jackie, do a letter to Pedro. 'Dear Pedro, we spoke a couple of weeks ago,' blah-blah. Then drop him down a hole. Too little, too late, too many bees round the honeypot—that one, okay? Tell you what, Kate—add *this.*"

But instead of adding *this,* Roper interrupts himself to telephone the *Iron Pasha*'s skipper in

Fort Lauderdale about the new paintwork on the hull. Or Claud the stablemaster about his fodder bills. Or Talbot the boatmaster about the bloody awful state of the jetty on Carnation Bay. Or his antiques dealer in London to discuss that decent-looking pair of Chinese dogs that are coming up at Bonham's next week, could be just right for the two seaward corners of the new conservatory, provided they're not too bilious green.

"Oh, Thomas, *super!* How *are* you—no headaches or anything ghastly? Oh, *good."* Jed is in the butler's pantry, seated at a pretty Sheraton desk, talking menus with Miss Sue the house-keeper and Esmeralda the cook while she poses for the imaginary photographer from *House & Garden.* She has only to see Jonathan enter to make him indispensable: "Now, Thomas. *Honestly,* what do *you* think? Listen. Langoustines, salad, lamb—or salad, langoustines, lamb? . . . Oh, I'm *so* glad. Well, that's exactly what *we* thought, isn't it, Esmeralda? . . . Oh, Thomas, can we *possibly* pick your brains about *foie gras* with Sauternes? The Chief *adores* it, I *loathe* it and Esmeralda is saying, *very* sensibly, why not just let them carry on with champagne? . . . Oh, Thomas"—dropping her voice so she can pretend to herself that the servants can't hear—"Caro Langbourne is *so* upset. Sandy's being an abso-lute *pig* again. I wondered whether a sail might cheer her up, if you've *really* got the energy. If she goes on at you, don't worry, just sort of close your ears, do you mind? . . . And, Thomas, *while* you're about it, could you *bear* to ask Isaac where the *hell* he's hidden the trestle tables? . . . And, Thomas, Daniel is absolutely determined to give Miss Molloy a *surprise* birthday party, if you can believe it, on the eighteenth. If you've got *any* ideas about that at *all,* I'll love you for absolutely *ever. . . .*"

But when Roper is not in residence, menus are forgotten, workmen sing and laugh—and so in his soul does Jonathan—and happy conversations break out everywhere. The buzz of bandsaws vies with the thunder of the landscapers' bulldozers, the whine of drills with the chime of builders' hammers, as everyone tries to get everything done in time for the Chief's return. And Jed, walking pensively with Caroline Langbourne in the Italian gardens, or sitting with her for hours on end in her bedroom in the guesthouse, keeps herself at a careful distance and does not promise to love Jonathan even for an afternoon, let alone for absolutely ever.

For ugly things are stirring in the Langbourne nest.

. . .

THE *Ibis,* a sleek young sailing dinghy available for the pleasure of Crystal guests, is becalmed. Caroline Langbourne sits in the prow, staring back to land as if never to return. Jonathan, not bothering with the tiller, is lounging in the stern with his eyes closed.

"Well, we can row, or we can whistle," he informs her languidly. "Or we can swim. I vote we whistle."

He whistles. She does not. Fish plop, but no wind comes. Caroline Langbourne's soliloquy is addressed to the shimmering horizon.

"It's a *very* odd thing to wake up one morning and *realize,*" she says—Lady Langbourne, like Lady Thatcher, has a way of singling out the unlikeliest words for punishment—"that one has been living *and* sleeping and virtually wasting one's *years,* let alone one's private money, on somebody who not only doesn't *give* a damn about you but behind *all* his legal flimflam and hypocrisy is *actually* the most complete and utter *crook.* If I *told* anybody what I knew—and I've only told Jed a *bit* because she's *extremely* young—*well,* they wouldn't believe the half of it. Not a *tenth.* They couldn't. Not if they're decent people."

The close observer keeps his eyes tight shut—and his ears wide open as Caroline Langbourne charges on. *And sometimes,* Burr had said, *just when you're thinking God's handed in His notice, He'll turn round and slip you a bonus so big you'll not believe your luck.*

· · ·

BACK IN WOODY'S HOUSE, Jonathan sleeps lightly and is wide awake the moment he hears the shuffle of footsteps at his front door. Tying a sarong round his waist, he creeps downstairs, all prepared to commit murder. Langbourne and the nanny are peering through the glass.

"Mind if we pinch a bed off you for the night?" Langbourne drawls. "Palace is in a bit of an uproar. Caro's blown her top, and now Jed's having a go at the Chief."

Jonathan sleeps fitfully on the sofa while Langbourne and his paramour noisily do the best they can upstairs.

. . .

JONATHAN AND DANIEL lie face down, side by side, on the bank of a stream high on Miss Mabel Mountain. Jonathan is teaching Daniel to catch a trout with his bare hands.

"Why's Roper in a bait with Jed?" Daniel whispers, so as not to alarm the trout.

"Keep your eyes upriver," Jonathan murmurs in return.

"He says she should stop listening to a lot of junk from a woman scorned," says Daniel. "What's a woman scorned?"

"Are we going to catch this fish or not?"

"Everybody knows Sandy screws the whole world and his sister, so what's the fuss?" Daniel asks, in near-perfect imitation of Roper's voice.

Relief arrives in the form of a fat blue trout nosing its way dreamily along the bank. Jonathan and Daniel return to earth, bearing their trophy like heroes. But a pregnant silence hangs over

Crystalside: too many secret lives, too much unease. Roper and Langbourne have flown to Nassau, taking the nanny with them.

"Thomas, that's totally unfair!" Jed protests too brightly, having been summoned with huge shouts to admire Daniel's catch. The strain is telling in her face: pinches of tension pucker her brow. It has not occurred to him till now that she is capable of serious distress.

"Bare *hands?* However did you do it? Daniel won't sit still even to have his hair cut, will you, Dans, darling? Plus he absolutely *loathes* creepy crawlies. Dans, that's super. Bravo. Terrif."

But her forced good humor does not satisfy Daniel. He sadly replaces the trout on its plate. "Trouts aren't crawlies," he says. "Where's Roper?"

"Selling farms, darling. He told you."

"I'm sick of him selling farms. Why can't he buy them? What will he do when he hasn't got any left?" He opens his book on monsters. "I like it best when it's Thomas and us. It's more normal."

"Dans, that's *very* disloyal," says Jed, and studiously avoiding Jonathan's eye, she hastens away to offer more comfort to Caroline, who strides alone on the beach, contemplating the vileness of man.

. . .

"JEDS! Party! Thomas! Let's cheer this bloody place up!"

Roper has been back since dawn. The Chief always flies at first light. All day long the kitchen staff has been toiling, planes have been arriving, the guesthouse has been filling up with MacDanbies, Frequent Fliers and Necessary Evils. The illuminated swimming pool and the gravel sweep are freshly groomed. Torches have been lit in the grounds and the sound system on the patio belts out nostalgic melodies from Roper's celebrated collection of 78s. Girls in their flimsy nothings, Corkoran in his Panama hat, Langbourne in his white dinner jacket and jeans, form eightsomes, pass partners, drawl and squeal. The barbecue crackles, the Dom is flowing, servants scurry and smile, the Crystal spirit is restored, even Caroline joins in the fun. Jed alone seems unable to kiss her sorrows goodbye.

"Look at it this way," says Roper—never drunk but the better for his own hospitality—to a blue-rinse English heiress who gambled away everything one had at Vegas, darling, such fun but thank God one's houses were in trust, and thank God too for darling Dicky. "If the world's a dungheap, and you build yourself a spot of Paradise and put a girl like this in it"—Roper flings an arm round Jed's shoulders—"in my book you've done the place a favor."

"Oh, but Dicky, darling, you've done us *all* a favor. You've put *sparkle* into our lives. *Hasn't* he, Jed, darling? Your man's a perfect marvel, and you're a very lucky little girl and never you forget it."

"Dans! Come here!"

Roper's voice has a way of producing silence. Even the American bond salesmen stop talking. Daniel trots obediently to his father's side. Roper releases Jed and places a hand on each of his son's shoulders and offers him to the audience for their inspection. He is speaking on impulse. He is speaking, Jonathan immediately realizes, to Jed. He is clinching some running dispute between them that cannot be resolved without the backing of a sympathetic audience.

"Tribes of Bonga-Bonga Land starving to death?" Roper demands of the smiling faces. "Crops failing, rivers dried up, no medicines? Grain mountains all over Europe and America? Milk lakes we don't use, nobody gives a toss? Who are the killers, then? It's not the chaps who make the guns! It's the chaps who don't open the larder doors!" Applause. Then louder applause when they see that it matters to him. "Bleeding hearts up in arms? Color supplements wingeing about the uncaring world? Tough titty! Because if your tribe hasn't got the guts to help itself, the sooner it's culled the better!" He gives Daniel a friendly shake. "Look at this chap. Good human material. Know why? Keep still, Dans. Comes from a long line of survivors. Hundreds of years, strongest kids survived, weaklings went under.

Families of twelve? Survivors bred with the survivors and made *him*. Ask the Jews—right, Kitty? Kitty's nodding. Survivors, that's what we're about. Best of the pack, every time." He turns Daniel round and points him at the house. "Off to bed, old boy. Thomas'll come and read to you in a minute."

For a moment Jed is as uplifted as the rest of them. She may not join in the applause, but it is clear from her smile and the way she squeezes Roper's hand that, however briefly, his diatribe has granted her a lightening of the guilt, or doubt, or perplexity, or whatever it is these days that clouds her customary pleasure in a perfect world.

But after a few minutes, she slips silently upstairs. And does not come down again.

. . .

CORKORAN AND Jonathan sat in the garden of Woody's House, drinking cold beer. A red halo of dusk was forming over Miss Mabel Island. The cloud rose in a last ferment, remaking the day before it died.

"Lad called Sammy," Corkoran said dreamily. "That was his name. Sammy."

"What about him?"

"Boat before the *Pasha.* The *Paula,* God help us. Sammy was one of the crew."

Jonathan wondered whether he was about to receive Corkoran's confession of lost love.

"Sammy from Kentucky. Matelot. Always

shinning up and down the mast like someone out of *Treasure Island.* Why's he do that? I thought. Showing off? Impress the girls? The boys? Me? Rum. Chief was into commodities in those days. Zinc, cocoa, rubber goods, tea, uranium, any bloody thing. Sit up all night sometimes, selling forwards, buying backwards, sideways, buying long, selling short, bulling, bearing. Insider stuff, of course, no point in taking risks. And this little bugger Sammy, nipping up and down the mast. Then I twigged. Hullo, I thought. I know what you're up to, Sammivel, my son. You're doing what I'd do. You're spying. Waited till we were anchored for the evening, as usual, sent the crew ashore, as usual. Then I fished out a ladder and pottered up the mast myself. Nearly killed me, but I found it straightaway, tucked into an angle beside the aerial. Couldn't see it from the ground floor. Bug. Sammy'd been bugging the Chief's satcom, shadowing him on the markets. Him and his buddies on shore. They'd pooled their savings. By the time we nabbed him, they'd turned seven hundred bucks into twenty grand."

"What did you do to him?"

Corkoran shook his head. "My problem is, old love," he confessed, as if it were something Jonathan might solve for him, "every time I look into your Pan eyes, all my chimes and whistles tell me it's young Sammy with his pretty arse shinning up the whatnot."

. . .

IT IS nine o'clock the next morning. Frisky has driven across to Townside and is sitting in the Toyota, trumpeting the horn for extra drama.

"Hands off cocks and pull on socks, Tommy boy, you're on parade! Chief wants a quiet tit-ah-tit. Forthwith, immediately, and get your finger out!"

. . .

PAVAROTTI WAS in full lament. Roper stood before the great fireplace, reading a legal document through his half-lenses. Langbourne was sprawled on the sofa, one hand draped over his knee. The bronze doors closed. The music stopped.

"Present for you," said Roper, still reading.

A brown envelope addressed to Mr. Derek S. Thomas lay on the tortoiseshell desk. Feeling its weight, Jonathan had a disconcerting memory of Yvonne, pale-faced in her Pontiac beside the highway.

"You'll need this," Roper said, interrupting himself to shove a silver paper knife toward him. "Don't hack it about. Too damned expensive."

But Roper did not resume his reading. He went on watching Jonathan over his half-lenses. Langbourne was watching him too. Under their double gaze, Jonathan cut the flap and extracted a New Zealand passport with his own photograph inside it, the particulars in the name of Derek

Stephen Thomas, company executive, born Marlborough, South Island, expiry three years off.

At the sight and touch of it he was for a moment ridiculously affected. His eyes blurred, a lump formed in his throat. Roper protects me. Roper is my friend.

"Told 'em to put some visas in it," Roper was saying proudly, "make it scruffy." He tossed aside the document he had been reading. "Never trust a new passport, my view. Go for the old 'uns. Same as Third World taxi drivers. Must be some reason why they've survived."

"Thanks," Jonathan said. "Really thanks. It's beautiful."

"You're in the system," Roper said, thoroughly gratified by his own generosity. "Visas are real. So's the passport. Don't push your luck. Want to renew, use one of their consulates abroad."

Langbourne's drawl was in deliberate counterpoint to Roper's pleasure. "Better sign the fucking thing," he said. "Try out some signatures first."

Watched by both men, Jonathan wrote Derek S. Thomas, Derek S. Thomas, on a sheet of paper until they were satisfied. He signed the passport, Langbourne took it, closed it and handed it back to Roper.

"Something wrong?" said Langbourne.

"I thought it was mine. To keep," said Jonathan.

"Who the hell gave you that idea?" said Langbourne.

Roper's tone was more affectionate. "Got a job for you, remember? Do the job, then off you go."

"What sort of job? You never told me."

Langbourne was opening an attaché case. "We'll need a witness," he told Roper. "Somebody who can't read."

Roper picked up the phone and touched a couple of numbers. "Miss Molloy? Chief here. Mind stepping down to the study a moment?"

"What am I signing?" Jonathan said.

"Jesus, *fuck,* Pine," said Langbourne in a pent-up murmur. "For a murderer on the run, you're pretty bloody picky, I must say."

"Giving you your own company to manage," said Roper. "Bit of travel. Bit of excitement. Lot of keeping your mouth shut. Big piece of change at the end of the day. All debts paid in full, with interest."

The bronze doors opened. Miss Molloy was tall and powdery and forty. She had brought her own pen of marbled plastic, and it hung round her neck on a brass chain.

The first document appeared to be a waiver in which Jonathan renounced his rights to the income, profits, revenue or assets of a Curaçao-registered company called Tradepaths Limited. He signed it.

The second was a contract of employment

with the same company, whereby Jonathan accepted all burdens, debts, obligations and responsibilities accruing to him in his capacity as managing director. He signed it.

The third bore the signature of Major Lance Montague Corkoran, Jonathan's predecessor in the post. There were paragraphs for Jonathan to initial and a place for him to sign.

"Yes, darling?" said Roper.

Jed had stepped into the room. She must have talked her way past Gus.

"I've got the Del Oros on the line," she said. "Dine and stay and mah-jongg in Abaco. I tried to get through to you but the switchboard says you're not taking calls."

"Darling, you know I'm not."

Jed's cool glance took in the group and stopped at Miss Molloy. *"Anthea,"* she said. "What*ever* are they doing to you? They're not signing you up to marry Thomas, are they?"

Miss Molloy turned scarlet. Roper gave an uncertain frown. Jonathan had never seen him at a loss before.

"Thomas is coming aboard, Jeds. Told you. Setting him up with a bit of capital. Giving him a break. Felt we owed him one. All he did for Dans and so on. We talked about it, remember? Hell's going on, Jeds? This is business."

"Oh, well, that's *super.* Congratulations, Thomas." She looked at him at last. Her smile was distancing, but no longer so theatrical. "Just be awfully careful you don't do anything you don't want, won't you? Roper's *terribly* persuasive. Darling, can I tell them yes? Maria's so *madly* in love with you, I'm sure it'll break her heart if I don't."

. . .

"ANYTHING ELSE going on?" Burr asked, when he had listened in near silence to Jonathan's account of these events.

Jonathan affected to search his memory. "The Langbournes are having a marital tiff, but I gather that's par for the course."

"It's not unknown in this neck of the woods either," said Burr. But he still seemed to be waiting for more.

"And Daniel's going back to England for Christmas," said Jonathan.

"Nothing else?"

"Not of any moment."

Awkwardness. Each man waiting for the other to speak.

"Well tread water and act natural," said Burr grudgingly. "And no more wild talk about breaking into his holy of holies, right?"

"Right."

Yet another pause before they both rang off.

I live my life, Jonathan told himself with deliberation as he jogged down the hill. I am not a puppet. I am nobody's servant.

EIGHTEEN

JONATHAN HAD planned his forbidden assault on the state apartments as soon as he learned that Roper had decided to sell some more farms and that Langbourne would be accompanying him and Corkoran would be stopping off in Nassau to attend to Ironbrand business.

His resolve was confirmed when he heard from Claud the stablemaster that on the morning following the men's departure, Jed and Caroline proposed to take the children on a pony trek of the island's coast path, setting off at six and returning to Crystal in time for brunch and a swim before the midday heat.

From that moment his dispositions became tactical. On assault day minus one he took Daniel on his first difficult climb up Miss Mabel's north face—more truthfully up the face of a small quarry cut into the steepest part of the hillock—which required three pitons and a roped traverse before they arrived triumphant at the eastern end of the airstrip. At the peak he gathered a bunch of sweet-scented yellow freesias, which the natives called shipping flowers.

"Who are they for?" Daniel asked while he

munched his chocolate, but Jonathan managed to dodge the question.

Next day he rose at his usual early hour and jogged a stretch of the coastal path to make sure the trekking party had set out as planned. He came face-to-face with Jed and Caroline on a windy bend, with Claud and the children straggling behind.

"Oh, Thomas, will you by *any* chance be going up to Crystal later?" Jed asked, leaning forward to pat her Arab's neck as if she were starring in a cigarette advertisement. *"Great.* Then could you be *frightfully* kind and tell Esmeralda that Caro can't eat *anything* with milk fat because of her diet?"

Esmeralda was fully aware that Caroline could eat no milk fat, because Jed had told her so in Jonathan's hearing. But Jonathan was learning to expect the unexpected from Jed these days. Her smiles were distracted, her behavior was more contrived than ever and small talk came hard to her.

Jonathan continued jogging till he reached his hide. He did not uncache the handset, because his will was his own today. But he did help himself to his subminiature camera got up as a Zippo lighter, and to the camera he added the bunch of lock picks that were not disguised as anything, and clutching them in his fist so that they didn't chime while he ran, he returned to Woody's

House and changed, then walked through the tunnel to Crystal, feeling the tingling of prebattle across his shoulders.

"Fuck you doin' with them shippin' flowers, Mist' Thomas?" the guard at the gate demanded of him good-humoredly. "You been up there robbin' poor Miss Mabel? Why, *shit.* Hey, Dover, come over here and put your stupid face in these shippin' flowers. You ever smell anything so beautiful? The shit you did! You never smelt nothin' in your life 'cept your young lady's cherry pie."

Reaching the main house, Jonathan had the giddying sensation of having returned to Meister's. It was not Isaac but Herr Kaspar who received him at the door. It was not Parker standing on the top of the aluminum ladder changing light bulbs but Bobbi the odd-job man. And it was Herr Kaspar's nymphet niece, not Isaac's daughter, who was languidly squirting insecticide into the potpourri. The illusion passed, and he was restored to Crystal. In the kitchen Esmeralda was conducting a seminar on world affairs with Talbot the boatman and Queenie from the laundry.

"Esmeralda, would you please find me a vase for these? Surprise present for Dan. Oh, and Miss Jed says to remind you that Lady Langbourne can't eat *any* milk products *at all.*"

He was so arch about saying this that his audience burst into fits of uncontrollable laughter, which followed Jonathan up the marble stair-case as, vase in hand, he headed for the second floor, apparently on his way to Daniel's quarters. Reaching the door to the state apartments, he paused. The flow of cheerful chatter from down-stairs ran on. The door was ajar. He pushed it and stepped into a mirrored hallway. The door at the end of it was closed. He turned the handle, think-ing Ireland and booby traps. He stepped inside, nothing blew up. He closed the door and looked round him, ashamed of his exhilaration.

The sunlight, filtered by net curtains, lay like ground mist on the white carpet. Roper's side of the enormous bed was not slept in. Roper's pil-lows were still puffed up. On his bedside table lay current copies of *Fortune, Forbes, The Economist,* and back numbers of catalogues from auction houses round the world. Memo pads, pencils, a pocket recorder. Shifting his gaze to the other side of the bed, Jonathan observed the imprint of her body, the pillows crushed as if by restlessness, the tissue of black silk that was her nightdress, her utopian magazines, the pile of coffee table books on furniture, great houses, gardens, great horses, more horses, books on Arab bloodstock and En-glish recipes, and how to learn Italian in eight days. The smells were of infancy—baby powder, bubble bath. A luxurious trail of yesterday's clothes was spread haphazard over the chaise longue; and through the open doorway to the bathroom, he saw yesterday's swimsuit hanging in triangles from the shower rail.

His eye quickening, he began reading the whole page at once: her dressing table, cluttered with mementos of nightclubs, people, restaurants, horses; photographs of laughing people arm in arm, of Roper in bikini shorts, his maleness much in evidence, Roper at the wheel of a Ferrari, of a racing boat, Roper in white peaked cap and ducks, standing on the bridge of the *Iron Pasha;* the *Pasha* herself dressed overall, berthed majestically in New York harbor, the outline of Manhattan soaring behind her; book matches, girlfriends' handwritten letters spilling from an open drawer; a child's address book with a photograph of soulful bloodhounds on the cover; notes to herself scribbled on bits of yellow paper and stuck to the edges of her mirror: "Diving watch for Dan's birthday?" "Phone Marie re Sarah's hock!" "S. J. Phillips re R's *cufflinks!!"*

The room felt airless. I'm a tomb robber, but she's alive. I'm in Herr Meister's cellar with the lights on. Bolt before they wall me in. But escape was not what he had come for. He had come for involvement. With both of them. He wanted Roper's secrets, but he wanted hers more. He wanted the mystery of what joined her to Roper, if it did; of her ludicrous affectations; and of why you touch me with your eyes. Setting the flower vase on a coffee table, he picked up one of her pillows, held it to his face and smelled the wood smoke from singing Aunt Annie's hearth. Of course. That's what you did last night. You sat up with Caroline in front of the fire and talked while the children slept. So much talk. So much listening. What do you say? What do you hear? And the shadow on your face. You're a close observer yourself these days, eyes staying on everything too long, including me. You're a child again, seeing everything for the first time. Nothing is familiar to you anymore, nothing is safe for you to depend on.

He pushed the mirrored door to Roper's dressing room and entered not her childhood but his own. Did my father own a military chest like this, with brass handles to lug it through the olive groves of Cyprus? This folding campaign table stained with ink and sundowners? This pair of crossed scimitars hanging in their scabbards from the wall? Or these dress slippers with their braided monograms like regimental crests? Even the rows of handmade suits and dinner jackets, wine red to black to white, the handmade shoes braced by wooden trees, white buckskins, patent evening pumps, had an unmistakable air of uniforms waiting for the signal to advance.

A soldier again, Jonathan checked for hostile signs: suspicious wires, contacts, sensors, some tempting trap to consign him to kingdom come. Nothing. Just the framed school groups from thirty years ago, snapshots of Daniel, a heap of small change in half a dozen currencies, a list of fine wines from Berry Bros. & Rudd, the annual accounts of his London club.

Does Mr. Roper go to England much? Jonathan had asked Jed at Meister's while they waited for the luggage to be loaded into the limousine.

Good Lord no, Jed replied. *Roper says we're* terribly *nice, but absolute wood from here up. Anyway, he can't.*

Why not? Jonathan asked.

Oh, I don't know, said Jed too carelessly. *Tax or something. Why don't you ask him?*

· · ·

THE DOOR to the inner office stood before him. The inmost room, he thought. The last secret is yourself—but which self: his or mine or hers? The door was of solid cypress, set in a steel frame. He listened. Distant chatter. Vacuum cleaners. Floor polishers.

Take your time, the close observer reminded himself. Time is care. Time is innocence. Nobody is coming upstairs to find you. Bedding at Crystal is changed at midday, after the clean sheets have had a chance to air in the sun: Chief's orders, diligently executed by Jed. We are obedient people, Jed and I. Our monasteries and convents were not in vain. He tried the door. Locked. One conventional lock, pipestem. The room's seclusion is its own security. Anyone found near it will be shot on sight. He reached for his picks and heard Rooke's voice in his ear. *Never pick a lock if you can find the key: first rule of burglary.* He swung away from the door and ran his hand along a couple of shelves. He lifted the corner of a rug, then a pot plant, then patted the pockets of the nearest suits, then the pockets of a dressing gown. Then he lifted a few of the nearer shoes and turned them upside down. Nothing. To hell with it.

He fanned out the picks and selected the one he thought likeliest to fit. It was too fat. He selected a second and, about to insert it, had a schoolboy terror of scratching the polished brass escutcheon. *Vandal! Who dragged you up?* He dropped his hands to his sides, breathed slowly a few times to reassemble his operational calm, and began again. Gently in . . . pause . . . gently back a fraction . . . in again. Stroke her, don't force her, as we say in the army. Listen to her, feel her pressures, hold your breath. Turn. Gently . . . back another fraction . . . now turn harder . . . and a little harder still. . . . *You are about to break the pick! You are about to break the pick and leave it in the lock! Now!*

The lock yielded. Nothing broke. No one emptied his Heckler in Jonathan's face. He removed the pick intact, returned it to its wallet and the wallet to his jeans pocket, and heard the squeak of the Toyota's brakes as it pulled up in the stableyard. Go cold. *Now.* The close observer stole to the window. Mr. Onslow Roper has returned unexpectedly from Nassau. Players from across the border are coming to collect their weapons. But it was only the day's bread arriving from Townside.

But nice listening, he told himself. Calm, attentive, panic-free listening. Well done. Your father's boy.

He was in Roper's den.

And if you step out of line, you'll wish you'd never been born, says Roper.

No, says Burr. *And Rob says no too. His holy of holies is out of bounds, and that's an order.*

. . .

PLAIN. A soldier's plainness. Everyman's decent moderation. No embroidered throne, no tortoiseshell desk, no nine-foot bamboo sofas with cushions that send you straight to sleep, no silver goblets, no Sotheby catalogues. Just a plain, boring little office for making deals and money. A plain leatherette-topped office desk with filing trays on a collapsing stand, pull it and they all take one pace forward. Jonathan pulled and that was what they did. One steel tubular chair. One round dormer window staring like a dead eye at its own blank piece of sky. Two swallowtail butterflies. How the hell did *they* get in here? One bluebottle, very noisy. One letter, lying on top of other letters. The address, Hampden Hall, Newbury. The signature, Tony. The topic, the writer's straitened circumstances. The tone both begging and threatening. Don't read it, photograph it. Calmly extracting the remaining papers from the tray, he laid them out like playing cards face up on the desk, removed the base of the Zippo lighter, armed the camera inside and peered through the tiny eyepiece. *Spread the fingers of both hands for range and thumb your nose,* Rooke had said. He thumbed his nose. The lens was fish-eye. All the pages were in shot. Aim up, aim down. Shoot. Change the papers. Keep my sweat away from the desk. Thumb my nose again to check the range. Calmly. Now just as calmly, *freeze.* He stood at the window, frozen. Observe, but not too closely. The Toyota is driving off, Gus at the wheel. Go back to work. Slowly.

He completed the first tray, replaced the papers, took the papers from the second. Six closely written pages of neat Roperscript. The crown jewels? Or a long letter to his ex-wife about Daniel? He laid them out in order, left to right. No, not a letter to Paula. These are names and numbers, lots of both, written on graph paper in ballpoint pen, the names on the left, the numbers set beside them, each digit carefully entered in its square. Gambling debts? Household accounts? Birthday list? Stop thinking. Spy now, think later. He took a step back, wiped the sweat from his face and breathed out. As he did so, he saw it.

One hair. One long, soft, straight, beautiful chestnut strand of hair that should have been in a locket or a love letter or lying on a pillow and smelling of wood smoke. For a moment he was furious, the way explorers are furious when they reach some hellish end point only to find the hated rival's cookpot there ahead of them. You lied to me! You *do* know what he does! You're hand in glove with him on the biggest dirty deal of his career! The next moment it pleased him to think that Jed had been making the same journey as himself, without benefit of Rooke or Burr or Sophie's murder.

After that he was terrified. Not for himself, for her. For her frailty. For her clumsiness. For her life. You bloody fool, he told her, leaving your handwriting all over the job! Have you never seen a beautiful woman with her face punched off? A small dog ripped from stem to stern?

Curling the telltale hair round the tip of his little finger, Jonathan poked it into the sweat-soaked pocket of his shirt, returned the second file to its tray and was spreading out the papers from the third as he heard the scuffle of horses' hooves from the direction of the stableyard, accompanied by children's voices raised in protest and rebuke.

Methodically, he restored the papers to their rightful home and walked to the window. As he did so, he heard from within the house the sounds of fast-running feet, then Daniel howling for his mother as he came storming through the kitchens to the hall. Then Jed's voice yelling after him. And in the stableyard he saw Caroline Langbourne and her three children, and Claud the stable-master holding Jed's Arab, Sarah, by the bridle, and Donegal the groom holding Daniel's pony, Smoky, who stood with his head hung in dudgeon as if he were disgusted by the whole display.

· · ·

BATTLE BRIGHT.

Battle calm.

His father's son. Bury him in uniform.

Jonathan slid the camera into the pocket of his shirt and checked the desk for careless traces. With his handkerchief he wiped the desktop, then the sides of the filing trays. Daniel was yelling louder than Jed, but Jonathan couldn't hear what either of them was saying. In the stableyard one of the Langbourne children had decided it was time to join the chorus of complaint. Esmeralda had come out of her kitchen and was telling Daniel not to be a silly boy now, what would his Papa say? Jonathan stepped into the dressing room, closed the steel-lined door to the den and relocked it with the pick, which took a little longer than it should have done because of his anxiety about violating the escutcheon. By the time he reached the bedroom he could hear Jed stomping up the stairs in her riding boots, declaring to anyone who cared to hear that she would never *never* take Daniel riding again in her bloody *life*.

He thought of retreating to the bathroom or

returning to Roper's dressing room, but hiding didn't seem to solve anything. A luxurious inertia was descending over him, a desire to embrace delay that reminded him of making love. So that by the time Jed appeared in the doorway in her riding gear, minus her crop and hard hat but flushed with heat and anger, Jonathan had placed himself before the coffee table and was arranging the shipping flowers because they had lost something of their perfection on the journey upstairs.

At first she was too angry with Daniel to be surprised by anything. And it impressed him that her anger made her real.

"Thomas, *honestly,* if you've got *any* influence over Daniel at all, I wish you'd teach him *not* to be so absolutely *bloody* wet when he hurts himself. One silly little fall, *no* damage to *anything* except his pride, and he makes an absolute— Actually, Thomas, what the *fuck* are you doing in this room?"

"I brought you some shipping flowers. From our climb yesterday."

"Why couldn't you have given them to Miss Sue?"

"I wanted to arrange them myself."

"You could have arranged them and given them to Miss Sue downstairs."

She glared at the unmade bed. At her yesterday's clothes flung over the chaise longue. At the open bathroom door. Daniel was still yelling.

"*Shut up, Daniel!*" Her eyes returned to Jonathan. "Thomas, *actually,* flowers or no flowers, I think you've got a *fucking* cheek."

It's the same anger. You simply switched it from Daniel to me, he thought, while he went on tinkering distractedly with the flowers. He suddenly felt deeply protective of her. The lock picks were lying like a ton weight against his thigh, the Zippo camera was practically falling out of his shirt pocket, his story about the shipping flowers, dreamed up for Esmeralda's benefit, was wearing pretty thin. But it was Jed's appalling vulnerability that he was thinking of, not his own. Daniel's howling had stopped while he listened for the effect.

"Why don't you call up the bullyboys, then?" Jonathan suggested, not to her so much as to the flowers. "Personal attack button right there beside you on the wall. Or pick up the house phone if you prefer. Dial nine, and I'll pay for my fucking cheek in the approved manner. Daniel isn't making a scene because he hurt himself. He doesn't want to go back to London and he doesn't like sharing you with Caroline and her kids. He wanted you for himself."

"Get out," she said.

But the calm was on him, and so was his concern for her, and between them they gave him the supremacy. The rehearsing and blank shots were over. It was live-ammunition time.

"Close the door," he ordered her, keeping his voice low. "It's not a good moment to talk, but there's something I have to say to you, and I don't want Daniel hearing it. He gets enough through your bedroom wall as it is."

She stared at him, and he could see the uncertainty working in her face. She closed the door.

"I'm obsessed by you. I can't get you out of my head. I don't mean I'm in love with you. I sleep with you, I wake up with you, I can't clean my teeth without cleaning yours as well and most of the time I'm quarreling with you. There's no logic to it, there's no pleasure to it. I haven't heard you express a single thought worth a damn, and most of what you say is affected bilge. Yet every time I think of something funny, I need *you* to laugh at it, and when I'm low, it's *you* I need to cheer me up. I don't know who you are, if you're anyone at all. Or whether you're here for the beer or because you're wildly in love with Roper. And I'm sure you don't know either. I think you're a total mess. But that doesn't put me off. Not at all. It makes me indignant, it makes me a fool, it makes me want to wring your neck. But that's just part of the package."

They were his own words. He was speaking for himself and nobody else. Nevertheless, the ruthless orphan in him could not resist shifting a little of the blame onto her shoulders. "Perhaps you shouldn't have nursed me so nicely. Lifting me up. Sitting on my bed. Let's say it's Daniel's fault for getting himself kidnapped. No, let's say it's mine for getting myself beaten up. And yours for making those spaniel eyes at me."

She shut her offending eyes and seemed to go to sleep for a moment. She opened them and lifted her hand to her face. And he was afraid that he had hit her too hard and invaded the tender ground that each of them guarded against the other.

"That's the most fucking impertinent thing *anyone* has said to me *ever,*" she said uncertainly, after quite a pause.

He let her dangle.

"Thomas!" she said, as if appealing for his help.

But he still did not come to her aid.

"*Jesus,* Thomas . . . oh, *fuck.* Thomas, this is *Roper*'s house!"

"It's Roper's house, and you're Roper's girl for as long as you can take it. My senses tell me you won't be able to take it much longer. Roper's a crook, as Caroline Langbourne has no doubt been telling you. He's not a buccaneer, or a Mississippi gambler, or a romantic adventurer, or however you decided to cast him when you picked each other up. He's an arms crook and at least a bit of a murderer." He took an outrageous step. He broke all Burr's rules and Rooke's in a single sentence. "That's why people like you and me end up spying on him," he said. "Leaving traces an inch deep all over his office. 'Jed was here.' 'Jed Marshall, her mark, her hair stuck in his papers.' He'd kill you for that. That's what he does. Kills." He paused to observe the effect of his backhanded confession on her, but she had frozen. "I'd better go and talk to Daniel," he said. "What's he supposed to have done to himself, anyway?"

"God knows."

She did a strange thing as he left. She was still at the door, and as he approached her, she took a step back to let him pass, which might have been normal courtesy. Then on some impulse that she could probably not have explained, she reached in front of him, turned the door handle and gave the door a shove, as if his hands were laden and he needed help.

Daniel was lying on his bed, reading his book on monsters.

"Jed just overreacted," he explained. "All I did was act up a little. But Jed went *berserk.*"

NINETEEN

IT WAS evening of the same day, and Jonathan was still alive, the sky was still in its place, no security gorillas fell on him out of the trees as he made his way back through the tunnel to Woody's House. The cicadas ticked and sobbed, the sun disappeared behind Miss Mabel's Mountain, dusk fell. He had played tennis with Daniel and the Langbourne children, he had swum with them and sailed with them, he had listened to Isaac on the subject of the Tottenham Hotspurs and to Esmeralda on evil spirits and to Caroline Langbourne on men, marriage and her husband.

"It isn't the *unfaithfulness* I mind, Thomas, it's the lying. I don't know why I'm telling you this, except you're *straight*. I don't care *what* he says about you, we *all* of us have our problems, but I know *straightness* when I see it. If he'd *only* say to me, 'I'm having an affair with Annabelle'— or *whoever* he's having an affair with at the time— 'and what's more I'm going to go *on* having an affair with her,' well, *I'd* say, 'All right. If that's the way we're playing it, so be it. Just don't expect *me* to be faithful while *you're* not.' I can *live* with that, Thomas. We have to if we're women. I *just* feel so furious I've let him have *all* my money and practically kept him for years, *and* let Daddy pay for the children's education, *only* to find that he's been lavishing money on any little trollop he happens to meet, leaving *us,* well, *not* penniless, but certainly not *flush.*"

During the rest of the day, he had spotted Jed twice: once in the summerhouse, wearing a yellow caftan and writing a letter, once walking with Daniel in the surf, her skirts pulled to her waist while she held his hand. And as Jonathan left the house, passing deliberately beneath her bedroom balcony, he heard her talking on the telephone to Roper: "No, darling, he didn't hurt himself at all, it was just fuss, and he got over it very quickly and did me an absolutely super painting of Sarah doing her airs above the ground right on top of the stable roof, you'll absolutely adore it. . . ."

And he thought: Now you tell him, *That was the good news, darling. But guess who I found skulking in our bedroom when I got upstairs. . . .*

. . .

IT WAS only when he reached Woody's House that time refused to pass. He let himself in cautiously, reasoning that if the protection had been alerted, their most likely course of action would be to go to his house ahead of him. So he entered by the back door and patrolled both floors before he felt able to extract the tiny steel cassette of film from his camera and, with a sharp knife from the kitchen, make a bed for it inside the pages of his paperback copy of *Tess of the D'Urbervilles.*

After that, things happened very much one by one.

He had a bath and thought: About now, you'll be having your shower, and nobody will be there to hand you your towel.

He made himself a chicken soup from left-overs that Esmeralda had given him, and he thought: About now, you and Caroline will be sitting on the patio eating Esmeralda's grouper with lemon sauce, and you'll be listening to another chapter of Caroline's life while her children are doing crisps and Coke and ice cream and watching *Young Frankenstein* in Daniel's play-room, and Daniel lies reading in his bedroom with the door shut, hating the pack of them.

Then he went to bed, because it seemed a good place to think about her. And remained in bed until twelve-thirty, at which time the naked close observer slid soundlessly to the floor and picked up the steel poker that he kept beneath it, because he had heard a furtive footfall on his doorstep. They've come for me, he thought. She's blown the whistle to Roper, and they're going to do a Woody on me.

But another voice in him spoke differently, and it was the voice he had been listening to ever since Jed had discovered him in her bedroom. So that by the time she tapped on his front door, he had put away the poker and knotted a sarong round his waist.

She too had dressed for the part: in a long dark skirt and a dark cape, and it would not have surprised him if she had turned up the Father Christmas hood, but she hadn't; it hung becomingly behind her. She was carrying a flashlight, and while he rechained the door she set it down and drew the cape more tightly round her. Then stood facing him with her hands crossed dramatically at her throat.

"You shouldn't have come," he said, quickly drawing the curtains. "Who saw you? Caroline? Daniel? The night staff?"

"No one."

"Of course they did. What about the boys at the lodge?"

"I tiptoed. No one heard me."

He stared at her in disbelief. Not because he thought she was lying but because of the sheer foolhardiness of her behavior. "So what can I get you?" he said in a tone that implied: since you've come.

"Coffee. Coffee, please. Don't make it specially."

Coffee, please. Egyptian, he remembered.

"They were watching television," she said. "The boys in the lodge. I could see them through the window."

"Sure."

He put on a kettle, then lit the pine logs in the grate, and for a while she shivered and frowned at the sputtering logs. Then she looked round the room, getting the idea of the place, and of him, taking in the books he had managed to assemble, and the spruceness of everything— the flowers, the watercolor of Carnation Bay propped on the chimneypiece beside Daniel's painting of a pterodactyl.

"Dans did a painting of Sarah for me," she said. "To make amends."

"I know. I was passing your room when you were telling Roper. What else did you tell him?"

"Nothing."

"Are you sure?"

She flared. "What do you expect me to tell him? Thomas thinks I'm a cheap little trollop without a thought in my head?"

"I didn't say that."

"You said worse. You said I was a mess and he was a murderer."

He handed her a mug of coffee. Black. No sugar. She drank some, both hands round the mug. "How the fuck did I get into this?" she asked. "Not you. Him. This place. Crystal. The whole shit."

"Corky said he bought you at a horse sale."

"I was shacked up in Paris."

"What were you doing in Paris?"

"Fucking these two men. The story of my

life. I fuck all the wrong people and miss out the right ones." She took another pull of coffee. "They had a flat on the rue de Rivoli. They scared the hell out of me. Drugs, boys, booze, girls, me, the whole bit. One morning I woke up and there was this flat full of bodies. Everyone had passed out." She nodded to herself as if to say, yes, that was it, that was the crunch. "Okay, Jemima, you don't collect two hundred quid, you just go. I didn't even pack. I stepped over the bodies and went to this bloodstock auction in Maison Lafitte that I'd read about in the *Trib*. I wanted to see horses. I was still half-stoned, and that was all I could think of: horses. That's all we ever did till my father had to sell up. Ride and pray. We're Shropshire Catholics," she explained gloomily, as if confessing the family curse. "I must have been smiling. Because this dishy middle-aged man said, 'Which one would you like?' And I said, 'That big one in the window.' I was feeling . . . light. Free. I was in a movie. That feeling. I was being funny. So he bought her. Sarah. The bidding was so quick I didn't really follow it. He had some Pakistani with him and they were sort of bidding together. Then he just turned to me and said, 'She's yours. Where do you want her sent?' I was scared stiff, but it was a dare, so I thought I'd see it through. He took me to a shop in the Élysées, and we were the only people. He'd had the riffraff cleared out before we got there. We were the only customers. He bought me ten thousand quids' worth of tat and took me to the opera. He took me to dinner and told me about an island called Crystal. Then he took me to his hotel and fucked me. And I thought: With one leap she clears the pit. He's not a *bad* man, Thomas. He just does bad things. He's like Archie the driver."

"Who's Archie the driver?"

She forgot him for a while, preferring to stare at the fire and sip her coffee. Her shivering had stopped. Once, she winced and drew in her shoulders, but it was her memory, not the cold, that was troubling her. *"Jesus,"* she whispered. "Thomas, what do I *do?"*

"Who's Archie?"

"In our village. He drove an ambulance for the local hospital. Everyone loved Archie the driver. He came to all the point-to-points and looked after people if they were hurt. He scraped up the bodies at the kids' gymkhanas, everything. Nice Archie. Then there was an ambulance strike, and Archie went and picketed the hospital gates and wouldn't let in the casualties because he said the drivers were all blacklegs. And Mrs. Luxome, who cleaned for the Priors, died because he wouldn't let her in." Another shudder passed over her. "Do you always have a fire? Seems silly, a fire in the tropics."

"You have them at Crystal."

"He really likes you. You know that?"

"Yes."

"You're his son or something. I kept telling him to get rid of you. I felt you coming closer, and I couldn't stop you. You're such a creep. He doesn't seem to see it. Perhaps he doesn't want to. I suppose it's Dan. You saved Dan. Still, that doesn't last forever, does it?" She drank. "Then you think: Okay, fuck it. If he won't see what's happening under his nose, that's his tough luck. Corky's warned him. So's Sandy. He doesn't listen to them."

"Why've you been going through his papers?"

"Caro told me a whole lot of stuff about him. Dreadful things. It wasn't fair. I knew some of it already. I'd tried not to, but you can't help it. Things people say at parties. Things Dan picks up. Those dreadful bankers, boasting. I can't *judge* people. Not *me*. I always think *I'm* in the hot seat, not them. The trouble is, we're so bloody straight. My father is. He'd rather starve than cheat the taxman. Always paid his bills the day they came in. That's why he went bust. Other people didn't pay *him,* of course, but he never noticed that." She glanced at him. Her glance became a look. *"Jesus,"* she whispered again.

"Did you find anything?"

She shook her head. "I couldn't, could I? I didn't know what to look for. So I thought, fuck it, and I asked him."

"You *what?*"

"I tackled him with it. One night after dinner. I said, 'Is it true you're a crook? Tell me. A girl's got a right to know.' "

Jonathan took a deep breath. "Well, that was honest at least," he said, with a careful smile. "How did Roper take it? Did he make a full confession, swear never to do wrong again, blame it all on his cruel childhood?"

"He went tight-faced."

"And said?"

"Said I should mind my bloody business."

Echoes of Sophie's account of her conversation with Freddie Hamid at the cemetery in Cairo invaded Jonathan's concentration.

"And you said it *was* your business?" he suggested.

"He said I wouldn't understand, even if he told me. I should shut up and not talk about things I didn't understand. Then he said, This isn't crime, this is politics. I said, *What* isn't crime? *What's* politics? Tell me the worst, I said. Give me the bottom line so that I know what I'm sharing."

"And Roper?" Jonathan asked.

"He says there isn't a bottom line. People like my father just think there is, which is why people like my father are suckers. He says he loves me and that's good enough. So I get angry and say, It may have been good enough for Eva Braun, but it isn't good enough for me. I thought he'd belt me. But he just took note. Nothing surprises him, do you know that? It's facts. One fact more, one fact less. Then you do the logical thing at the end of it."

Which was what he did to Sophie, thought Jonathan. "What about you?" he asked.

"What about me?" She wanted brandy. He hadn't any, so he gave her Scotch. "It's a lie," she said.

"What is?"

"What I'm living. Someone tells me who I am, and I believe them and go with it. That's what I do. I believe people. I can't help it. Now you come along and tell me I'm a mess, but that's not what he tells me. He says I'm his virtue. Me and Daniel, we're what it's all for. He said it straight out one night, in front of Corky." She took a gulp of Scotch. "Caro says he's pushing drugs. Did you know that? Some huge shipment, in exchange for arms and God knows what. We're not talking about sailing close to the wind. Not cutting a few corners or having a quiet joint at a party, she says. We're talking fully fledged, organized megacrime. She says I'm a gangster's moll—that's another version of me I'm trying to sort through. It's a thrill a minute being me these days."

Her gaze was on him again, straight and unblinking. "I'm in deep shit," she said. "I walked into this with my eyes wide shut. I deserve everything I get. Just don't tell me I'm a mess. I can do the sermons for myself. Anyway, what the fuck are *you* up to? You're no paragon."

"What does Roper say I'm up to?"

"You got into some heavy trouble. But you're a good chap. He's fixing you up. He's sick of Corky bitching about you. But then he didn't catch you prowling in our bedroom, did he?" she said, flaring again. "Let's hear it from you."

He took a long time to answer. First he thought of Burr, then he thought of himself and all the rules against talking. "I'm a volunteer," he said.

She pulled a sour face. "For the police?"

"Sort of."

"How much of you is you?"

"I'm waiting to find out."

"What will they do to him?"

"Catch him. Put him on trial. Lock him up."

"How can you *volunteer* for a job like that? Jesus."

No training covered this contingency. He gave himself time to think, and the silence, like the distance between them, seemed to join rather than divide them.

"It began with a girl," he said. He corrected himself. "A woman. Roper and another man arranged to have her killed. I felt responsible."

Shoulders hunched, the cape still gathered to her neck, she peered round the room, then back to him.

"Did you love her? The girl? The woman?"

"Yes." He smiled. "She was my virtue."

She took this in, uncertain whether to give it her approval. "When you saved Daniel, at Mama's, was that a lie too?"

"Pretty much."

He watched it all going through her head: the revulsion, the struggling to understand, the mixed moralities of her upbringing.

"Dr. Marti said they nearly killed you," she said.

"I nearly killed them. I lost my temper. It was a play that went wrong."

"What was her name?"

"Sophie."

"I need to hear about her."

She meant here, in this house, now.

. . .

HE TOOK HER up to the bedroom and lay alongside her without touching her while he told her about Sophie, and eventually she slept while he kept watch. She woke and wanted soda water, so he fetched some from the fridge. Then at five o'clock, before it was light, he put on his jogging gear and led her back along the tunnel to the gatehouse, not letting her use the flashlight but making her walk a pace behind him on his left side, as if she were a raw recruit he was leading into battle. And at the gatehouse he put his head and shoulders right into the window for one of his chats with Marlow the night guard, while Jed flitted by, he hoped unseen.

His anxiety was not eased when he returned to find Amos the Rasta sitting on his doorstep, needing a cup of coffee.

"You have a fine, upliftin' experience with your soul last night, Mist' Thomas, *sir?*" he inquired, pouring four heaped spoonfuls of sugar into his cup.

"It was an evening like any other, Amos. How about you?"

"Mist' Thomas, sir, I ain't smelt no fresh fire smoke at one a.m. of a Townside morning not since Mist' Woodman liked to entertain his lady friends to music and fine lovin'."

"Mr. Woodman would have done a lot better, by all accounts, to read an improving book."

Amos broke out in a wild chuckle. "There's only one man 'cept you on this island ever reads a *book,* Mist' Thomas. And he's ganja stupid and stone blind."

· · ·

THAT NIGHT, to his horror, she came to him again.

She was not wearing her cape this time but her riding gear, which she had evidently decided gave her some sort of immunity. He was appalled but not particularly surprised, for by then he had recognized Sophie's resolution in her, and he knew he could no more send her away than stop Sophie from going back to Cairo to face Hamid. So a quiet came over him, and it became a quiet shared. She took his hand and led him upstairs.

She guided him around his own bedroom, opening drawers and showing a distracted curiosity
about his shirts and underclothes. Something was
badly folded, so she folded it better. Something
was lost, and she found a partner for it. She drew
him to her and kissed him very exactly, as if she
had decided in advance how much of herself she
could afford to give him, and how little. When
they had kissed, she went downstairs again and
stood him under the overhead light and touched
his face with her fingertips, verifying him, photo-
graphing him with her eyes, making pictures of
him to take away with her. And in the incongruity
of the moment he remembered the old emigré
couple dancing at Mama Low's on the night of
the kidnapping, how they had touched each
other's faces in disbelief.

She asked for a glass of wine, and they sat on
the sofa drinking it and relishing the quiet they
had discovered they could share. She drew him to
his feet and kissed him once more, laying all her
body along him and spending a lot of time looking at his eyes as if to check them for sincerity.
Then she left him because, as she put it, that was
the most she could cope with until God pulled
another trick.

When she had gone, Jonathan went upstairs
to watch her from his window. Then he put his
copy of *Tess* in a brown envelope and addressed
it in illiterate capitals to THE ADULT SHOP, care of

a box number in Nassau given him by Rooke in the days of his youth. He dropped the envelope in the mailbox on the seafront for collection and shipment to Nassau by Roper jet next day.

. . .

"ENJOY OUR ALONENESS, did we, old love?" Corkoran inquired.

He was back in Jonathan's garden, drinking cold beer out of a can.

"Very much, thank you," said Jonathan politely.

"So one hears. Frisky says you enjoyed it. Tabby says you enjoyed it. Boys on the gate say you enjoyed it. Most of Townside seems to think you enjoyed it."

"Good."

Corkoran drank. He was wearing his Etonian Panama hat and his disgraceful Nassau suit, and he was talking out to sea. "And the Langbourne brood didn't cramp our style at all?"

"We managed a couple of expeditions. Caroline's a bit down-in-the-mouth, so the kids were rather pleased to get away from her."

"So *kind* we are," Corkoran reflected. "Such a *sport*. Such a proper *pet*. Just like Sammy. And I never even had the little sod." Pulling down the brim of his hat, he crooned *Nice work if you can get it* as if he were a mournful Ella Fitzgerald. "Message from the Chief for you, Mr. Pine. H hour is upon us. Prepare to kiss Crystal and everybody else goodbye. Firing squad assembles at dawn."

"Where am I going?"

Jumping to his feet, Corkoran marched down the garden steps to the beach as if he couldn't stand Jonathan's company anymore. He picked up a stone and, despite his bulk, skimmed it across the darkening water.

"In *my fucking place* is where you're going!" he shouted. "Thanks to some very classy foot-work by some shitty little queens unfriendly to the cause! Of whom I strongly suspect you to be the creature!"

"Corky, are you talking through your arse?"

Corkoran pondered the question. "Don't know, old love. Wish I did. Could be anal. Could be spot on." Another stone. "Prophet in the wil-derness, me. The Chief, though he'd never admit it, is a fully paid-up, unredeemable romantic. Roper believes in the light at the end of the pier. The trouble is, so did the fucking moth." Yet another stone, accompanied by an angry grunt of exertion. "Whereas Corky here is a dyed-in-the-wool skeptic. And my personal and professional view of you is, you're poison." Another stone. And another. "I *tell* him you're poison, and he won't believe me. He invented you. You plucked his baby from the flames. Whereas Corky here, thanks to persons unnamed—friends of yours, I suspect—is used goods." He drained his beer can and tossed it onto the sand while he searched for another pebble, which Jonathan obligingly handed him. "Well, let's face it, heart, one is going a *tad* to seed, isn't one?"

"I think one is becoming a *tad* deranged, actually, Corky," said Jonathan.

Corkoran brushed his hands together to get the sand off them. *"Jesus,* the effort of being criminal," he complained. "The people and the noise. The *sleaze.* The places one doesn't want to be. Don't you find the same? Of course you don't. You're above it. That's what I keep telling the Chief. Does he listen? Does he, my Khyber Pass."

"I can't help you, Corky."

"Oh, don't worry. I'll sort it out." He lit a cigarette and exhaled gratefully. "And now *this,"* he said, waving a hand at Woody's House behind him. "Two nights running, my spies tell me. I'd like to peach to the Chief, of course. Nothing would please me more. But I can't do it to our lady of Crystal. Can't speak for the others, though. Someone will bubble. Someone always does." Miss Mabel Island became a black stencil against the moon. "Never could do evenings. Hate the fuckers. Never could do mornings either, for that matter. Nothing but bloody deathbells. You get about ten minutes in a good day, if you're Corky. One more for the Queen?"

"No, thanks."

· · ·

IT WAS never going to be an easy departure. They assembled on Miss Mabel's airstrip in the early light like so many refugees, Jed wearing dark glasses and deciding to see nobody. On the plane, still with her dark glasses, she sat hunched in a back row, with Corkoran on one side of her and Daniel on the other, while Frisky and Tabby flanked Jonathan up front. When they landed at Nassau, MacArthur was hovering at the barrier. Corkoran handed him the passports, including Jonathan's, and everybody was waved through, no problems.

"Jed's going to be sick," Daniel announced as they climbed into the new Rolls. Corkoran told him to shut up.

The Roper mansion was stucco Tudor and creepery and wore an unexpected air of neglect.

In the afternoon, Corkoran took Jonathan on a grand shopping spree in Freetown. Corkoran was in an erratic mood. Several times he paused to refresh himself at nasty little bars, while Jonathan drank Coke. Everyone seemed to know Corkoran, some people a little too well. Frisky trailed them at a distance. They bought three very expensive Italian business suits—trousers to be adjusted by yesterday, please, Clive, darling, or the Chief will be *furious*—then half a dozen town shirts, socks and ties to match, shoes and belts, a lightweight navy raincoat, underclothes, linen handkerchiefs, pajamas and a fine leather sponge bag with an electric razor and a pair of handsome hairbrushes with silver T's: "My friend won't accept *anything* that isn't done to a T—will you, heart?" And when they got back to the Roper mansion, Corkoran completed his creation by producing a pigskin wallet full of mainline credit cards in the name of Thomas, a black leather attaché case, a gold wristwatch by Piaget and a pair of gold cufflinks engraved with the initials DST.

So that by the time everyone was assembled in the drawing room for Dom, Jed and Roper glowing and relaxed, Jonathan was the very model of a modern young executive.

"What do we think of him, loves?" Corkoran demanded with a creator's pride.

"Bloody good," said Roper, not much caring.

"Super," said Jed.

After Dom, they went to Enzo's restaurant on Paradise Island, which was where Jed ordered lobster salad.

· · ·

AND THAT WAS all it was. One lobster salad. Jed had her arm round Roper's neck while she ordered it. And kept her arm there while Roper passed her order to the proprietor. They were side by side because it was their last night together, and as everybody knew, they were these terrific lovers.

"Darlings," said Corkoran, raising his wine to them. "Perfect pairing. So incredibly beautiful. Let no man put asunder." And he swallowed a glassful at a gulp, while the proprietor, who was Italian and mortified, regretted there was no more lobster salad.

"Veal, Jeds?" Roper suggested. *"Penne*'s good. *Pollo?* Have a *pollo.* No, you won't. Full of garlic. Put you out of bounds. Fish. Bring her a fish. Like a fish, Jeds? Sole? What fish you got?"

"Any fish," said Corkoran, "should appreciate the sacrifice."

Jed had fish instead of lobster.

Jonathan also had fish and pronounced it sublime. Jed said hers was gorgeous. So did the MacDanbies, commandeered at no notice to make up Roper's kind of numbers.

"Doesn't look gorgeous to me," said Corkoran.

"Oh, but Corks, it's *far* better than lobster. My absolute favorite."

"Lobster on the menu, whole island stiff with lobster, why the hell haven't they got it?" Corkoran insisted.

"They just goofed, Corks. We can't all be geniuses like you."

Roper was preoccupied. Not in a hostile way. He just had things on his mind, and his hand in Jed's lap. But Daniel, soon to go back to England, chose to challenge his father's detachment.

"Roper's got the black monkey on his back," he announced to an unfortunate silence. "He's got this mega-megadeal coming off. It's going to put him beyond reach."

"Dans, put a sock in it," said Jed smartly.

"What's brown and sticky?" Daniel asked. No one knew. "A stick," he said.

"Dans, old chap, shut up," said Roper.

But Corkoran was their destiny that night, and Corkoran had launched himself on a story about this investment consultant chum of his called Shortwar Wilkins, who at the outbreak of the Iran-Iraq thing had advised his clients that it would all be over in six weeks.

"What happened to him?" Daniel demanded.

"Gentleman of leisure, I'm afraid, Dan. Pooped, most of the time. Bums money from his chums. Bit like me in a couple of years' time. Remember me, Thomas, when you drive by in your Roller and chance to see a familiar face sweeping out the gutters. Toss us a sovereign, for old times' sake, will you, heart? Good health, Thomas. Long life, sir. May *all* your lives be long. Cheers."

"And to you too, Corky," said Jonathan.

A MacDanby tried to tell *his* story about something or other, but Daniel again interrupted:

"How do you save the world?"

"You tell me, old heart," said Corkoran. "Dying to know."

"Kill mankind."

"Dans, *shut up,*" said Jed. "You're being horrid."

"I only said *kill mankind!* That's a *joke!* Can't you even understand a *joke?*" Raising both arms, he fired an imaginary machine gun at everybody round the table. "Bah-bah-bah-bah-bah! *There! Now* the world's safe. No one in it."

"Thomas, take Dans for a walk," Roper ordered down the table. "Bring him back when he's sorted out his manners."

But while Roper was saying this—without too much conviction, since Daniel on this evening of departure was deserving of indulgence—a lobster salad went by. Corkoran saw it. And Corkoran grabbed the wrist of the black waiter who was carrying it and wrenched him to his side.

"Hey, *man,*" the startled waiter cried, then grinned sheepishly round the room in the hope that he was part of some weird happening.

The proprietor was hastening across the room. Frisky and Tabby, seated at the gunmen's table in the corner, had risen to their feet, unbuttoning their blazers. Everybody froze.

Corkoran was standing. And Corkoran with unexpected power was bearing down on the waiter's arm and making the poor man twist against his inclination so that the tray tipped alarmingly. Corkoran's face was brick red, his chin was up and he was shouting at the proprietor.

"Do you speak English, sir?" he demanded,

loud enough for the whole restaurant to hear. *"I do. Our lady here ordered lobster, sir. You said there was no more lobster. You are a liar, sir. And you have offended our lady and her consort, sir. There was more lobster!"*

"Was ordered in advance!" the proprietor protested, with more spirit than Jonathan had credited him with. "Was special order. Ten o'-clock this morning. You want be sure of lobster? *You* order special. Let go this man!"

Nobody at the table had moved. Grand opera has its own authority. Even Roper seemed momentarily unsure whether to intervene.

"What is your name?" Corkoran asked the proprietor.

"Enzo Fabrizzi."

"Leave it out, Corks," Roper ordered. "Don't be a bore. You're being a bore."

"Corks, *stop* it," said Jed.

"If there is a dish our lady wants, Mr. Fabrizzi, whether it's lobster, or liver, or fish, or something very ordinary like steak, or a piece of veal—you *always* give it to our lady. Because if you don't, Mr. Fabrizzi, I shall buy this restaurant. I am vastly rich, sir. And you will sweep the street, sir, while Mr. Thomas here purrs past in his Rolls-Royce."

Jonathan, resplendent in his new suit at the further end of the table, has risen to his feet and is smiling his Meister's smile.

"Time to break the party up, don't you

think, Chief?" he says, awfully pleasantly, strolling to Roper's end of the table. "Everyone a bit travel weary. Mr. Fabrizzi, I don't remember when I had a better meal. All we *really* need now is a bill, if your people could kindly run one up."

Jed stands to go, looking nowhere. Roper lays her wrap over her shoulders. Jonathan pulls back her chair, and she smiles her distant gratitude. A MacDanby pays. There is a muffled cry as Corkoran lunges at Fabrizzi with serious intent— but Frisky and Tabby are there to restrain him, which is fortunate because by now several of the restaurant staff are spoiling to avenge their comrade. Somehow everybody makes it to the pavement as the Rolls pulls alongside.

I'm not going anywhere, she had said vehemently, as she held Jonathan's face and stared into his solitary eyes. *I've faked it before, I can fake it again. I can fake it for as long as it takes.*

He'll kill you, Jonathan had said. *He'll find out. He's certain to. Everybody's talking about us behind his back.*

But, like Sophie, she seemed to think she was immortal.

TWENTY

QUIET AUTUMN RAIN is falling in the Whitehall streets as Rex Goodhew goes to war. Quietly. In the autumn of his career. In the mature certainty of his cause. Without drama or trumpets or large statements. A quiet outing of his fighting self. A personal but also an altruistic war against what he has come inevitably to refer to as the Forces of Darker.

A war to the death, he tells his wife, without alarms. My head or theirs. A Whitehall knife fight, let's stay close. If you're sure, darling, she says. I am. His every move carefully considered. Nothing hasty, nothing too young, too furtive. He is sending clear signals to his hidden enemies in Pure Intelligence. Let them hear me, let them see me, he says. Let them tremble. Goodhew plays with open cards. More or less.

It is not only Neal Marjoram's disgraceful proposition that has spurred Goodhew into action. A week ago, he was nearly crushed to death cycling to his office. Selecting his favorite scenic route—first west across Hampstead Heath, respecting the permitted cycle paths, thence by way of Saint John's Wood and Regent's Park to

Whitehall—Goodhew found himself wedged between two high-sided vans, one a dirty white color with flaking lettering he couldn't read, and the other green and blank. If he braked, they braked also. If he pedaled harder, they accelerated. His perplexity turned to anger. Why did the drivers eye him so coldly in their wing mirrors, then eye each other as they edged ever closer, boxing him in? What was this third van doing behind him, blocking his escape?

He shouted, "Look out! Move over!" but they ignored him. The van behind was riding tight against the rear bumpers of the other two. Its windscreen was grubby, obscuring the driver's face. The vans on either side had drawn so close that if he had turned the handlebar, it would have knocked against one or the other of them.

Rising in his saddle, Goodhew drove his gloved fist against the panel of the van to his left, then pushed himself away from it to recover his balance. The dead eyes in the wing mirror studied him without curiosity. He attacked the van to his right in the same way. It responded by inching nearer.

Only a red traffic light saved him from being crushed. The vans stopped, but Goodhew, for the first time in his life, rode over on red, narrowly escaping death as he skimmed in front of the polished nose of a Mercedes.

· · ·

THE SAME AFTERNOON, RexGoodhewrewriteshis will. Next day, using his in-house wiles, he circumnavigates the laborious machinery of his own ministry—and his master's private office—and sequesters part of the top floor, a rambling set of attic rooms, already a museum piece, packed with electronic stay-behind equipment installed against the day, just around the corner, when Britain will be overrun by Bolshevism. The likelihood is now past, but the gray men of Goodhew's Administration Section have yet to be advised of this, and when Goodhew requests the floor for secret purposes, they could not be more helpful. Overnight, millions of pounds' worth of obsolete equipment is sent to rot in a lorry park in Aldershot.

Next day Burr's little team becomes the tenant of twelve musty attic rooms, two malfunctioning lavatories the size of tennis courts, a denuded signals room, a private staircase with a marble balustrade and holes in the linoleum treads, and a steel door by Chubb, with a turnkey's peephole. On the day after, Goodhew has the place electronically swept and removes all telephone lines susceptible to River House tampering.

In the matter of extracting public money from his ministry, Goodhew's quarter-century before the Whitehall mast is not in vain. He becomes a bureaucratic Robin Hood, fiddling the government's accounts in order to ensnare its wayward servants.

Burr needs three more staff and knows where he can find them? Hire them, Leonard, hire them.

An informant has a tale to tell but needs a couple of thousand up front? Pay him, Leonard, give him whatever he needs.

Rob Rooke would like to take a brace of watchers with him to Curaçao? Is a brace enough, Rob? Wouldn't a foursome be a safer bet?

Gone as if they had never been are Goodhew's niggling objections, the quips, the fey asides. He has only to pass through the steel door to Burr's new attic eyrie for the persiflage to fall from him like the cloak it always was. Each evening, at the close of the day's official play, he presents himself for what he modestly calls his night work, and Burr is pressed to match the energy with which he goes about his business. On Goodhew's insistence, the dingiest room has been set aside for him. It lies at the end of a deserted corridor, its windows give onto a parapet colonized by pigeons. Their billing and cooing would have driven a lesser man crazy, but Goodhew barely hears them. Determined not to trespass on Burr's operational territory, he emerges only to grab another handful of reports or make himself a cup of rose hip tea and exchange courteous pleasantries with the night staff. Then back to his desk and his review of the enemy's latest dispositions.

"I intend to sink their Operation Flagship

with all hands, Leonard," he tells Burr with a twitch of his head that Burr has not seen him do before. "Darker won't have a Mariner left when I've done with him. And your Dicky Blasted Roper will be safe behind bars, you mark my words."

Burr marks them but is uncertain of their truth. It is not that he doubts Goodhew's strength of purpose. Nor does he have any problem believing that Darker's people deliberately set out to harass, scare or even hospitalize their adversary. For months, Burr himself has been maintaining a careful watchfulness over his own movements. Whenever possible he has driven his children to school in the mornings, and always arranged for their collection in the evenings. Burr's concern is that, even now, Goodhew is unaware of the scale of the octopus. Three times in the last week alone, Burr has been denied access to papers that he knows to be in current circulation. Three times in vain he has protested. On the last occasion he presented himself in person to the Foreign Office Registrar in his lair.

"I fear you are misinformed, Mr. Burr," said the registrar, who wore an undertaker's black tie, and black protectors on the sleeves of his black jacket. "The file in question was cleared for destruction many months ago."

"You mean it's Flagship classified. Why don't you say so?"

"It's *what,* sir? I don't think I follow you. Do you mind explaining yourself more clearly?"

"Limpet is my case, Mr. Atkins. I personally opened the file that I am now requesting. It's one of half a dozen Limpet-related files opened and cross-referred by my department: two subject, two organization, two personal. There's not one of them that's been in existence above eighteen months. Who ever heard of a registrar authorizing the destruction of a file eighteen months after it went into action?"

"I'm sorry, Mr. Burr. Limpet may indeed be your case. I have no reason to disbelieve you, sir. But as we say in Registry, just because you own the case, you don't always own the file."

. . .

NEVERTHELESS, the flow of information continues at an impressive rate. Both Burr and Strelski have their sources:

The deal is firming up . . . the Panama connection is on line . . . six Panama-registered container ships on charter to Ironbrand of Nassau are heading across the South Atlantic bound for Curaçao, estimated date of arrival five to eight days from now. Between them they carry close to four hundred containers en route for the Panama Canal . . . the description of their freight varies from tractor parts to agricultural machinery to mining equipment to miscellaneous luxury goods. . . .

Handpicked military trainers, including four French paras, two Israeli ex-colonels of special forces, and six ex–Soviet Spetsnaz, met in Amsterdam last week for a munificent farewell *rijstafel* in the city's best Indonesian restaurant. Afterwards they were flown to Panama. . . .

Tales of large orders of matériel by Roper's nominees have been circulating in the arms bazaars for several months, but there has been a new gloss, which is to say that Palfrey's predictions of a switch in Roper's shopping list have found independent confirmation. Strelski's Brother Michael alias Apostoll has been talking to a fellow cartel lawyer named Moranti. The said Moranti operates out of Caracas and is held to be the mainstay of the shaky alliance between the cartels.

"Your Mr. Roper is going patriotic," Strelski announces to Burr over the secure telephone. "He's buying American."

Burr's heart sinks, but he plays unconcerned. "That's not patriotic, Joe! A Brit should be buying British."

"He's selling a new message to the cartels," says Strelski, undeterred. "If their perceived enemy is Uncle Sam, they're best off using Uncle Sam's toys. That way they have direct access to spares, they have captured enemy weapons they can assimilate, they are familiar with the enemy's techniques. British Starstreak HVMs, shoulder-held, British flag grenades, British tech, that's part of the package. Sure. But their mainstream toys, they have to be a mirror image of the perceived enemy. Some Brit, the rest American."

"So what do the cartels say?" Burr asks.

"They love it. They're in love with American technology. British too. They love Roper. They want the best."

"Does anybody explain what brought on this change of heart?"

Burr detects a concern comparable with his own below the surface of Strelski's voice.

"No, Leonard. Nobody explains a fucking thing. Not to Enforcement. Not in Miami. Maybe not in London either."

The story was confirmed a day later by a dealer of Burr's acquaintance in Belgrade. Sir Anthony Joyston Bradshaw, well known as Roper's signer in the shadier marketplaces, had the previous day switched a three-million-dollar pilot order for Czech Kalashnikovs to a similar order for American Armalites, destined theoretically for Tunisia. The guns were to be lost in transit and rerouted as agricultural machinery to Gdansk, where storage and onward transportation on a Panama-bound container ship had been arranged. Joyston Bradshaw had also expressed interest in British-built ground-to-air rockets but was allegedly demanding an inordinate side commission for himself.

But while Burr grimly noted this development, Goodhew appeared unable to grasp its implications:

"I don't care whether they're buying American guns or Chinese peashooters, Leonard. I don't care whether they're stripping the British bare. It's drugs for arms whichever way you look at it, and there's not a court on earth will condone it."

Burr noticed that as Goodhew said this he flushed and seemed to have difficulty keeping his temper.

. . .

STILL, the information pours in:

No location for the exchange of goods has so far been agreed upon. Only the two principals will know the final details in advance. . . .

The cartels have set aside the port of Buenaventura on the west coast of Colombia as the point of departure for their shipment, and past practice suggests that the same port will be used as the reception point for the incoming matériel. . . .

Well-armed if incompetent units of the Colombian army in the cartels' pay have been dispatched to the Buenaventura area to provide cover for the transaction. . . .

A hundred empty army trucks are mustered in the dockside warehouses—but when Strelski requests a sight of the satellite photographs that could confirm or deny this information, so he tells

Burr, he hits a brick wall. The espiocrats of Langley decree that he does not possess the necessary clearance.

"Leonard, will you please tell me something. What the fuck is Flagship in all this?"

Burr's head reels. It is his understanding that in Whitehall, code name Flagship is doubly restricted. Not only is it confined to those who are Flagship cleared, it is graded *Guard,* keep away from Americans. So what on earth is Strelski doing, an American, being refused access to code name Flagship by the barons of Pure Intelligence in Langley, Virginia?

"Flagship is nothing but a fence to keep us out," Burr fumes to Goodhew, minutes later. "If Langley can know about it, why can't we? For Flagship read Darker and his friends across the pond."

Goodhew is deaf to Burr's indignation. He pores over shipping maps, draws himself routes in colored crayons, reads up on compass bearings, stopover times and port formalities. He buries himself in works on maritime law and beards a grand legal authority he was at school with: "Now, what do you know, Brian, if anything," Burr hears him piping down the bare corridor, "about interdiction at sea? *Certainly* I'm not going to pay your ridiculous fees! I'm going to give you a *very* bad lunch at my club and steal two hours of your *grossly* inflated professional time in

the interest of your country. How's your wife putting up with you now you're a lord? Well, give her
my sympathy and meet me on Thursday prompt
at one."

You're coming on too strong, Rex, thinks
Burr. Slow down. We're still a long way from
home.

. . .

NAMES, Rooke had said: names and numbers.
Jonathan is providing them by the score. To
the uninitiated his offerings might seem at first
glance trivial: nicknames culled from place cards
at the dinner table, fugitive conversations partly overheard, the glimpse of a letter lying on
Roper's desk, Roper's jottings to himself about
the who, the how much, the how and when.
Taken singly, such snippets made poor fare
beside Pat Flynn's clandestine photographs of
Spetsnaz-turned-mercenaries arriving at Bogotá
airport; or Amato's hair-raising accounts of Corkoran's secret rampages in the Nassau flesh-
pots; or intercepted bank drafts from respectable financial houses, showing tens of millions
of dollars homing on Roper-related offshore companies in Curaçao.

Yet properly assembled, Jonathan's reports
provided revelations that were as sensational as
any great dramatic coup. After a night of them,
Burr declared that he felt seasick. After two,
Goodhew remarked that he would not be sur-

prised to read of his own high-street bank manager showing up in Crystal with a suitcase full of clients' cash.

It was not so much the tentacles of the octopus as its ability to enter the most hallowed shrines that left them aghast. It was the involvement of institutions that even Burr had till now presumed inviolate, of names above reproach.

For Goodhew, it was as if the very pageantry of England was dying before his eyes. Dragging himself homeward in the small hours, he would pause to stare feverishly at a parked police car and wonder whether the daily stories of police violence and corruption were true after all, not the invention of journalists and malcontents. Entering his club, he would spot eminent merchant bankers or stockbrokers of his acquaintance and—instead of flapping a hand at them in cheery greeting, as he would have done three months ago—would study them from under lowered brows across the dining room, asking them in his mind: Are you another of them? Are *you?* Are *you?*

"I shall make a démarche," he declared at one of their late-night threesomes. "I've decided. I'll convene Joint Steering. I'll mobilize the Foreign Office for a start; they're always good for a fight against the Darkists. Merridew will stand up and be counted, I'm sure he will."

"Why should he?" said Burr.

"Why shouldn't he?"

"Merridew's brother is top man in Jason Warhole, if I remember rightly. Jason's put in for five hundred bearer bonds in the Curaçao company at half a million a crack last week."

. . .

"DREADFULLY sorry about this, old boy," Palfrey whispered, from the shadows that seemed always to surround him.

About what, Harry?" said Goodhew kindly.

Palfrey's haunted eyes glanced past him at the doorway. He was sitting in a North London pub of his own choosing, not far from Goodhew's house in Kentish Town. "Panicking. Ringing your office. Distress rocket. How did you get here so fast?"

"Bike, of course. What's the matter, Harry? You look as though you've seen a ghost. They haven't been threatening *your* life too, have they?"

"Bike," Palfrey repeated, taking a pull of Scotch and immediately wiping his mouth with a handkerchief as if to remove the guilty traces. "About the best thing anyone can do, bike. Fellows on the pavement can't keep up. Fellows in cars have to keep going round the block. Mind if we go next door? Noisier."

They sat in the games room, where there was a jukebox to drown their conversation. Two

muscular-looking boys with crew cuts were playing bar billiards. Palfrey and Goodhew sat side by
side on a wooden settle.

Palfrey struck a match and had difficulty
bringing the flame to his cigarette. "Things are
hotting up," he murmured. "Burr's getting a bit
warm. I warned them, but they wouldn't listen.
Time to take the gloves off."

"You *warned* them, Harry?" Goodhew
said, mystified as ever by the complexity of Palfrey's systems of betrayal. "Warned whom? Not
Darker? You don't mean you warned Darker, do
you?"

"Got to play both sides of the net, old boy,"
said Palfrey, wrinkling his nose and casting another nervous glance around the bar. "Only way
to survive. Got to keep up your credibility. Both
ends." A frantic smile. "Tapping my phone," he
explained, pointing at his ear.

"Who is?"

"Geoffrey. Geoffrey's people. Mariners.
Flagship people."

"How do you know?"

"Oh, you don't. Can't tell. No one can. Not
these days. Not unless it's sort of Third World. Or
the police doing it with their feet. No way." He
drank, shaking his head. "It's hitting the fan, Rex.
Getting a bit big." He drank again, quick sips. He
muttered "Cheers," forgetting he had said Cheers
already. "They tip me the word. Secretaries. Old

buddies from Legal Department. They don't *say* it, you see. Don't have to. Not, 'Excuse me, Harry, my boss is tapping your phone.' It's hints." Two men in motorcycle leathers had begun a game of shove-halfpenny. "I say, would you mind if we went somewhere else?"

There was an empty trattoria opposite the cinema. The time was six-thirty. The Italian waiter despised them.

"The boys have done over my flat too," Palfrey said, sniggering as if he were relating a smutty joke. "Didn't pinch anything. My landlord told me. Two chums of mine. Said I'd given them the key."

"Had you?"

"No."

"Have you given a key to anyone else?"

"Well, you know. Girls and things. Most of 'em give 'em back."

"So they *have* been threatening you; I was right." Goodhew ordered spaghetti and a bottle of Chianti. The waiter pulled a sour face and yelled through the kitchen door. Palfrey's fear was all over him. It was like a breeze, plucking at his knees and taking his breath away before he spoke.

"Bit hard to unlock oneself, actually, Rex," Palfrey explained apologetically. "Habits of a lifetime, I suppose. Can't get the toothpaste back in the tube once you've sat on it. Problem." He ducked his mouth to the brim of his glass to catch the wine before it spilled. "Need a helping hand, as it were. Sorry about that."

As so often with Palfrey, Goodhew felt he was listening to a faulty broadcast of which the meaning came only in garbled bursts. "I can't promise you anything, Harry. You know that. There are no free dispensations in life. Everything has to be earned. I believe that. I think you do too."

"Yes, but you've got the guts," Palfrey objected.

"And you've got the knowledge," said Goodhew.

Palfrey's eyes popped wide in amazement. "That's what *Darker* said! Bang on! Too much knowledge. Dangerous knowledge. My bad luck! You're a marvel, Rex. Bloody clairvoyant."

"So you've been talking to Geoffrey Darker. What about?"

"Well, him to me, really. I just listened."

"When?"

"Yesterday. No, Friday. Came and saw me in my room. Ten to one. Just putting on my mac. 'What are you doing for lunch?' Thought he was going to invite me. 'Well, just a vague date at my club,' I said. 'Nothing I can't cancel.' So he said, 'Good. Cancel it.' So I canceled. Then we talked. In the lunch hour. In my office. Nobody around. Not even a glass of Perrier or a dry biscuit. Good tradecraft, though. Geoffrey always had good tradecraft."

He grinned again.

"And he said?" Goodhew prompted.

"He said"—Palfrey took a huge breath, like somebody about to do a length under water—"he said it was time for good men to come to the aid of the party. Said the Cousins wanted a clear run on the Limpet thing. They could take care of their Enforcement people all right, but they counted on us to take care of ours. Wanted to be sure I was aboard."

"And you said?"

"I was. Hundred percent. Well, I am. Aren't I?" He bridled. "You're not suggesting I should have told him to stuff it, are you? Christ!"

"Of course I'm not, Harry. You must do what is best for you. I understand that. So you said you were aboard. What did he say then?"

Palfrey relapsed into an aggressive sullenness. "He wanted a legal reading of the River House's demarcation deal with the Burr agency by Wednesday five p.m. The deal I drafted for you. I undertook to provide it."

"And?"

"That's all there is. Wednesday five p.m. is my deadline. The Flagship team will be holding a meeting the next morning. He'll need time to study my report first. I said, No problem."

The abrupt halt, on a high note, accompanied by a lifting of the brows, gave Goodhew pause. When his son made the same gesture, it meant that he was concealing something. Goodhew had a similar suspicion about Palfrey.

"Is that all?"

"Why shouldn't it be?"

"Was Darker pleased with you?"

"Very, as a matter of fact."

"Why? You'd only agreed to obey orders, Harry. Why should he be pleased with you? Did you agree to do something else for him?" Goodhew had the strange sense that Palfrey was urging him to press harder. "Did you tell him something perhaps?" he suggested, smiling in order to make confession more attractive.

Palfrey gave an anguished grin.

"But, Harry—what could you possibly have told Darker that he didn't know already?"

Palfrey was really trying. It was as if he was taking repeated runs at the same hurdle, determined to clear it sooner or later.

"Did you tell him about *me?*" Goodhew suggested. "You couldn't have done. It would have been suicide. Did you?"

Palfrey was shaking his head. "Never," he whispered. "Scout's honor, Rex. Wouldn't cross my mind."

"Then what?"

"Just a theory, Rex. Presumption, that's all. Hypothesis. Law of probabilities. Not secrets, nothing bad. Theories. Idle theories. Chit-chat. Pass the time of day. Chap standing in my room. Lunchtime. Staring at me. Got to tell him *something.*"

"Theories based on what?"

"The submission I prepared for you. About the sort of criminal case against Roper that would stick under English law. I worked on it in your office. You remember."

"Of course I remember. What was your theory?"

"There was this American secret annex that got it all going, prepared by their Enforcement people in Miami. The summary of evidence to date. Strelski, that the chap? Roper's original pitch to the cartels, the broad elements of the deal, all very shrouded, very top secret. Yours and Burr's eyes only."

"And your eyes too, of course," Goodhew suggested, pulling back from him in a presentiment of disgust.

"I played this game, you see. The one you can't help playing when you read a report like that. Well, we all do, don't we? Can't help it. Natural curiosity. Can't stop your *mind* going . . . spot the snitch. These long passages with only three chaps in the room. Two sometimes. Wherever they were, there was always this reliable source peaching on them. Well, I know modern technology is the cat's whiskers, but this was ridiculous."

"So you spotted the snitch."

Palfrey looked really proud, like a man who has finally put his courage together and done his duty for the day.

"And you told Darker whom you'd spotted," Goodhew suggested.

"The Greek chap. Hand in glove with the cartels and ratting on them to Enforcement as soon as their backs were turned. Apostoll. Lawyer, just like me."

. . .

INFORMED BY Goodhew that same night of Palfrey's indiscretion, Burr faced the dilemma every agent-runner dreads most.

His first response typically was from the heart. He drafted an urgent personal signal to Strelski in Miami, saying he had reason to believe that "unfriendly Purists are now conscious of the identity of your Brother Michael." He changed "conscious" to "witting" out of deference to the American espiocrats' jargon and sent it. He forbore from suggesting that the leak was British. Strelski could work that out for himself. His duty by Strelski done, the descendant of Yorkshire handloom weavers sat stoically in his attic room, staring through the skylight at the orange Whitehall sky. No longer was Burr eating out his heart for a sign, any sign, of his agent. Now it was his duty to decide whether to pull his agent out or swallow the risk and carry on. Still pondering, he ambled down the long corridor and perched himself, hands in pockets, on the radiator in Goodhew's office, while the pigeons argued on the parapet.

"Shall we do worst case?" Goodhew suggested.

"Worst case is, they put Apo under a bright light and he tells them he had orders from us to discredit Corkoran as a signer," said Burr. "Then they target my boy as the new signer."

"Who is *they* in this scenario, Leonard?"

Burr shrugged. "Apo's clients. Or the Purists."

"But good heavens, Leonard, Pure Intelligence is on our side. We have our differences, but they wouldn't endanger *our* source merely because of a turf war between . . ."

"Oh yes they would, Rex," Burr said kindly. "That's who they are, you see. That's what they do."

· · ·

ONCE AGAIN Burr sat in his room, contemplating his choice alone. A gambler's green desk lamp. A weaver's skylight to the stars.

Roper: two more weeks and I can have you. I'll know which ship, I'll know the names and numbers and the places. I'll have a case against you that not all your privilege and your smart insider friends and not all the legal sophistry in the business can buy off.

Jonathan: the best joe I ever had, the only

one whose code I never cracked. First I knew you as an inscrutable face. Now I know you as an inscrutable voice: *Yes, fine, thanks, Leonard. . . . Well, Corkoran does suspect me, but poor chap, he can't quite work out what he suspects me of. . . . Jed? Well, she is still in favor, so far as one can judge, but she and Roper are such behaviorists, it's jolly hard to tell what goes on underneath. . . .*

Behaviorist, thought Burr grimly. My God, if *you're* not a behaviorist, who is? What about your little spot of temperament at Mama Low's?

The Cousins will do nothing, he decided in a spurt of optimism. An agent identified is an agent gained. Even if they succeed in identifying Jonathan, they'll sit on their thumbs and wait to see what he produces.

The Cousins are sure to act, he told himself, as the pendulum swung the other way. Apostoll is their expendable asset. If the Cousins want to deserve favor with the cartels, they'll make them a present of Apostoll. If they think we're getting too close for comfort, they'll blow Apostoll and deprive us of our source. . . .

Chin in hand, Burr gazed up at the skylight, watching the autumn dawn appear between the torn ridges of cloud.

Abort, he decided. Spirit Jonathan to safety, change his face, give him yet another name, put up the shutters and go home.

And spend your life wondering which of the

six ships currently on charter to Ironbrand contain the arms haul of a lifetime?

And where the exchange of merchandise took place?

And how hundreds, perhaps thousands of millions of pounds' worth of bearer bonds vanished without trace into the well-tailored pockets of their anonymous bearers?

And how tens of tons of top-grade refined cocaine at airstrip prices went conveniently missing somewhere between the west coast of Colombia and the Free Zone of Colón, to resurface in sensibly controlled quantities, never too much at a time, on the joyless streets of Middle Europe?

And Joe Strelski and Pat Flynn and Amato and their team? All their miles in the saddle? For nothing? Handed to Pure Intelligence on a plate? Not even to Pure Intelligence, but to some sinister brotherhood within it?

The secure phone rang. Burr grabbed the receiver. It was Rooke, reporting from Curaçao on his field handset.

"The man's jet landed here an hour ago," he announced, with his built-in reluctance to mention names. "Our friend was of the party."

"How did he look?" Burr asked eagerly.

"Fit. No scars that I could see. Nice suit. Smart shoes. Had a crusher either side of him, but that didn't seem to cramp his style. Pink of condition, if you ask me. You said to ring you, Leonard."

Burr stared round him at the maps and sea charts. At the aerial photographs of tracts of jungle ringed in red. At the heaps of files littering the old deal desk. He remembered all the months of labor, now hanging by a thread.

"We stay with the operation," he said.

He flew to Miami next day.

TWENTY-ONE

THE FRIENDSHIP between Jonathan and Roper that, as Jonathan now realized, had been budding throughout the weeks at Crystal burst into flower the moment the Roper jet cleared Nassau International Airport. You might have thought the two men had agreed to wait for this shared moment of release before they acknowledged their good feelings for each other.

"Christ," Roper shouted, gleefully unfastening his seat belt. "Women! Questions! Kids! Thomas, good to have you aboard. Megs, bring us a pot of coffee, darling. Too early for shampoo. Coffee, Thomas?"

"I'd love some," said the hotelier. And added winningly: "After Corky's performance last night, I could do with rather a lot of it."

"Hell was all that stuff about you having a Roller?"

"I've no idea. I think he must have decided I was going to steal yours."

"Ass. Sit over here. Don't lurk across the aisle. Croissants, Megs? Red jelly?"

Meg was the stewardess, from Tennessee.

"Mr. Roper, now when did I ever forget the croissants?"

"Coffee, hot croissants, bread rolls, jelly, all round. Get that feeling sometimes, Thomas? *Free?* No kids, animals, servants, investors, guests, inquisitive women? Got your world back? Free to *move?* Weight on your back, women are, if you let 'em. Happy bunny today, Megs?"

"Sure am, Mr. Roper."

"Where's the juice? Forgotten the juice. Typical. Sacked, Megs. Fired. Better leave now. Jump."

Unperturbed, Meg set out their two breakfast trays, then brought the fresh orange juice and coffee and hot croissants and red jelly. She was a woman of about forty with the trace of a harelip and a bruised but gallant sexuality.

"Know something, Thomas?" she asked. "He *always* does this to me. It's like he has to psych himself up before he earns his next million. Do you know I have to *make* the red jelly. I sit home, I make red jelly for him. That's all I do when we're not flying. Mr. Roper won't eat anybody's red jelly but mine."

Roper let out a raw laugh. "Next *million?* Hell are you talking about, woman? Million wouldn't pay for the soap on this plane! Best red jelly in the world. Only reason she's still here." He crushed a bread roll in his fist, using all his fingers at once. "Good living's a duty. Whole point of it all. Living well's the best revenge. Who said that?"

"Whoever he was, he got it absolutely right," said Jonathan loyally.

"Set a high standard, let chaps strive for it. Only way. Turn the money over, world goes round. You worked in smart hotels. You know the score. Jelly's off, Megs. Fizzy. Right, Thomas?"

"To the contrary, it's to die for," Jonathan replied firmly, with a wink for Meg.

Laughter all round. The Chief is on a high; so is Jonathan. Suddenly they seem to have everything in common, including Jed. Gold lace lines the cloudbanks, sunlight streams into the plane. They could be on their way to heaven. Tabby is in the tail seat. Frisky has placed himself forward by the bulkhead, covering the pilots' door. Two MacDanbies sit in the middle of the plane, tapping at their laptop computers.

"Women ask too many questions, right, Megs?"

"Not me, Mr. Roper. Never."

"Remember that hooker I had, Megs? Me sixteen, her thirty, remember?"

"I surely do, Mr. Roper. She gave you your first lesson in life."

"Nervous, you see. Virgin." They were eating side by side, able to confide without the threat of eye contact. "Not her. Me." Another shout of laughter. "Didn't know the form, so I played the earnest-student type. Decided she had to have a

problem: 'Poor you, where did it all go wrong?'
Thought she was going to tell me her old dad had
the big C and her mum had run off with the
plumber when she was twelve. Looks at me. Not
a friendly look at all. 'What's your name?' she
says. Little Staffordshire terrier. Broad-arsed.
Five foot nothing. 'I'm Dicky,' I said. 'Now, you
listen to me, Dicky,' she says. 'You can fuck my
body, and that'll cost you a fiver. But you can't
fuck my mind, because that's private.' Never forgot it, did I, Megs? Marvelous woman! Should
have married her. Not Megs. The tart." His
shoulder nudged up against Jonathan's again.
"Want to know how it works?"

"If it's not a state secret."

"Fig leaf operation. You're the fig leaf. Straw
man, the Germans call it. Joke is, you're not even
straw. You don't exist. All the better. Derek
Thomas, merchant venturer, regular guy, quick
on his feet, personable, wholesome. Decent record
in commerce, no skeletons, good crits. It's Dicky
and Derek. Maybe we've done deals before. Nobody's business but ours. I go to the clowns—the
brokers, the venture boys, flexible banks—and I
say: 'Got a very smart cookie here. Brilliant plan,
quick profits, needs backing, mum's the word. It's
tractors, turbines, machine parts, minerals, it's
land, it's what the hell. Introduce you to him later
if you're good. He's young, he's got the connections, don't ask where, very resourceful, politi-

cally hip, good with the right people, opportunity of a lifetime. Didn't want you missing out. Double your money in four months max. You'll be buying paper. If you don't want paper don't waste my time. We're talking bearer bonds, no names, no pack drill, no connection with any other firm including mine. It's another trust-Dicky deal. I'm in but I'm not there. Company's formed in an area where no accounts need to be prepared or filed, no British connection, not our colony, somebody else's mess. When the deal's done, company ceases trading, pull the plug on it, close the accounts, see you sometime. Very tight circle, few chaps as possible, no silly questions, take it or leave it, want you to be one of the few.' All right so far?"

"Do they believe you?"

Roper laughed. "Wrong question. Does the story play? Can they sell it to their punters? Do they like the cut of your jib? Are you a pretty face on the prospectus? Play our cards right, answer's yes every time."

"You mean there's a *prospectus?*"

Roper let out another rich laugh. "Worse than a bloody woman, this chap!" he told Meg contentedly as she poured more coffee. "Why, why, why? How, when, where?"

"I never do that, Mr. Roper," said Meg severely.

"You never do, Megs. You're a good scout."

"Mr. Roper, you are patting my behind again."

"Sorry, Megs. Must have thought I was at home." Back to Jonathan. "No, there's no pro-spectus. Figure of speech. By the time we've printed the prospectus, with any luck we won't have a company."

. . .

ROPER RESUMED his briefing, and Jonathan heard him and replied to him from within the cocoon of his other meditations. He was thinking of Jed, and his images of her were so vivid it was a wonder that Roper, sitting a few inches from him, did not receive some telepathic inkling of them. He felt her hands on his face while she studied him, and he wondered what she saw. He remembered Burr and Rooke in the training house in London, and as he listened to Roper describing the energetic young executive Thomas, he realized that once again he was conniving in the manipulation of his character. He heard Roper say Langbourne had gone ahead to smooth the way, and wondered whether this might be the moment to warn him that Caroline was betraying the cause behind his back and so earn further credit in Roper's estimation. Then he decided Roper knew this anyway: how else would Jed have been able to tax him with his sins? He pondered, as he pondered constantly, the intrac-table mystery of Roper's notions of right and wrong, and he remembered how, in Sophie's judgment, the worst man in the world was a moralist who gained stature in his own eyes by disregarding his perceptions. *He destroys, he makes a great fortune, so he considers himself divine,* she declared in angry mystification.

"Apo will recognize you, of course," Roper was saying. "The bloke he met at Crystal—used to work at Meister's—chum of Dicky's. No problem there that I can see. Anyway, Apo's the other side."

Jonathan turned quickly to him, as if Roper had reminded him of something.

"I wanted to ask you, actually, who *is* the other side? I mean, it's great to be selling, but who's the buyer?"

Roper let out a false shout of pain. "We've got one, Megs! Doubts me! Can't leave a good thing alone!"

"Now, I don't blame him one bit, Mr. Roper. You can be very mean when you want to be. I've seen it before, you know I have. Mean and devious, and very, *very* charming."

Roper dozed, so Jonathan obediently dozed too, listening to the chirrup of the MacDanbies' laptops over the roar of the engines. He woke, Meg brought the ritual champagne and smoked-salmon canapés, there was more talk, more laughter, more doze. He woke again, to find the plane circling above a Dutch toy town shrouded in a white heat haze. Through the haze he saw the slow bursts of artillery fire as the flare stacks of Willemstad's oil refinery burned off their surplus gas.

"I'll be hanging on to your passport for you, if you don't mind, Tommy," Frisky said quietly as they walked across the shimmering runway. "Just pro tem, right? How are you off for cash at all?"

"I haven't any," said Jonathan.

"Oh, right, then. We needn't bother. Only, those credit cards old Corky gave you, they're more for show, you see, Tommy. You wouldn't get a lot of joy not *using* them, know what I mean?"

Roper had already been spirited through customs and was shaking hands with people who respected him. Rooke was sitting on an orange bench, reading the inside pages of the *Financial Times* through the horn-rimmed glasses he wore only for distance. A traveling team of girl missionaries was singing *"Jesu, Joy of Man's Desiring"* in baby sound, conducted by a man with one leg. The sight of Rooke brought Jonathan halfway back to earth.

. . .

THEIR HOTEL WAS a horseshoe of red-roofed houses at the edge of town, with two beaches and an outdoor restaurant that looked onto a choppy, windswept sea. In the center house—the proudest of them—in a run of large rooms on the top floor, the Roper party made its village, with Roper in one corner suite and Derek S. Thomas, executive, in the other. Jonathan's drawing room had a balcony with a table and chairs, and his bedroom had a bed big enough for four, and pillows that did not smell of wood smoke. He had a bottle of Herr Meister's complimentary champagne, and a bunch of complimentary green grapes, which Frisky ate in handfuls while Jonathan settled in. And he had a telephone that was not buried two feet underground and rang while he was still unpacking. Frisky watched him pick up the receiver.

It was Rooke, asking to speak to Thomas.

"Thomas speaking," Jonathan said in his best executive voice.

"Message from Mandy. She's on her way up."

"I don't know Mandy. Who is this?"

Pause while Rooke on the other end of the line affects to do a double take. "Mr. *Peter* Thomas?"

"No. I'm Derek. Wrong Thomas."

"Sorry about that. Must be the one in 22."

Jonathan rang off and muttered "Idiot." He showered, dressed and returned to the drawing room, to find Frisky slouched in an armchair, combing the in-house magazine for erotic stimulus. He dialed room 22 and heard Rooke's voice saying hullo.

"This is Mr. Thomas in 319. I've got some laundry to be collected, please. I'll leave it outside the door."

"Right away," said Rooke.

He went to the bathroom, took a bunch of handwritten notes that he had wedged behind the tank, wrapped them in a dirty shirt, put the shirt in the plastic laundry bag, added his socks, handkerchief and underpants, scribbled a laundry list, put the list in the bag and hung the bag on the outside door handle of his suite. Closing the door, he glimpsed Millie from Rooke's training team in London stomping down the corridor in a stern cotton dress to which was pinned a name badge saying "Mildred."

· · ·

THE CHIEF says to kill time till further orders, Frisky said.

So to Jonathan's delight they killed time—Frisky armed with a cellular phone and Tabby trailing sulkily behind for added killing power. But Jonathan, for all his fears, felt lighter of heart than at any time since he had set out from the Lanyon on his odyssey. The improbable prettiness of the old buildings filled him with a joyful nostalgia. The floating market and the floating bridge enchanted him exactly as they were supposed to. Like a man released from prison, he gazed dotingly on the boisterous throngs of sun-pink tourists and listened in marvel to the native chatter of Papiamento mingling with the startled accents of the Dutch. He was among real people again. People who laughed and stared and shopped and jostled and ate sugar buns in the street. And knew nothing, absolutely nothing, of his business.

Once, he spotted Rooke and Millie drinking coffee at a pavement restaurant and, in his new mood of irresponsibility, nearly gave them a wink. Once, he recognized a man called Jack who had shown him how to use impregnated carbon to make secret writing at the training house in Lisson Grove. Jack, how are you? He glanced round, and it was not Frisky's head or Tabby's that was bobbing along beside him in his imagination, but Jed's chestnut hair fluttering in the breeze.

I don't get it, Thomas. Do you love somebody for what he does *for a living? I'm not into that.*

What if he robs banks?

Everybody robs banks. Banks rob everybody.

What if he killed your sister?

Thomas, for Christ's sake.

If you could just call me Jonathan, he said.

Why?

It's my name. Jonathan Pine.

Jonathan, she said. Jonathan. *Oh shit! It's like being sent back to the beginning at a gymkhana and made to start all over again.* Jonathan . . . *I don't even like it.* Jonathan . . . Jonathan . . .

Maybe it'll grow on you, he suggested.

Returning to the hotel, they walked into Langbourne in the lobby, surrounded by a group of dark-suited moneymen. He was looking angry, the way he might look when his car was late or someone refused to sleep with him. Jonathan's good humor only added to his irritation.

"Have you seen Apostoll hanging around anywhere?" he demanded without so much as a hullo. "Bloody little man's gone missing."

"Not a dickybird," said Frisky.

The furniture had been cleared from Jonathan's drawing room. Bottles of Dom Pérignon lay in a tray of ice on a trestle table. A couple of very slow waiters were unloading plates of canapés from a trolley.

"You press the flesh," Roper had said, "you kiss the babies, look wholesome."

"What if they come at me with business talk?"

"They won't. Clowns'll be too busy counting the money before they get it."

"Could you possibly bring some ashtrays," Jonathan asked one of the waiters. "And open the windows if you don't mind. Who's in charge?"

"Me, sir," said the waiter who wore the name Arthur.

"Frisky, give Arthur twenty dollars, please."

With ill grace, Frisky handed over the money.

. . .

IT WAS Crystal without the amateurs. It was Crystal without Jed's eye to catch across the room. It was Crystal opened to the public and swamped by high-powered Necessary Evils—except that tonight Derek Thomas was the star. Under Roper's benign eye, the polished former night manager shook hands, flashed smiles, remembered names, made witty small talk, worked the room.

"*Hullo,* Mr. Gupta, how's the tennis? Why, Sir *Hector,* how jolly nice to see you again! Mrs. *Del Oro,* how *are* you? How's that brilliant son of yours doing at Yale?"

A buttery English banker from Rickmansworth took Jonathan aside to lecture him on the value of commerce to the emerging world. Two pumice-faced bond sellers from New York listened impassively.

"I'll tell you bluntly—I'm not ashamed of it—I've said it before to these gentlemen, I'll say it again now. With your Third World today, what matters is how they *spend* the stuff, not how they *make* it. Plow it back. Only rule of the game. Improve your infrastructure, raise your social standards. Beyond that, anything goes. I mean it. Brad here agrees with me. So does Sol."

Brad spoke with his lips so close together that Jonathan at first didn't realize he was speaking at all. "You, *ah,* have expertise at all, Derek? You, *ah,* an engineer, sir? Surveyor? Something of, *ah,* that kind?"

"Boats are my best thing, really," said Jonathan cheerfully. "Not Dicky's sort. Sailing boats. Sixty foot's about as far as I like to go."

"Boats, huh? I love 'em. He, *ah,* likes boats."

"Me too," says Sol.

The party ended with another orgy of hand-shakes. Derek, it's been an inspiration. You bet. Take care, now, Derek. You bet. Derek, there's a job for you in Philly anytime you say. . . . Derek, anytime you're in Detroit. . . . You bet. . . . Enraptured by his performance, Jonathan stood on the balcony smiling at the stars, scenting the oil on the dark sea wind. What are you doing now? Supper with Corkoran and the Nassau set—Cynthia who breeds Sealyhams, Stephanie who tells fortunes? Discussing yet more menus for the winter cruise with barely affordable Delia, the *Iron Pasha*'s coveted chef? Or are you lying with your head in the white silk cushion of your arm, whispering, *Jonathan, for Christ's sake, what's a girl to* do?

"Time for the nosebag, Tommy. Can't keep the gentry waiting."

"I'm not hungry, actually, Frisky."

"I don't expect anybody is, Tommy. It's like church. Come on."

. . .

DINNER IS in an ancient fort on a hilltop overlooking the harbor. Seen from here at night, little Willemstad is as big as San Francisco, and even the blue-gray cylinders of the refinery have a stately magic. The MacDanbies have taken a table for twenty, but only fourteen can be raised. Jonathan is being recklessly amusing about the cocktail party; Meg and the English banker and his wife are laughing themselves sick. But Roper's attention is elsewhere. He is staring down into the harbor, where a great cruise ship decked with fairy lights is moving between anchored cargo vessels toward a distant bridge. Does Roper covet it? Sell the *Pasha,* get something a decent size?

"Substitute lawyer's on his way, damn them," Langbourne announces, returning yet again from the telephone. "Swears he'll be here in time for the meeting."

"Who are they sending?" says Roper.

"Moranti from Caracas."

"That thug. Hell's happened to Apo?"

"They told me to ask Jesus. Joke of some sort."

"Anyone else decided not to show?" Roper asks, his eyes still fixed upon the cruise ship.

"Everyone else is on cue," Langbourne replies tersely.

Jonathan hears their conversation, and so does Rooke, seated with Millie and Amato at their table next to the protection. The three of them are poring over a guidebook of the island, pretending to wonder where they'll go tomorrow.

· · ·

JED WAS floating, which was what always happened to her when her life got out of sync: she floated, and she kept floating till the next man, or the next crazy house party, or the next family misfortune, provided her with a change of direction, which she then variously described to herself as fate, or running for cover, or growing up, or having fun, or—less comfortably these days—doing her own thing. And part of floating was to do everything at once, rather like the whippet she had had when she was young, who believed that if you ran fast enough round a corner, you were sure to put up something you could chase. But then the whippet was content that life should be a succession of patternless episodes, whereas Jed had for too long been wondering where the episodes in her own life were leading.

So in Nassau, from the moment Roper and Jonathan had left, Jed went straight to work doing everything. She went to the hairdresser and the dressmaker, she invited simply everybody to the house, she entered herself for the Windermere ladies' tennis competition and accepted every invitation that came her way, she bought files to contain her household bumf for the winter cruise, she telephoned the *Pasha*'s chef and housekeeper and drew up menus and placements, even though she knew that Roper was certain to countermand her instructions because in the end he liked to do it all himself.

But the time scarcely moved.

She prepared Daniel for his return to England; she took him shopping and got in friends his age, even though Daniel loathed them and said so; she organized a barbecue for them on the beach, all the time pretending that Corky was *quite* as much fun as Jonathan—I mean, *honestly,* Dans, isn't he a *scream?*—and doing her *absolute* best to ignore the fact that ever since they had left Crystal, Corkoran had sulked and puffed and shot pompous scowls at her *exactly* like her elder brother William, who fucked every girl in sight, including all her friends, but thought his little sister should go virgin to the grave.

But Corkoran was even *worse* than William. He had appointed himself her chaperon, her watchdog and her jailer. He squinted at her letters almost before she had opened them, he earwigged her phone calls and tried to elbow his way into every bloody corner of her day.

"Corks, darling, you *are* being a bore, you know. You're making me feel like Mary Queen of Scots. I know Roper wants you to look after me, but couldn't you *possibly* go and play on your own for *some* of the day?"

But Corkoran stuck doggedly at her side, sitting in the drawing room in his Panama hat and reading the newspaper while she telephoned; hanging around the kitchen while she and Daniel made fudge; writing out the labels for Daniel's homebound luggage.

Until finally, like Jonathan, Jed retreated deep inside herself. She gave up small talk, she gave up—except when she was with Daniel—her wearying efforts to appear on top of life, she gave up counting the hours and allowed herself instead to roam the landscape of her inmost world. She thought of her father and what she had always considered to be his useless and outdated sense of honor, and she decided it had actually meant more to her than all the bad things that had happened on account of it: such as the sale of the debt-ridden family house and the horses, and her parents' move to their present dreadful little bungalow on the old estate, and the perpetual rage of Uncle Henry and all the other trustees.

She thought of Jonathan and tried to fathom what it meant to her that he was working for Roper's ruin. She wrestled, as her father would have done, with the rights and wrongs of her dilemma, but all she could really come up with was that Roper represented a catastrophic wrong turning in her life, and that Jonathan had some brotherly claim upon her that was unlike any other claim she had ever felt; and that she even found it companionable when he saw through her, provided he was also confident of the good parts of her, because those were the parts she wanted to get out and dust and put back into service. For instance, she wanted her father back. And she wanted her Catholicism back, even if it woke the tearaway in her every time she thought about it. She wanted firm ground under her feet, but this time she was prepared to work for it. She would even listen sweetly to her bloody mother.

Finally came Daniel's day of departure, which by then she seemed to have been waiting for all her life. So Jed and Corkoran together took Daniel and his luggage to the airport in the Rolls, and as soon as they arrived Daniel needed to dawdle alone at the newsstand in order to buy sweets and reading material and do whatever small boys do when they're going back to their bloody mothers. So Jed and Corkoran waited for him in the middle of the concourse, both suddenly miserable at the prospect of his departure, the more so since Daniel was on the verge of serious tears. And then to her surprise she heard Corkoran speaking to her in a conspiratorial whisper.

"Got your passport, heart?"

"Corks, darling, it's *Daniel* who's leaving, not *me*. Remember?"

"Have you got it or not? Quick!"

"I've always got it."

"Then go with him, heart," he begged, taking out his handkerchief and fussing his nose with it in order not to look as though he was talking. "Jump for it now. Corks never said a word. All your own work. Seats galore. I asked."

But Jed didn't jump for it. It never crossed her mind, which was something she was at once extremely pleased about. In the past she had tended to jump first and ask questions afterwards. But that morning, she discovered that she had answered the questions in her mind already, and she wasn't going to jump anywhere if it meant jumping further away from Jonathan.

. . .

JONATHAN WAS dreaming deliciously when the phone rang, and still dreaming as he lifted it. Nonetheless, the close observer was swift in his reaction, stifling the first ring, then switching on the light, then grabbing a notepad and pencil in anticipation of Rooke's instructions.

"Jonathan," she said proudly.

He pressed his eyes shut. He jammed the phone to his ear, trying to contain the sound of her voice. Every practical instinct in him told him to say, "Jonathan who? Wrong number," and ring off. *You stupid little fool!* he wanted to scream at her. *I told you, don't ring, don't try and get in touch, just wait. So you ring, you get in touch and you bubble my real Christian name straight into the listeners' ears.*

"For Christ's sake," he whispered. "Get off the line. Go to sleep."

But the conviction in his voice was fading, and it was too late now to say wrong number. So he lay with the telephone at his ear, listening while she repeated his name, *Jonathan, Jonathan,* practicing it, getting the hang of it in all its shades, so that nobody would send her back to the beginning of the course to start her round again.

. . .

THEY'VE COME for me.

It was an hour later, and Jonathan could

hear footsteps trying to be silent outside his door. He sat up. He heard one step, and it was sticky on the ceramic tiles, and he knew it was a bare foot. He heard a second, and it was on the carpet that ran down the center of the corridor. He saw the corridor light go on and off in his keyhole as a body slipped past, he thought from left to right. Was Frisky sizing up to burst in on him? Had he gone to fetch Tabby so that they could do the job together? Was Millie returning his laundry? Was a barefoot boot boy collecting shoes to clean? The hotel does not clean shoes. He heard the click of a bedroom lock across the corridor and knew it was a barefoot Meg coming back from Roper's suite.

He felt nothing. No censure, no easing of his conscience or his soul. *I screw,* Roper had said. So he screwed. And Jed led the pack.

· · ·

HE WATCHED the sky lighten in his window, imagining her head gently turning against his ear. He dialed room 22, let it ring four times and dialed again but didn't speak.

"You're bang on course," Rooke said quietly. "Now hear this."

Jonathan, he thought, as he listened to Rooke's instructions. *Jonathan, Jonathan, Jonathan . . .* when is all this going to blow up in your face?

TWENTY-TWO

NOTARY MULDER'S office had rosewood furniture and plastic flowers and gray Venetian blinds. The many happy faces of the Dutch royal family beamed down from the paneled walls, and Notary Mulder beamed with them. Langbourne and the substitute lawyer, Moranti, sat at a table, Langbourne his usual sullen self, leafing through a folder of papers, but Moranti watchful as an old pointer dog, following Jonathan's every movement with his shaggy brown eyes. He was a broad-headed Latin in his sixties, white-haired and brown-skinned, with a pitted face. Even motionless, he brought something disturbing to the room: a whiff of popular justice, of peasant struggles for survival. Once, he let out a furious grunt and smashed his big paw on the table. But it was only to pull the paper across the table to inspect it, then shove it back. Once, he tilted back his head and peered into Jonathan's eyes as if he were examining them for colonialist sentiments.

"You are an English, Mr. Thomas?"

"New Zealander."

"You are welcome to Curaçao."

Mulder by contrast was plump and Pickwickian in a risible world. When he beamed, his cheeks twinkled like red apples. And when he stopped beaming, you wanted to hurry forward and ask him tenderly what you had done wrong.

But his hand shook.

Why it shook, who shook it, whether it shook from debauchery, or disability, or drink, or fear, Jonathan could only guess. But it shook as if it were someone else's hand. It shook as it received Jonathan's passport from Langbourne, and as it painstakingly copied the false details onto a form. It shook as it returned the passport to Jonathan instead of Langbourne. It shook again as it set the papers on the table. Even his pudgy forefinger shook as it indicated to Jonathan the place where he should sign his life away and the place where just initials would do the job.

And when Mulder had made Jonathan sign every sort of document he had ever heard of, and many he had not, the shaking hand produced the bearer bonds themselves, in a tremulous bundle of weighty-looking blue documents issued by Jonathan's very own Tradepaths Limited, each numbered and embossed with a ducal seal and engraved in copperplate like bank notes, which in theory they were, since their purpose was to enrich the bearer without revealing his identity. And Jonathan knew at once—he needed no confirmation from anybody—that the bonds were of Roper's own design: for gas, as he would say; to raise the ante; to impress the clowns.

Then, on Mulder's cherubic nod, Jonathan

signed the bonds too, as sole signatory to the company's bank account. And in the afterglow, he signed a little typed love letter to Notary Mulder, reaffirming him in his appointment as Curaçaoan resident manager of Tradepaths Limited in accordance with the local law.

And suddenly they were finished, and all that remained was for them to shake the hand that had performed so much hard work. Which they duly did—even Langbourne shook it—and Mulder, the rubicund schoolboy of fifty, waved them down the steps with vertical motions of his chubby hand, practically promising to write to them each week.

"I'll just have that passport back, Tommy, if you don't mind," said Tabby with a wink.

· · ·

"BUT DEREK AND I have already met, I think, Dicky!" the Dutch banker caroled to Roper, who was standing before the place where the marble fireplace would have been, if Curaçaoan banks had had fireplaces. "Not only last night, I think! We are old friends from Crystal, I would say! Nettie, bring Mr. Thomas some tea, please!"

For a moment the close observer's mind refused to engage. Then he remembered a night at Crystal, and Jed seated at her end of the table in low blue satin and pearls against her skin, and this same oafish Dutch banker who now stood before him boring everybody with his connections with great statesmen of the day.

"But of course! Good to see you again, Piet," the smooth hotelier exclaimed, a little late, offering his signer's hand. And then, as if he had never set eyes on them before, Jonathan found himself shaking hands with Mulder and Moranti for the second time in twenty minutes. But Jonathan made nothing of this, and neither did they, because he was beginning to understand that in the theater he had entered, one actor could play many parts in a single working day.

They sat down, using all four sides of the table, Moranti watching and listening like an umpire, and the banker at the head doing the talking, because he apparently saw it as his first duty to acquaint Jonathan with a mountain of useless information.

The share capital of a Curaçaoan offshore company could be denominated in any currency, said the Dutch banker. There was no limitation on foreign ownership of shares.

"Great," said Jonathan.

Langbourne's lazy eyes lifted to him. Moranti's didn't flinch. Roper, who had his head back and was studying the old Dutch moldings on the ceiling, pulled a private grin.

The company was exempt from all capital gains, all withholding, gift or estate taxes, said the banker. Transfer of shares was unrestricted. There was no transfer tax and no *ad valorem* stamp duty.

"Well, *that's* a relief," said Jonathan, in the same enthusiastic tone as before.

Mr. Derek Thomas was under no legal requirement to appoint external auditors, the banker said gravely, as if this elevated him to a higher monastic order. Mr. Thomas was at liberty at any time to move his company's seat to another jurisdiction, provided receptive legislation applied in the jurisdiction of his choice.

"I'll bear that in mind," said Jonathan, and this time, to his surprise, the impassive Moranti broke into a sunny smile and said "New Zealand," as if he had decided that the place had a good ring to it after all.

A minimum of six thousand U.S. dollars was required as paid-up share capital, but the requirement in this case was met, the banker continued. All that remained was for "our good friend Derek here" to put his name to certain pro forma documents. The banker's smile stretched like an elastic band as he indicated a black desk pen that stood nose down on a teak stand.

"I'm sorry, Piet," said Jonathan, puzzled but still smiling. "I didn't quite catch what you said back there. *What* requirement is met, exactly?"

"Your company is fortunate to be in an excellent state of liquidity, Derek," said the Dutch banker, in his best informal manner.

"Oh, splendid. I didn't realize. Then perhaps you'll allow me to take a look at the accounts."

The Dutch banker's eyes stayed on Jonathan. Only the slightest inclination of his head referred the question to Roper, who finally removed his gaze from the ceiling.

"Course he can see the accounts, Piet. It's Derek's company, for heaven's sake, Derek's name on the paper, Derek's deal. Let him see his accounts, if he wants to. Why not?"

The banker extracted a slim, unsealed orange envelope from a drawer of his desk and passed it across the table. Jonathan lifted the flap and drew out a monthly statement declaring that the current account of Tradepaths Limited of Curaçao stood at one hundred million U.S. dollars.

"Anyone else want to see it?" Roper asked.

Moranti's hand came out. Jonathan passed him the statement. Moranti examined it and passed it to Langbourne, who pulled a bored face and returned it unread to the banker.

"Give him the bloody check and let's get this over," said Langbourne, tilting his blond head at Jonathan but keeping his back to him.

A girl who had been hovering in the background with a folder under her arm processed ceremoniously round the table till she reached Jonathan. The folder was of leather and smudgily embossed by local craftsmen. Inside it lay a check made out to the bank, drawn on the account of Tradepaths, in the sum of twenty-five million U.S. dollars.

"Go on, Derek, sign it," said Roper, amused by Jonathan's hesitation. "Won't bounce. Kind of money we leave under the plate—right, Piet?"

Everyone laughed except Langbourne.

Jonathan signed the check. The girl put it back in the folder and closed the panels for decency. She was of mixed blood and very beautiful, with huge, puzzled eyes and a churchy demureness.

. . .

ROPER AND JONATHAN were sitting apart on a sofa in the window bay while the Dutch banker and the three lawyers did business of their own.

"Hotel all right?" Roper asked.

"Fine, thanks. Rather well run. It's hell staying in hotels when you know the trade."

"Meg's a good sport."

"Meg's terrific."

"Clear as mud, I should think, all this legal bollocks?"

"I'm afraid it is."

"Jed sends love. Dans won a pot at the kids' regatta yesterday. Chuffed him no end. Taking the replica back to his mother. Wanted you to know."

"That's marvelous."

"Thought you'd be pleased."

"I am. It's a triumph."

"Well, save your powder. Big night tonight."

"Another party?"

"Could call it that."

There was a last formality, and it required a tape recorder and a script. The girl operated the recorder, the Dutch banker coached Jonathan in the part.

"In your normal voice, please, Derek. Just as you were speaking here today, I think. For our records. Would you be so awfully kind?"

Jonathan first read the two typed lines to himself, then read them aloud: *"This is your friend George speaking to you. Thank you for staying awake tonight."*

"And again, please, Derek. Maybe you are a little bit nervous. Just relax, please."

He read it again.

"Once more, please, Derek. You are somewhat tense, I think. Maybe those large sums have affected you."

Jonathan smiled his most affable smile. He was their star, and stars are expected to show a little temperament. "Actually, Piet, I think I've rather given it my best shot, thank you."

Roper agreed. "Piet, you're being an old woman. Switch the bloody thing off. Come on, Señor Moranti. Time you had a decent meal."

The handshaking again: everyone to everyone in turn, like dear friends at the changing of the year.

. . .

"So WHAT d'you reckon?" Roper asked, through his dolphin smile, as he lay sprawled in a plastic chair on the balcony of Jonathan's suite. "Worked it out yet? Or still over your head?"

It was the nervous time. Time to be waiting

in the truck with your face blacked, exchanging casual intimacies to keep the adrenaline at bay. Roper had propped his feet on the balustrade. Jonathan was arched forward over his glass, gazing at the darkening sea. There was no moon. A steady wind was flicking the waves. The first stars were pricking through the stacks of blue-black cloud. In the lighted drawing room behind them, Frisky, Gus and Tabby were making murmured conversation. Only Langbourne, draped on a sofa and reading *Private Eye,* seemed unaware of the tension.

"There's a Curaçaoan company called Tradepaths, and it owns a hundred million U.S. dollars, less twenty-five," Jonathan said.

"Except," Roper suggested, his smile widening.

"Except it doesn't own a damn thing because Tradepaths is a wholly owned subsidiary of Ironbrand."

"No, it's not."

"Officially Tradepaths is an independent company, no connection with any other firm. In reality it's your creature and can't move a finger without you. Ironbrand can't be seen to be investing in Tradepaths. So Ironbrand lends the investors' money to a tame bank, and the tame bank happens to invest the money in Tradepaths. The bank's the cutout. When the deal's done, Tradepaths pays off the investors with a handsome profit, everybody goes away happy and you keep the rest."

"Who gets hurt?"

"I do. If it goes wrong."

"It won't. Anyone else?"

It occurred to Jonathan that Roper required his absolution.

"Somebody does, for sure."

"Put it another way. Who gets hurt who wouldn't get hurt anyway?"

"We're selling guns, aren't we?"

"So?"

"Well, presumably they're being sold to be used. And since it's a disguised deal, one might reasonably assume they're being sold to people who shouldn't have them."

Roper shrugged. "Who says? Who says who shoots who in the world? Who makes the bloody laws? The big powers? Jesus!" Unusually animated, he flung a hand at the darkening seascape. "You can't change the color of the sky. Told Jed. Wouldn't listen. Can't blame her. She's young like you. Give her ten years, she'll come round."

Emboldened, Jonathan went over to the attack. "So who's buying?" he demanded, repeating the question he had put to Roper on the airplane.

"Moranti."

"No, he's not. He hasn't paid you a cent. You've put up a hundred million dollars—or the investors have. What's Moranti putting up?

You're selling him guns. He's buying them. So where's his money? Or is he paying you in something that's better than money? Something you can sell for much, much more than a hundred mil?"

Roper's face was sculptured marble in the darkness, but it wore the long, bland smile.

"Been there yourself, haven't you? You and the Aussie you killed. All right, you deny it. Didn't see it big enough, your trouble. See it big or don't see it at all, my view. You're a smart chap all the same. Pity we didn't meet earlier. Could have done with you in a few other places."

A phone rang in the room behind them. Roper turned sharply, and Jonathan followed his gaze in time to see Langbourne standing with the receiver to his ear, looking at his wristwatch while he talked. He replaced the receiver, shook his head at Roper and returned to the sofa and *Private Eye*. Roper settled back into his plastic chair.

"Remember the old China trade?" he asked nostalgically.

"I thought that was in the 1830s."

"You've read about it, though, haven't you? You've read everything else, far as I can see."

"Yes."

"Remember what those Hong Kong Brits were running up the river to Canton? Dodging the Chinese customs, funding the empire, building themselves fortunes?"

"Opium," said Jonathan.

"For tea. Opium for tea. Barter. Came home to England, captains of industry. Knighthoods, honors, whole shebang. Hell's the difference? Go for it! That's all that matters. Americans know that. Why don't we? Tight-arsed vicars braying from the pulpit every Sunday, old nellies' tea parties, seedcake, poor Mrs. So-and-so's died of the whatnots? Screw it. Worse than bloody prison. Know what Jed asked me?"

"What?"

" 'How bad are you? Tell me the worst!' Christ!"

"What did you say?"

" 'Not bloody well bad enough!' I told her. 'There's me and there's the jungle,' I told her. 'No policemen on the street corner. No justice handed down by chaps in wigs familiar with the law. *Nothing*. I thought that was what you liked.' Shook her a bit. Serves her right."

Langbourne was tapping on the glass.

"So why are you present at the meetings?" Jonathan said. They were standing up. "Why keep a dog and bark yourself?"

Roper laughed loudly and clapped a hand on Jonathan's back. "Don't trust the dog, that's why, old boy. Any of my dogs. You, Corky, Sandy—wouldn't trust any o' you in an empty henhouse. Nothing personal. Way I am."

. . .

TWO CARS WERE waiting among the lighted hibiscus of the hotel forecourt. The first was a Volvo, driven by Gus. Langbourne took the front seat, Roper and Jonathan the back. Tabby and Frisky followed in a Toyota. Langbourne had a briefcase.

They crossed a high bridge and saw the lights of the town below them, and the black Dutch waterways cutting through the lights. They descended a steep ramp. The old houses gave way to shanties. Suddenly the dark felt dangerous. They were driving on a flat road, water to their right, floodlit containers piled four high to their left, marked with names like Sealand, Nedlloyd and Tiphook. They turned left, and Jonathan saw a low white roof and blue posts and guessed it was a customhouse. The paving changed and made the wheels sing.

"Stop at the gates and put your lights out," Langbourne ordered. "All of them."

Gus stopped at the gates and doused the car's lights. Close behind them, Frisky in the Toyota did the same. A barred white gateway stood before them, with warning notices in Dutch and English. Then the lights around the gate went out too, and with the darkness came silence. In the distance, Jonathan saw a surreal landscape of cranes and forklift trucks cross-lit by arc lamps, and the pale outlines of big ships.

"Let 'em see your hands. No one move," Langbourne ordered.

His voice had acquired authority. This was his show, whatever the show was. He opened his door an inch and worked it, making the courtesy light wink twice inside the car. He closed the door, and again they sat in darkness. He lowered his window. Jonathan saw an outstretched hand reach in. It was white and male and powerful. It was attached to a bare forearm and the short sleeve of a white shirt.

"One hour," Langbourne said, upward into the darkness.

"That's too long," a gruff, accented voice objected.

"We agreed one hour," Langbourne said implacably. "One hour or nothing."

"Okay, okay."

Only then did Langbourne pass an envelope through the open window. A pinlight torch went on; the contents were swiftly counted. The white gates swung back. Still without headlights, they drove forward, closely followed by the Toyota. They passed an ancient anchor embedded in concrete and entered an alley of many-colored containers, each marked with a letter combination and seven digits.

"Left here," Langbourne said. They swung left, the Toyota after them. Jonathan ducked his head as the arm of an orange crane swooped down on them out of the sky.

"Now right. *Here,*" said Langbourne.

They swung right, and the black hull of a

tanker rose out of the sea toward them. Right again, and they were skirting a row of half a dozen moored ships. Two were grand and newly painted. The rest were scruffy feeder ships. Each had a lighted gangway to the waterfront.

"Stop," Langbourne ordered.

They stopped, still in darkness, the Toyota on their tail. This time they waited only a few seconds, before another pinlight appeared in the windscreen: first red, then white, then back to red.

"Open all the windows," Langbourne told Gus. He was worried about hands again. "On the dash where they can see them. Chief, shove 'em on the seat in front of you. You too, Thomas."

With unaccustomed meekness Roper did as he was told. The air was cool. The smell of oil mingled with the smells of sea and metal. Jonathan was in Ireland. Then he was in Pugwash docks, stowed aboard the filthy freighter, waiting to steal ashore by darkness. Two white flashlights appeared either side of the car. Their beams scanned the hands and faces, then the car floor.

"Mr. Thomas and party," Langbourne announced. "Come to inspect some tractors, pay the other half."

"Which is Thomas?" said a man's voice.

"Me."

A pause.

"Okay."

"Everybody get out slowly," Langbourne ordered. "Thomas, behind me. Single file."

Their guide was lank and tall and seemed too young to be carrying the Heckler that swung at his right side. The gangway was short. Reaching the deck, Jonathan saw across the black water to the lights of the town again, and the flare stacks of the refinery.

The ship was old and small. Jonathan guessed forty thousand tons at most, converted from other lives. A wooden door stood open in a raised hatch. Inside, a bulkhead lamp glowed over a spiral flight of steel stairs. The guide once more went first. The echo of their feet was like the tramp of a chain gang. By the poor light Jonathan made out more of the man who was leading them. He wore jeans and sneakers. He had a blond forelock, which he flipped back with his left hand when it got in his way. The right hand still held the Heckler, the forefinger crooked snugly round the trigger. The ship too was beginning to reveal herself. She was fitted for mixed cargo. Capacity around sixty containers. She was a tub, a roll-on-roll-off workhorse at the end of her usefulness. She was a throwaway if things went wrong.

The party had come to a halt. Three men stood facing them, all white, all fair, all young. Behind them was a steel door, closed. Jonathan guessed on no evidence that they were Swedes. Like the guide, they carried Hecklers. It was now apparent that the guide was their leader. Something about his ease, his choice of posture as he joined them. His hacked and dangerous smile.

"How is the aristocracy these days, Sandy?" he called. Jonathan could still not place his accent.

"Hullo, Pepe," said Langbourne. "In the pink, thanks. How's yourself?"

"You all students of agriculture? You like tractors? Machine parts? You want to grow crops, feed all the poor people?"

"Let's just get on with the fucking job," Langbourne said. "Where's Moranti?"

Pepe grabbed the steel door and pulled it open at the same moment that Moranti appeared out of the shadows.

My Lord Langbourne is a weapons freak, Burr had said. *Played gentleman soldier in half a dozen dirty wars . . . prides himself on his killing skills . . . in his spare time he dabbles as a collector, same as the Roper . . . it makes them feel better to think they're part of history.*

. . .

THE HOLD constituted most of the belly of the ship. Pepe was playing host, Langbourne and Moranti walked beside him, Jonathan and Roper followed, then came the help: Frisky, Tabby and the three ship's hands with their Hecklers. Twenty containers were chained to the deck. On the lashing straps, Jonathan read a medley of transfer points: Lisbon, the Azores, Antwerp, Gdansk.

"This one we are calling the Saudi box," Pepe announced proudly. "They make it side-opening so Saudi customs can get inside and sniff around for booze."

The customs seals were steel pins banged into each other. Pepe's men hacked them apart with cutters.

"Don't worry, we got spares," Pepe confided to Jonathan. "Tomorrow morning everything look fine again. Customs don't give a shit."

The side of the container was slowly lowered. Guns have their own silence. It is the silence of the dead to come.

"Vulcans," Langbourne was saying, for the edification of Moranti. "High-tech version of the Gatling. Six twenty-millimeter barrels fire three thousand rounds a minute. State of the art. Ammo to match, more to follow. Each bullet's as big as your finger. One burst sounds like a horde of killer bees. Choppers and light aircraft don't stand a chance. Brand-new. Ten of 'em. Okay?"

Moranti said nothing at all. Only the barest nod betrayed his satisfaction. They moved to the next container. It was end-loaded, which meant they could view the contents only from the front. But what they saw was already enough.

"Quad fifties," Langbourne announced. "Four coaxially mounted point-five-oh-caliber machine guns designed to fire simultaneously at a single target. Shred any aircraft you like with a single burst. Trucks, troop transports, light armor—the Quad'll take 'em out. Mount 'em on a two-and-a-half-ton chassis, they're mobile and they hurt like hell. Also brand-new."

With Pepe leading, they crossed to the starboard side of the ship, where two men were gingerly extracting a cigar-shaped missile from a fiberglass cylinder. This time Jonathan had no need of Langbourne's expertise. He had seen the demonstration films. He had heard the tales. *If the Micks ever get their hands on these, you're dead,* the bomb-happy sergeant major had promised. *And they will,* he added cheerfully. *They'll nick them off Yankee ammo dumps in Germany, they'll buy them for a bloody fortune off the Afghans, the Izzies or the Pals, or whoever else the Yanks have seen fit to hand them out to. They're supersonic, man-packed, they're three to a carton, they're Stingers by name and they're Stingers by nature . . .*

The tour continued. Light anti-tank guns. Field radios. Medical gear. Uniforms. Ammunition. Meals Ready to Eat. British Starstreaks. Boxes made in Birmingham. Steel cannisters made in Manchester. Not everything could be examined. There was too much stuff, too little time.

"Likee?" Roper asked Jonathan quietly.

Their faces were very close. The expression on Roper's was intense and strangely victorious, as if his point were somehow proved.

"It's good stuff," Jonathan said, not knowing what else he was supposed to say.

"Bit of everything in each shipment. That's the trick. Boat goes astray, you lose a bit of everything, not all of something. Common sense."

"I suppose it is."

Roper wasn't hearing him. He was in the presence of his own accomplishment. He was in a state of grace.

"Thomas?" It was Langbourne, calling from the aft end of the hold. "Over here. Signing time."

Roper went with him. On a military clipboard, Langbourne had a typed receipt for turbines, tractor parts and heavy machinery as per attached schedule, inspected and certified to be in good order by Derek S. Thomas, managing director for and on behalf of Tradepaths Limited. Jonathan signed the receipt, then initialed the schedule. He gave the clipboard to Roper, who showed it to Moranti, then passed it back to Langbourne, who handed it to Pepe. A cellular telephone lay on a shelf beside the door. Pepe picked it up and dialed a number from the piece of paper that Roper was holding out to him. Moranti stood a little distance from them, with his hands curled to his sides and stomach out, like a Russian at a cenotaph. Pepe passed the phone to Roper. They heard the banker's voice saying hullo.

"Piet?" said Roper. "Friend of mine wants to give you an important message."

Roper handed the phone to Jonathan, together with a second piece of paper from his pocket.

Jonathan glanced at the paper, then read aloud. "This is your friend George speaking to you," he said. "Thank you for staying awake tonight."

"Put Pepe on the line, please, Derek," said the banker's voice. "I would like to confirm some nice news for him."

Jonathan handed the receiver to Pepe, who listened, laughed, rang off and clapped a hand on Jonathan's shoulder.

"You're a generous fellow!"

His laughter stopped as Langbourne drew a typed sheet of paper from his briefcase. "Receipt," he said curtly.

Pepe grabbed Jonathan's pen and, watched by all of them, signed a receipt to Tradepaths Limited for the sum of twenty-five million U.S. dollars, being the third and penultimate payment for the agreed consignment of turbines, tractor parts and heavy machinery delivered to Curaçao as per contract for onward transit on the SS *Lombardy.*

. . .

IT WAS four in the morning when she rang.

"We're leaving for the *Pasha* tomorrow," she said. "Me and Corky."

Jonathan said nothing at all.

"He says I'm to bolt. Forget the cruise, bolt while there's still a chance."

"He's right," Jonathan murmured.

"It's no *good* bolting, Jonathan. It doesn't work. We both know that. You just meet yourself again in the next place."

"Just get out. Go anywhere. Please."

They lay still again, side by side on their separate beds, listening to each other's breathing.

"Jonathan," she whispered. *"Jonathan."*

TWENTY-THREE

EVERYTHING HAD been going swimmingly with Operation Limpet. Burr, from his grim gray desk in Miami, said so. So did Strelski, next door along from him. Goodhew, telephoning twice a day on the secure line from London, had no doubt of it. "The powers that be are coming round, Leonard. All we need now is the summation."

"Which powers?" said Burr, suspicious as ever.

"My master for one."

"Your *master?*"

"He's turning, Leonard. He says so, and I have to give him the benefit of the doubt. How can I go over his head if he's offering me his full support? He took me to his heart yesterday."

"I'm glad to hear he's got one."

But Goodhew, these days, was in no mood for such sallies. "He said we should stay in much closer touch. I agree with him. There are too many people about with vested interests. He said there was a whiff of something rotten in the air. I couldn't have put it better myself. He would like to go on record as one of those who wasn't afraid to track it down. I shall see he does. He didn't mention Flagship by name, neither did I. Sometimes it pays better to be reticent. But he was greatly taken by your list, Leonard. The list did the trick. It was bald, it was uncompromising. There was no getting round it."

"*My* list?"

"The list, Leonard. The one our friend photographed. The backers. The investors. The runners and starters, you called it." There was an imploring note in Goodhew's voice that Burr wished he couldn't hear. "The smoking gun, for heaven's sake. The thing that nobody ever finds, you said, except that our friend did. Leonard, you're being willfully obtuse."

But Goodhew had misread the cause of Burr's confusion. Burr had known immediately which list. What he couldn't understand was the use that Goodhew had made of it.

"You don't mean you've shown the *list of backers* to your minister, do you?"

"Good heavens, not the raw material, how could I? Just the names and numbers. Properly recycled, naturally. They could have come from a telephone intercept, a microphone, anything. We could have filched it from the post."

"Roper didn't dictate that list or read it over the phone, Rex. He didn't put it in a letter box. He wrote it on a yellow legal pad, and there's only one of it in the world and one man who took a photograph of it."

"Don't split hairs with me, Leonard! My master is appalled, that's my point. He recognizes that a summation is close and heads must roll. He feels—so he tells me, and I shall believe him until I am proved wrong—he has his pride, Leonard, as we all do, our own ways of avoiding unpleasant truths until they are thrust upon us—he feels that the time has come for him to get off the fence and be counted." He attempted a valiant joke. "You know his way with metaphors. I'm surprised he didn't throw in some new brooms rising from the ashes."

If Goodhew was expecting a peal of jolly laughter, Burr did not provide it.

Goodhew became agitated: "Leonard, I had no alternative. I am a servant of the Crown. I serve a minister of the Crown. It is my duty to inform my master of the progress of your case. If my master tells me he has seen the light, I am not employed to tell him he's a liar. I have my loyalties, Leonard. To my principles as well as to him and to you. We're having lunch on Thursday after his meeting with the Cabinet Secretary. I'm to expect important news. I'd hoped you'd be pleased, not sour."

"Who else has seen the list of backers, Rex?"

"Other than my master, nobody. I drew his attention to its secrecy, naturally. One can't go on telling people to keep their mouths shut; one can cry wolf too often. Obviously the substance of it will go before the Cabinet Secretary when they meet on Thursday, but we may be sure that's where it will stop."

Burr's silence became too much for him.

"Leonard, I fear you are forgetting first principles. All my efforts over the last months have been devoted to achieving greater openness in the new era. Secrecy is the curse of our British system. I shall not encourage my master or any other minister of the Crown to hide behind its skirts. They do quite enough of that as it is. I won't hear you, Leonard. I won't have you fall back into your old River House ways."

Burr took a deep breath. "Point taken, Rex. Understood. From now on, I'll observe first principles."

"I'm glad to hear it, Leonard."

Burr rang off, then called Rooke. "Rex Goodhew gets no more unrefined Limpet reports from us, Rob. That's with immediate effect. I'll confirm in writing by tomorrow's bag."

· · ·

NEVERTHELESS, everything else had been going well, and if Burr continued to fret over Goodhew's lapse, neither he nor Strelski lived with any sense of impending doom. What Goodhew had called the summation was what Burr and Strelski called the hit, and the hit was what they now dreamed of. It was the moment when the drugs and arms and players would all be in the same place and the money trail would be visible and—assuming the joint team had the necessary rights and permissions—its warriors would fall out of the trees and shout "Hands up!" and the bad guys would give their rueful smile, and say "It's a fair cop, Officer"—or , if they were American, "I'll get you for this, Strelski, you bastard."

Or so they facetiously portrayed it to each other.

"We let it ride as far as it can go," Strelski kept insisting—at meetings, on the telephone, over coffee, striding on the beach. "The further down the line they are, the fewer places they have to hide, the nearer we are to God."

Burr agreed. Catching crooks is no different from catching spies, he said: all you need is a well-lit street corner, your cameras in position, one man in a trench coat with the plans, the other in a bowler with the suitcase full of used bills. Then, if you're very lucky, you've got a case. The problem with Operation Limpet was: Whose street? Whose city? Whose sea? Whose jurisdiction? For one thing was already clear: neither Richard Onslow Roper nor his Colombian trading partners had the smallest intention of completing their business on American soil.

* * *

ANOTHER SOURCE of support and satisfaction was the new Federal Prosecutor who had been assigned to the case. His name was Prescott, and he was more exalted than the usual federal prosecutor: he was a Deputy Assistant Attorney General, and everybody whom Strelski checked him out with said Ed Prescott was the best Deputy Assistant Attorney General there was, just the best, Joe, take it from me. The Prescotts were old Yale people, of course, and a couple of them had Agency connections—how could they not have?—and there was even a rumor, which Ed had never specifically denied, that he was in some way related to old Prescott Bush, George Bush's father. But Ed—well, Ed had never bothered with that stuff, he wanted you to know. He was a serious Washington player with his own agenda, and when he went to work he left his parentage outside the door.

"What happened to the fellow we had till last week?" Burr asked.

"Guess he got tired of waiting," Strelski replied. "Those guys don't hang around."

Bemused as ever by the American pace of hiring and firing, Burr said no more. Only when it was too late did he realize that he and Strelski were harboring the same reservations but, out of deference to each other, refusing to express them. Meanwhile, like everybody else, Burr and Strelski flung themselves upon the impossible task of persuading Washington to sanction an act of interdiction on the high seas against the SS *Lombardy,* registered in Panama, sailing out of Curaçao and bound for the Free Zone of Colón, known to be carrying fifty million dollars' worth of sophisticated weaponry described in the ship's manifest as turbines, tractor parts and agricultural machinery. Here again Burr afterwards blamed himself—as he blamed himself for pretty much everything—for spending too many hours succumbing to the tweedy charm and old-boy manners of Ed Prescott in his grand offices downtown, and too few in the joint planning team's operations room, attending to his responsibilities as a case officer.

Yet what else was he to do? The secret airwaves between Miami and Washington were busy day and night. A procession of legal and less legal experts had been mustered, and it was not long before familiar British faces started to appear among them: Darling Katie from the Washington embassy, Manderson from naval liaison staff, Hardacre from Signals Intelligence and a young lawyer from the River House who, according to rumor, was being groomed to replace Palfrey as legal adviser to the Procurement Studies Group.

Some days Washington seemed to empty itself into Miami; on others, the prosecutor's office was reduced to two typists and a switchboard operator, while Deputy Assistant Attorney General Prescott and his staff decamped to do battle on the Hill. And Burr, determinedly ignorant of the niceties of American political infighting, drew comfort from the hectic activity, assuming, rather like Jed's whippet, that where you have so much circumstance and movement, you must surely have progress too.

· · ·

SO REALLY there had been no heavy augurs, only the minor alarms that are part and parcel of a clandestine operation: for instance, the nagging reminders that vital data such as selected intercepts and reconnaissance photographs and area intelligence reports from Langley were somehow jamming in the pipeline on their way to Strelski's desk; and the eerie feeling, known separately to Burr and Strelski but not yet shared, that Operation Limpet was being run in tandem with another operation, whose presence they could feel but not see.

Otherwise the only headache was as usual Apostoll, who, not for the first time in his mercurial career as Flynn's supersnitch, had done a disappearing act. And this was all the more tiresome because Flynn had flown to Curaçao specially in order to be on hand for him and was now sitting about in an expensive hotel, feeling like the girl who has been stood up at the ball. But even on this score, Burr felt no cause for alarm. Indeed, if Burr was honest, Apo had a case. His handlers had been pushing him hard. Perhaps too hard. For weeks, Apo had been voicing his resentment and threatening to down tools until his amnesty was signed and sealed. It was not surprising, as the heat gathered, if he preferred to keep his distance rather than run the risk of attracting another six life sentences as an accessory before and after what looked like being the biggest drugs-and-arms haul in recent history.

"Pat just called Father Lucan," Strelski reported to Burr. "Lucan hasn't had a peep out of him. Pat neither."

"Probably wants to teach him a lesson," Burr suggested.

The same evening, the monitors turned in a bonus intercept, picked up on a random sweep of phone calls out of Curaçao:

Lord Langbourne to the offices of Menez & García, attorneys, of Cali, Colombia, associates of Dr. Apostoll and identified front men for the Cali cartel. Dr. Juan Menez takes the incoming call.

"Juanito? Sandy. What's happened to our friend the Doctor? He hasn't shown."

Eighteen-second silence. "Ask Jesus."

"What the hell does that mean?"

"Our friend is a religious person, Sandy. Maybe he has taken a retreat."

It is agreed that in view of the proximity of Caracas to Curaçao, Dr. Moranti will step in as a replacement.

And once again, as both Burr and Strelski admitted afterwards, they were shielding each other from their true thoughts.

Other intercepts described the frantic efforts of Sir Anthony Joyston Bradshaw to call Roper from a succession of public telephones scattered round the Berkshire countryside. First he tried to use his AT&T card, but a recorded voice told him it was no longer operative. He demanded the supervisor, paraded his title, sounded drunk, and was courteously but firmly cut off. The Ironbrand offices in Nassau were scarcely more helpful. On the first run, the switchboard refused to accept his collect call; on the second, a MacDanby accepted it but only in order to freeze him off. Finally he bullied his way to the skipper of the *Iron Pasha,* now berthed in Antigua:

"Well, where is he, then? I tried Crystal. He's not at Crystal. I tried Ironbrand and some cheeky bugger told me he was selling farms. Now *you* tell me he's 'expected.' I don't fucking *care* whether he's expected! I want him *now!* I'm *Sir* Anthony Joyston Bradshaw. It's an *emergency.* Do you know what an emergency is?"

The skipper suggested he try Corkoran's private number in Nassau. Bradshaw had already tried it, without success.

Nevertheless, somewhere, somehow, he found his man and spoke to him without troubling the monitors, as later events abundantly revealed.

The call from the duty officer came at dawn. It had the absolute calm of Mission Control when the rocket is threatening to blow itself to smithereens.

"Mr. Burr, sir? Could you get down here right away, sir? Mr. Strelski's on his way already. We have a problem."

. . .

STRELSKI MADE the journey alone. He would have preferred to take Flynn, but Flynn was still eating his heart out in Curaçao, and Amato was helping him, so Strelski went along for both of them. Burr had offered to come, but Strelski was having a certain difficulty with the British involvement in this thing. Not with Burr—Leonard was a pal. But being pals didn't cover the whole issue. Not just now.

So Strelski left Burr at headquarters, with the flickering screens and the appalled night staff and strict orders that nobody was to make a move of any sort, in any direction, not to Pat Flynn or the prosecutor or *anyone,* until he had checked this thing out and called through with a yes or a no.

"Right, Leonard? You hear me?"

"I hear you."

"Then good."

His driver was waiting for him in the car park—Wilbur, his name was, nice enough guy but basically had reached his ceiling—and together they drove with flashing lights and sirens wailing through the empty center of town, which struck Strelski as pretty damn stupid when, after all, what was the hurry and why wake everybody up? But he didn't say anything to Wilbur because, deep down, he knew that if he had been driving he would have driven the same way. Sometimes you do those things out of respect. Sometimes they're the only things left to do.

Besides, there *was* a hurry. When things start happening to key witnesses, you may safely say there is a hurry. When everything has been going a little too wrong for a little too long—when you have been living further and further out on the margin while everyone has been bending over backward to convince you that you are right there at the center of influence: Christ, Joe, where would we *be* without you?—when you have been overhearing just a little too much strange political theorizing in the corridors—talk of *Flagship,* not just as a code name but as an *operation*—talk of *moving goalposts* and *getting a little order into our own backyard*—when you have been treated to just five too many smiling faces, and five too many helpful intelligence reports and none that is worth shit—when nothing is changing around you, except that the world you thought you were moving in is quietly easing away from you, leaving you feeling like one man on a raft in the middle of a slow-moving crocodile-infested river going in the wrong direction—and, Joe, for Christ's sake, Joe, you are just *the* best officer Enforcement *has*— well, yes, you may safely say there is something of a hurry to find out who the fuck is doing what to whom.

Sometimes you watch yourself lose, thought Strelski. He loved tennis, and he loved it best when they gave you the TV close-ups of the guys drinking Coke between games, and you could see the face of the winner getting ready to win and the face of the loser getting ready to lose. And the losers looked the way he felt just now. They were playing their shots and working their hearts out, but in the end the score's the score, and the score at the dawn of this new day was not very good at all. It looked like set and match to the princes of Pure Intelligence on both sides of the Atlantic.

They passed the Grand Bay Hotel, Strelski's favorite watering hole when he needed to believe that the world was elegant and calm. They turned up the hill, away from the waterfront and the marina and the park. They drove through a pair of electrically controlled wrought-iron gates into a place that Strelski had never entered—a piss-elegant block called Sunglades, where the drug-rich cheat and fuck and have their being, with black security guards and black porters, and a white desk and white elevators, and a feeling, once you have passed through the gates, of having arrived somewhere more dangerous than the world the gates are trying to protect you from. Because being as rich as this in a city like this is so dangerous it's amazing that everyone here hasn't woken up dead in his emperor-sized bed long ago.

Except that, on this dawn, the forecourt was

jammed with police cars and TV vans and ambu-
lances and all the apparatus of controlled hys-
teria, which is supposed to quell a crisis but
actually celebrates it. The clamor and the lights
added to the sense of dislocation that had been
dogging Strelski ever since the husky-voiced policeman had called through with the news, because "we note you have an interest in this guy."
I'm not here, he thought. I've dreamed this scene
already.

He recognized a couple of men from Homicide. Curt greetings. Hi, Glebe. Hi, Rackham.
Good to see you. Jesus, Joe, what kept you? Good
question, Jeff; maybe somebody just wanted it
that way. He recognized people from his own
agency. MaryJo, whom he had once screwed, to
their mutual surprise, after an office party, and a
serious boy called Metzger, who looked as though
he needed fresh air fast, but in Miami there isn't
any.

"Who's up there, Metzger?"

"Sir, the police have about everyone they
know up there. It's bad, sir. Five days without AC
right up there next to the sun—it's really disgusting. Why did they turn the AC off? I mean, that's
just barbarous."

"Who told you to come here, Metzger?"

"Homicide, sir."

"How long ago was that?"

"Sir, one hour."

"Why didn't you call *me*, Metzger?"

"Sir, they said you were tied up in the ops room but on your way."

They, thought Strelski. *They* sending another signal. *Joe Strelski: fine officer but getting a little old for casework. Joe Strelski: too slow to be taken aboard the Flagship.*

The center elevator took him to the top floor without pausing on the way. It was the penthouse elevator. The architect's idea was this: you arrived in this starlit glass gallery that was also a security chamber, and while you stood in the gallery wondering whether you would be fed to the pit bulls or given a gourmet dinner and a nubile hooker to wash it down, you could admire the swimming pool and the Jacuzzi and the roof garden and the solarium and the fornicatorium and the other essential furbishments of a modest dope lawyer's life-style.

A young cop in a white mask needed to see Strelski's ID. Strelski showed it to him, rather than waste words. The young cop offered him a mask for himself, as if Strelski had just joined the club. After that there were photographic lights and people in coveralls to be steered around, and there was the stench, which was somehow more pungent through the mask. And there was saying "Hi" to Scranton from Pure Intelligence, and "Hi" to Rukowski from the prosecutor's office. And there was wondering how the fuck Pure Intelligence got to arrive on the scene ahead of you. And there was saying "Hi" to anyone who looked as if he might block your path, until you somehow elbowed your way to the most brightly lit part of the auction house, which was what the crowded apartment was like, except for the stench: everyone looking at the objets d'art and making notes and calculating prices, and not a lot of attention being paid to anyone else.

And when you had reached your destination, you could see, not a likeness, or a waxwork, but the authentic originals of Dr. Paul Apostoll and his current or late mistress, both undressed, which was how Apo liked to spend his leisure hours— always on his knees, as they used to say, and usually on his elbows—both greatly discolored, kneeling facing each other, their hands and heels tied and their throats cut, and their tongues pulled through the incision to make what is called a Colombian necktie.

Burr had known at the moment when Strelski took the message, long before he knew what the message said. Just the awful relaxation in Strelski's body as the message hit him was enough, and the way Strelski's eyes instinctively found Burr's and then dismissed them, preferring some other subject to fix on while he listened to the rest. The glance and the glance-away said everything. They were accusing and valedictory, both at once. They said: You did it to me, your people. And: From now on, it's a nuisance we're sitting in the same room.

While Strelski was listening, he jotted down a couple of notes, then he asked who had made the identification, and absently scribbled something else. Then he tore off the piece of paper and shoved it in his pocket, and Burr supposed it was an address and, from Strelski's stony face as he stood up, that he was going there and that it was a filthy death. Then Burr had to watch while Strelski strapped on his shoulder holster, and reflect how in the old days, in different circumstances, he would have asked Strelski why he needed a gun to visit a corpse, and Strelski would have found some supposedly Anglophobic answer, and they'd have got along.

So as Burr remembered the moment forever afterwards, he was actually being told of two deaths at once: Apostoll's, and that of their own professional companionship.

"Cops say a man's been found dead in Brother Michael's apartment up in Coconut Grove. Suspicious circumstances. I'm going to check it out."

And then the warning, given to everyone except Burr, yet directed at Burr particularly:

"Could be anyone. Could be his cook, his driver, his brother, who the fuck. Nobody moves till I say. Hear me?"

They heard him but, like Burr, knew it wasn't his cook, his driver or his brother. And now Strelski had called from the scene of the crime, and yes, it was Apostoll, and Burr was doing the things he had prepared in his mind to do as soon as the confirmation came, in the order he had planned. His first call was to Rooke, to tell him that the Limpet operation must as of now be considered compromised. And that accordingly Jonathan should be given the emergency signal for the first phase of the evacuation plan, which required him to escape from the company of Roper and his entourage and go to ground, preferably in the nearest British consulate, but, failing that, in a police station, where he should give himself up as the hunted criminal Pine as a prelude to fast-lane repatriation.

But the call was too late. By the time Burr tracked Rooke down in the passenger seat of Amato's surveillance van, the two men were admiring the Roper jet lifting into the rising sun as it took off for Panama. True to his known behavior pattern, the Chief was flying at first light.

"Which airport in Panama, Rob?" Burr asked, pencil in hand.

"Destination to the control tower was *Panama,* no details. Better ask air surveillance."

Burr was already doing so, on another line.

After that Burr called the British Embassy in Panama and spoke to the economic secretary, who happened also to represent Burr's agency and had a line to the Panamanian police.

Lastly he spoke to Goodhew, explaining that

there was evidence on Apostoll's body that he had been tortured before he was murdered, and that the possibility that Jonathan was blown must be regarded, for operation purposes, as a certainty.

"Oh, yes, well, I see," said Goodhew distractedly. Was he unmoved, or was he in shock?

"It doesn't mean we can't go for Roper," Burr insisted, realizing that by breathing hope into Goodhew he was trying to keep up his own courage.

"I agree. You mustn't let go. Grip, that's the thing. You've plenty of it, I know."

It always used to be *we,* thought Burr.

"Apo had it coming to him, Rex. He was a snitch. He was living on borrowed time. That's the name of the game. If the Feds don't eat you, the crooks will. He knew that all along. Our job is to pull out our man. We can do that. It's not a problem. You'll see. It's just a lot happening at once. Rex?"

"Yes, I'm still here."

Wrestling with his own turmoil, Burr was filled with a feverish pity for Goodhew. Rex shouldn't be subjected to this stuff! He's got no armor, he takes it too much to heart! Burr remembered that in London it was afternoon. Goodhew had been lunching with his master.

"How did it go, then? What was this important news?" Burr asked, still trying to beg an optimistic word out of him. "Is the Cabinet Secretary coming over to our side at last?"

"Oh, yes, thank you, yes, very pleasant," said Goodhew, terribly politely. "Club food, but that's what one joins clubs for." He's under anesthetic, thought Burr. He's wandering. "There's a new department being set up, you'll be glad to hear. A Whitehall Watch Committee, the first of its kind, I'm told. It stands for everything we've been fighting for, and I shall be its head. It will report directly to the Cabinet Secretary, which is rather grand. Everyone's given it their blessing; even the River House has pledged full support. I'm to make an in-depth study of all aspects of the secret overworld: recruitment, streamlining, cost effectiveness, load sharing, accountability. Pretty well everything I thought I'd done already, but I'm to do it again and better. I'm to start at once. Not a moment to be lost. It will mean giving up my present work, naturally. But he did rather imply there was a knighthood at the end of the rainbow, which will be nice for Hester."

Air surveillance was back on the other line. The Roper jet had dropped below radar level as it approached Panama. The best guess was it had turned northwest, heading toward the Mosquito Coast.

"So where the hell is it?" Burr shouted in his despair.

"Mr. Burr, sir," said a boy called Hank. "It disappeared."

. . .

BURR STOOD alone in the monitoring room in Miami. He had been standing there so long the monitors had ceased to notice him. They had their backs to him, and their control panels to play with, and their hundred other things to worry about. And Burr had the earphones on. And the thing about earphones is, there is no compromise, no sharing, no talking the material down. It's you and the sound. Or the lack of it.

"This one's for you, Mr. Burr," a woman monitor had told him briskly, showing him the switches on the machine. "Looks like you got yourself a problem there."

That was the extent of her sympathy. Not that she was an unsympathetic woman; far from it. But she was a professional, and other matters needed her attention.

He played the tape once, but he was so stressed and fuddled that he decided not to understand it at all. Even the label confused him. *Marshall in Nassau to Thomas in Curaçao.* Who the devil was Marshall when he was at home? And what on earth was he doing calling *my joe* in Curaçao in the middle of the night, just when the operation was beginning to spread its wings?

For who would ever have supposed, at first glance, with so much else to think of, that a *Marshall* was a girl? And not only a girl, but a Jemima alias Jed alias Jeds, calling from the Roper's Nassau residence?

Fourteen times.

Between midnight and four a.m.

Ten to eighteen minutes between each call.

The first thirteen times politely asking the hotel switchboard for Mr. Thomas, please, and being told, after due attempts to connect her, that Mr. Thomas was not answering his telephone.

But on the fourteenth shot, her industry is rewarded. At three minutes to four in the morning, to be precise, Marshall in Nassau is connected with Thomas in Curaçao. For twenty-seven minutes of Roper telephone time. Jonathan at first furious. Rightly. But then less furious. And finally, if Burr read the music right, not furious at all. So that by the end of their twenty-seven minutes, it's nothing but *Jonathan . . . Jonathan . . . Jonathan . . .* and a lot of huffing and puffing while they get off listening to each other's breathing.

Twenty-seven minutes of lovers' bloody vacuum. Between Roper's woman, Jed, and Jonathan, my joe.

TWENTY-FOUR

"FABERGÉ," Roper said, when Jonathan asked him where they were going.

"Fabergé," Langbourne replied out of the corner of his mouth.

"Fabergé, Thomas," Frisky said, with not a very nice smile, as they buckled themselves into their seats. "You've heard of Fabergé the famous jeweler, haven't you? Well, then, that's where we're going, isn't it, for a nice bit of R and R."

So Jonathan had retreated into his own thoughts. He had long been aware that he was one of those people who are condemned to think concurrently rather than consecutively. For instance, he was comparing the greens of the jungle with the greens of Ireland and reckoning that the jungle beat Ireland into a cocked hat. He was remembering how in army helicopters the ethic had been to sit on your steel helmet in case the bad guys on the ground decided they would shoot your balls off. And how this time he had no helmet—just jeans and sneakers and very unprotected balls. And how as soon as he had entered a helicopter in those days, he had felt the prickle of combat start to work in him as he sent a last goodbye to Isabelle and hugged his rifle to his cheek. And how helicopters, because they scared him, had always been places of philosophical reflection of the corniest kind for him, such as: I am on my life's journey, I am in the womb but heading for the grave. Such as: God, if you get me out of this alive, I'm yours for—well, life. Such as: Peace is bondage, war is freedom, which was a notion that shamed him every time it took him over, and had him casting round for somebody to punish—such as Dicky Roper, his tempter. And he was thinking that whatever he had come for, he was now approaching it, and Jed would not be earned, or worth earning, and Sophie would not be appeased, till he had found it, because his search was for-and-on-behalf-of both of them.

He stole a look at Roper, sitting across the aisle with his head back and his sleep mask on, and it occurred to him that until recently their relationship had been of a rather formal kind— health, passports, company structures, menus, Dan and so on—and that if they had been German they would still be calling one another *Sie*. But that now, with action in the air and the same women in common, Jed and Sophie, a bond of mutual dependence was forming between them. And that Roper was aware of this also—even if he didn't know the full reason—hence the little extra confidences, glances and asides. And that he had never seen anybody riding into a battle zone in a sleep mask.

He stole a look at Langbourne, seated behind

Roper reading his way through a lengthy contract, and he was impressed, as he had been in
Curaçao, by the way Langbourne sprang to life as
soon as he caught the whiff of cordite. He would
not say he liked Langbourne the better for it, but
he was gratified to discover that there was something on earth apart from women that was capable of rousing him from his supine state—even if
it was only the advanced techniques of human
butchery.

"Now, Thomas, don't you let Mr. Roper fall
into any bad company," Meg had warned from
the steps of her plane as the men humped their
luggage to the waiting helicopter. "You know
what they say about Panama: it's Casablanca
without the heroes, isn't that so, Mr. Roper? So
don't you-all go being heroes, now. Nobody appreciates it. Enjoy your day, Lord Langbourne.
Thomas, it's been a pleasure having you aboard.
Mr. Roper, that was not a seemly embrace."

They were climbing. As they climbed, the
sierra climbed with them until they entered
bumpy cloud. The helicopter didn't like cloud,
and it didn't like the altitude, and its engine was
wheezing and braying like a bad-tempered old
horse. Jonathan put on his plastic earmuffs and
was rewarded with the howl of a dentist's drill
instead. The air in the cabin turned from ice-cold
to intolerable. They lurched over a coxcomb of
snowcaps and flipped downward like a sycamore

seed until they were flying over a pattern of small islands, each with its half-dozen shanties and red tracks. Then sea again. Then another island, coming at them so fast and low that Jonathan was convinced that the clustered masts of the fishing boats were about to smash the helicopter to pieces or send it cartwheeling down the beach on its rotaries.

Now they are splitting the earth in two, sea one side, jungle the other. Above the jungle, the blue hills. Above the hills, white puffs of gun smoke. And underneath them roll the ordered ranks of slow white waves between tongues of dazzling green land. The helicopter banks tightly as if dodging unfriendly fire. Square banana groves like paddy fields merge with the sodden moorland of Armagh. The pilot is following a sanded yellow road leading to the broken-down farmhouse where the close observer blew two men's faces off and made himself the toast of his regiment. They enter a jungle valley; green walls envelop them as Jonathan is overcome by a dreadful need of sleep. They are climbing up the hillside, shelf by shelf, over farms, horses, villages, living people. Turn back; this is high enough. But they don't. They continue until zero is upon them and life below untraceable. To crash here, even in a big plane, is to have the jungle close over you before you hit the ground.

"They seem to prefer the Pacific side,"

Rooke had explained in Curaçao, eight hours and a lifetime ago, speaking over the house telephone from room 22. "Caribbean side's too easy for the radar boys to track. But once you're in the jungle it makes no difference anyway, because you won't exist. The head trainer calls himself Emmanuel."

"It isn't even a letter on the map," Rooke had said. "The place is called Cerro Fábrega, but Roper prefers to call it Fabergé."

Roper had taken off his sleep mask and was looking at his watch as if checking the airline's punctuality. They were in free fall over zero. The red-and-white posts of a helicopter pad were sucking them downward into the well of a dark forest. Armed men in battle gear were staring up at them.

If they take you with them it will be because they daren't trust you out of their sight, Rooke had said prophetically.

And so indeed had Roper explained before going aboard the *Lombardy*. He won't trust me in an empty henhouse until my signing hand has signed me off.

The pilot cut his engines. A squat Hispanic man in jungle uniform trotted forward to receive them. Beyond him, Jonathan saw six well-camouflaged bunkers, guarded by men in pairs who must have had orders not to leave the shadow of the trees.

"Hullo, Manny," Roper shouted as he

hopped cheerfully onto the tarmac. "Starving. You remember Sandy? What's for lunch?"

. . .

THEY PROCESSED cautiously down the jungle path, Roper leading and the stubby colonel chattering to him as they went, turning to him with all his thick body at once, lifting his cupped hands to grapple him each time he made a point. Close behind them walked Langbourne, who had slipped into a low-kneed jungle march; then came the training staff. Jonathan recognized the two loose-limbed Englishmen who had appeared at Meister's calling themselves Forbes and Lubbock and known to Roper as the Brussels boys. Then came two look-alike Americans with gingery hair, deep in converse with a flaxen man called Olaf. After them came Frisky and two Frenchmen he evidently knew from other lives. And behind Frisky came Jonathan and Tabby and a boy called Fernández, with a scarred face and only two fingers on one hand. If we were in Ireland, I'd reckon you were bomb disposal, thought Jonathan. The scream of birds was deafening. The heat scalded them each time they entered sunlight.

"We are in most steep country of Panama, please," said Fernández in a soft enthusiastic voice. "Nobody can walk this place. We have three-thousand-meter-high, very steep hill, all jungle, no road, no path. Terebeño farmers come, they burn tree, grow plantain one time, go away. No terror."

"Great," said Jonathan politely.

A moment's confusion, which Tabby was for once quicker than Jonathan to solve. "Soil, Ferdie," he corrected him kindly. "Not *terra. Soil.* The *soil* is too *thin.*"

"Terebeño farmers very sad people, Mr. Thomas. Once they fight everybody. Now they must marry to tribe they do not like."

Jonathan made sympathetic noises.

"We say we are prospector, Mr. Thomas, sir. We say we look oil. We say we look gold. We say we look *huaca,* gold frog, gold eagle, gold tiger. We are peaceful people here, Mr. Thomas." Great laughter, in which Jonathan obligingly took part.

From beyond the jungle wall Jonathan heard a burst of machine gun fire, followed by the dry smack of a grenade. Then a moment's silence before the babel of the jungle returned. That's how it used to be in Ireland, he remembered: after a bang, the old noises held their breath until it was safe to speak again. The vegetation closed over them, and he was in the tunnel at Crystal. Trumpet-shaped white flowers, dragonflies and yellow butterflies brushed against him. He remembered a morning when Jed wore a yellow blouse and touched him with her eyes.

He was returned to time present by a detachment of troops jogging past him down the hill at light-infantry speed, sweating under the weight of shoulder-held rocket launchers, rockets and machetes. Their leader was a boy with dead blue eyes and a bushwhacker's hat. But the eyes of his Spanish Indian troops were fixed in angry pain on the way ahead, so that all Jonathan knew of them as they scurried past was the praying exhaustion of their camouflage-dappled faces and the crosses round their necks and the smell of sweat and mud-soaked uniforms.

They entered alpine cool, and Jonathan was transferred to the forests above Mürren, headed for the foot of the Lobhorn for a one-day climb. He felt intensely happy. The jungle is another homecoming. The path led beside steaming rapids; the sky was overcast. As they crossed a dried river-bed, the veteran of many assault courses glimpsed ropes, trip wires, shell cases and netting, blackened pampas and blast marks on the tree trunks. They scrambled up a slope between grass and rock, reached a brow and looked down. The camp that lay below them was at first glance deserted. Fire smoke rose from the cookhouse chimney, to the sound of plaintive Spanish singing. All able-bodied men are in the jungle. Only the cooks, cadre and men on the sick list have leave to stay behind.

"Under Noriega, many paramilitary was being trained here," Fernández was saying in his methodical way, when Jonathan tuned back to him. "Panama, Nicaragua, Guatemala, Americano, Colombia. Spanish people, Indian people, all was trained here very good. To fight Ortega. To fight Castro. To fight many bad people."

It was not till they walked down the slope and entered the camp that Jonathan realized that Fabergé was a madhouse.

· · ·

A COMMANDING officer's lookout point dominated the camp, and it was backed by a triangular white wall daubed with slogans. Below it stood a ring of cinder-block houses, each with its function painted in obscene figures on the door: the cookhouse with a topless female cook, the bathhouse with its naked bathers, the clinic with its bloody bodies, the schoolhouse for technical instruction and political enlightenment, the tiger house, the snakehouse, the monkey house, the aviary and, on a small rise, the chapel house, its walls illuminated with a bulbous Virgin and Child watched over by jungle fighters with Kalashnikovs. Painted effigies stood waist-high among the houses, staring with truculent eyes down the concrete paths: a fat-bellied merchant in tricorn hat, blue tailcoat and ruff; a rouged fine lady of Madrid in her mantilla; an Indian peasant girl with bare breasts, her head turned in fear, eyes and mouth open, as she frantically works the handle of a mystic well. And protruding from the windows and fake chimneys of the houses, flesh-pink plaster arms, feet and frenzied faces, blood-spattered like the severed limbs of victims cut down while trying to escape.

But the maddest part of Fabergé was not the wall daubings or the voodoo statues, not the magic words of Indian dialect sprinkled between Spanish slogans or the rush-roofed Crazy Horse Saloon with its barstools and jukebox, and naked girls cavorting on the walls. It was the living zoo. It was the demented mountain tiger crammed beside a chunk of rotting meat in a cage barely his own size. It was the tethered bucks and crated jungle cats. It was the parakeets, eagles, cranes, kites and vultures in their filthy aviary, beating their clipped wings and raging at the dying of the light. It was the despairing monkeys mute in their cages and the rows of green ammunition boxes covered with wire mesh, each box containing a separate species of snake so that jungle fighters could learn the difference between friend and foe.

"Colonel Emmanuel love very much animal," Fernández explained as he showed his guests to their quarters. "To fight we must be children of the jungle, Mr. Thomas."

The windows of their hut were also barred.

· · ·

IT IS mess night at Fabergé, miniatures to be worn. The regimental guest of honor is Mr. Richard Onslow Roper, our patron, colonel in chief, comrade in arms and love. All heads are turned to him, and to the no-longer-languid lordling seated at his side.

They are thirty strong, they are eating chicken and rice and drinking Coca-Cola. Candles in jars, not Paul de Lamarie candlesticks, light their faces down the table. It is as if the twentieth century has emptied its garbage truck of leftover warriors and vanished causes into a camp called Fabergé: American veterans sickened first by war and then by peace; Russian Spetsnaz, trained to guard a country that disappeared while their backs were turned; Frenchmen who still hated de Gaulle for giving away North Africa; the Israeli boy who had known nothing but war, and the Swiss boy who had known nothing but peace; the Englishmen in search of military nobility because their generation somehow missed the fun (if only we could have had a British Vietnam!); the huddle of introspective Germans torn between the guilt of war and its allure. And Colonel Emmanuel, who according to Tabby had fought every dirty war from Cuba to Salvador to Guatemala to Nicaragua and points between in order to please the hated Yanqui: well, now Emmanuel would balance the score a little!

And Roper himself—who had summoned this ghostly legion to the feast—floated over it like some presiding genius, now commandant, now impresario, now skeptic, now fairy godfather.

"The *Mooj?*" Roper repeats amid laughter,

picking up on something Langbourne has said about the success of American Stinger missiles in Afghanistan. "The *Mujahedin?* Brave as lions, mad as hatters!" When Roper talks about war, his voice is at its calmest and the pronouns reappear. "They'd pop out of the ground in front of Sov tanks, bang away with ten-year-old Armalites and watch their bullets bounce off 'em like hailstones. Peashooters against lasers, *they* didn't care. Americans took one look at 'em and said: Mooj need Stingers. So Washington finagles Stingers to 'em. And the Mooj go crazy. Take out the Sovs' tanks, shoot down their combat helicopters. *Now* what? *I'll* tell you what! The Sovs have pulled out, no more Sovs, and the Mooj have got Stingers and are rarin' to go. So everyone else wants Stingers because the Mooj have got 'em. When we had bows and arrows we were apes with bows and arrows. Now we're apes with multiple warheads. Know why Bush went to war against Saddam?"

The question is directed at his friend Manny, but an American veteran replies.

"The oil, for Chrissakes."

Roper is not satisfied. A Frenchman has a second try.

"For the money! For the sovereignty of Kuwaiti gold!"

"For the *experience,*" says Roper. "Bush wanted the experience." He pointed a finger at the Russians. "In Afghanistan, you boys had eighty thousand battle-hardened officers fighting a flexible modern war. Pilots who'd bombed real targets. Troops who'd come under real fire. What had Bush got? War-horse generals from Vietnam and boy heroes from the triumphant campaign against Grenada, population three men and a goat. So Bush went to war. Got his knees brown. Tried out his chaps against the toys he'd flogged to Saddam, back in the days when the Iranians were the bad guys. Big handclap from the electorate. Right, Sandy?"

"Right, Chief."

"Governments? Worse than we are. They do the deals, we take the fall. Seen it again and again." He pauses, and perhaps he thinks he has spoken enough. But nobody else does.

"Tell them about Uganda, Chief! You were tops in Uganda. Nobody could touch you. Idi Amin used to eat out of your hand." It is Frisky, calling from the far end of the table, where he sits among old friends.

Like a musician doubtful whether to give an encore, Roper hesitates, then decides to oblige.

"Well, Idi was a wild boy, no question. But he liked a steadying hand. Anyone but me would have led Idi astray, flogged him everything he dreamed of and a bit more. Not me. I fit the shoe to the foot. Idi would have gone nuclear to shoot his pheasants if he could have done. You were there too, McPherson."

"Idi was a one-off, Chief," says a nearly wordless Scot at Frisky's other side. "We'd have been goners without you."

"Tricky spot, Uganda—right, Sandy?"

"Only place I ever saw a fellow eating a sandwich under a hanged man," Lord Langbourne replies, to popular amusement.

Roper does a Darkest Africa voice. " 'Cummon, Dicky, let's watch dem guns o' yours doin' their job.' Wouldn't go. Refused. 'Not me, Mr. President, thank you. You may do with me what you will. Good men like me are scarce.' If I'd been one of his own chaps he'd have wasted me on the spot. Goes all bubble-eyed. Screams at me. 'It's your duty to come with me!' he says. 'No, it's not,' I say. 'If I was selling you cigarettes instead of toys, you wouldn't be taking me down to the hospital to sit at the bedsides of chaps dying of lung cancer, would you?' Laughed like a drain, old Idi did. Not that I ever trusted his laughter. Laughter's lying, a lot of it. Deflection of the truth. I never trust a chap who makes a lot of jokes. I laugh, but I don't trust him. Mickey used to make jokes. Remember Mickey, Sands?"

"Oh, too bloody well, thank you," Langbourne drawls, and once more earns the merriment of the house: these English lords, you've got to hand it to them, they're something else!

Roper waits until the laughter fades: "All those war jokes Mickey used to tell, had 'em all in stitches? Mercenaries wearing strings of chaps' ears round their necks and stuff? Remember?"

"Didn't do him a lot of good, though, did it?" says the lord, further delighting his admirers.

Roper turns back to Colonel Emmanuel. "I told him, 'Mickey,' I said, 'you're pushing your luck.' Last time I saw him was in Damascus. The Syrians loved him too much. Thought he was their medicine man, get 'em anything they needed. If they wanted to take out the moon, Mickey would get 'em the hardware to do it. They'd given him this great luxury apartment downtown, draped it with velvet curtains, no daylight any-where—remember, Sandy?"

"Looked like a laying-out parlor for Moroc-can fags," says Langbourne, to the helpless mirth of all. And again Roper waits till all is quiet.

"You walked into that office from the sunny street, you were blind. Very serious heavies in the anteroom. Six or eight of them." He waves a hand round the table. "Worse-looking than some of these chaps, if you can believe it."

Emmanuel laughs heartily. Langbourne, playing the dude for them, lifts an eyebrow. Roper resumes:

"And Mickey at his desk, three telephones, dictating to a stupid secretary. 'Mickey, don't fool yourself,' I warned him. 'Today you're an hon-ored guest. Let 'em down, you're a dead honored guest.' Golden rule, back in those days: Never have an office. Soon as you've got an office, you're a target. They bug you, read your papers, shake you out and if they stop loving you they know where to find you. Whole time we worked the markets, never had an office. Lived in lousy hotels—remember, Sands? Prague, Beirut, Tripoli, Havana, Saigon, Taipei, bloody Mogadishu? Remember, Wally?"

"Certainly do, Chief," says a voice.

"Only time I could bear to read a book was when I was holed out in one of those places. Can't stand the passivity as a rule. Ten minutes of a book, I've got to be up and doing. But out there, killing time in rotten cities, waiting for a deal, nothing else to do but culture. Somebody asked me the other day how I earned my first million. You were there, Sands. You know who I mean. 'Sitting on my arse in Nowheresville,' I told him. 'You're not paid for the deal. You're paid for wasting your time.' "

"So what happened to Mickey?" Jonathan asks down the table.

Roper glances at the ceiling as if to say, Up there.

It is left to Langbourne to supply the punch line. "Hell, I never saw a body like it," he says in a kind of innocent mystification. "They must have taken *days* over him. He'd been playing all ends against the middle, of course. Young lady in Tel Aviv he'd grown a bit too fond of. Some might say it served him right. Still, *I* thought they were a bit hard on him."

Roper is standing up, stretching. "Whole thing's a stag hunt," he announces contentedly. "You trek, you wear yourself out. Things pull you down, trip you up, you press on. And one day you get a glimpse of what you're after, and if you're bloody lucky you get a shot at it. The right place. The right woman. The right company. Other chaps lie, dither, cheat, fiddle their expenses, crawl around. We *do*—and to hell with it! Good night, gang. Thanks, cook. Where's the cook? Gone to bed. Wise chap."

· · ·

"SHALL I TELL you something really, really funny, Tommy?" Tabby inquired, as they bunked down for the night. "Something you're going to really enjoy?"

"Go ahead," said Jonathan hospitably.

"Well, you know the Yanks have got these AWACS down at Howard Air Base outside Panama City, for catching the drugs boys? Well, what they do is, they go up very, very high and watch all the little planes buzzing round the coca plantations over in Colombia. So what the *Colombians* do is, being crafty, they keep this permanent little bloke drinking coffee in a café opposite the airfield. And every time a Yankee AWACS goes up, this bloke's on the blower to Colombia, tipping off the boys. I like that."

. . .

IT WAS another part of the jungle. They landed and the ground crew winched the helicopter into the trees, where a couple of old transport planes were parked under netting. The airstrip was cut alongside a stretch of river, so slender that until the last moment Jonathan was sure they would belly-flop into the rapids, but the metaled runway was long enough to take a jet. An army personnel carrier collected them. They passed a checkpoint and a notice saying BLASTING in English, though who would ever read and understand it was a mystery. The early sunlight made a jewel of every leaf. They crossed a sappers' bridge and drove between boulders sixty feet high till they came to a natural amphitheater filled with jungle echoes and the sound of tumbling water. The curve of the hillside made a grandstand. From it you looked down into a bowl of grassland broken by patches of forest and a winding river, and embellished at the center with a film set of cinder-block houses and seemingly brand-new cars parked along the curb: a yellow Alfa, a green Mercedes, a white Cadillac. Flags flew from the flat rooftops, and as the breeze lifted them Jonathan saw that they were the flags of nations formally committed to the repression of the cocaine industry: the American Stars and Stripes, the British Union Jack, the black, red and gold of Germany and, rather quaintly, the white cross of Switzerland. Other flags had evidently been improvised for the occasion: DELTA, read one, DEA another, and, on a small white tower all its own, U.S. ARMY HQ.

Half a mile from the center of this mock town, set amid pampas grass and close to the river's path, lay a mock military airfield with a crude runway, yellow wind sock and dapple-green control tower made of plywood. Carcasses of mothballed aircraft littered the runway. Jonathan recognized DC-3s, F-85s and F-94s. And along the river bank stood the airfield's protection: vintage tanks and ancient armored personnel carriers painted olive drab and emblazoned with the American white star.

Shielding his eyes, Jonathan peered at the ridge overlooking the north side of the horseshoe. The control team was already assembling. Figures in white armbands and steel helmets were talking into handsets, peering through binoculars and studying maps. Among them, Jonathan made out Langbourne with his ponytail, wearing a flak jacket and jeans.

An incoming light aircraft skimmed low over the ridge on its way to land. No markings. The quality was beginning to arrive.

· · ·

IT'S HAND-OVER DAY, thought Jonathan.

It's the troops' graduation ceremony before Roper collects.

It's a turkey shoot, Tommy boy, Frisky had

said, in the over-familiar manner that he had recently adopted.

It's a firepower demo, Tabby had said, to show the Colombian boys what they're getting for their you-know-what.

Even the handshakes had a finite quality. Standing at one end of the grandstand, Jonathan had a clear view of the ceremonials. A table of soft drinks had been set up, with ice in field containers, and as the VIPs arrived, Roper himself took them to the table. Then Emmanuel and Roper between them presented their honored guests to the senior trainers and, after more handshakes, led them to a row of folding khaki chairs set in the shade, where hosts and guests arranged themselves in a half-circle, talking self-consciously to each other in the way that statesmen exchange pleasantries at a photo opportunity.

But it was the other men, the men who sat out of focus in the shadows, who commanded the close observer's attention. Their leader was a fat man with his knees apart and farmer's hands curled on his fat thighs. Beside him sat a wiry old bullfighter, as thin as his companion was fat, with one side of his face scarred white as if it had been gored. And in the second row sat the hungry boys, trying to look assured, in over-oiled hair and watered leather boots, and Gucci bomber jackets and silk shirts and too much gold, and too much bulk inside the bomber jackets, and too much killing in their fraught, half-Indian faces.

But Jonathan is allowed no more time to scrutinize them. A twin-engined transport aircraft has appeared over the northern ridge. It is marked with a black cross, and Jonathan knows at once that today black crosses are the good guys and white stars the bad guys. Its side door opens, a stick of parachutists blossoms against the pale sky, and Jonathan is rolling and spinning with them as his mind becomes a pageant of army memories from childhood till here. He is at parachute camp in Abingdon, making his first balloon jump and thinking that dying and getting divorced from Isabelle don't have to be the same thing. He is on his first field patrol, crossing open country in Armagh, clutching his gun across his flak jacket and believing he is finally his father's son.

Our paras land well. A second and a third stick join them. One team scurries from chute to chute, gathering up the equipment and supplies, while another team gives covering fire. For there is opposition. One of the tanks at the edge of the airfield is already shooting at the men—which is to say its barrel is belching flame, and buried charges are exploding around the paras as they hasten into the pampas grass for cover.

Then suddenly the tank is firing no more and will never fire again. The paras have taken it out.

Its turret is askew, black smoke oozes from its interior, one of its tracks has snapped like a watch strap. In quick succession the remaining tanks get the same treatment. And after the tanks the parked aircraft are sent skidding and reeling across the runway until, buckled and quite dead, they can move no more.

Light anti-tank weapons, Jonathan is thinking; two to three hundred meters effective range; the favored weapon for killer patrols.

The valley splits again as defensive machine gun fire pours out of the buildings in a belated counterstrike. Simultaneously the yellow Alfa Romeo lurches to life and, remotely guided, races down the road in a bid to escape. Cowards! Chicken! Bastards! Why don't you stay and fight? But the black crosses have their answer ready. From the pampas, firing on settings of ten and twenty bursts, the Vulcan machine guns drive streams of heavy tracer into the enemy positions, cutting through the concrete blocks, plugging them with so many holes that they resemble giant cheese graters. Simultaneously the Quads, in bursts of fifty, lift the Alfa clean off the road and hurl it into a coppice of dry trees, where it explodes and bursts into flames, setting light to the trees also.

But no sooner is this peril past than a new one besets our heroes! First the ground explodes, then the sky goes mad. But do not fear: once more our men are prepared! Drones—aerial targets—are the villains. The Vulcan's six barrels can achieve an elevation of eighty degrees. They achieve it now. The Vulcan's radar range finder is co-mounted, her ammunition load is two thousand shells, and she is firing them in bursts of a hundred at a time, so loudly that Jonathan has set his face in a grimace of pain as he presses his hands over his ears.

Belching smoke, the drones disintegrate and, like scraps of so much burning paper, tumble sedately into the jungle's depths. On the grandstand it is time for Beluga caviar served from iced tins, and chilled coconut juice, and Panamanian Reserva rum, and single malt Scotch on the rocks. But no shampoo—not yet. The Chief plays long.

. . .

THE TRUCE is over. So is lunch. The town may finally be taken. From the pampas grass a brave platoon advances frontally on the hated colonialists' buildings, shooting and drawing fire. But elsewhere, covered by the distraction, less conspicuous assaults are being launched. Waterborne troops with blackened faces are advancing down the river on inflatable dinghies, barely visible among the reeds. Others, in special combat gear, are stealthily scaling the outside of the U.S. Army HQ. Suddenly, on a secret signal, both teams attack, tossing grenades through windows, leaping after them into the flames, emptying their auto-

matic weapons. Seconds later, all remaining
parked cars are immobilized or commandeered.
On the rooftops, the hated flags of the oppressor
are lowered and replaced by our own black cross.
All is victory, all is triumph, our troops are super-
men!

But wait! What is this? The battle is not yet
won!

Attracted by the growl of a plane, Jonathan
again glances up at the ridge, where the control
team sits tensely over its maps and radios. A white
jet aircraft—civilian, sparkling new, unmarked,
twin-engined, two men clearly visible in the cock-
pit—skims over the hilltop, dives steeply and
zooms low over the town. What is it doing here?
Is it part of the show? Or is it the real Drug
Enforcement Agency, come to watch the fun?
Jonathan looks round for somebody to ask, but
all eyes, like his, are fixed upon the plane, and
everyone is as mystified as he is.

The jet departs, the town lies still, but on the
ridge the controllers are still waiting. In the pampas grass also, Jonathan spots five men huddled in
a fire group and recognizes the two look-alike
American trainers among them.

The white jet is returning. It sweeps over the
ridge, but this time it ignores the town and begins
instead a rather vague ascent. Then from the pampas grass comes a furious, extended hiss, and the
jet vanishes.

It does not break up, or shed a wing, or reel giddily into the jungle. There is the hiss, there is the explosion, there is the fireball that is so quickly over that Jonathan wonders whether he has seen it at all. And after that, there are the tiny sparkling embers of the aircraft's skin, like golden raindrops, disappearing as they fall. The Stinger has done its work.

For a dreadful moment Jonathan really does believe that the show has ended with a human sacrifice. In the grandstand Roper and the distinguished guests are hugging and congratulating each other. Roper is popping Dom. Colonel Emmanuel is assisting him. Swinging round to the ridge, Jonathan sees delighted members of the control team congratulating each other also, wrestling hands, ruffling each other's hair and slapping each other on the back, Langbourne among them. Only when he looks higher does he see two white puffs of parachute half a mile back in the jet's flight path.

"Likee?" Roper inquired in his ear.

Like a nervous impresario, Roper was moving among the other spectators collecting opinions and congratulations.

"But who on earth were they?" Jonathan demanded, still reluctant to be mollified. "Those crazy pilots? What about the plane? That was millions of dollars of stuff!"

"Couple of clever Russkies. Hell-bent.

Slipped down to Cartagena airport, pinched a jet, put her on automatic pilot second time round and bailed out. Hope the poor owner doesn't want it back."

"That's outrageous!" Jonathan declared as his indignation gave way to laughter. "That's the most disgraceful thing I ever heard!"

He was still laughing when he found himself caught in the cross-gaze of the two American trainers, who had just arrived from the valley by jeep. Their similarity was eerie: the same freckled smile, the same gingery hair and the same way of resting their hands on their hips while they studied him.

"You British, sir?" asked one.

"Not particularly," said Jonathan pleasantly.

"You're Thomas, aren't you, sir?" said the second. "That Thomas Something or Something Thomas? Sir."

"Something like that," Jonathan agreed, more pleasantly still, but Tabby close beside him heard the undertow in his voice and placed a restraining hand discreetly on his arm. Which was unwise of Tabby, because in doing so he enabled the close observer to relieve him of a wad of American dollars nestling in the side pocket of his bush jacket.

Yet even at this gratifying moment, Jonathan cast an uneasy glance after the two Americans in Roper's train. Disenchanted veterans? Settling a grudge with Uncle Sam? Then get yourselves a couple of disenchanted faces, he told them, and stop looking as if you ride first class and charge the company for your time.

. . .

INTERCEPTED handwritten fax relayed to the Roper jet, marked MOST URGENT, from Sir Anthony Joyston Bradshaw in London, England, to Dicky Roper care of the SS *Iron Pasha,* Antigua, received 0920 hours and transmitted to the jet at 0928 hours by the *Iron Pasha*'s skipper, with a covering note apologizing if he had taken the wrong step. Sir Anthony's handwriting bulbous and illiterate, with misspellings, underlinings and the occasional eighteenth-century flourish. The style telegraphic.

Dear Dicky,

Re our conversation two days ago, have discussed matter with Thames Authority an hour ago and have assertained that offending information is documentary in your hand, and irrifutable. *Am also led to beleive that the* late Dr. Law *was used by unfriendly elements to squeeze out previous signatory in favor present incumbent.* Thames *are taking evasive action, suggest you do same.*

In view of this crucial *assistance trust you will send another* immediate ex gratia *care of usual bank, to cover further essential expenses your urgent interest.*

Best, Tony.

This intercept, which had not been passed to Enforcement, was surreptitiously obtained by Flynn from a source in Pure Intelligence sympathetic to his cause. In his chagrin following the death of Apostoll, Flynn had difficulty overcoming his native mistrust of the English. But after a half-bottle of ten-year-old Bushmills single malt, he felt strong enough to slip the document into his pocket and, having driven pretty much by instinct to the operations center, present it formally to Burr.

· · ·

IT WAS months since Jed had flown on a commercial flight, and at first she found the experience liberating, like riding on the top of a London bus after all those dreary taxi rides. I'm back in life, she thought; I've stepped out of the glass coach. But when she made a joke of this to Corkoran, who sat beside her as they headed for Miami, he sneered at her condescension. Which surprised as well as hurt her, because he had never been rude to her before.

And at Miami airport he was equally unpleasant, insisting that he pocket her passport while he went in search of a luggage trolley, then turning his back on her while he addressed two flaxen-haired men hanging around the departure desk for the onward flight to Antigua.

"Corky, who in heaven's name are they?" she asked him when he returned.

"Friends of friends, my dear. They will be joining us on the *Pasha.*"

"Friends of whose friends?"

"Of the Chief's, actually."

"Corky, they can't possibly be! They're absolute bruisers!"

"They're additional protection, if you wish to know. The Chief has decided to raise the strength of the security to five."

"Corky, why on *earth?* He's always been *perfectly* content with three before."

Then she saw his eyes and was scared, because they were vindictive and triumphant. And she realized that this was a Corkoran she didn't know: a slighted courtier on his way back to favor, with long-held grievances to settle with interest.

And on the plane he didn't drink. The new protection were flying in the back, but Jed and Corkoran sat in first class, where he renounced all alcohol rather than drink himself into a stupor, which was what she expected him to do. Instead, he ordered himself mineral water with ice and a slice of lime, and slurped it while he admired his reflection in the window.

TWENTY-FIVE

JONATHAN WAS also a prisoner.

Perhaps he had always been one, as Sophie had suggested. Or perhaps he had been one ever since he had been spirited to Crystal. But an illusion of freedom had always been conceded him. Till now.

The first warning came at Fabergé, as Roper and his party were about to take their leave. The guests had left. Langbourne and Moranti had left with them. Colonel Emmanuel and Roper were exchanging last bear hugs as a young soldier came running up the track, calling and waving a piece of paper above his head. Emmanuel took the paper, glanced at it and handed it to Roper, who pulled on his spectacles and took a pace away to read in greater privacy. And as Roper read, Jonathan saw him shed his customary lassitude and stiffen; then methodically fold the paper and put it in his pocket.

"Frisky!"

"Sir!"

"A word."

Parade-ground style, Frisky marched face-tiously over the bumpy ground to his master and came to attention. But when Roper took him none too gently by the arm and murmured an order in his ear, Frisky must have wished he hadn't been so damn funny. They entered the helicopter. Frisky went purposefully ahead and brusquely beckoned Jonathan to take the seat beside him.

"I've got the runs, actually, Frisk," Jonathan said. "Jungle tummy."

"Sit where you're fucking told," Tabby advised from behind him.

And on the plane Jonathan sat between them, and whenever he went to the lavatory Tabby stood outside. Roper meanwhile sat alone at the bulkhead, acknowledging nobody but Meg, who brought him fresh orange juice and, halfway into the journey, an incoming fax, which Jonathan saw to be handwritten. Having read it, Roper folded it into an inside pocket. Then he put on his eye mask and appeared to sleep.

At Colón airport, where Langbourne was waiting for them with two chauffeur-driven Volvos, Jonathan was again made unmistakably aware of his altered status.

"Chief. I need to talk to you at once. Alone," Langbourne yelled up from the runway, almost before Meg had got the door open.

So everyone waited aboard while Roper and Langbourne conferred at the foot of the gangway.

"Second car," Roper ordered, when Meg

had allowed the rest of the passengers to emerge. "All of you."

"He's got jungle tummy," Frisky warned Langbourne aside.

"Fuck his tummy," Langbourne retorted. "Tell him to contain himself."

"Contain yourself," said Frisky.

It was afternoon. The police box was empty; so was the control tower. So was the airfield, except for the white Colombian-registered private jets parked in rows beside the wide runway. Langbourne and Roper got into the front car, and as they did so, Jonathan noticed a fourth man, in a hat, seated beside the driver. Frisky opened the back door of the second car, Jonathan got in. Frisky got in after him. Tabby sat the other side of him, leaving the passenger seat empty. No one spoke.

On a huge billboard, a girl in frayed shorts spread her thighs round the latest brand of cigarette. On another she teasingly licked the erect aerial of a transistor radio. They entered the town, and a stench of poverty filled the car. Jonathan remembered Cairo and sitting beside Sophie while the wretched of the earth groveled in the rubbish. In streets of former grandeur, between shanties built of planks and corrugated iron, stood old timbered houses crumbling with decay. Bright-colored washing hung from the rotting balconies. Children played in the blackened arcades and floated plastic cups in the open drains. From colonial porches, workless men, twenty at a time, stared expressionlessly at the passing traffic. From the windows of an abandoned factory, hundreds of immobile faces did the same.

They had stopped for lights. Frisky's left hand, low behind the driver's seat, was drawing a bead with an imaginary revolver on four armed policemen who had stepped off the curb and were walking toward the car. Tabby read his gesture at once, and Jonathan felt him ease against the backrest and unfasten the middle buttons of his bush jacket.

The policemen were huge. They wore pressed uniforms of light khaki, lanyards and medal ribbons, and Walther automatics in burnished leather holsters. Roper's car had parked a hundred yards down the road. The traffic lights turned green, but two of the policemen were blocking the car's way while a third talked to the driver and the fourth scowled into the car. One of the men at the front was inspecting the Volvo's tires. The car rocked as another tested the suspension.

"I think the gentlemen would like a nice present, don't you, Pedro?" Frisky suggested to the driver.

Tabby was patting the pockets of his bush jacket. The police wanted twenty dollars. Frisky gave the driver ten. The driver gave them to the policeman.

"Some bugger nicked my cash off of me at the camp," Tabby said as they drove again.

"Want to go back and find him?" Frisky asked.

"I need a lavatory," said Jonathan.

"You need a fucking cork, is what you need," said Tabby.

Following close behind Roper's car, they entered a North American enclave of lawns, white churches, bowling centers and army brides in curlers pushing prams. They emerged on a seafront lined with pink 1920s villas with giant television aerials, razor-wire fences and high gates. The stranger in the front car was looking for house numbers. They rounded a corner and kept looking. They were in a grassy park. Out to sea, container ships, cruise ships and tankers waited to take their turn on the Canal. The front car had pulled up before an old house set in trees. The driver was tapping the horn. The door of the house opened, a slender-shouldered man in a white jacket tripped down the path. Langbourne lowered his window and called to him to take the car behind. Frisky leaned forward and opened the passenger door. Jonathan glimpsed a studious Arab-looking young man in spectacles. He took his place without speaking.

"How's the runs?" said Frisky.

"Better," said Jonathan.

"Well, keep them that way," said Tabby.

They entered a stretch of straight road. Jonathan had been to an army school like this. A high stone wall festooned with cables ran along their right side. It was topped with a triple strand of barbed wire. He remembered Curaçao and the road to the dockyard. Billboards appeared to their left: Toshiba, Citizen and Toyland. So this is where the Roper buys his toys, thought Jonathan absurdly. But it wasn't. It was where he collected his reward for all the hard work and hard cash he had invested. The Arab student lit a cigarette. Frisky coughed ostentatiously. The front car swung through an archway and stopped. They stopped behind it. A policeman appeared at the driver's window.

"Passports," the driver said.

Frisky had Jonathan's and his own. The Arab student in the front raised his head far enough for the policeman to recognize him. The policeman waved them through. They had entered the Free Zone of Colón.

Sleek shopfronts for jewelry and furs recalled Herr Meister's lobby. The skyline was ablaze with trade names from across the world and the pure blue glass of banks. Shiny cars lined the streets. Lurid container lorries backed and shunted and belched exhaust fumes over the crowded sidewalks. Shops are forbidden to sell retail, but everyone was selling retail. Panamanians are forbidden to buy here, but the streets were thronged with them, in all their different races, and most had come by taxi because taxi drivers have the best arrangements at the gate.

Every day, Corkoran had told Jonathan, the official workers arrive in the zone bare-necked, bare-wristed and bare-fingered. But when evening comes they look as though they are going to a wedding, in their shining bracelets, necklaces and rings. From all over Central America, he said, shoppers fly in and out unmolested by immigration or customs, some spending a million dollars in a day and depositing millions more for next time round.

The front car entered a dark street of warehouses, and they followed it nose to tail. Spots of rain rolled like fat tears down the windscreen. The hatted stranger in the front car was studying names and numbers:

Khan's Comestibles, Macdonald's Automotor, the Hoi Tin Food & Beverage Company, the Tel Aviv Goodwill Container Company, El Akhbar's Fantasias, Hellas Agricultural, Le Baron of Paris, Taste of Colombia Limitada, Coffee & Comestibles.

Then a hundred yards of black wall and one sign saying Eagle, which was where they got out.

"Are we going indoors? Maybe they've got one there," said Jonathan. "It's getting urgent again," he added, for Tabby's benefit.

· · ·

TENSION now, as they stand in the unlit side street. A fast tropical dusk is gathering. The sky is aglow with colored neon, but in this canyon of walls and dingy alleys, the dark is already real. Everyone's eyes are on the hatted man. Frisky and Tabby stand either side of Jonathan, and Frisky's hand is on Jonathan's upper arm: not grasping it exactly, Tommy, just making sure nobody gets lost. The Arab student has gone ahead to join the forward group. Jonathan sees the man in the hat enter the blackness of a doorway. Langbourne, Roper and the student follow him.

"Mush," Frisky murmurs. They walk forward.

"If you could just find me a loo," Jonathan says. Frisky's hand tightens on his arm.

Inside the doorway, reflected light glows at the end of a brick corridor lined with posters too dark to read. They reach a T junction, turn left. The light brightens, leading them to a glazed door with plywood tacked over the upper panes of glass to hide the writing underneath. A smell of chandlery pervades the still air: rope and flour and tar and coffee and linseed oil. The door stands open. They enter a luxurious anteroom. Leather chairs, silk flowers, ashtrays like glass bricks. On a center table, glossy trade magazines about Colombia, Venezuela and Brazil. And in a corner, a discreet green door with a bucolic lady and gentleman going for a walk on a ceramic tile.

"Quick, then," says Frisky, shoving Jonathan forward, and Jonathan keeps his jailers waiting for two and a half infuriating minutes by his watch while he sits on the lavatory and scribbles on a piece of writing paper spread on his knee.

They pass to the main office and it is large and white and windowless, with recessed lighting and a ceiling made of perforated tiles, and a conference table with empty chairs drawn up to it, and pens and blotters and drinking glasses laid like places for dinner. Roper and Langbourne and their guide stand at one end. The guide, now that he can be seen, turns out to be Moranti. But something has happened to his body, some quickening of urgency or hate, and his face has the slashed grimness of a Halloween lantern. At the other end of the room, by a second door, stands the farmer whom Jonathan remembers from this morning's military display, and at his arm the bullfighter, with one of the richly dressed boys in a leather bomber jacket beside him. The boy is scowling. And round the walls, six more boys, all wearing jeans and sneakers, all honed and fit after their extended stay at Fabergé, all pressing the smaller variety of Uzi submachine gun discreetly to their sides.

The door behind them closes, the other opens and it is the door to a real warehouse: not a steel-lined abyss like the hold of the *Lombardy* but a place with some pretension to taste, with stone-slab floors, and iron pillars that fan into palm trees as they reach the ceiling, and dusty art deco lampshades hanging from the girders. On the side of the warehouse that borders the street, closed garage doors. Jonathan counts ten of them, each with its own lock and number and its own bay for a container and a crane. And at the center, cardboard boxes by the thousand, piled in brown cubist mountains, with forklift trucks standing at their feet to trundle them the sixty meters to the containers on the street side. Only occasionally is a commodity displayed: a cluster of outsized pottery urns, for instance, waiting to be specially packed; a pyramid of video recorders; or bottles of Scotch whisky, which in a previous existence might have worn a less distinguished label.

But the forklift trucks, like everything else about the place, are idle: no watchman, no dogs, no night shift toiling at the packing bays or scrubbing down the floor; just the friendly smell of chandlery and the clip and squeak of their own feet on the flagstones.

· · ·

As ON the *Lombardy,* protocol now dictated the order of progression. The farmer led with Moranti. The bullfighter and his son walked after him. Then came Roper and Langbourne and the Arab, and finally Frisky and Tabby, with Jonathan pressed between them.

And there it stood.

Their prize, their rainbow's end. The biggest cubist mountain of them all, stacked roof-high in its own fenced enclosure and guarded by a ring of fighters with submachine guns. Each box numbered, each box bearing the same pretty-colored label of a laughing Colombian boy juggling coffee beans above his big straw hat, a Third World model of a happy child, with perfect teeth and a cheerful shining face, drug-free, loving life, juggling his way into the future. Jonathan took a quick reckoning, left to right, up and down. Two thousand boxes. Three thousand. His arithmetic deserted him. Langbourne and Roper stepped forward together. As they did so, Roper's features came into the stiff arc of the overhead light, and Jonathan saw him as he had seen him the very first time, stepping into the glow of the chandelier at Meister's, tall and at first glance noble, brushing the snow off his shoulders, waving at Fräulein Eberhardt and looking every inch the buccaneering dealmaker of the eighties, even if it was the nineties: *I'm Dicky Roper. My chaps booked some rooms here. Rather a lot of 'em . . .*

What had changed? All this time and all these miles later, what had changed? The hair a mite more gray? The dolphin smile a fraction stiffer at the corners? Jonathan saw no change in him at all. At every point where he had learned to read the Roper signals—the occasional flicking of a hand, the smoothing of the horns of hair above the ears, the ruminative tilting of the head while the great man affected to consider—Jonathan saw no hint of transformation.

"Feisal, table over there. Sandy, pick a box, pick twenty, different places. You chaps all right back there, Frisky?"

"*Sir.*"

"Hell's Moranti gone? There he is. Señor Moranti, let's get this thing on the road."

The hosts had formed a group apart. The Arab student was seated with his back to the audience, and while he waited he unloaded things from the recesses of his jacket and set them out on the table. Four of the fighting boys had taken the doors. One held a cellular telephone to his ear. The rest moved quickly toward the cubist mountain, passing between the ring of guards who remained facing outward like a shooting party, clutching their submachine guns across their chests.

Langbourne pointed at a box in the middle of the heap. Two boys tugged it out for him, dumped it on the ground beside the student, and pulled up the lid, which was not sealed. The student delved in the box and drew out a rectangular package bound in sackcloth and plastic and adorned with the same happy Colombian child. Placing it on the table before him, masking it with his body, he bowed low over it. Time stopped. Jonathan was reminded of a priest at Holy Communion, helping himself to the host and the wine with his back turned, before bringing them to his communicants. The student bowed more deeply, entering a phase of particular devotion. He sat back and gave Roper a nod of approval. Langbourne selected another box, from another part of the mountain. The boys tore it from its place. The mountain slipped and recovered. The ritual was repeated. And repeated. Perhaps thirty boxes were tested in this way. Nobody fidgeted his gun or spoke. The boys at the door were motionless. The only sound was the shuffle of the boxes. The student glanced at Roper and nodded.

"Señor Moranti," said Roper.

Moranti took a small step forward but didn't speak. The hatred in his eyes was like a curse. Yet what did he hate? The white colonialists who for so long had raped his continent? Or himself for stooping to this transaction?

"Reckon we're getting there. Quality's no problem. Let's do quantity, shall we?"

Under Langbourne's supervision, the fighters loaded twenty random boxes onto a forklift and drove them to a weighbridge. Langbourne read the weight from the illuminated dial, made a reckoning on his pocket calculator and showed it to Roper, who appeared to agree with it, for he again called something affirmative to Moranti, who turned on his heel and with the farmer at his side led the procession back to the conference room. But not before Jonathan had seen the forklift truck taking its load to the first of two containers standing open-topped in the bays numbered eight and nine.

"It's coming on again," he told Tabby.

"I'm going to kill you in a minute," said Tabby.

"No, you're not. I am," said Frisky.

. . .

THERE REMAINED the paperwork, which as everybody knew was the sole responsibility of the plenipotentiary chairman of the house of Tradepaths Limited of Curaçao, assisted by his legal adviser. With Langbourne beside him and the contracting parties under the guidance of Moranti opposite him, Jonathan signed three documents, which, so far as he could make out: acknowledged receipt of fifty tons of first-quality preroasted Colombian coffee beans; certified the accuracy of waybills, bills of lading and customs declarations in respect of the same cargo, freight on board the SS *Horacio Enriques,* presently on charter to Tradepaths Limited, ex Colón Free Zone and bound for Gdansk, Poland, in containers number 179 and 180; and instructed the master of the SS *Lombardy,* presently docked in Panama City, to accept a fresh Colombian crew and proceed without delay to the port of Buenaventura on the western coast of Colombia.

When Jonathan had signed everything the requisite number of times in the requisite places, he put down his pen with a small slap and glanced at Roper as if to say, "That's that."

But Roper, until recently so forthcoming, seemed not to see him, and as they walked back to the cars he strode ahead of everyone, contriving to suggest that the real business lay ahead, which was by now Jonathan's view as well, for the close observer had entered a state of readiness that exceeded anything he had experienced. Seated between his captors, watching the lights slip by, he was gripped by a stealth of purpose that was like a new-found talent. He had Tabby's cash, and it amounted to a hundred and fourteen dollars. He had the two envelopes that he had prepared while he was sitting in the lavatory. In his head he had the numbers of the containers, the number of the waybill and even the number of the cubist mountain, for a battered black plate had dangled over it like a cricket scoreboard at cadet school: consignment number 54 in a warehouse underneath the Eagle sign.

They had reached the waterfront. Their car pulled up for the Arab student to get out. He vanished into the darkness without a word.

"We're reaching crunch time, I'm afraid," Jonathan announced calmly. "In about thirty seconds I shan't be responsible for the consequences."

"For fuck's sake," Frisky breathed. The car in front was already accelerating.

"It's due about now, Frisky. The choice is yours."

"You filthy bugger," said Tabby.

Making signs with his hands and yelling "Pedro," Frisky induced the driver to flash his headlights at the car ahead, which stopped again. Langbourne leaned his head out of his window to shout what the fuck's the matter now? A lighted petrol station winked across the road.

"Tommy here's got his tummy again," Frisky said.

Langbourne turned back into the car to consult Roper, then reappeared. "Go with him, Frisky. Don't let him out of your sight. Move it."

It was a new petrol station, but the plumbing was not up to the standard of the rest. One tiny stinking unisex cubicle with no seat was the best it could offer. While Frisky waited outside the door, Jonathan made energetic noises of distress and, once more using his bare knee as a rest, wrote his last message.

. . .

THE WURLITZER BAR at the Riande Continental Hotel in Panama City is very small and pitch dark, and on Sunday nights it is presided over by a matronly round-faced woman who, when Rooke was able to make her out in the gloom, bore an odd similarity to his wife. And when she saw that he was not the kind who needed to talk, she filled a second saucer of nuts and left him to sip his Perrier in peace while she resumed her horoscope.

In the lobby, American soldiers in fatigues dawdled in glum groups amid the colorful bustle of nocturnal Panama. A short staircase led to the door of the hotel casino, with its courteous notice forbidding the carrying of arms. Rooke could make out ghostly figures playing baccarat and yanking at one-armed bandits. In the bar, not six feet from where he sat, reposed the magnificent white Wurlitzer organ itself, reminding him of cinemas in the days of his childhood, when an organist in a radiant jacket emerged from the dungeons on his white dreamboat, playing songs an audience could hum.

Rooke took little real interest in these things, but a man who is waiting without hope must have something to distract him, or he becomes too morbid for his health.

At first he had sat in his room, keeping close to the telephone because he was afraid the clatter of the air conditioner would drown its ring. Then he switched off the air conditioner and tried opening the French windows to his balcony, but the din from the Via España was so frightful that he quickly closed them again and lay on the bed and stewed for an hour without air from either the balcony or the air conditioner, but he became so drowsy that he nearly nodded off. So he phoned the switchboard and said he was going down to the poolside *now* and they should hold any call that came for him till he got there. And as soon as he reached the poolside he gave the maître d' ten dollars and asked him to alert the concierge and the telephone exchange and the doorman to the fact that Mr. Robinson of room 409 was dining at the poolside, table 6, should anyone inquire.

Then he sat and stared at the illuminated blue water of the empty pool, and at the empty tables, and upward at the windows of the surrounding high-rise buildings, and across to the house telephone on the poolside bar, and at the boys at the barbecue who were cooking his steak, and at the band that was playing rumbas just for him.

And when his steak came he washed it down with a bottle of Perrier water because, although he reckoned he had as good a head as the next man, he would as soon have gone to sleep on sentry duty as drink alcohol while he was playing the thousand-to-one chance that a blown joe would somehow get through the lines.

Then around ten o'clock, as the tables began to fill, he feared that the effect of his ten dollars might be wearing off. So, having called the switchboard on the house line, he took himself to the bar, where he now sat. And that was where he was when the barmaid who looked like his wife put down the telephone and smiled sadly at him.

"You Mr. Robinson, 409?"

Rooke was.

"You got a visitor, darling. He very personal, very urgent. But he a man."

· · ·

HE WAS A MAN, he was a Panamanian, he was small and Asian and silk-skinned, with heavy eyelids and a black suit and an air of sanctity. His suit was polished to a regimental brightness, like the suits worn by office messengers and undertakers. His hair was waved, his dimpled white shirt was spotless and his visiting card, which was made in the form of a sticky label to be fixed beside your telephone, announced him in Spanish and English as Sánchez Jesús-María Romarez II, driver of limousines day and night, English spoken but not, alas, as well as he would wish, señor; his English, he would say, was of the people but not of the scholar—a deprecating smile to heaven—and had been acquired mostly from his American and British clients, though fortified, it was true, by his early attendances at school, though these, alas, had been fewer than he would have wished, for his father was not a rich man, señor, and neither was Sánchez.

At which sad admission, Sánchez fixed his gaze dotingly on Rooke and got down to business.

"Señor Robinson. My friend. Please, sir. Forgive." Sánchez put a pudgy hand inside the breast of his black suit. "I have come to collect you five hundred dollar. Thank you, sir."

Rooke by now was beginning to fear he was

being set up as the victim of an elaborate tourist trap, of which the upshot would be that he was to purchase pre-Columbian artifacts, or a night with the wretched man's sister. But instead Sánchez handed him a thick envelope with the word *Crystal* embossed on the flap, over what appeared to be a diamond. And from it Rooke drew a handwritten letter from Jonathan in Spanish, wishing the bearer joy of the enclosed one hundred dollars and promising him five hundred more if he would personally deliver the enclosed envelope into the hands of Señor Robinson at the Riande Continental Hotel in Panama City.

Rooke held his breath.

In his secret elation, a new fear had taken hold of him: namely that Sánchez had dreamed up some idiot plan to keep him on the hook in order to increase the reward—for instance, by dumping the letter in a safe-deposit for the night, or entrusting it to his *chiquita* to keep under her mattress in case the gringo attempted to wrest it from him by force.

"So where's the second envelope?" he asked.

The driver touched his heart. "Señor, it is right here in my pocket. I am an honest driver, sir, and when I saw the letter lying on the floor in the back of the Volvo, my first thought was to drive full speed onto the airfield regardless of regulations and restore it to whichever of my noble clients had been so careless as to leave it there, in the hope but not necessarily the expectation of compensation, for the clients in my car were not of the quality of the clients of my colleague Domínguez, in the car in front. My clients, if I may say so, sir, without disrespect to your good friend, were altogether of a humbler nature—one was so insulting as to refer to me as a Pedro. But then, sir, as soon as I had read the inscription on the envelope, I recognized that my loyalties lay elsewhere. . . ."

Sánchez Jesús-María obligingly suspended his narrative while Rooke went to the concierge's desk and cashed five hundred dollars' worth of traveler's checks.

TWENTY-SIX

AT HEATHROW it was eight in the morning of a
sodden English winter's day, and Burr was wearing his Miami clothes. Goodhew, at the arrivals
barrier, wore a raincoat and the flat cap he used
for bicycling. His features were resolute, but his
eyes were overbright. The right eye, Burr noticed,
had developed a slight twitch.

"Any news?" Burr demanded when they had
barely shaken hands.

"What of? Who? They tell me nothing."

"The jet. Have they tracked it yet?"

"They tell me nothing," Goodhew repeated.
"If your man presented himself in shining armor
at the British Embassy in Washington, I would
hear nothing. Everything's handed down through
channels. The Foreign Office. Defence. The River
House. Even Cabinet. Everyone's a halfway
house to someone else."

"That's twice they've lost that plane in two
days," Burr said. He was heading for the cab
rank, spurning trolleys, lugging his heavy suitcase
by hand. "Once is carelessness, twice is deliberate.
It left Colón at nine-twenty at night. My boy was
on it, so was Roper, so was Langbourne. They've
got AWACs up there, radar on every atoll, you

name it. How can they lose a thirteen-seater jet?"

"I'm out of it, Leonard. I try to keep an ear to the ground, but they've taken the ground away. They keep me busy all day long. You know what they call me? The Comptroller of Intelligence. With a *p*. They thought I would appreciate the ancient spelling. I'm surprised to learn that Darker has a sense of humor."

"They're throwing the book at Strelski," Burr said. "Irresponsible handling of informants. Exceeding his brief. Being too nice to the Brits. They're practically accusing him of Apostoll's murder."

"Flagship," Goodhew muttered under his breath, like a rubric.

A different coloring, Burr noticed. High points of red on the cheeks. A mysterious whiteness round the eyes.

"Where's Rooke?" he asked. "Where's Rob? He should be back by now."

"On his way, I hear. Everybody on his way. Oh, yes."

They joined the taxi queue. A black cab pulled up; a policewoman told Goodhew to get a move on. Two Lebanese tried to push ahead of him. Burr blocked their way and opened the cab door. Goodhew began reciting as soon as he had sat down. His tone was remote. He might have been reliving the traffic accident he had so narrowly missed.

"Devolution is *old hat,* my master tells me

over the smoked eel. Private armies are *loose cannons on the deck,* he tells me over the roast beef. The small agencies should keep their autonomy, but henceforth they must accept *parental guidance* from the River House. A new Whitehall concept has been born. Joint Steering is dead. Long live Parental Guidance. Over the port we talk about how to *streamline,* and he congratulates me and tells me I'm to be put in charge of streamlining. I shall *streamline,* but I shall do it under parental guidance. That means, to suit Darker's whim. *Except.*" He leaned suddenly forward, then turned his head and stared at Burr full face. *"Except,* Leonard. I am still secretary of Joint Steering and shall remain so until my master in his wisdom deems otherwise or I resign. There are sound men there. I've been counting heads. We mustn't condemn the barrel because of a few bad apples. My master is persuadable. This is still England. We are good people. Things may go amiss from time to time, but sooner or later honor prevails and the right forces win. I believe that."

"The weapons on the *Lombardy* were American as forecast," Burr said. "They're buying Best Western, with a bit of British where it's any good. *And* training in it. *And* demonstrating it to their customers up at Fabergé."

Goodhew turned stiffly back to the window. Somehow he had lost the freedom of his movements. "Countries of origin provide no clue," he

retorted with the exaggerated conviction of someone defending a feeble theory. "It's the peddlers
who do the mischief. You know that perfectly
well."

"There were two American trainers up at the
camp, according to Jonathan's notes. He's only
talking about officers. He suspects they've got
American NCOs as well. High-powered identical
twins, they were, who had the bad manners to ask
him his business. Strelski says they must be the
Yoch brothers from Langley. Used to work
Miami, recruiting for the Sandinistas. Amato
spotted them in Aruba three months back, drinking Dom Pérignon with Roper while he was supposed to be selling farms. Exactly one week later,
Sir Anthony Joyston Bradshaw, our distinguished
knight, starts buying American instead of East
European and Russian with Roper's money.
Roper never hired American trainers before; he
wouldn't trust them. Why's he got them there?
Who are they working for? Who are they reporting to? Why's American Intelligence got so sloppy
suddenly? All these radar windows appearing
everywhere? Why didn't their satellites report
all that military activity up on the Costa Rican
border? Combat helicopters, war wagons, light
tanks? Who's talking to the cartels? Who told
them about Apostoll? Who said the cartels could
have their fun with him and deprive Enforcement
of their supersnitch while they're about it?"

Still staring out of the window, Goodhew was refusing to listen. "Take one crisis at a time, Leonard," he urged in a clenched voice. "You've got a boatful of arms, never mind where they come from, headed for Colombia. You've got a boatful of drugs headed for the European continent. You've got a villain to catch and an agent to save. Go for your objectives. Don't be distracted. That's where I went wrong. Darker . . . the list of backers . . . the City connections . . . the big banks . . . the big financial houses . . . Darker again . . . the Purists . . . Don't be sidetracked by all that: you'll never get there; they'll never let you touch them, you'll go mad. Stick to the possible. The events. The facts. One crisis at a time. Haven't I seen that car before?"

"It's the rush hour, Rex," said Burr gently. "You've seen them all." And then, just as gently, like a consolation to a beaten man: "My boy pulled it off, Rex. He stole the crown jewels. Names and numbers of the ships and containers, location of the Colón warehouse, waybill numbers, even the boxes they've stored the dope in." He patted his breast pocket. "I didn't signal it through; I didn't tell a soul. Not even Strelski. There's Rooke and me and you and my boy. We're the only ones who know. This isn't Flagship, Rex. This is still Limpet."

"They've taken my files," Goodhew said, not hearing again. "I kept them in the safe in my room. They've gone."

Burr looked at his watch. Shave at the office. No time to go home.

. . .

BURR IS calling in promises. On foot. Working the Golden Triangle of London's secret over-world—Whitehall, Westminster, Victoria Street. In a blue raincoat borrowed from a janitor, and a paper-thin fawn suit that looks as though he has slept in it, which he has.

Debbie Mullen is an old friend from Burr's River House days. They went to the same sec-ondary school and triumphed in the same exams. Her office is down one flight of steps, be-hind a blue-painted steel door marked NO ENTRY. Through glass walls, Burr can watch clerks of both sexes laboring at their screens and talking on telephones.

"Well, look who's been on holiday," says Debbie, eyeing his suit. "What's up, Leonard? We heard they were taking down your brass plate and sending you back across the river."

"There's a container ship called the *Horacio Enriques,* Debbie, registered Panama," says Burr, allowing his native Yorkshire accent to thicken, in order to emphasize the bond between them. "Forty-eight hours ago she was berthed in Colón Free Zone, bound for Gdansk, Poland. My guess is she's already in international waters, headed for the Atlantic. We have information she's carrying a suspect load. I want her tracked and listened to, but I don't want you to put out a search request."

He gave her his old smile. "It's owing to my source, you see, Deb. Very delicate. Very top secret. It's got to be all off the record. Can you be a pal and do that for me?"

Debbie Mullen has a pretty face and a way of laying the knuckle of her right forefinger against her teeth when she ponders. Perhaps she does this to conceal her feelings, but she cannot conceal her eyes. First they open too wide, then they focus on the top button of Burr's disgraceful jacket.

"The *Enrico* what, Leonard?"

"*Horacio Enriques,* Debbie. Whoever he is. Panama registered."

"That's what I thought you said." Removing her gaze from his jacket, she delves in a tray of red-striped folders till she comes to the one she is looking for and hands it to him. It contains a single sheet of blue paper, embossed and crested and of appropriate ministerial weight. It is headed "The Horacio Enriques" and consists of one paragraph of overlarge type:

The above-named vessel, the subject of a highly sensitive operation, is likely to come to your notice while changing course without apparent reason or performing other erratic maneuvers at sea or in harbor. All information received by your section which relates to her activities, whether from overt or secret sources, will be passed SOLELY AND IMMEDIATELY *to H/ Procurement Studies, the River House.*

The document is stamped TOP SECRET FLAG-SHIP GUARD.

Burr hands the folder back to Debbie Mullen and pulls a rueful smile.

"Looks as though we've crossed the wires a bit," he confesses. "Still, it all goes into the same pocket in the end. Have you got anything on the *Lombardy* while I'm about it, Debbie, also hanging about in those waters, most likely at the other end of the Canal?"

Her gaze has returned to his face and stayed there. "You a Mariner, Leonard?"

"What would you do if I said yes?"

"I'd have to telephone Geoff Darker and find out whether you'd been telling porky-pies, wouldn't I?"

Burr is really stretching his charm. "You know me, Debbie. Truth's my middle name. How about a floating gin palace called the *Iron Pasha,* property of an English gentleman, four days out of Antigua headed west? Anybody been listening to her at all? I need it, Debbie. I'm desperate."

"You said that to me once before, Leonard, and I was desperate too, so I gave it to you. It didn't do either of us any harm at the time, but it's different now. Either I'll ring Geoffrey, or you'll go. It's you to choose."

Debbie is still smiling. So is Burr. He keeps his smile in place all the way down the lane of clerks until he reaches the street. Then the London damp hits him like a clumsy punch and turns his self-control to outrage.

Three boats. All going in different bloody directions! My joe, my guns, my dope, my case—and none of it my business!

But by the time he reaches Denham's stately office he is his outwardly dour self again, the way Denham would like him best.

. . .

DENHAM WAS a lawyer and Harry Palfrey's unlikely predecessor as legal adviser to the Procurement Studies Group in the days before it became Darker's manor. When Burr launched his bloody battle against the illegals, Denham had urged him forward, picked him up when he got hurt and sent him back to try again. When Darker made his successful putsch and Palfrey padded after him, Denham put on his hat and quietly walked back across the river. But he had remained Burr's champion. If Burr ever felt confident of an ally among the Whitehall legal mandarins, Denham was his man.

"Oh, hullo, Leonard. Glad you rang. Aren't you freezing cold? We don't supply blankets, I'm afraid. Sometimes I rather think we should."

Denham played the fop. He was lank and shadowy, with a schoolboy shock of hair turned gray. He wore broad-striped suits and outrageous waistcoats over two-toned shirts. Yet deep down, like Goodhew, he was some sort of an abstainer.

His room should have been splendid, for he had the rank. It was high, with pretty moldings and decent furniture. But the atmosphere was of a classroom, and the carved fireplace was stuffed with red cellophane coated in a film of dust. A Christmas card eleven months old showed Norwich cathedral in the snow.

"We've met. Guy Eccles," said a chunky man with a prominent jaw who sat reading telegrams at the center table.

We've met, Burr agreed, returning his nod. You're Signals Eccles, and I never liked you. You play golf and drive a Jaguar. What the hell are you doing, muscling in on my appointment? He sat down. Nobody had quite asked him to. Denham was trying to turn up the Crimean War radiator, but either the knob had stuck or else he was turning it the wrong way.

"I've a bit of a load to get off my chest, Nicky, if it's all the same to you," said Burr, deliberately ignoring Eccles. "Time's running against me."

"If it's about the Limpet thing," said Denham, giving the knob a last wrench, "Guy might be rather good to have around." He perched himself on a chair arm. He seemed reluctant to sit at his own desk. "Guy's been hopping back and forth to Panama for months," he explained. "Haven't you, Guy?"

"What for?" said Burr.

"Just visiting," said Eccles.

"I want interdiction, Nicky. I want you to move heaven and earth. This is what we were in business for, remember? We sat up nights, talking about just this moment."

"Yes. Yes, we did," Denham agreed, as if Burr had made a valid point.

Eccles was smiling at something he was reading in a telegram. He had three trays. He took the telegrams from one tray and, when he had read them, chucked them into one of the others. That seemed to be his job today.

"It *is* about feasibility, however, isn't it?" Denham said. He was on the arm of the chair still, his long legs stretched straight before him, his long hands thrust into his pockets.

"So's my paper. So's Goodhew's submission to Cabinet, if it ever gets there. Where there's a will—remember, Nicky? We won't hide behind the arguments—remember? We'll get every country involved round a table. Face them off. Challenge them to say no. International hardball, that's what you used to call it. We both did."

Denham loped to the wall behind his desk and plucked a cord from the folds of a heavy muslin curtain. A large-scale map of Central America appeared, covered by a transparent skin.

"We have been *thinking* about you, Leonard," he said archly.

"It's action I'm after, Nicky. I've been doing a lot of thinking of my own."

A red boat was pinned off the port of Colón abreast of half a dozen gray ones. At the southern end of the Canal, projected routes to east and west of the Gulf of Panama were overlaid in different colors.

"We haven't been idle while you've been so industrious, I assure you. So ship ahoy. The *Lombardy,* her gunwales awash with arms. We hope. Because if they're not, we're in the most frightful shit, but that's another story."

"Is this the latest position anyone's got for her?" said Burr.

"Oh, I think so," said Denham.

"It's the latest *we've* got, that's for sure," said Eccles, dropping a green telegram into the center tray. He had a lowland Scottish accent. Burr had forgotten about it. Now he remembered. If there was one regional accent that grated on his ear like fingernails on a blackboard, it was lowland Scots.

"The Cousins' wheels grind exceeding slow these days," Eccles remarked, after a small suck of the front teeth. "It's that Vandon woman, Barba-ra. Everything has to be in triplicate for her." He gave his teeth a second suck of disapproval.

But Burr kept talking only to Denham, because he was anxious not to lose his temper. "There's two speeds, Nicky. Limpet speed and the other one. American Enforcement's being given the runaround by the Cousins."

Eccles did not look up from his reading as he spoke. "Central America is the Cousins' bailiwick," he said, in his borderer's brogue. "The Cousins watch and listen; we get the take. No point in setting two dogs after one hare. Not cost-effective. Not at all. Not these days." He tossed a telegram into a tray. "Bloody waste of money, in fact."

Denham was talking before Eccles had quite finished. He seemed concerned to hurry things along.

"So let's assume she's where she is when last reported," he proposed enthusiastically, poking at the *Lombardy*'s stern with his twig-like fore-finger. "She's *got* her Colombian crew—not yet confirmed, but we'll assume it—she's headed for the Canal and Buenaventura. All *exactly* as your marvelous source reports. Bravo him, her or it. If things happen in the ordinary way—and one *assumes* that she'll want to look as ordinary as poss—she'll hit the Canal sometime today. Right?"

Nobody said "Right" back.

"The Canal's a one-way street. *Down* in the mornings. *Up* in the afternoons. Or is it t'other way round?"

A tall girl with long brown hair walked in and without a word to anybody swept her skirts under her and sat herself primly before a computer screen as if she were about to play the harpsichord.

"It varies," Eccles said.

"Nothing to stop her turning tail and pissing off to Caracas, I suppose," Denham continued as his finger prodded the *Lombardy* into the Canal. "Sorry, Priscilla. *Or* up the road to Costa Rica or wherever. Or down this way and hit Colombia from the western side, long as the cartels can guarantee a safe harbor. They can guarantee most things. But *we're* still thinking Buenaventura, because you told us to. Hence the lines on my nice map."

"There's a fleet of army lorries lined up in Buenaventura to receive them," Burr said.

"Not confirmed," said Eccles.

"It bloody well is," said Burr, without lifting his voice in the least. "We had it from Strelski's late source via Moranti, plus there's independent corroboration from satellite photographs of lorries moving down the road."

"Lorries move up and down that road all the time," said Eccles. And stretched both arms above his head as if Burr's presence were draining him of energy. "Anyway, Strelski's late source is discredited. There's a serious school of thought says he was full of shit from the start. All these snitches fabricate. They think it'll earn them more remission."

"Nicky," Burr said to Denham's back.

Denham was pushing the *Lombardy* into the Gulf of Panama.

"Leonard," he said.

"Are we boarding her? Are we pulling her in?"

"You mean, are the Americans?"

"Whoever. Yes or no?"

Shaking his head at Burr's obduracy, Eccles posted yet another telegram ostentatiously into a tray. The girl at the computer had tucked her hair behind her ears and was pressing keys. Burr could not see her screen. The tip of her tongue had appeared between her teeth.

"Yes, well, that's the *bugger,* you see, Leonard," said Denham, all enthusiasm again. "Sorry, Priscilla. For the Americans—thank God—not for us. If the *Lombardy* hugs the coast"—his striped arm made a bowler's arc until it reached a route that followed the complex coastline between the Gulf of Panama and Buenaventura—"then, so far as *we* can see, she's got the Americans by the proverbial short-and-curlies. The *Lombardy* will then be sailing straight from Panamanian national waters into Colombian national waters, you see, so the poor old Americans won't get a look in."

"Why not arrest her in Panamanian waters? The Americans are all over Panama. They own the bloody place, or think they do."

"Not so at all, I'm afraid. If they're going to pounce on the *Lombardy* with all guns blazing, they'll need to sail in behind the Panamanian Navy. Don't laugh."

"It was Eccles laughing, not me."

"And in order to get the Panamanians to the starting line, they've got to prove that the *Lombardy* has committed a crime under Panamanian law. She hasn't. She's in transit from Curaçao and on her way to Colombia."

"But she's stuffed with illegal bloody guns!"

"So you say. Or your source does. And of course one terribly hopes you're right. Or he, she or it is, rather. But the *Lombardy* wishes the Pans no ill and she also happens to be Pan registered. And the Pans are *frightfully* reluctant to be seen providing flags of convenience and then inviting the Americans to tear them down. Very hard, in fact, to persuade the Pans to do *anything* at the moment. *Post-Noriega tristis,* I'm afraid. Sorry, Priscilla. Sullen hatred is more like it. Nursing some very wounded national pride."

Burr was standing. Eccles was watching him dangerously, like a policeman who has spotted trouble. Denham must have heard him stand, but he had taken refuge in the map. The girl Priscilla had stopped pressing keys.

"All right, hit her in Colombian waters!" Burr almost shouted, jabbing a finger at the coastline north of Buenaventura. "Lean on the Colombian government. We're helping them clean up their shop, aren't we? Rid themselves of the curse of the cocaine cartels? Busting their dope laboratories for them?" His voice slipped a little. Or perhaps it had slipped a lot and he only heard a little. "The Colombian government is not going to be exactly overjoyed to see weapons pouring into Buenaventura to equip the cartels' new army. I mean, have we forgotten everything we talked about, Nicky? Has yesterday been declared a top-secret area or something? Tell me there's some logic in this somewhere."

"If you think you can separate the Colombian government from the cartels, you're living in cloud-cuckoo-land," Denham retorted, with more steel than he seemed to possess. "If you think you can separate the cocaine economy from the economies of Latin America, you're barking."

"Wanking," Eccles corrected him, with no apology to Priscilla.

"A lot of people down that way regard the coca plant as a *double* blessing bestowed on them by God," Denham resumed, launching himself on a paean of self-exculpation. *"Not only* does Uncle Sam *choose* to poison himself with it, but he *enriches* the oppressed Latinos while he's about it! What could possibly be jollier? The Colombians will be *frightfully* willing to cooperate with Uncle Sam in a venture like this, of *course*. But they just may not *quite* get their act together in time to stop the shipment. *Weeks* of diplomacy necessary, one's afraid, and a *lot* of people on holiday. And they *will* want a guarantee of costs for when they pull her into port. All that unloading, the overtime, the unsociable hours." The sheer force of his harangue was producing calm. It is not easy to fulminate and listen at the same time. "And they'll want legal indemnification in case the *Lombardy* is clean, naturally. *And* if she isn't, which I'm delighted to believe, there'll be unseemly haggling about whose guns they are once they're confiscated. *And* who gets to keep them, and sell them back to the cartels when it's all over. *And* who goes to prison where, and how long for, and with how many hookers to keep him happy in the meantime. *"And* how many thugs he's allowed to have look after him, and how many telephone lines to run his business, and order his assassinations, and talk to his fifty bank managers. *And* who gets paid off when he decides he's done enough time, which will be in about six weeks. *And* who gets disgraced, and who gets promoted, and who gets a medal for bravery when he escapes. Meanwhile, one way or another, your guns will be safely in the hands of the chaps who've been trained to use them. Welcome to Colombia!"

Burr mustered the last of his self-control. He was in London. He was in the land of make-believe power. He was standing in its hallowed headquarters. He had left the most obvious solution till last, perhaps because he knew that in the world where Denham lived, the obvious was the least likely course.

"Okay, then." He rapped the center of Panama with the back of his hand. "Let's grab the *Lombardy* when she goes up the Canal. The Americans *run* the Canal. They *built* it. Or have we got another ten good reasons for sitting on our arses?"

Denham was enthusiastically appalled.

"Oh, my dear man! We'd be infringing the most sacred article of the Canal Treaty. Nobody—not the Americans, not even the Pans—has a right of search. Not unless they can prove that the vessel they're after presents a physical danger to the Canal. I suppose if it's full of bombs that could go off, you'd have a case. *Old* bombs, they'd have to be, not new ones. If you could *prove* they were going to go off. You'd have to be jolly sure. If they're properly packed, you're scuppered. *Can* you so prove? It's an all-American thing, anyway. We're only observing, thank God. Leaning a bit where it's helpful. Staying out of their light when it's not. We'll *probably* make a démarche to the Pans if we're asked. In concert with the Americans, of course. Just to give strength to their elbow. Might even make one to the Colombs, if State twists our arm. Nothing much to be lost, not at the moment."

"When?"

"When what?"

"When will you try and mobilize the Panamanians?"

"Tomorrow probably. Could be the next

day." He glanced at his watch. "What *is* today?" It seemed important to him not to know. "Depends how tied up the ambassadors are. When's Carnival, Priscilla? I forget. This is Priscilla. Sorry not to have done the honors."

Tapping softly at her keyboard, Priscilla said, "Not for *eons.*" Eccles had more telegrams.

"But you went *through* all this, Nicky!" Burr implored in one last appeal to the Denham he thought he had known. "What's changed? Joint Steering held policy meetings galore! You had every bloody contingency cooked three ways! If Roper does this, we do this. Or that. Or that. Remember? I saw the minutes. You and Goodhew agreed it all with the Americans. Plan A, Plan B. What happened to all that work?"

Denham was unperturbed. "Very hard to negotiate a *hypothesis,* Leonard. Particularly with your Latin. You should try my desk for a few weeks. You've got to present him with facts. Your Latin won't budge until it's real."

"Won't till it's not, either," murmured Eccles.

"Mind you," said Denham encouragingly, "from all one *hears,* the Cousins are absolutely busting a gut to make this one stick. The little *we* do isn't going to alter the price of fish one farthing. And of course Darling Katie will be pulling out *all* the stops in Washington."

"Katie's fantastic," Eccles agreed.

Burr had one last, terribly mistaken shot. It came from the same locker as other rash acts that he occasionally committed, and as usual he regretted it as soon as he had spoken.

"What about the *Horacio Enriques?*" he demanded. "Only a small point, Nicky, but she's headed for Poland with enough cocaine on her to keep the whole of Eastern Europe stoned for six months."

"Wrong hemisphere, I'm afraid," said Denham. "Try Northern Department, one floor down. Or Customs."

"How are you so sure she's your ship?" Eccles asked, smiling again.

"My source."

"She's got twelve hundred containers aboard. You going to look in all of them?"

"I know the numbers," said Burr, not believing himself as he spoke.

"You mean your source does."

"I mean I do."

"Of the containers?"

"Yes."

"Bully for you."

At the main door, while Burr was still raging against all creation, the janitor handed him a note. It was from another old friend, this time at the Ministry of Defence, regretting that, owing to an unforeseen crisis, he could not after all make their promised meeting at midday.

. . .

PASSING ROOKE'S DOOR, Burr smelled after-shave. Rooke was sitting stiff-backed at his desk, changed and immaculate after his journey, a clean handkerchief in his sleeve, a copy of the day's *Telegraph* in his pending tray. He might never have left Tonbridge.

"I telephoned Strelski five minutes ago. The Roper jet's still missing," Rooke said before Burr had a chance to ask. "Air surveillance have produced some cockeyed story about a radar black hole. Bunkum, if you ask me."

"Everything's happening as they planned it," Burr said. "The dope, the weapons, the money, all heading nicely for their destinations. It's the art of the impossible, perfected, Rob. All the right things are illegal. All the lousy things are the only logical course. Long live Whitehall."

Rooke signed off a paper. "Goodhew wants a summary of Limpet by close of play today. Three thousand words. No adjectives."

"Where have they taken him, Rob? What are they doing to him at this minute? While we sit here worrying about adjectives?"

Pen in hand, Rooke continued studying the papers before him. "Your man Bradshaw's been cooking the books," he remarked in the tone of one clubman censuring another. "Ripping off the Roper while he does his shopping for him."

Burr peered over Rooke's shoulder. On the

desk lay a summary of the illegal purchases of American weapons by Sir Anthony Joyston Bradshaw in his capacity as Roper's nominee. And beside it lay a full-plate photograph taken by Jonathan, showing penciled figures from Roper's filing tray in the state apartments. The discrepancy amounted to an informal commission of several hundred thousand dollars in Bradshaw's favor.

"Who's seen this?" Burr asked.

"You and I."

"Keep it that way."

Burr summoned his secretary and in an angry rush dictated a brilliant précis of the Limpet case, no adjectives. Leaving orders that he was to be informed of every development, he went back to his wife, and they made love while the children bickered downstairs. Then he played with the children while his wife did her rounds. He returned to his office and, having examined Rooke's figures in the privacy of his room, called up a set of intercepted faxes and telephone conversations between Roper and Sir Anthony Joyston Bradshaw of Newbury, Berkshire. Then he drew Bradshaw's voluminous personal file, starting in the sixties when he was just another new recruit to the illegal arms business, part-time croupier, consort of wealthy older women, and the unloved but zealous informant of British Intelligence.

For the rest of the night Burr remained at his desk before the mute telephones. Three times Goodhew called for news. Twice Burr said,

"Nothing." But the third time he turned the tables:

"Your man Palfrey seems to have gone off the air a bit too, hasn't he, Rex?"

"Leonard, that is not a subject we discuss."

But for once Burr was not interested in the niceties of source protection.

"Tell me something. Does Harry Palfrey still sign the River House's warrants?"

"Warrants? What warrants? You mean warrants to tap telephones, open mail, put in microphones? Warrants must be signed by a minister, Leonard. You know that very well."

Burr swallowed his impatience. "I mean, he's still the legal wallah there. He prepares their submissions, makes sure they fall within the guidelines?"

"That is one of his tasks."

"And occasionally he *does* sign their warrants. When the Home Secretary's stuck in traffic, for instance. Or the world's ending. In dire cases, your Harry is empowered to use his own judgment and square it with the minister later. Right? Or have things changed?"

"Leonard, are you wandering?"

"Probably."

"Nothing has changed," Goodhew replied, in a voice of restrained despair.

"Good," said Burr. "I'm glad, Rex. Thank you for telling me." And he returned to the lengthy record of Joyston Bradshaw's sins.

TWENTY-SEVEN

THE CRISIS MEETING of the full Joint Steering Committee was set for ten-thirty next day, but Goodhew arrived early to make sure everything in the basement conference room was as it should be, and set out agenda sheets and the minutes of the previous meeting. Life had taught him that you delegated these things at your peril.

Like a general before the decisive battle of his life, Goodhew had slept lightly, and the dawn had found him clear-minded in his purpose. His soldiers were many, he was convinced. He had counted them, he had lobbied them, and to sharpen their allegiance he had presented each of them with a copy of his original paper to the Steering Committee, entitled "A New Era," in which he had so famously demonstrated how the United Kingdom was more secretively governed, had more laws for the suppression of information and more unaccountable methods of concealing the nation's business from its citizens than any other Western democracy. He had warned them, in a covering note to Burr's report, that the committee faced a classic testing of its powers.

The first person to arrive in the conference

room after Goodhew himself was his mawkish schoolfriend, Padstow, the one who had made a point of dancing with the plainest girls in order to give them confidence.

"I say, Rex, you remember that personal top-secret and whatnot letter you sent me, to cover my rear end while your man Burr was staging his frolics in the West Country? For my very own file?" As usual, Padstow's lines could have been written by P. G. Wodehouse on a bad day.

"Of course I do, Stanley."

"Well, you don't have a copy, by any chance, do you? Only I can't quite lay the old hands on it. I could have absolutely sworn I put it in my safe."

"As I remember, the letter was handwritten," Goodhew replied.

"But you didn't sort of bung it under a copier before you sent it round?"

Their conversation was curtailed by the arrival of two assistant secretaries from the Cabinet Office. One gave Goodhew a reassuring smile; the other, Loaming, was too busy dusting his chair with his handkerchief. *Loaming's one of them,* Palfrey had said. *He's got some theory about the need for a world underclass. People think he's joking.* They were followed by the heads of the Armed Services Intelligence branches, then by two barons from Signals and Defence, respectively. After them again came Merridew of the Foreign Office Northern Department. His sidekick was a grave woman called Dawn. Word of Goodhew's new appointment had been thoroughly leaked. Some arrivals shook his hand. Others mumbled awkward encouragement. Merridew, who had played wing forward for Cambridge to Goodhew's fly half for Oxford, went so far as to pat his upper arm—at which Goodhew, in an exaggerated piece of histrionics, affected frightful pain and cried, "Oh, oh, I think you've broken it, Tony!"

But the forced laughter was cut dead by the arrival of Geoffrey Darker and his reassuring deputy, Neal Marjoram.

They steal, Rex, Palfrey had said. *They lie ... they conspire ... England's too small for them ... Europe's a Balkan Babel ... Washington's their only Rome ...*

The meeting begins.

. . .

"OPERATION LIMPET, Minister," Goodhew declares as dully as he knows how. Goodhew, as usual, is secretary; his master is ex officio chairman. "Several quite pressing issues to be resolved, I'm afraid. Action this day. The situation is set out in Burr's summary; nothing has changed that we know of, as of an hour ago. There is also the competence of interested departments to be settled."

His master appears to have lapsed into a mood of sullen resentment. "Where the hell *is* Enforcement?" he grumbles. "Pretty odd, isn't it, an Enforcement case, no one from Enforcement here?"

"Enforcement is still a co-opted agency, I regret to say, Minister, although some of us have been struggling to have it upgraded. Only chartered bodies and heads of department are represented at full Steering sessions."

"Well, I think we should have your man Burr here. Damn silly, if he's been running the show, knows it inside out and we haven't got him here to talk about it. Isn't it? Well, isn't it?" Looking round.

Goodhew has not expected such a golden opportunity. Burr, he knows, is sitting only five hundred yards away. "If that is your view, Minister, will you allow me to summon Leonard Burr to this meeting, and will you allow me to record that a precedent has now been established whereby co-opted agencies engaged in matters central to your committee's deliberations may be *regarded* as chartered, pending their elevation to chartered status?"

"Objection," Darker snaps. "Enforcement's the thin end of the wedge. If we let Burr in, we'll end up with every Mickey Mouse agency in Whitehall. Everybody knows these small outfits are up for grabs. They start trouble, then they haven't got the clout to end it. We've all seen Burr's background paper. Most of us know the case from other angles. The agenda says we're going to be talking command and control. The last thing we need is the *subject* of our discussions sitting here, listening in."

"But, Geoffrey," says Goodhew lightly, *"you are the constant subject of our discussions."*

The minister mutters something like "Oh, all right, leave things as they are for the moment," and the first round is a draw, with both protagonists slightly bloodied.

. . .

A FEW MINUTES of English chamber music while the heads of Air and Naval Intelligence describe their respective successes in tracking the *Horacio Enriques.* When they have completed their reports they proudly circulate full-plate photographs.

"Looks like a perfectly ordinary tanker to me," says the minister.

Merridew, who detests espiocrats, agrees. "Probably is," he says.

Somebody coughs. A chair creaks. Goodhew hears a kind of nasal bray from higher up the scale than he is ready for, and recognizes it as the familiar sound of a senior British politician prefacing a point of argument.

"Why is this one *ours,* anyway, Rex?" the minister wishes to know. "Bound for Poland. Panamanian ship, Curaçaoan company. Not our baby at all, far as I can see. You're asking me to push it upstairs to number 10. I'm asking why we're sitting here talking about it at all."

"Ironbrand's a British company, Minister."

"No, it's not. It's Bahamian. Isn't it Bahamian?" Business, while the minister, with the mannerisms of a much older man, makes a show of rummaging through Burr's three-thousand-word summary. "Yes. It's Bahamian. Says so here."

"Its directors are British, the men committing the crime are British, the evidence against them was gathered by a British agency under the aegis of your ministry."

"Then give our evidence to the Poles, and we can all go home," says the minister, very pleased with himself. "Splendid plan, if you ask me."

Darker smiles in icy admiration of the minister's wit, but prefers to take the unprecedented step of correcting Goodhew's English. "Can we say *testimony,* please, Rex? Rather than evidence? Before we all get carried away."

"I am not carried away, Geoffrey, nor shall I be, unless it is feet first," Goodhew retorts too loudly, to the discomfort of his supporters. "As to passing our evidence to the Poles, Enforcement will do that at its discretion, and not before a decision has been agreed on how to proceed against Roper and his accomplices. Responsibility for seizing the shipment of arms has already been ceded to the Americans. I do not propose to cede the rest of our responsibility to the Poles unless those are my instructions from the minister. We are talking of a rich and well-organized crime syndicate in a very poor country. The perpetrators chose Gdansk because they think they can control it. If they're right, it will make no difference what we tell the Polish government; the cargo will be landed anyway, and we shall blow Burr's source for nothing except the pleasure of warning Onslow Roper that we are on his trail."

"Perhaps Burr's source is blown already," Darker suggests.

"Always a possibility, Geoffrey. Enforcement has many enemies, some across the river."

For the first time, Jonathan's ghostly shadow has fallen across their table. Goodhew has no personal knowledge of Jonathan, but he has shared enough of Burr's travail to share it again now. And perhaps this awareness fuels his sense of outrage, for once more he undergoes a startling change of color as he resumes his argument, his voice a little above its customary level.

Under the agreed rules of Joint Steering, he says, every agency however small is sovereign in its sphere.

And every agency however large is obliged to provide support in aid of every other agency, while respecting its rights and freedoms.

In the Limpet case, he continues, this principle has come under repeated fire from the River House, who are demanding control of the operation on the grounds that such control is demanded by its counterpart in the United States—

Darker has interrupted. It is Darker's strength to possess no middle gears. He has smoldering silence. He has, in extremis, the capacity to reverse his position when a battle looks irretrievably lost. And he has attack, which is what he uses now.

"What do you mean, *demanded by its counterpart in the United States?*" he cuts in scathingly. "Control of Limpet has been *granted* to the Cousins. The Cousins *own* the operation. The River House doesn't. Why not? It's like to like, Rex. Your own pedantic rule. *You* drafted it. Now you've got to live with it. If the Cousins are running Limpet over there, so should the River House be over here."

Having struck, he sits back, waiting for a chance to strike again. Marjoram waits with him. And although Goodhew behaves as if he has not heard, Darker's onslaught has stung him. He moistens his lips. He glances at Merridew, an old accomplice, hoping he will say something. Merridew is silent. Goodhew returns to the charge but makes a fatal error. That is to say, he departs from the march route he has mapped for himself and speaks *ex tempore.*

"But when we invite *Pure Intelligence,*" Goodhew resumes, with too much ironic emphasis, "to explain to us just *why* the Limpet case needs to be taken out of Enforcement's hands"—

he looks angrily round him and sees his master affecting boredom, staring at the white brick wall—"we are asked to share in a mystery. It is called *Flagship,* an operation so secret, and so wide-flung, apparently, that it permits of almost any act of vandalism in the civil service calendar. It is called *geopolitics.* It is called . . ." He seems to wish he could escape the rhythms of his rhetoric, but he is launched and unable to pull back. How dare Darker stare at him like this? That smirking Marjoram! Those crooks! "It is called *normalization. It is called chain reactions too intricate to describe. Interests that cannot be divulged."* He hears his voice shaking but cannot stop it. He remembers urging Burr not to go this very path. But he can't help himself. "We are told of some *larger picture* that we cannot see because we are too *lowly.* In other words, Pure Intelligence must swallow up Limpet and be damned!" There is water in Goodhew's ears, and water in front of his eyes, and he has to wait a moment before his breathing settles down.

"Okay, Rex," says his master. "Nice to hear you in form. Now let's talk turkey. Geoffrey, you sent me a minute. You say this whole Limpet thing as perceived by Enforcement is a load of baloney. Why?"

Goodhew unwisely leaps in: "Why did I not see a copy of this minute?"

"Flagship," Marjoram replies in the dead silence. "You're not Flagship cleared, Rex."

Darker offers a more detailed explanation, not to ease Goodhew's pain but to increase it: " 'Flagship' is the code name for the American end of this, Rex. They gave us a very tight need-to-know as a condition of cutting us in. Sorry about that."

. . .

DARKER HAS THE FLOOR. Marjoram hands him a file. Darker opens it and licks a prim finger and turns a page. Darker has timing too. He knows when eyes are on him. He could have been a bad evangelist. He has the gloss, the stance, the curiously prominent rump. "Mind if I ask you a few questions, Rex?"

"I believe it is a maxim of your service that only the answers are dangerous, Geoffrey," Goodhew counters. But levity is not his ally. He sounds ill-tempered and silly.

"Did the same source who told Burr about the dope tell him about the arms shipment to Buenaventura?"

"Yes."

"Did the same source get this whole thing going in the first place? Ironbrand—drugs for arms—a deal's being cooked up?"

"That source is dead."

"Really?" Darker sounds interested rather than concerned. "So that all came from Apostoll, did it? The dope lawyer who was playing all ends against the middle so that he could buy himself out of prison?"

"I am not prepared to discuss sources by name in this manner!"

"Oh, I think it's all right when they're dead. Or bogus. Or both."

Another stage pause while Darker considers Marjoram's file. The two men have a peculiar affinity with each other.

"Is Burr's source the one that's been putting out all the hair-raising stuff about the alleged involvement of certain British finance houses in this whole deal, then?" Darker inquires.

"A single source provided that information and has provided much else besides. I do not think it appropriate that we should discuss Burr's sources any further," says Goodhew.

"Sources or single source?"

"I refuse to be drawn."

"Is the single source live?"

"No comment. Live, yes. That's all I'm saying."

"He or she?"

"Pass. Minister, I must object."

"So you're saying that one live source—he or she—fingered the deal to Burr, fingered the dope to Burr, fingered the weapons to Burr, the ships, the money laundering and the participation of British finance. Yes?"

"You are missing the point—I suspect deliberately—that a great number of technical sources have supplied collateral at almost every turn, and all of it has substantiated the intelligence provided by Burr's live source. Unfortunately, much of the technical product has recently been denied to us. I intend to raise that matter formally in a moment."

"*Us* meaning Enforcement?"

"In this case, yes."

"Always a problem, you see, when one's handing hot material to these little agencies you're so fond of, to know whether they're secure."

"I would have thought their smallness made them *more* secure than much larger agencies with questionable connections!"

Marjoram takes over, but it could easily have been Darker speaking still, for Darker's eyes remain fixed on Goodhew's, and Marjoram's voice, though silkier, has the same accusatory tone.

"Nevertheless, there have been times when there has been *no* collateral," Marjoram suggests, with a tremendously sympathetic smile round the table. "Times when the source has, as you might say, spoken alone. Has given you things that were in effect *not* checkable. 'Here you are,' as it were. 'Take it or leave it.' And Burr has taken it. And so have you. Yes?"

"Since you deny us so much of the recent collateral, we have learned to make do without it. Minister, is it not in the nature of *any* source who produces original material that his product will not be provable in every particular?"

"Bit academic, all this, actually," the minister complains. "Can we get on to the gritty, Geoffrey? If I'm shoving this upstairs, I'll have to collar the Cabinet Secretary before Question Time."

Marjoram smiles in assent but does not change his tactic by a whit. "Quite a source, I must say, Rex. And quite a lot of mischief if he's leading you by the nose. Or she is; sorry. Not sure *I'd* like to take a flier on him if *I* was advising the PM, all the same. Not without knowing a bit more about him or her. Boundless faith in one's agent's all very fine in the field. Burr had a bit too much of it sometimes, back in the days when he worked for the River House. We had to keep him on a tight rein."

"The little I know of the source convinces me entirely," Goodhew retorts, digging himself deeper into the mire. "The source is loyal and has made immense personal sacrifices for the sake of his or her country. I urge that the source be listened to and believed, and his intelligence acted upon today."

Darker takes back the controls. He looks first at Goodhew's face, then at his hands where they rest on the table. And Goodhew in his increasingly fraught state has the disgusting notion that Darker is thinking it would be amusing to pull out his fingernails.

"Well, that's impartial enough for anyone," Darker says, with a glance at the minister to make sure he has heard the witness condemning himself out of his own mouth. "Haven't heard such a resounding declaration of blind love since . . ." He turns to Marjoram. "What's the man's name again—the escaped criminal? He's got so many names now I can't remember which is the right one."

"Pine," says Marjoram. "Jonathan Pine. Don't think he's got a middle name. There's been an international warrant out for him for months."

Darker again. "You're not telling me Burr's been listening to this man Pine, are you, Rex? You can't be. No one falls for him. Might as well believe the wino on your street corner when he tells you he's short of the fare home."

For the first time, both Marjoram and Darker are smiling together, a little incredulously, at the thought that somebody as bright as dear old Rex Goodhew could have made such a monumental blunder.

. . .

GOODHEW HAS the sensation of being alone in a great empty hall, awaiting some kind of prolonged public execution. From far away he hears Darker trying to be helpful to him by explaining that it is pretty standard, in a case where action is to be contemplated at the highest level, for intelligence services to come clean about their sources.

"I mean, look at it their way, Rex. Wouldn't *you* want to know whether Burr has bought the crown jewels or a fabricator's load of old bones?

Not as if Goodhew was exactly flush with sources, is it? Probably paid the bloke his whole annual budget in one shot." He turns to the minister. "Among his other skills, this man Pine forges passports. He came to us about eighteen months ago with some story about a shipment of high-tech weaponry for the Iraqis. We checked it out, didn't like it and showed him the door. We thought he might be a bit loco, to be frank. A few months ago he cropped up as some kind of fac-totum to Dicky Roper's household out in Nassau. Part-time tutor to their difficult son. Tried to ped-dle anti-Roper stories round the intelligence ba-zaars in his spare time."

He glances at the open file in order to make sure he is being as fair as possible.

"Got quite a record. Murder, multiple theft, dope-running and illegal possession of various passports. I hope to God he's not going to get into the witness box and say he did it all for British Intelligence."

Marjoram's index finger helpfully points out an entry lower down the page. Darker spots it and gives a nod to show that he is grateful to be reminded.

"Yes, that's an odd little story about him too. While Pine was in Cairo, it seems he ran up against a man called Freddie Hamid, one of the Hamid brothers of evil fame. Pine worked in his hotel. Probably pushed his dope for him as well.

Our man Ogilvey out there tells us there are quite strong pointers to suggest that Pine killed Hamid's mistress. Beat her to death, apparently. Took her to Luxor for a weekend, then killed her in a jealous rage." Darker shrugged and closed the file. "We *are* talking of somebody who is seriously unstable, Minister. I don't think the PM should be asked to authorize drastic action based on Pine's fabrications. I don't think you should either."

Everyone looks at Goodhew, but most look away again in order not to embarrass him. Marjoram particularly seems to feel for him. The minister is talking, but Goodhew is tired. Perhaps that's what evil does to you, he thinks: it tires you.

"Rex, you *have* to fight your corner on this one," the minister is complaining. "Has Burr done a deal with this man or not? I hope he hasn't had anything to do with his *crimes?* What have you promised him? Rex, I insist you remain. There have been far too many cases recently of British Intelligence employing criminals on terms. Don't you dare bring him back to this country, that's all. Did Burr tell him who he was working for? Probably gave him my phone number while he was about it. Rex, come back." The door seems an awfully long way off. "Geoffrey says he's been some kind of special soldier in Ireland. About all we need. The Irish will be *really* grateful. For Christ's sake, Rex, we've hardly started on the agenda. Major decisions to take. Rex, this is very untidy. Not your scene at all. I'm nobody's man, Rex. Goodbye."

. . .

THE AIR in the outside stairwell is blessedly cool. Goodhew leans against the wall. Probably he is smiling.

"I expect you'll be looking forward to your weekend, sir, won't you?" the janitor says respectfully.

Touched by the man's good face, Goodhew hunts for a kindly answer.

. . .

BURR WAS WORKING. His body clock was stuck in mid-Atlantic, his soul was with Jonathan in whatever hell he was enduring. But his intellect, his will and his inventiveness were concentrated upon the work before him.

"Your man blew it," Merridew commented, when Burr called him to hear how the Steering Committee meeting had gone. "Geoffrey walked all over him in hobnail boots."

"That's because Geoffrey Darker tells bloody lies," Burr explained carefully, in case Merridew needed educating. Then he went back to work.

He was in River House mode.

He was a spy again, unprincipled and uncontrite. The truth was what he could get away with.

He sent his secretary on a Whitehall forage, and at two o'clock she returned, calm but slightly breathless, bearing the stationery samples he had instructed her to scrounge.

"Let's go," he said, and she fetched her shorthand pad.

Mostly, the letters he dictated were addressed to himself. A few were addressed to Goodhew, a couple to Goodhew's master. His styles were various: Dear Burr, My dear Leonard, To the Director of Enforcement, Dear Minister. In the more elevated correspondence, he wrote "Dear So-and-so" by hand at the top, and scribbled whatever kiss-off occurred to him at the bottom. Yours, Ever, Yours aye, My best to you.

His handwriting also varied, in both its slope and its characteristics. So did the inks and writing instruments he awarded to the various correspondents.

So did the quality of the official stationery, which became stiffer the higher he moved up the Whitehall ladder of beings. For ministerial letters he favored pale blue, with the official crest die-stamped at the head.

"How many typewriters have we got?" he asked his secretary.

"Five."

"Use one for each correspondent, one for us," he ordered. "Keep it consistent."

She had already made a note to do so.

Alone again, he telephoned Harry Palfrey at the River House. His tone was cryptic.

"But I must have a reason," Palfrey protested.

"You can have it when you show up," Burr retorted.

Then he rang Sir Anthony Joyston Bradshaw in Newbury.

"Fuck should I take orders from you, Christ's sake?" Bradshaw demanded haughtily, in a quaint echo of Roperspeak. "No executive powers, lot of wankers on the touch line."

"Just be there," Burr advised.

Hester Goodhew telephoned him from Kentish Town to say that her husband would be staying home for a few days: winter was never his best time, she said. After her, Goodhew himself came on the line, sounding like a hostage who has been rehearsed in his lines. "You've still got your budget till the end of the year, Leonard. Nobody can take that away from you." Then, rather horribly, his voice cracked. "That poor boy. What will they do to him? I think of him all the time."

So did Burr, but he had work to do.

· · ·

THE INTERVIEWING room at the Ministry of Defence is white and sparse and prison lit and prison scrubbed. It is a brick-lined box with a blacked-out window and an electric radiator that stinks of burned dust whenever it is switched on. The absence of graffiti is alarming. Waiting, you wonder whether the last messages are painted out after the occupant is executed. Burr arrived late by design. When he entered, Palfrey attempted to look at him disdainfully over the top of his trembling newspaper, and smirked.

"Well, I did *come,*" he said truculently. And stood. And made a show of folding up his paper.

Burr closed and carefully locked the door behind him, set down his briefcase, hung his coat on the hook and slapped Palfrey very hard across the side of the face. But dispassionately, reluctantly almost. As he might have hit an epileptic to ward off a fit, or his own child to calm him in a crisis.

Palfrey sat down again with a plop, on the same bench where he had been sitting earlier. He held his hand to the offended cheek.

"Animal," he whispered.

To a point, Palfrey was right, except that Burr's wildness was under iron control. Burr had the real black mood on him, and not his closest friends, not his wife, had seen him with the real black mood. Burr himself had seen it seldom. He didn't sit, but crouched fat-arsed and chapel style at Palfrey's side, so that their heads could stay nice and close together. And to help Palfrey listen, he grabbed the poor fellow's drink-stained tie at the knot in both hands while he spoke, and it made a rather fearful noose.

"I've been very, very kind to you, Harry Palfrey, up till now," he began, in a mainstream speech that benefited from not having been prepared. "I've not queered your pitch. I've not peached. I've looked on indulgently while you gumshoed back and forth across the river, into bed with Goodhew, selling him out to Darker, playing all the ends against the middle, just the way you always did. Still promising divorce to every girl you meet, are you? Of course you are! Then hurrying home to renew your marriage vows to your wife? Of course you are! Harry Palfrey and his Saturday night conscience!" Burr tightened the hangman's knot of Palfrey's tie against the poor man's Adam's apple. " 'Oh, the things I have to do for England, Mildred!' " he protested, playing Palfrey's part. " 'The cost to my integrity, Mildred! If you but knew the tenth of it, you'd not sleep for the rest of your life—except with me, of course. I *need* you, Mildred. I need your warmth, your consolation. Mildred, I love you! . . . Just don't tell my wife; she wouldn't understand.' " A painful lunge of the knot. "You still peddling that crap, Harry? Back and forth across the border, six times a bloody day? Ratting, re-ratting, re-re-ratting, till your furry little head's sticking out of your puzzled little arse? Of *course* you are!"

But it was not easy for Palfrey to give a rational response to these questions, because of Burr's unyielding, double-handed, closing grip on his silk tie. It was a gray tie, silvery, which made the stains more prominent. Perhaps it had served Palfrey for one of his many marriages. It seemed incapable of breaking.

Burr's voice became a mite regretful. "Ratting days are over, Harry. The ship's sunk. Just one more rat, and that's your lot." Without at all relaxing his grip on Palfrey's necktie, he put his mouth close to Palfrey's ear. "You know what this is, Harry?" He lifted the thick end of the tie. "It's Dr. Paul Apostoll's tongue, pulled through his throat, Colombian style, thanks to Harry Palfrey's ratting. You *sold* Apostoll to Darker. Remember? Ergo, you *sold* my agent Jonathan Pine to Darker also." He was tightening his grip on Palfrey's throat with every *sold.* "You *sold* Geoffrey Darker to Goodhew—except you didn't *really,* did you? You *pretended* to, then you doubled on yourself and *sold* Goodhew to Darker instead. What are you getting out of it, Harry? *Survival?* I wouldn't bet on it. In my book you're due about one hundred and twenty pieces of silver out of the reptile fund, and after that it's the *Judas tree.* Because, knowing what I know and you don't, but what you are about to know, you are finally, terminally ratted *out.*" He relinquished his grip and rose abruptly to his feet. "Can you still read? Your eyes are looking poppy. Is that terror or penitence?" He swung to the door and grasped the black briefcase. It was Goodhew's. It had scuff lines where it had ridden on the carrier of Goodhew's bicycle for a quarter of a century, and the remnants of the official crest, worn off. "Or is it alcoholic myopia affecting our vision these days? Sit *there!* No, *here!* The light's better."

And on the *there* and *here* Burr flung Palfrey like a rag doll, using his armpits to lift him and sitting him down very heavily each time. "I'm feeling rough today, Harry," he explained apologetically. "You'll just have to bear with me. I think it's the thought of young Pine sitting there being burned alive by Dicky Roper's beauties. I must be getting too old for the job." He slapped a file on the table. It was stamped FLAGSHIP in red. "The purport of these papers that I wish you to peruse is, Harry: you are singly and collectively fucked. Rex Goodhew is not the buffoon you took him for. More under his flat hat than we ever knew. Now read on."

Palfrey read on, but it cannot have been an easy read, which was what Burr had intended when he went to such lengths to rob him of his repose. And before Palfrey had quite finished reading he started weeping, so copiously that some of his tears blotted the signatures and Dear Ministers and Yours evers that topped and tailed the faked correspondence.

While Palfrey was still weeping, Burr produced a Home Office warrant, which so far bore nobody's signature at all. It was not a plenary warrant. It was merely a warrant of interference, authorizing the listeners to impose a technical fault on three telephone numbers, two in London and one in Suffolk. This simulated fault would have the effect of misrouting all calls made to the three numbers to yet a fourth number, of which the coordinates were given in the appropriate space. Palfrey stared at the warrant; Palfrey shook his head and tried to make noises of refusal through his clogged mouth.

"Those are Darker's numbers," he objected. "Country, town, office. I can't sign that. He'd kill me."

"But if you *don't* sign, Harry, *I'll* kill you. Because if you go through channels and take this warrant to the appropriate minister, the said minister will go running to his Uncle Geoffrey. So we're not doing that, Harry. You personally are going to sign the warrant on your own authority, which is what you're empowered to do in exceptional circumstances. And I personally am going to send the warrant to the listeners by very safe messenger. And you personally are going to spend a quiet social evening with my friend Rob Rooke in his office, so that you personally don't run the temptation of ratting in the meantime out of habit. And if you *do* make any fuss, my good friend Rob will most likely chain you to a radiator until you repent yourself of your many sins, because he's a hulk. Here. Use my pen. That's the way. In triplicate, please. You know what these civil servants are. Who do you talk to over at the listeners, these days?"

"No one. Maisie Watts."

"Who's Maisie, Harry? I'm not in touch these days."

"Queen bee. Maisie makes it happen."

"And if Maisie's out to lunch with her Uncle Geoffrey?"

"Gates. Pearly, we call him." A weak grin. "Pearly's a bit of a boy."

Burr picked Palfrey up again and dropped him heavily before a green telephone.

"Call Maisie. Is that what you'd do in an emergency?"

Palfrey whistled a kind of yes.

"Say there's a very hot authorization on its way by special courier. She's to handle it herself. Or Gates is. No secretaries, no lower decks, no answering back, no raised eyebrows. You want slavish, mute obedience. Say it's signed by you, and the highest ministerial confirmation in the land will follow soonest. Why are you shaking your head at me?" He slapped him. "I don't like you shaking your head at me. Don't do it."

Palfrey managed a tearful smile while he held a hand to his lip. "I'd be jokier, Leonard, that's all. Specially if it's as big as this. Maisie likes a laugh. So does Pearly. 'Hey Maise! Wait till you

get a load of this one! It'll blow your socks off!'
Clever gal, you see. Gets bored. Hates us all. Only
interested in who's next up the guillotine steps."

"Then that's how you play it, isn't it?" said
Burr, putting a friendly hand on Palfrey's shoulder. "Just don't fox with me, Harry, or the next
one up the steps is you."

All eagerness to oblige, Palfrey lifted the receiver of the green Whitehall internal telephone
and, under Burr's gaze, dialed the five digits that
every River rat learns at his mother's knee.

TWENTY-EIGHT

DEPUTY ASSISTANT ATTORNEY GENERAL Ed
Prescott was a man's man, as Yale men of his
generation tend to be, and when Joe Strelski entered his big white office in downtown Miami
after being kept waiting half an hour in the anteroom, Ed gave him the news as one man should to
another, cutting out the bullshit, straight from the
shoulder the way a man likes it, whether he's old
New England stock like Ed, or plain Kentucky
hillbilly like Strelski. Because frankly, Joe, those
boys have fucked me over too: dragged me here
from Washington to do this thing, had me turn
down some very attractive work at a time when
everyone, and I mean everyone, even the guys
right up there, needs the work. Joe, I have to say
it to you—these people have not been square with
us. So I want you to appreciate we're together in
this. It's been a year of your life, but by the time
I've put my house back in order it will have been
a year of my life too. And at my age, Joe—well,
hell, how many years do I have?

"I'm sorry for you, Ed," said Strelski.

And if Ed Prescott caught the undertone,
he preferred to let it pass him by, in the interest

of being two men together, solving a shared dilemma.

"Joe, just exactly how much did the Brits tell you about this undercover man they had, this Pine, this fellow with the names?"

Strelski did not fail to notice the past tense.

"Not too much," said Strelski.

"So how much?" said Prescott, man-to-man.

"He wasn't a professional. He was some kind of volunteer."

"A walk-in? I never trusted walk-ins, Joe. In the days when the Agency paid me the compliment of consulting me from time to time, back in the Cold War, which seems like a century ago, I always counseled caution toward these would-be Soviet defectors clamoring to make us a present of their wares. What else did they tell you about him, Joe, or did they keep him wrapped in a flattering shroud of mystery?"

Strelski's manner was deliberately deadpan. With men like Prescott that was all you could do: parry until you had worked out what he wanted you to say, then either say it, or plead the Fifth, or tell him to shove it up his ass.

"They told me they had structured him in some way," he replied. "They'd given him extra background to make him more attractive to the target."

"*Who* told you, Joe?"

"Burr."

"Did Burr tell you the nature of this background at all, Joe?"

"No."

"Did Burr indicate to you how much background was there already, and how much came out of the makeup box?"

"No."

"Memory is a whore, Joe. Think back. Did he tell you that the man was alleged to have committed a homicide? Maybe more than one?"

"No."

"Smuggled drugs? In Cairo as well as Britain? Maybe in Switzerland also? We're checking."

"He was not specific. He said they had fitted the guy out with this background, and that now that he had this background we could have Apostoll badmouth one of Roper's lieutenants and figure Roper would take to the new guy as a signer. Roper uses signers. So they gave him a signer. He likes his people flaky. So they gave him flaky."

"So the Brits were witting to Apostoll. I don't think I knew that."

"Sure they were. We made a meeting with him. Burr, Agent Flynn and myself."

"Was that wise, Joe?"

"It was collaboration," said Strelski with a tightening of his voice. "We were into collaboration, remember? It's come apart at the seams a little. But in those days we had joint planning."

Time stopped while Ed Prescott took a tour around his very large office. Its darkened windows were of inch-deep armored glass, turning the morning sunlight into afternoon. The double doors, closed against intruders, were of reinforced steel. Miami was enduring a season of home invasions, Strelski remembered. Teams of masked men held up everybody in the house, then helped themselves to whatever caught their eye. Strelski wondered whether he would go to Apo's funeral this afternoon. The day is young. See what I decide. After that he wondered whether he would go back to his wife. When things got this lousy, that was what he always wondered. Sometimes being away from her was like being out on parole. It wasn't freedom, and sometimes you seriously wondered whether it was any better than the alternative. He thought of Pat Flynn and wished he had Pat's composure. Pat took to being an outcast like other people take to fame and money. When they told Pat not to bother with coming into the office till this thing was cleared up, Pat thanked them, shook all their hands, had a bath and drank a bottle of Bushmills. This morning, still drunk, he had called Strelski to warn him of a new form of AIDS that was afflicting Miami. It was called Hearing Aids, Pat said, and came from listening to too many assholes from Washington. When Strelski asked him whether he happened to have heard any news about the *Lombardy*—for instance, whether anybody had seized it, sunk it or married it—Flynn had given the best rendering of an Ivy League exquisite that Strelski could remember: "Oh now, Joe, you bad boy, you know better than to ask a man a secret thing like that, with *your* clearance." Where the hell does Pat get all those voices from? he wondered. Maybe if I drank a bottle of Irish a day, I could do some too. Deputy Assistant Attorney General Ed Prescott was trying to put more words into his mouth, so he supposed he'd better pay attention.

"Burr was evidently not as forthcoming about his Mr. Pine as you were about your Dr. Apostoll, Joe," he was saying, with enough reproach in his voice to sting.

"Pine and Apostoll were different types of sources. They were not comparable in any way," Strelski retorted, pleased to hear himself loosening up. It must have been Flynn's joke about Hearing Aids.

"Like to explain that a little, Joe?"

"Apostoll was a decadent creep. Pine was— Pine was an honorable guy who took risks for the right side. Burr was very strong on that. Pine was an operative, he was a colleague, he was family. Nobody ever called Apo family. Not even his daughter."

"Was this Pine the same man who practically dismembered your agent, Joe?"

"He was under tension. It was a big piece of

theater. Maybe he overreacted, took his instructions a little too much to heart."

"Is that what Burr told you?"

"We tried to work it out that way."

"That was generous of you, Joe. An agent in your employ takes a beating to the tune of twenty thousand dollars' worth of medication plus three months' sick leave and a pending lawsuit, and you tell me his assailant maybe overreacted a little. Some of these Oxford-educated Englishmen can be very persuasive in their arguments. Did Leonard Burr ever strike you as a disingenuous person?"

Everyone is in the past, thought Strelski. Including me. "I don't know what that means," he lied.

"Lacking in candor? Insincere? Morally fraudulent in some way?"

"No."

"Just no?"

"Burr's a good operator and a good man."

Prescott took another tour round the room. As a good man himself, he seemed to have difficulty wrestling with the harsher facts of life.

"Joe, we have a couple of problems with the Brits right now. I'm speaking at the Enforcement level. What your Mr. Burr and his confederates promised us here was a squeaky-clean witness in the form of Mr. Pine, a sophisticated operation, some big heads on a platter. We went along with that. We had fine expectations of Mr. Burr, and of Mr. Pine. I have to tell you that at the Enforcement level the British have not lived up to their promises. In their dealings with us, they have shown a duplicity which some of us might not have expected of them. Others, with longer memories, on the other hand, might."

Strelski supposed he should join Prescott in some general damnation of the British, but he didn't feel inclined. He liked Burr. Burr was the kind of fellow you could rustle horses with. He'd learned to like Rooke, although he was a tight-ass. They were a pair of nice guys, and they had run a good operation.

"Joe, this class act of yours—forgive me, of Mr. Burr's—this honorable guy, this Mr. Pine, has a criminal record going back for years. Barbara Vandon in London and friends of hers up in Langley have dug up some very unsettling background material on Mr. Pine. It seems he is a closet psychopath. Unfortunately, the British pandered to his appetites. There was a quite bad killing in Ireland, something with a semi-automatic. We haven't gotten to the bottom of it, because they hushed it up." Prescott gave a sigh. The ways of men were devious indeed. "Mr. Pine kills, Joe. He kills and he steals and he runs dope, and it's a mystery to me that he never used that knife he pulled on your agent. Mr. Pine is also a cook, a night owl, a close-combat expert and a painter. Joe, that is the classic pattern of a psychopathic fantasist. I do not like Mr. Pine. I would not trust him with my daughter. Mr. Pine had a psychopathic relationship with a doper's hooker in Cairo, and ended up beating her to death. I would not trust Mr. Pine on the stand as my witness, and I have the gravest, and I mean the gravest, reservations about the intelligence he has hitherto supplied. I've seen it, Joe. I've studied it at the many points where his testimony stands alone and uncorroborated yet indispensable to the credibility of our case. Men like Mr. Pine are the secret liars of society. They will sell their own mothers and believe themselves to be Jesus Christ while they do it. Your friend Burr may be capable, but he was an ambitious man who was breaking his ass to get his own outfit off the ground and have it compete with the big players. Such men are the natural prey of the fabricator. I do not believe that Mr. Burr and Mr. Pine made a wholesome pair. I don't say they consciously conspired, but men in secret conclave can psych one another up in ways that make them cavalier with the truth. If Dr. Apostoll were still with us—well, he was a lawyer, and even if he was a little crazy, it was my belief that he would hold up pretty well in the stand. Juries always have a place in their hearts for a man who has returned to God. However, that is not to be. Dr. Apostoll is no longer available as a witness."

Strelski was trying to help Prescott off the hook. "It never happened, right, Ed? How's about we agree the whole case was a piece of horseshit? There's no dope, no guns, Mr. Onslow Roper never broke bread with the cartels, mistaken identity, you name it."

Prescott pulled a rueful smile as if to say he did not think that he would go that far. "We are talking about what's demonstrable, Joe. That's a lawyer's job. The lay citizen has the luxury of believing in the truth. A lawyer has to be content with the demonstrable. Put it that way."

"Sure." Strelski was smiling too. "Ed, may I say something?" Strelski leaned forward in his leather chair and opened his hands in a gesture of magnanimity.

"Go right ahead, Joe."

"Ed, relax, please. Don't strain yourself. Operation Limpet is dead. Langley killed it. You're just the mortician. I understand that. Operation Flagship lives, but I'm not Flagship cleared. My guess is, you are. You want to screw me, Ed? Listen, I've been screwed before; you don't have to take me to dinner first. I've been screwed so many times, with so many variations, I'm a veteran. This time it's Langley and some bad Brits. Not to mention a few Colombians. Last time it was Langley and some bad somebody else, maybe they were Brazilians—no, dammit, they were Cubans, and they'd done us a few favors in the dark days. Time before that it was Langley and some very, very rich Venezuelans, but I think there were also some Israelis besides—to be honest, I forget—and the files got lost. And I think there was an Operation Surefire, but I wasn't Surefire cleared."

He was furious but wonderfully comfortable. Prescott's deep leather armchair was a dream; he could lounge in it forever, just breathing in the luxury of a nice penthouse office without the unpleasantness of a lot of people getting in his way or a naked snitch kneeling on the bed with his tongue pulled down his chest.

"The other thing you want to tell me, Ed, is I can kiss but I can't tell," Strelski resumed. "Because if I tell, somebody will have my ass and take away my pension. Or if I *really* tell, somebody may feel obliged reluctantly to shoot my fucking head off. I understand those things, Ed. I have learned the rules. Ed, will you do me a favor?"

Prescott was not accustomed to listening without interrupting, and he never did anyone a favor unless he could count on one in return. But he knew anger when he saw it, and he knew that anger given time subsides, whether in people or in animals, so he regarded his role as essentially a waiting one and kept his smile going and answered rationally, as he would if he were in the presence of a raving lunatic. He knew also that it was essential not to show alarm. There was always the red button on the inside of his desk.

"If I can, Joe, for you, anything," he replied handsomely.

"Don't change, Ed. America needs you as you are. Don't give up any of your friends in high places or your connections with the Agency or your wife's arm's-length lucrative directorships of certain companies. Keep fixing things for us. The decent citizen knows too much already, Ed. Any more knowledge could seriously endanger his health. Think television. Five seconds of any subject is enough for anybody. People have to be normalized, Ed, not destabilized. And you're the man to do it for us."

. . .

STRELSKI DROVE HOME carefully through the winter sunlight. Anger brought its own vividness. Pretty white houses along the waterfront. White sailing yachts at the end of emerald lawns. The postman on his midday round. A red Ford Mustang was parked in his drive, and he recognized it as Amato's. He found him sitting on the deck wearing a funereal black tie and drinking Coke from the icebox. Stretched beside him on Strelski's rattan sofa, dressed in a Bogside black suit complete with waistcoat and black derby, lay a comatose Pat Flynn, an empty bottle of Bushmills single malt whiskey, ten years old, clutched to his bosom.

"Pat's been socializing with his former boss again," Amato explained, with a glance at his recumbent comrade. "They had like early breakfast. Leonard's snitch is aboard the *Iron Pasha*. Two guys helped him off the Roper jet at Antigua, two more guys helped him onto the seaplane. Pat's friend is quoting from reports compiled by very pure persons in Intelligence who have the honor to be Flagship cleared. Pat says maybe you'd like to pass the word of this to your friend Lenny Burr. Pat says to give Lenny his best respects. He enjoyed the experience of Mr. Burr despite the subsequent difficulties, tell him."

Strelski glanced at his watch and went quickly indoors. Speech on this phone was not secure. Burr picked up his end at once, as if he were waiting for it to ring.

"Your boy's gone sailing with his rich friends," Strelski said.

. . .

BURR WAS THANKFUL for the pelting rain. A couple of times he had pulled onto the grass verge and sat in the car with the torrent booming on the roof while he waited till it eased. The downpour bestowed a temporary pardon. It restored the handloom weaver to his attic.

He was running later than he had meant to.

"Take care," he had said meaninglessly, as he consigned the abject Palfrey to Rooke's custody. Take care of Palfrey, perhaps he was thinking. Or perhaps: Dear God, take care of Jonathan.

He's on the *Pasha,* he kept thinking as he drove. He's alive, even if he'd rather not be. For a while, that was all Burr's brain could do for him: Jonathan's alive, Jonathan's in torment, they're doing it to him *now.* Only after this period of due anguish, as it seemed to Burr, was he able to apply his considerable powers of reasoning and, little by little, count up what crumbs of consolation he could find.

He's alive. Therefore Roper must want to keep him that way. Otherwise he would have had Jonathan killed as soon as he had signed his last piece of paper: another unexplained corpse on the Panamanian roadside, who cares?

He's alive. A crook of Roper's stamp does not bring a man to his cruise yacht in order to kill him. He brings him because he needs to ask him things, and if he needs to kill him afterwards, he does it at a decent distance from the boat, with a proper respect for the local hygiene and the sensitivities of his guests.

So what does Roper want to ask him that he doesn't already know?

Perhaps: How much has Jonathan betrayed of the fine detail of the operation?

Perhaps: What is now the precise risk to Roper—of prosecution, of the frustration of his grand scheme, of exposure, scandal, outcry?

Perhaps: How much protection do I still enjoy among those who are protecting me? Or will they be tiptoeing out of the back door as soon as the alarms begin to sound?

Perhaps: Who do you think you are, worming your way into my palace and stealing my woman from under me?

An arch of trees rose over the car, and Burr had a memory of Jonathan seated in the cottage at the Lanyon the night they dispatched him on his mission. He is holding Goodhew's letter to the oil lamp: *I'm sure, Leonard. I, Jonathan. And I'll be sure tomorrow morning. How do I sign?*

You signed too bloody much, Burr told him gruffly in his mind. And it was me who egged you on.

Confess, he begged Jonathan. *Betray me, betray us all. We've betrayed you, haven't we? Then do it back to us and save yourself. The enemy's not out there. He's here among us. Betray us.*

He was ten miles out of Newbury and forty miles out of London, but he was in the depths of rural England. He climbed a hill and entered an avenue of bare beech trees. The fields to either side were freshly plowed. He smelled silage and remembered winter teas before the hob in his mother's kitchen in Yorkshire. We are honorable people, he thought, remembering Goodhew. Honorable English people with self-irony and a sense of decency, people with a street spirit and a good heart. What the hell's gone wrong with us?

A broken bus shelter reminded him of the tin hut in Louisiana where he had met Apostoll, betrayed by Harry Palfrey to Darker, and by Darker to the Cousins, and by the Cousins to God knew whom. Strelski would have brought a pistol, he thought. Flynn would have waded ahead of us, cradling his machine gun in his arms. We would be gun people, feeling safer for our guns.

But guns aren't the answer, he thought. Guns are a bluff. I'm a bluff. I'm unlicensed and unloaded, an empty threat. But I'm all I've got to wave at Sir Anthony Bloody Joyston Bradshaw.

He thought of Rooke and Palfrey sitting silently together in Rooke's office and the telephone between them. For the first time he almost smiled.

He spotted a signpost, turned left into an unpaved drive and was assailed by the false conviction that he had been here before. It's the conscious meeting the unconscious, he had read in some smart magazine: between them they give you the sense of déjà vu. He didn't believe that junk. Its language moved him to near violence, and he was feeling near violent now, just at the thought of it.

He stopped the car.

He was feeling too violent altogether. He waited for the feeling to subside. Christ almighty, what am I becoming? I could have strangled Palfrey. He lowered his window, put back his head and drank the country air. He closed his eyes and became Jonathan. Jonathan in agony, with his head back, unable to utter. Jonathan crucified, nearly dead and loved by Roper's woman.

A pair of stone gateposts loomed before him, but no notice saying Lanyon Rose. Burr stopped the car, took up the telephone, dialed Geoffrey Darker's direct line at the River House and heard Rooke's voice say "Hullo."

"Just checking," said Burr, and dialed the number of Darker's house in Chelsea. He heard Rooke again, grunted and rang off.

He dialed Darker's number in the country, with the same result. The intervention warrant was in operation.

Burr drove through the gates and entered a formal park run wild. Deer stared stupidly at him over the broken railing. The drive was thick with weeds. A grimy sign read JOYSTON BRADSHAW ASSOCIATES, BIRMINGHAM, with the BIRMINGHAM crossed out. Below it somebody had daubed the misspelled word *Enquieries* and an arrow. Burr passed a small lake. On the far side of it, the outlines of a great house appeared against the restless sky. Broken greenhouses and neglected stables clustered behind it in the dark. Some of the stables had once been offices. External iron staircases and gangways led to rows of padlocked doors. Of the main house, only the porch and two ground-floor windows were lit. He switched off the engine and took Goodhew's black briefcase from the passenger seat. He slammed the car shut and mounted the steps. An iron fist protruded from the stonework. He pulled it, then pushed it, but it didn't move. He grasped the door knocker and hammered on the door. The echoes were drowned in a tumult of howling dogs and a man's gravel voice lifted roughly against them:

"Whisper, shut up! Get down, damn you! All right, Veronica, I'll take it. That you, Burr?"

"Yes."

"You alone?"

"Yes."

The clatter of a chain being slipped from its runner. The turning of a heavy lock.

"Stay where you are. Let 'em smell you," the voice ordered.

The door opened; two great mastiffs snuffled at Burr's shoes, dribbled on his trouser legs and licked his hands. He stepped into a vast dark hallway reeking of damp and wood ash. Pale rectangles marked the places where pictures had once hung. A single light bulb burned in the chandelier. By its glow, Burr recognized the dissolute features of Sir Anthony Joyston Bradshaw. He wore a frayed smoking jacket and a town shirt with no collar.

The woman, Veronica, stood apart from him in an arched doorway, gray-haired and indeterminately aged. A wife? A nanny? A mistress? A mother? Burr had no idea. Beside her stood a small girl. She was about nine and wore a navy blue dressing gown with gold embroidery on the collar. Her bedroom slippers had gold rabbits on the toes. With her long fair hair brushed down her back, she looked like a child of the French aristocracy on her way to the scaffold.

"Hullo," Burr said to her. "I'm Leonard."

"Off to bed, Ginny," Bradshaw said. "Veronica take her to bed. Got some important business to discuss, darling, mustn't be disturbed. About money, you see. Come on. Give us a kiss."

Was Veronica darling, or was the child? Ginny and her father kissed while Veronica from her archway watched. Burr followed Bradshaw down a long ill-lit corridor to a drawing room. He had forgotten the slowness of big houses. The journey to the drawing room took as long as crossing a street. Two armchairs stood before a wood fire. Stains of damp ran down the walls. Water from the ceiling plopped into Victorian pudding bowls on the floorboards. The mastiffs arranged themselves cautiously before the fire. Like Burr, they kept their eyes on Bradshaw.

"Scotch?" Bradshaw asked.

"Geoffrey Darker's under arrest," Burr said.

. . .

BRADSHAW TOOK the blow like an old boxer. He rode it, he barely winced. He held still, his puffy eyes half-closed as he calculated the damage. He glanced at Burr as if expecting him to come again, and when Burr didn't he shuffled forward a half step and threw a series of rolling, untidy counterpunches.

"Bollocks. Utter codswallop. Crap. *Who* arrested Darker? You? You couldn't arrest a drunken tart. *Geoffrey?* You wouldn't dare! I know you. I know the law too. You're a flunkey. You're not even police. You couldn't arrest Geoffrey any more than a"—he was lost for a metaphor—"fly," he ended feebly. He tried to laugh. "Stupid bloody trick," he said, turning his back while he addressed a tray of drink. *"Christ."* And shook his head to confirm this while he poured himself Scotch from a superb decanter that he must have forgotten to sell.

Burr was still standing. He had set the briefcase beside him on the floor. "They haven't got to Palfrey yet, but he's pinned out on the board," he said with absolute composure. "Darker and Marjoram have been taken into custody pending charges. Most likely there'll be an announcement tomorrow morning, could be afternoon if we can keep the press off. In one hour's time exactly, unless I give instructions to the contrary, uniformed police officers are going to come to this house in big, very shiny, very noisy cars and, in the full view of your daughter, and whoever else you've got, take you down to Newbury police station in handcuffs and detain you. You'll be dealt with separately. We're throwing in fraud for extra spice. Double accounting, deliberate and systematic evasion of Customs and Excise regulations, not to mention collusion with corrupt government officials and a few other charges we propose to think up while you languish in a prison cell, preparing your soul for a seven-year stint after remission and trying to shift the blame to Dicky Roper, Corkoran, Sandy Langbourne, Darker, Palfrey and whoever else you can shop to us. But we don't need that kind of collaboration, you see. We've got Roper in the bag too. There's not a port in the Western Hemisphere but there's a big burly man waiting on the dockside with extradition papers at the ready, and the only real question is, do the Americans snatch the *Pasha* while she's at sea, or do they let everyone have a nice holiday because it's likely to be their last for a very long time indeed?" He smiled. Vindictively. Sportingly. "The forces of light have won the day for once, Sir Anthony, I'm afraid. That's me and Rex Goodhew and some rather clever Americans, if you were wondering. Langley led Brother Darker up the garden path. What they call a sting operation, I believe. You don't know Goodhew, I suppose. Well, you'll get to know him in the witness box, I've no doubt. A natural actor, Rex turned out to be. Could have made a fortune on the stage."

Burr was watching Bradshaw dial. First he

had watched him fumble in a huge marquetry desk, flinging aside bills and letters while he rummaged. Then he had watched him holding an exhausted Filofax to the pale light of a standard lamp while he licked his thumb and turned the pages until he came to *D*.

Then he watched him stiffen and inflate with angry self-importance as he barked into the telephone.

"I want Mr. Darker, please. Mr. *Geoffrey* Darker. *Sir* Anthony Joyston Bradshaw would like to speak to him on an urgent matter. So be rather snappy, will you?"

Burr watched the self-importance drain out of him and his lips begin to separate.

"Who's that? Inspector *what?* Well, what's wrong? Give me Darker. It's urgent. *What?"*

And then, as Burr heard Rooke's confident, slightly regionalized accents on the other end of the line, he saw the scene in his mind's eye: Rooke in his office, standing at the telephone, which was what he liked to do, his left arm straight at his side and chin tucked right in—the parade-ground position for talking on the telephone.

And little Harry Palfrey, whey-faced and dreadfully cooperative, waiting for his turn.

Bradshaw rang off, making a confident show of it. "Burglary on the premises," he announced. "Police in possession. Normal procedure. Mr. Darker is working late at his office. He has been contacted. Everything totally normal. Told me."

Burr smiled. "That's what they always say, Sir Anthony. You don't think they're going to tell you to pack up and bolt, do you?"

Bradshaw stared at him. "Bollocks," he muttered, returning to the lamp and his phone book. "Bullshit, whole thing. Some stupid game."

This time he dialed Darker's office, and yet again Burr saw the scene in his mind: Palfrey picking up the telephone for his finest hour as Rooke's loyal agent; Rooke standing over him while he listened on the extension, Rooke's big hand helpfully on Palfrey's arm and his clear, uncomplicated gaze encouraging Palfrey in his lines.

"I want Darker, Harry," Bradshaw was saying. "I need to talk to him right away. Absolutely vital. Where is he? . . . Well, what do you mean, you don't know? . . . Fuck's sake, Harry, what's the matter with you? There's been a burglary at his house, the police are there, they've been on to him, spoken to him, where is he? . . . Don't give me that operational shit. *I'm* operational. *This* is operational. *Find* him!"

For Burr a long silence. Bradshaw has the earpiece flat against his ear. He has turned pale and frightened. Palfrey is saying his great lines. Whispering them, the way Burr and Rooke rehearsed him. From the heart, because for Palfrey they are true.

"Tony, get off the line, for Christ's sake!" Palfrey urges, doing his furtive voice and scrubbing his nose with the knuckles of his spare hand. "The balloon's gone up. Geoffrey and Neal are for the high jump. Burr and company are throwing the book at us. Chaps running in the corridors. Don't call again. Don't call anyone. Police in the lobby."

Then, best of all, Palfrey rings off—or Rooke does it for him—leaving Bradshaw frozen at his post, and the dead phone at his ear, and his mouth open in the interests of better hearing.

"I brought the papers, if you want to see them," Burr said comfortably as Bradshaw turned to stare at him. "I'm not supposed to, but they do give me a certain pleasure, I'll admit. When I said seven years, I was being pessimistic. It's my Yorkshire blood not wanting to exaggerate, I suppose. I think you'll get more like ten."

His voice had gathered volume but not pace. He was unpacking the briefcase while he spoke, ponderously, like an insinuating magician, one rumpled file at a time. Sometimes he opened a file and paused to study a particular letter before he put it down. Sometimes he smiled and shook his head as if to say, Would you believe it?

"Funny how a case like this can turn itself round on a sixpence, just in an afternoon," he mused while he toiled. "We flog away, me and my lads and lasses, and nobody wants to know. Up against a brick wall, every time. We've had a cast-iron case against Darker for, oh"—he allowed himself another pause for smiling—"as long as *I* can remember, anyway. As for Sir Anthony, well, *you* were in our sights while I was a beardless lad at grammar school, I should think. You see, I really hate you. There's lots of people I want to put behind bars and never shall, it's true. But you're in a category of your own, you are; always have been. Well, you know that, really, don't you?" Another file caught his eye, and he allowed himself a moment to flip through it. "Then all of a sudden the phone goes—lunchtime as usual, but by a mercy I'm on a diet—and it's somebody I've hardly heard of from the Director of Public Prosecutions' office. 'Hey, Leonard, why don't you slip down to Scotland Yard, get yourself a couple of hungry police officers and go and pull that fellow Geoffrey Darker in? It's about time we cleaned up Whitehall, Leonard, got rid of all these bent officials and their shady contacts on the outside—men like Joyston Bradshaw, for instance—and made an example to the outside world. The Americans are doing it, so why can't we? Time we proved we're serious about not arming future enemies—all that junk.' " He pulled out another file, marked TOP SECRET, GUARD, EYES ONLY, and gave it an affectionate pat on the flank. "Darker's under what we're calling voluntary house arrest at the moment. Confession time, really, except we don't call it that. We always like to stretch *habeas corpus* when we're dealing with members of the trade. You have to bend the law from time to time, otherwise you don't get anywhere."

· · ·

NO TWO BLUFFS are the same, but one component is necessary to all of them, and that is the complicity between the deceiver and the deceived, the mystical interlocking of opposing needs. For the man on the wrong side of the law, it may be the unconscious need to get back on the right side. For the lone criminal, a secret longing to rejoin the pack, any pack, if only he can be a member. And in the worn-out playboy and scoundrel who was Bradshaw—or so at least the attic weaver prayed as he watched his adversary read, turn forward, turn back, take another file and read again—it was the habitual search for exclusive treatment at any price, for the ultimate deal, for revenge against those who lived more successfully than he did, that made him the willing victim of Burr's deception.

"For Christ's sake," Bradshaw muttered at last, handing back the files as if they made him sick. "No need to go over the top. Got to be a middle ground. Must be. Reasonable man, always have been."

Burr was less forthcoming. "Oh, I don't think I would call it middle ground at all, Sir Anthony," he said, with a resurgence of his former anger as he took back the files and stuffed them into the briefcase. "I'd call it a fixture postponed until the next time round. What you do is, you telephone the *Iron Pasha* for me, have a quiet word with our mutual friend."

"What sort of word?"

"This sort. Tell him the shit's hit the fan. Tell him what I've told you, what you've seen, what you've done, what you've heard." He glanced out of the uncurtained window. "Can you see the road from here?"

"No."

"Pity, because they're out there by now. I thought we might see a little blue light winking at us across the lake. Not even from upstairs?"

"No."

"Tell him we've rumbled you all ways up, you've been quite careless and we've traced your phony end users back to source and we're following the careers of the *Lombardy* and the *Horacio Enriques* with interest. Unless. Tell him the Americans are warming up a cell for him at Marion. They want to bring their own charges. Unless. Tell him his high friends at court aren't friends anymore." He handed Bradshaw the telephone. "Tell him you're scared to death. Weep, if you still can. Tell him you can't take prison. Let him hate you for your weakness. Tell him I nearly strangled Palfrey with my bare hands, but that was because I thought he was Roper for a moment."

Bradshaw licked his lips, waiting. Burr crossed the room and placed himself in the darkness of a far window.

"Unless what?" Bradshaw asked nervously.

"Then tell him this," Burr resumed, speaking with great reluctance. "I'll drop all charges. Against you and against him. This time round. His ships get a free run. Darker, Marjoram, Palfrey—they're going where they belong. But not him and not you and not the cargoes." His voice rose. "And tell him I'll follow him and his terrible generation to the ends of the earth before I give up on him. Tell him I'm going to breathe clean air before I die." He lost himself for a moment, and recovered. "He's got a man called Pine on his boat. You may have heard of him. Corkoran telephoned you from Nassau about him. The River rats dug up his past for you. If Roper lets Pine go within one hour from you putting down the phone"—again he faltered—"I'll bury the case. He has my word."

Bradshaw was staring at him with a mixture of astonishment and relief. "Jesus Christ, Burr. Pine must be some catch!" A happy thought struck him. "I say, old boy—you're not on a piece of the action yourself, by any chance, are you?" he asked. Then he caught Burr's eye, and the hope faded.

"You'll tell him I'll want the girl too," Burr said, almost as an afterthought.

"What girl?"

"Mind your bloody business. It's Pine and it's the girl. Alive and unharmed."

Hating himself, Burr began reading out the satcom number of the *Iron Pasha.*

. . .

IT WAS LATE the same night. Palfrey walked, not noticing the rain. Rooke had put him into a cab, but Palfrey had paid it off. He was somewhere near Baker Street, and London had become an Arab town. In the neon-lit windows of small hotels, dark-eyed men stood about in desultory groups, fidgeting their beads and gesticulating to each other while the children played with their new train sets and veiled women spoke among themselves. Between the hotels stood the private hospitals, and at the steps of one of these Palfrey paused in the lighted entrance, perhaps wondering whether to admit himself and then, deciding not, walked on.

He wore no coat or hat, he carried no umbrella. A cab slowed as it went past him, but the distraction in Palfrey's face could not be appealed to. He was like a man who had mislaid something essential to his purposes: his car perhaps—which street had he left it in?—his wife, his woman—where had they arranged to meet? Once, he patted the pockets of his sodden jacket, for keys or cigarettes or money. Once, he went into a pub that was about to close, put a five-pound note on the bar and drank a double Scotch without water and left, forgetting his change and muttering the word "Apostoll" out loud—though the only witness to testify to this afterwards was a theological student, who thought he was declaring himself an apostate. The street had him again, and he pursued his quest, looking at everything yet somehow rejecting it—no, you're not the place, not here, not here. An old whore with dyed blond hair called at him good-humoredly from a doorway, but he shook his head—not you either. Another pub had him, just as the barman was calling for last orders.

"Fellow called Pine," Palfrey told a man to whom he raised his glass in a distracted toast. "Very much in love." The man silently drank with him because he thought Palfrey looked a bit cut up. Somebody must have pinched his girl, he thought. A little runt like him, no wonder.

Palfrey chose the island, a triangle of raised pavement with a railing round it that seemed to be uncertain whether its job was to fence people in or fence them out. But the island was still not what he had been looking for, apparently, perhaps more some kind of vantage point or a familiar landmark.

And he didn't enter the protection of the railing. He did what kids do in the playground, said another witness: he put his heels on the outside curb and hooked his arms behind him over the railing, so that for a thoughtful while he seemed to be attached to the outside of a moving round-about that wasn't moving, while he watched the empty late-night double-decker buses racing past him in their hurry to get home.

Finally, like someone who has got his bearings, he straightened himself up and put back his rather wasted shoulders until he resembled an old soldier on Remembrance Day, chose a particularly fast oncoming bus, and threw himself under it. And really on that particular stretch of road, at that time of night, and the streets like a skating rink from the pouring rain, there was absolutely nothing the poor driver could do. And Palfrey would have been the last to blame him.

A will, handwritten but legally phrased, if somewhat battered, was found in Palfrey's pocket. It forgave all debts and appointed Goodhew his executor.

TWENTY-NINE

THE *Iron Pasha,* 1,500 tons, 250 feet long, steel-built by Feadship of Holland in 1987 to the specifications of her present owner, interior by Lavinci of Rome, powered by two 2,000-horsepower MWM diesel engines and equipped with Vosper stabilizers, Inmarsat satellite-telecommunications-systems radar, including an anti-collision set and Radar Watch—not to mention fax, telex, a dozen cases of Dom Pérignon and a live holly tree in a tub in anticipation of the Christmas festivities—sailed out of Nelson's Dockyard, English Harbour, Antigua, the Antilles, on the morning tide, bound for her winter cruise of the Windward and Grenadine islands, and ultimately, by way of the islands of Blanquilla, Orchila and Bonaire, for Curaçao.

A smattering of the better names and faces from Antigua's fashionable St. James's Club had assembled at the dockside to see her off, and there was much sounding of air horns and ships' whistles as the ever-popular international entrepreneur Mr. Dicky Onslow Roper and his elegantly attired guests stood astern of the departing vessel, waving their farewells to cries of "God speed" and "Have a simply marvelous time, Dicky, you've deserved it" from the shore. Mr. Roper's personal pennant, portraying a glittering crystal, fluttered from the mainmast. Society-watchers were gratified to observe such familiar favorites of the jet set as Lord (Sandy to his intimates) Langbourne on the arm of his wife, Caroline, thus discounting rumors of a breakup, and the exquisite Miss Jemima (Jed to her friends) Marshall, Mr. Roper's constant companion since more than a year and renowned hostess of the Roper Xanadu in the Exumas.

The other sixteen guests constituted a carefully selected company of international makers and shakers and included such social heavyweights as Petros (Patty) Kaloumenos, who had recently attempted to purchase the island of Spétsai from the Greek government, Bunny Saltlake, the American soup heiress, Gerry Sandown, the British racing driver, and his French wife, and the American film producer Marcel Heist, whose own yacht, the *Marceline,* was presently under construction in Bremerhaven. No children were of the company. Guests who had never sailed on the *Pasha* before were likely to spend their first days swooning over her luxurious appointments: her eight staterooms, all with king-sized beds, hi-fi, telephone, color television, Redouté prints and historic paneling; her softly lit Edwardian salon in red plush, with antique gaming table and eighteenth-century bronze heads, each in its domed recess of solid walnut; her maple dining room, with sylvan paintings after Watteau; her pool, Jacuzzi and solarium; her Italian afterdeck for informal dining.

Of Mr. Derek Thomas of New Zealand, however, the gossip columnists wrote nothing at all. He featured on no Ironbrand public relations handout. He was not on deck waving to the friends on shore. He was not at dinner, delighting his companions with his sensitive conversation. He was in the *Pasha*'s nearest thing to Herr Meister's fine-wine cellar, chained and gagged and lying in the dark, in a bloody solitude relieved by visits from Major Corkoran and his assistants.

· · ·

THE COMBINED STRENGTH of the *Pasha*'s crew and staff was twenty, including captain, mate, engineer, assistant engineer, a chef for the guests and a chef for the crew, a head stewardess and housekeeper, four deckhands and a ship's purser. The company also included a pilot for the helicopter and another for the seaplane. The security team was augmented by the two German-Argentinians who had flown with Jed and Corkoran from Miami and, like the ship it protected, was lavishly equipped. The tradition of piracy in that region is by no means extinct, and the ship's arsenal was capable of sustaining a prolonged firefight at sea, deterring marauding aircraft or sinking a hostile vessel venturing alongside. It was stored in the forward hold, where the security team also had its quarters, behind a seaproof steel door that in turn was protected by a grille. Was that where Jonathan was being kept? After three days at sea, such was Jed's distraught conviction. But when she asked Roper he seemed not to hear her, and when she asked Corkoran he threw up his chin and made a stern frown.

"Stormy waters, old love," said Corkoran through set lips. "Be seen not heard, my advice. Bed and board and a low profile. Safer for all. Don't quote me."

The transformation she had observed in Corkoran was by now complete. A ratlike intensity had replaced his former sloth. He smiled seldom and issued snappish orders at male members of the crew, whether they were plain or pretty. He had pinned a row of medal ribbons to his mildewed dinner jacket and was given to grandiose soliloquies about world problems whenever Roper was not there to shut him up.

· · ·

THE DAY of Jed's arrival in Antigua was the worst in her life. She had had plenty of other worst days till now—her Catholic guilt had supplied her with a whole bunch. There had been the day the mother superior marched into the dormitory and told her to pack her things, her taxi was waiting at the door. That was the same day her father ordered her to go to her bedroom while he took priestly advice on how to handle a sixteen-year-old virgin whore caught stark naked in the potting shed with a village boy doing his unsuccessful best to deflower her. There had been the day in Hammersmith when two boys she had refused to sleep with had got drunk and decided to make common cause, taking it in turns to hold her down while the other raped her. And there had been the too-wild days in Paris before she stepped over the sleeping bodies, straight into Dicky Roper's arms. But the day she boarded the *Pasha* in English Harbour, Antigua, had knocked the others off the scoreboard.

On the plane, she had managed to ignore Corkoran's veiled insults by escaping into her magazines. At Antigua airport he had thrust his hand officiously under her arm, and when she tried to shake free he had clutched her in a claw-like grip while the two blond boys trod on her heels. In the limousine, Corkoran rode up front and the boys sat too close either side of her. And as she climbed the *Pasha*'s gangway, all three made a phalanx round her, no doubt to demonstrate to Roper—if he was watching—that they were obeying orders. Frog-marched to the door of the state apartments, she was obliged to wait while Corkoran knocked.

"Who is it?" Roper demanded from within.

"A Miss Marshall, Chief. Safe and moderately sound."

"Show her in, Corks."

"With luggage, Chief, or was it without?"

"With."

She stepped inside and saw Roper sitting at the desk with his back to her. And he remained there, still with his back to her, while a steward parked her luggage in the bedroom and withdrew. He was reading something, checking it with a pen as he went along. A contract, a whatever. She waited for him to finish, or put it down and turn to her. Even get up. He didn't. He reached the end of the page, scribbled something—she thought his initials—then passed the next page and went on reading. It was a thick, typed document, blue, with a red ribbon and a red-ruled margin. There were quite a few pages to go. He's writing his will, she decided. *And to my former mistress Jed I leave absolutely sod all. . . .*

He was wearing his navy blue tailored silk dressing gown with rolled collar and crimson piping, and usually, when he put it on, it meant either that they were about to make love, or just had. While he read he occasionally shifted the angle of his shoulders inside it, as if he sensed she was admiring them. He had always been proud of his shoulders. She was still standing. She was six feet from him. She was wearing jeans and a knit vest and several gold necklaces. He liked her to wear gold. The carpet was puce and brand-new. Very expensive, very deep. They had chosen it together from samples, in front of the fire at Crystal. Jonathan had lent his advice. This was the first time she had seen it in position.

"Am I disturbing you?" she asked, when he had still not turned his head.

"Hardly at all," he replied, while his head remained bowed over the papers.

She sat on the edge of a chair, clutching her tapestry bag on her lap. There was such over-control in his body, and such harnessed tension in his voice, that she presumed that at any moment he was going to get up and hit her, probably all in one movement: a spring and a sweeping backhand swipe that would knock her into the middle of next week. She'd once had an Italian boy who'd done that to her as a punishment for being witty. The punch had carried her clean across the room. It should have felled her outright, but her riding balance helped her, and as soon as she had grabbed her things from the bedroom, she let the punch carry her out of the house.

"I told them lobster," Roper said, as he again initialed something on the document before him. "Reckoned you were owed one after Corky's little number at Enzo's. Lobster all right for you?"

She didn't answer.

"Chaps tell me you've been having a bit of a tumble with Brother Thomas. Likee? Real name's Pine, by the way. Jonathan to you."

"Where is he?"

"Thought you'd ask that." Turn a page.

Raise an arm. Fuss the half-lens reading glasses. "Been going on long, has it? Quickies in the summerhouse? Knickers off in the woods? Bloody good at it, both of you, I must say. All those staff around. I'm not stupid either. Didn't spot a thing."

"If they're telling you I slept with Jonathan, I didn't."

"Nobody said much about sleep."

"We are not lovers."

She had said the same to the mother superior, she remembered, but it hadn't cut much ice. Roper paused at his reading but still didn't turn his head.

"So what are you?" he asked. "If not lovers, what?"

We're lovers, she conceded stupidly. It made not one whit of difference whether they were physical lovers or some other kind. Her love for Jonathan and her betrayal of Roper were accomplished facts. The rest, as in the potting shed, was technical.

"Where is he?" she demanded.

Too busy reading. A shift of the shoulders as we amend something with our six-foot-long Mont Blanc.

"Is he on the boat?"

A sculptured stillness now, her father's pensive silence. But her father was afraid the world was going to the devil and, poor love, hadn't the least idea how to stop it. Whereas Roper was helping it on its way.

"Says he did it all by himself," Roper said. "That true? Jed didn't do any of it. Pine's the baddie, Pine did it all. Jed's snow white. Too thick to know what she's about, anyway. End of statement for the press. All his own work."

"What work?"

Roper shoved his pen aside and stood, still contriving not to look at her. He crossed the room to the paneled wall and pressed a button. The electric doors of the drinks cupboard rolled back. He opened the refrigerator, fished out a bottle of the Dom, uncorked it and filled himself a glass. Then, as a kind of compromise between looking at her and not, he spoke to her reflection in the mirrored interior of the cupboard, what he could see of it between a row of wine bottles and the vermouths and Camparis.

"Want some?" he asked, almost tenderly, lifting the bottle of Dom and offering it to her reflection.

"What work? What's he supposed to have done?"

"Won't say. Asked him to, but he won't. What he's done, who for, who with, why, starting when. Who's paying him. Nothing. Could save himself a hell of a lot of aggro if he did. Gallant chap. Good choice you made. Congratulations."

"Why should he have *done* anything? What are you doing to him? Let him go."

He turned and walked toward her, looking at her directly at last, with his pale, washed eyes, and this time she was certain he would hit her, because his smile was so unnaturally at ease, his manner of such studied unconcern, that there had to be a different version of him inside. He was still wearing his reading glasses, so he had to lower his head to look at her over the top of them. His smile was sporting, and very close to her.

"Simon-pure, is he, your lover boy? Lily-white, is he? Mister Clean? Utter balls, dear. Only reason I took him in was because some hired lout held a pistol at my boy's head. You telling me he wasn't part of the caper? Horseshit, sweetheart, frankly. You find me a saint, I'll pay the candle. Till then, I'll keep my money in my pocket." The chair she had chosen was dangerously low. His knees as he bowed over her were at the level of her jaw. "Been having my thoughts about you, Jeds. Wondering whether you're quite as dumb as I supposed. Whether you and Pine aren't in it together. Who picked who up at the horse sale, eh? Eh?" He was tweaking her ear, making a mischievous joke of it. "Bloody clever chaps, women. Clever, *clever* chaps. Even when they're pretending they haven't got anything between their ears. Make you think you chose *them,* fact is they chose *you.* Are you a plant, Jeds? Don't *look* a plant. Look a bloody pretty woman. Sandy thinks you're a plant. Wishes he'd had a tumble with you himself. Corks wouldn't be *surprised* if you were a plant"—he gave an effeminate simper—"and your fancy boy ain't saying *nuttin'.*" He was tweaking her ear to the rhythm of each accented word. Not painful tweaks. Playful ones. "Level with us, Jeds, will you, darling? Share the *joke.* Be a *sport.* You're a *plant,* aren't you, sweetheart. A plant with a lovely arse, aren't you?"

He moved his hand to her chin. Taking it between his thumb and forefinger, he raised her head to look at her. She saw the merriment in his eyes that she had so often mistaken for kindness, and she supposed that once again the man she had been loving was somebody she had put together out of the bits of him she wanted to believe in, while she ignored the bits that didn't fit.

"I don't know what you're talking about," she said. "I let you pick me up. I was scared. You were an angel. You never did me wrong. Not till now. And I gave you my best shot. You know I did. Where is he?" she said, straight into his eyes.

He released her chin and walked away down the room, holding his champagne glass wide.

"Good idea, girl," he said approvingly. "Well done. Spring him. Spring your lover boy. Put a file in his French loaf. Shove it through the bars on visiting day. Pity you haven't brought Sarah along with you. Two of you could ride away on her into the sunset." No change of tone. "You don't know a fellow called Burr at all, do you, Jeds, by any chance? First name Leonard?

North Country oaf? Smelly armpits? Gospel trained? Come your way at all? Ever have a tumble with him? Probably called himself Smith. Pity. Thought you might have."

"I don't know anyone like that."

"Funny thing. Nor does Pine."

They dressed for dinner, back-to-back, choosing their clothes with care. The formal madness of their days and nights aboard the *Pasha* had begun.

. . .

The menus. Discussion with the steward and the cooks. Mrs. Sandown is French, and her opinion on everything is therefore regarded by the kitchen as gospel, never mind she eats only salads and swears she knows nothing about food.

Laundry. When guests are not eating they are changing, bathing and copulating, which means that every day they must have clean sheets, towels, clothes and table linen. A yacht sails on its food and its laundry. A whole section of the service deck is got up with banks of washing machines, dryers and steam irons, which two stewardesses tend from dawn till dusk.

Hair. The sea air does terrible things to people's hair. At five every evening the guest deck is humming to the sound of hair dryers, and it is their peculiarity to fail when guests are halfway through their toilet. Therefore at ten to six exactly, Jed may count on the sight of a belligerent, half-dressed lady guest lurking in the gangway with her hair stuck up like a lavatory brush, brandishing a defunct hair dryer and saying, "Jed, darling, could you *possibly?*"—because the housekeeper is by now supervising the final touches to the dinner table.

Flowers. Every day, the seaplane visits the nearest island to fetch flowers, fresh fish, seafood, eggs and newspapers, and to post letters. But the flowers are what Roper cares about most, the *Pasha* is famous for its flowers and the sight of dead flowers, or flowers not adequately arranged, is likely to cause serious tremors below decks.

Recreation. Where shall we put in, swim, snorkel, whom shall we visit, shall we dine out for a change, send the helicopter or the seaplane for the Somebodys, take the Somebody Elses ashore? For the guests on the *Pasha* are not a static population. They change from island to island according to their negotiated length of stay, bringing new blood, new banalities, a new approach to Christmas: how *terribly* behind one is with one's preparations, darling, I haven't even *thought* about my presies, and isn't it time you and Dicky got married, you look so absolutely *yummy* together?

And Jed in the madness goes along with this mad routine, waiting for a chink. Roper's references to putting files into bread loaves is not inaccurate. She would fuck all five guards and

Langbourne and even Corkoran, if he were so disposed, in order to get alongside Jonathan.

. . .

MEANWHILE, as she waits, all the rituals of her strict childhood and convent school—the rules of grit your teeth and smile—entwine her in their humiliating embrace. While she obeys them, nothing is real, but also nothing comes adrift. For both these blessings she is grateful, and the possibility of a chink remains. When Caroline Langbourne treats her to a discourse on the pleasures of marriage to Sandy now that the slut of a nanny is safely back in London, Jed smiles dreamily and says, "Oh, Caro, darling, I'm so awfully pleased for you both. And for the children, naturally." When Caroline adds that she probably said some absolutely *barmy* things about the business deals Dicky and Sandy were getting up to, but she'd talked it all through with Sandy and she really *had* to admit she'd seen things *rather* blacker than they were—and honestly, how *can* one make one's pennies these days without getting one's fingers the *weeniest* bit grubby?—Jed is pleased about that too and assures Caro that she can't remember a *thing* that Caro said about all that anyway, with Jed and business it's just in one ear and out the other and thank God for it. . . .

And at night she sleeps with Roper, waiting for the chink.

In his bed.

Having dressed and undressed in his presence, worn his jewelry and charmed his guests.

The encounter most often comes at dawn, when her will, like the will of the dying, is at its weakest. He reaches for her, and Jed in some dreadful eagerness at once returns his call, telling herself that in doing so she is drawing the teeth of Jonathan's oppressor, taming him, bribing him, making peace with him for Jonathan's salvation. And waiting for the chink.

Because that is what she is trying to buy from Roper all the time, in this mad silence they are sharing, following their first exchange of gunfire: a chance to get past his guard. They can laugh together about something as crucial as a bad olive. Yet, even in their sexual frenzies, they no longer mention the one subject that still joins them: Jonathan.

Is Roper too waiting for something? Waiting herself, Jed believes he is. Why else does Corkoran tap on the stateroom door at all odd hours, poke his head round, shake it and withdraw? In her nightmares, Corkoran doubles as Jonathan's executioner.

· · ·

SHE KNOWS where he is now. Roper hasn't told her, but it has been an amusing game for him, looking on while Jed spots the clues and pieces them together. And now she knows.

First she notices the unnatural grouping at

the forward end of the boat, on the lower deck beyond the guest cabins: a clogging of people, an air of accident. It is nothing she can put her finger on, and anyway that section of the boat has always been hazy to her. In the days of her innocence, she heard it referred to as the security area. Another time as the hospital. It is the one part of the boat that belongs to neither guests nor crew. And since Jonathan himself is also neither, Jed sees the hospital as the fitting place to put him. Hovering with intent around the kitchen, Jed observes trays of invalid food, not ordered by herself. They are laden when they go forward. They are empty when they return.

"Is someone ill?" she demands of Frisky, stopping him in his path.

Frisky's manner is no longer deferential, if it ever was. "Why should there be?" he says pertly. The tray aloft. One-handed.

"Then who's eating slops? Yogurt, chicken broth—who's that for?"

Frisky affects to notice for the first time what is on his tray. "Oh, that's Tabby, that is, miss." He has never in his life called her "miss" before. "Got a bit of the toothache, Tabby has. Had a wisdom tooth out in Antigua. Lot of bleeding. He's on the painkillers. Yeah."

She has begun to work out who visits him and when. It is an advantage of the rituals that control her that the smallest irregular movement on the ship is her concern; she knows by instinct whether the pretty Filipino stewardess has slept with the captain or the bosun or—as happened briefly one afternoon while Caroline was sunbathing on the afterdeck—with Sandy Langbourne. She has observed that it is Roper's three trusties— Frisky, Tabby and Gus—who sleep in the cabin above the private stairway to what she now believes is Jonathan's cell. And that the German-Argentinians across the gangway may suspect, but do not share the secret. And that Corkoran— the new, puffed up, officious Corkoran—makes the journey twice a day at least, setting out with an air of circumstance and returning churlish.

"Corky," she beseeches him, trading on past friendship. "Corks, darling, please—for God's sake—how is he? Is he ill? Does he know I'm here?"

But Corkoran's face is shaded by the darkness he has visited. "I warned you, Jed. I gave you every chance," he retorts huffily. "You wouldn't hear me. You were willful." And goes his way like an offended beadle.

Sandy Langbourne is also an occasional visitor. His chosen hour is after dinner during his evening prowl of the decks in search of more diverting company than his wife.

"You bastard, Sandy," she whispers at him as he saunters past her. "You utter spoilt bloody shit."

Langbourne remains unaffected by this onslaught. He is too beautiful and bored to care.

And she knows that Jonathan's other visitor is Roper, because Roper is unusually pensive when he returns from the forward area. Even if she has not seen him go there, she can tell by his manner when he reappears. Like Langbourne, he favors evenings. First stroll on deck, chat to the skipper or call one of his many stockbrokers, currency dealers and bankers round the globe: how about taking a flier on Deutschies, Bill? Swissies, Jack? the yen, the pound, the escudo, Malaysian rubber, Russian diamonds, Canadian gold? Then gradually, by these and similar staging posts, he is drawn as if by magnetic attraction toward the forward part of the boat. And vanishes. When he reappears, his expression is overcast.

But Jed knows better than to beg or weep or scream or cause a scene. If there is one thing that makes Roper dangerous, it is a scene. It is the unwarranted invasion of his self-esteem. It is bloody women sniveling at his feet.

And she knows, or thinks she knows, that Jonathan is doing what he tried to do in Ireland. He is killing himself with his own courage.

· · ·

IT WAS BETTER than Herr Meister's cellar, but it was also far, far worse. There was no going round and round the black walls. But that was because he was chained to them. He was not neglected; his presence was known to a succession of attentive people. But these same people had stuffed his mouth with chamois leather and taped it with adhesive, and although there was an understanding that they would remove these inconveniences whenever he gave the signal that he wished to talk, they had already demonstrated to him that if he gave the signal frivolously there would be consequences. Since then, he had developed a firm policy not to talk at all, not even a "good morning" or "hullo," because his terror was that—since he was somebody who tended on occasion to confide, if only in his character as hotelier—this tendency would become his undoing, and "hullo" would turn into "I sent Rooke the numbers of the containers and the name of the boat," or whatever other stray confession sprang to mind in the agony of the moment.

Yet what confession did they want from him? What more did they need to know that they didn't know already? They knew he was a plant and that most of the stories about him were invention. If they did not know how much he had betrayed, they knew enough to change or abort their plans before it was too late. So why the urgency? Why the frustration? Then gradually, as the sessions grew more ferocious, Jonathan came to recognize that his confession was something they felt that they were owed by right. He was their spy. They had unmasked him. Their pride demanded a contrite statement from the gallows.

But they were reckoning without Sophie. They didn't know about his Secret Sharer. Sophie who had been there ahead of him. And was there now, smiling at him over her coffee, please, Egyptian. Forgiving him. Amusing him: seducing him a little, urging him to live by daylight. When they beat his face—a prolonged and careful beating, but a devastating one—he wryly compared faces with her, and for a distraction he told her all about the Irish boy and the Heckler. But nothing maudlin; she was utterly against it; they never went in for self-pity or lost their sense of humor. *You killer this woman?* she teased him, lifting her plucked dark eyebrows and laughing her mannish laugh. No, he *hadn't* killered her. They had put that discussion behind them long ago. She had listened to his account of his dealings with Ogilvey, she had heard him out, now smiling, now frowning in distaste. "I think you did your duty, Mr. Pine," she declared when he had finished. "Unfortunately there are many kinds of loyalty, and we cannot serve them all at once. Like my husband, you believed you were a patriot. Next time you will make a better choice. Perhaps we shall make it together." When Tabby and Frisky worked on his body—mostly by chaining him in attitudes that produced prolonged and excruciating pain—Sophie reminded him how her body had been broken too: in her case, clubbed until it was destroyed. And when he was deep down and half asleep and wondering how he would make it back to the top of the crevasse, he regaled her with accounts of difficult climbs he had made in the Oberland—a north face of the Jungfrau that had gone seriously wrong; bivouacking in a hundred-mile-an-hour wind. And Sophie, if she was bored, never showed it. She listened with her great brown eyes steadfastly upon him, loving and encouraging him: *I am sure that you will never again give yourself away so cheaply, Mr. Pine,* she had told him. *Our good manners can sometimes disguise our courage from us. Have you something to read on the plane back to Cairo? I think I shall read. It will help me to remember that I am myself.* And then, to his surprise, he was back in the little flat in Luxor, watching her pack up her overnight bag, one object at a time and very deliberately, as if she were selecting companions for a much longer journey than the trip to Cairo.

And of course it was Sophie who had encouraged him to keep his silence. Had she herself not died without betraying him?

When they had pulled off the adhesive and removed the chamois bung, it was on Sophie's advice that he asked to speak to Roper personally.

"That's the way, then, Tommy," said Tabby, out of breath from his exertions. "You have a natter with the Chief. Then we can all have a nice beer together like the old days."

And Roper in his own good time strolled

down to see him, dressed in his cruise gear—including the white buckskin shoes with crêpe soles that Jonathan had noticed in his dressing room at Crystal—and sat on the chair across the room from him. And it passed through Jonathan's mind that this was now the second time that Roper had seen him with his face in a mess, and that Roper's expression on both occasions had been identical: the same wrinkling of the nose, the same critical assessment of the damage and of Jonathan's chances of survival. He wondered how Roper would have looked at Sophie if he had been around while they were beating her to death.

"All right, Pine?" he asked pleasantly. "No complaints? They looking after you all right?"

"Beds are a bit lumpy."

Roper laughed good-humoredly. "Can't have everything, I suppose. Jed misses you."

"Then send her to me."

"Not her scene, I'm afraid. Convent girl. Likes a sheltered life."

So Jonathan explained to Roper that during his initial conversations with Langbourne, Corkoran and others, the suggestion had repeatedly been aired that Jed was in some way involved in Jonathan's activities. And he wished to say categorically that whatever he had done, he had done it alone, unaided at any point by Jed. And that far too much had been made of a couple of social visits to Woody's House that had taken place when Jed was being bored to death by Caroline Langbourne and Jonathan was lonely. After that, he regretted he could not answer any further questions. Roper, normally so swift to take a point, seemed for a while stuck for words.

"Your people kidnapped my boy," he said at last. "You lied your way into my house, stole my woman. You tried to screw up my deal. Hell do I care whether you talk or not? You're dead."

So it's punishment, not just confession, thought Jonathan, as they bunged up his mouth again. And his sense of kinship with Sophie, if it was possible, grew stronger. I didn't betray Jed, he told her. And I won't, I promise. I shall remain as steadfast as Herr Kaspar with his wig.

Herr Kaspar wore a *wig?*

But didn't I tell you? Good heavens! Herr Kaspar is a Swiss hero! He gave up twenty thousand tax-free francs a year, just in order to be loyal to himself!

You are right, Mr. Pine, Sophie agreed gravely, when she had listened attentively to everything he had to tell her. You must not betray Jed. You must be strong like Herr Kaspar, and you must not betray yourself either. Now you will put your head on my shoulder, please, the way you do with Jed, and we shall sleep.

. . .

AND FROM THEN ON, as the questions continued without benefit of answer, now singly, now in a hail, Jonathan occasionally saw Roper back in the same chair, though no longer wearing the white buckskin shoes. And always Sophie stood behind him, not in a vengeful way but just to remind Jonathan that they were in the presence of the worst man in the world.

"They'll kill you, Pine," Roper warned, a couple of times. "Corky will go over the top and that'll be that. These queers never know where to draw the line. Quit before it's too late, my advice." After that, Roper would sit back, wearing that look of personal frustration that comes over all of us when we seem unable to help a friend.

Then Corkoran would reappear and, leaning eagerly forward in the same chair, would fire his questions like commands, and count to three while he waited to be obeyed. And on *three,* Frisky and Tabby went to work again, until Corkoran was tired, or appeased.

"Well, if you'll excuse me, old heart, I'll slip into my sequined sari, pop a ruby in my navel and tuck into a few peacock's tongues," he said as he bowed his way, smirking, to the door. "Sorry you can't be part of the fun. But if you won't sing for your supper, what can one do?"

Nobody, not even Corkoran, stayed long. If a man refuses to speak, and sticks to his resolve, the show acquires a certain sameness. Only Jonathan, roaming his internal world with Sophie, was blessed with any sense of profit. He owned nothing he did not want to own, his life was in order, he was free. He congratulated himself on having discharged his institutional commitments. His father, his mother, his orphanages and singing Aunt Annie, his country, his past and Burr—all had been paid in full and on the nail. As to his sundry female creditors, they could no longer touch him with their accusations.

And Jed? Well, there was something rather wonderful in paying in advance for sins that he had yet to commit. He had deceived her, of course—Mama Low's, getting himself smuggled into the castle, offering a faulty version of himself—but he had a sense that he had also rescued her, which was Sophie's view entirely.

"And you don't think too shallow?" he asked Sophie, in the way young men consult wise women about their loves.

She pretended to be cross with him. "Mr. Pine, I think you are playing a little bit the flirt. You are a lover, not an archaeologist. Your Jed has a nature that has not been touched. She is beautiful, so she is used to being fawned on and adored, and occasionally misused. That is normal."

"I have not misused her," Jonathan replied.

"But you have not fawned on her either. She is not confident of you. She comes to you because she wishes your approval. But you withhold it. Why?"

"But, Madame Sophie, what do you think she does to *me?*"

"You are joined by a friction that you both resent. That is also normal. It is attraction's dark side. You have both got what you wanted. Now it is time to find out what to do with it."

"I'm just not ready for her. She's banal."

"She is not banal, Mr. Pine. And I am sure you will never be ready for anybody. However, you are in love, and that is that. Now let us get some sleep. You have work to do, and we shall need all the strength we can muster if we are to complete our journey. Was the fizzy-drink treatment as bad as Tabby promised?"

"Worse."

. . .

HE NEARLY DIED AGAIN, and when he woke, Roper was there with his interested smile. But Roper was not a climber and did not understand the fixity of Jonathan's determination: why else do I climb mountains, he explained to Sophie, if not to reach the peak? On the other hand, the hotelier in him had every sympathy for a man who has run away from feeling. Jonathan really wanted to reach out his hand to Roper, and as a gesture of friendship pull him down here into the abyss, just so that the Chief could get an idea of what it was like: you who are so proud of believing in nothing, and me down here with my faith in everything intact.

Then he dozed off for a while, and when he woke, he was in the Lanyon, walking on the cliffs with Jed, not wondering anymore who would be round the corner, waiting for him, but content with himself and with the person at his side.

But he still refused to speak to Roper.

His refusal was becoming more than a vow. It was an asset, a resource.

The very act of withholding was giving him renewal.

Every word he didn't speak, every juddering fist or foot or elbow that rocked him off to sleep, every new and separate pain, went into him like fresh supplies of energy to be hoarded against a future day.

When the pain became unbearable, he had visions of raising himself toward it to receive and store away its life-giving powers.

And it worked. Under the cover of his agony, the close observer in Jonathan assembled his operational intelligence and prepared his plan for the deployment of his secret energy.

Nobody carries a gun, he thought. *They are following the law of all good prisons. Warders do not carry guns.*

THIRTY

SOMETHING AMAZING had happened.

Something good or terrible. Either way it was
decisive, it was terminal, it was the end of life as
Jed had so far known it.

The phone call had roused them in the
early evening. Person-to-person and confidential,
Chief, the skipper had said cautiously. It's Sir
Anthony, Chief; I'm not sure whether you want
me to put it through. Roper growled and rolled
on his side to take it. He was wearing his robe
again. They were lying on the bed after making
love, though God knew it was not love they had
been making but something closer to hate. His
old appetite for screwing in the afternoons had
recently revived. So had hers. Their appetite for
each other seemed to grow in inverse proportion
to their affection. She was beginning to wonder
whether sex had anything to do with love at all.
"I'm a good fuck," she had told him afterwards,
staring at the ceiling. "Oh, you *are,*" he had
agreed. "Ask *anyone.*" Then this phone call,
with his back to her: Oh, blast him, yes, I'll take
it. Then the stiffening of his back, a freezing of
the dorsal muscles through the silk, an uneasy

shifting of the buttocks, the legs settling on each other for protection.

"Tony, you're out of court. Are you pissed again? . . . *Who* is? Well, put him on. Why not? . . . All right, talk, if you want. I'll listen. Nothing to do with me, but I don't mind listening. . . . Don't give me sob stories, Tony, not my kind of music. . . ." But soon these surly interjections grew shorter, and the spaces between them longer, until Roper was listening in total silence, and his body lay alert and dead still.

"Just a minute, Tony," he ordered suddenly. "Hold it." He turned to her, not bothering to put his hand over the mouthpiece. "Run a bath," he told her. "Go into the bathroom, close the door, run the taps. Now."

So she went into the bathroom and turned on the taps and lifted the rubberized extension, but of course he heard the water running and bawled at her to get off the line. So after that she turned the taps to a trickle and pressed her ear to the keyhole, until the door exploded in her face and sent her flying across the Dutch-tiled floor, part of their recent decoration scheme. Then she heard Roper call, "Go on, Tony. Little local difficulty."

After that she listened to him listening, but that was all she heard. She got into the bath and remembered how once it was his pleasure to get in the other end and shove a foot between her legs while he read the *Financial Times* and in return she would tease him with her toes and try and give him an erection. And sometimes he would haul her back to bed for another round, soaking the sheets with bathwater.

But this time he just stood in the doorway.

In his robe. Staring at her. Wondering what the hell to do about her. About Jonathan. About himself.

His face was set in that stony stay-away-from-me frown that he wore very rarely, and never in front of Daniel: the one that made and broke whatever was necessary for his preservation.

"You better get dressed," he said. "Corkoran will be here in two minutes."

"What for?"

"Just dress."

Then he went back to the phone, started to dial a number and changed his mind. He laid the receiver back on its cradle with such immense control that she knew he wanted to smash it into fragments, and the whole boat with it. He put his hands on his hips and stared at her while she dressed, as if he didn't like what she was putting on.

"Better wear sensible shoes," he said.

And that was when her heart stopped, because on board nobody ever wore anything but deck shoes or bare feet, except in the evenings, when dress shoes could be worn by the women, though they were not allowed stiletto heels.

So she dressed and pulled on a pair of sensible rubber-soled suede lace-ups she had bought at Bergdorf's during one of their trips to New York, and when Corkoran knocked on the door, Roper took him into the drawing room and spoke to him alone for as much as ten minutes, while Jed sat on the bed thinking of the chink she had still not found, that magic formula for Jonathan's salvation and her own. But it wouldn't come to her.

She had fantasized about blowing up the boat with the arsenal stored in the forward hold—a kind of *African Queen* job with everyone aboard, including Jonathan and herself; about poisoning the guards, or staging a dramatic denunciation of Roper's crimes before the assembled dinner guests, culminating in a search for the hidden prisoner; or simply holding Roper to ransom with a carving knife. Several other solutions that work so well in movies had occurred to her, but the truth was, the staff and crew were watching her all the time, several of the guests had remarked that she was in a nervous state, there were rumors she was pregnant, and there was not a single passenger on the boat who would believe her, do anything, or—even if she did convince them she was right—give a damn.

Roper and Corkoran came out of the drawing room and Roper threw on some clothes, not before stripping naked in front of them, a thing that had never bothered him, in fact he rather liked it, and for a bad moment she feared that he was going to leave her alone with Corkoran for some reason, and she couldn't think of a good one. To her relief Corkoran moved with him to the door.

"Stay in here and wait," Roper said as they left. As an afterthought he turned the lock on her, a thing he had not done before.

First she sat on the bed, then lay on it, feeling like a prisoner of war not knowing whether the right side or the wrong side is going to storm the camp. But *somebody* was storming it, she was certain. Even locked inside the stateroom, she could catch the tension of the murmured instructions to the staff, the quickening of light feet in the corridor. She felt the pulse of engines, and the boat leaned a little. Roper has selected a new course. She looked out of the porthole and saw the horizon turning. She stood up, saw to her surprise that she was wearing blue jeans instead of one of the million-dollar numbers Roper insisted on for cruises, and she remembered the magic of a last day of term, when you could get out of your hated gray convent uniform and put on something really daring, like a cotton frock, for the glorious moment when your parents' car came hobbling over Mother Angela's speed bumps to take you away.

But nobody except herself had told her she was leaving. It was her own idea, and all she could do was will it into reality.

She decided to put together an escape kit. If she needed sensible shoes, then she must need sensible other things too. So she grabbed her shoulder bag from the top shelf of her wardrobe and put in her sponge bag and toothbrush and some spare underclothes. She pulled open the drawers of the desk and to her amazement found her passport—Corkoran must have given it to him. When she came to her jewelry, she determined to be high-minded. Roper had always loved to give her jewels, and there had been a possessors' code about which jewel and which occasion should be remembered: the rose diamond necklace for their first night together in Paris; the emerald bracelet for her birthday in Monaco; the rubies from Christmas in Vienna. Forget them, she told herself with a shudder: leave the memories in the drawer. Then she thought: To hell, it's only money, and grabbed three or four pieces as currency for their future life together. But no sooner had she put them in her shoulder bag than she fished them out and dumped them on Roper's dressing table. I'll never be your jewelry girl again.

She had no problem, however, helping herself to a couple of Roper's handmade shirts, and silk underpants in case Jonathan was out of stock. And a pair of Gucci espadrilles that Roper was rather fond of, which looked as though they might be Jonathan's size.

Her courage spent, she flopped back onto the

bed again. It's a trick. I'm not going anywhere. They've killed him.

. . .

JONATHAN HAD always known that when the end came—whatever end they had decided on—they would come to him as a pair. His educated guess was that the pair would be Frisky and Tabby, because torturers, like anybody else, have their own protocols: this is my job, that is your job and the big jobs go to the biggest people. Gus had always been an adjunct. They had made a pair when they dragged him to the lavatory, they had made a pair when they sponged him down, which they seemed to do for their own fastidious reasons, not for his: they had never got over the time in Colón when he had threatened to soil himself, and when they were angry with him, they never failed to tell him what a filthy little bastard he was.

So when Frisky and Tabby threw open the door and switched on the blue overhead storm light, and Frisky the left-hander made for Jonathan's right side, leaving his left arm free for emergencies, and Tabby knelt to the left of Jonathan's head—fussing with his keys as usual, never having the right one ready in advance—everything was exactly the way the close observer had predicted, except that he had not expected them to be quite so frank about the purpose of their visit.

"We're all very, very fed up with you, I'm

afraid, Tommy. The Chief particularly," said Tabby. "Which is why you're going on a journey. Sorry about this, Tommy. You had your chance, but you would be stubborn."

Which said, Tabby dealt Jonathan a half-hearted side-kick in the stomach, in case he was thinking of being a bother.

But Jonathan was long past the bothersome stage, as they could see. In fact there was an awkward moment when Frisky and Tabby seemed to wonder whether the bother was over for good, because when they saw him slumped forward with his head slewed sideways and his mouth open, Frisky dropped to his knees and yanked up Jonathan's eyelid with his thumb and peered into his eye.

"Tommy? Come on. Can't have you missing your own funeral, can we?"

Then they did a wonderful thing. They let him lie there. They unchained him and they ungagged him, and while Frisky sponged his face down and put a fresh plaster across his mouth but no bung, Tabby pulled off what was left of his shirt and got him into a fresh one, arm by arm.

But if Jonathan was playing floppy as a rag doll, already his secret store of energy was emptying itself into every part of his body. His muscles, bruised and half-paralyzed by cramp, were screaming out to him for the relief of action. His smashed hands and crumpled legs were glowing, his blurred vision was clearing even while Frisky mopped his eyes.

He waited. He remembered the advantage of that extra moment of delay.

Lull them, he thought, as they hauled him to his feet.

Lull them, he thought again, as he slung an arm round each of their shoulders for support and let his weight hang on them as they dragged him down the corridor.

Lull them, he thought, as Frisky went crookedly ahead of him up the spiral staircase and Tabby propped him up from below.

Oh, God, he thought, as he saw stars stretched across black sky, and a great red moon floating on the water. Oh, God, give me this last moment.

They stood on the deck, the three of them, like a family group, and Jonathan could hear Roper's thirties music echoing through the early darkness from the taverna at the stern, and the jolly sounds of chatter as the evening revelries began. The forward end of the boat was unlit, and Jonathan wondered whether they intended to shoot him: one shot at the height of the music, who would hear?

The boat had changed course. A stretch of shore lay only a couple of miles off. There was a road. He could see the row of streetlights below the stars, more like mainland than island. Or perhaps a row of islands, who could tell? Sophie, let's do this together. Time to say a fond goodbye to the worst man in the world.

His guards had come to a halt, waiting for something. Slumped between them, an arm still clutched round each of their shoulders, Jonathan waited too, pleased to notice that his mouth had started bleeding again inside the plaster, which would have the double effect of loosening it and making him look even more smashed up than he was.

Then he saw Roper. He'd probably been there all the time, and Jonathan hadn't spotted him in his white dinner jacket against the white of the bridge. Corkoran was there too, but Sandy Langbourne hadn't made it. Probably screwing one of the maids.

And between Corkoran and Roper he could see Jed, or if he couldn't, God had put her there. But yes, he could see Jed, and she could see him, she saw nothing except him, but Roper must have told her to keep quiet. She was wearing plain jeans and no jewelry, which pleased him unnaturally: he really hated the way Roper hung his money on her. She was looking at him and he was returning her look, but what with his face in the mess it was, she couldn't know that. Probably, with all the extra moaning and sagging he was doing, she wasn't feeling very romantic.

Jonathan slumped still lower in the arms of

his guards, and they obligingly stooped and grasped him more firmly round the waist.

"I think he's going," Frisky murmured.

"Where to?" Tabby said.

And that was the cue for Jonathan to drive their two heads together with more force than he had ever commanded in his life. The power began in his leap as he seemed to rise in flight from the hole where they had chained him. It swarmed through his shoulders as he flung wide his arms, then closed them in one huge and terrible hand-clap, then a second: temple against temple, face against face, ear against ear, skull against skull. It ran through his body as he thrust the two men away from him, then hurled them onto the deck and with the side of his right foot kicked each head in turn, one scything blow for each, then a second to the throat. Then he stepped forward, stripping the plaster from his face as he advanced on Roper, who was giving him orders, the way he had at Meister's.

"Pine. Shouldn't have done that. Don't come any nearer. Corks, show him your gun. Putting you ashore. Both o' you. Done your job and failed. Total waste of time, whole stupid game."

Jonathan had found a length of ship's railing and was clutching it with both hands. But he was only resting. He wasn't weakening. He was giving his secret reinforcements time to group.

"Stuff's all delivered, Pine. Tossed 'em a boat

or two, couple of arrests—what the hell? You don't think I do this kind of thing alone, do you?" Then he repeated what he had told Jed. "This isn't crime. This is politics. No good being high-and-mighty. Way of the world."

Jonathan had started toward him again, though his steps were wide and faltering. Corkoran cocked his gun.

"You can go home, Pine. No, you can't. London's pulled the rug from under. There's a warrant out for you in England too. Shoot him, Corks. Do it now. Head shot."

"Jonathan, stop!"

Was it Jed or Sophie calling him? Plain walking was no longer easy for him. He wished he could get back to the handrail, but he had reached the center of the deck. He was wading. The deck was swaying. His knees were failing. Yet the will in him would not let go. He was determined to grapple with the unreachable, put blood on Roper's beautiful white dinner jacket, smash his dolphin smile, make him scream *I kill, I do wrong, there is good and bad and I am bad!*

Roper was counting, the way Corkoran had liked to count. Either he was counting awfully slowly or Jonathan's sense of time was failing. He heard *one* and he heard *two,* but he didn't hear *three,* and he wondered whether this was another way of dying: they shoot you, but you go on with your life exactly as before; it's just that no one knows you're there. Then he heard Jed's voice, and it had the authoritarian ring that had always particularly annoyed him:

"Jonathan, for Christ's sake, *look!*"

Roper's voice came back, like a faraway radio station picked up by chance. "Yes, look," he agreed. "Look here, Pine. Look what I've got. I'm doing a Daniel on her, Pine. But this time it isn't a game."

He managed to look, though things were getting hazy for him. And he saw that Roper, like a good commanding officer, had taken one step forward of his adjutant and was standing pretty much at attention in his smart white jacket, except that with one hand he was holding Jed by her chestnut hair and with the other he was holding Corkoran's pistol to her temple—typical of old Corky to sport an honest-to-God army-issue nine-millimeter Browning. Then Jonathan lay down, or fell down, and this time he heard Sophie and Jed in chorus, yelling at him to stay awake.

· · ·

THEY HAD FOUND a blanket for him, and when Jed and Corkoran had lifted him to his feet, Jed wrapped it round his shoulders in that nursy way she had demonstrated at Crystal. With Jed and Corkoran holding him, and Roper still in command of the gun in case of a second resurgence, they hauled him to the ship's side, passing what was left of Frisky and Tabby on their way.

Corkoran made Jed go first, then between them they helped Jonathan down the steps, while Gus in the launch was offering his hand. But Jonathan refused it and nearly fell into the water in consequence, which struck Jed as typical of his stubbornness, just when everyone was trying to help him. Corkoran was saying something interfering about the island being Venezuelan, but Jed told him to shut up, and he did. Gus was trying to give her instructions about the outboard, but she knew quite as well as he did about outboards and told him so. Jonathan, shrouded like a monk in his blanket, was crouching in the middle of the boat, trimming it out of instinct. His eyes, hardly visible inside their swellings, were raised to the *Pasha,* which towered over them like a skyscraper.

Jed looked up at the boat and saw Roper in his white jacket, peering down into the water for something he had lost. For a moment he looked exactly as she had seen him that first day in Paris: a clean-cut, amusing English gentleman, perfect for his generation. He vanished, and she fancied she heard the music from the afterdeck lift a little across the water as he went back to the dance.

THIRTY-ONE

IT WAS the Hosken brothers who saw it first. They were out pulling their lobster pots off Lanyon Head. Pete saw it and Pete didn't say a damn word. At sea Pete never did. Didn't say much on land either, come to think of it. They were having a lucky day with the lobsters. Four beauties they'd caught, ten pounds' weight the lot, my robins.

So Pete and his brother Redfers drove to Newlyn in their old post office van, and got cash for them, because they only ever dealt in cash. And on the drive back to Porthgwarra, Pete turned to Redfers and said, "See that light in Lanyon cottage this morning then?"

And it turned out that Redfers had seen it too, but not made anything of it. He had supposed it was some hippy in there, or New Ager or whatever they call them, one of those buggers from the bus camp over to Saint Just.

"Maybe some yuppie from up-country's gone and bought the place," Redfers suggested, as an afterthought, while they drove. "Been empty long enough. Near on a year. Nobody down here's going to find that bloody chunk of money."

Pete wouldn't have that at all. The suggestion offended something deep in him. "How can you buy a house if you can't find the bugger who owns it?" he asked his brother sharply. "That's Jack Linden's house. Nobody can't buy that house, except they find Jack Linden first."

"Perhaps it's Jack who's back in it, then," Redfers said, which was what Pete had been thinking too, but hadn't said. So Pete scoffed, and told Redfers he was daft.

For several days after that, neither brother found anything further to say on the subject, not to each other and not to anybody else. With a spell of sweet weather and the mackerel rising, and bream if you knew where to look for them, why should they bother about some light in Jack Linden's upstairs bedroom window?

It wasn't till one evening a week later, when they were taking a last look at a patch of shallow water Pete always liked a couple of miles southeast of the Lanyon, and caught the smell of wood smoke on the offshore wind, that they separately arrived at the same unspoken decision to stroll casually down the lane and find out who the hell was living there—most likely that stinking old gyppo, Slow-and-Lucky, and his bloody mongrel. If so, he got no business. Not in Jack Linden's house. Not Lucky. That wouldn't be appropriate.

Long before they reached the front door, they knew it wasn't Lucky or anyone like him.

When Lucky moved into a house, he didn't immediately cut the grass round the front path, or polish the brass doorhandle for you, boy. And he didn't put a pretty chestnut mare in your paddock—bloody hell, boy, she was so pretty she damn near smiled at you! Lucky didn't hang woman's washing on the clothes line either, even if he *was* a bit kinky. Or stand still as a bloody buzzard at the parlor window, more like a shadow than a man, but a familiar shadow for all the weight he'd lost, challenging you to come up the path so he could break your legs for you, same as he damn near done for Pete Pengelly that time they tried to lamp his rabbits.

He'd grown a beard, they noted, before they turned tail and scuttled back up the lane: a dirty big thick Cornish type of beard, more mask than bloody hair. God help us! Jack Linden in a Jesus beard!

But when Redfers, who was courting Marilyn these days, plucked up his courage and informed Mrs. Trethewey, his mother-in-law-to-be, that Jack Linden had come back to the Lanyon, not a ghost but flesh, she bit off his head for him:

"That's no more Jack Linden than I am," she retorted. "So don't you go being a silly boy, Redfers Hosken. That's a gentleman from Ireland and his lady, and they're going to breed horses and paint pictures. They've bought their house and paid their debts, and they're turning over a new leaf in life, which is high time you did the same."

"Looked like Jack to me," said Redfers, with more spirit than he felt.

Mrs. Trethewey fell quiet a moment, deliberating how much she could safely tell a boy of such patent limitation.

"Now you listen to me, Redfers," she said. "Jack Linden who came here a while back is far away over the hills. The person who lives at the Lanyon—well, I grant you he may be some kind of relative of Jack's, that's possible, and there's a similarity for those of us who didn't know Jack well. But I've had the police here, Redfers. A very persuasive gentleman from Yorkshire, with charm to burn, came all the way from London and spoke to certain people. And what may look like Jack Linden to some of us is an innocent stranger to those who are a little wiser. So I'll trouble you never to talk out of turn again, because if you do, you'll hurt two precious souls."

ACKNOWLEDGMENTS

I ACKNOWLEDGE with gratitude the help of Jeff Leen of *The Miami Herald* and Rudy Maxa, Robbyn Swan, Jim Webster of Webster Associates, Edward Nowell of Nowell Antiques, Billy Coy of Enron, Abby Redhead of ABS, Roger and Anne Harris of Harris's Restaurant, Penzance, Billy Chapple of St. Buryan, and friendly spirits in the U.S. Drug Enforcement Agency and the U.S. Treasury who for obvious reasons cannot be mentioned here. Nor would it be appropriate to name arms dealers who opened their doors to me, as opposed to those who ran a mile when they heard me coming, or a former British soldier in Ireland who allowed me to plunder his memory. The management of a certain great hotel in Zurich, true to its traditions, showed a sporting indulgence towards the foibles of an old guest. Scott Griffin piloted me in Canada, Peter Dorman and his colleagues at the Chicago House in Luxor showed me extraordinary courtesy, and opened my eyes to the splendors of ancient Egypt. Frank Wisner revealed to me a Cairo I shall never forget. The Mnushins lent me their piece of paradise. Kevin Buckley pointed me in good directions,

Dick Koster gave me the keys to Fabergé, Gerasimos Kanelopulos spoiled me in his bookshop, Luís Martinz gave me a precious piece of Panama's magic. Jorge Ritter showed me Colón and much more, Barbara Deshotels shepherded me in Curaçao. If I have failed to live up to their hospitality and wise words, the fault is in me, not in them. Of all the people along the way who gave me encouragement and a helping hand, John Calley and Sandy Lean are almost too close to thank, but without them the *Iron Pasha* might never have set sail.

(continued)

Will Weng, editor, *The New York Times Large Print Crossword Puzzles*, Volume 2 (paper)

Will Weng, editor, *The New York Times Large Print Crossword Puzzles*, Volume 3 (paper)

Eugene T. Maleska, editor, *The New York Times Large Print Crossword Puzzles*, Volume 4 (paper)

Eugene T. Maleska, editor, *The New York Times Large Print Crossword Puzzles*, Volume 5 (paper)

Eugene T. Maleska, editor, *The New York Times Large Print Crossword Puzzles*, Volume 6 (paper)

Eugene T. Maleska, editor, *The New York Times Large Print Crossword Puzzles*, Volume 7 (paper)

James A. Michener, *Mexico* (paper)

James A. Michener, *The Novel*

James A. Michener, *The World is My Home* (paper)

Richard North Patterson, *Degree of Guilt*

Maria Riva, *Marlene Dietrich* (2 volumes, paper)

Mickey Rooney, *Life Is Too Short*

William Styron, *Darkness Visible*

Margaret Truman, *Murder at the National Cathedral*

Margaret Truman, *Murder at the Pentagon*

Donald Trump with Charles Leerhsen, *Trump: Surviving at the Top*

Anne Tyler, *Saint Maybe*

John Updike, *Rabbit at Rest*

Lois Wyse, *Grandchildren Are So Much Fun I Should Have Had Them First*